Simplicissimus,
The German Adventurer

Simplicissimus,
The German Adventurer

by
Hans Jacob Christoffel von Grimmelshausen

Translated by
JOHN C. OSBORNE

With a Foreword by
LYNNE TATLOCK

The German Simplicißimus

That is:

The Description of the Life of a Peculiar Wanderer
Named Melchior Sternfels von Fuchshaim,
Including Where and in What Manner He Came
into This World, What He Saw, Learned,
Experienced and Put Up With Therein;
Also Why He Voluntarily Left It.

Exceedingly Amusing and in Many Ways Useful to Read.

Brought to Light
by
German Schleifheim
of Sulsfort

Monpelgart
Printed in the Shop of Johann Fillion
In the Year 1669.

Newfound Press
THE UNIVERSITY OF TENNESSEE LIBRARIES, KNOXVILLE

Newfound Press is a digital imprint of the University of Tennessee Libraries. Its publications are available for non-commercial and educational uses, such as research, teaching and private study. The author encourages the "fair use" of these materials as defined in current U.S. Copyright Law. You may reproduce Newfound Press materials by printing, downloading, or making copies without prior permission as long as the original work is credited. For all other uses, contact:

Newfound Press
University of Tennessee Libraries
1015 Volunteer Boulevard
Knoxville, TN 37996-1000
www.newfoundpress.utk.edu

Cover illustration is frontispiece from the 1669 edition, courtesy of the Beinecke Rare Book and Manuscript Library, Yale University.

ISBN-13: 978-0-9797292-5-6
ISBN-10: 0-9797292-5-4

Grimmelshausen, Hans Jakob Christoph von, 1625-1676.
[Abenteuerliche Simplicissimus. English]
        Simplicissimus : the German adventurer / by Hans Jacob Christoffel von Grimmelshausen ; translated by John C. Osborne ; with a foreword by Lynne Tatlock.
        440 p. ; 28 cm.
        Translation of: Abenteuerliche Simplicissimus.
        Includes bibliographical references.
        1. Thirty Years' War, 1618-1648 -- Fiction.   2. Simplicissimus (Fictitious character) -- Fiction. I. Osborne, John C., 1928-   II. Title.
PT1731.A7 E5 2008

Book design by Jayne Rogers and Martha Rudolph

Contents

Foreword

Reading "Simplicissimus" in Translation in 2008

Lynne Tatlock
Hortense and Tobias Lewin Distinguished Professor in the Humanities
Washington University in St. Louis

WITH THE ONLINE EDITION OF JOHN C. OSBORNE'S HITHERTO unpublished translation, *Simplicissimus, The German Adventurer*, the Newfound Press at the University of Tennessee makes readily available to an English-speaking audience worldwide Hans Jacob Christoffel von Grimmelshausen's masterpiece. A searing coming to terms with the Thirty Years' War and the chaos that it drew in its wake, this early novel is arguably the most important German literary work of the seventeenth century.

Translating *Simplicissimus*

Ever humbling, the art of translation demands compromise, judgment, and creativity. Translating a literary text, especially one as complex as Hans Jacob Christoffel von Grimmelshausen's *Simplicissimus*, presents multiple challenges that the unschooled reader cannot begin to suspect. How one translates is, furthermore, inevitably influenced by the venue of publication and the norms and expectations of the historical moment, be they those of a broad reading public or those within academic circles. The following sometimes critical overview of *Simplicissimus* in translation is written in deep appreciation of the difficulties faced by each translator who took on the daunting task of rendering Grimmelshausen's masterpiece into English for a specific time and a specific audience.

John Osborne's translation of the *edition princeps* of *Der abenteuerliche Simplicissimus* (printed by Wolff Eberhard Felssecker in Nuremberg, dated 1669) here sees the light of day in electronic form almost one hundred years after Hans Jacob Christoffel von Grimmelshausen's *Simplicissimus* was belatedly translated into English for the first time and published in the United Kingdom. The first English translator, A.T.S. Goodrick, who identified himself on the title page of a later edition as "sometime fellow and tutor of St. John's College, Oxford" (Routledge, 1924), justified his translation of 1912 as more important as "a contribution to the history...or the sociology of the momentous period to which the romance of 'Simplicissimus' belongs, than as a specimen of literature"

(1912, 1). Goodrick characterizes the book's chief interest for the then-modern reader as lying "in the pictures or rather photographs of contemporary manners and characters which it presents" (1912, 1), thus implying that Grimmelshausen's novel could be taken at face value as a lively documentation of the Thirty Years' War and its aftermath.

Working principally with Tittmann's edition of *Simplicissimus*, published in 1877, as the basis for his translation, Goodrick did not have at his disposal the wealth of scholarship (beginning with Jan Hendrik Scholte's important scholarly edition of the novel [Saale: Niemeyer, 1938]) that has brought contemporary scholars to a deeper understanding of this complex seventeenth-century text. Furthermore, ideas about the novel as it had developed in England shaped his expectations of Grimmelshausen's text—both in what he praised and in what he disdained or disregarded.

Goodrick may not have fully understood the nature of the book he translated, a hybrid text composed of disparate kinds of writing, some of it original and some not, a work that operates in multiple modes of representation including allegory and emblem. He did not know, for example, the full extent of Grimmelshausen's reliance on, indeed pirating of, other texts, of his tendency to cut and paste. Nor did he understand the importance of this ubiquitous practice for the seventeenth-century writer. The vivid description of the Battle of Wittstock in chapter 27 of book 2, for example, that can tempt modern readers to speak of realism, borrows liberally from an encyclopedic work of the seventeenth century, the *Theatrum Europaeum*. Goodrick did know, however, that the concluding chapter of book 5 of the novel quotes at length Aegidius Albertinus's translation from 1599 of Atonius de Guevara's *Menosprecio de corte y alabanza de aldea* (1539; Scorn of the Court and Praise of the Village). Yet this borrowing appears to have offended his sense of the originality and integrity of the book. He simply omitted this key reflection on vanity, a central theme of *Simplicissimus*, with the words: "The first part of the chapter is a fair translation, extended to many pages, of Quevara's [sic] somewhat trite reflections on the vanity of a worldly life.... The only part of the chapter which concerns the story is as follows" (1912, 403). Elsewhere he elected not to translate a chapter because he found it "uninteresting": "Chap. xix. is an uninteresting excursus on certain communities of Anabaptists in Hungary" (1912, 389), he writes, missing the point that the interest in the utopian community of the Anabaptists is entirely consonant with one of the central concerns of a novel that opens with a lament about social climbing as symptomatic of the chaotic times.

Goodrick elected to translate Grimmelshausen into an archaic English that in 1912 powerfully evoked the seventeenth century. The English of this translation, however, sounds very quaint in 2008, though it is not as archaic subsequently as the opening sentence leads the reader to expect, "There appeareth in these days of ours ... a certain disease which causeth those who do suffer from it ... forthwith to give themselves out as gentlemen and nobles of ancient descent" (Goodrick 1912, 1) .

Appearing in several different editions under two different titles, Goodrick's translation remained the lone, and thus definitive, English translation for fifty years. However, by the time it was republished yet again in 1962, this time with the University of Nebraska Press, it had a rival: Walter Wallich's *The Adventures of a Simpleton* which appeared with The New English Library Limited in that same year.

Like Goodrick, Wallich abridges the text according to his own lights. Noting the need to pare the book down to a size manageable in one volume, Wallich writes in his postcript: "The cuts have been made in such a way as to preserve the continuity of the story, omitting mainly a highly fantastical journey to the centre of the earth, a certain amount of moralizing, and a peroration near the end which Grimmelshausen lifted bodily—with due acknowledgements—from the Spanish divine Guevara" (Wallich, 249). Precisely this moralizing is, however, central to the vision of the text and the mentality of the age that produced it. Moreover, what Wallich calls the "journey to the centre of the earth," the famous Mummel Lake adventure from book V, belongs to one of several allegorical episodes that provide sharp commentary on the social formations and mores of the day.

Wallich's translation heralded a small boom in new translations of *Simplicissimus*. Two years later in 1964, a second new translation, *Simplicius Simplicissimus* by Hellmuth Weissenborn and Lesley MacDonald with engravings by Hellmuth Weissenborn, appeared in London with Calder. According to Weissenborn, the translation aims "to render the work in a style acceptable for this century, without expurgation, but retaining the vigour, truthfulness and occasional coarseness of the language" (9). Nevertheless, the translators chose to shorten "a few repetitive passages," in essence yielding to the temptation to improve on Grimmelshausen to make him more palatable to modern tastes (Weissenborn, 9). Conflating the novel with its creator, Weissenborn characterizes the work in his introduction as "full of natural strength, born from an unspoiled and open heart" (Weissenborn, 10). A third abridged translation by George Schulz-Behrend followed a year later in 1965. Behrend's lively and highly readable, but significantly abridged, translation was re-published with Camden House in 1993.

A special American translation of *Simplicissmus* in a limited edition (1981) aimed at book collectors constitutes an interesting interlude in the publishing history of Grimmelshausen's fascinating novel. Eighteen engravings by the illustrator Fritz Eichenberg, reproduced in the volume, provided the impetus for this new translation.

Previous English translations had, according to the translator, John P. Spielberg, omitted many of the episodes that Eichenberg had chosen to illustrate with his wood engravings. This translation therefore includes the *Continuatio*, which was published separately in 1669 and is understood as a sixth book of sorts of *Simplicissimus*. Spielberg reminds his readers that translation is "one of the commonest forms of treachery" (xxiii) and declares his intention to "provide as complete a translation of the original as my capacity to understand it will allow, and to let the story with all its digressions tell itself in language as straightforward as I can command" (xxiii). Yet he too in the end abridges the text somewhat, omitting "a few sentences which would require extensive explanatory notes." Spielberg presumably had a strong sense of this edition as an art book and therefore held that the book with its illustrations needed to speak for itself without scholarly notes.

In 1986 the University Press of America published the first unabridged English translation of the five books of the first edition of *Simplicissimus* including as well a translation of the *Continuatio*. This modestly produced yet usefully annotated edition, has long been out of print. The translator, Monte Adair, aims in his choice of language, like Schulz-Behrend in his abridged translation, for readability, thereby domesticating Grimmelshausen's seventeenth-century prose to conform, for example, with the demands of English syntax. To do so, he shortens sentences and reduces the use of subordinate clauses. Adair's translation, though readable and reliable, does not match Schulz-Behrend's for lively turn of phrase.

Dedalus, the last publishing house to republish Goodrick's translation, launched a new translation of *Simplicissimus* by Mike Mitchell in 1999. Mitchell correctly remarks in his introduction of Grimmelshausen's stylistic range that it is "wide, from the simple piety of the hermit to satire, occasional moralising, displays of erudition, classical learning and practical knowledge, extended allegory and fantasy. But most of the book is in a plain, vigorous language which is not afraid of crude vulgarity and even the occasional awful pun. This makes the story come vividly alive and keeps it moving and is one of the reasons why it is still readable today" (9). Aimed at a general reading public, Mitchell's translation provides readers with no explanatory notes. Mitchell obviously strove for readability, producing a text in modern English that is easy and enjoyable to read. An argument can be made for the desirability of such a naturalized or domesticated translation. Osborne, however, pursued a different strategy when he chose to translate Grimmelshausen's masterpiece, and it is instructive to compare his choices with Mitchell's.

Osborne's translation of the five original books of Grimmelshausen's novel aspires to meet the needs of a general as well as a scholarly readership. It includes historical information and explanation even more extensive, for example, than that provided in the most widely circulating German edition of *Simplicissimus*, the Reclam edition by Hans Heinrich Borchert. Osborne's notes, like the translation itself, are potentially valuable not only for readers who know no German but also for students and scholars who can read *Simplicissimus* in the original German.

Osborne, in his unabridged *Simplicissimus*, strives to remain faithful to the original in style and effect. His translation is, for example, the only one to reproduce the lengthy opening paragraph of the book as a single sentence—as it was in the original. While it is true that German syntax allows for longer and more complex sentences than does English, seventeenth-century prose pushes the limits even of German; Grimmelshausen's prose is expansive, overladen, breathless, and sometimes awkward. Osborne's translation gives us not only a feel for the abundance and exuberance of this writing, but also a sense of its occasional opacity and complexity. Indeed, Osborne pushes the limits of English to give us a sense of how Grimmelshausen stretches his own language. Among other things, Osborne's English occasionally adheres to German word order, thereby giving the reader a sense of a text that is not easily digestible, but instead foreign and dense. We read, for example, in book 1 chapter 2 "Oh the life of nobility which then I led!" Osborne has placed the verb in the final position in keeping with German. Mitchell by contrast naturalizes the syntax, writing "what a fine life it was that I led in those far off days" (19). Similarly, Osborne opens chapter 7 of book 1 with the words "In what manner I was helped come back to my senses I do not know," lightly imitating German syntax with the placement of the subordinate clause at the head of the sentence, whereas Mitchell domesticates the sentence: "I do not know what it was that brought me round" (30). Whereas Mitchell and others, presumably in pursuit of readability, tend to collapse the doubling typical of Grimmelshausen and other baroque writers, Osborne retains it. Therefore in the opening sentence, Osborne writes "scratched and scraped" (bk 1:1) to reproduce Grimmelshausen's "zusammengeraspelt und erschachert," whereas Mitchell writes "scratched together" (17); Spielberg "scraped together" (3); and Schulz-Behrends, creatively reaching for the doubling, "by hook or crook scraped together" (1993, 1); Adair, "scrapped and haggled" (1), and Wallich "scraped together" (1). Osborne, in contrast to Mitchell, also pointedly preserves the Latinity of the original that was typical of seventeenth-century German prose. Where Osborne preserves the Latin "in summa summarum" (bk 1:1) "musicus" (bk 1:4) and "centauris" (bk 1:12), for example, Mitchell writes "in short" (17), "musician" (19) and "centaurs" (24) respectively. Where Osborne retains the odd locution "like the *primum mobile*" (bk 1:13), providing a note of explanation, Mitchell omits it (24). Similarly,

Osborne also reproduces the use of foreign words besides Latin, typical of German seventeenth-century prose, whereas Mitchell does not, as for example, in "nobilistes" (French; bk 1:1), which Mitchell translates as "nobles" (17) and "*Jalemi* songs" (Greek; bk 1:5), which Mitchell translates as "dirges" (19).

As can be seen from these few examples and as will become quickly clear to any reader, Osborne mediates *Simplicissimus* for the modern reader in a learned, lightly archaic and foreign-sounding, yet readable English. His *German Adventurer* thus speaks across 350 years in a language that is both alien and familiar, signaling its origins in a time, locality, and mentality different from our English-speaking present.

Interpreting *Simplicissimus*

Grimmelshausen's extraordinary novel, by virtue of its very hybridity, has given rise to a plethora of studies from a wide range of approaches during the last fifty years. Its at least superficial affinity to Spanish picaresque novels has demanded its consideration in a broader European context and thus commanded close attention both to its narrator and the social satire that he mediates. The episodes in which the protagonist, Simplicius, literally plays the role of the fool or jester have also led scholars to understand the novel in the European tradition of the literature of folly.

The narration of a life in the first person that constitutes this novel has inspired literary historians interested in narratology, furthermore, to examine the book as fictionalized autobiographical writing and to evaluate its claims to truth-telling. Is Simplicius, our narrator, a creditable guide to his own life? To what extent does he share in the vice of the world he depicts and thus become suspect? What does the gap between the knowledge of the narrator and his once-naïve self tell us about his moral development and the outlook of the book as a whole? For some scholars, the (auto)biographical mode even signals a precursor to the German *Bildungsroman* of the following century as it came to be embodied in Johann Wolfgang von Goethe's *Wilhelm Meister's Years of Apprenticeship* (1795/96).

The arcane allusions and use of allegory in the novel have led to still other approaches that have uncovered multiple levels on which the novel can be read. Along these lines, a number of scholars have argued strenuously for a *sensus astrologicus*. According to this view, the novel reveals a planetary structure that is closely tied to its central thematic of constancy and inconstancy. Still other scholars have understood the novel to carry a Christian eschatological message figured in the emblematics of the novel.

Much attention has been devoted to the striking and enigmatic frontispiece, the so-called phoenix copper. It has been argued that this engraving indicates to readers who know how to interpret it properly how the book itself is to be read. Scholars have based this view on the fact that *Simplicissimus* appeared without an introduction in a historical moment in print culture when the introduction was ubiquitous in similar publications. The introduction normally served to explain, justify, and apologize for the work in question and thus to influence the reception of the book. The phoenix copper has been thought to serve precisely these purposes. More recent scholarship has spoken of the function of Grimmelshausen's frontispiece in terms of the performativity of seventeenth-century book illustration, that is, of the frontispiece as advertising the book and staging its contents.

Grimmelshausen's frontispiece displays the characteristic tri-partite structure of the emblem: *pictura*, *inscriptio*, and *subscriptio*, that is, image, motto (usually printed above the image), and subscription (a prose or verse quotation beneath the picture). In choosing this form for the frontispiece, Grimmelshausen selected a symbolic mode ubiquitous in seventeenth-century high culture. As Peter Daly formulates it, "emblems are composed of symbolic pictures and words; a meaningful relationship between the two is intended; the manner of communication is connotative rather than denotative."[1] The emblem is thus at once representation and interpretation.

A range of possibilities has been suggested for the ways the emblematic phoenix copper can elucidate the contents of *Simplicissimus*. The obvious hybridity of the monstrous figure, alluded to in the verse beneath the picture, has been understood to introduce the work as a satire, a genre understood in Horatian poetics to be marked by its assembly of disparate parts. The disparate parts also point to the wanderings of the picaresque figure through the four elements, perhaps a hint at the arcane ways of knowing in which the novel deals. The figure's face and his composite parts have also been understood both as borrowed from contemporary representations of the Devil and demons and thus to signal that the novel is to be read as a warning not to imitate the title character's behavior. Still other critics have pointed to the resemblance of the head and face to those of the satyr and have thus argued for the chimera as an allusion to the satirical intent of the novel. The gesture of the figure's left hand, too, has been seen both as figuring the satirist's scorn and as pointing to the things of the world depicted in the book as well as indicating how to read them and thus Grimmelshausen's book as a whole. Obvious references to the plot and theme of the novel in the images displayed in the book depicted in the frontispiece are the props of royalty, the weapons of war, and the fool's cap. The figure's little finger and index finger span the space between the innocent and unknowing child in swaddling and the tree of knowledge. Knowledge of the world of course leads Grimmelshausen's simpleton into error and sin; self-knowledge potentially brings him to salvation.

Simplicissimus, with its farcical episodes of cross dressing and interest in fashion and disguise, male bonding, and social hierarchy, additionally offers a wealth of material for scholars interested in the history of gender—in particular masculinity—and its representations. A look at Simplicius's failure to live up to the roles and responsibilities dictated by his social estate and his gender suggests new ways in which the eponymous hero must be not only viewed critically but as symptomatic of a world in crisis as a result of thirty years of warfare. With a work as complex, comprehensive, lively—and quite simply entertaining—as is *Simplicissimus*, there remains more to be learned. We can be certain that the next fifty years will bring new insights into this old yet perennially fresh text.

Bibliography of Translations in English in Chronological Order

Editions of Alfred Thomas Scrope Goodrick's Translation

The Adventurous Simplicissimus: being the description of the life of a strange vagabond, Melchior Sternfels von Fuchshaim. Translated by A. T. S. Goodrick. London: Heinemann, 1912.

Simplicissimus, The Vagabond. Translated by A. T. S. Goodrick. Introduced by William Rose. London: George Routledge & Sons, 1924; New York: E.P. Dutton & Co., 1924.

The Adventurous Simplicissimus. Translated by A. T. S. Goodrick. Preface by Eric Bentley. Lincoln, NE: University of Nebraska Press, 1962.

Simplicissimus. Translated by S. Goodrich [sic] (1912). Introduced by David Blow. Dedalus European Classics. Sawtry: Dadalus/Hippocrene, 1989. Reprint, Sawtry: Dedalus, 1995.

Other Translations

The Adventures of a Simpleton. Translated by Walter Wallich. London: The New English Library Limited, 1962; New York: Ungar, 1963.

Simplicius Simplicissimus. Translated by Hellmuth Weissenborn and Lesley MacDonald. Illustrated by Hellmuth Weissenborn. London: Calder, 1964.

The Adventures of Simplicius Simplicissimus. Translated by George Schulz-Behrend. Indianapolis, IN: Bobbs-Merrill, 1965.

The Adventures of Simplicissimus. Translated by John P. Spielman. Illustrated by Fritz Eichenberg. New York: Limited Editions Club, 1981.

An Unabridged Translation of Simplicius Simplicissimus. Translated, introduced and edited by Monte Adair. Landham, MD: University Press of America, 1986.

The Adventures of Simplicius Simplicissimus. Translated and introduced by George Schulz-Behrend. 2nd rev. ed. Columbia, S.C.: Camden House, 1993.

Simplicissimus. Translated and introduced by Mike Mitchell. Sawtry, Cambs: Dedalus, 1999.

Selected Bibliography of Secondary Works in English

Ashcroft, Jeffrey. "Ad Astra Volandum: Emblems and Imagery in Grimmelshausen's Simplicissimus." *MLR* 68 (1973): 843-62.

Aylett, Robert P. T. *The Nature of Realism in Grimmelshausen's "Simplicissimus" Cycle of Novels*. Europäische Hochschulschriften 1, Deutsche Sprache und Literatur 479. Bern: Lang, 1982.

___. "Lies, Damned Lies, and Simplex's Version of the Truth: Grimmelshausen's Unreliable Narrator." *Daphnis* 18 (1989): 159-77.

Battafarono, Italo Michele. "Grimmelshausen's 'Autobiographies' and the Art of the Novel." In Otto, *Companion Volume*, 45-91.

Bertsch, Janet. *Storytelling in the Works of Bunyan, Grimmelhausen, Defoe, and Schnabel*. Rochester, NY: Camden House, 2004.

Breuer, Dieter. "In Grimmelshausen's Tracks: The Literary and Cultural Legacy." In Otto, *Companion Volume*, 232-65.

Gillespie, Gerald. "From Duplicitous Delinquent to Superlative Simpleton: Simplicissimus and the German Baroque." In: *The Picaresque: A Symposium on the Rogue's Tale*, edited by Carmen Benito-Vessels and Michael Zappala, 107-22. Newark: University of Delaware Press, 1994. 107-22.

Greene, Shannon Keenan. "'To see from these black lines': The Mise en Livre of the Phoenix Copperplate and Other Grimmelshausen Illustrations." In Otto, *Companion Volume*, 333-56.

Haberkamm, Klaus. "Allegorical and Astrological Forms in the Works of Grimmelshausen with Special Emphasis on the Prophecy Motif." In Otto, *Companion Volume*, 93-145.

Hess, Peter. "The Poetics of Masquerade: Clothing and the Construction of Social, Religious, and Gender Identity in Grimmelshausen's *Simplicissimus*." In Otto, *Companion Volume*, 299-331.

Heckman, John. "Emblematic Structures in *Simplicissimus* Teutsch" *MLN* 84 (1969): 876-90.

Leblans, Anne. "Grimmelshausen and the Carnivalesque: The Polarization of Courtly and Popular Carnival in *Der abenteuerliche Simplicissimus*." MLN 105 (1990): 494-511.

Menhennet, Alan. *Grimmelshausen the Storyteller. A Study of the "Simplician" Novels.* Columbia, S.C.: Camden House, 1997.

Metzger, Michael and Erika Metzger. "The Thirty Years War and its Impact on Literature." In: *German Baroque Literature: The European Perspective*, edited by Gerhard Hoffmeiser, 38-51. New York: Ungar, 1983.

Negus, Kenneth. *Grimmelshausen*. Twayne World Author Series 291. New York: Twayne Publishers, 1974.

Otto, Karl F., Jr., ed. *A Companion to the Works of Grimmelshausen*. Rochester, NY: Camden House, 2003.

Paas, John Roger. "Applied Emblematics. The Figure on the Simplicissimus Frontispiece and its Places in Popular Devil-Iconography." *Colloquia Germanica* 13 (1980): 303-20.

Schade, Richard E. "Simplicius in Paris: The Allegory of the Beautiful Lutenist." *Monatshefte* 88.1 (Spring 1996): 31-42.

____."Text and Image. Representation in Grimmelshausen's Continuatio." *German Quarterly* 64 (1991): 138-48.

____. "Todsündendidaktik. On Its Function in Representational and Literary Art (Hans Sachs, Heinrich Julius, Grimmelshausen)." *Daphnis* 15. 2-3 (1986): 551-84.

____. "A War Story of Deceit, Gambling, and Sex: Simplicissimus at the Siege of Magdeburg (1636)." *Germanisch-Romanische Monatsschrift* 53.2 (2003): 155-81.

Spahr, Blake Lee. "Grimmelshausen's Simplicissimus: Astrological Structure?" *Daphnis* 1 (1977): 7-29.

Schweitzer, Christoph E. "Grimmelshausen and the Picaresque Novel." In Otto, *Companion Volume*, 147-64.

Schweitzer, Christoph E. "Problems in the Editions of Grimmelshausen's Works." In Otto, *Companion Volume*, 25-42.

Tatlock, Lynne. "Ab ovo: Reconceiving the Masculinity of the Autobiographical Subject." In: *The Graph of Sex and the German Text. Gendered Culture in Early Modern Germany 1500-1700*, edited by Lynne Tatlock and Christiane Bohnert, 383-412. Chloe 19. Amsterdam and Atlanta: Rodopi, 1994.

___. "Engendering Social Order: From Costume Autobiography to Conversation Games in Grimmelshausen's Simpliciana." In Otto, *Companion Volume*, 269-96.

___. ed. *Seventeenth Century German Prose*. The German Library 7. New York: Continuum, 1993.

Wagener, Hans. "Johann Jacob Christoffel von Grimmelshausen." In *German Baroque Writers, 1661-1730*, edited by James Hardin, 121-39. *Dictionary of Literary Biography* 168. Detroit, MI: Gale Research, 1996.

I thank Karl F. Otto, Jr., for his careful review of an earlier draft of this essay.

Preface

I FIRST MET JOHN C. OSBORNE IN KNOXVILLE IN 1965 WHEN I CAME TO THE University of Tennessee from the University of Oregon to be a full professor in the Department of Germanic and Slavic Languages, and eventually department head. John had been hired the year before as an associate professor, and he and I thus began a collegial association which was to last until my retirement, twenty-seven years later. John was heard to boast that in all these years we had not had a single altercation—I don't know if he realized how much this was due to my patience! John had come here from the University of Chicago, where he had been an assistant professor after securing his Ph.D. from Northwestern University in 1962.

John had gone to Duke as an undergraduate, and had spent his junior year in Switzerland. After college he became a U. S. Government interrogator in post-bellum Germany before continuing his studies at Northwestern. John Osborne played a major role in the success of an expanding German program. He not only planned and taught a number of graduate courses in German literature, but also he directed a record number of M.A. and Ph.D. theses. By the time he retired, Osborne had directed 25 M.A. theses and six doctoral dissertations, and, in all, served on fifty-two master's and seventeen doctoral thesis committees. On top of that he was in charge of developing holdings for the library, which still has a very respectable collection.

Robert Hiller, Osborne's collaborator at the University of Chicago, joined the University of Tennessee, and the two started translating works by H. J. C. von Grimmelshausen, Germany's greatest writer of the Baroque Era, the seventeenth century. His best known work was *Simplicissimus,* but he also wrote a number of shorter works that were more or less companion volumes. Bob and John started with *Die Land Störtzerin Courasche,* which was a good choice, as it was the inspiration for Bertolt Brecht's play *Mutter Courage,* well known in this country. It was published by the University of Nebraska Press in 1965 as *The Runagate Courage.* Next came *Der seltzame Springinsfeld,* which won the Fist Basilius Award given by Wayne State University. In 1981 Wayne State University Press published the work as *The Singular Life Story of Heedless Hopalong.*

There are two other smaller works among the Simplician Writings, *Das wundersame Vogelnest I* and *II*. A translation of the first by Hiller and Osborne was discovered among the Osborne papers, neatly typed and annotated, called, as one might expect, *Wondrous Bird's Nest I*. So far as is known, it had never been submitted for publication. *Bird's Nest II* seemed to be extant only in the original in John's minuscule and sometimes difficult handwriting. It has been typed and edited for publication.

After Bob Hiller retired, John continued alone and translated the entire *Simplicissimus*. A copy in the Osborne papers shows that it had been sent to Bob with a note, "Here it is. Tell me what you think." I suspect Bob never read it, as soon afterward he died of a heart attack. In 1987 Osborne won a University of Colorado Kayden Award for best literary translation of the year. Other Osborne publications include an article on Grimmelshausen with Hiller, a bibliography of German Romanticism, and a translation of a German history of Russian intellectual history with Martin Rice.

When in 1987 I stepped down from the headship, I moved to the office next to John's. John had a little radio in his office on which he played classical music all the time he was alone there. I told him I'd never be able to stand listening to that all day long and to my surprise he never played it when I was in my office after that. Maybe he was the patient one after all.

I retired in 1992, and John joined me in retirement in 1994. In the ensuing years he and his wife, Martha Lee (a professor of philosophy and head of Women's Studies at UT), did a lot of traveling to Europe and once to Egypt. Unfortunately, in 1997 he found out he had cancer. He received treatment for it in the Houston medical complex, and was able to live five more years before he succumbed on November 19, 2002. He was able to enjoy a virtually normal quality of life until a few weeks before his death.

John was one of the most intelligent men I have known. His knowledge of literature surpassed that of anybody else's in our department or anywhere else I have been. He was a very hard worker in every phase of academic life. We enjoyed, I think, mutual respect and a sort of affection for each other which I greatly prized.

Henry Kratz
Knoxville, Tennessee

A Note from Newfound Press:

Henry Kratz and Martha Lee Osborne, John Osborne's widow, submitted this manuscript to Newfound Press on March 16, 2006. We asked Professor Kratz to write a personal context for the work which follows. A professor of German at the University of Tennessee and a respected scholar of languages, Henry Kratz died on April 14, 2008.

Introduction

SIMPLICISSIMUS THE ADVENTURER (*DER ABENTHEUERLICHE Simplicissimus*), by Hans Jacob Christoffel von Grimmelshausen, is generally considered the greatest German novel of the seventeenth century, and apart from its literary value also contains a wealth of information about life in Germany in the Thirty Years' War. This work is accompanied and complemented by four shorter novels, *The Runagate Courage* (*Die Landstörzerin Courasche*), *The Strange Hopalong* (*Der seltzame Springinsfeld*), and *The Wondrous Bird's Nest I* and *II* (*Das wunderbarliche Vogel-Nest I* and *II*). These works together are known as the Simplician writings.

Simplicissimus the Adventurer is a picaresque narrative purporting to be the autobiography of the title character. According to his own account, Simplicissimus is a foundling of noble birth, who comes into the world on June 22, 1622, the date of the battle of Höchst during the Thirty Years' War (1618-1648). While still a small child he is forced to flee into the forest when his foster parents' home is attacked by marauding soldiers. For two years he lives in innocence and piety with an anchorite, who in reality is his natural father. When the anchorite dies, the boy wanders to the Protestant fortress of Hanau. In the garrison there he is dressed in fool's clothes because he is simple and naïve, but he soon learns the evil ways of the world and becomes an accomplished dissembler. While at play outside the fortress walls he is seized by an Imperialist raiding party, and after many hardships and adventures he reaches Westphalia, where his talent for taking booty makes him renowned as "the huntsman of Soest." Now his only thoughts are of material gain. For a time he lives in princely fashion in Cologne, but his fortunes change and he flees to Paris. After serving as apprentice to a quacksalver he becomes a famous opera singer and much sought-after gallant. But this life of ease and luxury is soon over, and he returns to Germany ailing and impoverished. He again joins the army, this time as a musketeer, then becomes the companion of highwaymen, and finally is appointed commander of a company of soldiers. When his best friend is wounded, Simplicissimus accompanies him to a watering place (Sauerbrunnen), where the friend dies. Simplicissimus then settles down as a farmer, but this is clearly not the life for him and he again sets out on adventures that take him to Moscow, whence he returns to Germany by way of Egypt, Italy, and Switzerland. Home once more, he realizes the vanity of his quest for worldly fame and fortune. Like his father before him, he withdraws from the world to end his days as an anchorite.

Simplicissimus made its first appearance, presumably, at the Frankfurt spring book fair of 1668, then it went through five editions, at least two of which went into a second printing. Perhaps the best indication of its popularity is the number of other literary works which attempted to capitalize on its success. By 1675 fifteen different books had been published which treated characters from *Simplicissimus*, or were supposed to be written by Simplicissimus or one of the Simplician characters, or mentioned the words "Simplicissimus" or "Simplician" prominently in the title; and by 1700 more than thirty such works had appeared.

The real name of the author of *Simplicissimus* and other Simplician novels was not known until well into the nineteenth century, in 1838. The author himself was in no small measure responsible for this situation, for he delighted in attributing his works to persons with fanciful names, all of which were anagrams of one another. *Simplicissimus* allegedly was composed by one German Schleifheim von Sulsfort, and Philarchus Grossus von Trommenheim is listed as the author of both *Courage and Hopalong*. The first part of *The Wondrous Bird's Nest* is attributed to Michael Rechulin von Sehmsdorf, but the second part has in place of an author's name a string of initials - A C EEE FF G HH II LL MM NN OO RR SSS T UU - the letters from which, more or less, the preceding names are composed. The authors of other Simplician writings bear yet other anagrammatic names: Simon Lengfrisch von Hartenfels, Erich Steinfels von Grufensholm, and Israel Fromschmidt von Hugenfelz.

A century of painstaking research has proved that the life of Grimmelshausen was quite different from that of his hero. So far as can be ascertained, Hans Jacob Christoffel von Grimmelshausen was born in or near Gelnhausen, a village in the Spessart, in either 1621 or 1622. While he was yet a child his father died and his mother remarried and moved away, leaving him in the care of his paternal grandparents, who were well-to-do but by no means wealthy. At the age of six or seven Grimmelshausen began attending the Lutheran school at Gelnhausen, receiving instruction in reading, writing, arithmetic, Latin, and the tenets of the Augsburg Confession. His formal schooling ended in September, 1634, when Protestant Gelnhausen was taken and plundered by Catholic Imperial troops. Apparently his grandparents took him to the Protestant fortress of Hanau in early December, but in January while he was playing outside the fortifications the lad was seized by an Imperial raiding party. A month or so later he was captured by anti-Imperialist Hessian troops and taken to Cassel. In the summer of 1636 he apparently was present at the second siege of Magdeburg and at the battle of Wittstock. During the winter of 1636-1637 he is presumed to have been at the Imperial winter quarters in Soest, where he joined a regiment of dragoons under the command of the Imperial field marshal, Count Götz, and participated in the campaigns of 1637 and 1638 along the Upper Rhine. During the spring of 1638 Götz' army set out to succor the garrison at Breisach, then under siege by Protestant forces. En route Götz took Offenburg, a fortified city on the Kinzig River not far from the Rhine, but the attempt to relieve Breisach failed. After wintering with the army in Suabia, Grimmelshausen returned to Offenburg and enlisted as a musketeer in the regiment of Lieutenant Colonel Hans Reinhard von Schauenburg. In 1640 he was assigned as scribe to the regimental secretary and served in this capacity until 1647; he was then transferred to another Imperial fortress, Wasserburg, and served as regimental secretary under von Schauenburg's brother-in-law, Colonel Johann Burkard von Elter, until the end of the war.

Grimmelshausen's connection with the von Schauenburgs did not end with the war. After his return to Offenburg and his marriage on August 30, 1649, to an officer's daughter, Katharina Henninger, he was appointed steward (*Schaffner*) of the hereditary von Schauenburg domains in and around Gaisbach, a village in the Rench valley near Oberkirch. Grimmelshausen began his stewardship as the servant of three masters, Hans Reinhard, his former commanding officer, and two other von Schauenburgs, Carl Bernhard and Claus. He fell out of favor with Claus, but continued to serve the other two until 1655, when he gave up Carl's stewardship, presumably because his work for Hans Reinhard was almost more than he could manage. His duties included keeping all accounts, attending to minor legal matters concerning financial transactions, and collecting the fees, duties, and taxes due the lords of the estate. He was, in addition, Hans Reinhard's private secretary and in his behalf undertook inspections of the widely scattered von Schauenburg properties. For all these services he apparently was paid the modest sum of about thirty sovereigns a year.

In 1653 Grimmelshausen succeeded in acquiring a rundown piece of property in Gaisbach, the "Spitalbühne"—it appears in his works as "Hybspinthal"—where the foreword to *Satyrischer Pilgram* and the Dedication to *Dietward und Amelind* allegedly were composed. He built two houses on the Spitalbühne, occupying one of them, and at the same time continued to maintain a residence in Gaisbach at Hans Reinhard's steward's house. In 1657 he acquired a permanent home in Gaisbach by trading his unoccupied house on the Spitalbühne for the steward's house belonging to Phillip Hannibal von Schauenberg, son and heir of the now deceased Claus. As part of the bargain, Grimmelshausen received the privilege of maintaining a public house in the large room on the ground floor.

As was customary at the time, he had speculated with the properties and income of the family he served, and his debts to them gradually increased until at last, on September 7, 1660, Grimmelshausen relinquished his post as steward, possibly at Hans Reinhard's request. Until 1662 he seems to have supported himself and his growing family by plying the innkeeper's trade "at the sign of the Silver Star"; then he was entrusted with a stewardship by a wealthy Strassburg doctor, Johann Küffer the Younger, who had acquired some property near Gaisbach and was setting himself up as a country squire. This time too his stewardship ended with hard feelings, and the year 1666 saw him once more employed as innkeeper. Now, however, in order to earn more money for his ever increasing family (all told he had ten children), Grimmelshausen began to spend much of his time in the second-floor study of the steward's house, composing some of the works which were to make him famous.

On March 16, 1667, he was appointed chief magistrate (*Schultheiss*) of Renchen, a village of about seven hundred people, seat of one of the six courts under the jurisdiction of the Oberkirch district, one of the eleven districts making up the secular possessions of the bishopric of Strassburg. As well as presiding over the court, the chief magistrate was charged with collecting taxes, carrying out the orders of the community's governor (*Obervogt*), guarding public funds set aside for Renchen's orphans and wards, and ensuring public safety and obedience to the laws and ordinances. Grimmelshausen continued to serve in this post until his death on August 16, 1676.

John C. Osborne
Knoxville, Tennessee

Simplicissimus, The German Adventurer

BOOK I

Describes the rustic origins of Simplicius and how he was brought up in keeping therewith

Amongst the common folk[1] there has manifested itself in this age in which we live (which many believe to be the last one) a malady whose sufferers—when they lie ill with it and have scratched and scraped together sufficient money so that they can have, besides a few coppers in their purse, a ridiculous looking suit of clothes in the new fashion, bedizened with a thousand different kinds of silk ribbons, or have come to be, by a stroke of good fortune, well known and men of parts—forthwith maintain that they are gentlemen to the manor born and noblemen of ancient lineage, even though it often turns out that their forefathers were day laborers, carters, and porters, their cousins ass drivers, their brothers jailers and constables, their sisters harlots, their mothers bawds or even witches, and, *in summa summarum,*[2] their entire family, back to their thirty-two great-great-great-grandparents, as soiled and sullied as ever the Sugar Boy gang[3] in Prague was; indeed, these new *nobilistes*[4] are themselves often as black as if they had been born and bred in Guinea. Now to these foolish folk I should not like to be compared, even though, to tell the truth, it is indeed a fact that I have often thought that I surely must needs have been descended from a great lord, or at least from a gentleman, because by nature I would be inclined to pursue the life of an aristocrat had I but the means and wherewithal to do so. But all jesting aside, my family origins and upbringing can indeed be compared to those of a prince, if one but be willing to overlook one great difference. What difference? My Pa[5] (for that is what a father is called in the Spessart Forest)[6] had a fine palace of his own like any other nobleman, indeed, one so nice as not every king can build with his own hands, nor will ever in all eternity undertake to build. It was daubed with clay and roofed not with barren slate, cold lead, and red copper, but with straw, on which noble grain grows. And so that he, my Pa, might properly blazon forth his nobility and wealth, he did not, as other great lords are wont to do, have the wall around his castle constructed of field stones, which are found by the road or dug up in barren places, much less of common bricks, which can be manufactured and fired in a short while; rather, he took for this purpose the wood of the oak, which useful and noble tree[7] furnishes the beams in smokehouses from which sausages and fat hams are hung and which takes over a hundred years to attain its full maturity. Where is the monarch who emulates him in this?

His rooms, halls, and chambers he had let smoke completely blacken on the inside, for the sole reason that black is the most steadfast color in the world and that this sort of painting takes for its perfection more time than an artful painter requires for his excellent works of art. The tapestries were the most delicately woven ones on the entire earth, for they were made for us by the very weaver[8] who ages ago made so bold as to compete in spinning with Minerva herself. His windows were dedicated to St. Papyrus[9] for no other reason than that he knew that it takes more time and effort to make paper,[10] if one reckon the time from the sowing of the hemp or flax seed till the paper has been completely manufactured, than it takes to manufacture the best and most transparent glass from Murano,[11] because his station made him choose to believe that everything which is accomplished through much effort is valuable and all the more precious, and whatever is precious is most proper for a nobleman. Instead of pages, lackeys, and stableboys he had sheep, goats, and swine, each nicely and properly attired in its own livery, which retinue also often waited upon me on the pasture till I drove them home. His arsenal or armory was sufficiently stocked with plows, hoes, axes, mattocks, shovels, pitchforks, and hayforks, with which weapons he exercised every day, for hoeing and plowing were his *disciplina militaris,*[12] as they were for the ancient Romans in times of peace. Yoking oxen was his general *commando;*[13] hauling manure, his construction of fortifications; plowing his military campaign; and cleaning stables, his princely pastime and sport. In such wise he made war upon the entire globe, as far as he could reach, and at every harvest took rich booty from it. To all this I attach no great importance, and I do not at all boast about it, lest I be derided along with the other new *nobilistes* of my ilk, for I do not esteem myself to be any better than my Pa, who had this dwelling of his in a very pleasant spot, namely in the Spessart Forest, which is so desolate that it is a wilderness still peopled by its original inhabitants: wolves. And in the interest of brevity I do not, at this juncture, give any particulars about Pa's family, heritage, and name, because it is not my purpose here[14] anyway to swear an oath that I am of the nobility. It will suffice if the Reader knows that I was born in the Spessart Forest.

Now just as my Pa's household, as will have been noted, was very noble, so also anyone with good sense can easily conclude that my upbringing was similar to and commensurate with it; and anyone who so thinks will not be deceived either, for by my tenth year I had already comprehended the *principia*[15] of my Pa's princely *exercitia,*[16] while in regard to book-learning I could pass for the famous Amphistides,[17] of whom Suidas reports that he could not count above five, for my Pa chanced to be much too highminded and therefore followed the usual custom of our times, which is that folk of gentle birth do not trouble themselves much about book-learning or, as they call it, "wasting their time in school," because they have people to do their ink-squiggling for them. For the rest, I was an excellent *musicus* on the bagpipe, on which I could make beautiful *Jalemi* songs;[18] but as regards *theologia*[19] I refuse to believe that at that time there was anyone of my age in all Christendom who was my equal, for I knew nothing about man or God, heaven or hell, angel or devil, nor could I distinguish between good and evil. It is therefore not difficult to imagine that, given this *theologia*, I lived like Adam and Eve in the Garden of Eden, who in their innocence knew nothing of sickness, death, and dying, much less of life after death. O wonderful life of nobility (you might well call it a life of no ability) wherein one does not even trouble oneself about medicine! Using *theologia* as a norm, one can also judge how much I knew about *studio legum*[20] and all the arts and sciences, as many as there be in the world. Indeed, I was so perfect and complete in my want of knowledge that it was impossible for me to know that I did not know anything at all. I say again: O the life of nobility which then I led! But my Pa did not desire to let me enjoy this life of bliss any longer, but rather deemed it fitting that I in keeping with my noble birth, should also behave and live like a nobleman, for which reason he began to draw me on to higher things and to charge me with more difficult *lectiones*.[21]

CHAPTER 2

Describes the first stage of nobility to which Simplicius rose, together with an encomium to shepherds, with appended excellent instructions

He bestowed upon me the most splendid post that there is, not only at his court but in the entire world namely, the office of herdsman. First, he entrusted me with his swine, secondly with his goats, and finally with his whole flock of sheep, that I should tend them, feed them, and protect them from the wolves by means of my bagpipe (the sound of which alone, as Strabo[22] writes, makes the sheep and lambs in Arabia fat). At that time I was quite like David, except that instead of a bagpipe he had but a harp, which was not a bad beginning for me, but rather a good omen that in time, had I any good fortune, I should become a world-renowned man; for since the beginning of the world,[23] persons of high estate have at some time in their lives been herdsmen, as we read in Holy Scripture of Abel, Abraham, Isaac, Jacob, his sons, and Moses[24] himself, who was obliged to tend his father's sheep before he became the general and *legislator* over 600,000 men in Israel. "Aye," some may object, "those were holy men devoted to God, not peasant lads from the Spessart Forest who knew nothing of God." I must own that to be true, but should my innocence at that time be held against me? Amongst the heathens of yore one also finds such *exempla* as are found amongst God's chosen people. Amongst the Romans there were aristocratic families who were without doubt named Bubulcus, Statilus, Pomponius, Vitulus, Vitellios, Annius, Caprus,[25] and the like because they worked with the animals which were so named, and perhaps they even tended those animals too. Indeed, Romulus and Remus[26] were themselves herdsmen. Spartacus,[27] of whom the entire Roman Empire was so terrified, was a herdsman. And? Others who were herdsmen were (as Lucian[28] asserts in his *dialogo Helenae*) Paris,[29] the son of King Priam, and Anchises,[30] the father of the Trojan prince Aeneas; handsome Endymion,[31] for whose love chaste Luna herself vied, was also a herdsman; *item*, grisly Polyphemus.[32] Aye, the gods themselves (as Phornutus[33] says) were not ashamed of this profession: Apollo[34] tended the kine of Admetus, King of Thessaly; Mercury,[35] his son Daphnis, Pan,[36] and Proteus[37] were herdsmen of the first order and are therefore still the patrons of herdsmen in silly poets' works. Mesha,[38] King in Moab, was, as we read in the second book of Kings, a herdsman. Cyrus,[39] the powerful king of the Persians, was not only brought up by Mithridates, a herdsman; he himself tended herds too. Gyges[40] was a herdsman and later, through the power of a ring, a king. Ismael Sophi,[41] a Persian king, likewise tended cattle in his youth, so that Philo the Jew[42] speaks excellent well on the matter in his *vita Moysis* when he says: the office of herds- man is preparation for and the beginning of ruling over men; for just as the *bellicosa* and *martiala ingenia*[43] are first taught and practiced in the hunt, so those who are to be educated to rule ought first to be trained in the lovely and amiable office of the herdsman; all of which my Pa must needs have well understood, and which to this very day gives me no slight hope for future grandeur.

But to return to my flock:[44] You must know that I knew as little about wolves as I did about my own lack of knowledge. Therefore my Pa was all the more assiduous in his *instructio*. He said: "Boy, be alert! Don' let them sheep go a-runnin' too fur from one another, an' play the bagpipe loud, so the wolf don' come and do no harm, 'cuz he be a four-laiged rogue and thief who'll gobble up man 'n' beast, an 'if'n you don' take care I'll beat yer bottom!" I answered with equal civility: "Pa, tell me what this here wolf look like. I ain't never seen no wolf." "Eh, ya stupid rascal," he replied, "ye'll stay a fool yer whole life long. I wunner what'll ever come o;' ya, yer already such a big lummox an' don' even know yet what a four-laiged rogue the wolf be." He gave me yet more instructions and at last grew angry, for which reason he went off grumbling, because he was of the opinion that my slow wit would not be able to grasp his subtle instructions.

CHAPTER 3

Reports of the fellow-suffering of a loyal bagpipe

So I fell to making such a racket[45] with my bagpipe that you might well have poisoned the toads in the herb-garden with it, so that I thought myself safe from the wolf, which was ever on my mind. And since I remembered that my Ma (that is what a mother is called in the Spessart Forest and on Vogelsberg Mountain)[46] had often said that she feared that the hens would some day die from my music, I thought it proper to sing too, so that the *remedium* for the wolf might be all the more powerful, and in fact I sang a song which I had learned from my Ma herself:

The Peasant's Song[47]

O Peasantry, so oft maligned,

And yet the best of all mankind,

If one but closely look at you,

One must give you your proper due.

What would the world look like right now

If Adam had not toiled with plow?

The man today of noble birth

Descends from one who tilled the earth.

All of the earth is for your use.

Whatever foods your fields produce,

What feeds the folk in ev'ry land

Must first go through the peasant's hand.

The Emperor, whom God did give

Us as a shield, he too must live

From what you grow; the soldier too,
Who oft inflicts great harm on you.

You grow the meat on which we dine,
You grow the grapes which give us wine,
You grow the grain which gives us bread.
Your plow assures that we're well fed.

The eart were wasteland ev'rywhere
If peasants were not dwelling there.
This earth were dismal, dire and drear
If there were no more peasants here.

To honor you is only fair.
You nourish mankind ev'rywhere.
Fair Nature gives you her love too,
And God approves of what you do.

You're hale and hearty, strong and stout.
What peasant e'er came down with gout?
For gout's a nobleman's disease,
Which kills them as live lives of ease.

You're free of Pride, the worst disease,
Especially in times like these,
And that you might escape its snare,
God gave you one more cross to bear:

The baneful things which soldiers do
Turn out to be a boon for you:
That you may not to Pride incline,
The soldier says: "What's yours is mine!"

This far and no further did I get with my song, for I, together with my flock of sheep, was surrounded in a trice as it were by a troop of cuirassiers[48] who had lost their way in the great forest and had been put back on the right path by my music and shepherd-cries.

"Oho!" thought I. "These are the fellows, all right! These are the four-legged rogues and thieves about which Pa told you." For at first I took horse and rider (as the American Indians did[49] the Spanish cavalry heretofore) to be a single creature, and therefore I could not but think that they must be wolves. And therefore I wished to chase these dreadful *centauris*[50] away and be rid of them again, but I had scarce blown up my bagpipe for this purpose when one of them grabbed me by the wing and hurled me so violently onto an empty plow-horse, which they had taken, together with others, as booty, that I could not but fall off on the other side on top of my dear bagpipe, which began to shriek as pitiably as if it had wished to move the entire world to pity; but it was of no avail, even though it did not spare even its last gasp in lamenting my fall; I was simply compelled to get back up on the horse, no matter what my bagpipe said or sang; and what vexed me the most was that the troopers claimed that I had hurt the bagpipe when I fell upon it, which was why it had screamed bloody murder. And so my mare[51] took me along at a steady trot, like the *primum mobile*, till we reached my Pa's farm. Wondrous strange notions were flitting about in my brain, for I fancied, because I was sitting upon this beast, the likes of which I had never seen before, that I too would be changed into such an iron fellow, but because this transformation did not take place, other crotchets came to my mind; I thought that these strange critters were there for the sole purpose of helping me drive home the sheep, since none of them ate up any of my sheep, but instead hurried along as if of one mind, and in fact towards my Pa's farm by the most direct way. Therefore I looked around sharply for my Pa, to see whether he and my Ma were not going to come soon to meet us and to bid us welcome, but in vain, for he and my Ma, together with our Ursula, who was Pa's only daughter, had fled out the back door and were not of a mind to await the arrival of these guests.

CHAPTER 4

Simplicius' palace is conquered, plundered, and destroyed, and the soldiers do terrible damage in it

Though I did not intend to take you, peace-loving Reader, along with these troopers to my Pa's house and home, because rather bad things will happen there, the course of my history nevertheless requires that I leave to esteemed posterity the story of what atrocities[52] were now and again perpetrated during this German war of ours,[53] and particularly that I demonstrate by my own example that all such evils often must have been ordained by the goodness of the Almighty for our own good. For, dear Reader, who would have told me that there is a God in heaven, had soldiers not destroyed my Pa's house and, by capturing me, compelled me to go out amongst the people of the world, from whom I received sufficient instruction in this matter? Shortly before, I could neither know nor imagine anything but that my Pa, my Ma, I, and the rest of the household were all alone on earth, because no other human being was known to me, nor any other human habitation but the one I went into and out of each day. But soon afterwards I learned how human beings came into this world and that they were obliged to leave it again. I was a human being in shape only, and a Christian in name only, and otherwise no more than a beast! But the Almighty looked with pitying eyes upon my innocence and resolved to bring me to know both Him and myself, and though He had thousands of ways to accomplish this, He without doubt wished to avail Himself only of that one in which my Pa and Ma, as an example to others, would be punished for the dilatory way in which they had brought me up.

The first thing that these troopers did was to stable their horses. After that each had his special task to perform, and each task augured nothing but death and destruction; for while some of them began to slaughter the animals and to boil and bake their flesh, so that it looked as if a merry banquet were going to be held there, there were others who stormed through the house, upstairs and down; indeed, not even the privy was spared, for they searched it as if the Golden Fleece of Colchis[54] were concealed in it. Others packed up in large bundles our cloth, clothes, and all manner of household goods, as if they were going to set up a shop somewhere to sell second-hand wares; and what they did not mean to take along was smashed to pieces. Some thrust their swords into the hay and straw, as if they did not have enough sheep and swine to stick; some shook the down out of the mattresses and filled them instead with bacon, dried meat, and even household stuff, as if they would then be better to sleep upon; others smashed in the stove and the windows, just as if they were proclaiming an everlasting summer. They beat the copper and pewter houseware flat and packed up the bent and ruined pieces of it. The bedsteads, tables, chairs, and benches they burned, even though many cords of dry firewood were stacked in the yard. Earthenware pots and bowls were broken up, either because the troopers preferred to eat roasted meat or because they had in mind to eat but one meal there. Our maid was man handled in the stable in such wise that she could scarce stand up and walk out of it, which is certainly a shame to report! The hired man they tied up and laid on the ground, thrust a piece of wood into his mouth to hold his jaws open, and poured a milk-pail full of vile liquid manure down his throat; this they called a "Swedish punch,"[55] and with it they compelled him to lead a party of them to other places, where they took away people and animals and brought them to our farm, amongst which folk were also my Pa, my Ma, and our Ursula.

Then they set to unscrewing the flints from their pistols and to screwing in their place the peasants' thumbs, and to torturing the poor rascals, just as if they were witches headed for the stake; in fact, they had already thrust one peasant they had captured into a bake-oven and were after him with fire, despite the fact that he had not yet confessed to anything. Around the head of another one they put a rope and twisted it tight with a stick till the blood spewed from his mouth, nose, and ears. *In summa*, each had his own special way of torturing the peasants, and thus each peasant had his own particular torture. But my Pa,[56] to my way of thinking at the time, was the luckiest one, because he confessed with laughter what others were obliged to say with pain and heart-rending laments, and no doubt this honor was accorded him because he was the head of the household, for they set him down by the fire, bound him so that he could move neither his hands nor his feet, and rubbed onto the soles of his feet moistened salt, which our old nanny goat was obliged to lick off again and thereby tickle him so that he nearly died laughing. That looked like such fun to me that I, either to keep him company or because I knew no better, could not but laugh most heartily along with him. In the midst of this laughter he confessed what they desired of him and revealed the location of a hidden treasure, which was much richer in gold, pearls, and jewelry than one might have supposed a peasant to possess. Of the women, maids, and girls I know nothing in particular to report, because the troopers did not let me watch how they dealt with them. I do know, however, that now and again one heard some of them scream pitiably inside the house, and I judge indeed that my Ma and Ursula fared no better than the others. Amidst this misery I turned the roasting spit, and in the afternoon I helped water the horses, during which task I came upon our maid in the stable, who looked so terribly tousled that I did not recognize her, and she spoke to me in a faint voice: "Boy, run away, else the troopers will take you with them. See that you get away from here; surely you can see how badly...." That was all she was able to say.

CHAPTER 5

How Simplicius ran away and was frighted by rotted trees

Then I straightway fell to considering my unfortunate condition, which I saw with my own eyes, and to pondering how I might best make good my escape. But whither should I go? My wit was much too slight to suggest anything to me in that regard, but I did succeed, on towards evening, in running away into the forest. But now, whither should I go from there? The footpaths and the forest were as little known to me as the road to China through the frozen sea beyond Nova Zembla.[57] To be sure, the pitch-black night covered me for my protection, but to my unenlightened mind it still seemed all too light. Therefore I hid myself in a clump of bushes where I could hear not only the screams of the peasants, who were being tortured, but also the singing of the nightingales, which little birds did not deem it necessary to feel compassion for the peasants, whom some folks are wont to call "birds" too, or to stop their lovely singing because of the peasants' misfortune. Therefore, without a care in the world I laid me down and went to sleep. But when the morning star flickered in the east, I saw my Pa's house engulfed in flames, and no one willing to put the fire out. I ventured forth in the hope of coming upon someone from my Pa's household, but I was straightway espied by five troopers, who screamed to me: "Young 'un! Come over here or, the divil take me, I'll fill you so full o' hot lead that smoke'll come out o'yer mouth!" I, for my part, stood stock-still, my mouth agape, because I knew not what the trooper desired or meant, and as I was looking at them this way, like a cat at a new barndoor, and they could not get to me because of a swamp which lay between us, which undoubtedly sorely vexed them, one of them fired his carbine at me, from which abrupt fire and unexpected bang, which Echo made all the more terrifying with manifold reverberations, I was so frightened that I forthwith fell to the ground. I was so frightened that I did not bat an eyelash, and though the troopers rode on their way and without doubt left me there for dead, that whole day long I had not the courage to get up. But when night overtook me again I did stand up and wander forth into the forest till I saw a dead tree shimmering from afar, which again filled me with fear, and I therefore turned around posthaste and kept walking till I espied another tree of that sort, from which I likewise ran away again, and in this manner I passed the night, running back and forth from one dead tree to another. At last sweet Dawn came to my aid by commanding the trees to leave me in peace in her presence, but this was still of no help to me, for my heart was full of fear, my limbs full of fatigue, my empty stomach full of hunger, my mouth full of thirst, my brain full of foolish notions, and my eyes full of sleep. I nevertheless kept on walking, I knew not whither, and the further I walked, the deeper into the forest and the further from people I came. At that time I endured and experienced (but without remarking it at all) the result of being without good sense and knowledge. Had a mindless beast been in my place, it would have better known what it should have done to preserve itself, and yet I did have enough of my wits about me, when night once more overtook me, to crawl into a hollow tree and make it my resting place for the night.

CHAPTER 6

A short chapter, and so pious that Simplicius falls into a swoon

I had scarce settled down to go to sleep when I heard a voice which said: "O what great love Thou hast for us ungrateful mortals! Alas, Thou art my sole consolation! My hope, my riches, my God!" and so much more of the like that I could not mark or understand all of it.[58]

These were indeed words which should rightly have cheered, consoled, and delighted a Christian who was in the condition I was in at that time. But, O simplemindedness and ignorance! I could not make head nor tail of them, and it was all completely Greek to me, a language of which I could not only not understand anything, but also one whose strangeness terrified me. But when I heard that the hunger and thirst of him who was speaking it were to be stilled, my unbearable hunger counseled me to invite myself to be his guest. Therefore I mustered up the courage to step out of my hollow tree and to approach the voice I had heard. Then I espied a tall man with long greyblack hair which was all tangled up and hanging down to his shoulders; he had an unkempt beard shaped almost like a Swiss cheese;

his face, to be sure, was pale yellow and haggard, yet still rather lovely to look upon; and his coat was mended and patched with more than a thousand pieces of all kinds of cloth; around his neck and body he had wound a heavy iron chain such as St. William wears,[59] and to my eyes he appeared in other respects so horrid and frightening that I fell to trembling like a leaf; and what increased my fear was the fact that he was pressing to his breast a crucifix about six feet tall, and because I knew not what it was, I could come to no other conclusion but that this old man must needs be the wolf[60] of which my Pa had told me shortly before. In this anxiety I whisked out with my bagpipe, which was the only treasure I had saved from the troopers; I blew up the bag, pressed the keys, and let a mighty sound be heard, to drive away this dreadful wolf, at which sudden and unusual music in so desolate a place the hermit was at first not a little startled, thinking without doubt that perchance a demonic spirit had come to torment him, as had happened to St. Anthony the Great,[61] and to disrupt his devotions. But as soon as he recovered he, taking me to be his tempter, jeered at me in the hollow tree into which I had again retreated; indeed, he was so confident that he walked towards me in order to properly deride the enemy of the human race. "Ha!" said he. "Thou art a proper fellow to beleaguer saints without divine decree, etc." More I did not understand, for his approach aroused in me such horror and fright that I was bereft of my senses and fell into a swoon then and there.

CHAPTER 7

Simplicius is treated like a friend in humble quarters

In what manner I was helped come back to my senses I do not know, but this I do well know: that when I did come back to my senses the old man had my head in his lap and had opened my jacket in the front. When I saw the hermit so close to me, I fell to screaming terribly, as if he had been at that very moment about to tear my heart out of my body. He, however, said: "Be quiet, my son. I am not going to do anything to you. Do not be afraid. etc." But the more he comforted and caressed me, the more I screamed: "O, you're going to eat me up! O, you're going to eat me up! You're the wolf and wish to eat me up!" "Not at all, my son." said he. "Do not be afraid. I am not going to eat you up." This battle lasted a long while, till I finally let myself be so far persuaded as to go into his hut with him. In it Poverty herself was the court stewardess, Hunger the cook, and Want the master of the kitchen. There my stomach was revived with vegetables and a drink of water, and my spirits, which were completely distraught, were raised up and set aright again by the old man's comforting friendliness. Therefore I easily let myself be deluded by the charm of sweet Sleep into paying my debt to Nature. The hermit saw my need to sleep, and so he let me have a place alone in his hut, because but one person could lie down in it. At about midnight I awoke again and heard him singing the following song, which I later learned by heart:

> Sweet bird of night, thou nightingale,
> Come, let thy dulcet tones regale
> The world with joyous singing!
> Come, praise Him who made me and thee,
> For others, sleeping peacefully,
> Have put aside their singing.
> > So lift thy voice now,

> Sweet and clear, in songs of cheer,
> In songs of love
> To our Lord God in Heav'n above!
> And though the sun no longer shines,
> Though darkness now the world confines,
> We still shall keep on singing
> Of God's beneficence and might,
> So even in the dark of night
> His praises still are ringing!
> > So lift thy voice now, etc.

> And echoes, ringing through the dale,
> Now wish to join thee, nightingale,
> And let God hear their ringing.
> They frighten mortal sleep away,
> To which we are in thrall each day,
> So we can hear them singing.
> > So lift thy voice now, etc.

The stars in heaven, shining bright,

Are praise to God this starry night;

To Him they're honor bringing.

The owl, who cannot sing at all,

Proves by her rasping, hooting call:

God's praise she too is singing!

    So lift thy voice now, etc.

So come, my darling little bird,

And we shall show by song and word:

To sleep we'll not be clinging!

For till the dawn comes fresh and clear

O'er these dark virgin forests here

God's praises we'll keep singing!

    So lift thy voice now, etc.

While this song lasted, it did truly seem to me as if the nightingale, and the owl and Echo too, had joined in the singing, and if I had ever heard the hymn "O Morning Star, How Fair and Bright!"[62] or were able to make up the melody to it on my bagpipe, I should have whisked out of the hut to join in the music-making, because this *harmonia* sounded so sweet to me; but I fell asleep and did not wake up again till well into the day, at which time the hermit was standing before me and saying: "Get up, child. I shall give you something to eat and then show you the way through the forest so that you may get back to where there are people and to the next village well before nightfall." I asked him: "What are those? 'People' and 'village'?" "Good heavens!" answered the hermit. "Are you a stupid or a clever boy?" "No," said I, "my Ma's and Pa's boy is who I am, not Stupid's or Clever's boy." The hermit, sighing and crossing himself, was astonished and said: "All right, my dear child, I have been chosen to instruct you better, for the sake of God." Then our queries and responses fell out as is shown in the following chapter.

CHAPTER 8

How Simplicius, by means of exalted eloquence, gives evidence of his excellence

Hermit: What is your name?

Simplicius: My name is Boy.

Hermit: I can well see that you are not a girl. What did your father and mother call you?

Simplicius: I don't have any father and mother.

Hermit: Then who gave you that shirt you're wearing?

Simplicius: O, my Ma.

Hermit: Then what did your Ma call you?

Simplicius: She called me "boy" and "rascal" and "clumsy oaf" and "gallows-bird."

Hermit: And who was your Ma's husband?

Simplicius: Nobody.

Hermit: With whom did your Ma sleep at night?

Simplicius: With my Pa.

Hermit: And what did your Pa call you?

Simplicius: He called me "boy" too.

Hermit: And what is your Pa's name?

Simplicius: His name is "Pa."

Hermit: Well, what did your Ma call him?

Simplicius: "Pa," and also "Sir."

Hermit: Did she never call him by any other name?

Simplicius: Yes, she did.

Hermit: Well, what name was it?

Simplicius: "Lout," "boor," "drunken pig," and other names too, when they fell quarreling.

Hermit: You are truly an ignorant fool not to know either your parents' name or your own.

Simplicius: O? Well you don't know them either.

Hermit: Do you know how to pray?

Simplicius: Of course! I pray the bagpipe.

Hermit: I am not asking about that, but whether you know the Lord's Prayer.

Simplicius: Yes, I do.

Hermit: Well then, let me hear you say it.

Simplicius: Our Father witch art in heaven, hollow be Thy   name, Thy kingdom comes, Thy will done in heaven and earth, give us debts as we give our debtors, lead us not into evil temptation, but deliver us from the kingdom and the power and the glory, world without end Amen.

Hermit: Have you never been to church? Do you not know anything about Jesus?

Simplicius: Of course I do! My Pa always had cheeses. I liked the ones best that he hung in the smokehouse with the hams.

Hermit: Not cheeses, Jesus! Jee! Jee!

Simplicius: Oh, I know what you mean. Ox words!

Hermit: Ox words?

Simplicius: Yes. "Gee" is what you say to the ox to go this away, and "haw" to tell it to go that away.

Hermit: Heavens above! Do you know nothing about our Lord God?

Simplicius: Of course I do. He stood by our parlor door at home, on the house-altar. My Ma brought him back from a fair and pinned him up there.

Hermit: O merciful God! Now I realize for the first time what a great act of mercy and beneficence it is for him to whom Thou impartest knowledge of Thyself, and how no one to whom Thou doest not give it may be called a human being. O Lord, vouch safe me so to honor Thy holy name that I become worthy to thank Thee as fervently for this sublime act of mercy as Thou hast been generous in granting it to me. Hark you, Simplicius! (for I know not what else to call you). When you say the Lord's Prayer, you must speak it this way: Our Father, which art in Heaven, hallowed be Thy name. Thy kingdom come, Thy Will be done, on earth as 'tis in heaven. Give us this day our daily bread, and—

Simplicius: —and cheese to go on with too! Isn't that right?

Hermit: Ah, my dear child! Be quiet and learn. You have much more need of this than of cheese. 'Tis not the place of boys like you to interrupt an old man, but rather to be silent, to listen, and to learn. If I but knew where your parents dwelt, I should gladly take you back to them, and at the same time teach them how they ought to bring up their children.

Simplicius: I know not whither I ought go—our house is burnt down, and my Ma ran away and came back with Ursula,[63] and my Pa too, and our maidservant was sick and lying in the stable.

Hermit: Who burned your house down?

Simplicius: Uh, the iron men who came, sitting on these things, as big as oxen, but they had no horns; these here men slaughtered our sheep and cows and swine, and then I ran away too, and after that the house was burned down.

Hermit: But where was your Pa?

Simplicius: O, the iron men tied him up, then our old nanny goat licked his feet, and my Pa could not but laugh, and he gave these here iron men lots of white pennies, big ones and little ones, and pretty yellow ones too, and other beautiful glittering things, and pretty strings full of little white peas.

Hermit: When did this happen?

Simplicius: Why, when I was supposed to be tending the sheep. They tried to take away my bagpipe too.

Hermit: When were you supposed to be tending the sheep?

Simplicius: Didn't you hear? When the iron men came. And after that our Ann said I should run away, else the soldiers—she meant the iron men—would take me away with them. And then I ran away and came hither.

Hermit: And whither do you wish to go now?

Simplicius: I really don't know. I wish to stay here with you.

Hermit: Keeping you here would not be fitting for me or for you. Eat! Then I shall take you back to where there are people.

Simplicius: Do tell me, what manner of things be "people"?

Hermit: "People" are human beings, like you and me. Your Pa, your Ma, and your Ann are human beings, and when there are many human beings collected together, they are called "people."

Simplicius: Aha!

Hermit: Now go and eat.

This was our discourse, during which the hermit often looked upon me and heaved deep sighs. I know not whether he did that because he had such great pity for me because of my simplemindedness and ignorance, or for a reason which I did not learn till some years later.

CHAPTER 9

Simplicius turns from a bestia into a Christian human being

I fell to eating and left off prattling, which lasted no longer than till I had filled my belly and the old man bade me be on my way. Then I sought out the very tenderest words which, in my boorish uncouthness, could think of, all of which were meant to move the hermit to keep me with him. Now even though it did prove burdensome to him to tolerate my annoying presence, he nevertheless did resolve to suffer me to remain with him, more in order that he might instruct me in the Christian religion than that I might assist him in his now advanced age with my services. His greatest fear was that a boy of my tender years might not be able to endure for long such a hard way of life.

A period of about three weeks was my probationary year,[64] just at the time when St. Gertrude[65] was with the gardeners in the fields, and so I let myself be used in their *professio* too. I behaved so well that the hermit took a particular liking to me, not because of the work, to be sure, which I was already accustomed to doing before, but because he saw not only that I listened intently to his instructions, but also that the tablet of my heart, soft as wax and still devoid of writing, revealed itself to be equally adept at grasping them. For these reasons he also became all the more zealous in initiating me into all that was good. He began his lessons with the fall of Lucifer; from thence he came to the Garden of Eden, and after we, together with our forefathers, were expelled from it, he passed through the law of Moses, and by means of the Ten Commandments and their explications (of which he said that they were a true guiding principle by which to apprehend the will of God and to lead, following them, a life holy and pleasing to God), he taught me to distinguish virtue from vice, to do good and to shun evil. Finally he came to the Gospel and told me of Christ's birth, passion, death, and resurrection. Last of all, he concluded with the Day of Judgment and painted for me a picture of heaven and hell. And all these things, with relevant particulars, yet not with a host of unnecessary details, but rather in the way it seemed to him that I might best grasp and comprehend them. When he was finished with one *materia* he set out upon another and was able, with infinite patience, to adapt his lessons to my questions and to proceed with me so skillfully that he could not have better imparted them to me. His life and his words were a never-ending sermon for me which, through the grace of God, my mind, which was really not all that dull and dense, did not let pass without bearing fruit, in such measure that in those three weeks I had not only comprehended everything which a Christian ought to know, I had also gained such fondness for this instruction that I could not sleep nights for thinking about it.

Since that time I have[66] pondered upon the matter many times and have found that Aristotle[67] reached the correct conclusion in his *lib. 3. de Anima* when he compared the soul of the human being to an empty tablet upon which nothing is writ and upon which one can note down all manner of things, and that all this was done by the highest Creator so that this smooth tablet, by means of diligent *impressio* and exercise, might be brought to completeness and perfection; for which reason also Aristotle's commentator, Averroes, in *lib. 2. de Anima*[68] (where the *philosophus* says that the *intellectus* is all *potentia* and that nothing is brought *in actum* but through *scientiam*; that is, man's mind is capable, to be sure, but nothing can be put into it without diligent exercise), reaches this clear conclusion: namely, this *scientia* or exercise is the *perfectio* of the soul, which soul, in and of itself, nowhere has anything to it. This Cicero[69] confirms in *lib. 2. Tuscul. quaest.* when he compares the soul of a human being without instruction, knowledge, or intellectual exercise to a field which is, to be sure, by its nature fruitful, but which will nevertheless bear no fruit unless one till it and sow it with seed.

All this I demonstrated by my own example, because I so soon comprehended everything which the pious hermit presented to me since he found the smooth tablet of my soul completely empty and without any images already impressed upon it that might have hindered putting something else onto it. But I still retained, measured against other people, my unalloyed simplicity, for which reason the hermit (because neither he nor I knew my true name) called me "Simplicius."

At the same time I also learned to pray, and when he resolved to accede to my persistent desire to remain with him, we built a hut for me like his, of wood, twigs, and earth, shaped almost like the tents which musketeers put up in the field, or like the turnip sheds of peasants in some parts, indeed so low to the ground that I could scarce sit upright in it. My bed was of dry leaves and grass, and just as large as the hut itself, so that I know not whether I should call this dwelling, or burrow, a covered resting place or a hut.

CHAPTER 10

In what manner he learned in the wild forest to read and write

The first time I saw the hermit reading the Bible I could not imagine with whom he might be carrying on such an intimate and, to my mind, very earnest conversation. I well saw that his lips were moving, but I saw no one who was speaking with him, and though I knew nothing about reading and writing, I did note from his eyes that he was engrossed in something in this book. I kept my own eyes glued to the book, and when he put it aside I made for it, opened it up, and at first grasp laid eyes upon the first chapter of the Book of Job and the picture at the beginning of it, which was a fine woodcut and was beautifully illuminated. I asked the figures in the picture strange things, and because no answer to me was forthcoming, I grew impatient and was saying, just as the hermit slipped up behind me: "You little ragamuffins! Has the cat got your tongues? Were you not able, but a moment ago, to chatter away with my father (for that is what I was obliged to call the hermit)? I well see that you are driving home my poor Pa's sheep and have set fire to the house. Stop! Stop! I'll put out this fire for sure!" With that I got up to fetch water, because the need for it seemed to me to be present. "Whither away, Simplicius?" said the hermit, who I did not know was behind me. "O, Father!" said I. "There are soldiers there too. They have sheep and are about to drive them off. They took them from the poor man with whom you were just talking, and his house is already ablaze too, and if I don`t put it out soon, it will burn down!" With these words I pointed with my finger to what I saw in the picture. "Just stay here," said the hermit, "there is really no danger." I answered, as politely as I knew how: "Are you blind? You keep them from driving off the sheep, and I'll go fetch water." "But these pictures are not alive," said the hermit, "they are merely made in order to depict for us things which happened long ago." I answered: "But you were just talking with them. How can they not be alive?"

The hermit could not but laugh at this, against his will and contrary to his wont,[70] and he said: "My dear child, these pictures cannot talk, but what they are and what they are doing I can see from these black lines, which is called 'reading,' and when I read that way, you think I am talking with the pictures, but that is not so." I answered: "If I am a human being like you, then I must needs also be able to see in the black lines what you can. How am I to make sense of what you say? My dear Father, do instruct me how I am to understand this." Then he said: "Well, all right, my son, I shall teach you so that you will be able to talk with these pictures as well as I do, but it will take time, during which I must exercise patience and you diligence." Then he wrote for me on pieces of birch bark an alphabet shaped like the printed letters in the book, and when I knew the letters, I learned to spell, then to read, and finally to write, better than the hermit himself could, because I wrote everything like the printed letters.

CHAPTER II

Tells of food, household articles, and other necessary things which one requires for life in this world

For about two years, namely till the hermit died, and somewhat longer than a half a year after his death, I remained in this forest. It therefore seems to me a good idea to tell the curious Reader, who often wishes to know things of even the slightest importance, something about our doings, actions, and transactions, and how we passed our life.

Our food was all kinds of garden vegetables: turnips, cabbage, beans, peas, and the like. Nor did we scorn beechnuts, wild apples, pears, cherries—indeed, hunger often made acorns palatable to us. Our bread, or to put it more accurately, our cakes we made of pounded maize and baked in hot ashes. In the winter we caught birds with springes and snares, and in the spring and summer God bestowed upon us baby birds in their nests. We often made do with snails and frogs, nor were we averse to fishing with weir-baskets and fishing lines, since there flowed not far from our dwelling a brook teeming with fish and crayfish, all of which things were obliged to convoy our crude vegetables down into our stomachs. One time we caught a young wild pig, which we kept in a pen, fed acorns and beechnuts, fattened up, and finally devoured, because the hermit knew that it could not be a sin to enjoy what God has created to this end for the entire human race. Of salt we used little, and of spices none at all, for we durst not arouse our thirst, because we had no winecellar. What little salt we required was given us by a parson who lived about fifteen miles away from us, a man of whom I shall have much more to tell.

As concerns our tools and utensils, there were enough of them on hand, for we had a shovel, a mattock, an ax, a hatchet, and an iron pot to cook in, which articles were, to be sure, not our own, but borrowed from the parson. Each of us had a dull, worn-out knife. This was our property, and other than that we had nothing. Nor did we have need of either dishes, plates, spoons, forks, kettles, pans, griddles, spits, saltcellars, or other table- and kitchenware, for our pot also served as our dish, and our hands were our forks and spoons, and if we desired to drink, we did it from the spring through a reed, or we lapped water from the spring like Gideon's warriors.[71] Of any kind of cloth, wool, silk, cotton, and linen, for either beds, tables, or tapestries, we had nothing but what we had on our backs, because we considered that we had enough if we could protect ourselves from rain and frost. Otherwise we had no fixed regimen or routine in our household, except on Sundays and holy days, when we set out on our way at midnight so that without anyone noticing it we might reach the parson's church, which was somewhat off to the side of a village, and wait for church service. In that church we betook ourselves onto the top of a broken pipe organ, from which spot we could look down upon the altar and up to the pulpit. The first time I saw the parson climb up into it, I asked my hermit what he meant to do in that big tub. And after church service was over, we went home just as furtively as we had come, and when we reached our dwelling, weary of foot and limb, we sank our good teeth into our wretched fare. Then the hermit passed the rest of the time in prayer and in instructing me in things of a godly nature.

On workdays we did what most needed doing, as the occasion demanded, and such as the time of year and our condition required. Sometimes we worked in the garden, other times we gathered rich soil from shady places and from hollow trees, to use instead of dung to improve our garden, and other times we wove baskets or fish creels, or we chopped firewood, fished, or did other things of the like to avoid idleness. And during all these chores the hermit did not leave off most staunchly instructing me in all that was good. Mean-while I learned in this hard life to endure hunger, thirst, heat, cold, and heavy labor, and, first and foremost, to know God and how one ought best to serve Him, which was the most important thing of all. To be sure, my loyal hermit did not wish to let me know anything beyond that, for he believed that for a Christian to achieve his goal and purpose it sufficed if he but diligently prayed and worked, which is why it came about that, even though I was rather well versed in spiritual matters, understood my Christianity quite well, and spoke the German language as beautifully as if I were *Orthographia*[72] herself, I nevertheless remained the most naive of mortals, so much so that when I left the forest and went into the outside world I was such a wretched booby there that there was nothing I had the wits to do.

CHAPTER 12

Takes note of a beautiful way to die in a state of blessedness and to have oneself buried at slight expense

I had passed about two years there and had scarce become accustomed to the rigorous life of a hermit when my best friend on earth took up his mattock, gave me a shovel, and led me by the hand, as he was wont to do every day, to our garden, where we were wont to say our prayers. "Now, Simplicius, my dear child," said he, "because, praise God, the time is at hand when I shall depart this world, pay my debt to nature, and leave you behind in this world, and particularly because I can roughly foresee the future events of your life and well know that you will not long tarry in this wasteland, I wish to strengthen you in the path of virtue upon which you are embarked, and to impart to you as instruction several precepts by which you ought to live your life, infallible guiding principles by which to achieve eternal salvation, so that you will be found worthy in that other life to look, like all the holy elect, upon the face of God throughout all eternity."

These words made my eyes as wet with tears as the enemy's stratagem once made the city of Villingen[73] wet with the waters of the Brisach River. In short, these words were so unbearable to me that I could not bear them, and I said: "Most beloved Father, are you then going to leave me alone in this wild forest? Is the..." More I could not bring forth, for my heart's torment became so violent, because of the excessive love I bore my good father, that I sank down at his feet as if dead. He, for his part, pulled me to my feet again, consoled me as well as time and situation permitted, and rebuked me, as it were, for my shortcoming by asking whether I desired to oppose what the Almighty had ordained. "Do you not know," he continued, "that neither heaven nor hell can do that? Therefore, do not behave this way, my son! What burden do you make so bold as to put upon my weak body (which is desirous of rest for itself)? Do you think to oblige me to live longer in this vale of tears? O no, my son, let me go, since you will not be able to compel me, either with weeping or with tears, and even less with my consent, to continue longer in this life of misery after it is God's express will that I leave it. Instead of crying out to no avail, obey my last words, which are that the longer you live, the more you should seek to know yourself, and even if you were to live to be as old as Methuselah,[74] continue to strive for this goal; because the reason that most people are damned is that they have not known what they were or what could or should become of them." He further, as a staunch friend, advised me that I should at all times shun

29

bad company, for the harm it does is beyond words to describe. He gave me an example of it, saying: "If you put a drop of malmsey[75] wine into a vessel full of vinegar, it will instantly turn to vinegar, but if you pour that much vinegar into malmsey, it will disappear in the wine. My dearest son," said he, "remain steadfast, for he who perseveres unto the end will be saved. But should it happen, contrary to my hopes, that because of human frailty you fall, then get up again quickly by means of honest penitence."

This scrupulous pious man commended to me only these few precepts, not, of course, because he knew no more, but because I seemed to him, primarily because of my youth, not to be sufficiently capable of comprehending more in the state I was in, and because a few words are easier to retain in the memory than a long tirade; and if they are weighty and meaty, they are of greater profit when they are pondered upon than a long sermon which one has understood down to the last word but is wont to soon forget again.

These three things—to know oneself, to shun bad company, and to remain steadfast—this pious man without doubt deemed good and necessary because he himself had practiced them and in so doing did not fail. For after he had come to know himself, he shunned not only bad company but the entire world, and he persevered in this resolve till the end, on which without doubt salvation depends, and in what manner this end came follows herewith.

Now after he had commended to me those precepts, he fell to digging his own grave with his mattock. I helped as best I could, doing as he commanded, and yet did not conceive what he had in mind. Meanwhile he said: "My dear and, truly, only son (for I have begat no creature other than you, to the honor of our Creator), when my soul has gone to its appointed resting place, do last honors and your final duty to my body. Cover me up again with the earth which we have just dug from this pit." Then, taking me into his arms, he kissed me and pressed me to his breast much harder than would have seemed possible for a man as frail as he appeared to be. "My dear child," said he, "I commend you to God's protection, and I die all the more cheerful in spirit because I hope that He will grant you it." I, for my part, could do nothing but lament and weep. I clung to the chain which he wore around his neck and thought to hold him by it so that he should not leave me. He, however, said: "My son, leave me be, so that I may see whether this grave is long enough for me." Then he took off the chain, together with the cloak, and lay down in the grave, just like one who is about to go to sleep, saying: "Ah, Almighty God, take back the soul which Thou hast given me. Lord, into Thy hands I commend my spirit, etc." Then he softly closed his lips and his eyes. I, however, stood there like a bump on a log and did not think that his dear soul had really departed his body, since I had often seen him in trances of that sort.

I, as was my wont when this sort of thing occurred, waited several hours beside the grave in prayer, but when my most beloved hermit made no move to get up again, I climbed down into the grave to him and fell to shaking him, kissing him, and caressing him, but there was no life in him any more, because grim, inexorable Death had robbed poor Simplicius of his dear companion. With my tears I wet, or to put it better, I embalmed the lifeless body, and after I had run hither and thither for a long while, crying out wretchedly, I began, with more sighs than shovelfuls of earth, to cover him up, and when I had scarce covered his face, I climbed down into the grave again and uncovered it again so that I might see and kiss it one more time. This I did the entire day, till I was finished and till I had in this wise concluded all by myself the *funeralia*, *exequias*, and *luctus gladiatorios*, because neither bier nor coffin, pall, candles, gravediggers, nor mourners, nor any clergy were present who might have sung the dead man to his rest.[76]

CHAPTER 13

Simplicius lets himself be pushed hither and thither like a reed in the wind

Several days after the hermit died I betook myself to the parson I mentioned above and reported my master's death to him, and at the same time begged counsel from him as to what I should do in these present circumstances. Now despite the fact that he strongly advised me not to remain in the forest any longer, I nevertheless bravely set forth to follow in my predecessor's footsteps, doing during the entire summer what a pious *monachus*[77] ought to do. But just as all things by Time are changed, so the grief which I bore for the hermit also abated little by little, and the extremely harsh winter cold outside me at the same time extinguished inside me the heat of my firm resolve. The more I began to waver, the more I neglected to say my prayers, because instead of contemplating things heavenly and divine, I let myself be overwhelmed by a desire to see the world; and when in this manner I became unfit to live the godly life in the forest any longer, I resolved to go to the parson again, to hear whether he would still counsel me, as before, to leave the forest. To this end I set off towards his village, and when I got there I found it in full blaze, for a party of troopers of horse had just plundered it, set it afire, killed some of the peasants, driven many away, and taken a few prisoner, amongst whom was the parson himself. O Lord!

How full of trials and tribulations human life is! Scarce has one misfortune passed than we are beset by another! I am not surprised that the heathen philosopher Timon[78] erected many gallows in Athens on which people might hang themselves and thus, by a brief and terrible deed, end their wretched lives. The troopers had just got ready to set out upon their way and were leading the parson along by a rope. Some were screaming "Shoot the scoundrel!" while others desired to have money from him. He, however, lifted his hands up to heaven and pleaded in the name of God and all His avenging angels for Christian mercy and forbearance, but in vain; for one of them rode him down and at the same time dealt him such a blow to the head that he fell flat on his face and commended his soul to God. The other remaining peasants whom they had captured fared not a whit better.

Now just when it looked as if these troopers in their tyrannical cruelty had completely lost their wits, there came such a swarm of armed peasants out of the forest as if some one had poked a stick into a wasps' nest. They began to scream so terribly, to attack so ferociously, and then to shoot so at the soldiers that my end stood on hair,[79] because I had never before witnessed any diversion of this sort, for the peasants of the Spessart Forest and Vogelsberg Mountain are truly no more apt to let anyone crow over them on their own dunghills than are the folks of Hessia, the Sauerland,[80] and the Black Forest. At that the troopers ran away and left behind not only the cattle they had taken but also tossed away bag and baggage, thereby throwing their entire booty to the wind so that they might not themselves become the booty of the peasants, but some of them did fall into their hands.

This fine diversion very nearly cured me of my desire to see the world, for I thought that if that be how things are in the world, the wilderness is far more amenable. But I also desired to hear what the parson had to say about it. Because of the wounds and the blows he had received he was quite faint, weak, and feeble, but he did put it to me that he could neither counsel nor assist me, because he himself had now fallen into such a plight that he must needs take up the beggar's staff to seek and solicit his daily bread, and even if I were to remain still longer in the forest, I should not have his assistance to comfort me, because, as I could see with my own eyes, both his church and the parsonage were in flames. Then I quite sadly betook myself to my dwelling in the forest, and since on this journey I was little comforted, but on the other hand came to be much more devout, I resolved to myself never to leave the wilderness again, for which reason I was already pondering whether I could live without salt (which the parson had provided me before) and could thus make do without all other human beings.

CHAPTER 14

A quaint comoedia[81] about five peasants

And so that I might act upon my resolve and become a true forest hermit, I put on the hair shirt my hermit had left behind and girded his chain over it, not, to be sure, because I had need of them to mortify my unruly flesh, but so that I might resemble my predecessor in appearance as well as behavior and with this clothing protect myself from the raw winter cold.

The second day after the aforementioned village had been plundered and burnt, just as I was sitting in my hut and, whilst saying my prayers, was roasting carrots in the fire to sustain myself with, about forty or fifty musketeers surrounded me. Even though they were astonished at my appearance, they nevertheless ransacked my hut, searching for what was not to be found there, for I had nothing but books, which they threw in a heap, because they were of no value to them. Finally, when they looked at me more closely and saw by my feathers what manner of poor bird they had caught, they could easily tot up the account and see that there was poor booty to be hoped for from me. After that they were surprised at my hard life and had great pity for my tender years, particularly the officer who was commanding them; indeed, he used me honorably, and he politely requested that I show him and his men the way back out of the forest, in which they had been wandering around lost for a long while. I did not refuse this request, but led them by the most direct way to the village where the parson had been so badly used, because I knew no other way. Before we came out of the forest, however, we saw about ten peasants, some armed with muskets and others busy burying something. The musketeers rushed up to them screaming "Halt! Halt!" but they answered with their firearms, and when they saw that they were outnumbered by the soldiers, they quickly ran away so that the tired musketeers could not overtake a one of them. The musketeers therefore decided to dig up again what the peasants had been interring. That was all the easier to do because they had left lying on the ground the mattocks and shovels they had been using; and they had dug but a few shovelfuls when they heard a voice from down below which said: "O, you arrant knaves! O, you arch-villains! Do you think Heaven will let your unchristian cruelty and knavery go unpunished? No! There is still many an honest fellow alive who will avenge your inhumanity, so that no more of your fellowmen will be obliged to lick your arses!" At this the soldiers looked at one another in surprise, because they knew not what they ought do. Some thought they had found a ghost, but I thought I was dreaming. Their officer bade them keep digging, and they straightway came upon a barrel, broke it open, and found in it a fellow who had neither nose nor ears any more, and yet was still alive. As soon as he had recovered a little and recognized several of the troopers in the group, he told how the day before, when some of his regiment were out foraging, the peasants had taken six of them prisoner, five of whom they had shot to death but an hour before. They had been compelled to stand in single file, and because he was the sixth and last in the file and the bullet, after having penetrated through five bodies, had not reached him, they had cut off his nose and ears, but before that they had compelled him to lick the arses (*s. v.*) of five of them. Now when he had seen himself so completely degraded by these rogues, who were devoid of honor and forgetful of God, he had said the vilest things to them he could think of, even though they intended to let him off with his life, and he had called them by their right names, in the hope that one of them might perchance lose his temper and put a musket ball into him. But in vain. Instead, after he had made them angry, they had stuck him into the barrel here and had buried him alive this way, saying that since he so eagerly desired to die, as a joke they were going to accede to his wishes in this regard.

While he was thus bemoaning the suffering he had endured, another party of soldiers came diagonally across the field on foot. They had come upon those same peasants, taken five of them prisoner, and shot the rest to death. Among the prisoners were four whose bidding the so badly abused trooper had shortly before been so disgracefully obliged to do. Now when, by the passwords they called out to one another, the two parties recognized one another to be from the same army, they joined forces and heard again from the trooper what had befallen him and his comrades. Then one would have had the surprise of one's life to see how the peasants were tortured. Some wished, in their first fury, to shoot them dead, but others said: "No, we must first properly torture these wanton birds and make them pay what they owe for the way they used this trooper." Meanwhile the peasants received such stout blows to the ribs with muskets that they could not but spit blood. At last one soldier stepped forward and said: "Gentlemen, because it is a disgrace to the entire *soldateska*[82] that these five peasants so horribly tortured this wretch (thereby pointing to the trooper), it is only fair that we expunge this blot upon our escutcheon and make these rogues lick the trooper's arse a hundred times in return." Contrarily, another one said: "This fellow is unworthy that such an honor be accorded him, for had he not been a sluggard, he would never have performed that disgraceful service, to the disgrace of all honest soldiers, but would rather have first died a thousand deaths." Finally it was unanimously agreed that each of these peasants whose arses had been licked clean should make amends for that by licking the arses of ten soldiers, saying each time: "Herewith I expunge and wash away the disgrace which soldiers believe they incurred when a sluggard licked our arses." Only when that was done were they going to resolve what they would further do to the peasants after they had performed this fine task. Then they set to work, but the peasants were so stubborn that they could not be compelled to do it, either by promising them that they would get off with their lives or by any kind of torture. One trooper took the fifth peasant, whose arse had not been licked, a little ways off to the side and said to him: "If you will deny God and all His saints, I'll let you run off whither you wish." To this the peasant answered that in all his days he had cared nothing for saints, and also had hitherto had yet little to do with God Himself, and then he swore *solenniter*[83] that he did not know God and desired to have no part of His kingdom. Then the soldier fired at his forehead a musket ball, which, however, had no more effect than if it had been shot at a steel mountain. Then he drew his short broadsword, saying: "Aha! So you are one of that ilk![84] I promised to let you run off whither you desired, look you, but now, since you do not desire to go to heaven, I am going to dispatch you to hell!" And with that he split his head in twain down to his jawbone. When he fell down there, the soldier said: "This is how one must avenge oneself and punish these wicked rogues, in both this world and the next."

Meanwhile the other soldiers had laid hands upon the remaining four peasants, whose arses *had* been licked. They tied them over a fallen tree, with hands and feet tied together so nicely that they turned their arses (*s. v.*)[85] straight up in the air, and after they had pulled their breeches down, they took several yards of fuse cord, tied knots in it, and sawed back and forth like a fiddler so harshly through their buttocks that the red blood fell to flowing. "This," said they, "is the way to dry out your licked-clean arses, you rogues!" The peasants, of course, screamed terribly, for they did not leave off sawing till skin and flesh was away, clear down to the bone. Me, however, they let go back to my hut, because the last-mentioned party well knew the way back to their army; so I cannot know everything they finally did to the peasants.

CHAPTER 15

Simplicius is despoiled and has a wondrous dream about the peasantry, and how things go in time of war

When I came back home I found that my tinder box and all my household goods, together with all the paltry victuals which I had grown in my garden throughout the summer and had saved to eat during the coming winter, were all of them gone. "What am I to do now?" I thought. At that time Necessity assuredly did teach me to pray. I mustered together what few wits I had, so as to deliberate upon what I should now do or not do; but inasmuch as my knowledge of the world was slight and superficial, I could not conclude what the right thing was for me to do. The best thing I did was that I commended my soul unto God and resolved to place my trust in Him alone, else I must needs have despaired and perished. Besides, the things which I had seen and heard that day preyed upon my mind without surcease. I thought not so much about the victuals and my self-preservation as about that *antipathia*[86] which prevails betwixt soldiers and peasants, but my paltry wit sufficed only to conclude that there must without doubt be two different kinds of human beings in the world who were not descended as a single race from Adam but were rather divided into the wild and the tame, like other mindless beasts, because they persecuted one another so cruelly.

Amidst these thoughts I fell asleep from vexation and from the cold, with my stomach plagued by hunger.[87] Then it seemed to me, as in a dream, as if all the trees which stood around my dwelling on a sudden changed and took on a completely different appearance. On every treetop sat a nobleman, and all the branches were bedecked not with leaves but with all manner of fellows,[88] some with long lances, others with muskets, pistols, partizans,[89] and flags, and some with fifes and drums. This was diverting to behold, because all of them were so nicely and neatly separated from one another by rank. The roots of the tree, however, were made up of people who counted for naught, such as artisans, day laborers, and mostly peasants and the like, which folk nevertheless gave the tree its strength and replenished it when at times the tree lost its strength. Indeed, they replaced from amongst their own the leaves which fell off, to their own even greater ruin; and all the while they sighed about those who were sitting in the tree, and not without good cause either, for the entire weight of the tree was upon them and so pressed them down that all their money came tumbling out of their purses, even those locked with seven seals. And when it did not tumble out, then *commissarii*[90] so cudgeled them with rods, which they called "confiscation for the army," that sighs came forth from their hearts, tears from their eyes, blood from beneath their fingernails, and marrow from their bones. And yet there were among them some who were lighthearted; they never had a care in the world, took nothing seriously, and tribulations evoked from them not words of solace but witty remarks.

CHAPTER 16

What soldiers nowadays do and omit to do, and how difficult it is for one of lowly birth to achieve preferment in the army

Thus the roots, beset by nothing but hardship and lamentation, were obliged to bear and sustain these trees, and those on the lowermost branches were obliged to do the same with much greater effort, labor, and privation; but they were usually more cheerful than the roots, but at the same time also spiteful, tyrannical, and for the most part godless, and always a heavy and unbearable burden for the roots. Around them were written these rhymes:

> Hunger and thirst,[91] cold and heat,
> Toil and poverty, vict'ry and defeat,
> Injustice, atrocities, turmoil, and strife:
> That's the common soldier's life.

These rhymes were all the more in accord with the truth because they matched the soldiers' deeds;[92] for glutting themselves with food and drink, suffering hunger and thirst, roaring and whoring, gambling and rambling, carousing and sousing, murdering others and being murdered in turn, beating others to death and being beaten to death in turn, tormenting others and being tormented in turn, hunting others and being hunted in turn, frightening others and being frightened in turn, robbing others and being robbed in turn, plundering others and being plundered in turn, fearing others and making others fearful in turn, causing others misery and suffering miserably in turn, defeating others and being defeated in turn, and, *in summa*, ruining and harming others and being ruined and harmed in turn was all they did and were, in which deeds they let hinder them neither winter nor summer, neither snow nor ice, neither heat nor cold, neither rain nor wind, neither hill nor dale, neither field nor morass, neither ditches, passes, seas, walls, fire, water, nor battlements, neither father nor mother, brothers nor sisters, neither danger to their own bodies, souls, and consciences, indeed, neither loss of life or of salvation or of anything else one can name. Instead, they kept right on plying their trade, till little by little they finally perished, died, went to their graves, and gave up the ghost in battles, sieges, assaults, campaigns, and even in garrison (which is, after all, heaven on earth for a soldier, particularly when he happens upon fat peasants), except for some few who, having failed to diligently flay peasants and steal them blind, turned out to be the very finest beggars and runagates.[93] Just above these wretched folk sat such old chicken thieves[94] as had managed to survive on the lowest branches for some years at the utmost peril to their persons, had kept plugging away, and had had the good fortune to escape death thus far. They looked solemn and somewhat more reputable than the ones on the lowest branches, because they had climbed up one *gradum*;[95] but above them were yet higher folk, who also had a higher opinion of themselves, because they were wont to command the lowest ones. These men were called doublet-drubbers, because with their cudgels and hell-bards[96] they were wont to belabor the backs as well as the heads of pikemen,[97] and to give musketeers[98] birch oil to lubricate their weapons with. Above these, the trunk of the tree had a segment, or different part, which was a smooth section, without branches, and lubricated with singular *materialia*[99] and with the wondrous soap of ill will, so that no fellow, unless he be of the nobility, could climb up it, neither through bravery nor skill nor knowledge, no matter how well he might be able to climb, for it was more smoothly polished than a marble column or a steel mirror. Above this spot sat those with flags,[100] some of them young and others rather on in years. The young ones had been lifted up by their kinsmen, while some of the older ones had in part climbed up by themselves, either on a silver ladder which is called "Palmgrease," or on some other bridge which Fortune, for want of anyone better, had constructed for them. Further up sat yet higher ones,[101] who also had their troubles, cares, and vexations, but they enjoyed the advantage that they could lard their purses best of all with what they cut out of the roots of the tree with a knife which they called "Requisition." They were most dexterous and skillful when a *commissarius* came along and emptied a pail full of gold over the tree to nourish it, in that they caught most of it as it was falling down and let as good as nothing reach the people lowest on the tree. Therefore, more of the lowest ones were wont to die of hunger than at the hands of the enemy, from which two dangers the ones highest up in the tree seemed to be exempted. Therefore there was an endless scrambling and climbing in this tree, because everyone desired to sit on the uppermost delightful spots; but there were some lazy, slovenly rascals, not worthy to eat of military rations, who troubled themselves little about an upper position and were obliged to do, one way or the other, what their duty required of them. The lowliest ones who did harbor ambitions hoped for the fall of the ones above so that they might sit in their places, and when one out of ten thousand of them managed to get that far, then it did not happen till they had reached the irksome age at which they were better suited for roasting apples in the fireplace than for facing the foe on the field of battle. And even when one of them was in this advantageous position and performed his duties well, he was envied by others, or else robbed of both rank and life by an unexpected whiff of gunpowder. Nowhere was the going rougher for them than at that smooth place, for any officer who had a good sergeant or sergeant major did not wish to lose him, which must needs happen if they made him an ensign. Therefore, instead of old soldiers, they much preferred to make ensigns of ink-squigglers,[102] valets, pages who had come of age, impoverished noblemen, some kinsman or other, or some other toady or starveling who snatched bread from the mouths of them who merited it.

CHAPTER 17

Though in time of war the nobleman, and rightly so, is given preference over him of low birth, many from the contemptible estate do come to high honors

This so vexed a sergeant major[103] that he began to rail at it in a high dudgeon, but Sir Lovelord said: "Do you not know that always and everywhere officers' positions have been filled by noble personages, because they are best suited for this? Old graybeards do not defeat the enemy, else one might as well hire a herd of billy goats to do the work. As the saying goes:

A younger ram,[104] if it be fit,

Can be a flock's bellwether;

And better than an older ram

> Will keep the flock together.
>
> You, shepherd, know, despite its youth
>
> This young ram won't desert you.
>
> A person shows bad judgment when
>
> He makes of age a virtue.

Tell me, you old dodderer, whether noble-born officers are not held in higher respect by the *soldateska* than those who were common farmhands before they joined the army? And what becomes of military discipline if there is no respect for officers? Can a general not place more trust in a nobleman than in a peasant lad who ran away from father and farm and was unwilling to do anything even for his own parents? A true nobleman would rather die with honor than put a blot upon his family's escutcheon by being committing treason, by deserting, or something of the like. Moreover, the nobility[105] deserves preference in all ways, as is to be seen in *leg. dig. Honor. de honor.*, in which John de Platea[106] expressly demands that preference be given the nobility in the filling of officers' positions and that noblemen should quite rightly be preferred to *plebeiis*.[107] Indeed, this is customary in all codes of law, and is confirmed in Holy Scripture, for 'Beata terra,[108] cujus Rex nobilis est' it says in Ecclesiasticus 10, which is a splendid testimonial to the preference which the nobility deserves. And even though one of you is a good soldier, knows the smell of gunpowder, and can devise stratagems for all occasions, that does not mean that he is capable of commanding others. This virtue, by contrast, is innate to the nobility or is inculcated into them from childhood on. Seneca[109] says: 'Habet hoc proprium generosus animus, quod concitatur ad honesta, et neminem excelsi Ingenii Virum humilia delectant et sordida,' which same thought Faustus Poeta[110] expressed in the following distich:

> Si te rusticitas vilem genuisset agrestis
>
> Nobilitas animi non foret esta tui.

Moreover, the nobility has more means than does the peasantry to help with money those who are under their command, and to bring undermanned companies up to full strength. And it would not be right, as the well-known proverb says, should one place a peasant above a nobleman. Also, peasants would become much too arrogant if one straightway made them masters, for as the saying goes:

> Never doth shear so sharp the sword[111]
>
> As when a peasant become a lord.

Had peasants, through long-established and commendable tradition, had in their possession officers' positions and other high posts, they would surely not be quick to let a nobleman get into one. Moreover, even though we would often like to help you soldiers of fortune[112] (as you are called), so that you might be elevated to higher honors, by the time we have tested you and deemed you worthy of something better, you are generally so old and decrepit that we must needs have reservations about promoting you in rank; for by then the fire of your youth is burned out, and the only thing you have in mind is simply how you can cultivate and pamper your sick bodies, which are ravaged by the many hardships they have suffered and are no longer of use for service in war, no matter who may be fighting and garnering the honor. Contrarily, a young hound is much happier to take up the chase than an old lion."

The sergeant major answered: "What fool would be willing to serve if he durst not hope to be promoted in rank on the basis of merit, and thus to be rewarded for his faithful service? The devil take a war of that sort! In this world the important thing is whether one shows one's merit or not. I have heard our old commanding officer say many times that he desired under his command no soldier who did not firmly believe that through meritorious service he might become a general. And thus all the world must needs acknowledge that those nations which let common but competent soldiers advance in rank and who take their valor into account are generally victorious, which one well sees in the case of the Persians and the Turks. As the saying goes:

> A lamp will give you light,[113] but it must be afforded
> Good olive oil to drink for its rejuvenation.
> Thus faithful service must receive fair compensation:
> A soldier will fight best when valor is rewarded."

Lovelord answered: "When a man's good qualities are seen, then he will surely not be overlooked, for which reason one finds nowadays many who exchanged the plow, the needle, the cobbler's last, or the shepherd's staff for the sword, who displayed their merit and who rose far above the common nobility, to the rank of count and baron. Who was Johan de Werdt?[114] Who was the Swedes' Stablejack?[115] Who were the Hessians' Little Jim[116] and St. Andreas?[117] Of their kind many are known, not all of whom, for the sake of brevity, I shall name. It is therefore nothing new in the present time, and it will doubtless also be true in the future, that men who are commoners by birth but are honest will achieve high honors through service in time of war, which also happened amongst the ancients.

Tamerlane[118] became a mighty king and terrible scourge of the entire world, and yet before that he was merely a swineherd; Agathocles,[119] King of Sicily, was a potter's son; Thelephas, a cartwright, became king in Lydia; Emperor Valentinian's father[120] was a rope maker; Mauritius Cappadox,[121] an indentured servant, came to be emperor after Tiberius;[122] John Zemisces[123] came from the schools to the throne of the empire. Thus Flavius Vobiscus[124] attests that Bonosus Imperator[125] was a poor schoolmaster's son; Hyperbolus,[126] the son of Chermides, was first a lantern maker and after that Prince in Athens; Justinus,[127] who ruled before Justinian, was a swineherd before he became emperor; Hugo Capet,[128] a butcher's son, was later King of France; Pizarro[129] was likewise a swineherd and later, in the West Indies' lands, Count, whose weight they were obliged to equal in hundredweights of gold."

The sergeant major answered: "All that is no more than grist for my mill. But meanwhile I well see that the doors to the one honor or the other are kept barred to us by the nobility. They put a nobleman, when he is scarce dry behind the ears, into the sort of post that we can never hope to dream of, even though we have done more than many a *nobiliste* whom they are now putting forward for the post of commanding officer. And just as there is amongst the peasantry many a noble *ingenium*[130] who for want of means is not set to studying in school, many a valiant soldier grows old under his musket who more rightly merited a command and could have better performed greater services for his generalissimo."

CHAPTER 18

Simplicius plunges into the world for the first time and suffers ill fortune

I had no desire to listen any longer to the old jackass, but rather granted him the plight of which he complained, because he had often beaten his poor soldiers like dogs. I turned back to the trees which the entire land was full of and saw how they swayed back and forth and banged together. Then the fellows in them came rattling down in droves; the rumblings of war and the tumblings of the warriors occurred at the same instant. In a moment the quick were the dead; in an instant one lost an arm, the second a leg, and the third even his head. As I was looking upon this, it seemed to me as if all those trees which I had seen were simply one tree, which covered all *Europa*[131] with its branches, and on its crown sat the god of war, Mars. To my mind this tree could have cast shade over the entire world, but it was buffeted, as if by north winds, by envy and hatred; by suspicion and ill will; by pride, arrogance, and greed; and by other fine virtues of that sort. It appeared quite thin and transparent, for which reason someone had carved the following rhymes into its trunk:

> The mighty oak,[132] when rent by savage wind's harsh breath,
>
> Doth break its branches off and die a lingering death.
>
> Through feuds and civil wars and internecine strife.
>
> The world's put out of joint, and pain and death are rife.

By the powerful rattling of these injurious winds and the shattering of the tree itself I was awakened from my sleep and saw myself still alone in my hut. Therefore I began to think about what I should do. It was impossible for me to remain in the forest, because everything had been so completely taken from me that I could no longer maintain myself there. Nothing was left but a few books, which were scattered hither and yon and in a jumble. As I was picking them up, with tears in my eyes, and at the same time fervently imploring God that He might lead and conduct me to wherever I ought to go, I found by chance a letter which my hermit had written while he was still alive. It read thusly: "My dear Simplicius! When you find this letter, then go forthwith out of the forest and deliver yourself and the parson from present harm, for he has done much good for you. God, Whom you should keep your eyes upon always and fervently pray to, will lead you to a place which will be most fitting for you. However, always keep your eyes upon Him, and make every effort to always serve Him as if you were still with me in the forest. Remember and do without surcease my last bidding, and you will be able to persevere. *Vale!*"[133]

I kissed this little letter and the hermit's grave a thousand times and set out to look for people till I found them, and therefore I kept going straight on for two days, and when darkness overtook me I sought a hollow tree in which to spend the night. My sustenance consisted of nothing but beechnuts, which I picked up from the ground on the way. On the third day, however, I came to a rather open field not far from Gelnhausen;[134] there I enjoyed a downright festive meal, because all over the fields were haystacks which, to my good fortune, the peasants had not been able to bring in because they had been chased off by the battle at Nördlingen;[135] in one of these I bedded down for the night, because it was bitter cold, and I satisfied my hunger with kernels I rubbed out of the wheat, which tasted better than anything I had eaten for a long time.

CHAPTER 19

How Simplicius is taken to Hanau and Hanau is taken with Simplicius

When day broke I filled my belly again with wheat, then betook myself to Gelnhausen,[136] and there found the city gates open, which gates were partly burned and yet still half barricaded with piles of dung. I went in, but could not lay eyes upon a single living soul; instead, the streets were strewn here and there with dead bodies, some of which were completely stripped, some down to their shirts. This heartrending sight was a terrible spectacle for me, for as anyone can well imagine for himself, in my simplemindedness I could not divine what manner of misfortune must needs have put the place into such a state. I found out shortly afterwards that the Imperials had made a surprise attack upon some of the Duke of Weimar's[137] troops there. I had got scarce two stone's throw into the city when I had already seen enough of it. Therefore I turned around again, went to the side of it through the meadow and came to a highway which took me to the splendid fortress of Hanau.[138] As soon as I caught sight of the first watch at the city gate, I tried to pass through, but two musketeers straightway came up to me, seized me, and took me into their *corps de garde*.[139]

But first, before I tell what else happened to me, I must tell you, dear Reader, about my droll appearance on that occasion, for my clothing and gestures were passing strange, odd, and queer, so that the governor of the city even had my picture painted. First of all, for three and a half years my hair had neither been cut nor combed nor waved nor curled in either the Greek, the German, or the French fashion;[140] rather, it was still standing up so daintily upon my head in its natural disarray, with more than a year's dust in it instead of being bestrewn with hair-stuff, talc, or powder (as they call the stuff which fools of both sexes use), that with my pale visage I peered out from beneath it like a barn owl about to snap at something or intent upon catching a mouse. And because I was always wont to go bareheaded and my hair was naturally curly, it looked as if I were wearing a Turkish turban on my head. The remainder of my attire was commensurate with my chief adornment, for I had on my hermit's cloak, if I durst still call it a cloak, because the cloth from which it had originally been cut had disappeared completely, and nothing was left of it but the mere form, which was still presented to the eye by more than a thousand little patches of cloth of all colors, sewed to the cloth at random during repeated mendings. Over this cloak, worn to a frazzle and yet so oft repaired, I wore the hair shirt as a doublet (because I was using the sleeves as a pair of stockings and had cut them off for this purpose), and my entire body was girt with iron chains in front and in back, in nice crosswise fashion, as they are wont to paint St. William,[141] so that I looked almost like one of those fellows who have been captives of the Turks and go about the land to beg for their friends still in captivity. My shoes were cut from wood, and the shoestraps were woven from the bark of linden trees. My feet themselves, however, were as blood red in appearance as if I had on a pair of stockings of the color favored by the Spanish, or else as if I had dyed my skin with fernambuck. I do believe that if a juggler, a mountebank, or a peddler had had me at the time and had exhibited me as a Samoyed[142] or a Greenlander, he would have encountered many a fool who would have paid a farthing to look upon me. Now even though anyone in his right mind should have been able to conclude without difficulty from my haggard and famished appearance and my tattered clothes that I had not run away from a cookshop or from a lady's boudoir, much less from some great lord's retinue, I was nevertheless rigorously interrogated at the watch. And while the soldiers were gawking at me, I for my part was looking at the bizarre appearance of their officer, whose questions I was obliged to answer. I knew not whether he was a he or a she, for he wore his hair and beard in the French fashion: on each side he had long braids hanging down like a horse's tail, and his beard had been so wretchedly abused and so mutilated that between his nose and his mouth there were only some few hairs coming out which were so short that one could scarce see them. No less did his wide breeches put me into no slight doubt concerning his sex, since they were to my eyes much more like a woman's skirt than a pair of man's breeches. I thought to myself: "If this be a man, then he ought to have a true beard, because this fop is no longer as young as he pretends to be. But if it be a woman, then why does the old whore have so much stubble around her mouth? Surely it is a woman," I thought, "for no honorable man would ever let his beard be so wretchedly mistreated; even rams are so greatly ashamed when their beards are clipped that they will not set foot a-mongst a strange flock." And since I was still in doubt and knew not what the current fashion was, in the end I took him to be a man and a woman at the same time.

This mannish woman or this womanish man (as he seemed to me to be) had my person thoroughly searched, but they found nothing upon me but a little book made of birch bark into which I had written my daily prayers and had also put the letter which my pious hermit, as reported in the previous chapter, had left behind for me as a *valete*.[143] This he took from me, but because I did not wish to lose it I fell to my knees before him, clasped him around both knees, and said: "O, my dear hermaphrodite! Please let me keep the little prayer book!" "You fool!" he answered. "Who in the devil told you my name was Herman?" Then he commanded two soldiers to take me to the governor of the city, for whom he sent along the aforementioned book, because this fool, as I straightway perceived, could himself neither read nor write.

So they led me into the city, and everyone came running up as if a sea monster were being put on display. And just as everyone desired to look upon me, each one also made something unusual of me. Some took me to be a spy, others to be a madman, others to be a wild man, and yet others to be a spirit, a spook, or some other miraculous thing which might portend something special. There were also some who took me to be a fool, which persons would have shot nearest the mark if I had not known about our dear Lord God.

CHAPTER 20

In what manner he was delivered from prison and torture

When I was brought before the governor[144] he asked me whence I came. I answered that I did not know. He asked further: "Well, whither are you going?" I again answered: "I do not know." "What in the devil do you know then?" he asked further. "What is your trade?" I answered as before that I did not know. He asked: "Where is your home?" And when I again answered that I did not know, his face changed expression, I do not know whether from anger or astonishment. But because everyone is wont to suspect the worst, and particularly since the enemy was in the vicinity, which enemy, as already reported, had but the night before taken Gelnhausen and destroyed a regiment of dragoons[145] there, he came down upon the side of those who took me to be a traitor or an enemy spy, and then ordered them to search my person. And when he learned from the soldiers of the watch who had brought me to him that this had already been done and that nothing had been found upon me but the little book, which at the same time they handed to him, he read a few lines in it and asked me who had given me the little book. I answered that it had been mine from the beginning, because I had made it myself and written into it. He asked: "But why on birch bark, of all things?" I answered: "Because the barks of other trees are not suitable." "You rascal!" said he. "I'm asking you why you did not write on paper." "O!" I answered. "We had no paper in the forest." The governor asked: "Where? In what forest?" I again answered with my old refrain that I did not know.

Then the governor turned to several of the officers who were waiting upon him and said: "This is either a rogue of the first order or a complete fool. Of course, he can- not be a fool because he can write." And as he was talking he leafed through my little book so violently, to show them my beautiful handwriting, that the hermit's letter could not but fall out of it. This he had an officer pick up. I, however, grew pale at this, because I held it to be my greatest treasure and relic, which reaction the governor well remarked and therefore grew even more suspicious of treason, particularly after he had opened the letter and read it, for he said: "I recognize this handwriting and know that it was writ by an officer well known to me, but I cannot recollect which one." And the contents seemed quite strange and unintelligible to him too, for he said: "This is without doubt a message in code which no one can understand but a person who knows the key to the code." Me, however, he asked what my name was, and when I answered "Simplicius" he said: "O, yes! You're a right fine fellow! Away with him, away with him, and forthwith put him into irons, hands and feet." And so the two soldiers went off with me to the new lodgings assigned to me, namely the jail, and turned me over to the provost, who, in accordance with his instructions, adorned my hands and feet with iron bonds and chains, as if I had not enough to bear with the ones I already had bound around my body.

These first steps to welcome me were not yet enough for the outside world; rather, hangman and bailiff came with gruesome instruments of torture, which truly did make my situation gruesome, despite the fact that I had my innocence to console me. "O, God!" said I. "How much I deserve this! Simplicius ran away from the service of God and into the world, so such a monster of Christianity as I am should receive the proper reward which I deserve for my wantonness. O, unhappy Simplicius! Whither has your ingratitude brought you? Look you, scarce had God brought you to knowledge of Himself and into His service, when you run away from His service and turn your back upon Him! Could you not have continued to eat acorns and beans as before, in order to serve your Creator unhindered? Did you not know that your loyal hermit and preceptor fled the world and chose the wilderness for himself? O, you blockhead! You left the wilderness in hope of satisfying your shameful lust to see the world. And now, look you, whereas you thought to feast your eyes, you must needs perish and go to ruin in this perilous labyrinth. Could you not before, you stupid booby, imagine that your blessed predecessor would not have exchanged the world's joys for the harsh life he led in the wilderness if he had thought it possible to achieve in this world true peace of mind, genuine calmness of spirit, and eternal salvation? Poor Simplicius, now go to, and receive your just deserts for the vain thoughts you have harbored and for your presumptuous folly! You have no right to complain and to console yourself with your innocence, because you rushed headlong to your martyrdom and subsequent death." Thus I reproached myself for my sins, begged God for forgiveness, and commended my soul unto Him. Meanwhile we were approaching the tower where they incarcerated criminals, but when the need is highest, the God's help is nighest; for when I was surrounded by beadles and was standing before the prison, together with a large throng of people, to wait till it was opened and I was put into it, my parson, whose village had been plundered and burned shortly before, also desired to see what was afoot (for he was also under house arrest for the time being). When he looked out the window and espied me, he cried out very loudly: "O, Simplicius! Is that you?" When I saw and heard him, I could do nothing but lift up my hands towards him and cry: "O, Father! O, Father! O, Father!" He, however, asked what I had done. I answered that I did not know; they had surely brought me hither because I had run out of the forest. But when he learned from bystanders that they took me to be a traitor, he bade them do nothing to me till he had reported to the governor concerning who I was, for this would serve to exonerate both me and himself and to prevent the governor from doing violence to us both, since he knew me better than any other person on earth.

CHAPTER 21

Fickle Fortune smiles upon Simplicius

He was permitted to go to the governor, and more than a half-hour later I was fetched also and placed in the servants' quarters, where two tailors, a cobbler with shoes, a shopkeeper with hats and stockings, and another one with all manner of cloth had already arrived, so that I might be outfitted as soon as possible. They took off my cloak, together with the chains and the hair shirt, so that the tailors could take my measurements; following that a barber appeared with sharp lye and sweet-smelling soaps, and just as he was about to practice his art upon me, another order came which frightened me terribly, because it said that I should put my habit back on again. This was not meant as ill as I feared, for straightway there came in a painter with his tools,[146] namely, minium and cinnabar for my eyelids; lacquer, indigo, and ultramarine for my coral-red lips; orpiment, king's yellow, and massicot for my white teeth (which I was fletching from hunger); lamp black, coal black, and umber for my yellow hair; white lead for my horrible eyes; and all manner of colors for my rainbow-hued cloak. He also had a whole handful of brushes. He fell to looking at me, sketching me, painting the background coat, cocking his head to one side in order to compare precisely his work with my form. One moment he changed the eyes, another the hair, in a trice the nostrils, and, *in summa*, everything which he had not done right in the beginning, till in the end he had drawn a natural looking figure which was that of Simplicius. Only then was the barber permitted to whisk down upon me. He washed my head and tinkered with my hair for a full hour and a half. Following that he cut it in the fashion then current, for I had hair to spare. After that he put me into the bath and cleansed my haggard, emaciated body of more than a three- or four-year coat of dirt. Scarce was he finished when they brought me a white shirt, shoes and stockings, together with a neckpiece, or collar, and a hat with a plume; and the breeches were also beautifully adorned and edged with galloons, but the doublet was still missing, on which, to be sure, the tailors were working with haste. The cook arrived with a hearty cup of broth, and the serving-maid with a glass of wine. There sat Milord Simplicius like a young count, accommodated in the finest way. I fell to eating valiantly, despite the fact that I knew not what they meant to do with me, for I as yet knew nothing about the condemned man's last meal; therefore the taste of this splendid beginning of the meal made me feel more mellow and mild than I could ever tell of, boast of, and put into words. Indeed, I find it difficult to believe that I ever, a single time in all my days, felt greater pleasure than at precisely that time. Now when the doublet was finished, I put it on too, and in these new clothes presented to the eye such an ungainly figure that it looked like a *trophaeum*,[147] or as if they had put finery on a fence-post, because the tailors had purposely made the clothes too large for me because of the hope which was harbored that I would in a short while put on weight, which manifestly did happen too, because of such good victuals. The clothes I wore in the forest, together with the chains and all appurtenances, were, on the other hand, put into the curiosities' cabinet alongside the other rarities and antiquities, and my portrait in life-size was placed next to them.

After the evening meal milord was laid into a bed the likes of which had never fallen my lot, either in my Pa's house or at the hermit's; but my belly so grumbled and rumbled the entire night through that I could not sleep, perhaps for no other reason than because it either did not yet know what was good to eat, or because it was astonished at the delicious new foods which had fallen its lot. One way or the other, however, I remained in bed till the dear sun shone again (for it was cold) and considered what manner of strange experiences I had had for several days now, and how the dear Lord had so loyally helped me get through them and had brought me to such a fine place.

CHAPTER 22

Who the hermit was whose companionship Simplicius had enjoyed

That same morning the governor's steward charged me to go to the parson and hear what his master had talked about with him concerning me. He gave me an escort who brought me to him. The parson led me into his *museum*,[148] sat down, bidding me sit also, and said: "My dear Simplicius, the hermit with whom you lived in the forest was not only the brother-in-law of the governor here but was also his patron in the war and his most valued friend. As the governor was so kind as to tell me, from youth on this man was never wanting in any virtue, neither in bravery befitting a heroic soldier nor in religiosity and piety, which two virtues, in fact, are seldom to be found in the same person conjoined. His religious bent and calamitous events finally impeded the course of his happiness in this world, so that he scorned and put aside his patent of nobility and considerable properties in Scotland,[149] where he was born, because all the doings of the world seemed to him vapid, vain, and reprehensible. In a word, he hoped to exchange his high station in this world for a greater *gloria*[150] in the next one, because his noble spirit felt only disgust for all worldly splendor, and his thoughts and aspirations were directed solely towards such a wretched life as the one in which you encountered him in the forest and afforded him companionship till his death. In my opinion, he was led astray to do this by reading many papist books about the lives of the hermits of old.

"And I shall also not conceal from you how he came to the Spessart Forest and to that wretched hermit's life, so that in the future you will be able to tell others about it. The second night after the bloody battle of Höchst[151] was lost, he came, solitary and alone, to the door of my parsonage towards morning, just after I and my wife and children had fallen asleep, because we had not slept a wink the entire night before and half that same night, because of the noise in the countryside which both those who were taking flight and those who were in pursuit of them were making. He knocked politely at first, and following that violently enough, till he awakened me and my sleep-drunk household, and after I, at his behest and after an exchange of a few words which were quite decorous on both sides, opened the door, I saw the cavalier dismount from his spirited steed. His fine clothes were as bespattered with the blood of his enemies as they were adorned with gold and silver, and because he was still holding his naked sword in his hand, fear and trepidation came

50

over me; but when he sheathed it and uttered nothing but courteous words, I had cause to wonder that so fine a gentleman would request of a simple village pastor lodging for the night in such a friendly manner. Because of his handsome person and noble bearing I addressed him as General Mansfeld[152] himself, but he said that on this occasion he was to be compared to Mansfeld only in unhappiness, and indeed was to be preferred to him in this regard. Three things he lamented: namely, his lost lady, who was great with child; the lost battle; and the fact that he had not had the good fortune to lose his life in it fighting for the Evangelical cause,[153] as other honest soldiers had. I wished to console him but soon saw that he, in his magnanimity, had no need of consolation. After that I gave him what the house had to offer and had a soldier's bed of fresh straw made for him, because he was unwilling to lie upon any other one, although he was much in need of rest. The first thing which he did the following morning was to make me a present of his horse and to distribute amongst my wife, children, and servants his money (which he had with him in gold, in no small sum, together with several precious rings). I knew not what manner of man I was dealing with, because soldiers are much rather wont to take than to give. Therefore I had reservations about accepting such expensive gifts and objected that I did not merit them from him, nor did I know how I might ever deserve them; in addition, I said that if anyone were to see such riches, and particularly the valuable horse, which could not be hid, in the possession of me and mine, then many people would conclude that I had helped rob or even murder him. He said, however, that I should not give a care to this—he was going to insure me against danger with a document writ by his own hand; indeed, he said, he did not even wish to be wearing his shirt, much less his clothes, when he left the parsonage, and with that he revealed to me his resolve to become a hermit. I did everything I could to dissuade him from it, because it seemed to me that this project savored of the papacy, and I reminded him that he could better serve the Evangelical cause with his sword. But it was in vain, for he disputed so long and so much with me, till I agreed to everything and equipped him with those books, pictures, and household articles which you found with him, though he desired, in return for all he had given me, only the woolen blanket under which he had slept upon the straw that night. From it he had a cloak made. And I was also obliged to trade with him my wagon chains, which he always wore, for a golden chain, on which he carried the *contrefait*[154] of his beloved, with the result that he retained neither gold nor goods. My servant took him to the most desolate spot in the forest and helped him put up his hut there. In what manner he passed his life there, and wherewith I at times assisted him and lent him a helping hand, you know as well—indeed, perhaps better than I.

"Now recently, after the battle at Nördlingen[155] was lost and I, as you know, was completely plundered and at the same time badly injured, I fled hither to safety because I already had my best things here anyway. And when my cash monies were about to run out, I took three rings and the golden chain which I mentioned, with the *contrefait* which hung on it—which I had from the hermit—and his signet ring, which was also amongst the things, and took them to a Jew in order to turn them into silver. The Jew, however, because of their value and beautiful workmanship, offered them for sale to the governor, who straightway recognized the coat of arms on the signet ring, and the *contrefait*, and sent for me and asked where I had got this jewelry. I told him the truth, produced the hermit's handwritten note, or letter of transferral, and related the entire story, also how he had lived and died in the forest. But he was not willing to believe this and instead placed me under house arrest till he might better learn the truth; and as he was about to send out a scouting party to inspect the hermit's dwelling and to have you fetched hither, I saw you being led to the tower. Because the governor now no longer had cause to doubt my testimony, since I had cited as corroboration the place where the hermit had lived, *item*[156] you and other living witnesses, particularly my sexton, who often let you and the hermit into the church before daybreak, and especially since the letter which he found in your prayer book gives excellent testimony not only to the truth of what I said but also of the saintliness of the blessed hermit, he thus desires to do well by you and me because of his late brother-in-law. You need but decide now what you wish him to do for you. If you wish to study, he will pay the expenses for it; if you have the desire to learn a trade, he will have you taught one; but if you wish to stay with him, then he will keep you like his own child, for he said he would take in even a dog if it should come to him from his late brother-in-law." I answered that it was all one to me what the governor did with me.

CHAPTER 23

Simplicius becomes a page; item, how the hermit's wife was lost

The parson kept me in his lodgings till ten o'clock before he went with me to the governor to tell him my decision, and he waited so long so that he could be his guest at the noonday meal, because the governor then entertained without specific invitation; for at that time Hanau was being blockaded, and times were so hard for the common man, what with the folks who had fled to the fortress to take refuge there, that even some folks who flattered themselves that they were above the common herd did not disdain to pick up off the streets frozen turnip peelings which the wealthy had chanced to throw away. And he did have such good fortune too that he got to sit next to the governor himself at the head of the table. I, however, waited upon the guests with a plate in my hand, as the steward had instructed me, in which I was about as skillful as a jackass is at playing chess. But the parson, with his tongue alone, made up for what the clumsiness of my body could not. He said that I had been brought up in the wilderness, had never been amongst people, and therefore should be considered excused because I could not yet know how I should comport myself in society. The loyalty which I had shown the hermit and the hard life I had endured with him were such as to evoke wonderment and were by themselves sufficient reason not only to tolerate my awkwardness but even to give me preferment over the finest boys of noble birth. He further related that I was the hermit's one and only joy, because my face, as he had often said, looked so like that of his beloved, and that he had often been surprised at my steadfastness and my inalterable resolve to stay with him, and at many other virtues for which he had praised me. *In summa*, he could not express adequately with what fervent ardor the hermit had recommended me to him, the parson, shortly before his death, and had owned that he loved me as much as if I were his own child.

This so tickled my ears that it seemed to me I had already received delight enough to make up for everything which I had endured with the hermit. The governor asked whether his late brother-in-law had known that he was at the time the commanding officer at Hanau. "Indeed!" said the parson. "I told him of it myself. But he (with a cheerful face, to be sure, and a slight smile) listened to it as impassively as if he had never heard the name Ramsey[157] before, so that even now when I ponder upon the matter, I cannot but be astonished at this man's steadfastness and firm resolve, namely, how he could bring himself not only to renounce the world but also to put quite out of his mind his best friend, who was, after all, near at hand!" Tears filled the eyes of the governor, who otherwise was not softhearted and womanish in spirit, but was rather a brave and valorous soldier. He said: "Had I known that he was still alive and where he might be found, I should have had him brought to me, even against his will, so that I might repay him for what he did for me, but since Fortune begrudges me this, I shall provide for his son in his stead. Alas!" he said further. "That honest cavalier had good cause to lament the loss of his wife, who was great with child, for she was captured by a party of Imperial horse that was pursuing the fleeing enemy, and also in the Spessart Forest, in fact. When I learned of this and knew not but what my brother-in-law had been killed in the battle at Höchst, I straightway sent a trumpeter[158] to the other side to ask after my sister and to ransom her, but I accomplished nothing, except that I learned that that same party of horse had been attacked and dispersed in the Spessart Forest by some peasants, and that in this skirmish my sister had been lost by them again, so that to this very day I know not whither she went."

This and the like was the table talk of the governor and the parson, about my hermit and his beloved, which couple's fate was all the more to be deplored because they had had but one year together. I, however, thus became the governor's page, and such a fellow as the people, particularly the peasants, when I was to announce them to my master, were already calling Milord Youngster, though one seldom sees a youngster who has been a milord but indeed milords who were once youngsters.

CHAPTER 24

Simplicius excoriates the folk and sees in the world many idols

At that time there was nothing of value about me but my pure conscience and my genuinely pious spirit, which were attended and accompanied by noble Innocence and Simplicity. Of vices I knew nothing at all but that I had chanced to hear the names of them or had read of them, and when I saw one of them actually committed, it was to me a terrible and seldom thing, because I had been brought up and taught to keep the presence of God ever in mind and to live most earnestly in accordance with His divine will; and because I knew what His will was, I was wont to weigh people's actions and character against it, and in doing this it seemed to me that I saw nothing but abominations. Lord God! How astonished I was at first when I considered the law and the Gospel, together with the admonitions of Christ, and then regarded the deeds of them who claimed to be His disciples and followers. Instead of candor and forthrightness, which every true Christian ought to practice, I found in all worldly folk nothing but hypocrisy, and such countless other follies that I even doubted whether I had Christians before me; for I could easily detect that many knew what the solemn will of God was, but I detected in them, on the other hand, no solemn effort to accomplish it.

And so my mind was filled with a thousand different crotchets and strange thoughts, and I was sorely tempted because of the command of Christ[159] when he says: "Judge not, that ye be not judged." Nevertheless, there came to my memory the words of St. Paul,[160] which he writes to the Gal. in Chapter 5: "Now the works of the flesh are manifest, which are these: adultery, fornication, uncleanness, lasciviousness, idolatry, witchcraft, enmity, strife, envy, wrath, contention, emulations, seditions, hatred, murder, drunkenness, revelings and the like, of which I tell you, as I have told you in time past, that they which do such things shall not inherit the kingdom of God." Then I thought: "After all, everyone is doing that openly. Why should I then not also conclude candidly from the words of the apostle that no one will achieve salvation either?"

Along with pride and greed (together with their hangers-on), gluttony, lechery, and fornication were a daily occurrence amongst those of means. And what seemed to me the most horrid abomination of all was that some, particularly the common soldiers, whose vices are not wont to be punished most severely, merely made light of both their godlessness and of the divine will of God. For example, I once heard one of them who had broken the marriage vows and even desired to be praised for the deed he had done say these godless words: "It serves the patient cuckold right that he's wearing a pair of horns on account of me, and if I'm to confess the truth, I did it more to offend the man than to pleasure the woman, so that I might avenge myself upon him." "What barren vengeance," answered an honest soul who was standing there, "by which one sullies one's own conscience and acquires the shameful name given to them as break the marriage vows!" "Break the marriage vows!" he answered with a derisive laugh. "I did not break them, I but bent them a little, for she and I were but following our natural bent. The marriage vows were not broken, for they are still man and wife. One breaks a marriage only when one runs off with a woman, thereby putting man and wife asunder." And then he straightway explained, in accordance with his devil's catechism, the seventh commandment, which expresses this view more clearly by saying "Thou shalt not steal." He uttered many more such words, so that I sighed to myself and thought: "O, you blasphemous sinner! You say that you merely bend marriages and that our Dear Lord breaks them because through death he puts asunder man and wife." "Do you not think," I said to him, from excess zeal and vexation, even though he was an officer, "that with these godless words you sin even more than by breaking the marriage vows?" He, however, answered me: "You dunce! Shall I box you on the ears a few times?" And I do believe that I should have got some brisk ones if the fellow had not been obliged to fear my master. And so I kept silent and after that saw that it was no seldom occurrence at all that single folk cast their eyes upon wedded ones, and wedded folk upon single ones.

When I was still studying with my hermit the way to achieve eternal life, I wondered why God had forbidden His people, under pain of harsh punishment, to worship false idols, for I imagined to myself that anyone who had recognized the true, eternal God would surely never ever honor and worship any other god, and then I concluded in my stupidity that this commandment was unnecessary and had been given in vain. But alas! Fool that I was, I knew not what I thought I knew, for as soon as I entered the world I saw that despite this commandment nearly everyone had a particular idol of his own. Indeed, some had more idols than the ancient and modern heathens themselves. Some had theirs in the money chest, in which they placed all confidence and trust. Many a man had his at court and placed all his faith in him, even though the idol was but a court favorite and often as dissolute a sluggard as his worshiper himself was, because his airy divinity consisted solely in the prince's favor, which was as fickle as April weather. Others had theirs in their *reputatio*[161] and imagined that if they but preserved it, they would themselves be demigods. Yet others had theirs in their heads, namely, those to whom God had given sound wits, so that they were adept at grasping certain arts and sciences; these set to one side the Kind One Who had given them good wits and relied upon the gift which He had bestowed upon them, in the hope that it would give them everything they required. There were also many whose idol was their own belly, to which they daily made sacrifices, as the heathens did to Bacchus[162] and Ceres[163] in times gone by; and when the belly showed itself refractory, or other human ailments announced their presence, then these wretched people made a god of the *medicus*[164] and sought the preservation of their life in the apothecary shop, from which, to be sure, they were, more often than not, dispatched to their death. Many fools made goddesses of sleek sluts; they gave them fanciful names, worshiped them day and night with many thousand sighs, and composed songs to them which contained nothing but their praises, along with a humble plea that they have mercy and pity upon their folly and become such fools as they themselves were. On the other hand, there were women who had set up their own beauty as their god. "It will surely get me a husband," they thought, "no matter what God may say about it!" This idol was sustained and worshiped daily with all manner of paints, salves, lotions, powders, and all manner of other stuff with which they besmeared themselves. I saw people who took well-situated houses to be gods, for they said that as long as they had dwelt in them good fortune and health had been vouchsafed them, and the money had come raining in the windows, as it were; which folly I found most surprising, because I saw the true reason why the householders earned so much money. I knew a fellow who for some years could not sleep because of the tobacco trade, because he gave to it his heart, mind, and every waking thought, which ought to have been devoted to God alone. He wasted many thousand sighs upon it, by day as well as by night, because he prospered from it. But what happened? This madman died and vanished like tobacco smoke itself. Then I thought: "O, you wretched man! Had the salvation of your soul and the honor of our true God been as important to you as that idol which stands in front of your shop in the shape of a Brazilian with a roll of tobacco under his arm and a pipe in his mouth, I should be confident that without the slightest doubt you would have earned the right to wear a splendid wreath of honor in the other world." Another associate[165] of these fools had even worse gods, for when at a party everyone was telling in what manner he had nourished himself and survived during the time of terrible hunger and famine, he bluntly said that snails and frogs had been his lord god, for if there had been none of them, he must needs have died of hunger. I asked him what God Himself, Who had given him these *insecta*[166] as sustenance, had meant to him. But the fool could not answer, and I could not but be all the more surprised, because I have never read anywhere that the idolatrous Egyptians of old, or the American Indians of most recent times, ever proclaimed that sort of varmint a god, as this coxcomb did.

I once went with a distinguished gentleman into a curiosities cabinet in which there were rare and beautiful things. Of the paintings none pleased me more than an *Ecce homo*,[167] because of its pity-arousing depiction, by which it enraptured those who beheld it and spurred them to sympathy. Next to it hung a paper chart painted in China upon which were painted the idols of the Chinese seated in their majesty, some of them depicted like devils. The master of the house asked me which piece in his curiosities cabinet pleased me best. I pointed to the *Ecce homo*, but he said I was in error; the Chinese painting was rarer and therefore more valuable; he would not give it up for ten such *Ecce homos*. I answered: "Does what passes your lips come from your heart?" He said: "I should certainly think so!" Then I said to him: "Then the god of your heart is one whose *contrefait* your lips assert to be most valuable." "You madman!" said he. "I hold rarity in esteem." I answered: "What is rarer and more wonderful than that God's Son Himself suffered for our sake, as this picture shows us?"

CHAPTER 25

To strange Simplicius everything in the world seems strange, and he for his part seems that way to the world too

Now as much as these and yet a greater multitude of other sorts of idols were venerated, just as much, on the other hand, was God in His truly divine majesty scorned, for while I saw no one who desired to keep His word and commandment, I did see many, on the other hand, who opposed Him in all things and surpassed in wickedness the publicans (who, in the time when Jesus still walked the earth, were public sinners). Christ says: "Love your enemies,[168] bless them that curse you, do good unto them that hate you, pray for them which insult and persecute you, that ye may be children of your Father which is in heaven; for if ye love them which love you, what reward have ye? Do not even the publicans the same?" But I not only found no one who desired to obey this command of Christ, rather every one did just the opposite. The motto was "Kin are mostly less than kind"; and nowhere was there more envy, hatred, jealousy, strife, and contention than betwixt brothers, sisters, and other blood relatives, particularly when it fell to them to share an inheritance. And everywhere the craftmen's guilds hated one another too, so that I could not but palpably see and conclude that the public sinners, publicans, and tax collectors, who were despised because of their evil and godless ways, were far superior to us present-day Christians in regard to practicing brotherly love, since Christ Himself gives testimony that they loved one another. Therefore I considered: if we have no reward when we do not love our enemies, what manner of great punishment must then be in store for us if we hate even our friends? Where there should have been the greatest love and loyalty, I found the utmost disloyalty and the most powerful hatred. Many a master flayed his loyal servants and subjects, but on the other hand, some subjects were rogues in their dealings with their masters. I saw continuing squabbling betwixt many married folk; many a tyrant treated his honest wife worse than a dog, and many a loose slut deemed her virtuous husband a fool and an ass. Many brutish masters cheated their hard-working servants of the wages due them, and scrimped on both food and drink; on the other hand, I saw many faithless servants who through theft or negligence brought their virtuous masters to ruin. Merchants and craftsmen vied with one another in playing the Jew,[169] and through all manner of schemes and swindles they sucked the peasant dry of what he had earned by the sweat of his brow; on the other hand, some peasants were so utterly godless that they even made the effort, if they were not decently cunning enough at evil, to deceive others, or even their own masters, by pretending to be simpleminded. I once saw a soldier give another one a brisk blow on the cheek, and I presumed that the man who had been struck would turn the other cheek (because I had never yet been present at a brawl). But I was in error, for the man who had been insulted drew his sword and gave the other man a sound blow on the head in return. I screamed to him at the top of my lungs, saying: "Alas, my good man, what are you doing?" "You take me for a sluggard?" he answered. "The devil take me if I do not take my revenge or lose my life! Ha! A man would have to be a rogue to let someone treat him like a *couillon*!"[170] The uproar betwixt the two combatants grew louder, because the supporters of each, together with the crowd standing there and others who came running up, also got embroiled with one another. Then I heard them swear[171] so wantonly by God and their immortal souls that I could not believe that they held these to be their most precious treasures. But that was mere child's play, for they did not stop at such petty children's oaths, but rather one straightway heard: "May thunder, lightning, and hail strike me dead!" "May the devil take me and tear me into not one but into a hundred thousand pieces and take me away through the air with him!" The holy sacraments likewise could not but be trotted out, not merely sevenfold, but in such exaggerated expressions as "I swear by a hundred thousand sacraments!" "By tons of sacraments!" "By galleys full of sacraments!" and "By moats full of sacraments!" so that again my hair stood on end. I again thought of Christ's command[172] when he says: "Swear not at all, neither by heaven, for it is God's throne, nor by the earth, for it is His footstool; neither by Jerusalem, for it is the city of the great King. Neither shalt thou swear by thy own head, because thou canst not make one hair white or black. But let thy communication be 'Yea' and 'No'; for whatsoever is more than these cometh of evil." All this, and what I saw and heard, I pondered upon, and I firmly concluded that these brawlers were not Christians at all, and I therefore sought other companions.

What seemed most terrible of all to me was when I heard some these braggarts boast of their wickedness, sins, shame, and vices, for at divers times, indeed daily, I heard them say": "'ods blood! did we ever get drunk yesterday! I got dead drunk three times in one day and puked as many times." "'ods wounds! Did we ever torment the peasants, those rogues!" "'ods bodikins! Did we ever take booty!" "'ods poison! Did we ever have fun with the women and maidens!" *Item*, "I cut him down with my sword as if the hail had struck him down." "I shot him so that his eyeballs rolled back in his head." "I cheated him so nicely that the devil might have took him." "I tripped him up so nicely that he might have broke his neck." These and such-like unchristian words filled my ears every day, and in addition I saw and heard people committing sins "by God," which is surely to be lamented. The practice was most common amongst the soldiers, namely, when they said: "By God, we're going to go on patrol, to plunder, to steal, to shoot dead, to kill, to attack, to take prisoners, to set afire," and whatever their other terrible works and deeds may be. Thus usurers also make so bold as to close their sales "by God" so that they may flay and scrape in accordance with their devilish greed. I once saw two knaves[173] hanged who were going to rob a house at night, and when they put the ladder against the house and one of them was about to climb into the window "by God!" the watchful householder threw him down again to "go to the devil," from which he broke his leg and was therefore captured, and some days later hanged, together with his comrade. Now when I heard, saw, and considered things of that sort, and as was my wont whisked out the Holy Scriptures, or else naively admonished against it, people took me to be a fool. Indeed, I was so often derided for my good intentions that I finally also grew indignant and resolved to say nothing at all, which resolve I could not keep, out of Christian love for my fellowman. I wished that everyone had been brought up by my hermit, since I was of the opinion that many folks would then look at the doings in the world through my eyes and would see the world the way Simplicius then saw it. I had not enough wit to understand that if there were none but people like Simplicius in the world, one would not see so many vices either. Meanwhile, it is certain that a man of the world who is accustomed to all vices and follies and who commits them himself cannot realize in the least what manner of evil path he and his ilk are walking down.

CHAPTER 26

A strange new way of wishing one another good luck and of greeting one another

Now when I thought I had reason to doubt whether I was living amongst Christians or not, I went to the parson and related to him everything I had heard and seen, and what my thoughts were, namely, that I held the people to be mere mockers of Christ and of His word, and not Christians, with the request that he do help me out of this nightmare, so that I might know what I ought to hold my fellow human beings to be. The parson answered: "Of course they are Christians, and I should not advise you to call them otherwise." "My God!" said I. "How can that be? For when I point out to the one or the other of them the transgression which he is committing against God, I am mocked and derided." "Do not be surprised at that," answered the parson. "I believe that if our pious early Christians who lived at the time of Christ, indeed, if the apostles themselves, were to be resurrected and to come to the world today, they would ask the same question as you and would indeed, like you, be taken by everyone to be fools. What you have hitherto seen and heard is a common thing, and mere child's play compared to what otherwise goes on and is perpetrated in the world, secretly and openly, with violence against God and man, but let that not vex you. You will find few Christians such as the late Sir Samuel[174] was."

Now while we were thus talking with one another, they led across the square some men who had been captured by the other side, which interrupted our discourse, because we too looked at the captives. Then I heard an absurdity the likes of which I should never have dreamt of, but it was merely a new fashion in greeting and welcoming one another; for one man from our garrison who had heretofore also served the Emperor knew one of the prisoners, went up to him, gave him his hand, pressed the other's hand with sheer joy and affection, and said: "Damme! Are you still alive, you whoreson knave? Fuchris-sakes, look how the devil has brought us together here! 'od damme, I thought you'd long since been hanged!" Then the other one answered: "'ods bodikins, you old whoreson rogue! Is it really you? The devil take you, how did you get here? I should never in all my days have thought I would come upon you again; instead I thought the devil would have long since come to fetch you!" And when they parted from one another, one said to the other not "God be with you!" but "Good luck! Good luck! Perhaps we can get together tomorrow, and then we'll get roaring drunk together."

"Is that not a fine godly greeting?" said I to the parson. "Are those not wonderful Christian wishes? Do these fellows not have a holy resolve for tomorrow? Who would recognize them to be Christians, or listen to them without being astonished? If they speak to one another that way out of Christian love, then how will it go when they quarrel with one another? Parson, if these are sheep from Christ's flock and you are His appointed shepherd, then it would behoove you to lead them to a better pasture." "Yes, my dear child," answered the parson, "amongst godless soldiers that is just how it goes, God have mercy! Even if I were to say something to them, it would do no more good than if I were preaching to the deaf, and I should have nothing for my pains but these godless fellows' perilous hatred." I was surprised; I chatted a while longer with the parson and went to wait upon the governor, for I had leave to look about the city at certain times and to go to the parson, because my master had got wind of my simplemindedness and thought it would abate if I got about in the world, saw and heard things, and if others schooled me or, as they say, got rid of my rough edges and knocked me into shape.

CHAPTER 27

The secretarius is smoked out of the chancellory by a foul stench

My master's partiality to me increased with each passing day, and with each passing day became greater, because with each passing day I came to look more and more like not only his sister, who had been the wife of the hermit, but also him himself, since the good food and idle days in a short while made me sleek. This partiality I enjoyed with everyone, for whosoever had some business with the governor also showed himself partial to me, and the *secretarius*[175] in particular rather liked me. Since he was obliged to teach me to cipher, he had much amusement from my simplemindedness and ignorance. He had but recently come from his studies and was therefore full of schoolboy pranks, which gave him the appearance of having one oar too many or too few out of the water. He often persuaded me that black was white and white was black. Therefore it happened that at first I believed everything he said and in the end nothing at all he said. I once reproached him for his dirty inkwell, but he answered that this was the best thing he had in the entire chancellery, for from it he plucked out whatever he desired: the finest ducats, clothes, and, *in summa*, what means he possessed he had fished out of it little by little. I refused to believe that such splendid things were to be got out of such a small contemptible thing. He, however, said that the *spiritus papyri*[176] (that is what he called ink) was capable of doing this, and that the inkwell was called a well because it held such large things. I asked how in the world one could get them out, since one could scarce stick two fingers into it. He answered that he had an arm in his head which was compelled to do this labor; he also hoped soon to pluck a rich and beautiful maiden from it, and if he had good fortune, he ventured to believe he would soon get his own land and subjects out of it, which had indeed happened before on occasion. I could not but be astonished at this cunning skill and asked whether yet other people possessed this same art. "Of course." he answered. "All chancellors, doctors, *secretarii*, procurators or lawyers, *commissarii*,[177] *notarii*,[178] merchants, and tradesmen, and countless others, who generally become wealthy men from it, if they but fish diligently." I said: "Then the peasantry and hard-working folks are stupid to eat their daily bread which they earn by the sweat of their brow and not to learn this art too." He answered: "Some know not how profitable this art is; and therefore they do not desire to learn it. Some would like to learn it, but the arm in their head or other means are wanting. Some learn the art and have

62

arm enough, but they do not have the skill which the art requires if one desires to become rich from it. Others know and possess the skill in everything which appertains to it, but they live upon barren soil and have no opportunity, as I do, to practice the art properly."

As we were discoursing in this manner about the inkwell (which in fact reminded me of the never-empty purse of Fortunatus)[179] I chanced to take in hand the book which listed all the titles of the nobility and how they should be addressed, in which book I found, to my way of thinking at the time, more foolish things than I had ever before laid eyes upon. I said to the *secretario*: "These are all the progeny of Adam and made of the same clay, and indeed but ashes and dust. Whence, then, does so great a difference in them come? 'Your Excellency,' 'Your Holiness,' 'Most Serene Highness'! Are these not divine attributes? Here one of them is 'Gracious'; there another one is 'Serene'! And why must the word 'Highness' always be added? Everyone knows that some people are taller than others, but a few inches diffence does not make for 'Highness'! And why do they have here 'Your Eminence' but not 'Your Eninence'? And what happened to 'Your Oh-inence' 'Your Pee-inence,' 'Your Que-inence'? And what manner of foolish words are these: 'Right Reverend'? Is that to distinguish him from 'Wrong Reverend' or from 'Left Reverend'?" The *secretarius* could not but laugh at me and made an effort to explain the one and the other title, and all the words particularly; but I persisted that the titles were not right, for it would be much more to one's credit if he were entitled "Friendly" rather than "Eminent"; *item*, if the word "Noble" itself signified none but highly praiseworthy virtues, then why was a "Noble Sir" of lower rank than a "Your Lordship" (which words designated a prince or count)? And that the members of the nobility are "Well Born" is an outright falsehood. Any nobleman's mother could attest to that if she were asked how well she felt at her son's birth.

Now while I was thus making sport of these honorifics, there unexpectedly escaped from me such terrible belly-gas that both the *secretarius* and I were frighted at it. In a trice it announced its presence both to our noses and in the entire room, as if its arrival had not already been heard clearly enough. "You swine!" said the *secretarius* to me. "Get you gone to the other swine in the pigpen, with whom you are better able to join in song, you fart, than to converse with honorable folk!" But he and I were both obliged to vacate the premises and leave them to the foul stench. And contrary to the old saw which says that it is an ill wind that blows no good, this ill wind caused me to be banished from the chancellery.

CHAPTER 28

One who envies Simplicius teaches him fortunetelling, and another pretty little trick too

I fell into this misfortune quite innocently, however, for the unusual foods and medicines which they gave me every day to rectify my shrunken stomach and knotted intestines incited in my belly many powerful storms and strong winds which tormented me extraordinarily when they sought to break out by violence. And since I did not realize that it was wrong to let Nature have her way in this regard, particularly since it would have been impossible to resist such inner force in the long run anyway, and my hermit had never given me any instruction in the matter (for these guests were few and far between with us), nor had my Pa forbidden me to let these little fellows go their way, I let them take the air and let everything pass which desired to be on its way, till I lost my credit with the *secretario*, as I have related. To be sure, his patronage might easily have been dispensed with, had I got into no more trouble, but I fared like any virtuous man who goes to a nobleman's court, where the snake takes up arms against Nasica,[180] Goliath against David,[182] the Minotaur against Theseus,[183] Medusa against Perseus,[184] Circe against Ulysses,[185] Aegisthus against Menelaus,[186] Paludes against Coraebus,[187] Medea against Peleas,[188] Nessus against Hercules,[189] and, even worse, Althea against her own son, Meleagrus.[181,190]

Besides me, my master had, as his other page, a first-rate scamp who had already been with him for a few years. To him I gave my heart, because he was the same age as I. I thought: "He is Jonathan and you are David."[191] But he vied with me because of the great partiality which my master bore for me and which daily increased. He feared I might perchance even step into his shoes, and he therefore secretly regarded me with eyes full of hatred and envy and pondered upon ways in which he might trip me up and through my fall prevent his own. But I had the eyes of a dove,[192] and I was also of a completely different cast of mind. Indeed, I confided to him all my secrets, which consisted of nothing but childishly naive and innocent things, for which reason he could nowhere find a way to harm me. One time we had been chatting for a long while in bed before we went to sleep, and because we were talking about fortune-telling, he promised to teach me it for nothing, and then bade me put my head under the covers, for he persuaded me that he must needs impart the art to me in this manner. I did exactly as I was told and paid close attention, waiting for the arrival of the fortune-telling spirit. 'ods bodikins! It gained entry to my nose, and indeed so strongly that I was obliged to put my entire head outside the covers again. "What is it?" asked my teacher. I answered: "You're fartin'!" "And you," he answered, "are now a fartin'teller, for you were able to tell that I was fartin'." This I did not feel to be an insult, for at that time I had no gall, but instead desired to know of him by what manner of trick one could get rid of these fellows so quietly. My comrade answered: "That trick is easy. You need but lift your left leg, like a dog pissing on a corner stone, and say to yourself *je pete*,[193] *je pete*, *je pete*, and at the same time press as hard as you can. Then they'll go slinking away as silently as thieves." "That's good." said I. "And even if it stinks[194] afterwards, they'll think the dogs have befouled the air, particularly if I've lifted up my left leg nice and high." Alas, I thought, had I but known this trick when I was in the chancellery today!

CHAPTER 29

Two eyes from a calf's head fall to the lot of Simplicius

The next day my master had arranged for his officers and other good friends a banquet fit for a king, because he had received the glad tidings that his troops had taken the strong fortress of Braunfels[195] without losing a single man; so I was obliged, as was my office, to help carry in food like everyone else waiting the table, to pour wine, and to wait upon the guests with plate in hand. The first day a large fat calf's head[196] (of which it is customarily said that no poor man dare eat one) was handed me to carry to the table. Now because it was boiled till it was very tender, one eye, with all the substance belonging to it, was hanging out rather far, which to me was a delightful and seductive sight. And because the smell of both the fresh bacon broth and the ginger strewn upon it was so enticing to me, I felt such an appetite that my mouth watered till it was full. *In summa*, the eye smiled at my eyes, my nose, and my mouth at the same time and bade me, as it were, to be so kind as to incorporate it into my voracious stomach. I did not let myself be tugged by the coat tails for long, but fulfilled my desires. In the hallway I so masterfully lifted out the one eye with the spoon which I had just received that day, and without hesitation so quickly dispatched it to its appointed place that no one became aware of it till the *piece de resistance*[197] of the meal came to the table and betrayed me and itself. For when they were about to carve it, my master straightway saw why the carver held back in surprise. He certainly did not wish to be the butt of ridicule because they had made so bold as to serve him a one-eyed calf`s head! The cook was obliged to come to the table, and those who had borne it in were questioned with him. Finally the finger pointed to poor Simplicius, namely, because the head with both eyes intact had been given to him to take to the table; but what happened after that no one could say. My master, with a terrible scowl to my way of thinking, asked what I had done with the calf's eye. Quickly I whisked my spoon out of my pocket again, gave the calf's head a second *coup de grace*,[198] and showed them, in a manner both short and sweet, what they wished to know, since in a trice I downed the second eye just as I had the first one. "*Par dieu!*"[199] said my lord and master. "This *actus*[200] is better than ten calves!" The gentlemen present praised this *dictum*[201] and called my deed, which I had done out of naivete, a wondrously shrewd invention and a portent of my future valor and fearless resolve, so that this time I not only happily escaped punishment by repeating the very act by which I had merited it, but also received from some amusing wags, toadies, and court fools the following praise: I had acted wisely, they said, in lodging both eyes in the same place, so that they might afford each other the aid and companionship to which, after all, they had been originally destined by Nature. My master said, however, that I should not play this trick upon him a second time.

CHAPTER 30

How the people little by little got tipsy and finally, without knowing it, blind drunk

At this meal (I imagine it happens at other ones too) they came to the table in quite Christian fashion. They said grace very quietly, and to all appearances very devoutly too. This quiet devoutness continued as they partook of the soup and the first course, with them eating just as if they were in a Capuchin monastery. But scarce had each one said "To your good health!" three or four times when everyone grew much louder. I could not describe how, as time passed, each one's voice little by little grew louder, unless I were to compare the entire company to an orator who begins softly at first and in the end thunders out his words. They brought dishes called "appetizers," because they were spiced and designed to whet their appeite for drink, so that they could drink all the more, *item*, "side dishes," so called because they were supposed to taste rather good alongside the drinks; not to mention all manner of French *potages*[202] and Spanish *ollas potridas*.[203] These foods, through thousands of artful culinary techniques and countless admixtures, had been so peppered, laced with herbs, seasoned, mixed, spiced, and prepared to stimulate drinking, in such wise that they were completely changed from what they were when Nature originally produced them, that Cnaeus Manlius[204] himself, even if he had just come straight from Asia and had his best cooks with him, would nevertheless not have recognized what they were originally. I thought to myself: "Why could these not also destroy the senses of a person who enjoys them and the drink which goes with them (for which purpose, primarily, they had been prepared), or even turn that person into a *bestia*?[205] Who knows whether Circe employed any different means than these when she transformed Ulysses'[206] crew into swine? I saw at once that with these courses the guests glutted themselves like swine, then drank like fish, all the while behaving like jackasses, and in the end they all of them puked like tanners' dogs! In vessels the size of milk-pails they poured down their gullets the noble wines of Hochheim, Bacharach, and Klingenberg, which straightway caused their effect to be felt up above, in their heads. Then I saw to my astonishment how everyone was transformed, namely, how sensible folk who were shortly before in full possession of all five of their senses now quite on a sudden fell to acting like fools and to uttering the silliest things in the world. As time went on, the great follies which they committed and the great toasts which they drank to one another became ever more extravagant, so that it appeared that follies and toasts were vying with one another to see which of them could outdo the other. Finally their contest turned into revolting swinishness. Quite in keeping with my nature at that time, I knew not whence their giddiness came, since the effect of wine—drunkenness—was in fact still unknown to me, which then put diverting crotchets and fancies into my odd ponderings. I well saw their strange *minas*,[207] but I knew not the origin of their condition. Till then each one had emptied his plate with good appetite, but when their stomachs were full, it became more difficult for them than it is for a coachman who with a rested team moves along well on a plain but cannot drive it up a mountain. And when their heads too were full of wine, their inability to think clearly was replaced by something else: for the one, by the courage which he had imbibed with the wine; for a second one, by a sincere desire to drink a toast to his friend; or for a third one, by the honest effort to prove his mettle as a nobleman. And when these, in the long run, could not suffice either, each exhorted the others to pour down the wine by the measure, in toasts to great lords, or his dear friends, or his beloved, at which the eyes of many of them filled with tears and the sweat of panic broke out upon their faces. But the drunken carousing must needs go on! Indeed, in the end they made noise with drums, fifes, and fiddles, and shot off their pistols as an accompaniment, without doubt because the wine was compelled to invade and take their stomachs by force. I wondered whither they were able to pour it all, because I did not yet know that before it rightly got warm inside them they gave it back up with great pain from the very place into which they had shortly before poured it, at the utmost peril to their health.

My parson was at this banquet also, and like the others, because he was a human being like the others, he was pleased to excuse himself from the table. I went off after him and said: "My dear Parson, why do the people act so strange? Why is it that they stagger so hither and thither? It well nigh seems to me that they no longer rightly have their wits about them. They have eaten and drunk their fill and swear that the devil should take them if they can drink another drop, and yet they do not cease to glut themselves with drink! Are they obliged to do it, or are they wasting food and drink so uselessly of their own free will, to spite God?" "My dear child," answered the parson, "'wine in, wits out,' as the saying goes. This is nothing yet compared to what is coming. Tomorrow towards dawn will scarce be time for them to part from one another, for even though their stomachs are packed full, they've not yet got right merry." "But will their stomachs not burst," said I, "if they keep shoveling food and drink into them so immoderately? Can their souls, which are in God's image, survive in such fatted-swine bodies, in which they are imprisoned without any godly emotion, just as if they were locked in dark prisons and varmint-ridden thieves' towers? Their noble souls, I say, how can they torment them so? Are not their senses, of which their souls ought to be making use, buried as if in the guts of mindless beasts?" "Hold your tongue!" answered the parson. "Else you may be dealt grievous blows. This is no time to be giving a sermon, else I should do it, and better than you!" When I heard this, I continued to observe in silence how they wantonly wasted food and drink, despite the fact that poor Lazarus, whom they might have refreshed with them, was, in the form of many hundreds of refugees from the Wetterau region[208] whose hunger peered forth from their eyes, wasting away upon our doorstep because his cupboard was bare.

CHAPTER 31

How Simplicius fails badly when he tries to perform his trick, and how they beat time to churchsong on his body

While I was waiting upon the table with my plate in my hand and my mind plagued with all manner of crotchets and odd notions, my stomach was not leaving me in peace either. It rumbled and grumbled without surcease and thereby gave it to be understood that there were some little fellows in there who desired fresh air. I thought to rid myself of the rumbling, to open the passageway, and in so doing to avail myself of the trick which my comrade had taught me but the night before. Following his instructions I lifted my left leg, together with the thigh, high into the air, pressed with all the strength I could muster, and was about to say to myself at the same time my *je pete* thrice. But when this enormous fellow whisked out of my behind and, contrary to my expectations, made such a terrible sound, I was so frightened that I no longer knew what I was about. On a sudden I became as frightened as if I were standing upon the ladder to the gallows and the hangman had already started to put the noose around my neck, and in this precipitous fear I was so confused that I no longer had command of my own limbs, for which reason my mouth too grew rebellious at the sound of this abrupt noise and was unwilling to give precedence in any way to my behind, nor to let it do all the talking, even though it, created for talking and screaming, was supposed to be mumbling its words to itself. Therefore my mouth, to spite my behind, let what I had in mind to say to myself be heard quite loudly, and indeed as frightfully as if someone were about to cut my throat. The more horribly the wind from below gave off explosions, the more terribly the "*je pete*" came out above, as if my stomach`s entrance and exit were vying with one another to see which of them was capable of thundering away in the most frightful voice. In this wise I did incur alleviation in my gut, but also the displeasure of my master, the governor. At this unexpected explosion all his guests well nigh grew sober again. I, however, because I could not, despite all my efforts and labor, control any of my wind, was strapped to a washtub and beaten so badly that I remember it to this very day. This was the first bastonading I had ever received since the first breath I ever took, because I had so abominably befouled the air which, after all, we were all obliged to share. Then they brought incense tablets and candles, and the guests took out their musk-boxes and balsam-boxes, and even their snuff; but the best *aromata*[209] were of well nigh no use. Thus, I had from this *actu*,[210] which I played better than the best actor in the world, peace in my stomach but blows on my backside, whilst the guests had their noses full of the stench and the waiters their troubles making the room smell good again.

CHAPTER 32

Deals again with nothing else but drunken carousing and how one can rid oneself of parsons

When this was over I was obliged to wait upon the table again as before. My parson was still there and was, like others, urged to drink, but he did not rightly wish to do it, but rather said that he did not desire to drink like a beast. Contrarily, one fine toper demonstrated to him that he, the parson, drank like a beast, whereas he, the toper, and those others present, drank like human beings. "For," said he, "a beast drinks but as much as tastes good to it and quenches its thirst, because it does not know what is good, nor do they like to drink wine. We human beings, however, are pleased to make use of drink and to let the noble juice of the grape slide down our gullets, as did our forbears also." "That is all well and good," said the parson, "but it behooves me to take every measure to observe moderation." "Indeed," answered the other, "and an honest man keeps his word!" and then had a measure of wine poured for him to quaff when he drank to the parson's good health. But the parson escaped and left the toper behind with his pail of wine.

Now when he had been got rid of, everything became topsy-turvy, and it began to appear as if this banquet was meant to be the specified time and occasion for people to avenge themselves upon one another by drinking themselves into a stupor, to bring shame upon one another, or else to play tricks upon one another; for when one of them was so far gone that he could neither sit up, walk, nor stand, the others said "Now we're even! You did the same to me before. Now you're paid back!" and so forth, etc. And anyone who was able to endure and to tope the best was quick to boast about it and thought himself a prince of a fellow. Finally they were all staggering about as if they had eaten henbane. It was really a quaint diversion to see them, and yet no one was astonished at it, as I was. One sang, the other wept; one laughed, the other moaned; one cursed, the other prayed; one cried loudly "Courage!" and the other was no longer able to say anything at all; one was quiet and peaceful, the other desired to banish the devil by brawling; one slept and kept silent, the other chattered so much that no one could get a word in edgewise. One related his amorous adventures, the other his terrible deeds in battle; some talked of the church and of religious matters, others of the *ratio status*,[211] politics, the affairs of the world and of the Empire; some of them ran hither and thither and could not stay in one spot, others were lying down and could not lift even a finger, much less walk or stand upright; some were

70

eating like plowhands and as if they had not touched food for a week, others were puking up again what they had swallowed down that day. In short, all they did and omitted to do was so funny, foolish, odd, and at the same time so sinful and godless that the foul smell which had escaped me and for which I had also been beaten so cruelly was to be accounted as nothing in comparison to it. Finally a serious quarrel began at the lower end of the table. Then people threw glasses, beakers, bowls, and plates at one another's heads and struck one another not only with fists but with chairs, chair-legs, swords, and all manner of other objects, so that the red blood flowed down over their ears, and my master straightway put an end to the quarrel again.

What the governor did when he became abominably drunk

Now when it was peaceful again, the master-topers took the musicians, together with the ladies, and strolled to another house, the great hall of which was chosen for and dedicated to another folly. My master, however, sat down on his couch, because he felt ill, either from anger or from overindulging. I left him lying where he lay, so that he might rest and sleep, but I had scarce got to the doorway when he attempted to whistle for me but could not do it. He called out to me, saying nothing but "Simpls!" I sprang to his side and found his eyes rolled back in his head like a beast's when its throat is cut. I stood there before him like a bump on a log and knew not what ought to be done. But he pointed to the *tresoir*²¹² and babbled: "Br, bri, bring that thing here, you scoundrel! Ha, ha, hand me the *lavoir*! I'm, I'm go-, goin, goin' to puke!" I hastened and brought the washbasin, and when I got to him both his cheeks were puffed out like a trumpeter's. He seized me quickly by the arm and compelled me to stand so that I could not but hold the *lavoir*²¹³ directly under his mouth, which on a sudden popped open with the most painful gagging and spewed forth such foul *materi*²¹⁴ into the aforementioned *lavoir* that I well nigh fainted from the intolerable stench, particularly because (*sal. ven.*)²¹⁵ some pieces sprayed into my face. I was almost about to join him in his activity, but when I saw how he paled I desisted out of fear and was afraid that his soul would escape him together with his puke, because he broke out into a cold sweat, and his face looked like that of a man who is dying.

71

But straightway when he had recovered again, he bade me fetch some fresh water so that he might rinse out his wine-bag again.

After that he commanded me to take away the puke, which, because it was lying in a silver *lavoir*, did not seem to me to be anything disgusting, but rather a bowl full of appetizers, which most assuredly does not deserve to be thrown away. Besides, I knew that my master had not collected anything bad in his stomach, but instead splendid and delicate pasties, and also all manner of baked things, wild fowl, game, and meat, which one could still easily recognize and distinguish. I scurried off with it but knew not whither, or what I should do with it; and I durst not ask my master. I went to the court steward, whom I showed this fine *tractament*[216] and asked what I should do with the puke. He answered: "You fool! Take it to the tailor so that he can make a fine gown of it!" I asked where the tailor was. "No," he answered, since he saw how simpleminded I was, "take it to the doctor so that he may inspect it and see what condition our master is in." This fool's errand I should have gone on, had the steward not feared the consequences of it. He therefore bade me take the stuff to the kitchen, with the charge that the maids should save it and pepper it, which in all seriousness I did, and for that reason was teased mightily by those sluts.

CHAPTER 34

How Simplicius ruined a dance

My master was just going out when I got rid of my *lavoir*. I walked along behind him to a large house, where I saw in the great hall so many gentlemen, ladies, and single persons whirling about so quickly that it was teeming with people. They were tripping about and yowling so much that I thought they had all gone stark raving mad, for I could not divine what they might intend with this raging and storming. Indeed, the sight of them[217] seemed so terrible to me that my end stood on hair,[218] and the only thing I could imagine was that all of them must needs be bereft of their wits. When we came closer I saw that they were our guests, who had still had their wits about them that very forenoon. "My God!" I thought to myself. "What are these poor folk doing? Alas! A madness has surely befallen them." Soon it occurred to me that it might perchance be evil spirits who were in disguises and were mocking the entire human race with their frivolous running about and monkey-business, for I thought: "Had they human souls and God's image in them, they would surely not act so inhuman." When my master came to the entry-hall and was about to enter the great hall, the raging was just coming to an end, but they were still bending and bowing their heads and scraping and sliding their feet over the floor, so that it seemed to me as if they were attempting to wipe out the footprints which they had made during their raging. From the sweat which poured down their faces, and from their huffing and puffing, I could deduce that they had been working themselves to death, but their cheerful faces gave it to be understood that they did not regard these labors to be onerous.

I would surely have liked to know whither indeed this foolishness was meant to lead, and I therefore asked my comrade and bosom friend, who but shortly before had taught me fortune-telling, what the meaning of this raging was, or as what this raging, tripping, and trotting was to be regarded. He told me, swearing that it was the gospel truth, that those present had made a compact to stamp in the floor of the hall[219] by force. "Why else," said he, "do you think they are hopping about so wildly? Did you not see that to amuse themselves they have already broken out the windows? The very same thing will happen to this floor." "Oh Lord!" I answered. "Then we must needs perish, and in falling, together with them, break every bone in our bodies!" "Yes," said my comrade, "that is the purpose they have in mind, and they are working like the devil to do it. You'll see that when they venture into mortal peril, each one seizes a pretty lady or maiden, for it is said that pairs of folk who fall whilst holding on to one another that way are generally not hurt." Since I believed all this, I was overcome with such anxiety and fear for my life that I no longer knew where I should stay; and when the musicians, whom I had not yet espied, were heard in the bargain, and the men ran for the ladies the way soldiers run for their firearms and posts when they hear the sound of the drums, and when each seized a lady by the hand, it really seemed to me as if I already saw the floor collapsing and myself and many others plunging head over heels through it. And when they began to jump about so that the entire building trembled, because they had begun to play a popular melody, I thought "Now your life is at an end!" My only thought was that the entire building would suddenly collapse. Therefore, in extremest anxiety I seized by the arm, abruptly and like a bear, a lady of high nobility and excellent virtue with whom my master was just then conversing, and I clung to her like a burr. And when she gave a start, not knowing what manner of foolish notions were going through my head, I acted the role of the *homme desperat*[220] and fell to screaming in desperation as if someone were about to murder me. And as if that were not enough, something also escaped me and into my breeches that gave off an indescribably foul stench, the likes of which my nose had not perceived in a long while. On a sudden the musicians left off playing, the men and women left off dancing, and the honorable lady to whose arm I was clinging was offended, because she thought that my master had arranged this to embarrass her. Then my master commanded them to beat me and afterwards lock me up somewhere, because I had already played several pranks upon him that day. The quartermaster soldiers who were supposed to execute the order not only took pity upon me, they also could not stay close to me because of the stench, and therefore they spared me the blows and locked me up under the stairs in a goose coop. Since that day[221] I have pondered much on this affair and have come to the conclusion that those *excrementa*[222] which escape us in moments of fear and terror give off a much worse smell than when one has taken a strong purgative.

NOTES — BOOK I

CHAPTER 1: *Describes the rustic origins of Simplicius and how he was brought up in keeping therewith*

1.   Amongst the common folk…born and bred in Guinea: this satire on the parvenu and pretender to noble birth, as Scholte pointed out, is taken, in some parts verbatim, from Garzoni, Discourse 19 (p. 119 f.), not from Martin Freudenhold's "Guzman", as Rudolf von Payer had thought (Freudenhold also borrowed from Garzoni); Scholte (p. 119 f.) presents in parallel texts the pertinent passages from all three works.

2.   in summa: in sum, to sum up, in a word.

3.   the Sugar Boy gang in Prague: a notorious band of thieves, headed by a man named Zuckerbastl, which I have rendered as "Sugar Boy"; Grimmelshausen here departs from his model, which compares the "new noblemen" to Brontes and Sterops, the soot-blackened cyclopes who toiled in Vulcan's blacksmithy. Bobertag (DNL 33, xxviii) pointed out that reference is made to the same gang in Nikolaus Ulenhart's translation of Cervantes' Rinconete y Cortadillo, which appeared, together with the same translator's version of Lazarillo des Tormes, in 1617 under the title Zwo kurtzweilige, lustige und lächerliche Historien…. Ulenhart moved the scene of the action in Cervantes' novella, which he entitled "History von Isaac Winckelfelder und Jobst von der Schneid," to Prague. The passage in question occurs when the two protagonists are observed in the act of stealing and are then informed by the observer, himself a professional thief: "If a man wishes to be safe, he should sign on with a man here whom the criminal element commonly call Sugar Boy; he is the leader, the master, the ather, and the father-confessor of all those who desire to pass their lives and support themselves by stealing and other such-like things" (p. 245 f.). Grimmelshausen may have been prompted to use "Sugar Boy" in the simile by the fact that he is described in the Ulenhart version as dressed completely in black, with a black face (p. 56 f.). Carl Alt (p. 32 f.) pointed out yet other borrowings from Ulenhart's version (see below).

4.   nobilistes: noblemen.

5.   My Pa…: the following satire on "the noble life of the peasantry" is taken, in many instances verbatim from Garzoni's Discourse 19; Scholte (p. 120 f.) presents parallel texts.

6.   the Spessart Forest: a highland forest situated between the Main River and the Kinzig River.

7.   which useful and noble tree…fat hams are hung: in German the phrase is unclear; it reads "welcher nutzliche edle Baum / als worauff Bratwärste und fette Schunken wachsen" (literally "which useful noble tree on which sausages and fat hams grow").

8.   the very weaver…with Minerva herself: a spider. The allusion is to Arachne, a Lydian maiden who took such great pride in her spinning that she challenged Minerva (Athena) to compete with her; when Minerva could find no flaw in a piece of cloth woven by Arachne, she tore it to shreds; Arachne, in despair, then hanged herself, but Minerva saved her life and then turned her into a spider. Grimmelshausen could have read the tale in Garzoni, Discourse 52 (p. 381).

9.   St. Papyrus: the original German is "St. Nitglas" (St. Not-glass), a play on words on St. Nicholas and reference to the fact that the windows were made of oiled paper.

10.   it takes more time and effort to make paper…: in the so-called "Schermesser Episode"—in Chapter 11 of the Continuatio (Book VI of later Simplicissimus editions)—the making and fate of paper, from the planting of the flax seed to the use of waste paper in a privy, is treated (Garzoni, Discourse 52, was apparently the inspiration for the episode).

11.   Murano: a city near Venice, since the thirteenth century the site of the Venetian glass manufacturing industry. Garzoni (Discourse 63, p. 418) claims that "the art of glass blowing has now risen so high in Murano that there is nothing one can design which they cannot fabricate."

12.　　disciplina militaris: military exercises, military training.

13.　　general commando: general command.

14.　　because it is really not my purpose here…: the German here—"weil es ohne das allhier umb keine Adeliche Stifftung zu thun ist / da ich soll auff schwören"—is unclear, but presumably Grimmelshausen, as Alt (p. 32 f) noted, has taken over in garbled form a remark from Ulenhart's translation of Cervantes (p. 269) which is clear enough: "…(weil es an diesem Ort nicht umb Adeliche Stiffter zu thun / zu denen wir sollen auffgeschworen werden)…."

15.　　principia: principles.

16.　　exercitia: exercises.

17.　　Amplistides…Suidas…: this bit of erudition is taken verbatim from Garzoni, Discourse 15 (for parallel texts see Scholte, p. 121); Amplistides should read Amphistides (the name of one of the fool figures in Greek comedy who was extremely stupid); Suidas, the famous Greek lexicographer who flourished c. 970 A. D., mentioned this example of stupidity (Suidae Lexicon, ed. Bernhardy, vol I, col. 1081).

18.　　Ialemi songs: songs of lament, dirges; the term is derived from the Greek word for lament, dirge. Grimmelshausen's source is Garzoni, Discourse 40 (p. 348), where the context probably led him to presume that Ialemi songs were those whose music was unbearable bad or cacaphonous. In instances where Scholte did not find borrowings, I shall include the text 1) of the Source (S) and 2) of Grimmelshausen's edition princeps (ST). S: "Und man findet manchen Narren / welcher sich wol für einen Orpheum oder Amphionem darff außgeben / macht aber einen kalten und unlustigen Ialemi Gesang an / welcher solcherkünstlichen Stück halben / eine ewigen Namen hinderlassen / daß man / wie Paulus Manutius saget / solche Gesäng Ialemi Gesäng nennet / davon die Teutschen / so zwar haben hören leuten / wissen aber nicht in welchem Dorff / sagen / er gehe auff ein La, mi auß."; ST: "Sonst war ich ein trefflicher Musicus auff der Sackpfeiffen / mit deren ich schöne Ialemi-Gesäng machen konte:…"

19.　　theologia: theology.

20.　　studio legum: the study of law.

21.　　lectiones: lessons.

CHAPTER 2: *Describes the first stage of nobility to which Simplicius rose, together with an encomium to shepherds, with appended excellent instructions*

22.　　Strabo…: Grimmelshausen here borrows nearly verbatim from Garzoni, Discourse 40 (Scholte, p. 122, presents parallel texts). Strabo (c. 64 B.C.-24 A.D.) was the foremost Roman geographer.

23.　　since the beginning of the world…amiable office of herdsman: the source of this "Encomium to Herdsmen" is Garzoni, Discourse 54 (Scholte, p. 122 ff., presents parallel texts).

24.　　Moses…: the number (not mentioned at all in Garzoni, and thus apparently an interpolation made by Grimmelshausen) is actually given as 603,550 in the Bible (Numbers 1, 46).

25.　　Bubulcus, Statilus, Pomponius, Vitulus, Vitellios, Annius, Caprus: a strange mixture of Roman family names (Statilius, Pomponius, Vitellius, Annius) and surnames (Bubulcus, Vitulus, Capra), of which only four refer to herded animals: Bubulcus (plowman, one who plows with oxen, from bos, bovis, adj. bubulus - ox, bull, cow); Vitulus (bull calf); Vitellius (from Vitellus - little calf); and Capra (from capra - nanny goat, caper - billy goat). The reason for the confusion becomes clear when the sequence as it appeared in Grimmelshausen's source is considered (names are in the accusative plural): "Iunios, Bubulcos, Statilios, Tauros, Pomponios, Vitullos, Vitellios, Portios, Annios, Capros." While the punctuation here makes it appear as if all the names were of the same sort, the sequence in which they appear indicates that reference is being made to four Roman families by name and surname (nomen et cognomen), namely the family of Iunius Bubulcus, Statilius Taurus, Pomponius Vitulus, and Annius Capra. Marcus Terentius Varro, in De re rusticarum II, i, 10, cites the latter three as examples of families whose names derived from the terms for domestic animals. Vitellius was a well-known name because of the Roman emperor who bore it (reigned A.D. 69, between Otho and Vespasian); Portius, finally, is apparently a misprint of Porcius (from porcus - pig), a Roman family also cited by M. Terentius Varro. The confusion introduced by erroneous punctuation in Grimmelshausen's source is compounded, of course, by the fact that Grimmelshausen (or his editor) omitted from the sequence Iunios and Tauros.

26. Romulus and Remus: Romulus was the legendary founder of Rome who, together with his twin brother Remus, was suckled by a she-wolf, then discovered by Faustulus, a herdsman, and brought up among his companions.

27. Spartacus: originally a shepherd, he was sold into slavery and trained to be a gladiator. In about 73 B. C. he escaped and became the leader of a band of runaway slaves which soon grew so large that he was able, in 73-71 B.C., to defeat one Roman army after another. He was finally slain in a battle near the river Silarus.

28. Lucian…in his dialogo Helenae: Lucian (c. 120-180 A.D.), a Greek writer and greatest of the second-century sophists, flourished during the reign of Marcus Arelius. The dialogus Helenae, more rightly the dearum iudicium (Judgment of the Goddesses) is a separate dialogue but is traditionally printed as the twentieth of Lucian's Dialogues of the Gods; it portrays the "judgment of Paris" and of course mentions Paris, Priam, and Anchises and makes clear that they are herdsmen.

29. Paris: the second son of Priam, King of Troy, and Hecuba; Paris' abduction of Helen, the wife of Menelaus, brought about the Trojan War.

30. Anchises: because he rivaled the gods in beauty, Aphrodite (Venus) became enamored of him and bore him a son, Aeneas, who, after the fall of Troy, carried his blind father on his shoulders out of the burning city.

31. Endymion…Luna: Endymion was a youth famous for his beauty; while he was sleeping on Mount Latmus Selene (Luna), the moon goddess, became captivated by his beauty, came down to earth, kissed him, and lay down beside him.

32. Polyphemus: the son of Poseidon (Neptune); he was one of the Cyclops, gigantic monsters who had only one eye, and that in the center of the forehead. He captured Ulysses, who escaped with his men by blinding the giant. He is described in Acerra philologica II, 14 (p. 214 f.).

33. Phornutus: Lucius Annaeus Phornutus (Phurnutus), or Cornutus was a Stoic philosopher who flourished around 50 A. D.; his work on the gods was entitled, in the Latin translation of the original Greek, De natura deorum….

34. Apollo…Admetus: after Apollo, one of the major Greek gods, slew the Cyclops he was required to live as a mortal for nine years, during which time he tended the flocks of Admetus, who was king of Pherae in Thessaly.

35. Mercury: Roman god of commerce and financial gain (equivalent to the Greek god Hermes); see below, Notes to Book III, Chapter 4. Daphnis: son of Mercury (Hermes) and a nymph; he was deemed to be the founder of bucolic poetry.

36. Pan: Greek god of flocks and herdsmen; he is generally thought of as a son of Hermes (Mercury). See also Notes to Book III, Chapter 4.

37. Proteus: a man endowed with prophetic powers, he appears in early Greek legend as a subject of Poseidon (Neptune), whose flocks of seals he tended.

38. Mesha: 2 Kings 3, 4: "And Mesha king of Moab was a sheepmaster…."

39.   Cyrus…Mithridates: Cyrus (the Elder) was the founder of the Persian empire. According to legend his grandfather, even before Cyrus was born, ordered him killed after a dream seemed to portend that Cyrus would become ruler of all Asia; instead of carrying out the grandfather's order, the man to whom the new-born child was given took Cyrus to a herdsman, by whom the boy was then raised (Herodotus, Persian Wars I, 110f.); Mithridates should actually read Mitradates (cf. Herodotus, Persian Wars I, 110).

40.   Gyges: a Lydian king who reigned from 716 to 678 B.C.; according to legend Gyges, while a herdsman, found a ring which made its wearer invisible. The tale is retold in Acerra philologica I, 49 (p. 86 ff.) and in Garzoni, Discourse 58 (p. 403).

41.   Ismael Sophi: founder of a Persian dynasty (1487-1524).

42.   Philo the Jew…in his vita Moysis: Philo Judaeus (first century A. D.) discussed the life of Moses in two treatises which are generally entitled De vita Mosis (despite the fact that they were written in Greek); the quotation cited is found in I, 60).

43.   bellicosa and martiala ingenia: war-like and martial geniuses, i.e. great military leaders.

44.   But to return to my flock…: Kurz (p. 368) suspected that the expression was an allusion to "Pour revenir a nos moutons," which was well known from its use by Rabelais and by Moliere in his Farce de Pathelin.

CHAPTER 3: *Reports of the fellow-suffering of a loyal bagpipe*

45.   making such a racket…in the herb-garden with it: this rather strange trope is taken verbatim from Garzoni, Discourse 42 (p. 348); see also below, Notes to Book III, Chapter 3.

46.   Vogelsberg Mountain: der Vogelsberg is a mountain (772 meters high) which rises above the southern Hessian highlands.

47.   The Peasant's Song: Grimmelshausen's source has not yet been identified; concerning Grimmelshausen and the peasantry see Hans Dieter Gebauer, Grimmelshausens Bauerndarstellung, Marburg: Elwert, 1977 (Marburger Beiträge zur Germanistik 53).

48.   cuirassiers: light cavalrymen who wore as armor only a cuirass, a doublet of leather, or sometimes metal.

49.   as the American Indians did…: the source of this anecdote has not been determined. Könnecke (I, 149 f.) believed that Simplicissimus' perception of horse and rider as a single creature was inspired by a similar misapprehension on the part of Parzifal. The similarities between the early years of Simplicissimus and of the hero of Wolfram von Eschenbach's Parzifal have long been noted: both spend their boyhoods in the forest, far removed from all save the immediate family, and both are so naive as to seem perfect fools. Weydt (p. 202 ff.) reviews earlier comparisons of Simplicissimus and Parzifal and gives a comprehensive list of motif correspondances.

50.   centauris: centaurs: wild beasts who were half horse and half man.

51.   And so my mare…primum mobile: this far-fetched simile was doubtless inspired by a similar image used by Garzoni in Discourse 44 (p. 352): S: "Die Wirth halten sich auch nit allzeit zum besten / ziehen einen bißweilen eine Meren unter / die einen stättigen Trab hat / wie das primum mobile,…"; ST: "Also gieng meine Mehr mit mir dahin / in einem stetigen Trab / wie das Primum mobile,…" Garzoni, in his Discourse 6, defined a primum mobile as "the first movement…which the sun takes with it from sunrise till sunset, and which is taken again from sunset till sunrise, from which there arises one natural day." Grimmelshausen presumably had in mind the regular rising and falling, the up and down motion of one not

accustomed to riding on horseback. Willi Heining's surmise (p. 84) that the passage indicated Grimmelshausen's knowledge of alchemy is thus groundless.

CHAPTER 4: *Simplicius' palace is conquered, plundered, and destroyed, and the soldiers do terrible damage in it*

52.   atrocities…: Bechtold suggests (p. 36 f.) that the scene was inspired by a description of similar plundering in Moscherosch, Zauberbecher (p. 297).

53.   this German war of ours: in Grimmelshausen's historical source, Wassenberg, the Thirty Years' War is broken down into a series of wars, each named after the primary scene of the action or a major participant; since the "German war" does not appear as one of them, it would seem that this is Grimmelshausen's sardonic comment on the fact that after the fall of the "Winter King" in 1620 all the major military actions took place on German soil.

54.   the Golden Fleece of Colchis: the golden fleece was suspended from an oak tree in the grove of Ares in Colchis; Jason and his companions on the Argo (the argonauts) were sent by Pelias, the king of Thessaly, to get it away from the Colchian king Acetes. With the help of the king's daughter, Medea, Jason succeeded in taking possession of the golden fleece and escaping from Colchis with it. Grimmelshausen was probably familiar with the tale from its re-narration in Acerra philologica I, 87, p. 88 f.; Garzoni, p. 684; Herold's version of Diodorus Siculus, p. cc ff.

55.   "Swedish Punch": liquid excrement.

56.   But my Pa…nearly died laughing: this episode may have been inspired by a popular anecdote about Dracula, who inflicted a similar torture on his victims; the anecdote appears, among other places, in Zanach's Historische Erquickstunden I, 160.

CHAPTER 5: *How Simplicius ran away and was frightened by rotted trees*

57.   Nova Zembla: Novaya Zemlya ("new land"), two large islands extending from Russia northwest into the Arctic.

CHAPTER 6: *A short chapter, and so pious that Simplicius falls into a swoon*

58.   the encounter with the hermit: various works have been cited as models or inspiration for this episode: Bloedau (p. 27 f.) cites Balthasar Kindermann's Die unglückliche Nisette, Bechtold (p. 40 f.) the beginning of Part II of Guzman, Konopatzki (p. 44 f., 145) Paphnutius' description of his first encounter with St. Onuphrius, as related in the Vitae patrum I, "Vita sancti Onuphrii, eremitae, and Bechtold (p. 41 f.) the tale of the alchemist in Moscherosch, "Kauff-haus."

59.   a heavy iron chain such as St. William wears: Grimmelshausen scholars are not in complete agreement about which St. William is meant. While most who attempt to identify him at all believe he is William Duke of Aquitaine (8th century), Borcherdt identifies him (p. 357) as the St. William who lived in the twelfth century, was converted by St. Bernard, undertook, dressed in chains and a helmet, a pilgrimage to Rome and the Holy Land, and then lived in Sienna as a hermit until his death in 1157. The St. William whom Grimmelshausen has in mind is doubtless the legendary hero of the chansons de geste whom Wolfram von Eschenbach treated in his Willehalm and who represents the fusion of more than a dozen historical personages named William (Guillaume) who participated in the struggle against the invading Saracens in the eight century and in the subsequent French conquest of Catalonia. Two of these in particular contributed to the figure of legend: William of Orange (Guillaume d'Orange), later St. William of Gellone; and William Fairhair (Guillaume tete d'etoupe), who was Duke of Aquitaine. The former, who was in the service of Charlemagne, defended Narbonne against the Saracens, fought valiantly against them in the battle at Villedaigne, and in 803 took Barcelona from them; in 804 he founded

a monastery in Gellone (now called Saint Guilhem-le-Desert), to which he retired in 806 and where he died in 812. Duke William of Aquitaine (died 983) was as loyal to his master, Louis IV, as William of Orange had been to Charlemagne. The confusion of the two men in the popular imagination may have occurred because Louis the Pious, whom Charlemagne put under William of Orange's charge in 790, bore among other titles that of King of Aquitaine. In any event, the deeds and piety of William of Orange soon came to be attributed to Duke William of Aquitaine. The view that Grimmelshausen had this figure in mind is supported by the fact that above the picture of St. William in Aegidius Albertinus' Himmlische Cammer-Herren (p. 526), which shows him with a Bible in his right hand, a staff in his left, a helmet on his head, and chains wrapped around his waist, the saint is identified as "S. Willhelmus Hertzog" (Saint William, Duke). Konopatzki reproduces the picture (opposite p. 48).

60.   this old man must needs be the wolf….: Konopatzki (p. 46, 145) suggests that the mistaking of the hermit for a wolf was inspired by the anecdote in the Vitrum patrum about the herdsmen who came upon the hermit Acepsimas and took him to be a wolf because the weight of the chains he was wearing caused him to walk bent over as if he were going on all fours. It seems more likely that Grimmelshausen was prompted to link the hermit who reminded him of St. William to a wolf by the quatrain in German which was printed directly under his picture in Himmlische Cammer-Herren: "Ein Wolff zuvor Wilhelmus war / Hernach mild als ein Lämblein gar / Da Gottes Gnad sein Hertz berührt / Und ihn zur Sünden Büssung führt" ("Before William was a wolf, Afterwards mild as a little lamb, Since God's grace touches his heart and leads him to repent of his sins").

61.   St. Anthony the Great: a famous hermit in Egypt (died 356 A. D.) who several times successfully warded off the devil's efforts do disturb him during his religious devotions; the subject of the "temptation of St. Anthony" was a favorite theme of painters in medieval times and later.

CHAPTER 7: *Simplicius is treated like a friend in humble quarters*

62.   "O Morning Star, How Fair and Bright!": the hermit's song is identical in rhythm to the text of this popular protestant hymn (Wie schön leuchtet der Morgenstern), the text of which was written by Philipp Nicolai (1556-1608) in 1599 and set to music by Scheidemann; a number of other hymn texts (and at least one secular one) were set to the same music (Weydt, Nachahmung, 163-90 discusses them in detail); whether Grimmelshausen composed the text himself or, as seems more likely, copied it from an as yet unidentified source, has not yet been determined.

CHAPTER 8: *How Simplicius, by means of exalted eloquence, gives evidence of his excellence*

63.   Ursula: Könnecke (I, 153, and Footnote 5) established that the name did occur in Grimmelshausen's own family and that his mother-in-law was named Ursula.

CHAPTER 9: *Simplicius turns from a bestia into a Christian human being*

64.   my probationary year: the year which a novice was required to serve before he was permitted to take monastic orders.

65.   St. Gertrude: St. Gertrude of Nivelles (626-659) was the first abbess of the Nunnery of Nivelles, which was founded about 646 by her mother, Ita. St. Gertrude's feast day, as Grimmelshausen noted in his Perpetual Calendar (p. 60), was March 17.

66.   Since that time I have…found that…: the entire passage is taken almost verbatim from Garzoni's introductory essay, entitled "General Discourse on all the Sciences, Arts, and Trades"; Scholte (p. 124 f.) presents parallel texts.

67.   Aristotle…in his lib. 3. de Anima: Aristotle (384-322 B.C.), Greek philosopher, second in fame only to Plato.

68.   Averroes, in lib. 2. de Anima: Averroes (ibn Rushd, c. 1126-c.1198) was the most famous of the Islamic philosophers.

69.   Cicero…in lib. t. Tuscul. quaest.: M. Tullius Cicero (106-44 B.C.) was a famous Roman orator; the work referred to is his Tusculanarum disputationum, II, 5, 13.

CHAPTER 10: *In what manner he learned in the wild forest to read and write*

70.   The hermit could not but laugh…: the hermit's normal demeanor—calm and amiable equanimity—was that which was considered ideal at the time. A similar episode in The Singular Life Story of Heedless Hopalong (Chapter 3, p. 9) reveals that the mature Simplicissimus does attain this ideal of behavior: "Simplicius, however, who had been listening to this conversation, broke out laughing and laughed till he shook, which in fact was the first and last time I ever saw or heard him laugh, for otherwise he comported himself in a very grave manner, and although he spoke in a rough and manly voice, he was more gracious and amiable than he looked, albeit he was in fact right sparing with words."

CHAPTER 11: *Tells of food, household articles, and other necessary things which one requests for life in this world*

71.   like Gideon's warriors: Judges 7, 4 ff.

72.   Orthographia: the goddess of orthography (correct language).

CHAPTER 12: *Takes note of a beautiful way to die in a state of blessedness and to have oneself buried at slight expense*

73.   Villingen: in 1633 and 1634 Villingen, a city on the eastern edge of the Black Forest which was in the hands of the Imperial forces, was besieged three times by the Swedes; the second time (16 July-9 September 1634) the Swedes built a dam which backed up the Brigach River, on which Villingen was situated, so that the town was flooded. An account of the incident can be found in Theatrum Europaeum III, 100.

74.   Methuselah: an ancestor of Noah; Methuselah is said to have lived 969 years (Genesis 5, 27).

75.   malmsey: a strong sweet wine; it originally came from Monemvasia (Napoli die Malvosia, hence the German name "Malvoisier") in Morea.

76.   till I had…to his rest: the entire passage is based on Garzoni, Discourse 143 (p. 349-351). While funeralia (funeral ceremonies) and exequias (rites, obsequies) were copied correctly, either Grimmelshausen or his printer changed Garzoni's ludos gladiatoros (gladiatorial games) into the meaningless phrase luctus gladiatorios (S: "Es haben aber die Alten unterschiedliche Weisen gehabt / ihre Todten zu begraben / dabey sie auch vielerhand vnnd unterschiedliche Ceremonien gehalten / welche sie funeralia vnd exequias genennet /…"; ST: "biß ich fertig worden / und auff diese Weis die funeralia, exequias und luctus gladiatorios allein geendet /…") In enumerating the requisites for a proper funeral Grimmelshausen followed Garzoni verbatim except in two instances where he shortened his source: S: "Endlich bey dem Begräbnuβbedencket man den todten Cörper /dz Bahr / den Sarck / die Decke / die Liechter / die Leute / so in beleiten / die Todtenträger / vnd die Clerisey / so den Gesang verrichten."; ST: "weil ohne das weder Baar / Sarch / Decken / Liechter / Todtenträger noch Gelaits-Leut / und auch kein Clerisey vorhanden gewest / die den Todten besungen hätte."

CHAPTER 13: *Simplicius lets himself be pushed hither and thither like a reed in the wind*

77.   monachus: monk.

78.   Timon: Timon of Athens, a legendary misanthrope who was a contemporary of Pericles; the tale about Timon's gallows was wide spread. Grimmelshausen included the anecdote in the "Gegensatz" of The Satyrical Pilgrim I, 2; here it agrees almost verbatim with the rendition of the anecdote found in Boaistuau-Launay's Theatrum mundi (four-language version), p. 28 f., and Zanach's Historische Erquickstunden III, 4 f.

79.   my end stood on hair: Grimmelshausen uses such transpositions to indicate the speaker's fright and confustion; in The Singular Life Story of Heedless Hopalong the alleged author, Philarchus, becomes so distraught that he writes that "Day was not built in a Rome" (p. 1).

80.   Sauerland: the "Süderland" of Westphalia; it consists of the territory between the Sieg, Möhne and Ruhr and is a forested hill region with deep and narrow valleys.

CHAPTER 14: *A quaint comoedia about five peasants*

81.   comoedia: comedy, farce, merry episode.

82.   soldateska: soldiers, soldiery.

83.   solenniter: solemnly.

84.   So you are one of that ilk!: So you are one of those people who have sold their souls to the devil in return for the guarantee that no weapon can kill you. The belief was at the time wide spread that a person could be made "shotfree" (impervious to harm by weapons) by entering into a pact with the devil.

85.   s. v.: salva venia, i.e. with your indulgence, i.e. if you'll pardon my language.

CHAPTER 15: *Simplicius is despoiled and has a wondrous dream about the peasantry, and how things go in time of war*

86.   antipathia: antipathy, dislike.

87.   Amidst these thoughts…: the technique of the symbolic dream or vision (which now follows) is one which Moscherosch favored and employed repeatedly in his "Gesichte" (visions) in Philander von Sittewald. Bechtold (p. 43) believed that the "Tree of Mars" was patterned on the "Tree of Society" section in Moscherosch, "Zauberbecher."

88.   all manner of fellows: those with long lances are pikemen; those with muskets, musketeers or dragoons; those with pistols, probably troopers of horse; those with partizans, infantrymen; those with flags, ensigns (standard bearers), the lowest commissioned officer rank.

89.   partizans: a partizan was a long-handled spear with one or more lateral cutting projections; it was carried by infantrymen in the seventeenth century.

90.   commissarii: plural of commissarius, the quartermaster officer in charge of billeting and procuring provisions for the troops.

CHAPTER 16: *What soldiers nowadays do and omit to do, and how difficult it is for one of lowly birth to achieve*

preferment

in the army

91.   Hunger and thirst…: the source of the poem is as yet unknown.

92.   the soldiers' deeds: Bechtold (p. 43 f.) suggested that this passage might have been inspired by a similar description of the soldier's life in Moscherosch, "Soldatenleben."

93.   runagates: German "Landstörtzer"; vagabonds, tramps.

94.   such old chicken thieves: during the Thirty Years' War it was a matter of honor among foragers to steal only large cattle, and it was considered demeaning to steal anything as small as a chicken; see Hopalong's retort when Simplicissimus' Ma called him a "chicken thief": "Chicken thief? Don't think I wasted my time on such trifles, on such childish tricks! I stole only four-footed animals, and only healthy ones to boot, or I should not deign to take them." (The Singular Life of Heedless Hopalong, p. 54)

95.   gradum: grade, military rank.

96.   hell-bards: play on words on "halberds"; the halberd was a combination of a spear and a battle-ax, with a sharp blade ending in a point which was affixed to a staff about six feet long.

97.   pikemen: the pikeman, protected by a helmet and a breastplate, carried a sword and a pike some eighteen feet long; Hopalong probably summed up the universal attitude towards the pikeman when he said: "Now a musketeer, to be sure, is a poor, harried creature, but compared to a miserable pikeman he enjoys lordly good fortune. It is sad to contemplate, much less to tell, of the hardships these poor boobies are obliged to suffer, and you cannot really believe it unless you have been one yourself. And therefore I think that anyone who slays a pikeman when he could spare his life is murdering an innocent man and can never justify such homicide, for even though these poor dumb cattle (as they are contemptuously called) are assigned the task of protecting brigades against cavalry attack in the open field, they do not, on their own accord, do any harm at all, and anyone who runs into their long spears gets what he deserves. In summa, I have been in many hot encounters in my day, but I have seldom seen a pikeman kill anyone." (The Singular Life of Heedless Hopalong, p. 56 f.).

98.   musketeers: the musketeer carried a musket, or firelock, which was about six feet long and so heavy that it had to be rested on a fork or otherwise supported when fired; he also carried a bandolier with extra powder charges.

99.   materialia: substances.

100.   those with flags: the ensigns; since the soldiers at that time swore allegiance not to any particular country or person but to the flag (standard) of their unit, and because any fighting unit which captured a standard also automatically received all those who had sworn to it, the standard inevitably drew hot enemy attack and thus exposed the ensign, the lowest ranking commissioned officer to considerable danger.

101.   Further up sat yet higher ones…: the commissioned officers above the rank of ensign.

102.   ink-squitterers: army slang for "company clerks" because they did all the writing; the German verb from which the noun is derived is quite close in meaning to the now obsolete "squitter" ("to void thin excrement"), the thin excrement in this case being black ink.

CHAPTER 17: *Though in time of war the nobleman, and rightly so, is given preference over him of low birth, many from the contemptible estate do come to high honors*

103.   a sergeant major…Sir Lovelord: the abrupt introduction of the two disputants, like the name Lovelord (Adelhold) given to the nobleman, is typical of the practice of Moscherosch in his satires in the form of dreams or visions in Philander von Sittewald. A sergeant major was the highest non-commissioned rank. The subject of the dispute—whether military leaders should come from the ranks of the nobility or up through the ranks of the military—was discussed repeatedly in the seventeenth century.

104.   A younger ram…: the poem is taken verbatim from Julius Wilhelm Zinkgref's Sapientia picta, Plate LXIII, ("Iam regit argumentum").

105.   Moreover, the nobility…non foret esta tui: Source for the passage is Garzoni, Discourse 19; Scholte (Zonagri, p. 125 f.) presents parallel texts.

106.   John de Platea: Joannes de Platea (died 1427); according to Jöcher III, 1621, he wrote a book entitled De feudis.

107.   plebiis: commoners, people of base birth.

108.   Beata terra,…Eccliasticus 10: 'Blessed art thou, O land, when thy king is the son of nobles.' The quotation comes from Ecclesiastes 10, 17, not from Eccliasticus; Borcherdt (p. 361 f.) conjectures that Grimmelshausen's source, Garzoni, confused the appreviations "Eccle." and "Eccli."

109.   Seneca…et sordida: L. Annaeus Seneca (4 B.C.-65 A.D.), the famous Roman philosopher and orator; In English the quotation from Seneca would read: "'Tis the property of a noble soul that it is inspired by what is good; and no man of noble mind is delighted by things which are base and vile." In the German version of Garzoni which Grimmelshausen used, a German translation of the quotation was given, but Grimmelshausen chose to omit it.

110.   Fausta Poeta…non foret esta tui: Publio Fausto Andreline of Firli (c. 1462-1518), a humanist, university professor and poet who wrote in Latin, produced a number of literary works, among them Hecatodistichon (1512), from which this distich may come. In English the distich would read: "If thou wert born of low estate, of ignoble parents,/ Never wouldst thou possess mind and spirit sublime." Here too Grimmelshausen omitted the German translation which his source provided.

111.   Never doth sheer so sharp the sword…: this old saw and slight variations of it are quite common; as Kurz was first to point out (p. 372), a variation is found as early as Freidank's Bescheidenheit: "Nieman so nahe schiert, Als wa der bur herre wird." Strangely enough, I could find no equivalent proverb or saying in English.

112.   soldiers of fortune: men who are not of noble birth but choose the military as a profession and rise through the ranks to become officers.

113.   A lamp will give you light…: the poem is taken verbatim from Zinkgref's Sapientia picta, Plate XLII ("Nisi infundas oleum").

114.   Johann de Werdt: also written Jean de Wert (1600-1652); he was greatly admired by the common soldiers because he, a "soldier of fortune" par excellence, had risen from the rank of common trooper of horse to colonel and, after his victory at the battle of Nördlingen, to the rank of lieutenant field-marshal. He was an officer first in the army of the Duke of Bavaria and then, in 1646, was made a general in the allied Imperial army.

115.   Stablejack: Stallhans, or Staalhans, or, as spelled in military correspondence of the time (cf. Könnecke II, 214 f.) Stahlhansch (died 1644), a lieutenant colonel in the Swedish army; Riederer, in his edition of Grimmelshausen's works (II, 603), says he was the child of poor Finnish parents.

116.   Little Jim: in German "der kleine Jakob": the nickname of Jakob Mercier (died 1633), who rose through the ranks to become a colonel in the Hessian army.

117.   St. Andreas: Daniel St. Andree, colonel in the Hessian forces in Westphalia in 1637 (cf. Könnecke I, 221 and 250 ff.).

118.   Tamerlane: (1336-1405), Mongolian conqueror of central Asia.

119.   Agathocles: (361-289 B.C.), tyrant of Syracuse. According to Polybius (XII 15, 6) his father, Carcinos, was a potter.

120.   Valentinian's father: Valentinian I (321-375) was Roman emperor from 364 until his death. His father, Gratianus Funarius (which means "rope-maker") was of low birth; according to Ammianus Marcellinus (Rerum gestarum XXX 7, 2), as a boy he carried around rope for sale and fought off grown men who sought to take it away from him.

121.   Mauritius Cappadox: Mauricius of Cappadocia (539-602), Byzantine emperor (reigned 582-602); he was not an indentured servant at all, but rather the offspring of an old Roman family which had settled in Arabissus in Cappadocia (cf. Pauly l4, 2387 ff.)

122.   Tiberius: Tiberius II (Anicius Thrax, Flavius Constantinus), reigned from 578-582.

123.   John Zemisces: Joannes I Zimisces, emperor of Constantinople (969-976); actually, in his early youth he served with distinction in the Greek armies.

124.   Flavius Vobiscus: Flavius Vopiscus Syracusius (late 3rd century A.D.), one of the six "scriptores historiae Augustae" and biographer of Bonosus; according to Borcherdt (p. 363) the citation is found in II, 423 of Haurisius' edition Scriptores historiae Romanae.

125.   Bonosus Imperator: Quintus Bonosus Imperator, a Roman general in the Rhenish provinces; he led a rebellion against Rome and was declared emperor in the provinces, but when the Emperor Probus put down the revolt (in 280 or 281) Bonosus took his own life by hanging himself.

126.   Hyperbolus…Chermes: Hyperbolus, Athenian demagogue during the Peloponnesian War, was ostracized in 417 (or 415), whereupon he went to Samos; he was murdered by the oligarchs of Samos in 411 B.C. Sources disagree as to the name of his father; according to Theopompus of Chios the father's name was "Chremes"—not "Chermes" (cf. Pauly IX 254 ff.).

127.   Justinus…Justinian: Justinus I (Flaviuis Anicus, 450-527), East Roman emperor (518 to 527); he was succeeded by Justinian, surnamed the Great, Roman emperor in Constantinople (527-565) and the driving force behind the establishment of the Pandects and the Justinian Code. Justinus, born to poor parents, is said by Zonaras to have worked in his youth as a herdsman (Procopius says he worked as a farm hand). Cf. Pauly X, 1314.

128.   Hugo Capet: founder of the Capetian dynasty in France, and king from 987 to 996.

129.   Pizarro: Francisco Pizarro (1475-1541), discoverer and conqueror of Peru.

130.   ingenium: mind.

CHAPTER 18: *Simplicius plunges into the world for the first time and suffers ill fortune*

131.   Europa: Europe.

132.   The mighty oak…: the poem is taken verbatim from Zinkgref's Sapientia picta, Plate XXX ("A se confringi tur ipsa").

133.   Vale!: Farewell!

134.   Gelnhausen: a town on the upper course of the Kinzig River where the river descends from the hills into the Rhine-Main basin.

135.   the battle of Nördlingen: the battle, in which the Imperial army of King Ferdinand of Hungary, reinforced by Spanish troops, defeated the forces of Marshal Horn and Duke Bernhard of Weimar, took place on September 6-7, 1634. Grimmelshausen's other protagonists also experienced the battle. Courage, who was with the Imperials, lost a husband in the fray (Runagate Courage, p. 157); Hopalong, also with the Imperial army, fought in the battle and reports that he took good booty (The Singular Life Story of Heedless Hopalong, p. 62 ff.).

CHAPTER 19: *How Simplicius is taken to Hanau and Hanau is taken with Simplicius*

136.   Gelnhausen…Duke of Weimar's troops there: the town was taken and plundered by the Duke of Weimar's troops in September 1634, and again on January 15, 1635 (Könnecke I, 159). Grimmelshausen seems to have conflated the two events. Inasmuch as Gelnhausen was his birthplace, it seems likely that he experienced the earlier attack.

137.   Duke of Weimar: Duke Bernhard of Weimar (1604-1639)joined Gustav Adolf's army in 1631 after serving as an officer in the Danish army, and after Gustav's death in the Battle of Lützen became the primary military leader of the Protestant forces in Germany.

138.   the splendid fortress of Hanau: situated at the confluence of the Main and the Kinzig, some ten miles from Frankfurt/Main; the well fortified town and garrison was strategically important for the control of the Hessian plain.

139.   corps de garde: guard-room, headquarters of the watch.

140.   the Greek, the German, or the French fashion: as yet I have been unable to determine what these fashions in hairdressing were.

141.   as they were wont to paint St. William: see above, Notes to Chapter 6.

142.   Samoyed: one of a Siberian Mongolian people, related to the Finns; the Samoyeds were hunters and fishers.

143.   valete: farewell present.

CHAPTER 20: *In what manner he was delivered from prison and torture*

144.   the governor: at the time the governor was Jacob Freiherr von Ramsay (1589-1639), a major general in the Swedish army; he entered Swedish service in 1630 and was made commandant of the Hanau fortress in 1634, in which post he remained until 1638.

145.   dragoons: a dragoon was a mounted infantryman and thus combined the mobility of the cavalryman with the fire-power of the infantryman; he carried both pistols and a musket, so he could fight either on horesback or on foot, though he was classified as an infantryman.

CHAPTER 21: *Fickle Fortune smiles upon Simplicius*

146.   a painter with his tools: the paints, of course, do not match at all the colors they are supposed to produce; Grimmelshausen's source for this passage has not yet been found.

147.   trophaeum: used here in the original sense, i.e. a tree or stone pillar upon which accoutrements taken from the enemy were affixed, as a sign of victory.

CHAPTER 22: *Who the hermit was whose companionship Simplicius had enjoyed*

148.   museum: study, library.

149.   Scotland: Ramsay was by birth a Scot; Grimmelshausen here indicates that the hermit was of the same nationality, which conflicts, of course, with the clearly German name of the hermit, which is revealed in Book V, Chapter 8 .

150.   gloria: glory.

151.   the bloody battle of Höchst: in the Battle of Höchst, which was fought on June 22, 1622, General Tilly, the commander of the Imperial forces, defeated the Protestant army led by Duke Christian von Braunschweig. Courage reports that she took part in the battle and captured a major and took much booty (The Runagate Courage, p. 66).

152.   General Mansfeld: Count Ernst von Mansfeld (1585-1626).

153.   the Evangelical cause: the protestant cause, for which the hermit had fought unsuccessfully in the Battle of Höchst.

154.   contrefait: picture, portrait.

155.   the battle at Nördlingen: cf. above, Chapter 18.

156.   item: also, furthermore.

CHAPTER 23: *Simplicius becomes a page; item, how the hermit's wife was lost*

157.   Ramsey: see above, Chapter 20.

158.   a trumpeter: during the Thirty Years' War parleys with the enemy were customarily carried out by trumpeters.

CHAPTER 24: *Simplicius excoriates the folk and sees in the world many idols*

159.   the command of Christ: Matthew 7, 1.

160.   St. Paul: the quotation is from Galatians 5, 19 ff.; Willi Heining (p. 99 f.) determined that Grimmelshausen here quoted directly from the 1546 Luther translation of the Bible.

161.   reputatio: good name, good reputation.

162.   Bacchus: Roman god of wine.

163.   Ceres: Roman goddess of grain, agriculture.

164.   medicus: doctor, physician.

165.   associate: the German play on words, GeEsell (Gesell: comrade, and Esel: ass), is an old one. Burkhard Waldis, for example, employs it in his translation of Aesop (Fable 20, line 77), as Borcherdt points out.

166.   insecta: literally, insects; here, repulsive creatures.

167.   an Ecce homo: depiction of Christ with the crown of thorns.

CHAPTER 25: *To strange Simplicius everything in the world seems strange, and he for his part seems that way to the world too*

168.   Christ says: Love your enemies…: Matthew 5, 44-46.

169.   in playing the Jew: in engaging in sharp business practices. Grimmelshausen shares the casual anti-Semitic attitude of virtually all Christians of his time.

170.   couillon: scoundrel, rogue, troublemaker; from Vulgar Latin "coleone" (eunuch), which derived from Latin "coleus" (scrotum); it became in French "couillon," in German "cujon," and in Italian "coglione."

171.   Then I heard them swear…: Bechtold (p. 493) points out a similar description of soldiers' curses in Moscherosch, "Soldatenleben."

172.   Christ's command…"Swear not at all…: Matthew 5, 34.

173.   two knaves: this anecdote is elaborated upon in Vogelnest I.

CHAPTER 26: A strange new way of wishing one another good luck and of greeting one another

174.   the late Sir Samuel: apparently refers to the hermit, whose first name, one would have to assume, was "Samuel"; the hermit's first name, it should be noted, is never revealed (he is referred to by his title, "Captain", in Book V, Chapter 8). "Samuel," of course, could also refer to Samuel Greifnsohn von Hirschfeld (another of the many anagrams of his name which Grimmelshausen devised), who is identified in an afterword as the real author of Simplicissimus (cf. p.). It seems unlikely that "Samuel" is meant to refer to Samuel S. de Tecla (died 1650), as Borcherdt (p. 367) suggested.

CHAPTER 27: *The secretarius is smoked out of the chancellory by a foul stench*

175.   secretarius: Latin: secretary, clerk, company clerk (in the military), in charge of conducting correspondence for the commanding officer (in this case, the governor of the fortress); Grimmelshausen himself occupied this position in Offenburg toward the end of his military career.

176.   spiritus papyri: spirit of paper.

177.   commissarii: commisars, commissioners.

178.   notarii: notaries, law clerks.

179.   Fortunatus: hero of Fortunatus, a popular chapbook which first appeared in 1509; among the magic objects which the hero possessed was a purse which remained full of coins, no matter how many coins were taken from it.

CHAPTER 28: *One who envies Simplicius teaches him fortunetelling, and another pretty little trick too*

180.   where the snake..Meleagrus: this display of erudition is taken for the most part verbatim from Garzoni, Discourse 62 (Scholte, 127, prints both texts); Garzoni, however, writes "Medea against Peleager," thus omitting "against Perseus, Nessus against Hercules, and, what is more, Althea against her own son…. "; the omission, it might be noted, goes back to Garzoni's original Italian version. Whether Grimmelshausen or his publisher's editor filled in the omission correctly cannot be determined.

181.   the snake…Nasica: The pairing here makes no sense. "Nasica" might refer to Pub. Cornelius Scipio Nasica Serapio (2nd century B.C.), the leader in the assassination of Tib. Sempronius Gracchus (164-133 B.C.). It is possible, though

unlikely, that one of the Renaissance polyhistors (or a typesetter) mistook "Sempronius" for some form of "serpens" (snake, serpent); it seems more probable that there was an omission here too and that the "snake" was meant to be paired with Heracles (Hercules), who killed with his bare hands the two serpents which Hera sent into the chamber where he and his brother were sleeping (he was only a few months old at the time), and that Nasica was meant to be paired with Gracchus. Herold's version of Diodorus Siculus contains the tale of Hercules and the serpents (p. clxxv).

182. Goliath…David: see Samuel 17, 1-11, 17-58.

183. the Minotaur…Theseus: the Minotaur, a monster with the head of a man and the body of a bull, was the result of a liaison between Pasiphae, the wife of King Minos of Crete, and a bull. Minos shut the Minotaur up in the labyrinth, where it was fed on human flesh, namely that of seven boys and seven maidens from Athens who were delivered to Minos each year. This abomination came to an end when Theseus, the Athenian hero, entered the labyrinth and destroyed the Minotaur. The story can be found in German in Acerra philologica I, 34 (p. 62 f.) and Herold's version of Diodorus Siculus (p. ccxiii).

184. Medusa…Perseus: Medusa, the daughter of Phorcus, bore Neptune (Poseidon) a son, Pegasus, and as punishment for this Minerva (Athena) gave her eyes which could turn to stone anyone upon whom they looked. Perseus, using his shield as a mirror, was able to locate Medusa without looking at her directly, and he then put her to death by cutting off her head.

185. Circe…Ulysses: Circe, a sorceress dwelling on the island of Aeaea, turned all Ulysses' companions except Eurylachus into swine by giving them a drink from a magic cup. Ulysses, protected from the magic liquid by a root which Hermes had given him, forced Circe to restore his crew to their original form. The tale is recounted in Acerra philologica I, 87 (p. 161 f.), in Garzoni (p. 333), and in Moscherosch.

186. Aegisthus…Menelaus: this pairing is obviously an error. Aegisthus seduced Clytemnestra while her husband Agamemnon was away fighting in the Trojan War; he then slew Agamemnon upon his return. Agamemnon's son, Orestes, spurred on by his sister Electra, then avenged his father's murder by slaying both Aegisthus and Clytemnestra. The only connection between Aegisthus and Menelaus is that Menelaus was Agamemnon's brother. It is possible that Garzoni, or Garzoni's source, confused Menelaus with Orestes; it is also possible, of course, that Garzoni or his printer, dropped the words "against Orestes, Paris"; Paris was the seducer of Menelaus' wife Helen and thus Menelaus' arch-enemy, and he was defeated by Menelaus in single combat outside the walls of Troy, but Aphrodite saved him; Paris later died from a wound inflicted by Philoctetes.

187. Paludes…Coraebus: this pairing also makes no sense as it stands. Virgil (Aeneid II, 424) remarks that Coroebus (not "Coraebus"), who was the son of Mygdon of Phrygia (Virgil, Aeneid II, 341), freed Cassandra and fought on the side of Troy in the Trojan War, was killed in battle by Peneleus, one of the leaders of the Boetians. It is conceivable that "Peneleus" became confused with "Peleides," another name for Achilles, the foremost warrior of the Greeks, and thus logically an opponent of the side for which Coroebus was fighting.

188. Medea…Pelias: Medea, by betraying her father and killing her brother, made it possible for Jason to take the Golden Fleece which had been in their custody. Jason turned the Fleece over to his uncle, Pelias, who had sent Jason on the quest for it in order to get rid of him. When Pelias still refused to make Jason his heir, Medea exacted vengeance by persuading Pelias' daughters that they could restore their father to vigor and youth by cutting him up and boiling the pieces of his body. The cure was a failure. Herold (p. ccvii f.) tells this "Wunderthaat Medee."

189. Nessus…Hercules: When Hercules was going into exile together with his wife Deianira they came to the River Evenus; Hercules forded it, but he gave his wife to the centaur Nessus to carry across on his back. Nessus, however, sought to take Deianira by force, and when Hercules heard her screams he shot an arrow through Nessus' heart. Diodorus Siculus' account of the deed appears in Herold (p. cxcvii).

190.   Althea…Meleagrus: When Meleager was a week old, the Fates prophesied that he would die as soon as a piece of wood burning on the hearth was completely consumed. His mother, Althea, put out the firebrand and had it locked in a chest. When Meleager, in order to punish his mother's brothers, slew them, Althea avenged their death by throwing the piece of wood into the fire and thus bringing about the death of her own son. Herold (p. cxcvi f.) presents Diodorus Siculus' version of the tale. Inasmuch as the stories of Medea and Pelias, Heracles and Nessus, and Althea and Meleager should have been familiar to Grimmelshausen from Herold, it is quite possible that Grimmelshausen, realizing that "Medea against Peleager" made no sense, paired these two with their appropriate opponents and threw in Hercules and Nessus, whose story immediately follows that of Althea and Meleager, for good measure.

191.   Jonathan…David: the legendary friends in the Old Testament (1 Samuel 18).

192.   the eyes of a dove: the allusion is to two passages in the Song of Solomon (1, 15 and 4, 1).

193.   je pete: I'm breaking wind.

194.   if it stinks…: in Grimmelshausen's Vogelnest I the hero does in fact escape from a room by causing a stench which the occupants of the room blame on the dogs.

CHAPTER 29: *Two eyes from a calf's head fall to the lot of Simplicius*

195.   Braunfels: a city in Hessia near Wetzlar; the fortress there was taken by protestant forces on January 28, 1635 (cf. Theatrum Europaeum III, 404).

196.   calf's head: the model for Simplicius' feat, Bechtold (p. 61) asserts, is an anecdote in Moscherosch, "Rentkammer."

197.   piece de resistance: main dish.

198.   coup de grace: finishing stroke.

199.   par dieu!: By God!

200.   actus: trick, performance, feat.

201.   dictum: remark, assertion.

CHAPTER 30: *How the people little by little got tipsy and finally, without knowing it, blind drunk*

202.   potages: soups.

203.   ollas potridas: a stew of vegetables and various meats.

204.   Cnaeus Manlius: Cnaeus Manlius Vulso, Roman consul who amassed considerable wealth during the wars in Asia (188 B.C.); he and his soldiers are said to have spread Asiatic luxuries amongst the Romans.

205.   bestia: mindless beast.

206.   Circe…Ulysses: see above, Chapter 28.

207.   minas: miens, looks, facial expressions.

208.   the Wetterau region: district in Hessia.

CHAPTER 31: *How Simplicius fails badly when he tries to perform his trick, and how they beat time to churchsong on his body*

209.   aromata: aromatic substances.

210.   actu: stage performance.

CHAPTER 32: *Deals again with nothing else but drunken carousing and how one can rid oneself of parsons*

211.   ratio status: welfare of the state.

CHAPTER 33: *What the governor did when he became abominably drunk*

212.   tresoir: side-board.

213.   lavoir: washbasin.

214.   materi: substance.

215.   sal. ven.: salva venia: with your indulgence, i.e. if you'll pardon my language.

216.   tractament: French: feast, food.

CHAPTER 34: *How Simplicius ruined a dance*

217.   Indeed, the sight of them…: the notion that an onlooker who cannot hear the music playing could very easily take dancers to be raging maniacs is frequently expressed in the attacks on dancing which abound in the literature of the time. Grimmelshausen could have encountered it in Garzoni, Discourse 45 (p. 353), among other places.

218.   my end stood on hair: see above, Notes to Chapter 13.

219.   to stamp in the floor of the hall…: this notion may have been inspired by actual historical episodes which those inveighing against dancing were delighted to cite. Zanach (Historische Erquickstunden III, 375 ff.) tells of a dance given by the Archbishop of Salzburg at which the floor collapsed, killing many of the dancers; and Zeiller (Episteln I, 32 f.), citing as his source Martinus Crusius, Annal. suev. (III, i, 4), tells of a floor collapsing under the weight of the participants at a dance held in Nuremberg in 1225; nearly 70 people allegedly lost their lives in the accident.

220.   homme desparat: French: man about to despair.

221.   Since that day…purgative: the same opinion is expressed Guzman (Chapter 14).

222.   excrementa: excretions; fecal matter and liquid excretions. 2) Peter Lauremberg's Acerra philologica, which contained two chapters on figures from classical mythology and a number of the better known classical tales; a strong indication that he knew this work well is the near verbatim agreement of his remarks concerning Democritus and Heraclitus in The Singular Life Story of Heedless Hopalong (Chapter 3, p. 9) and Lauremberg's description in I, 75, p. 138 (S: Diese zwey Dinge / Lachen und Weinen / gehören zwar dem Menschen eygentlich zu / und keinem unfernünfftigen Thiere. Aber man muβnicht allzeit weinen / und nicht allzeit lachen / als diese beyde Männer gethan: Sondern weinen hat seine Zeit und lachen hat auch seine Zeit. Nun ist das Weinen dem Menschen mehr angebohren / als das Lachen: dann nicht allein alle Menschen / wann sie auff die wWelt kommen / weinen: (Man hat nur das einige Exempel des Königes Zoroastris, der / wie er geborn / alsbald gelachet.) Sondern es hat der Herr Christus unser Seligmacher / etliche mahl geweinet / als nemblich über Jerusalem / über den verstorbenen Lazarum: Aber daβ er jemahls gelachet / finden wir in der heiligen Schrifft nicht.";

Der seltzame Springinsfeld: "Simplicius antwortet / das Wainen gehöret dem Menschen so wohl als das Lachen eigentlich zu / aber gleichwol alzeit zulachen oder alzeit zu wainen wie diese beyde Männer gethan / wäre eine Thorheit / dann alles hat seine Zeit; gleichwohl aber ist das Wainen dem Menschen mehr als das Lachen angeborn / wainen (man hat nur das einige Exempel des Königs Zoroastris, der / wie er geborn / alsbald gelacht / so zwar von Nerone auch gesagt wird) sondesr es hat der Herr Christus unser Seeligmacher selbst etlichmahl gewainet; aber daβ wer iemahls gelacht / wird in H. Schrifft nirgends gefunden / …"). Weydt is in error when he asserts that Grimmelshausen constructed the Springinsfeldt passage from three passages from Harsdörffer's Heraclitus und Democritus.

Simplicissimus, The German Adventurer

BOOK II

How goose and gander mated

In my goose coop I conceived what I wrote in the first part of my book *BLACK AND WHITE*[1] about both dancing and toping, and it is therefore unnecessary to make any further report about them here. But I cannot pass over in silence the fact that at that time I still doubted whether the dancers were raging so wildly in order to stamp in the floor, or whether I had merely been persuaded that this was so. Now I shall further tell how I got out of the goose-coop prison. For three whole hours, namely, till the *praeludium Veneris*[2] (the dancing, I should have said) had ended, I was obliged to sit in my own offal, till a man sneaked up and fell to fumbling with the bolt. I pricked up my ears like a sow pissing in a puddle, and the fellow who was at the door not only opened it, he whisked into it just as quickly as I should have liked to be out of it; and in addition he dragged a woman with him by the hand, just as I had seen done at the dance. I had no way of knowing what was about to transpire, because I had well nigh grown inured to the many adventures which had befallen my foolish mind that day, and I had acquiesced to the fact that I could not but further endure with patience and in silence everything my Fate sent me. So I pressed close to the door with fear and trembling, awaiting the end. Straightway thereafter, there arose betwixt those two a whispering, of which, to be sure, I understood nothing but that one party was complaining about the foul smell, while the other party, for his part, was consoling the first one: "Assuredly, most beautiful lady," said he, "you may be certain that I am sorry from the bottom of my heart that frowning Fortune granted us no more honorable place in which to enjoy the fruits of our love. But I can assure you that your most charming presence makes this contemptible nook more delightful to me than the loveliest Paradise itself." Then I heard kissing and remarked strange postures, but I knew not what it was or might signify, and therefore I continued to keep quiet as a mouse. But when another odd noise began, and the goose coop, which was made only of slats nailed under the stairs, fell to creaking, and particularly when the woman acted as if this business were hurting her, I thought to myself: "These are two of those raging folk who helped stamp in the floor, and now they have betaken themselves hither to do the same thing here, and to deprive you of your life." No sooner had these thoughts taken possession of me than, I for my part, in order to escape death, took possession of the door, through which I whisked out, screaming bloody murder, which naturally sounded like the screams which had got me into this place; but I had presence of mind enough to lock the door again behind me and to seek the open house door instead. Now this was the first wedding I ever in all my days attended, despite the fact that I had not been invited to it. On the other hand, however, I was not obliged to give them a wedding present either, though the bridegroom afterwards charged me all the more, which I indeed honestly paid. Dear Reader, I tell this tale not so that you may laugh at it, but rather so that my *histori*[3] may be complete and so that you, dear Reader, may be reminded of what fine fruits are to be expected from dancing.[4] For one thing I do deem certain is that at dances many a deal is struck which an entire friendship must later be ashamed of.

CHAPTER 2

When it is a right good time to bathe

Now though I had happily escaped the goose coop in this manner, I then first became completely aware of my misfortune, for my breeches were full, and I knew not whither to go with this load. In my master's quarters everyone was still and sleeping. Therefore I durst not approach the sentry who was standing guard in front of the house. In the *corps de garde*[5] of the main watch they were unwilling to suffer my presence, because I stank much too badly. It was too cold, and thus impossible for me to stay out in the streets, so I knew not which way to turn. It was already far past midnight when it occurred to me that I ought to take refuge with the oft-mentioned parson. I followed my intent to knock at his door, and in so doing I was so importunate that the maid finally grudgingly let me in; but when she smelled what I was bringing in with me (for her nose straightway discovered my secret), she grew even angrier. Therefore she fell to upbraiding me, which her master, who had now almost slept his fill, soon heard. He called the two of us to come to his bedside, but as soon as he had perceived what was amiss and had wrinkled his nose a little, he said that there was never a better time to take a bath, no matter what the almanacs say, than in the condition in which I then found myself, and he commanded the maid to wash my breeches and hang them by the stove till it was full daylight, and me to put myself to bed, for he well saw that I was completely stiff from the cold. I had scarce warmed up when day began to dawn and the parson was already standing by my bed, to hear how I was and what the nature of my problems was, because I could not as yet, on account of my wet shirt and breeches, get out of bed and go to him. I told him everything, beginning with the trick which my comrade had taught me and how badly it had turned out. Following that I asserted that the guests, after he, the parson, had left the banquet, had quite lost their wits and (as my comrade had reported to me) had undertaken to stamp in the floor; *item*, into what a terrible panic I then fell, and in what manner I had attempted to save my life, but as a result had been locked in the goose coop; also, what words and deeds I witnessed there from the two persons who released me again, and in what manner I had locked the two of them up in my stead. "Simplicius," said the parson, "your affairs are in a dreadful state. You had a good situation—but I fear! I fear!—it is ruined. Just hurry up and get out of bed; and get out of my house so that I do not fall into your master's disfavor along with you because they found you in my quarters." And so I was obliged to depart with my garments still damp, and to learn for the first time how well off one is with many folks when one is in one's master's favor, and how one is looked at askance when that favor falters.

I went to my master's quarters, where everyone was sleeping dead to the world, except the cook and a few maidservants. The latter were cleaning the room where the people had caroused yesterday, while the former was preparing a breakfast, or rather a meal, from the leftovers. I came to the maidservants first. There broken glass, from drinking vessels and windowpanes, was lying all over. In some places it was full of what the guests had let fly from both above and below, and in other places there were large puddles of spilled wine and beer, so that the floor looked like a map on which someone had wished to portray and depict sundry bodies of water, islands, and dry or traversible lands. It stank in the entire room much worse than in my goose coop, and therefore I could not stay there long, but instead made my way to the kitchen, and by the fire let my clothes dry out completely on my body, awaiting with fear and trembling what Fortune would further do to me when my master had slept his fill. In addition, I pondered upon the world's folly and mindlessness, and called to mind everything which had befallen me the day before and that same night, and what I had seen, heard, and learned at first hand. The result of these thoughts was that I then deemed the needy and miserable life which my hermit had led to be a blessed one, and wished that he and I were in our former condition once more.

CHAPTER 3

The other page is rewarded for his tutorials, and Simplicius is chosen to be a fool

When my master got up, he sent his orderly to fetch me from the goose coop. He brought the tidings that he had found the door open and a hole cut behind the bolt with a knife, by which means the prisoner had freed himself. But before the report arrived my master was apprised by someone else that I had been seen in the kitchen not long since. Meanwhile the servants were obliged to run hither and thither to fetch to breakfast yesterday's guests, amongst whom was also the parson, who was obliged to appear earlier than the others, because my master desired to talk with him about me before the guests were at the table. He asked him first if he thought me to be of sound mind or insane, or whether I was simpleminded or malicious, and therewith told him everything: how disgracefully I had behaved the day and night before, which some of his guests had deemed and taken to be offensive, as if he had intentionally arranged it; *item*, that he had commanded that I be locked up in a goose coop in order to protect himself from the sort of embarrassment I might yet be able to cause him, from which coop, however, I had broken out and was now walking about in the kitchen like a squire who was no longer obliged to serve him. In all his days, he said, he had never encountered such a prank as I had played upon him yesterday in the presence of so many honorable folk; and he knew nothing to do with me but to order me whipped and, because I behaved so doltishly, he would send me packing.

In the meantime, while my master was thus complaining about me, the guests were assembling little by little, and when he had finished speaking the parson answered that if the Lord Governor would be so kind as to hear him out with patience for a little while, he would relate one thing and another about Simplicius and his affairs which would not only make clear his innocence but would also dispel any misconceptions held by those who were offended by his behavior.

While they were talking about me in this manner upstairs, downstairs in the kitchen the mad ensign, whom I had locked up in my stead together with another person, was negotiating with me, and by threats and by a sovereign which he gave me, he got me to promise to hold my tongue about his doings.

The tables were set, and like the day before were full of folks and foods. Wines flavored with wormwood, sage, elecampane, quince, and lemon, together with *hippocras*,[6] were given the task of soothing the heads and stomachs of the topers again, for well nigh all of them were martyrs of the devil. The first thing they spoke of was themselves, namely, how they had toasted one another yesterday till they were full to the gorge; and yet there was not one of them who would honestly admit that he himself had been full to the gorge, even though the evening before some of them had sworn by the devil that they could not drink another drop and yet had kept screaming over and over "Wine, milord!" Some, to be sure, said they had gotten nicely tipsy, while others contended that no one would drink full to the gorge after tipsiness set in. But when they were tired of both talking and hearing about their own follies, poor Simplicius was obliged to suffer. The governor himself reminded the parson to reveal some amusing things about me as he had promised.

The parson first off begged that no one hold it against him if he perchance must needs speak words which might be deemed ill befitting a man of the cloth. Then he began to tell his tale, first, for what reasons I was wont to be plagued by belly gasses; what manner of distress I had caused the *secretario* with them in the chancellery; what trick I learned, along with fortune- telling, to control them; and how badly this trick had stood the test when I tried it; *item*, how strange the dancing seemed to me because I had never seen anyone dance; what report about dancing I had heard from my comrade; and for what reasons I had seized the noble lady and as a result was put into the goose coop. And this he recounted in such refined turns of phrase that they could not but laugh till tears ran down their cheeks; and in so doing he so modestly made excuses for my naivete and ignorance that I was taken back into my master's good graces and was permitted to wait upon the table. But about what had befallen me in the goose coop, and how I got out of it, he was unwilling to say a word, because it seemed to him that he might offend certain saturnine blockheads who were of the opinion that men of the cloth should always be of sour mien. However, my master, to provide amusement for his guests, asked me what I had paid my comrade for teaching me such fine tricks, and when I answered "Nothing!" he said: "Then I shall pay him his tutor's fees for you," whereupon he ordered him to be tied spread-eagle over a tub and flogged, just as they had done with me the day before when I had tried to do the trick and found that it did not work.

My master now had sufficient report of my naivete and therefore desired to spur me on to provide more amusement for him and his guests. He saw clearly that the musicians would count for nothing as long as his guests had me to amuse them, for with my foolish sallies I seemed to everyone to be better than the music of seventeen lutes.[7] He asked me why I had cut a hole in the door of the goose coop. I answered: "Someone else may have done that." "Who?" he asked. I said: "Maybe the man who came to join me there." "Who came to join you?" I answered: "I dare not tell anyone that." My master was a quick-witted man and well saw what one must needs do to get at me. Therefore he pressed me and asked who had forbidden me to tell. I straightway answered: "The mad ensign." And after I remarked from everyone's laughter that I must have really put my foot into my mouth, and also saw that the mad ensign, who was sitting at the table, turned as red as a beet, I was unwilling to say anything else unless he let me. And it required no more than a gesture which my master made to the mad ensign in lieu of a command, and I was permitted to tell what I knew. Then my master asked me what the mad ensign was doing joining me in the goose coop. I answered: "He was bringing a damsel to me." "What else did he do?" said my lord and master. I answered: "It looked to me as if he was going to pass water in the coop." My lord and master asked: "And what did the damsel do then? Was she not embarrassed?" "Oh, not in the least, milord!" said I. "She hoisted her skirts (most esteemed, well-bred, honorable, and virtuous Reader! Please forgive my ill-mannered quill-pen for putting down everything in the crude words I uttered upon that occasion!) and she was going to take a shit!" At this all who were present broke out in such loud laughter that my master could hear nothing further, much less ask me anything more, and in fact it was not necessary to do so unless one desired to make a laughing-stock of the honorable and virtuous damsel (*scil.*).[8]

Then the court steward told those at the table that I had recently come back from the bulwark, or wall of the fortress, and said that I knew where thunder and lightning came from. I had seen on the back of some wagons some large blocks which were hollow inside; into them they had stuffed onion seeds and an iron turnip with its tail cut off; then they tickled the end of the blocks with a jagged spit, at which smoke, thunder, and hellfire came out the front. They came up with yet more anecdotes of that sort, so that throughout the entire meal they talked and laughed about almost nothing but me. The result of this was a general decision that would lead to my demise, which was that if they manipulated me properly, I would in time develop into a rare good court jester whom they could give as a present to the greatest potentate in the world and who could make even dying men laugh.

CHAPTER 4

About the man who pays, and what manner of military service Simplicius performed for the Crown of Sweden, from which service he received the name Simplicissimus

ow while they were carousing this way and were about to make merry as they had the day before, the watch, handing over a letter to the governor, announced the arrival of a *commissarius*[9] who was at the gate and had been dispatched by the war council of the Crown of Sweden[10] to muster the garrison and inspect the fortress. This cast a pall over all their pleasure and took the wind out of their joyous laughter, like the bellows of a bagpipe when the air goes out of it. The musicians and the guests dispersed in much the way tobacco smoke disappears: they left only their smell behind. My master himself scurried to the gate with the adjutant, who was carrying the keys, and with a deputation from the main watch and many lanterns, in order to let in the "ink-squiggler,"[11] as he called him. He wished, he said, that the devil had broken that man's neck into a thousand pieces before he ever got to the fortress. But as soon as he let him in and was welcoming him on the inner drawbridge, he came very close, if not all the way, to holding his stirrup for him so as to demonstrate his devotion to him. Indeed, the deference which the two showed to one another instantly became so great that when the *commissarius* dismounted and was accompanying my master on foot to his lodgings, each insisted upon walking to the left of the other, etc. "Ah!" I thought to myself. "What a wondrous spirit of hypocrisy governs men, since it makes one man turn the other into a fool." We approached the main watch in this manner, and the sentinel called out his "Who goes there?" even though he saw that it was my master. He did not wish to answer, but rather to leave the honor to the other man; hence the sentinel grew all the more vehement as he repeated his challenges. Finally, to the last "Who goes there?" the *commissarius* answered "The man who pays you!" Now as we were passing by the sentinel, with me bringing up the rear, I heard that same sentinel, who was a new recruit and had probably been a well-to-do peasant on Vogelsberg Mountain before, mutter these words: "You are a real lying bastard! 'The man who pays me!' The sonovabitch who takes my money away from me, that's what you be! You've sweated so much money out of me that I wish lightning would strike you dead before you get out of this town!" From this moment on I clung to the thought that this stranger in his short velvet coat must needs be a holy man, because not only did he remain unscathed by all the curses aimed at him, but

101

those who hated him showed him every honor, kindness, and favor. That very night he was entertained like royalty, gotten blind drunk, and then put into a splendid bed.

The following day everything was at sixes and sevens at the inspection. Simpleminded booby though I was, I was nevertheless smart enough to deceive the clever *commissarium* (for which post and office they surely do not take children), which deceit I learned to practice in less than an hour, because the whole trick was knowing how to count to five and nine, and to beat them on the drum, because I was still too small to play the role of a musketeer. To this end they outfitted me in borrowed garments and also with a borrowed drum (for the knee-pants I wore as a page were not suitable to this business); without doubt they had me use borrowed things because I myself was also borrowed from the court to serve as drummer boy. And so I successsfully passed the inspection. But since they did not trust a simpleminded soul like me to remember a strange name, which I was to answer to when it was called, whilst stepping out of ranks, I was obliged to remain Simplicius. My surname the governor himself supplied, commanding them to write |me down on the roster as "Simplicius Simplicissimus," thus making me, like a whore's child, the first member of my family, even though, as he himself confessed, I looked like his own sister. And after that I retained this name and surname till I learned my true names, and I played my role rather well under them, to the advantage of the governor and with but slight harm to the Crown of Sweden, which was the only military service I ever performed for the Swedes my whole life long, for which reason their enemies have no cause to hate me for it.

CHAPTER 5

Simplicius is taken to hell by four devils and plied with Spanish wine

When the *commissarius* had left again, the oft-mentioned parson secretly bade me come to his lodgings and said: "O Simplicius! Your tender years grieve me, and your future misery moves me to pity. Hark you, my child, and know that it is certain that your master has resolved to rob you of all your wits and make you into a fool, wherefore to such purpose he is already having a costume made for you. Tomorrow you must needs enter that school in which you are to unlearn how to reason. In that school they will without doubt torment you so terribly that unless God or natural means prevent it, you cannot but turn into a fool. But despite the fact that this is a precarious and perilous business, I have resolved, because of your hermit's piety and your own innocence, and out of loyal Christian love for my fellowman, to come to your aid with advice and the good remedies you will need, and to place at your disposal this medicine here. Therefore, do as I tell you, and take this powder, which will strengthen your mind so much that you shall be able to withstand everything easily, without injury to your wits. Also, you have here a salve. Smear it upon your temples, the crown of your head, the nape of your neck, and also in your nostrils. And use these two things when you go to bed tonight, for at no time will you be safe from being dragged out of bed. But see to it that no one becomes aware of my warning and of the medicines I have given you, else it might turn out ill for both you and me. And when they have you under this accursed treatment, do not pay heed to and believe anything of which they attempt to persuade you, but do act as if you believed everything. Say little, so that the people who are charged with treating you do not see that they are wasting their time and effort, else you will be subjected to different torments, even though I cannot tell in what manner they will deal with you. And when you have on your fool's costume and your cap with bells on it, come to see me again so that I may attend you with further counsel. In the meanwhile I shall pray to God on your behalf, that He may preserve your wits and your health." Then he presented me with the powder and salve which he had mentioned, and I strolled back home with them.

It happened just as the parson had said. No sooner was I sound asleep than four fellows disguised in frightful devils' masks came into my room and up to my bed.[12] They cavorted about like mountebanks and carnival fools. One of them had a red-hot pitchfork in his hands, and another one a torch, and the other two seized me, dragged me out of bed, danced back and forth with me for a while, and forced my clothes onto my body. I, for my part, acted as if I took them to be real live devils. I screamed bloody murder at the top of my lungs and made gestures which showed me to be near frightened to death. They, however, announced to me that I must needs go with them. Then they bound my head with a towel so that I could neither hear, nor see, nor scream. They led me in sundry roundabout ways, up and down many flights of stairs, and finally into a cellar in which a large fire was burning. And after they had taken the towel off again, they began to drink toasts to me with Spanish wine and malmsey. They had no difficulty persuading me that I had died and was now in the depths of hell, because I acted on purpose as if I believed all the lies they were telling me. "Go on and drink hearty," said they, "because you must needs stay with us forever more, and if you won't be a good comrade and drink with us, then you must go into this fire here!" The poor devils attempted to disguise their voices and speech so that I should not recognize them, but I straightway perceived that they were my master's orderlies, but I did not let on that I knew, but rather laughed up my sleeve that I was making fools of these fellows who were supposed to be making a fool of me. I drank my share of the Spanish wine, but they guzzled down more than I did, because such heavenly nectar seldom comes to such fellows, wherefore I might well swear that they had drunk their fill before I had. And when it seemed to me that the time was right, I staggered about, acting the way I had recently seen my master's guests act, and finally I refused to drink any more at all, but rather desired to sleep. They, however, poked at me with the pitchfork, which they always had lying in the fire, and chased me about from one corner of the room to the other, so that it appeared as if they themselves were possessed, which chase was either so that I should drink more, or at least so that I should not sleep. And whenever, during the chase, I fell down, as I on purpose often did, they dragged me to my feet again and acted as if they were going to throw me into the fire. And so I fared as a falcon does when it is kept awake to be trained, which was the heavy cross I was obliged to bear. To be sure, I could have outlasted them easily insofar as drunkenness and sleep were concerned, but all of them did not stay there at the same time; instead, they spelled each other. In the end, therefore, I could not but get the worst of it. Three days and two nights I spent in this smoky cellar, which had no light but that thrown by the fire. My head therefore fell to roaring and pounding as if it were about to explode, so that finally I was obliged to devise a way to rid myself of my misery, together with my tormentors. I did what the fox does when it believes that it can no longer outrun the hounds and pisses in their faces, for since Nature was at that very moment urging me to take a shit (*s. v.*), I stuck my finger down my throat at the same time so as to throw up, with the result that I paid the bill with such an unbearable stench that even my devils themselves could scarce stay in the same room with me any longer. Then they put me into a sheet and beat me so mercilessly that all my innards, together with my soul, felt like they were about to pop out, from which I became so beside myself and bereft of my senses that I lay there as if I were dead. Nor do I know what else they did to me, so completely dead to the world was I.

CHAPTER 6

Simplicius goes to heaven and is transformed into a calf

When I came to my senses again I was no longer in the dingy cellar with the devils but in a beautiful chamber, in the hands of three of the most disgusting old hags the earth has ever borne. At first, when I opened my eyes a little, I took them to be real demons from hell, and had I at that time already read the works of the old pagan poets, I should have taken them to be the Eumenides,[13] or at least one of them to be Tisiphone,[14] come from hell to rob me of my wits as she had Athamas, because I indeed already knew that I was there for the purpose of being turned into a fool. This hag had a pair of eyes like two will-o'-the-wisps, and between them a long, thin nose like a hawk, the end or tip of which actually reached down to her lower lip. I saw only two teeth in her mouth, but they were so very long, round, and thick that they might almost have been compared to the fingers on which married folk wear gold rings, and in color they might have been compared to gold itself; *in summa*, there was enough bone there for a whole mouthful of teeth, but it was quite badly distributed. Her face looked like Spanish leather, and her white hair hung down around her head in remarkable disarray, because they had but just moments before fetched her from her bed. I know of nothing comparable to her pendulous breasts but two shrunken cow-udders drained of two-thirds of their milk; and at the bottom of each hung a dark brown teat a half-finger long. Truly a frightening sight, which might have served no purpose other than as an excellent antidote against the mindless lust of lewd billy goats. The other two hags were not a whit prettier, despite the fact that they had pug noses like monkeys and had put on their clothes somewhat more neatly. When I had recovered a bit more, I saw that the one of them was our scullery maid, and the other two were the wives of two of our orderlies. I acted as if I could not move a muscle—and in fact, I surely did have no desire to go dancing—when these honorable old crones undressed me till I was naked as a jaybird and cleansed me like a young child of all the offal. This did do me much good. While they were working on me, they showed such great patience and admirable pity for me that I should almost have revealed to them how well my affairs still stood; but I thought to myself: "No, Simplicius, do not trust any old woman; rather, consider that you have victory enough if you at your tender age can deceive three crafty old sluts whom one could use as bait with which to trap the devil himself in an open field. From this skirmish you may find hope that you will achieve better things in your later years." Now when they were finished with me, they laid me into an excellent bed, in which I fell asleep the instant my head touched the pillow. They, for their part, went and took away with them their pails and other things with which they had bathed me, together with my clothes and all the filth. As far as I can tell, I slept more than twenty-four hours at one stretch, and when I awoke again, there stood at my bedside two beautiful youths with wings who were richly adorned with white shirts, taffeta cummerbunds, pearls, jewels, gold chains, and other fine-looking things.[15] One of them had a gilded bowl full of wafers, cookies, marchpane, and other confections; the other one, for his part, had a gilded goblet in his hands. These two, who gave themselves out to be angels, attempted to persuade me that I was now in heaven because I had so happily withstood purgatory and had escaped both the devil and his grandmother. Therefore, they said, I should but wish for whatever my heart desired, since everything I might wish for was present in sufficiency, or it was in their power to have it brought to me. I was tormented by thirst, and since I saw the goblet before me, I demanded but a drink, which was in fact handed me more than willingly. This was not wine, however, but a sleeping potion, which I drank in one draught and from which I again fell asleep as soon as it was warm in me.

The next day I awoke again (for otherwise I should still be sleeping) and found myself no longer in the bed, or in the room where I had been, but in my old goose-coop prison. Again there was a terrible darkness, as in the cellar before, and in the bargain I had on a garment of calfskin, the rough side of which was on the outside. The breeches were cut in the Polish or Swabian fashion,[16] and the doublet even more absurdly. Above, on my neck, was a cap like a monk's cowl, which was pulled down over my head and which was adorned with a fine pair of ass's ears. I could myself not but laugh at my unlucky star, because I saw from both my nest and my plumage what manner of bird I was meant to be. At that time I fell, for the first time, to searching my soul and to pondering upon what was best for me. I resolved to act as foolishly as I possibly could, and at the same time to await with patience what else Fate might have in store for me.

CHAPTER 7

How Simplicius reconciled himself to his bestial condition

I could have easily freed myself by means of the hole which the mad ensign had cut in the door before, but because I was supposed to be a fool, I did not do that, and not only did I act like a fool who had not enough wit to get out by himself, I also acted like a hungry calf yearning for its mother; and my high-pitched moos were indeed soon heard by the men who had been charged to listen for them, with the result that two soldiers came up to the goose coop and asked who was in there. I answered: "You fools! Don't you hear that it is a calf?" They opened the coop, took me out, and expressed amazement that a calf could speak, which roles they played with the forced posturing of a newly hired and unskillful actor who cannot play well the part of the person he is supposed to represent, so that I often thought that I myself would be obliged to help them with the farce. They discussed what they ought to do with me, and agreed to give me as a present to the governor, who, because I could talk, would give them more than a butcher would pay them for me. They asked me how things stood with me. I answered: "Badly enough!" They asked: "Why?" I said: "Because it is the custom here to lock honest calves up in goose coops. You fellows must know that if they want me to grow up to be a proper ox, they must bring me up as is fitting for an honorable bull." After this brief discourse they led me across the lane towards the governor's quarters. A large throng of boys followed us, and because they, as well as I, were crying like calves, a blind man could not but have concluded from the noise that they were driving a herd of calves along, but from the sight of it, it looked like a pack of fools, old and young.

And so I was given as a present to the governor by the two soldiers, just as if they had taken me as booty in a foray. He gave them an *honorarium* as a present, and me he promised the best things which I should have in his household. I recollected the story about the goldsmith's boy[17] and said: "Indeed, sir, but they must not lock me up in the goose coop again, for we calves cannot abide such usage if we are to grow and become fine heads of cattle." The governor assured me a better fate, and thought himself terribly clever because he had made such a droll fool of me. I, for my part, thought to myself: "Just you wait, my dear sir! I have withstood the trial by fire and I have been hardened. Now let us see which of us will be best able to play his role." Meanwhile a peasant who had taken refuge in the fortress was driving his stock to be watered; as soon as I saw that, I left the governor and amidst my calf cries hurried to the cows, just as if I desired to suck them. When I got to them they were much more frightened of me than of any wolf, even though I wore their kind of hide. Indeed, they, running off in all directions, went as mad as if a nest of hornets had been loosed upon them in August, so that their owner could not bring them back together in one place again, which was a fine prank. In a trice a crowd of people had assembled to watch this spectacle, and after my master had laughed as if he were about to burst, he finally said: "Show me one fool, and I'll show you a hundred more!" But I thought to myself: "And none other than you yourself is the one of the fools you're talking about!"

Now just as everyone from that time on called me "Calf," I, for my part, also called everyone by a particular mocking nickname. In the opinion of the people, and particularly of my master, these were for the most part quite clever, for I christened everyone as his qualities demanded. To put it *summariter*,[18] many a person took me to be a witless buffoon, and I held everyone else to be a witted one. This, in my opinion, is still the way of the world, since everyone is satisfied with his own wits and imagines that he is the cleverest person of all.

The above-described amusing diversion which I provided with the peasant's cattle made the forenoon, which passed all too quickly anyway, pass even more quickly, for at that time it was nigh on to the winter solstice. At the noonday meal I waited upon the table as I had before, but as I did so I did many odd things, and when I was supposed to eat, no one could get any human food and drink into me. I simply insisted upon having grass, which at that time was hard to come by. My master had a pair of fresh calfskins fetched from the butcher and had them put onto two small boys. These he put at the table with me, served us the first course, which was winter lettuce, and bade us eat hearty. Also, he had a live calf led in and given lettuce freshened with salt. I stared at all this |as if I were astonished by it, and those around me urged me to eat along with the other calves. "Indeed!" they said when they saw that I was so disinterested. "It's nothing new for calves to eat meat, fish, cheese, butter, and other things. Why, sometimes they even drink themselves into a stupor! These beasts know a good thing when they see it. Indeed," they went on, "nowadays things have gone so far that there's precious little difference betwixt them and human beings. Are you to be the only one not to join in with the rest?"

I was all the more quick to let them persuade me, because I was hungry, not because I had already seen with my own eyes that some human beings are more swinish than pigs, more ferocious than lions, more ruttish than billy goats, more envious than dogs, more unruly than horses, more uncouth than jackasses, more drunken than cattle, more cunning than foxes, more rapacious than wolves, more buffoonish than monkeys, and more poisonous than snakes and toads— human beings, all of whom ate human food, and yet differed only in their outer form from beasts, and for sure were by far not as innocent as a calf.[19] I took my feed with my fellow calves as my appetite demanded, and had a stranger unexpectedly seen us sitting there at the table together that way, he would without doubt have thought that old Circe[20] had been resurrected again to make men into beasts, which art my master at that time knew and practiced. In precisely the same way as at the noonday meal was I treated at the evening |meal. And just as my fellow diners and parasites, etc., ate so that I would eat, so they were also obliged to go to bed with me unless my master were willing to let me sleep the night in the cow stall. And I did this so that I might sufficiently make fools of them who thought that they had made a fool of me. And I came to this firm conclusion: that all-benevolent God gives and imparts to each and every person, in the condition to which He has assigned him, as much wit as he requires for his self-preservation, and that therefore many, with doctorate degrees or without, are vain to imagine that they alone are intelligent and the cream of the crop, because there are intelligent folks everywhere in the world.

CHAPTER 8

Tells of the remarkable memory[21] of some folks, and of the forgetfulness[22] of others

When I awoke in the morning my two calfly bedfellows were already gone, so I too got up and, when the adjutant fetched the keys to open the city gates, left the house and slipped off to my parson. To him I told everything, how I had fared both in heaven and in hell. And when he saw that I was suffering pangs of conscience because by pretending to be a fool I was deceiving many |folks, and particularly my master, he said: "You need not be concerned about that. The foolish world wishes to be deceived. Since they have left you your wits, use them to your own advantage. Imagine that you, like the phoenix,[23] have gone through fire from imprudence to prudence, and have thus been born again to a new human life. But know at the same time that you are not out of the woods yet, but have slipped into a fool's cap at peril to your sanity. These are strange times, and no one can know whether you can get out of it again without losing your life. A person can go to hell in a hurry, but to get out of it again requires some huffing and puffing. As yet you are by far not man enough to escape the dangers which await you, as you may imagine. Therefore, what you require is more caution and prudence than you required at the time when you still did not know what prudence and imprudence were. Remain humble, and await with patience the changes which the future will bring."

His discourse was on purpose so equivocal, I imagine, because he could tell by the look upon my face that I thought I was a fine fellow because I had slipped by with such masterful deception and great skill; and I, for my part, surmised from the look upon his face that he had become annoyed and vexed with me, for his expression indicated that, and of what good was I to him? Therefore I changed my tone and expressed to him my profound gratitude for the wonderful medicines which he had given me to preserve my wits; indeed, I made impossible promises to gratefully repay him, as my indebtedness to him demanded, for everything he had done for me. This tickled him pink, and also put him into a different mood, for then he straightway boasted that his medicaments were excellent, and he told me that Simonides Melicus[24] had invented an art, which Metrodorus Sceptius,[25] not without great effort, had perfected, by means of which he had been able to teach people to repeat word for word everything they had read or heard but one time. And this, he said, would not have transpired without using any brain-strengthening medicaments such as he had given me. "Yes, my dear parson," I thought to myself, "when I was with my hermit, I read in your own books something quite different about the source of the art of Sceptius and memorization." But I was so sly that I said nothing, for if I am to tell the truth, when I was supposed to become a fool, I became, for the first time in my life, sharp-witted and more cautious about what I said. He, the parson, continued, telling me how Cyrus[26] had been able to call every one of his thirty thousand soldiers by name, how Lucius Scipio[27] had been able to name all the citizens in Rome by theirs, and how Cynaeus,[28] the ambassador of Pyrrhus, had been able, on the day after he had arrived in Rome, to recite accurately the names of all of the senators and noblemen there. "Mithridates,[29] King in Pontus and Bithynia," he said, "had under him peoples who spoke twenty-two different languages, to all of whom he could administer justice in their native tongues and with each of whom individually, as *Sabell. lib. 10 cap. 9* reports, he could speak.[30] The learned Greek Charmides[31] told people by heart whatever anyone desired to know from any of the books in the entire library, even though he had read over them but one time. Lucius Seneca[32] could recite back two thousand names after they had been read to him, and, as Ravisius[33] reports, after two hundred students had spoken two hundred verses, he could recite them all back, beginning with the last one and ending with the first. Ezra,[34] as Eusebius[35] *lib. temp. fulg. lib. 8 cap. 7* writes, knew the Pentateuch by heart and dictated it word for word to scribes, who wrote it down. Themistocles[36] learned Persian in one year. Crassus[37] could in Asia talk in five different dialects of the Greek language and administer justice to his subjects in them. Julius Caesar[38] read, dictated letters, and gave audiences at the same time. Of Aelius Hadrianus,[39] Portius Latrone,[40] the Romans, and others I shall report nothing, but merely say of St. Jerome[41] that he knew Hebrew, Chaldean, Greek, Persian, Medean, Arabic, and Latin. The hermit Antonius[42] knew the whole Bible by heart, just from hearing it read. And Colerus[43] *lib. 18 cap. 21*, citing from Marcus Antonius Muretus,[44] writes of a Corsican who listened to the names of six thousand people and afterwards recited them back quickly and in correct order.

"I am telling you all this," he said further, "so that you will not think it impossible that a person's memory can be excellently strengthened and preserved by medicine, just as, on the other hand, it is weakened, and even obliterated, in many ways, for which reason Plinius[45] *lib. 7 cap. 24* writes that there is nothing about a human being as absurd as his memory, and that it can either disappear completely, or lose a great part of its strength, as a result of illness, shock, fear, anxiety, and grief. Of a scholar in Athens one reads that he forgot everything he had ever studied, even his ABC's, after a stone fell down upon his head. Another man, as a result of illness, got to the point where he forgot his own servant's name; and Messala Corvinus,[46] who had previously had a good memory, no longer knew his own name. Schrammhans[47] writes in *fasciculo Historiarum, fol. 60* (which, however, sounds as boastful as if Plinius himself had written it) that a priest once drank blood from his own veins and as a result forgot how to read and write, but otherwise retained his memory intact, and when, a year later, at the same place and the same time, he again drank of the same blood, he had been able to read and write again as before. To be sure, what Jo. Wierus[48] *de praestigiis daemon. lib. 3 cap. 18* writes is more credible: If one eats bears' brains one falls as a result into such fantasy and strong delusions that one believes himself to have turned into a bear, as he proves by the example of a Spanish nobleman who, after he had eaten bears' brains, ran around in the wild forest and was persuaded that he was a bear. My dear Simplicius, had your lord and master known this trick, you might have been transformed into a bear like Callisto[49] instead of into a bull like Jupiter."[50]

The parson told me much more on the same subject, gave me some more of his medicaments, and instructed me on how I should further behave. With that I made my way home again and brought along with me more than a hundred boys, who were running after me and all once more crying like calves. Therefore my master, who had just gotten up, went to the window, saw so many fools together at one time, and was so gracious as to laugh heartily at this spectacle.

CHAPTER 9

Perverse praise[51] for a fair lady

As soon as I came home I was obliged to go into the parlor too, because noble ladies were there with my master and would have liked to see and hear his new fool. I appeared and stood there like a mute, for which reason the lady whom I had seized at the dance before had cause to say that she had been told that this calf could speak, but now she realized that this was not true. I answered: "And I, for my part, was of the opinion that monkeys cannot speak, but I hear clearly that this is not the case." "What!" said my master. "Are you of the opinion that these ladies are monkeys?" I answered: "If they aren't already, they surely soon will be. Who knows how they may turn out? I did not expect to turn into a calf either, but I did." My master asked me what I saw about these ladies that made me think they were monkeys. I answered: "Our monkey goes about with his arse bare, and these ladies have already bared their breasts, while other maidens are wont to keep theirs covered." "You scamp!" said master. "You are a foolish calf, and you talk like what you are. These ladies are right to let what is worth seeing be seen. The monkey, however, goes about naked out of poverty. Now straightway make good your transgression, else you'll be soundly whipped and chased by dogs into the goose coop, which is what is done to calves who do not know how to mind their manners. Let us hear whether you know how to praise a lady as is fitting." Then I looked the lady up and down, from head to toe, and looked at her as full of ardor and love as if I desired to marry her. Finally I said: "Milord, I see clearly what's amiss here. The thieving tailor is to blame for it all. The cloth that should be at the top, around the neck, and was supposed to cover the breasts, he left it at the bottom of the skirt. That is why it drags along so far behind her. You ought to cut the rascal's hands off if he can't do any better at dressmaking than that. Milady," I said to her, "get rid of him if he is going to put you so to shame, and see that you get my Pa's tailor. His name is Master Paulie. He could make real pretty pleated skirts for my Ma, our Anne, and our Ursula which were completely even at the bottom all the way around. They surely did not drag in the dirt like yours. You really wouldn't believe what pretty clothes he could make for the sluts." My master asked me whether my Pa's Anne and Ursula were prettier than this lady. "O, not at all, milord!" said I. "This lady has hair that is as yellow as baby-shit, and the part in it is as white and as straight as if the skin had been capped with hog bristles. Indeed, her hair is so beautifully rolled up that it looks like hollow pipes, or as if she had a few pounds of candles or a dozen sausages hanging down on each side of her head. Ah! Just look what a beautiful smooth brow she has! Is it not more delicately arched than a fat buttock, and whiter than a skull that has been out in the weather for years and years? But it really is a shame that her delicate skin is so blotched by her hair powder, for if people who did not know any better were to see it, they might well think the lady had a bad case of scabies which was causing those scales, which would be all the more a shame because of her sparkling eyes, which glitter more brightly in their blackness than the soot on the damper of my Pa's stove, which glistened so terribly when our Anne stood in front of it with a wisp of straw to heat the room, as if there were not already enough fire in these eyes to set the entire world on fire. Her cheeks are so nice and rosy, but not as completely red as the new ribbons were a while back with which the Swabian wagoners from Ulm[52] decorated their bibs. And the deep red which she has on her lips exceeds that color by far, and when she laughs or speaks (I beg milord pay close heed to this), then one sees two rows of teeth in her mouth, so neatly lined up in rows and looking like sugar, as if they had been carved from one piece of white turnip. O, what a wonderful sight! I do not believe it would hurt a man if she bit him with them. And her neck is well nigh as white as curdled milk, and her little breasts, which are below it, are of the same color and without doubt as hard to the touch as a goat's udder that is bursting with too much milk. They surely are not as limp as the ones the old crones had who wiped my arse a while back when I went to heaven. O, milord, look at her hands and fingers! They are really so slender, so long, so supple, so flexible, and so delicately made, just like the ones the gypsy women had a while back and used to slip into your pockets when they wished to filch something from you. But what is all this compared to her whole body, which, to be sure, I cannot see bare? Is it not as delicate, as slender, and as graceful as if she had been having greenapple trots for a whole week?" At this such peals of laughter broke out that they could no longer hear me, nor could I go on talking. And in this wise I gave them blunt words as long as I pleased.

CHAPTER 10

Tells of nothing but heroes and famous artists

Then there followed the noonday meal, at which I again let them make good use of me, for I had resolved to speak out about all follies and to punish all vanities, a task for which my status as a fool was excellently well suited. No table companion was too exalted a person for me to reprimand and pluck up for his vices, and whenever there was anyone who bridled at it, either the others derided him, or my master represented to him that a person of sound mind generally does not grow angry at a fool. The mad ensign, who was my worst enemy, I straightway put into a pickle. But the first person who, at the behest of my master, confronted me with reasoned arguments was the *secretarius*, for when I called him a "title-smith," mocked him because of the vain titles which he employed in his work, and asked him what the title of the first man on earth was, he answered: "You talk like a mindless calf, because you do not know that after Adam and Eve there lived divers persons who so ennobled themselves and their families through their rare virtues—such as wisdom, heroic deeds, and the invention of useful arts—that they were also raised up by others above all earthly things, indeed above the stars and into the realm of the gods. Were you a human being, or had you at least read in histories like a human being, then you would also understand the difference which exists betwixt people, and you would therefore be quick to grant everyone his honorific; but since you are a calf and are neither worthy nor capable of human honor, you speak of the matter like a stupid calf and begrudge the noble human race that in which it delights." I answered: "I was once just as much a human being as you are, and I have read rather much and can therefore judge that you either do not understand this business correctly or are persuaded by self-interest to make it out to be different than you know it to be. Tell me, what manner of wonderful deeds are there, and what manner of praiseworthy arts have been invented that are sufficient to ennoble an entire family for several hundred years in a row, long after the heros and artists themselves have died off? Did not the hero's strength and the artist's wisdom and great ability die with them? If you do not understand this, and endow children with their parents' qualities, then I must needs contend that your father was a stupid codfish and your mother a flounder." "Ha!" answered the *secretarius*. "If it did any good for us to insult each other, I could reproach you that your Pa was an uncouth Spessart Forest peasant, and though it is true your homeland and family produces the biggest blockheads there are, you have nevertheless outdone even them, since you've turned into a mindless calf." "That is right," I answered, "that is what I have been maintaining, namely, that parents' virtues are not always inherited by their children, and that therefore children are not always worthy of their parents' honorifics. To be sure, it is no shame for me that I have been turned into a calf, because in this instance I have the honor of following in the footsteps of that great and powerful king, Nabuchodonesar.[53] Who knows whether it will not please God that I, like Nabuchodonesar, be turned into a human being again and that I in fact become even greater than my Pa was? I single out for praise only those persons who make themselves noble through their own virtues." "Well," said the *secretarius*, "assuming—but not conceding—that children should not always inherit their parents' honorifics, you must admit that those who have made themselves noble through their good conduct are deserving of all praise. If that be so, however, then it follows that it is right to honor the children because of their parents, for as the old saying goes, 'Like father, like son.' Who would not praise the progeny of Alexander the Great,[54] if there still be any of them around, for the great martial valor of their venerable ancestor? He demonstrated his desire to do battle in his youth, when he could not yet bear arms, by weeping for fear that his father might conquer everything and leave him nothing to subdue. Did he not, even before he was thirty years of age, conquer the world and wish that there were another one on which to wage war? Did he not, in a battle he fought with the Indians, grow so angry when he was deserted by his troops that he sweated blood? Did he not look as if he was completely surrounded by fiery flames, so that even the barbarians could not but grow so afraid of him that they left off fighting him? Who would not esteem him to be higher and nobler than other men, when Quintus Curtius[55] attests of him that his breath smelled like balsam blossoms, his sweat like musk, and his dead body like precious spices? I might also mention here Julius Caesar[56] and Pompey,[57] of whom the former fought in pitched battles fifty times, over and beyond the victories he earned in the civil wars, and slew and killed 1,152,000 men; the latter captured and vanquished 876 cities and towns, from the Alps to furthermost Spain, not to mention 940 ships taken from sea pirates. The fame of Marcius Sergius[58] I shall pass over in silence, and say but little about Lucius Siccius Dentatus,[59] who was guild-master in Rome when Spurius Turpeius and Aulus Eternius[60] were the mayors; he fought in 110 battles and eight times vanquished men who had challenged him to a duel; he could show on his body forty-five battle scars, all received facing the foe, and not a one on his back; with nine generalissimos he marched in triumphal marches into Rome (which triumphs they achieved primarily because of their valor). The military honor of Manlius Capitolinus[61] would not be less, had he not diminished it himself at the end of his life, for he could exhibit thirty-three battle scars, not to mention that he once single-handedly rescued the *Capitolium* with all its treasures from the French. Where are Hercules,[62] Theseus,[63] and others of whom it is well nigh impossible to recount and describe their immortal fame? Should not these be honored in their progeny?

"But I shall leave off war and weapons, and turn to the arts, which, to be sure, appear to be somewhat less significant, but which have nevertheless made their masters quite famous. What skill is found in Zeuxis,[64] who with his clever head and skillful hand deceived the birds in the air; *item*, Apelles,[65] who painted a Venus so lifelike, so beautiful, so perfect, and in all her lineaments so subtle and delicate that young swains actually fell in love with her? Plutarch[66] writes that Archimedes[67] pulled a large ship laden with merchants' wares across the marketplace of Syracuse by a single rope and with one hand, just as if he were leading a sumpter mule by the bridle, which task twenty oxen—much less two hundred calves of your ilk—could not have performed. And should this honest master not be endowed with a special honorary title, in keeping with his artistry? Who would not be willing to praise above other men the one who made for the Persian king Sapor[68] a device of glass which was so wide and high that he could sit in the middle and at the center of it and see underneath his feet the stars rise and set? Archimedes made a mirror with which he set fire to the enemy's ships in the middle of the sea. And Ptolemy[69] makes mention of a wondrous kind of mirror which reflected as many faces as there were hours in the day. Who would be unwilling to praise the man who first invented the alphabet? Indeed, who would be unwilling to raise above all others the artist who invented the noble art of printing, useful the entire world over? If Ceres[70] is held to be a goddess because she is said to have invented agriculture and grain-milling, why would it then be an injustice if one honored others with titles commensurate with their qualities? To be sure, it makes little difference if you, you uncouth calf, get this through your ox-skull or not. You are like the dog who was lying in the manger and would not grant hay to the ox because he himself could not eat it. You are incapable of honor, and for precisely this reason you begrudge it to those who are worthy of it." When I saw myself harried in this manner, I answered: "Heroic deeds would be highly praiseworthy if they were not accomplished at the expense of the lives and ruination of others. But what manner of fame is it that is besmirched with blood shed by so many innocent human beings? And what manner of nobility is it that is acquired and achieved through the ruination of so many thousands of other human beings? Insofar as the arts are concerned, what are they but sheer vanity and folly? Indeed, they are just as empty, vain, and useless as the honorifics themselves to which they may entitle one; for they serve either the greed or the lust or the sensuality or the corruption of others, like those terrible things I saw a while back on those flatbed wagons.[71] And we might well do without printing presses and printed books too, in accordance with the utterance and opinion of that holy man[72] who averred that the entire world was for him enough of a book in which to observe the miracles of his Creator and to recognize Almighty God in them."

CHAPTER 11

About the onerous and perilous life of a regent[73]

My master also desired to jest with me and said: "I see quite well that you are contemptuous of the honorifics of the nobility because you yourself do not believe that you will ever become a nobleman." I answered: "Milord, were I supposed to assume your honored post this very hour, I should really not accept it." My master laughed and said: "That I can believe, for oat straw is fitting for an ox. If you had any sense for the higher things in life, as noble minds are said to have, then you would consciously strive for high honors and posts. I, for my part, deem it no petty trifle when Fortune raises me above others." I sighed and said: "Alas! How onerous all your honors are! Milord, I assure you that you are the most wretched man in all Hanau." "How so? How so, Calf?" said my master. "Do tell me the reason, for I do not find it within myself." I answered: "If you do not know and feel that you are governor of Hanau and how burdened down you are with cares and anxiety on that account, then you are blinded by all-too-great lust for the honor you enjoy, or you are made of iron and are quite insensitive. To be sure, yours is the right to command, and anyone upon whom you look must obey you, but do they do so for nothing? Must you not care for every single one of them? Look you, you are now surrounded by enemies, and the safekeeping of this fortress is upon your shoulders alone. You must endeavor to figure how you may thwart your enemy, and at the same time you must take care that your schemes not be spied out. Has it not often been necessary for you to stand guard duty like a common soldier? Moreover, you must see to it that no shortage of money, munitions, provisions, and men occurs, for which reason you must keep the entire region under tribute by incessant requisitions and oppressions. When you send your men out for this purpose, what they mostly do is rob, plunder, steal, burn, and murder. Only a short while back, they plundered the town of Orb, occupied Braunfels, and burned Staden[74] to the ground. In the process, of course, they took booty for themselves, but you took upon yourself a grave responsibility in the eyes of God. I shall concede that you perhaps like the pleasure and honor which is yours, but do you know who is going to enjoy the treasures which you are amassing? And assuming that you hold on to these riches (which does seem unlikely), you must needs leave them in this world, and into the next world you will take with you nothing but the sin which you have incurred in gaining them. And if you have the good fortune to make use of your booty, you have still wasted the sweat and blood of the poor, who must now suffer want and misery, or even perish and die of hunger. O, how often do I see that your thoughts are scattered hither and yon because of the weight of your office, whereas I and other calves sleep peacefully and without the least affliction! If you do not have good fortune, then it will cost you your head whenever something or other is neglected which should have been done to safeguard the fortress and the people under your command. Look you, I am exempt from such worries! And because I know that I owe it to Nature to die, I do not worry that someone will storm my stall, or that I must needs skirmish with effort for my life. Should I die young, then I am exempted from the laborious life of a draft-ox. And without doubt they are plotting against you in a thousand different ways. Therefore your entire life consists of nothing but endless worrying and waking, for you must fear friend and foe, who are scheming to do to you what you think to do to others—to deprive you of either your life, or your money, or your reputation, or your command, or something else. The foe attacks you openly, and your would-be friends secretly envy you your good fortune. Nor are you at all safe from your subordinates either. I shall pass over in silence how your burning desires torment you daily and drive you hither and thither, how you plot to achieve greater fame and to make a greater name for yourself, to rise higher in rank, to amass more riches, to trick the enemy, to take by surprise the one town or the other, and, *in summa*, to do almost everything which distresses other folk and which is harmful to your own soul and displeasing God to His Divine Majesty! And what is worst of all, you are so indulged by your flatterers that you do not know yourself what you are, and you are so taken in and poisoned by them that you cannot see how perilous the path you are traveling is, for they acclaim as right everything you do, and by them all your vices are made out to be and proclaimed to be virtues. In their mouths your cruelty is justness, and when you have land and folk destroyed, they say you are a good soldier, and they goad you on to do harm to others so that they may remain in your good graces and fatten their own purses." "You sluggard!" said my master. "Who do you think you are, to preach to me like that?" I answered: "Dearest milord, do I not speak the truth when I say that you are already so ruined by your flatterers and thumb-twiddling toadies that nothing more can be done to help you? On the other hand, other folks see your vices quite clearly and adjudge you worthy of harsh criticism, not only in major and important affairs, but also sufficiently so in minor things of little import. Do you not have sufficient examples of this amongst famous persons who lived in times of yore? The Athenians muttered against Simonides,[75] just because he talked too loudly. The Thebans complained about their Paniculus because he spat in public.[76] The Lacedaemonians scolded their Lycurgus[77] for walking with his head bowed down. The Romans thought it unbecoming of Scipio[78] to snore so loudly when he slept; it seemed to them despicable that Pompey[79] scratched himself with but one finger; they made fun of Julius Caesar because he did not wear his sash in a dainty and pleasing way. The Uticans defamed their good Cato[80] because in their opinion he ate too fast, with food in both sides of his mouth; and the Carthaginians spoke maliciously of Hannibal[81] because he always went about with his chest uncovered and bare. What do you think now, dear milord? Do you really think that I would trade places with a man who has—aside from twelve or thirteen dinner guests, toadies, and parasites—more than a hundred, probably more than ten thousand people who are openly or secretly his enemies, who libel and slander him, who are jealous and envious of him? Moreover, what manner of happiness, what manner of pleasure, what manner of joy can really be had by a person under whose custody, care, and protection so many people live? Is it not necessary that you watch over all your subjects, care for them, and hear the grievance and complaint of each of them? Would not this alone be burdensome enough, even if you had neither enemies nor ill-wishers? I well see how much you must toil and moil, and how many annoyances you tolerate. Dearest milord, what will be your reward in the end? Tell me, what will you have from it? If you do not know, then let the Greek Demosthenes[82] tell you—Demosthenes, who, after he had boldly and loyally promoted and protected the common weal and the laws of the Athenians, was, contrary to all law and equity, banished from the land and sent into exile like a man who had perpetrated a terrible crime. Socrates[83] was given poison. Hannibal was so ill rewarded by his subjects that he was obliged to wander about the world a fugitive; and the same thing happened to the Roman, Camillus. And the Greeks similarly rewarded Lycurgus and Solon,[84] one of whom was stoned to death, and the other of whom was banished as a murderer after they had put out one of his eyes. So keep your command, together with the rewards you have from it! You must not share any of them with me, for if all goes well with you, you will at least have nothing to show for it but a bad conscience. If, however, you were to pay heed to your conscience, then you would soon be relieved of your command because you would be deemed an incompetent, no differently than if you too, like me, had been turned into a stupid calf."

CHAPTER 12

About the intelligence and knowledge of mindless beasts[85]

While I was thus discoursing, everyone looked at me, and all who were present were astonished that I should be able to make such a speech, which, as they asserted, would have been difficult enough for a man of sound mind, had he attempted to do it without working it out beforehand. I, however, concluded my speech and said: "That is the reason then, milord, why I do not desire to trade places with you. And, in fact, I do not need to do so, for the springs give me healthful water to drink instead of your precious wine, and He Who saw fit to let me be turned into a calf will also be able to so bless the fruits of the earth that they will not be any more unpleasing as food and sustenance for my life than they were for Nabuchodonesar's, and Nature has provided me with a good hide, whereas you are often disgusted with the finest foods, and the wine often gives you a splitting head and throws you into one illness or another."

My master answered: "I know not what to make of you! You seem to me to be much too sensible for a calf. I do well nigh believe that under your calfskin there is a scamp's skin!" I pretended to be angry and said: "Do you human beings really think that we beasts are complete fools? You must not imagine anything of the sort. I contend that if older beasts could talk as well as I do, they would soon make you think differently. If you think we are so stupid, then do tell me who taught wild doves, jays, blackbirds, and partridges how to purge themselves by eating bay leaves? And doves, turtledoves, and chickens to do it with dandelions? Who teaches dogs and cats that they should eat grass with dew on it if they wish to cleanse their full bellies? Who teaches turtles to heal themselves with hemlock when they are bitten? And the stag, when it is shot, how it should take recourse to *dictamno*, or wild penny-royal? Who instructed the weasel to use rue when it desires to fight a bat or some kind of snake? Who teaches the wild boar to recognize ivy and the bear to recognize mandrake, and tells them that they are good medicines for them? Who advised the eagle to seek and use an eaglestone when it is having difficulty laying its eggs? And who makes the swallow understand that it should medicate the rheumy eyes of its young with *chelidonio*?[86] Who has instructed the snake to eat fennel when it desires to slough off its skin and improve its eyesight? Who teaches the stork to purge itself? The pelican to let its own blood? And the bear to have itself bled by bees? Why, I might well nigh say that you human beings learned your arts and sciences from us beasts! You glut yourselves with food and drink till you fall ill and die. We beasts don't do that! A lion or a wolf, if it is getting too fat, will fast till it is thin, alert, and healthy again. Now who behaves more wisely? Over and beyond all this, observe the birds in the sky, observe the divers structure of their artful nests, and because no one can duplicate their work, you must surely concede that they are both more sensible and more ingenious than you human beings are. Who tells the summer birds when, on towards spring, they should come to us and hatch their young? And on towards fall when they should betake themselves away again and to warm lands? Who instructs them that for this purpose they must needs have a place to assemble? Who directs them, or who shows them the way, or do you human beings perchance lend them your compasses so that they not get lost on the way? No, my dear friends, they know the way without your help, and how long they must travel, and when they should depart from one place for another: so they require neither your compass nor your calendar. Further, look at the industrious spider, whose web is very nearly a miracle. See if you can find a single knot in it anywhere. What hunter or fisherman taught it to spread its net and, depending on how it employs the net, to listen in the furthermost corner of the net or in the very center of it for its prey to enter? You human beings are surprised at the raven, about which Plutarach attests that it kept dropping stones into a bowl half full of water till the water was high enough so that it could drink from it at its ease. What would you do if you were to dwell with and amongst the beasts, and to see and observe their other actions, and what they do and omit to do? Then you really would admit that it looks as if all animals have something akin to special natural powers and virtues of their own in all their *affectionibus*[87] and moods, and as if they had received lessons and instruction in when to be cautious, strong, generous, timid, or harsh. Each beast knows the other; they can distinguish other beasts from one another; they pursue those that are useful to them and flee those that are harmful; they avoid danger, gather what they require for their nourishment, and at times deceive even you human beings. Therefore, many *philosophi*[88] of old seriously considered the possibility, and were not ashamed to ask and to dispute, whether mindless beasts did not have good sense after all. But I do not care to say anything more on these matters. Go observe the bees, and see how they make wax and honey, and then come back and tell me what you think."

CHAPTER 13

Contains all manner of things; anyone who desires to know about them must read it himself, or have someone read it to him

Then various opinions about me were given by my master's guests. The *secretarius* maintained that I should be considered a fool because I esteemed and presented myself as a beast which possessed reason, and particularly since those who had too few wits or too many and who nevertheless considered themselves of sound mind were the very best and drollest fools. Others said that if they could dispel the illusion that I was a calf, or persuade me that I had turned into a human being again, then I could be considered sane and sensible enough. My master, for his part, said: "I take him to be a fool, because he bluntly tells everyone the truth to his face. On the other hand, his discourses are so constituted that they do not befit a fool." And all this they said in Latin so that I should not understand it. He asked me if I had had any schooling back when I was a human being. My answer was that I knew not what "schooling" was. "But, milord," I said further, "what manner of things be these 'schools' that you use when you go 'schooling'? Are they those flocks of fishes you catch in a seine?" To this the mad ensign answered: "I know what be the matter wi' this here laddie. He got the divil in him, he do! He be possessed! That be the divil what's a-talkin' out'n his mouth!" Therefore my master took the occasion to ask me whether, now that I had turned into a calf, I was still wont to say my prayers like other people, as I had before, and whether I still hoped to go to heaven. "Certainly!" I answered. "I still have my immortal soul. As you can easily imagine, it will not desire to go to hell, particularly since I have already fared so ill there. I am merely transformed, like Nabuchodonesar in olden times, and I might well, in good time, turn back into a human being again." "I hope you do! said my master with a deep sigh. From that I was easily able to conclude that he was overcome by remorse because he had made so bold as to make me into a fool. "But let us hear it!" he went on. "How are you wont to pray?" Then I knelt down, lifted my eyes and hands up to heaven as a good hermit does, and because my master's remorse, which I had remarked, brought great solace to my heart, I could not hold back my tears, and, after reciting the *Pater noster*,[89] I prayed, to all outward appearances with the utmost devotion, for the good of all Christendom, for my friends and my enemies, and that God might let me live in this temporal world in such a way that I might be worthy to sing His praises in eternal bliss, which prayer, with its piously conceived words, I had been taught by my hermit. At this, several softhearted onlookers almost fell to weeping themselves because they felt such great pity for me. Indeed, my master's eyes were filled with tears.

After the meal my master sent for the parson. To him he told everything that I had brought up and thereby gave the parson to understand that he was worried that something might be amiss with me, and that the devil might perchance have slipped under the coverlet with me, because while I had shown myself to be quite naive and ignorant before, now I was able to bring up things which were astonishing to people. The parson, who knew best how things stood with me, answered that they should have thought about that before they made so bold as to make me into a fool, that human beings were created in God's image, and that no one should use them like wild beasts, particularly when they are young. But, he said, he could never ever believe that the evil spirit had been allowed to join in the game, because I had always commended my soul to God in such fervent prayer. However, had the devil, contrary to all hopes, been ordained and allowed to do this, then it would be difficult to answer for it to God, particularly since there is no greater sin anyway than when one human being robs another of his sanity and, therefore, of the opportunity to praise and to serve God, for which purpose primarily he had been created. "I gave you, before you made him into a fool, the assurance that he had wits enough; that he could not, however, fit into the world because he had been brought up by his father, a loutish peasant, and by your brother-in-law in the wilderness in all simplicity. Had you at first had a little patience with him, he would surely in time have begun to improve. He was but a simple and virtuous child who was as yet unacquainted with the evil world. But I doubt not in the least that he can be restored to his former state if we can cure him of his delusion and bring him to the point where he no longer believes that he has been turned into a calf. We read of a man who firmly believed that he had turned into an earthenware jug and therefore begged his family to put him in a high place so that no one might bump into him and break him.[90] Another man went so far as to imagine that he was a rooster, and in his illness he crowed day and night. Yet another went so far as to think that he had already died and was wandering about as a ghost, and was therefore unwilling to take unto himself either medicine, or food, or drink any more, till finally a clever doctor hired two fellows who pretended to be ghosts but who ate and drank heartily, put these two into the company of the sick man, and persuaded him that nowadays ghosts are wont to eat and drink too, whereby he was then restored to his former state. I myself had in my parish a sick peasant who, when I went to visit him, complained to me that he had in his body between 125 and 150 gallons of water; if he could get rid of it, he thought, he might get well again, and he asked me either to cut him open so that it could run out of him, or to hang him up in smoke so that it would dry up. Then I spoke to him and persuaded him I could get the water out of him in a different way. Then I took a stopcock, such as is used with beer barrels and wine casks, tied to it one end of a length of gut, and I tied the other end to the bung of a wash tub which to this purpose I had had filled with water and brought there. Then I made as if I was sticking the stopcock into his stomach, which he had bound up all over with rags so that it might not explode. Then I let the water from the tub run out through the stopcock, at which the booby was overjoyed, took off the rags after the procedure was finished, and in a few days was restored to his former state again. In this manner another person was helped who imagined that he had all manner of horse tack, reins, and the like in his belly. To him the doctor gave a purgative and put these things at the bottom of the chamber pot, so that the fellow could not but believe that they had come out with his stool. And they tell of a madman who believed that his nose was so long that it reached to the ground. They attached a sausage to the end of his nose, cut off slices of it, one by one, till they got to the real nose, and when he felt the knife on his nose, he screamed that his nose was now again in its proper shape. Good Simplicius can also surely be helped, as these other people were."

"All that I do believe," answered my master, "but what concerns me is that he was so ignorant before, but can now talk about such things—and relate them so perfectly too—as older, more experienced, and more widely read folks than he is can scarce do. He told me many characteristics of beasts and described his own person as nicely as if he had spent his entire life in the sophisticated world, so that I could not but wonder at it and take his words to be almost an oracle or a warning from God."

"Milord," answered the parson, "there may be a natural explanation for this. I know that he is well-read, since both he and the hermit went through all the books I had, and there were in fact quite a number of them. And because the lad has a good memory, but now has an idle mind and is forgetful of his own identity, he can bring up things which he put into his mind before. And I do foresee that in time he can be restored to his former state." Thus the parson let the governor dangle betwixt fear and hope. He defended me and my cause in the best way and brought about good times for me and for himself access to my master. The final conclusion they reached was that they should observe me for a while longer; and this the parson did more for his own benefit than for mine, for by coming and going and acting as if he were laboring and taking great pains on my behalf, he curried the governor's favor. Therefore the governor took him into his service and made him the chaplain of the garrison, which was no small thing in such troubled times, and which I granted him with all my heart.

CHAPTER 14

What a noble life Simplicius continued to lead, and how the Croats spoiled it for him when they took him as part of their spoils

From then on I possessed the favor, good will, and love of my master completely, of which I can with truth boast. I wanted for nothing to make me happier but that my calf's clothes were still too much for me and my years still too few, though I did not know that. And the parson did not wish to have my wits restored to me yet either, because it seemed to him the time was not ripe, and it was not commensurate with his own best interests. And when my master saw that I delighted in music, he had me taught it, and at the same time put me in the hands of an excellent lute-player, whose art I soon pretty well comprehended and whom I even outstripped, because I could sing better than he could. And so I served to delight, amuse, entertain, and astonish my master. All the officers showed me deference, the wealthiest townsmen bestowed gifts upon me, and the servants as well as the soldiers wished me well because they saw how partial to me my master was. One gave me this present, and the other that one, because they knew that court jesters can often accomplish more with their masters than a well-documented petition can, and that was what they had in mind when they gave me presents, because some of them gave me things so that I should not speak ill of them, and some so that to their benefit I should speak ill of others. In this way I got together a rather goodly sum of money, most of which I gave to the parson for safekeeping, because I did not yet know of what use it was. And inasmuch as no one durst look askance at me, I had no vexations, cares, or troubles from any quarter. All my thoughts I devoted to my music and to how I might politely make the one or the other person aware of his shortcomings. Thus I grew like a calf in clover, and my physical size and strength increased palpably. People could soon tell by looking at me that I was no longer mortifying my flesh in the forest with water, acorns, beechnuts, roots, and herbs, but rather that the good food and the Rhenish wine and Hanau strong-beer was setting well with me, which in such wretched times was to be prized a gift of God, for at that time all of Germany was suffering from the flames of war, from hunger, and from pestilence, and Hanau itself was surrounded by enemies—all of which did not perturb me in the least. After the siege was lifted, my master planned to make a present of me to either Cardinal Richelieu[91] or Duke

Bernhard of Weimar,[92] for aside from the fact that he hoped to earn their great gratitude with me, he also contended that it was well nigh impossible for him to bear the sight of me any longer, because he saw me daily in this fool's habit, and with each passing day I more and more resembled his late sister. This the parson advised him not to do, for he insisted that the time had come for him to perform a miracle and make me back into a human being of sound mind. Accordingly, he advised the governor to have two calfskins prepared and to have them put on other boys, and then to command a third person to appear in the guise of a doctor, prophet, or wandering magician, to perform curious ceremonies during which he stripped both me and the other two boys of our calfskins, and to maintain that he could make people out of animals and animals out of people. In this way I could indeed be restored to my former state, and without particular effort I could be led to believe that I, like a number of others, had been turned into a human being again. When the governor was so gracious as to agree to this suggestion, the pastor communicated to me what he had arranged with my master and easily persuaded me to agree to it. But envious Fortuna was unwilling to let me slip out of my fool's costume so easily, or to let me continue to enjoy the good life I was leading, for while the tanners and tailors were working on the clothes required for this *comoedia*,[93] I was ambling about with some other boys on the ice outside the fortress walls, when, unexpectedly, from whither I know not, a party of Croats rode up, seized all of us, set us on some mountless farm horses they had just stolen, and rode off with us. To be sure, at first they were dubious about whether they should take me along, till finally one of them said in Bohemian: "Mee vameh doho blasna zebao, bo vadehmeh ho gbabo Obersto fee."[94] To him another one answered: "Prshees ambambo ano, mee ho magonie possadeime, vann rozumi niemezki, vonn budeh mit kratock filleh zebao." And so I was obliged to mount up and to learn that a single hour of misfortune can deprive a person of all his prosperity and can so remove him from all happiness and deliverance that he will pay for it for as long as he lives.

CHAPTER 15

Simplicius' life with the troopers and what he saw and experienced with the Croats

Now though the people of Hanau straightway sounded the alarm, mounted up, and rode out of the town and held the Croats up and troubled them somewhat with a skirmish, they nevertheless could not take any of their booty back from them, for these rascals took advantage of an opportunity to escape and took the road to Budingen,[95] where they foddered and gave the townsmen there the captive sons of the wealthy Hanau townsmen to be ransomed, and also sold the horses and other goods they had stolen. From there they set out again, well before it was dark, much less before it was day again, rode quickly through the forest towards the convent of Fulda,[96] and on the way took everything they could carry. The robbing and plundering did not hinder their rapid progress in the least, for they rode like the devil, of whom folks are wont to say that he can run and (s. v.)[97] take a shit at the same time, and not miss a trick along the way. And so, that very evening we arrived at the convent of Hirschfeld,[98] where they had their quarters, with a large amount of booty. All of it was divided up, and I went to Colonel Corpes. [99]

With this master everything, to my mind, was repugnant and strange. The dainty morsels of Hanau had been replaced by coarse black bread and scraps of beef or, when things really went well for me, a piece of stolen ham. For me wine and beer had turned into water, and instead of sleeping in a bed, I was obliged to make do with a pile of straw in the stable with the horses. Instead of playing the lute, which had entertained everyone in Hanau, I was obliged at times to crawl under the table with the other boys, howl like a dog, and let myself be raked with spurs, which was no fun at all for me. Instead of promenading about as I had in Hanau, I was permitted to ride out foraging, to curry horses, and to haul manure out of the stables. Foraging, however, was nothing but roaming out into the villages with great toil and effort, and often not without danger to life and limb, and threshing, grinding, baking, stealing, and taking whatever was to be found there, torturing and ruining the peasants, and indeed even raping their maids, wives, and daughters. And if the peasants were unwilling to put up with that, or if they chanced to make so bold as to rap the one or the other forager on the knuckles, and at that time there were many guests of that ilk in Hesse, then the foragers chopped them down when they got their hands on them, or at least sent their houses heavenward in smoke. My master had no wife (for warriors of his ilk are not wont to take wives along with them), no page, no valet de chambre, no cook, but on the other hand he had a heap of grooms and stableboys who attended to both him and his horses, and he was not ashamed to saddle his own horse, or to shake out fodder in front of it. He always slept upon a pile of straw or upon the bare ground and covered himself with his fur coat. Therefore upon his clothes one often saw lice crawling about, of which he was not in the least ashamed, but rather he went so far as to laugh when someone picked one of then off of him. He wore his hair short, and he had a wide Swiss beard which stood him in good stead, for he was wont to disguise himself in peasant clothes and to go out in them to scout the enemy. Now even though, as you have heard, he did not dine like a grandee, he was nevertheless honored, loved, and feared by his men and by others who knew him. We never stayed in one place; rather, we were here one day, there the next. One day we attacked, and the next we were attacked in turn. So we never ever paused in our efforts to diminish the Hessian forces, but Melander,[100] for his part, did not leave off us either, but captured and sent to Cassel[101] many a trooper of ours.

This restless life did not appeal to me at all, and therefore I often wished, in vain, that I were back in Hanau. The heaviest cross I had to bear was that I could not talk with the other lads and was now and then obliged to let nearly everyone push me, cheat me, beat me, and mistreat me. The greatest diversion which my colonel had from me was that I was obliged to sing to him in German and, like the other stableboys, to puff up my cheeks so that a vile sound would be made when he slapped the air out of them, which pastime seldom occurred, to be sure, but when it did I received such cuffs in the face that the red blood flowed, and I had enough of that to last me a lifetime.[102] Finally I fell to taking upon myself the cooking chores and to cleaning my master's musket, which he highly prized, because I was still of no use on foraging expeditions anyway. That went so excellently well for me that I finally earned my master's favor, for which reason he had another fool's costume made for me out of calfskins, with much longer ass's ears than I had worn before. And because my master was not finicky in his taste, I required all the less culinary skill; but since I often lacked salt, lard, and spices, I soon did grow weary of my trade and therefore cudgeled my brain night and day about how I might make good my escape, particularly since I had reached another spring. Now when I was ready to put this plan into effect, I took on the task of carrying far away from camp the sheep and cow entrails so that they would not make such a horrible stench any more, to which the colonel was agreeable. Now when I was busy doing that, I finally stayed away till it grew dark, and then I whisked off into the nearest forest.

CHAPTER 16

Simplicius takes good booty and then becomes a thieving forest hermit

To all appearances, however, the more time passed the worse my situation became, so that I began to think that I had been born under an unlucky star, for I was but a few hours away from the Croats when some highwaymen grabbed me. They without doubt thought that I was a fine catch, because in the dark of night they did not see my fool's costume, and two of their number straightway took me to a certain spot in the forest. When they had brought me thither, and it was still pitch black, one fellow right off desired to take my money from me, to which end he put down his gloves and his flintlock and fell to searching my person, asking: "Who are you? Do you have any money?" But as soon as he felt my hairy garment and the long ass's ears on my cap (which he took to be horns) and at the same time perceived bright sparks (which can generally be seen on animals' pelts when you stroke them in the dark), he was so frightened that he jumped back from me. This I straightway perceived, for which reason, I before he could recover or come to his senses, so stroked my costume with both hands that it shimmered as if I were full of burning sulphur inside, and I answered him in a terrifying voice: "I am the devil, and I am going to wring your neck and your comrade's so that your heads will be facing backwards!" This so frightened the two of them that both of them scurried away over stick and stone, as quickly as if hellfire were after them. The dark night could not stay their rapid course, and though they often bumped into saplings, stones, trees, and tree trunks, and even more often fell into a heap, they nevertheless quickly jumped to their feet again. This they kept doing till I could no longer hear them. Meanwhile I, however, kept laughing so terribly that the whole forest echoed with my laughter, which without doubt was a terrifying thing to hear in such a dark wasteland.

Now when I was setting out to depart, I stumbled over the flintlock. This I took with me, because I had learned to handle firearms when I was with the Croats. When I walked on, I bumped into a knapsack which, like my clothes, was made from calfskin. I picked it up likewise and found that a flintlock pouch well stocked with powder, lead, and all appurtenances was hanging down under it. I took all of it onto my back, put the firearm upon my shoulder like a soldier, and hid not far from there in some thick bushes, with the idea in mind to sleep there for a while. But as soon as day dawned, the entire party came to that same spot and fell to looking for the lost musket and knapsack. I pricked up my ears like a fox and kept quieter than a mouse; and when they did not find anything, they fell to making fun of the two who had fled from me. "O, you cowardly ninnies!" they said. "You ought to be ashamed to the bottom of your soul that you let a lone man frighten you, chase you off, and take your firearm!" But the one fellow swore that the devil might take him if that had not been the devil himself; indeed, he said, he had felt his horns and rough hide. And the other one behaved quite badly and said: "I care not whether it was the devil or his grandmother, so long as I get my knapsack back." One of them, whom I took to be the one of highest rank, answered this fellow, saying: "What do you think the devil desires your knapsack and your flintlock for? I'll wager my life that the fellow you so disgracefully let escape took both of them along with him." Another one argued against this fellow and said that it might also be that some peasants had been there in the interim and had found the things and taken them. Everyone finally agreed with this surmise, but the entire party still firmly believed that they had had the devil in their clutches, primarily because the one who had attempted to search me in the dark not only swore to this by all that was holy, he was also able to describe and stress powerfully my rough, sparking hide and my two horns, which are sure signs of the devil. And I do believe that if I had again let them see me unexpectedly, the entire party would have run away.

Finally, after they had searched for a sufficiently long while and had found nothing, they went on their way. I, however, opened the knapsack in order to eat breakfast, and the first thing I pulled out of it was a purse in which there were some three hundred and sixty ducats. Now there is no use asking whether I was pleased at this! But gentle Reader, be assured that the knapsack pleased me much more than this fine sum of money because I saw it to be as well stuffed with provisions. And inasmuch as coins of this sort, where common soldiers are concerned, are generally much too few and far between to be carried along on raiding parties, the thought occurred to me that the fellow must needs have just seized this money secretly on that very raid and had quickly shoved it into his knapsack so that he might not be obliged to share it with the others.

I then cheerfully ate my breakfast and soon found a delightful little spring at which I refreshed myself and counted my fine ducats. And even though it were to cost me my life if I were not to tell in what country or region I was at that time, I could not do so. In the beginning I stayed in the forest for as long as my provisions, from which I ate sparingly, held out, but when my knapsack was empty, hunger drove me into the peasants' houses. Then I crept by night into cellars and kitchens and took whatever victuals I found and could carry. These I dragged with me into a part of the forest which was the wildest of all. There I led once more, as before, a hermit's life in every regard, except that I stole a lot and prayed all the less, and had no one place to live but roamed about, here one day and there the next. It was very much to my advantage that it was the beginning of summer, and I could also kindle fire with my flintlock whenever I desired.

CHAPTER 17

How Simplicius went to the witches' dance[103]

While I was roaming about, sundry peasant folk came upon me now and again, but they always fled from me. I know not whether the cause was that they had been made skittish, chased off their lands, and constantly kept on the move by the war, or whether the highwaymen had spread abroad the story of the adventure which they had had with me, so that after that those who saw me likewise believed that the devil was really wandering about in the region. Therefore I could not but fear that my provisions might run out and that I might thereby fall into extreme peril, unless I was willing to eat roots and herbs once more, to which fare I was no longer accustomed. Deep in these thoughts I heard two woodcutters, which greatly pleased me. I followed the sound of the chopping, and when I saw them I took a handful of ducats from my purse, crept up to them, showed them the tempting gold, and said: "Gentlemen, if you will assist me, I shall give you a handful of gold." But as soon as they saw me and my gold, they forthwith took to their heels, leaving behind mallet and wedge, together with their cheese- and bread-bag, from which I filled my knapsack again, withdrew into the forest, and well nigh despaired of ever in all my days living amongst people again.

After turning things over in my mind for a long while, I thought to myself: "Who knows how you may fare in the future? But you do have money, and if you can bring it for safekeeping to decent folk, then you can live for a rather long while from it." And so it occurred to me that I should sew it up into my clothing. Therefore I made from my ass's ears, which so put folks to flight, two armlets, put my ducats from Hanau, together with the ones I had taken from the highwaymen, under house arrest in the aforementioned armbands, and tied them around my arms above the elbow. Now when I had put my treasure into safekeeping this way, I broke into some peasants' cottages and took from their stores what I required and could lay my hands on, and though I was still naive, I was nevertheless so

131

sly that I never went back to the same place from which I had already taken something. Therefore I was very lucky in my stealing and was never caught pilfering.

One time, at the end of May, when I was about to fetch my sustenance in the usual, though illegal, way and had gone to a farmhouse to this end, I went into the kitchen but soon perceived that people were still up (*nota:*[104] where there were dogs I did not go in). Therefore I opened wide a kitchen door which led into the yard so that if there were any danger I might scurry off immediately. And so I sat there quiet as a mouse till I might expect that the people had gone to bed. In the meanwhile I caught sight of a crack in the little sliding panel betwixt the kitchen and the living room. I crept up to it to see whether the people were not going to sleep soon, but my hopes were dashed, for they had just got dressed, and instead of a candle they had a blue flame[105] standing upon the bench, by the light of which they were smearing something onto sticks, brooms, pitchforks, chairs, and benches, and then they flew out the window upon them. I was frightfully astonished and felt great horror, but because I was accustomed to more terrifying things, and especially because I had never in my life read or heard anything about witches and warlocks, I was not particularly perturbed by it, primarily because it all happened so quietly; rather, after everyone had flown off I betook myself into the room too, considered what I might take along with me, and where I might look for it, and, deep in thought, I sat down astraddle a bench. Scarce had I sat me down when I, together with the bench, went out the window in a trice, leaving behind, as pay for the smearers and for the ingenious salve, my knapsack and flintlock, which I had taken off and laid aside. Sitting down, flying off, and dismounting all happened in the bat of an eye almost, for it seemed to me that I instantly came to a large throng of folks, unless it be that out of fear I paid no heed to how long this long journey took. These people were dancing a curious dance, the likes of which I had never in my life seen, for they had joined hands and made many circles inside each other, with their backs to one another, the way the Graces are painted, so that their faces were turned outward. The inner circle consisted of about seven or eight people, the second of probably twice as many, the third of more than the first two put together, and so forth, so that in the outermost circle there were more than two hundred people. And because one circle or ring danced to the left and the next one to the right, I could not see how many circles they made, or what they had in the middle which they were dancing around. It looked dreadfully strange, because their heads bobbed up and down and past one another so oddly. And their music was just as strange as the dance, and each person, I thought, was singing along while he danced, which created a singular *harmoniam.*[106] The bench which was carrying me thither landed by the minstrels, who were standing about outside the circle around the dance. Instead of flutes, pipes, and shawms, some of them had nothing but adders, vipers, and blindworms upon which they were blowing merrily. Some had cats, upon whose arses they were blowing, while they did the fingering upon their tails, which sounded like bagpipes. Others were fiddling upon horses' skulls as if upon the best violins, and yet others were playing the harp upon cow-ribs such as are found lying in carrion pits. And there was one there who was carrying under his arm a bitch whose tail he was turning around like a barrel organ handle, while he fingered it on the teats. And all the while the devils were trumpeting through their noses so that it resounded throughout the entire forest. And when this dance was soon finished, the entire infernal society fell to raving, screaming, yelling, bellowing, howling, raging, and fuming, as if they were all as mad as March hares. Now anyone can imagine what fear and terror I was in. In the midst of this hubbub there came up to me a fellow who had under his arm an enormous toad, easily as big as a kettle drum, whose guts had been pulled out his arse and stuffed back into his mouth, which looked so repulsive that the sight of it turned my stomach. "Look you here, Simplicius!" said he. "I know that you are a good lute player. Let us hear a pretty little piece!" I was so frightened that I well nigh fainted, for the fellow had called me by name, and in this terror I could not make a sound, and it seemed to me as if I were in the midst of a very bad dream; and therefore I prayed inwardly in my heart that I might wake up, but the fellow with the toad at whom I was staring was pulling his nose in and out like a Calcutta turkey and finally so pushed against my chest that I nearly suffocated from it. Therefore I fell to calling loudly to God, and the entire throng disappeared. In a trice it was pitch-black dark, and my heart was so filled with fear that I fell to the earth and crossed myself a good hundred times.

CHAPTER 18

Why it should not be thought that Simplicius is a teller of tall tales

Inasmuch as there are some folk, and, indeed, amongst them distinguished and learned people, who do not believe that witches and demons exist, much less that they fly back and forth through the air, I doubt not that there will be some who will say that Simplicius is telling a tall tale here. Now I have no desire to quarrel with such folk, because it takes no great skill to boast: rather, that is the most common pastime nowadays; so I cannot deny that I too could engage in it, for if I could not, I should be a poor booby indeed. But let those who deny that witches travel by broomstick consider the case of Simon the Magus,[107] who was lifted up into the air by the evil spirit and then, in answer to St. Peter's prayer, dropped to earth again. Nicolaus Remigius,[108] who was a valiant, learned, and sensible man and who had no small number of witches burned at the stake in the Duchy of Lorraine, tells of John Hembach that his mother, who was a witch, took him along to a witches' sabbath when he was sixteen years of age, so that he could play for their dance, since he had learned to play the pipes. To this end he climbed up a tree and was playing along and observing the dance closely (perhaps because it all seemed so odd to him). Finally he said: "Dear God forbid! Whence come so many foolish and mindless folks?" And scarce had he uttered these words when he fell out of the tree, sprained his shoulder, and called to them for help, but there was no one there but himself. When he later bruited this about, most people took it to be a fairy tale, till shortly after that Catherina Praevotia, who had been at that same dance, was arrested for witchcraft. She told the same thing about what had happened there, even though she had not heard the gossip which Hembach had spread abroad. Majolus[109] gives two examples, one about a hired man who doted upon his wife, and another about an adulterer who took from an adulteress a jar and smeared himself with the salve in it, and both of them went to the conclave of sorcerers. And there is also the tale about a hired hand who got up early and greased the wagon, but because in the darkness he had seized the wrong jar, the wagon rose up into the air so that they were obliged to pull it down again. Olaus Magnus[110] relates in his *lib. 3. Hist. de gentibus Septentrional. I. cap. 19* that Hading,[111] King of Denmark, rode back to his kingdom, out of which he had been driven by rebels, a great distance through the air, over the sea, on the back of the spirit of Odin,[112] who had transformed himself into a horse. And it is also sufficiently well known in what manner some wives and unmarried lasses in Bohemia caused the men who slept with them to be brought, against their will, to them over great distances, at night, on the backs of billy goats. What Torquemada[113] tells in his *Hexamerone* about one of his schoolmates can be read in that book. Ghirlandus[114] also writes of a distinguished gentleman who, when he noted that his wife was smearing salve upon herself and then leaving the house, once compelled her to take him with her to a gathering of sorcerers. When they were eating there, and there was no salt, he requested some, and got it with great effort, then saying: "Praise be to God, there comes the salt." Then the lights went out and everyone vanished. Now when it was daylight, he learned from some shepherds that he was near the city of Benevento, in the Kingdom of Naples, and thus a good five hundred miles from his home. Therefore, even though he was quite wealthy, he was still obliged to beg his way home; and when he got home he forthwith turned his wife over to the authorities as a witch, and she was burned at the stake. How Doctor Faust,[115] along with others who were not even sorcerers, rode through the air from one place to the other is sufficiently well known from his *histori*. And in fact, I myself knew a wife and a maidservant, both of whom are dead now as I write this, though the maidservant's father is still alive. On the hearth by the fire this maidservant was once smearing oil upon the shoes of her mistress, and when she was finished with one of them and set it aside in order to oil the other one too, the oiled one on a sudden flew up the chimney. But this story was hushed up. All of this I am telling only so that folks may really consider the possibility that sorceresses and warlocks at times do physically ride to their gatherings, and not so that people must needs believe that I went thither in the way I have described, for it is all one to me whether anyone believe it or not. And anyone who refuses to believe it can devise some other way by which I marched in such a short while from the convent of Hirschfeld or Fulda (I myself know not whither I had wandered about in the forests) to the Archbishopric of Magdeburg.[116]

CHAPTER 19

Simplicius comes to be a fool once more, just as he had been before

I shall now take up my *histori* again, and I assure you, dear Reader that I lay upon my belly till it was broad daylight because I had not the courage to get up. In addition, I was still dubious about whether or not I had dreamed the things of which I have told, and even though I was rather terror stricken, I was still brave enough to go to sleep, because I thought I could not lie in any worse place than in a wild forest, in which I had spent most of my time since I left my Pa, and to which I had therefore become rather accustomed. It was about nine o'clock in the morning when some foragers came by and awakened me. Not till then did I see that I was in the middle of an open field. They took me with them to some windmills and, after they had ground their grain there, then to their camp outside the walls of Magdeburg, where I was given to a colonel of foot, who asked me whence I came and to what sort of master I belonged. I related everything, down to the last detail, and because I could not find a name for the Croats, I described their clothes and gave examples of their language; and also I told that I had run away from them. About my ducats, I kept silent and what I told about my journey through the air and about the witches' dance they considered crotchets and foolish fancies, particularly since in my discourse I jumbled things up in other regards, too. Meanwhile a crowd of people gathered around me (for one fool creates a thousand more like himself). Amongst them was one who had been a prisoner in Hanau the year before and had accepted service there, but had after that come back to the Imperials. He knew me and straightway said: "Oho! This was the commandant's calf in Hanau!" The colonel asked him for more details concerning me, but the fellow knew nothing further about me, except that I knew how to play the lute; *item*, that the Croats of Colonel Corpes had taken me away from outside the walls of the fortress of Hanau; and then that the aforementioned commandant was distressed to lose me because I was a such a very fine fool. Then the colonel's lady sent word to another colonel's lady who knew how to play the lute rather well and therefore always carried one with her. She asked her for the use of her lute. It came and was given to me, with the charge that I should let them hear me play something. To my way of thinking, however, they ought first to have given me something to eat, because an empty belly does not go well together with a full one, such as the lute had. This was done, and after I had pretty well stuffed my craw and had at the same time swallowed a good-sized drink of Zerbst beer,[117] I let them hear what I could do, both with the lute and with my voice. All the while I said all manner of confusing things, anything that came into my head, so that with little effort I got the people to the point where they believed that I was indeed what my costume proclaimed me to be. The colonel asked me what I desired to do now, and when I answered that it was all one to me, we struck a bargain that I should stay with him and be a member of his retinue. He also desired to know where my ass's ears had got to. "If you knew where they were," I answered, "they would surely look good on you." And I did well to keep silent about them, because all my wealth was in them.

In a short while I became familiar with most of the high-ranking officers in the armies of both the Emperor and the Prince Elector of Saxony,[118] and particularly well known to the ladies, who decorated my cap, my sleeves, and my cropped ass's ears all over with silk ribbons of all sorts of colors, so that I well nigh believe that some of these present-day fops copied their fashion in clothing from me. Whatever money was given me by the officers, however, I shared generously, for I spent all of it, down to the last farthing, guzzling Hamburg and Zerbst beer with my comrades, which beers agreed with me excellently well, not to mention the fact that everywhere I went, there was plenty of food for me to cadge.

But when my colonel procured my own lute for me, for he thought he would keep me with him forever, I was no longer permitted to run free back and forth betwixt the two camps. Rather, he put me into the care of a guardian, who was to keep an eye upon me and whom I was to obey. This was a man after my own heart, for he was quiet, sensible, well educated, a man of few words, but worthwhile ones, and, best of all, exceeding God-fearing, well read, and versed in all manner of arts and sciences. I was obliged to sleep by night in his tent with him, and by day I was not let out of his sight. He had been a noble prince's councillor and court official, and had also been very wealthy, but because he had been completely ruined financially by the Swedes, and especially because his wife had died and his only son, because of their poverty, could no longer attend the university, but was serving as a muster-clerk in the army of the Prince Elector of Saxony, he stayed with this colonel and let them employ him as a master-of-horse,[119] to pass the time till the perilous course of the war along the Elbe River changed, and till the sun of his former good fortune might shine upon him once more.

CHAPTER 20

A rather long chapter dealing with dice-playing[120] and what goes with it

Because my guardian was more old than young, he also could not sleep without interruption the entire night through. This was the reason why he saw through my game in the first week and expressly learned that I was not the fool I made myself out to be; for before that he had also noted something and judged differently from my face, because he was well versed in *physiognomiam.*[121] One time I awoke at midnight and pondered upon my own life and the curious events in it, and I got up and as a way of giving thanks I related all the good things God had done for me and all the perils He had rescued me from. After that I lay down again with heavy sighs and slept the rest of the night.

My guardian heard everything but acted as if he were sound asleep, and this happened several nights in a row, so that he deemed himself sufficiently assured that I had more sense than many a man on up in years who imagines that he has much sense. But he did not speak to me about this in the tent, because its walls were too thin, and at this time, for certain reasons, he did not wish to let anyone else know this secret yet, and before he had assured himself of my innocence. One time when I was taking a walk behind the camp, which he was happy to permit so that he would have reason to come look for me and thereby have the opportunity to speak to me alone, he found me, as he desired, in a solitary spot giving audience to my thoughts, and he said: "My dear good friend, because I make so bold as to wish the best for you, I am happy that I can speak with you here alone. I know that you are not a fool, as you pretend to be, and further that you do not wish to remain in this wretched and contemptible state. Now if your welfare is dear to you, and if you are willing to place your trust in me, an honorable man, then you can tell me the state of your affairs, and then I, for my part, shall assist you where possible, in word and deed, to figure how you might perchance be helped, so that you may get out of your fool's costume."

At this I flung my arms around his neck and for sheer joy behaved as if he were a prophet come to deliver me from my fool's cap. And after we had sat down upon the ground, I told him the story of my entire life. He looked into the palms of my hands and was surprised at the curious events which had already befallen me and were yet to come, but he was by no means willing to counsel me to put off my fool's costume in the near future, because, he said, he saw by means of *chiromantia*[122] that my *fatum*[123] was threatened by imprisonment, which would bring with it peril to life and limb. I thanked him for his good opinion of me and for the counsel he had given me, and begged God that He reward him for his loyal friendship, and I begged him himself that he be and remain my faithful friend and father (because I had been forsaken by all others).

Then we got up and walked to the gaming area, where men were jousting with dice and swearing in the name of "thousands of galleys full of, schooners full of, tons of, and moats full of" you-know-what. The place was about as large as Old Market Square in Cologne. Everywhere cloaks were spread out upon the ground and tables set up, all of which were filled with gamesters. Every group had three square "rogue's bones" to which they entrusted their fortune, because they shared their money and could not but give some to one person and take some from another. And every cloak or table had a vice-master—I meant to say "dice-master," though dice do hold their prey as fast as in a vise. It was their task to be arbitrators, and they were supposed to see to it that no cheating occurred. They also supplied the cloaks, tables, and dice, therefore managed to take so many fees from the winnings that they generally made more money than any of the dice-players, but to no avail to themselves, for they generally gambled it away again, or if it was put to any better use, it went to the sutler or to the surgeon, because the badly battered pates of the dice-masters ofttimes required mending.

These foolish people were enough to strike you with wonder, because they all thought they were going to win, which was, after all, impossible, unless they took their stakes out of someone else's pocket; and even though they all did harbor this hope, the rule of thumb was nevertheless "every man for himself," because everyone concentrated upon his own luck; for some hit the mark and some missed it, some won and some lost. Therefore, some cursed too, some raged; some cheated, and others were rooked. Thus the winners laughed and the losers gnashed their teeth; some sold their clothes and whatever else of value they had, and others won their money right away from them; some demanded honest dice; others, for their part, desired false ones and slipped them unnoticed into the game; but others threw them out of the game again, smashed them, and bit them in two with their teeth, and ripped up the dice-masters' cloaks. Amongst the false dice were Dutch ones, which must be rolled so that they skitter along the table; they had two fives, on opposite sides, and two sixes, and were as sharp-ridged as the skinny asses they give soldiers to ride. Other dice were High German ones; these you must hold as high as the Bavarian Alps when you are about to toss them. Some were made of hartshorn, light on top and heavy on the bottom; others were loaded with quicksilver or lead, and yet others with chopped-up hair, tinder, straw, and charcoal. Some had sharp edges; on others the edges were filed off completely; some were long and club-shaped; and some looked like fat toads. And all of these sorts of dice were made for the sole purpose of cheating. They did what they were made to do; whether you tossed them so that they bounced or tossed them so that they skittered made no difference at all. And that is not to mention the dice with two fives and two sixes on them and, contrariwise, two aces and two deuces. With these rogue's bones they cheated, filched, and stole their money from one another, money which they themselves perhaps had stolen, or at least got hold of at hazard to life and limb, or else by sour toil and sweat.

Now as I was standing there and observing the gaming field, together with the gamesters in their folly, my guardian asked me how I liked this sport. I answered: "I do not like the way they blaspheme God with their terrible oaths, but otherwise I can say nothing as to its value or lack thereof, since it is a matter of which I have no knowledge and which I do not yet understand in the least." To this my guardian said further: "Well, know then that this is the worst and most loathesome of all spots in the entire camp, for here one man seeks to take another man's money and in so doing loses his own. The moment one so much as sets foot here with the idea of gaming, one has trangressed against the tenth commandment, which says 'Thou shalt not covet thy neighbor's house.' If you gamble and win, particularly by cheating and using false dice, then you transgress against the seventh and eighth commandments. Indeed, it can happen that you become the murderer of the man from whom you have won money, namely, if his losses are so great that he falls into poverty, into dire need and despair, or into other loathesome vices. It is no excuse when you say 'I put up my money too, and I won fair and square!' for you, you scoundrel, went to the gaming area with the intent to become rich at the expense of another. If you then game away your money, you have not atoned simply by virtue of the fact that you must needs be deprived of what is yours; rather, you have incurred, like the rich man in the parable, grievous sin, for which you must answer to God, namely, that you have so frivolously squandered what He gave you as sustenance for yourself and your family! A man who runs to the gaming table to gamble also runs the risk that he may lose not only his money but his life and, what is worst of all, even the salvation of his immortal soul. I am telling you all this for your information, my dear Simplicius, because you indicate that you have no knowledge of gaming, and so that you shall shun it your entire life long."

I answered: "My dear master, if gaming is really so terrible and perilous a thing, why then do the commanding officers permit it?" My guardian answered me: "I do not wish to say it is because some of the officers participate in it themselves. Rather, it is because the soldiers are no longer willing to forego it, indeed, are no longer able to do without it, for once a person has succumbed to gaming or has got into the habit or, better, has become possessed by the gaming devil, he little by little becomes so bent on gaming (whether he win or lose) that rather than do without it, he would sooner go without sleep, which is why one sees some men rattling the dice all night long and gaming instead of enjoying the finest food and drink, and keeping on with it till they game away the shirts off their backs. Gaming has been prohibited in the past at divers times, under penalty of imprisonment and death, and, at the orders of the general staff, it has been stopped, publicly and by force, by armed police, provosts, hangmen, and bailiffs. But none of it did any good, for the gamesters foregathered somewhere else, in secret nooks and crannies and behind hedges, won money from one another, fell out with one another, and broke one another's necks about it, so that because of all the murder and manslaughter, and also primarily because many a soldier was gaming away his firearm and his horse, even his daily rations, they were obliged to permit public gaming again, and even to set aside this specific place for it, so that the main watch would be near at hand to counter any mischief which might occur, which, of course, cannot always prevent the one or the other man from getting himself killed here. And because gaming is an invention of Satan himself, and brings him no small profit, he has also ordained and sent to swarm about the world special gaming-devils who have nothing else to do but to tempt men to gamble. Divers dissolute fellows sell their souls to them by means of certain pacts and covenants so that he permit them to win. And yet, you will not find one rich gamester in ten thousand; rather, they are on the contrary generally poor and needy, because their winnings are held in scant esteem and are therefore gambled away again or squandered in some other dissolute manner. This is where the all too true but lamentable saying comes from: 'The devil never lets gamesters loose, but he does let them lose'; for he robs them of their belongings, courage, and honor, and then does not let a gamester loose till he has finally deprived him of even his immortal salvation (unless God in His infinite mercy prevent it). If, however, a gamester is by nature of such merry humor and so magnanimous that he cannot be brought by any misfortune or loss to fall into melancholy, dejection, or other noxious vices arising therefrom, then the foul and wily fiend lets him win considerable sums, so that in the end he may get him into his net by having him waste his money, grow proud, glut himself with food and drink, and consort with whores and knaves."

I crossed and blessed myself at the thought that in a Christian army they allowed practices which were said to have been invented by the devil, particularly since they obviously and palpably resulted in so much harm and damage, both in this world and the next. But my guardian said that he had not told me even the half of it, and that anyone who desired to describe all the evils which arose from gambling would be attempting the impossible, because they say that the dice, when they leave the dice-player's hand, are in the devil's, so that I could imagine only that there runs along after every die (when it leaves the dice-player's hand and rolls along the cloak or table) a little devil who controls it and causes it to come up the number his master's interest demands. At the same time, my guardian said, I should consider that the devil did not so zealously espouse the cause of gaming for no good reason, but without doubt knew how to turn a handsome profit from it. "And at the same time, note further that just as there are wont to be standing near the gaming place some Jews and chafferers who are prepared to buy up for a cheap price whatever rings, clothes, and jewels the gamesters have won or lost and wish to still gamble away, so also there are devils lurking there so that they can arouse and nurture in those who have finished gaming, no matter whether they have won or lost, other thoughts ruinous to the soul. In the minds of the winners he of course builds frightful castles in the air, and into those who have gambled away their money and whose minds are confused anyway and are therefore all the more susceptible to his harmful whisperings, he without doubt puts nothing but such thoughts and schemes as are directed solely at ultimate ruin. I assure you, Simplicius, that I am of a mind to write an entire book about this *materi*,[124] as soon as I am living in peace and quiet with my loved ones again. There I shall describe the valuable time which gamesters waste, and, further, the terrible oaths with which they blaspheme God when they are gaming. I am going to tell of the insults which they hurl at one another, and also include many frightful examples and stories about what has happened at, by, and during games of chance, at which point I shall not forget to mention the duels and killings which have occurred as a result of them. Indeed, I shall depict and present to the reader's eyes the greed, wrath, envy, jealousy, falseness, deceit, selfishness, thievery, and, in a word, all the mindless follies of both dice-players and card-players in such vivid colors that people who read this book will feel as much abhorrence for gaming as if they had drunk sow's milk (which is given without their knowledge to gamesters to cure them of this illness of theirs); and I shall thereby demonstrate to all Christendom that our dear Lord is more blasphemed by a single party of gamesters than He is served by an entire army." I praised this project and wished him the opportunity to carry it out.

CHAPTER 21

A chapter somewhat shorter and more amusing than the previous one

With each passing day my guardian became fonder of me and I of him in return, but we kept our intimacy quite secret. I, of course, acted the fool, but I did not indulge in crude capers or buffoonery, so that my observations and behavior were simpleminded enough but nevertheless turned out more witty than foolish. My colonel, who had an enormous yen for the hunt, once took me along when he went out to catch partridges with a bird-net, which *inventio*[125] pleased me exceeding well. But because the pointer was so skittish that it generally flushed the birds before they could be netted, we could not catch many. Then I gave the colonel the following piece of advice: he should have a bitch covered by a falcon or a golden eagle (the way people are wont to do with horses and asses when they desire to have mules) so that the pups would have wings; with them the partridges could then be caught in flight. I also made the suggestion, because things were dragging along so with the conquest of the city of Magdeburg, that they should make a big long rope, as thick as a forty-gallon keg, draw it around the city, and hitch all the men and beasts in both camps to it, and in this wise pull the city to the ground in one day. A superabundance of such foolish notions and crotchets I thought up each day, because it was part of my trade, so that my workshop was never found empty, as it were. And my master's clerk, who was a bad sort and a thoroughgoing rogue, provided me with much *materi*[126] to sustain me on the path which fools are wont to follow, for whatever this jokester persuaded me was true, I not only believed myself but passed on to others when I happened to be engaged in a discussion and the topic of conversation took that direction.

One time when I asked him what manner of creature our regimental chaplain was, because his clothes were different from those of others, he said: "He is Master *Dicis non facis*,[127] which in our language means that he is a fellow who gives other men wives in holy wedlock but takes none himself. He is the archenemy of thieves because they do not talk about what they do, while he talks about what he does not do; and, on the other hand, the thieves are not at all fond of him either, because generally the time when they get best acquainted with his sort is when they are about to be hanged." When I later called the good and honorable *pater*[128] by that name he was mocked contemptuously and I was deemed an evil and scoundrelly fool and given a dose of birch oil for it. Further, the clerk persuaded me that they had torn down and burned the public houses of ill repute in Prague behind the city wall, and that the sparks and ashes from them had been dispersed like the seed of a weed, all over the world. *Item*, he said that from amongst the soldiery no valiant heroes or stouthearted fellows ever went to heaven, but rather only simpleminded ninnies, sluggards and the like, who were content with their wages: and no politic cavaliers *a la mode*[129] and *galantes dames*,[130] but only people with the patience of Job, henpecked husbands, tiresome monks, melancholy parsons, women who go to church every time the doors are open, poor beggar-whores, all manner of scum that is not worth the shot and powder to blow it up, and young children who were still shitting in their breeches. He also told me the lie that the sole reason why tavern keepers are sometimes called publicans is because in their profession they, more than any other people, make it clear in public whether they are going to heaven or to the devil. Concerning military matters he persuaded me that they sometimes also shoot with golden musket balls, and the more costly they are, the more damage they generally do. "Indeed," he said, "they drag along in golden chains as captives whole armies, together with the artillery, munitions, and baggage." Further, he persuaded me that more than half of the wives wore the breeches in the family, even though one could not see them, and that even though they could not perform witchcraft, nor were they goddesses like Diana,[131] many of them conjured larger horns onto their husbands' heads[132] than Acteon[133] ever bore, all of which I believed, so stupid a fool was I.

On the other hand, my guardian, when he was alone with me, entertained me with discourse of quite a different sort. He also acquainted me with his son, who, as has already been reported, was a muster-clerk with the army of the Elector of Saxony and was possessed of qualities far different from those of my colonel's clerk. Therefore my colonel was very fond of him and was also intent upon bargaining to get him away from his captain and making him his regimental clerk, which post his own aforementioned clerk had his eye upon.

With this muster-clerk, whose name, like his father's, was Richard Trueheart, I came to be such good friends that we swore to one another eternal brotherhood, by virtue of which we should never abandon one another in fortune or in misfortune, in joy or in sorrow. And because this happened with his father's knowledge, we maintained our union all the more firmly and unswervingly. Accordingly, nothing would have been more pleasing to us than to free me from my fool's costume in an honorable manner and to be of true service to one another, which, however, old Trueheart, whom I regarded and honored as a father, did not approve of, but rather said expressly that if I were to change my status in the near future, this act would bring me imprisonment and great peril to life and limb. And because he also prognosticated that he and his son would soon be the butt of great ridicule, and he thus thought that he had reason to live all the more carefully and cautiously, he was all the more unwilling to meddle in the affairs of a person whose impending great peril he could see with his own eyes, for he feared that he might share my upcoming misfortune if I revealed myself, because he had already long since been aware of my secret and knew me inside out, as it were, but had not informed his colonel of the truth about me.

Shortly after that, I perceived even more clearly that my colonel's clerk was terribly envious of my new brother, because he feared he might be promoted to the secretary post before him, for I well saw how peeved he was at times, how envy consumed him, and that he always sighed, burdened by thought, whenever he looked at either old Trueheart or his son. From that I judged and believed beyond the shadow of a doubt that he was plotting to trip up young Trueheart and bring him to a fall. To my brother, both because of my loyal affection for him and the indebtedness I bore him, I communicated what I suspected so that he might take precautions against this Judas. He, however, dismissed it with a shrug of the shoulders, for the reason that he was more than sufficiently superior to the clerk in the use of both the quill and the sword, and he enjoyed, moreover, the great favor and good will of the colonel in the bargain.

CHAPTER 22

A scoundrelly thief's trick to do another man in

ecause it is customary in war to make old tried-and-true soldiers the provosts,[134] we too had one of that ilk in our regiment, and, in fact, such an accursed rogue of the first order, rotten to the core, that it might well be said of him that he was far more experienced than was necessary; for he was a veritable necromancer, sorcerer, and devil- conjurer, and in his physical person not only as impervious to musket balls as if he were made of steel, but also, over and beyond that, the sort of fellow who could make others that way too, and even put whole squadrons of specter-cavalrymen[135] onto the battlefield.[136] His external appearance was naturally like that of Saturn, as poets and painters depict him for us, except that he had neither crutch nor scythe.[137] Now even though the poor soldiers who were captured and fell into his merciless hands deemed themselves all the more unfortunate because of this character of his and because of his constant presence, there were nevertheless people who liked to consort with this killjoy, particularly the clerk, Olivier, and the greater his envy of young Trueheart became, the stronger the intimacy between him and the provost grew. Therefore I could easily reckon for myself that the *conjunctio* of *Saturnus* and *Mercurius*[138] would bode no good for honest Trueheart.

At just that time my colonel was blessed with a baby son, and the christening supper, at which young Trueheart was asked to serve, was near fit for a king; and because out of politeness he was happy to attend, this was the opportunity Olivier had been waiting for to perpetrate the knavish trick which he had been plotting for a long while; for when everything was over, my colonel's large gold-plated goblet[139] was missing, which he should not have lost so easily, because it was still there after the strangers who were guests had already gone. The page said, in fact, that he had last seen Olivier with it, but he refused to admit this. Then the provost was fetched to clear the matter up, and at the same time he was commanded, if by his art he could solve the theft, to arrange his work so that the thief would be known to no one but the colonel, because other officers of his regiment had been present whom he would not like to publicly disgrace, should one of them prove to have committed this indiscretion.

Now because everyone knew himself to be innocent, we all went merrily into the colonel's large tent, where the sorcerer set to work. Everyone looked at one another and demanded to hear what was going to happen in the end, and whence the lost goblet would come. Now after he had murmured a few words, one, two, three, and even more young puppies sprang forth out of the breeches-pockets, sleeves, boots, and codpieces of the one person and the other, and out of wherever there was an opening in the clothes. These whisked quickly hither and thither about the tent hither and yon. All were exceeding beautiful, of many different colors, and each was marked in a special manner, so that it was a right merry spectacle to behold; and my tight Croat calf-breeches were conjured so full of young pups that I was obliged to take them off and, since my shirt had long since rotted on my back in the forest, to stand there naked. Finally one puppy, which was the most agile of them all, sprang out of young Trueheart's codpiece, and it had on a golden collar; this one devoured all the other puppies, of which there were so many scrambling about the tent that one could not set one foot in front of the other because of them. Now when this puppy had got rid of all the others, it grew smaller and smaller, till it finally actually changed into the colonel's table-goblet.

Now at this point not only the colonel but everyone else present could not but believe that none other than young Trueheart had stolen the goblet. Therefore the colonel said to him: "Look you, you ungrateful guest, did I, in return for all the good things I have done for you, deserve this thievery, of which I should never have believed you capable? Look you here, I had intended to make you my *secretarium* tomorrow, but now it would serve you right if I had you hanged this very day, which would unfailingly happen, were I not desirous of sparing your honest old father. Get you out of my camp this instant, and never let me lay eyes upon you again as long as you live!" Trueheart attempted to excuse himself but was paid no heed, because it was clear as day that he'd done the deed. And as he was going away, old Trueheart fell completely into a swoon, so that they were hard put to revive him, and the colonel himself was hard put to console him, saying that a virtuous father need not answer for the misdeeds of his prodigal child. And so, with the help of the devil, Olivier achieved what he had long been striving for but had not been able to attain by honorable means.

CHAPTER 23

Richard Trueheart sells himself for a hundred ducats

As soon as young Trueheart's captain learned of this affair, he relieved him of his post as clerk and burdened him down with a pike,[140] from which time on he was held in such contempt by many that even the dogs were of a mind to piss on him, for which reason he then often wished that he were dead. His father, for his part, grieved so much about it that he came down with a grave illness and reconciled himself to dying. And inasmuch as he had himself prognosticated beforehand that he must needs run risk to life and limb on July 26th (which day was in fact near at hand), he therefore got permission from the colonel for his son to come visit him one more time, so that he might talk with him about his inheritance and might reveal to him his last will and testament. I was not excluded from their reunion, but was instead the third party to their sorrow. There I saw that the son had no need to make any excuses to his father, because the latter well knew his son's character and good upbringing and was therefore sufficiently assured of his innocence. As a wise, sensible, and thoughtful man, he deduced without difficulty from the circumstances that Olivier had arranged for the provost to get his son into trouble, but what could he do against a sorcerer from whom he had worse to fear, should he venture to exact revenge? Moreover, he foresaw his own death and yet could not die in peace because he was going to leave his son in such disgrace, in which condition the son was all the less confident of continuing to live, since he wished all the more anyway to die before his father did. It was assuredly so heartrending to see the misery of these two that I could not but weep from the bottom of my heart. Finally their common and agreed-upon decision was to patiently leave their affairs to God, and the son should ponder upon ways and means by which he could get a discharge from his company and seek his fortune elsewhere. But when they examined this plan by the cold light of day, they lacked the money with which he might buy his freedom from his captain, and only when they fell to considering and lamenting what misery their poverty held them captive in, and how it cut them off from any hope of improving their present condition, did I remember my ducats, which I still had sewn up in my ass's ears. Therefore I asked how much money they had need of. Young Trueheart answered: "If someone came and gave us a hundred sovereigns, I am confident that it would take care of all my needs." I answered: "If that will help you, then be of good cheer, for I shall give you a hundred ducats." "O," he answered me in return, "how is that? Are you really a fool after all? Or so wicked as to make fun of us in our direst straits?" "No, no!" said I. "I'll give you the money." Then I took off my doublet and untied the ass's ear from round my arm, opened it, and made him himself count out and take unto himself a hundred ducats out of it. The rest, I kept, saying: "With these I shall support your sick father, whenever he may need them." Then they threw their arms around my neck, kissed me, and for sheer joy knew not what they were doing; and they desired to supply me with a handwritten document and in it assure me that I should be a co-heir of old Trueheart along with his son, or that they, should God help them recover what was rightfully theirs, would with great gratitude repay me this *summam*[141] with interest, neither of which offers I accepted, but rather commended myself to their undying friendship. Then young Trueheart desired to swear an oath to take vengeance upon Olivier or to die in the attempt, but his father forbade him this, assuring him that the man who slew Olivier would be finished off by me, Simplicius. "And yet," he said, "I rest well assured that neither of you will kill the other, because neither of you is destined to die in mortal combat." After that he enjoined us to swear together an oath to love one another unto our death, and to stand by one another through thick and thin. And young Trueheart was indeed able to buy his way free[142] for thirty Imperial sovereigns, in return for which his captain gave him honorable discharge, and with the rest of the money he betook himself at the first opportunity to Hamburg, there equipped himself with two horses, and let the Swedish army make use of his services as a freebooter,[143] meanwhile commending to me the care of his father.

CHAPTER 24

Two prophecies are fulfilled simultaneously

None of my colonel's people was better able to care for old Trueheart during his illness than I was, and because the sick man was more than well satisfied with me, this task was assigned me by the colonel's lady, who did him many kindnesses; and inasmuch as, because of such good nursing and on account of his son, he became sufficiently refreshed, his condition improved from day to day so that even before July 26th he had returned to complete health in almost every respect; but he desired to stay in his quarters and act as if he were ill, till that day, at which he obviously felt horror, had passed. Meanwhile he received visits from all manner of officers from both armies who desired him to tell them their future fortune and misfortune, for since he was a good *mathematicus*[144] and caster of horoscopes and at the same time also an excellent physiognomician and *chiromanticus*,[145] his predictions seldom went unfulfilled. In fact, he even named the date upon which the battle of Wittstock[146] afterwards occurred, since many men came to him who were threatened with violent death upon that same date. The colonel's lady he had assured that she would come down with child while still in camp, because Magdeburg[147] would not be surrendered to our side till six weeks had elapsed. To perfidious Olivier, who was all feigned cordiality in his presence, he said expressly that he must needs die a violent death and that I was destined to avenge his death, no matter when it might happen, and would in turn kill his murderer, for which reason in the following time Olivier held me in high esteem. He told me myself the entire future course of my life, in such detail as if it were already completed and he had been with me all through it, to which, however, I paid little heed, and yet afterwards I remembered many things he had told me, after they had happened or come true, and primarily that he warned me against water, because he feared that I would suffer my demise in it.

Now when July 26th arrived he quite fervently admonished me and a quartermaster musketeer (whom the colonel: at his request, had assigned to me for that day) to let no one come into his tent. And so he lay alone in it and prayed without interruption. But when it got to be afternoon, there came riding up a lieutenant from the troopers' camp who asked for the colonel's master-of-horse. He was sent to us and was straightway sent away by us, but he refused to be sent away and instead begged the quartermaster musketeer, amidst promises to make it worth his while, to let him see the master-of-horse, with whom he must needs speak that very evening. But because this was to no avail either, he fell to cursing and raging like a thunderstorm, saying that he had already ridden over so many times to see the master-of-horse and had never yet found him in, and now that he was here, yet again he was not going to have the honor of speaking a single word with him. Then he dismounted and could not be prevented from unbuttoning the tentflap, at which I bit him in the hand and got for my pains a sharp box on the ears. As soon as he saw my old guardian he said: "Let me beg you, sir, to forgive me for making so bold as to address a few words to you." "All right," answered the master-of-horse, "what do you desire, sir?" "Nothing," said the lieutenant, "but that I desire to beg you, sir, to be so kind as to cast my horoscope." The stablemaster answered: "I hope, my dear sir, that you will forgive me for not being able, because of my illness, to fulfill your request at this time, for this task requires many mathematical calculations, and my aching head will not be capable of doing them now. But if you will be so kind as to wait till tomorrow, I hope I shall be able to afford you satisfaction enough."

"Sir," the lieutenant then said, "just tell me for the time being what you see in my palm." "My dear sir," answered old Trueheart, "that art is quite uncertain and misleading. Therefore I beg you to spare me it. Tomorrow, on the other hand, I shall gladly do anything you desire of me." But the lieutenant would not be sent away and instead stepped up to the bedside of my father, held out his hand, and said: "Sir, I pray you, only a few words concerning the end of my life, with my assurance that if it should be something bad, I shall accept what you say as a warning from God to take all the more care. Therefore, I pray you, for God's sake, not to keep the truth from me." The honest old man then answered him bluntly, saying: "Well, all right. You should take care lest you be hanged this very hour." "What! You old rogue!" said the lieutenant, who was drunk as a loon. "How dare you talk to a gentleman that way?" With that he drew his sword and ran my dear old Trueheart through, right there in his bed. The quartermaster musketeer and I immediately began screaming bloody murder, so that everyone seized his weapons. The lieutenant, however, immediately took to his heels and without doubt would have escaped on horseback, had the Prince Elector of Saxony[148] himself, with many horse, not been riding by just then and chased and caught him. When he heard about what had happened, he turned to von Hatzfeld,[149] our general, and said this and nothing more: "It is bad discipline for an Imperial camp when even a sick man in his own bed is not sure of his life against murderers." That was a harsh statement and enough to cost the lieutenant his life, since our general forthwith had him hanged by his fine neck.

CHAPTER 25

From a lad Simplicius is transformed into a lass[150] and acquires divers lovers

From this true *histori*[151] it can be seen that not all prophecies ought to be ignored, as they are by oafs who cannot believe in anything. And one can also deduce from this that a man will scarce be able to avoid the end predestined for him, even though a long while or a short while before he has been told of his misfortune in prophecies of that sort. To the question which might arise as to whether it be necessary, profitable, and worthwhile for a man to have his fortune told and his horoscope cast, I can but answer that old Trueheart told me much that I often wished and still do wish that he had kept silent about, for the misfortunes which he reported to me I have never been able to avoid, and those which still await me are giving me grey hairs, because I fear they will befall me as the former ones did, whether I take care to prevent them or not. But so far as strokes of good fortune which are foretold for a person are concerned, it is my opinion that they are more often than not misleading, or at least do not come true as much as prophecies of misfortune do. What good did it do me that old Trueheart swore to me by all that is holy that I was born and bred of noble parents, since I knew no one other than my Pa and my Ma, who were uncouth peasants in the Spessart Forest? *Item*, what good did it do von Wallenstein, the Duke of Friedland, that they prophesied to him that he would be crowned king to the sound of music? Do we not know how he was sung to sleep at Eger?[152] Therefore, others may break their skulls worrying about this question; I am going to return to my *histori*.

When I had lost, as I have related, both my Truehearts, the entire camp outside the walls of Magdeburg became odious to me, which place I was wont, anyway, to call a city of canvas and straw with earthen walls. I became as sick and tired of my condition as if it had been stuffed down my craw with iron cookspoons. Finally I made up my mind not to let anyone use me as a fool any longer, and to rid myself of my fool's garb, even if in so doing I should lose life and limb. This I set about doing in the following very reckless way, because no better opportunity seemed to present itself to me.

Olivier, the *secretarius*,[153] who had become my guardian after old Trueheart's death, often let me ride on foraging expeditions with the grooms. Now one time when we came into a large village in which some of the baggage which had fallen to the troopers of horse was stored, and everyone was going into and out of the houses to look for what might perchance be there to take along, I too stole away and looked to see whether I might find some old peasant clothes which I could exchange for my fool's cap. But I did not find what I was looking for, but was obliged to make do with a woman's dress. I put it on because I saw that I was alone, and I threw my old clothes into a privy, imagining nothing but that now I had delivered myself from all my troubles. In this outfit I walked across the lane towards some of the officers' ladies, taking such mincing steps as perchance Achilles did when his mother recommended him to Lycomedes.[154] But I had scarce got outside the house when some foragers saw me and taught me to hop along more quickly, for when they screamed "Halt! Halt!" I but ran all the faster, reaching those officers' ladies before they did, at which ladies' feet I fell to my knees and begged them in the name of all women's honor and virtue to protect my virginity from these ruttish fellows. And my request was not only fulfilled, I was even taken on as a maidservant by the lady of a captain of horse, with whom I made do till Magdeburg; *item*, till Werberschanz and also Havelberg and Perleberg[155] were taken by our side.

This lady was not a girl any more, even though she was still young, and she became so smitten with my smooth face and straight limbs that finally, after lengthy efforts and much beating around the bush to no avail, she gave me to understand all too bluntly where the shoe pinched her. I, however, was at that time still much too conscientious; I acted as if I did not understand what she meant, and behaved in such wise that from my actions one might not esteem me to be anything but a virtuous virgin. The captain and his groom had come down with the same ailment. Therefore the captain bade his wife dress me better, so that she need not be ashamed of my ugly peasant smock. She did more than was bidden her to do and decked me out like a French doll, which caused the fire in all three of them to blaze even more hotly. Indeed, it finally got so hot that master and servant most eagerly desired of me what I could not do for them and was modestly refusing to do for the lady herself. At last the captain resolved to seize an opportunity when he could have from me by force what it was really impossible for him to get. This his wife perceived, and because she still hoped to conquer me in the end, she cut him off at every pass and frustrated his every scheme, so that he thought it must needs make him as mad as a March hare. One time, when my master and his lady were asleep, the groom stood outside the wagon in which I was obliged to sleep every night, lamenting to me his love with hot tears, and just as fervently pleading for mercy and pity. But I showed my heart to be harder than a stone and gave him to understand that I meant to preserve my virginity till I was married. Now when he offered at least a thousand times to marry me and yet heard in reply no answer but my assurance that it was impossible for me to wed him, he finally fell completely into despair, or at least pretended to, for he drew his sword, put the point of it to his chest and the hilt against the wagon, and acted as if he were now about to run himself through. I thought to myself, "the devil is a rogue," and consoled him by saying that tomorrow morning he would receive my final answer. With that he was content and went to sleep. I, however, stayed awake all the longer, considering my strange plight. I realized quite well that in the long run things would end badly for me, for with each passing day the captain's lady was growing more importunate in her enticements, the captain bolder in his advances, and the groom more desperate in his constant love; but I knew not how to find my way out of this labyrinth. Often I was obliged to pick lice off my lady in broad daylight, solely so that I might see her alabaster breasts and touch her tender body, which, because I was made of flesh and blood too, in the long run came to be difficult to abide. And if the lady left me in peace, then the captain tormented me, and when I ought to have had a night's rest free from both of them, then the groom plagued me, so that the woman's dress caused me more trouble than my fool's cap had. At that time I clearly recalled (but much too late) my late Trueheart's prophecy and warning and could not but think I was already in that prison, with peril to life and limb, about which he had told me, for the women's clothes were holding me prisoner, because in them I could not run away, and the captain would have used me badly, had he recognized me to be a boy and ever caught me chasing lice with his beautiful lady. What was I to do? I finally resolved to reveal myself that very night to the groom, as soon as day dawned, for I thought to myself: "His pangs of love will subside then, and if you let him have some of your ducats, he will help you to men's clothing again and thus to escape in them the straits you are in." It would have been a good plan, had Fortuna[156] but desired it to be, but she was against me.

Right after midnight my Johnny arose to fetch his answer and fell to rattling on the wagon, just as I had fallen into a deep, deep sleep. He called out, somewhat too loudly: "Sabina! Sabina! O, my darling, get up and keep your promise!" so that with his words he awakened the captain rather than me, because he, the captain, had his tent next to the wagon. This without doubt made him red with wrath, because he was already consumed with jealousy anyway, but he did not come out to interrupt our doings, but merely got up to see what course our affair would take. At last the groom awakened me with his importunity and urged me either to come out of the wagon and join him or to let him come in to me; but I scolded him severely, asking him if he thought me a whore and saying that my agreement of yesterday was contingent upon wedlock, outside of which he could never possess me. He answered that I should get up anyway, because day was about to break, so that I might make breakfast for the servants betimes. He would fetch the wood and water, he said, and start the fire for me. I answered: "If you are willing to do that, then I can sleep all the longer. Go on ahead. I'll follow soon." But because the fool refused to desist, I got up, more to do my work than to do any courting with him, since, it seemed to me, the desperate madness of yesterday had left him again. I could pass for a girl rather well when we were in the field, for with the Croats I had learned to cook, bake, and wash clothes, and in the field, soldiers' wives are not wont to spin anyway. But whatever other woman's work I could not do, such as brushing and braiding my lady's hair, for example, my lady was quite willing to overlook, for she well knew that I had not learned to do it.

Now as I was climbing down out of the wagon with my sleeves rolled up, my Johnny grew so inflamed at the sight of my bare arms that he could not leave without kissing me, and because I did not particularly resist, the captain, who was seeing it with his very own eyes, could not bear it and sprang out of the tent with his sword drawn, to give my lover a blow, but he ran off and forgot to come back. The captain, however, said to me: "You bloody whore! I'll teach you!" etc. More than that he could not say in his anger, and instead he beat upon me as if he had gone mad. I fell to screaming, so he was obliged to leave off, so that he not cause any alarm, for the two armies,[157] the Saxon and the Imperial, were at that time next to one another, because the Swedish army under General Banier[158] was approaching.

CHAPTER 26

How he is imprisoned as a traitor and sorcerer

Now when day dawned, my master turned me over to the stableboys, just as the two armies were setting out on the march. Now they were a swarm of ragamuffins, and therefore the chase which I was obliged to suffer was all the greater and more frightful. They rushed into the bushes with me, all the better to sate their bestial lusts, which is the practice of these children of the devil when a woman is handed over to them. And they were followed by many other fellows, who were watching this wretched diversion, amongst whom was also my Johnny. He did not let me out of his sight, and when he saw what they were going to do to me, he attempted to deliver me by force, even if it should cost him his head. He attracted a crowd of bystanders, because he said that I was his intended. They felt sympathy for me and him and desired to be of help to him. This, to be sure, did not set well with the boys, who thought they had more right to me did not desire to let such a fine catch out of their hands. Therefore they resolved to meet force with force. Then people on both sides fell to dealing out blows. The crowd and the noise grew greater with each passing moment, so that it looked almost like a tourney, at which every man does his best for the sake of a beautiful lady. Their terrible screams caught the attention of the provost, who arrived just as they tore my clothes off my body and saw that I was not a woman. His presence caused everyone to fall silent, because he was much more feared than the devil himself. Also, all of those who had laid hands onto one another dispersed. He briefly informed himself about the affair, and whereas I was hoping he would deliver me, he, to the contrary, took me prisoner, because it was uncommon and a very suspicious business that a man in woman's clothing should be found in the army. He and his men were walking along with me in this wise past the regiments (all of which were standing in the field and preparing to march), with the intention of handing me over to the judge advocate or provost marshal; but as we were passing my colonel's regiment I was recognized, addressed, clothed in rags by my colonel, and turned over as a prisoner to our old provost, who put irons onto my hands and legs.

It was terribly painful for me to march along this way in chains and fetters, and John Rumblygut would have tortured me nicely too if the *secretarius*, Olivier, had not given me food, for I durst not let my ducats, which I had got away with till then, come to light, unless I were willing to lose all of them, and to put myself into even greater peril in the bargain.

The aforementioned Olivier communicated to me that very evening the reason why I was being kept prisoner under such heavy guard, and our regimental magistrate straightway received orders to interrogate me, so that my testimony might be submitted all the sooner to the judge advocate general, for they took me to be not only a scout and a spy, but also a person who could perform witchcraft, because shortly after I had left my colonel's service they had burned several witches who, before they had died, had owned that they had seen me at their general assembly when they had been together to dry up the Elbe River so that Magdeburg might be taken all the sooner. The points to which I was supposed to answer were the following:

First, whether I had gone to school, or at least could read and write.

Second, why I had approached the camp outside the walls of Magdeburg in the costume of a fool, when I did, after all, have sufficient wits about me, both when I was in the service of the captain of horse and now.

Third, for what reason I had disguised myself in women's clothes.

Fourth, whether I, along with other demons, had been at the witches' dance.

Fifth, where my fatherland was, and who my parents were.

Sixth, where I had been before I came to the camp outside the walls of Magdeburg.

Seventh, where and to what end I had learned woman's work, such as washing, baking, cooking, etc. *Item*, where I had learned to play the lute.

Then I attempted to tell the story of my entire life, so that the circumstances of the curious events which had befallen me would rightly explain everything and would respond to these questions in a truthful and quite intelligible way; but the regimental magistrate was not all that curious, but vexed and fatigued from the march. Therefore he desired but short, clear answers to what was asked. Accordingly, I answered in the following manner, from which, however, one could not comprehend anything essential and basic, and in fact as follows:

To the first question: I had not, in fact, gone to school, but I could nevertheless read and write.

To the second: Because I had no other clothes I had been obliged to appear in fool's garb.

To the third: Because I was tired of my fool's garb and could not find any men's clothes.

To the fourth: Yes, but I had gone thither against my will and likewise could not perform witchcraft.

To the fifth: My fatherland was the Spessart Forest, and my parents were peasants.

To the sixth: At Hanau with the governor and with a Croat colonel named Corpes.

To the seventh: when I was with the Croats I was obliged, against my will, to learn to wash, bake, and cook; and at Hanau to play the lute, because it gave me pleasure.

When this testimony of mine was written down, he said: "How can you deny and say that you have not gone to school when you—when they still took you to be a fool—answered a priest during mass when he said 'Domine, non sum dignus'[159]—answering in Latin, too—that he need not say that, everyone already knew it?" "Sir," I answered, "other people taught me that back then, and persuaded me it was a prayer that one must say at mass when our chaplain is conducting the service." "Yes, yes!" said the regimental magistrate. "I can see that you're the sort whose tongue must be loosened by torture." I thought to myself: "God help me if they loosen my head in the bargain!"

Early the next morning came orders from the judge advocate general to our provost that he should keep a sharp eye upon me, for he was of a mind, as soon as the armies made camp, to interrogate me himself, in which case I would without doubt be obliged to be put to torture, unless God ordained differently. During this captivity I thought constantly of my parson in Hanau, and of the late Trueheart, because both had prophesied how I would fare when I got out of my fool's garb.

CHAPTER 27

How the provost fared at the Battle of Wittstock[160]

That same evening, when we had scarce made camp, I was taken to the judge advocate general, who had before him my testimony, together with writing materials, and he set to interrogating me more closely. I, for my part, told of my actions as they had really been, but I was not believed, and the judge advocate general could not determine whether he had before him a fool or a thoroughgoing scoundrel, because the questions and answers fell so nicely and the affair itself was passing strange. He bade me take a quill and write, to see what I could do and whether my handwriting was known, or at least of such character that something could be deduced by looking at it. I seized quill and paper as adroitly as a person who works with them every day and asked him what I should write. The judge advocate general (who was perhaps miffed because my interrogation was dragging on far into the night) answered: "Ha! Write, your mother is a whore." I wrote down "Your mother is a whore" and when these words were read they merely made things all the worse for me, for the judge advocate general said that he now really did believe that I was a true scamp. He asked the provost whether they had searched me and whether they had found anything in writing upon my person. The provost answered: "No, why should he have been searched when the deputy provost brought him to us very nearly completely naked?" But alas! That was to no avail. The provost was obliged to search me in the presence of all of them, and in accomplishing this with all care, O Misfortune! he finds the two ass's ears with the ducats tied around my arms. Then they said: "What further proof do we require? This traitor has without doubt taken it upon himself to perpetrate some great rascality, for why else would any sane man put himself into fool's garb, or a man disguise himself in women's clothes? Indeed, can he be supplied with such a large sum of money for any purpose other than perpetrating some important deed? And does he not himself say that he learned to pluck the lute at the court of the governor of Hanau, the pluckiest soldier in the world? Indeed, gentlemen, can you imagine what deceitful tricks he learned from those scoundrels? The next best way is to put him to the torture tomorrow as he deserves, and to rush him to the bonfire, particularly since he has been in the company of sorcerers anyway and merits no better fate." How I felt at that time anyone can easily imagine. To be sure, I knew I was innocent and I had great trust in God, but I nevertheless saw the peril I was in and lamented the loss of my fine ducats, which the judge advocate general had pocketed.

But before they could set in motion this severe trial against me, Banier's troops ran afoul of ours. At the very beginning the armies were fighting to gain an advantage, and straightway after that for the heavy artillery pieces, of which those on our side were lost immediately. Our provost, of course, was posted with his men and prisoners rather far behind the lines of *battaglia*,[161] but we were nevertheless so close to our brigade that we could recognize every man in it from the back by the clothes he was wearing; and when the Swedish squadron joined battle with ours, both we and those who were engaged in combat were in mortal peril, for in a trice the air was so full of whistling musket balls flying over us that it looked as if the salvo had been fired expressly for our benefit. The timid ducked down to escape it, as if they were attempting to climb into their own skins to hide, but those who had courage, and had been present at diversions of that sort before, let the salvo go over their heads and did not turn a hair. In the battle itself, however, everyone sought to prevent his own death by felling the man nearest to him.[162] The horrible shooting, the clatter of armor, the cracking of the pikes, and the screaming of both the wounded and the attackers, along with the trumpets, drums, and fifes, made a frightful music! There one saw nothing but dense smoke and dust, which seemed as if it desired to conceal the abominable sight of the wounded and the dead. In it one heard pitiable cries of woe from the dying and merry screams from those who were still full of courage. The horses themselves appeared as if they were growing livelier in defending their masters with each passing moment, so hot did they show themselves to be in doing this duty, which they were being goaded on to do. One saw some of them fall down dead under their masters, full of wounds which they had innocently received in reprisal for their loyal service; others fell on top of their riders and thus in death had the honor of being borne by those whom they, in their lifetime, had been obliged to bear; still others, after they had unburdened themselves of the valiant burden which had been commanding them, left human beings to their madness and rage, ran off, and sought their first freedom in the distant field. The earth, whose wont it is to cover the dead, was itself at that place bestrewn with dead who were branded in divers ways. Heads which had lost their natural owners lay in one place, and in another lay bodies which were wanting their heads; some, in gruesome and wretched wise, had their entrails hanging out, and on others the head was smashed and the brains oozing out of it. There one saw how bodies devoid of souls were robbed of their own blood and, on the other hand, how bodies still alive were covered with the blood of others. Arms which had been shot off lay there with the fingers still twitching, just as if they desired to go back into the fray; on the other hand, some fellows ran away who had not yet spilled a drop of blood; severed legs lay there which, even though unburdened of the weight they had borne, had nevertheless grown much heavier than they had been before. One saw maimed soldiers begging to be dispatched to their death and others, by contrast, begging for quarter and that their lives be spared. *Summa summarum*,[163] it was naught but one wretched and deplorable spectacle! After the victorious Swedes had first separated our vanquished troops into small units, they drove them from the field where they had fought with such ill fortune, dispersing them completely with their hot pursuit, during which turn of events my fine provost also took flight with his prisoners, even though we, with but one person capable of resisting, had merited no hostility on the part of the victors. And as the provost was threatening us with death and thus goading us on to flee with him, young Trueheart came galloping up with five other horse and greeted him with a pistol: "Look you there, you old dog!" said he. "Is there still time for you to make your little puppies? I'll pay you for your trouble!" But the musket ball did as little harm to the provost as it would have to a steel anvil. "Oho! So that's the sort of fellow you are!"[164] said Trueheart. "I'll not have come here to please you in vain. You are going to die, even if your soul be grafted to you!" And then he told a musketeer from the watch which the provost had with him that he would grant him no quarter unless he slew the provost with an ax, which the musketeer then did. And so the provost got his just deserts. I, however, was recognized by Trueheart, who ridded me of my chains and bonds, set me upon a horse, and had his groom lead me to safety.

CHAPTER 28

Concerning a battle in which the victor is captured whilst vanquishing his foes

Now just as the groom of my deliverer was leading me out of further peril, his master, contrarily, was being driven in dead earnest by the desire for honor and booty to plunge into the battle, with the result that he hewed his way so far into the fray that he was taken prisoner. After the victors had distributed the booty and buried their dead and my friend Trueheart was discovered to be missing, his captain of horse inherited me, together with his groom and horses, so I was obliged to let them use me as a stableboy, in return for which I had nothing but the promise that if I behaved myself well, when I got a little drier behind the ears he would then move me up, that is, make me a trooper of horse, with which promises then I was obliged to be content for the time being.

Immediately after that my captain was promoted to lieutenant colonel, and I was given the post with him which David had filled in olden times with King Saul, for in quarters I played the lute for him, and on the march I was obliged to walk along behind him wearing his cuirass, which was a burdensome thing for me. And even though this armor was invented to protect the person wearing it from the enemy, I found the opposite to be the case for me, because a brood of offspring of my own which I had hatched persecuted me under its protection all the more safely. Under it they frolicked, sported, and cavorted unhindered, so that it appeared as if I were wearing the armor to protect them, not me, since I could not reach under it with my hands and launch a raid upon them. I devised all manner of *strategemata*[165] by which to annihilate this *armada*,[166] but I had neither the time nor the opportunity to extirpate them by fire (as is done by putting clothes into ovens) or by water or by poison (since I well knew what effect quicksilver had on the skin). Much less could I procure means to get rid of them by wearing other clothes or white shirts; rather, I was obliged to drag them about with me and proffer them my body and my blood. When they then abused and misused me so under the armor, I would whip out one of the pistols as if I were about to exchange fire with them, but I merely took the ramrod and pushed them away from their grazing land with it. Finally I devised the art of wrapping a piece of fur around it and turning it into a fine trap for them. When I then ran this lousing-pole under the armor I fished them by the dozens out of their advantageous position and broke their necks, but it did little good.

One time my lieutenant colonel was commanded to take a *cavalcada*[167] under heavy escort to Westphalia, and had he had as many troopers as I had lice, he would have struck terror into the heart of the entire world; but because this was not the case, he was obliged to move with caution and, also for this reason, to keep under cover in the Gemmer March[168] (that is a forest betwixt Hamm[169] and Soest).[170] At that time my own war against my minions had reached a critical stage. They were tormenting me so severely with their tunneling work that I feared they might take up permanent lodgings betwixt my skin and my skeleton. It is no wonder that the Brazilians, in their rage and lust for revenge, gobble up their lice because they press them so! One time I thought I could bear the pain no longer, and while some troopers were eating, some sleeping, and some standing guard, I went off a little to the side under a tree to do battle with my foes. To this end I took off the armor, despite the fact that others put it on when they mean to fight, and I fell to such a slaughtering and murdering that both the swords on my thumbs were dripping with blood and were full, of dead bodies, or better, empty skins; and those I could not kill I sent into exile, letting them walk around the tree. Whenever this *rencontre*[171] comes to mind, I still feel bites all over my skin, just as if I were still in the midst of that battle. I thought, of course, that I ought not to rage so against creatures in whose veins my own blood flowed, and particularly since they were such loyal servants that they were willing to accompany their master to the rack and the gallows, and since I had often, in the field, lain so softly upon their multitudes on the hard ground; but I continued to tyrannize them anyway, so unmercifully that I even failed to note that the Imperials were mounting charges against my lieutenant colonel, till they finally came to me, liberated the poor lice, and took me myself prisoner, for they were not at all frightened by my valor, by means of which I had shortly before slain thousands and had outstripped that tailor who killed seven at one blow. I was given to a dragoon,[172] and the best booty he had from me was my lieutenant colonel's cuirass, which he sold for a rather good price to the commandant of Soest, where he was quartered. And so he became my sixth master in the war, because I was obliged to be his servant boy.

CHAPTER 29

How well a pious soldier fared in Paradise, till he died, and how after his death a chasseur took his place

Our housekeeper, unless she were willing to let me populate her house and herself with my minions, was of course obliged to rid me of them. She made short shrift of them, sticking my rags into the oven and burning them out as clean as an old tobacco pipe, so that with these varmints gone, my life was rosy once more. Indeed, no one can imagine how good I felt when I was free of this torment, in which I had sat for several months, as if I were sitting upon an anthill. On the other hand, I straightway had another cross to bear, because my master was one of those soldiers who are persuaded that they are going to heaven. He was quite satisfied with his army pay, and, for the rest, he would not hurt a flea. His entire fortune consisted of what he earned standing guard and from what he saved from his weekly pay. This, though it was not much, he held in higher regard than some folks do oriental pearls. Every farthing he sewed into his clothes, and so that he might have some farthings in reserve, his poor horse and I were obliged to help him save them up. That is the reason why I was obliged to crunch on dry pumpernickel and make do with water or, when things were going very well, near beer, which was little to my taste, particularly since my throat grew quite raw from the dry black bread and my entire body quite thin. But if I desired to eat better, I could steal my victuals, but with the express understanding that he not get wind of it. Were all soldiers like him, there would be no need of either gallows, stocks, hangmen, deputy provosts, or surgeons, sutlers, or drummers to play taps, for he did nothing even remotely like unto gambling, duelling, and glutting himself with food and drink. And when he was commanded to go somewhere on convoy or on a raiding party or on any other military mission, he walked along like an old woman with a cane. And I do believe that if this good dragoon had not possessed such heroic soldierly virtues, he would not have got me as a prisoner either, for he would have run after my lieutenant colonel and tried to take him captive. I had no hope of getting any clothes from him, because his own were covered with patches, like those of my hermit. Similarly, his saddle and tack were worth scarce threepence and his horse so feeble from hunger that neither Swede nor Hessian had any prolonged pursuit to fear from him.

All this moved his captain to send him on guard duty to Paradise—which was the name of a nunnery—not, of course, because he was of much use as a guard, but so that he might graze his fill and get his mount into good shape again, and particularly because the nuns had asked for a fellow who was pious, conscientious, and quiet. So he rode thither, and I walked along behind him, because unfortunately he had but one horse. "'ods bodikins, Simprick!" he said on the way (for he could not remember the name Simplicius). "When we get to Paradise, are we ever going to glut ourselves!" I answered: "The name is auspicious. God grant that the place lives up to its name." "You're right," he said (for he did not know what the word 'auspicious' meant), "you could call it 'hospicious,' because it is a fine hospice, and we'll be drinking the best beer by the keg there, and wanting for nothing! Just behave yourself. I am going to have a fine new coat made for myself pretty soon now; then you may have my old one. It will make a good coat for you." He was right to call it his old one, for I do believe that coat could remember the battle of Pavia,[173] so shabby and weather-beaten did it look. So his giving it to me gave me no great joy.

Paradise we found to be as we desired it to be, and, better still, we found in it not angels but beautiful maidens who plied us with food and drink, so that in a short while I was sleek and plump again, for there was the richest beer there, the best Westphalian ham and knackwurst, delicious and delicate beef which they boiled in brine and generally served cold. There I learned to spread black bread with a layer of salted butter as thick as your finger, and put a slab of cheese on top so that it slid down the gullet all the better. And when I came upon a leg of mutton spiked with garlic, and had a good tankard standing next to it, then I refreshed myself, body and soul, and forgot all the suffering which I had endured. *In summa*, this Paradise agreed with me as well as if it had been the real one. I had no cause for concern, except that I knew that this life would not last forever and that I was obliged to go about in rags.

And just as Misfortuna had not come to me singly when she had fallen to riding me before, so it now really seemed as if Fortuna desired to make amends for the past, for when my master sent me to Soest to fetch all the rest of his baggage, on the way I found a package and in it several bolts of scarlet for a coat, together with red satin for the lining. This I took along and exchanged in Soest at a draper's for ordinary green woolen cloth for a suit, together with all the trimmings, on the condition that he would have this garment made for me and that a new hat would be furnished me in the bargain. And since I still lacked a pair of new shoes and a shirt, I also gave the merchant the silver buttons and galloons which belonged to the coat, in return for which he procured for me what I still required, and thus I dandied myself up in brand new clothes. Thus attired I returned to Paradise to my master, who grumbled mightily because I had not brought the package which I had found to him. Indeed, he spoke to me of beatings, and it would not have taken much (if he had not been ashamed and if my clothes had fit him) for him to strip me and wear the new clothes himself, even though I imagined to myself that I had acted quite properly.

Meanwhile the old skinflint could not but be ashamed that his page was better dressed than he himself was. Therefore he rode to Soest, borrowed money from his captain, and with it outfitted himself in the best manner, promising to pay this back from his weekly pay for guard duty, which indeed he zealously did. Of course, he himself still had twice as much as he had borrowed, but he was much too sly to touch it, for had he done that, he would have lost the soft bed in which he could lie that winter in Paradise, and some other naked fellow would have been sent thither in his stead. In this way, however, the captain must needs leave him there if he desired to get back the money he had lent him. From this time on, we led the most slothful life in the world, and playing at bowls was the most work we did. When I had curried, fed, and watered my dragoon's nay, I plied the squire's trade and took walks. The nunnery was also provided with a guard by the Hessians, our opponents—a musketeer detached from the garrison at Lippstadt.[174] He was by trade a furrier and therefore not only a mastersinger[175] but also an excellent swordsman, and so that he should not forget his skills, he practiced daily with me for a long while with all weapons, at which I became so adept that I would not have hesitated to give him satisfaction, had he desired it. My dragoon, however, played with him at bowls rather than with swords, and in fact the stakes were never anything but who must needs drink the most beer at dinner, in which wise the losses of each of them were made good by the nunnery.

The convent had its own game preserve and therefore also kept its own gamekeeper, and because I too was clad in green, I became his companion and that fall and winter learned all he knew about hunting, in particular as concerned small game. For that reason, and because the name Simplicius was somewhat unusual and difficult for the common folk to remember or to pronounce, everyone called me "the little chasseur." Meanwhile I became acquainted with all the highways and byways there, which I afterwards put to excellent use. When the weather was bad and I could not roam about the fields and forests, I read all manner of books which the steward of the nunnery lent me. And as soon as the noble ladies became aware that besides my beautiful voice I could also play the lute and some few things on the clavichord, they paid all the more careful heed to my doings; and because I was in the bargain rather well proportioned and handsome of face, they took to be noble all my manners, my character, and whatever I did or omitted to do, so that now I was unexpectedly obliged to play the favored squire, who caused them surprise that he should be making do with such a slovenly dragoon for a companion. Now when in this way I had passed the winter in all these pleasures, my master was relieved of his duty there and given another post, at which he grew so morose at the thought of leaving this good life that he fell ill because of it, and because of a high fever he fell into, and especially because all the old wounds which he had received his entire life long in the war also played their part, he made short shrift of it, as a result of which I had someone to bury three weeks later. I wrote this epitaph for him:

> Here lies old Skinflint, a soldier brave and true,
>
> Who never spilled another's blood, as other soldiers do.

By rights and by custom the captain should have inherited and taken unto himself the deceased's horse and weapons, and the sergeant all his belongings, but because I was at that time a fresh and nearly full-grown youth and gave them the hope that in time I should not fear to stand up to anyone, they offered to turn all of it over to me if I were willing to continue to serve in my dead master's stead. I was all the happier to accept, because it was known to me that my master had sewn into his old breeches a rather sizable number of ducats, which he had been scraping together his entire life long. And when, to this end, I gave my name, namely Simplicius Simplicissimus, and the company clerk (who was named Cyriacus) could not write it down *orthographice*,[176] he said: "There be no devil in hell with a name like that!" And because I then quickly asked him whether there was one in hell who was named Cyriacus, and he could not answer, even though he thought himself to be a clever fellow, this so pleased my captain that he straightway from the beginning set great store by me.

CHAPTER 30

How the chasseur started out when he fell to plying the soldier's trade, from which a young soldier can learn a few things

Because the commandant at Soest lacked a fellow in his stable such as I seemed to him to be, he was unhappy to see that I had become a foot soldier, nor did he desist from making so bold as to attempt to get me back, to which purpose he cited my tender years, refusing to let me pass for a grown man.[177] And after he had presented these arguments to my master, he also sent for me and said: "Hark you, little chasseur, you are to be my servant." I asked what my duties were to be. He answered: "You are to care for my horses." "Sir," said I, "we two are ill suited to one another. I should prefer a master in whose service the horses carry me, but since I shan't be able to have such a one, I shall remain a foot soldier." He said: "You don't even have a beard yet!" "O no!" said I. "I dare say I can hold my own against a man who is eighty years old. The beard does not make the man, else billy goats would be highly prized." He said: "If your courage is as great as your mouth, then I shall let you pass for a man." I answered: "That can be tested in the next skirmish." And thereby I gave it to be understood that I was unwilling to let anyone use me as a stableboy. And so he let me be what I was and said that actions would speak louder than words.

Then I scurried off to get my dragoon's old breeches, and after I had performed surgery upon them, I procured me from their entrails another good war-horse and the best weapon I could lay hands upon, and I polished it till it shone like a mirror. I once more had clothes made for me out of green cloth, because the name "chasseur" very much pleased me. My old clothes, however, I gave to my page, because they had got too small for me. And so I rode along with him like a young nobleman, and indeed I thought myself far better than the common herd. I was so bold as to decorate my hat like an officer, with a mad bunch of plumes. Therefore I soon acquired enviers and enemies. Betwixt them and me rather harsh words were exchanged, and finally blows, but scarce had I shown two or three of them what I had learned in Paradise from the furrier when all of them not only left me in peace, they even sought out my friendship. All the while I let them use me both mounted and on foot in raiding parties, for I was well mounted and fleeter of foot than others of my age, and when it came to dealing with the enemy, I went straightway to the top, like cream in a milkpail, and always attempted to be in the forefront of the action. Because of that, I was in a short while well known to both friend and foe, and so famous that both sides thought highly of me, as a result of which the most dangerous schemes were given me to carry out, and to this end entire raiding parties were given me to command. And I fell to stealing like a Bohemian, and when I snatched anything worth mentioning, I gave my officers such generous shares of it that I was permitted to ply this trade even in forbidden places, because I was receiving help from all sides. The general of the other side, Count von Götz,[178] had three garrisons left in Westphalia, namely, at Dorsten,[179] Lippstadt,[180] and Coesfeld.[181] I was a great nuisance to them, for with small raiding parties I lay well nigh daily before the city gates of the one or the other town and snatched many a good piece of booty. And because I came through everywhere unscathed, the folk believed that I could make myself invisible and that I was as impervious to musket balls as iron and steel. Because I was feared like the plague, thirty men from the enemy were not ashamed to flee from me when they knew that

I was in the vicinity with only fifteen men. Finally it got to the point that when any town was to be required to pay tribute, I was obliged to accomplish this. From this my purse grew to be as great as my reputation. My officers and comrades loved their chasseur; the most distinguished partisans from the other side lived in fear of me; and the local folk I kept on my side through fear and love of me, for I knew how to punish my opponents and to reward handsomely those who did me the slightest service, for which reason I spent well nigh half my booty again upon entertaining and upon purchasing information. For these reasons no raiding party, no convoy, and no party of travelers left the other side's posts without my knowing about their departure. Then I conjectured what they planned to do and made my schemes accordingly, and because I, with the aid of Fortuna, carried several of these off well, everyone was surprised at my tender years, so much so that even many officers and doughty soldiers from the other side desired to lay eyes upon me. At the same time I showed myself so courteous and discreet towards my prisoners that they often cost me more than my booty was worth, and whenever, without violating my oath of fealty and my obligation to my master, I could do anyone from the other side a courtesy—particularly the officers, even if I did not know them—I did not hesitate to do so.

As a result of my behavior I should have been promoted to the rank of officer betimes, had my tender years not prevented it, for anyone of the age I was who desired to have a company must needs be a member of the nobility in good standing. Moreover, my captain could not promote me because there were no vacant officers' posts in his company, and he did not wish to give me to another captain, because in me he had more than a milch cow. I did, however, advance to lance corporal. This honor, namely, that I was given preference over old soldiers, though it was a matter of slight importance, and the praise which they daily heaped upon me were the spurs, as it were, which goaded me on to higher things. I schemed day and night how I might carry out some plot or the other in order to make myself yet greater. Indeed, often I could not sleep for such foolish scheming. And because I saw that I lacked the opportunity to demonstrate by deeds how courageous I was, I worried that I should not daily have the opportunity to test my mettle in combat with the other side. I often wished that there were a Trojan war or a siege like the one at Ostende[182] and, fool that I was, I did not consider that the pitcher goes to the well till it someday breaks. But that is just the way it is when a heedless young soldier has money, good fortune, and courage, for then come arrogance and pride, and because of the latter, instead of one page I kept two grooms, whom I outfitted excellently well and provided with mounts, by which action I burdened myself with all the officers' envy.

CHAPTER 31

How the devil stole the parson's bacon[183] and how the chasseur got himself into a trap

I must tell a few of the adventures which befell me now and again before I left the company of dragoons again, and even though they are not of importance, they really are diverting to hear, for I not only undertook great projects, I did not scorn small ones either, if I but suspected that I might achieve by them a reputation amongst the people. My captain was ordered with some fifty foot to go to the district of Recklinghausen[184] to carry out an ambush there, and because we thought that before we could put the scheme into effect we should be obliged to keep hidden in the underbrush for two or three days, each of us took along with him a week's provisions. When, however, the rich *caravana*[185] which we were on the lookout for did not arrive at the appointed time, we ran out of bread, which we could not steal unless we were willing to betray our presence and let our plan come to naught. Therefore hunger oppressed us mightily. And in this place I had no one beholden to me, as I did elsewhere, who might secretly bring something to me and my men. Therefore, in order to get food we were obliged to devise some other methods unless we were willing to go back home empty-handed. My comrade, a student who knew Latin and had but a short while before run away from school and let the army feed him, sighed in vain for the barley soup which till now his parents had prescribed for his best interests and which he had scorned and forsaken. And when he thought of the food he had eaten in days gone by, he also remembered the schoolbag he had carried when he was enjoying it. "Alas!" he said to me. "Is it not a shame that I did not study so many arts by which I could now feed myself. I know *re vera*[186] that if I were permitted to go to see the parson in that village, there would be an excellent *convivium*[187] with him." "I pondered upon these words a while and assessed our situation, and because those who knew the highways and byways hereabouts could not go out, lest they be recognized, while those who were not known in these parts knew of no opportunities to steal or secretly buy anything, I devised a scheme involving our student and presented it to the captain, even though it was in fact hazardous; but he had such faith in me, and our situation was so bad, that he consented to it.

I changed clothes with another fellow, and together with the student I ambled off to the aforementioned village by a roundabout way, even though it lay but a half hour's walk from us. In it we recognized the house next to the church to be the parson's home, because it was

167

built in town-style and abutted the wall which ran around the entire church grounds. I had already instructed my comrade what he should say, for he still had on his shabby student's clothes. I, however, gave myself out to be a journeyman painter, for I thought 1 would have no opportunity to practice that art in the village, because peasants do not decorate their houses with paintings. The clerical gentleman was courteous; after my traveling companion had addressed him in Latin with profound respect and had told a pack of lies about how on the road soldiers had plundered him and robbed him of his money and food for the journey, the parson offered him a piece of buttered bread along with a drink of beer. I, however, acted as if I were not with him and said I would be going to eat in the inn and then call him so that we might still that same day put a piece of the way behind us. So I went to the inn, more to spy out what I desired to get that same night than to still my hunger, and I had the good fortune to encounter on the way a peasant who was sealing up his bake-oven with two large loaves of pumpernickel in it, which were supposed to sit for twenty-four hours and bake through. I made short shrift of it with the innkeeper, because I already knew where bread was to be had. I bought some "studs" (that is so-called "white bread") to bring to my captain, and when I came to the parsonage to admonish my comrade that he should go, he had already spilled the beans and told the parson that I was a painter and was planning to journey to Holland to completely perfect my art there. The parson bade me a hearty welcome and requested that I go with him into the church, where he desired to show me several paintings which were to be repaired. So that I might not ruin the comedy completely, I was obliged to follow. Now he led me through the kitchen, and when he opened the night latch on the thick oaken door which led to the churchyard, *O mirum!*[188] I saw that the black heavens were full of lutes, flutes, and fiddles, by which I mean the hams, knackwurst, and sides of bacon which were hanging in the chimney. I looked at them reassuringly, because it seemed to me as if they were laughing along with me, and I wished that they were in the company of my comrades in the forest, but in vain, for they were so stubborn that in defiance of me they kept hanging there. Then I pondered upon means by which I might make them companions of the above-mentioned bake-oven full of bread, but I could not so easily devise anything because, as mentioned above, the churchyard was completely walled-in, and all the windows were well secured with iron grates, and also, in the churchyard lay two enormous large dogs which, I feared, would for sure not sleep at night if someone were to attempt to steal that on which they were granted the right to gnaw as a reward for faithfully guarding it.

Now when we came into the church, discussing all manner of paintings, and the parson was attempting to engage me to repair several of them and I was seeking all manner of excuses and pointing out that I was journeying to Holland, the sacristan, or sexton, said: "Fellow, you look to me more like one of those run-away soldier boys than a journeyman painter." I was no longer accustomed to talk like that, and yet I was obliged to put up with it. So I simply shook my head a little and answered him: "Fellow, just give me quickly brush and paints, and in a trice I shall have painted you a fool the likes of you." The parson made light of it and told us both it was not fitting to make assertions like that about one another in such a holy place, and thereby gave it to be understood that he believed both of us. Then he had us given another drink and let us go our way. I, however, left my heart behind with the smoked sausages.

Before nightfall we came back to our comrades, where I retrieved my clothes and weapons, told the captain what I had accomplished, and selected six stout fellows who were to help me bring back the bread. We came to the village at midnight and in all stealth took the bread out of the oven, because we had someone with us who knew how to cast a spell upon dogs so that they would not bark. And as we were about to go past the parsonage, I simply could not bring myself to go any further without the bacon. On a sudden I stood still and looked as best I could to see whether there might not be a way to get into the parson's kitchen, but I saw no entry other than the chimney, which this time must needs serve as a door for me. We carried the bread and weapons into the churchyard and into the mausoleum, and set up a ladder and rope taken from the shed, and because I could climb up and down chimneys as well as any chimney sweep (which I had learned from childhood on by climbing up in hollow trees), I and one other climbed up onto the roof, which consisted of layers of hollow tiles and was very nicely constructed for my project. I wound up my hair into a knot on top of my head, let myself down the chimney to my beloved bacon, with one end of the rope in my hand, and tied one ham after another and one side of bacon after another to the rope, which the man on the roof adroitly fished out onto the roof and gave to others to carry to the mausoleum. But what a catastrophe! When I had finished my work and tried to climb back up again, a rung broke under me so that poor Simplicius fell down, and the wretched chasseur found himself caught like a rat in a trap. My comrades on the roof let the rope down to pull me up, but it broke before they had lifted me from the floor. I thought to myself: "Well, chasseur, now you must be the object of a hunt, in which your hide, like Acteon's,[189] will be terribly scratched!" For the parson had been awakened by my fall and had commanded his cook to light a candle immediately. She came into the kitchen to me in her nightgown, with her skirt draped over her shoulders, and stood so close to me that she brushed against me with the skirt. She reached for a glowing coal, held the candle to it, and fell to blowing upon it. I, for my part, blew much harder than she did, at which the good slut took such fright that she dropped fire and candle and withdrew to where her master was. And so I gained respite to ponder by what means I might make good my escape, but nothing occurred to me. Down the chimney my comrades gave me to understand that they were willing to break into the house and take me out by force, but I did not let them, but instead commanded that they should look to their weapons and leave only Hopalong[190] up at the top of the chimney, and should wait and see whether I might be able to get away quietly and without a ruckus, so that our ambush would not fall through, but that if this should prove to be impossible, they should then do their best. *Interim*[191] the clergyman lit a candle, and his cook told him that there was a horrible spirit in the kitchen which had two heads (for she had perhaps seen the knot of hair on the top of my head and taken it for a second head). All this I heard, and therefore with my dirty hands, which I rubbed in the ashes, soot, and coals, I made my hands and face look so abominable that without doubt I no longer looked like an angel (as the nuns at Paradise had said before), and the sacristan, had he seen it, would have surely conceded that I was a quick painter. I began to make a terrible racket in the kitchen, throwing about all manner of pots and pans. I got my hands onto a pot-ring; this I hung around my neck, and the pot-hook I held in both hands to defend myself with if need be. The pious parson, however, did not let all this deter him, for he came marching in as if in a church procession, with his cook, who was holding two wax tapers in her hand and carrying a kettle of holy water over her arm. And he was armed with his surplice, together with his stole, and had his holy-water sprinkler in one hand and in the other a book from which he began to exorcise me, asking who I was and what business I had there. Now because he took me to be the devil himself, I thought it but right that I indeed behave like the devil, i.e. that I resort to lies; and I therefore answered: "I am the devil, and I am going to wring your neck and your cook's!" He continued with his exorcising, and with the strongest conjuration of all bade me be gone back to whence I came. I, however, answered in a quite frightening voice that this was impossible, even if I desired to. In the meantime Hopalong, who was an out-and-out rogue of the first order and understood no Latin, kept up his hocus-pocus on the roof, for when he heard how things stood in the kitchen, namely, that I was pretending to be the devil and that the clergyman indeed took me to be one, he fell to hooting like an owl, barking like a dog, neighing like a horse, bleating like a billy goat, and braying like an ass, and caused noises to be heard coming from the chimney which sounded one minute like a pack of cats rutting in February, and the next like a chicken trying to lay an egg, for this fellow could mimic the sound of all the animals, and when he desired to, he could howl like a whole pack of wolves. This frightened the parson and his cook near out of their wits, and I had pangs of conscience because I had let him exorcise me as if I were the devil, whom he actually did take me to be, because he had heard or read somewhere that the devil liked to appear in green clothes.

In the midst of the anxieties which had befallen us both, I saw, to my good fortune, that the night latch on the door leading to the churchyard had not caught and that only the bolt was shot. I quickly slid it open, whisked out the door and into the churchyard (where I then found my companions standing with their weapons at the ready), and left the parson to exorcise the devil as long as he might ever desire to. And after Hopalong had brought me my hat from the roof and we had put our provisions into sacks, we went back to our men, because we had nothing more to do in the village, except that we returned the ladder and the rope to the place from which we had taken them.

The entire raiding party restored itself with what we had stolen, and not a one of us got the hiccups either, such blessed folk were we! And all had sufficient cause to laugh at the trip I had taken. Only the student found it difficult to be pleased that I had stolen from a parson who had so completely stuffed his, the student's, face; indeed, he swore by all that was holy that he would gladly pay for the bacon he had eaten, as soon as he had the means in hand to do so, and yet he glutted himself like the rest of us, just as if he had hired on to do just that. So we lay at that same place for two more days in wait for those we had been expecting for so long. We did not lose a single man in the attack, and yet we took more than thirty prisoners and as magnificent booty as I have ever helped divide up. I had a double share because I had done the best: that was three beautiful Frisian stallions laden with what merchants' wares they could carry off in a hurry. And had we had time to look thoroughly for booty and to put it into safekeeping, each of us would have been rich enough, for his part, inasmuch as we left more behind than we took along, because we were obliged to scurry off in the greatest haste with what we could carry; and so, in fact, we withdrew further, in the interests of safety, to Rheine,[192] where we ate and divided the booty, because our troops were there. There I once more thought about the parson from whom I had stolen the bacon. The reader can imagine what a rash, wanton, and ambitious fellow I was, since it was not enough for me that I had robbed the pious clergyman and so terribly frightened him; in the bargain I desired to garner honor from the escapade. Therefore I took a sapphire set in a gold ring which I had snatched on that same raid and sent it from Rheine with a trustworthy courier to the parson, together with the following letter:

Most honored Sir, etc.

Had I of late in the forest had any food left to live on, I should have had no cause to steal Your Grace's bacon, during which occasion you presumably were very frightened. I swear before the Almighty that you suffered this anxiety against my will, and I hope therefore all the sooner for your forgiveness. Insofar as the bacon itself is concerned, however, it is meet that it be paid for, and therefore I am sending in lieu of payment this ring, which was surrendered by those for whose sake the goods must needs have been taken, with the request that Your Grace be so kind as to make do with it. At the same time I assure you that otherwise you in any event have a true and faithful servant in the man whom your sacristan took to be no painter and who is otherwise called the Chasseur.

To the peasant, however, whose bake-oven they had emptied, the members of the raiding party sent from the common booty sixteen Imperial sovereigns, for I had taught them that they must needs in such wise win to their side the country folk, who could often help a raiding party in dire need or, on the other hand, could betray it, sell it, and deprive its members of their heads. From Rheine we went to Münster,[193] and from there to Hamm and home to our quarters in Soest, where after a few days I received an answer from the parson which read as follows:

Noble Chasseur!

If the person from whom you stole the bacon had known that you were going to appear to him in the form of the devil, he would not have so often desired to see the famous chasseur with his own eyes. But just as the borrowed meat and bread was paid for much too dearly, the fright received is all the easier to get over, primarily because it was caused, against his will, by such a famous personage, who is herewith pardoned therefore with the request that he not hesitate to visit the man who did not hesitate to exorcise the devil. *Vale.*[194]

Everywhere I behaved this way and thereby made a great name for myself, and the more I paid out and entertained, the more booty flowed into my hands, and I thought I had made a good investment with this ring, though it was worth nigh on to a hundred Imperial sovereigns. And with this I come to the

END OF THE SECOND BOOK

N O T E S · B O O K I I

CHAPTER 1: *How goose and gander mated*

1.   my book BLACK AND WHITE: the first of Grimmelshausen's works to be published was Der Satyrische Pilgram I (The Satirical Pilgrim Part I), which he calls Black and White because of its subtitle: that is, Cold and Warm, White and Black..... It consisted of ten discourses (he called them "Sätze"), each of which consisted of three parts: a "Satz" (which gave the positive aspects of the subject); a "Gegensatz" (which considered the negative aspects); and a "Nachklang" (in which an attempt was made to resolve the differences). Most of the material was taken verbatim from Garzoni and others, and very little was original writing. The first volume appeared in 1666; a second volume, containing ten more discourses, appeared in 1667, the year before the publication of the editio princeps of Simplicissimus, and it contains perhaps the first explicit reference to Simplicissimus. Part I, Discourse 6 (Sechster Satz vom Tantzen) and Discourse 7 (Siebender Satz vom Wein) are the parts to which Grimmelshausen is referring here.

2.   praeludium Veneris: prelude of Venus, i.e., prelude to love-making.

3.   histori: story, tale.

4.   Dear Reader, I tell this tale...: the assignation in the goose-coop, according to Borcherdt (p. 371), is modeled on an episode in Guzman (III, 32).

CHAPTER 2: *When it is a right good time to bathe*

5.   corps de garde: guard-room.

CHAPTER 3: *The other page is rewarded for his tutorirals and Simplicius is chosen to be a fool*

6.   hippocras: a wine flavored with spices, so called because of its Latin name, "vinum Hippocraticum," which it was given because the wine was filtered through a "Hippocrates bag."

7.   the music of seventeen lutes: Grimmelshausen repeatedly uses the number "seventeen" to indicate a large number of items. As Koschlig (p. 31 f.) has pointed out, it occurs not only here, but also in Book III, Chapter 7, and twice in The Wondrous Bird's Nest. Weydt (p. 298) suspects that the reason may have been because of its connection with Grimmelshausen's day of birth, which Weydt believes was March 17, 1621. It might also be noted that the number plays an important role in the life of Joseph, one of Grimmelshausen's favorite Biblical figures: Joseph was seventeen when he was carried off to Egypt (Genesis 37, 2), and he spent seventeen years there (Genesis 47, 28).

8.   scil.: Latin: scilicet: you may understand or know; used by Roman authors to indicate that a statement was obvious, evident or clearly true; here Grimmelshausen uses it ironically, as it is used in Moscherosch (I, 130 and III, 179).

CHAPTER 4: *About the man who pays and what manner of military service Simplicius performed for the Crown of Sweden, from which service he received the name Simplicissimus*

9.   commissarius: agent (of the Swedish crown), here functioning as an inspector-general.

10.   Crown of Sweden: the Hanau garrison was part of the Swedish army.

11. ink-squiggler: see Notes to Book I, Chapter 16; here the term is used to indicate that the commissarius spends all his time at a desk and never engages in genuinely soldierly tasks.

CHAPTER 5: *Simplicius is taken to hell by four devils and plied with Spanish wine*

12. No sooner was I sound asleep...: Bechtold (p. 62) notes that this scene is modeled on an episode in Guzman (Book I, Chapter 14).

CHAPTER 6: *Simplicius goes to heaven and is transformed into a calf*

13. the Eumenides: in classical mythology the furies, goddesses of vengeance; in the later classical tradition they were three in number: Tisiphone, Alecto, and Megaera. Acerra philologica I, 86 (p. 160) and Moscherosch (VI, 307) identify them as Eumenides, Furies and Errinyes and give their names correctly.

14. Tisiphone...Athamas: Athamas, the son of Aeolus and Enarete, was king of Orchomenus in Boeotia. At Hera's orders he married Nephele, who bore him two children, but he was really in love with Cadmus' daughter Ino, who also bore him two sons. He thereby incurred the wrath of Hera, who caused him to go mad.

15. ...when I awoke again...: Bechtold (p. 62 f.) suggests that an anecdote in Moscherosch, "Complementum" (p. 672) may have served as a model for this scene.

16. in the Polish or Swabian fashion: precisely what these fashions were has not been determined.

CHAPTER 7: *How Simplicius reconciled himself to his bestial condition*

17. the story about the goldsmith's boy : the boy availed himself of a caustic response which is crude but often heard in that part of Germany: "Kiss my arse!"

18. To put it summariter: to put it in a nutshell.

19. some human beings are more swinish than pigs...: Bechtold (p. 64) thought the series was taken from or modeled on Moscherosch, "Wahrmund von der Tannen" (Preface to the First Vision). Such series of animal comparisons were common at the time, however; Garzoni, Discourse 3 (p. 57), includes one in a description of a prelate, and Aegidius Albertinus wrote one in his Hirnschleiffer (p. 29 f.).

20. old Circe: see above, Book I, Chapter 28.

CHAPTER 8: *Tells of the remarkable memory of some folks, and of the forgetfulness of others*

21. remarkable memory: lists of persons with remarkable memories abound in seventeenth-century writings, and all of them go back to similar lists offered by Latin writers whom the Renaissance polyhistors and encyclopedists mined for information. The classical source of the first seven men mentioned (Simonides, Metrodorus, Cyrus, Lucius Scipio, Cineas, Mithridates, and Charmadas) was Pliny's Naturalis historia VII, 24; Pliny also related the anecdote concerning the twelfth person mentioned, Julius Caesar (l.c. VII, 25). Quintilian (XI, 50) repeated the anecdotes about Cyrus and Charmadas and added new ones concerning Themistocles and Crassus (the tenth and eleventh persons listed), and the Elder Seneca, in the prologue to his Controversarium supplied the information given about himself and Porcius Latro. To these twelve persons Renaissance polyhistors added a number of others (Beyerlink's Magnum Theatrum Vitae Humanae lists more than thirty), among them Ezra (apparently from Josephus II, 5), St. Anthony and St. Jerome (from Augustine's prologue to De doctrina

Christiana and his epistle to Bishop Cyrillus), Aelius Hadrianus (presumably from Aelius Spartianus' Life of Hadrian, Chapter 20), and Muretus. Scholte suggested Garzoni, Discourse 60, as the source which Grimmelshausen then amplified somewhat and presented parallel texts (Scholte, p. 128 ff.)—Garzoni lists twelve of the seventeen examples). Borcherdt ("Miszellen zu Grimmelshausens Simplicissimus,: Euphorion 23, 289 f.) compared the list with similar lists in polyhistorical works by Ravisius Textor, Sabellicus, Solinus and Zwinger and came to the conclusion that Zwinger's Theatrum vitae humanae (Basel, 1565), which lists all the examples except Crassus, was probably the source Grimmelshausen used. More recently, Koschlig (p. 311 ff.) suggested that Grimmelshausen used as point of departure for the passage a list given by Johannes Colerus (see below), who is specifically referred to in the passage, but Colerus' list is so short—only four of the seventeen examples, i.e. two fewer than are given in Acerra philologica (1637), which Bobertaag deemed the starting point—and would entail so much editing that it seems unlikely that Grimmelshausen used it, for his tendency was to take over entire passages almost unchanged, including the scholarly citations they contained. The real source of the list is yet to be determined.

22.   forgetfulness: these examples, save for that given by Schrammhans, are originally from Pliny, Naturalis historia VII, 24.

23.   the phoenix : legendary bird which supposedly lived 500 years, then burned itself and arose rejuvenated from its own ashes. It is described in Acerra philologica II, 37 (p. 241 f.).

24.   Simonides Melicus: Simonides of Ceos, surnamed not Mellicus but Melicertes (556-468 B.C.), was deemed to be the inventor of mnemonics (the art of strengthening the memory); he was thought of as an Athenian because he lived in Athens until his patron there was murdered.

25.   Metrodorus Sceptius: (c. 140 B.C.), a philosopher at the court of Mithridates Eupator, who later had him executed.

26.   Cyrus: Cyrus the Great (reigned 558-529 B.C.), founder of the Persian Empire.

27.   Lucius Scipio: Pliny (Naturalis historia VII, 24) does not identify him more specifically; Borcherdt (p. 375) suggests that Lucius Scipio Asiaticus is meant.

28.   Cynaeus: Cineas served as ambassador of King Pyrrhus to the Romans in 280 B.C.

29.   Mithridates: Mithridates VI of Ponto, surnamed the Great (136-63 B.C.), celebrated because of his wars with the Romans.

30.   Sabell...: Marcus Antonius Coccius Sabellicus (1436-1506), best known for his poem De rerum et artium inventoribus ; the passage, according to Borcherdt (p. 375), is from his Exemplorum libri decem.

31.   Charmides: actually Charmadas (flourished c. 110 B.C.), a schoolman, pupil of Carneades.

32.   Lucius Seneca: see above, Book I, Chapter 17; the Seneca who mentions his own prodigious memory in his preface to Controversiarum liber I was not Lucius Seneca but his father, M. Annaeus Seneca, whose work came to be published together with that of his son.

33.   Ravisius: Joannes Ravisius Textor, i.e. Jean Tixier, seigneur de Ravisi (c. 1480-1524), Renaissance polyhistorian and philologist, author of Officina partim historiis, partim poeticiis referta disciplinis (Paris, 1520).

34.   Ezra: priest and scribe; one of the principal characters in the chronicler's history of Israel; he is said to have been sent to Jerusalem in 398 B.C. by the king of Babylon Artaxerxes II to restore the Pentateuch.

35.   Eusebius: surnamed Pamphili (c. 264-340); he was made bishop of Caesarea about 315; the author of an ecclesiastical history. Borcherdt (p. 375) notes that the citation is incorrect; the passage is in Chronicarum (Temporum), liber I, caput

SIMPLICISSIMUS, THE GERMAN ADVENTURER

18, 5. The citation as given reflects that of Zwinger, who used Bapt. Fulgosus' *De dictis et factis memorabilibus Pontificum, Imperatorum, Ducum, Principum, Episcoporum aliorumque collectanea* lib. IX (p. 843 in the Basel edition of 1541).

36.   Themistocles: (514-449 B.C.), celebrated commander of the Athenian fleet which defeated Emperor of Persia Xerxes in 480 B.C. at Salamis.

37.   Crassus: P. Licinius Crassus Dives Mucianus (2nd century B.C.); consul in 131 B.C., he died after being defeated by Aristiconus, who had occupied the kingdom of Pergamus, a territory which had been bequeathed to Rome. The classical source of the anecdote is Quintilian XI 2, 50.

38.   Julius Caesar: (100-44 B.B.), most famous of all Roman generals.

39.   Aelius Hadrianus: P. Aelius Hadrianus, usually called Hadrian (76-138 A.D.), Roman emperor from 117 to his death.

40.   Portius Latrone: Porcius Latro (flourished 17 B.C., died 4 B.C.), celebrated Roman orator and rhetorician, and close friend of the Elder Seneca.

41.   St. Jerome: Eusebius Sophronius Hieronymus (c. 320-420), the great Christian scholar of his time.

42.   Antonius: St. Anthony; see above Book I, Chapter 6.

43.   Colerus: Johannes Colerus (c. 1570-1639), scholar and expert on farming in all its aspects; his best known work was his Oeconomia ruralis et domestica. According to Borcherdt (p. 376), the work referred to here is Calendarium perpetuum et sex libri Oeconomici (p. 794 in the 1613 edition). For a detailed discussion of his influence on Grimmelshausen, see Koschlig, pp. 121-135 and 140-158.

44.   Marcus Antonius Muretus: (1526-1585), French philologist. The passage, according to Borcherdt (p.376) comes from Variorum lectionem, lib. III, caput l.

45.   Plinius: Gaius Plinius Secundus, usually called Pliny the Elder (c. 23-79 A.D.). The quotation comes from his Naturalis historiae, lib. 37.

46.   Messala Corvinus: M. Messala Corvinus (c. 70 B.C.-3 A.D.); his memory failed him about two years before his death.

47.   Schrammhans: Bobertag (DNL XXX, 121, Footnote 15) suggested that Grimmelshausen might have invented the name and pointed out that a lansequenet in an anecdote by Hans Sachs and the hero of several stories by Michael Lindner bore that name; Borcherdt (p. 376) was able to add little except the exact title of Lindner's work, Katzipori. While Grimmelshausen may have been familiar with the Schrammhans of Sachs and Lindner, he was in fact alluding to a real person, Johann Schramm, who in 1589 published a work entitled Fasciculus historiarum, das ist: Historien vnd Exempel, der alten Keyser, Könige und Herren, so in jrem Stande vnd Beruff den Regimenten, jhnen selbst, vnd andern nützlich oder schedlich gewesen... Aus welscher und lateinischer Sprache ins Deutsche gantz kurtz zusammengezogen... The anecdote referred to is indeed found on the page mentioned. Since no other anecdotes from Schramm's work appear to have been used by Grimmelshausen, and insmuch as he almost invariably includes authorial citations only when he is copying from a second source, it seems unlikely that he was familiar with the Fasciculus, but rather found it cited in some other work. Whether Grimmelshausen or his source was responsible for changing "Johann Schramm" into "Schrammhans" will remain uncertain until the source is determined. The reason for the change, however, does seem certain: the "bloodthirstiness" of Schramm's anecdote must have brought to mind one of the most bloodthirsty criminals of the 1660's, one Hans Hahn, of Wohlau in Silesia, whose nickname was "Schrammhans." His story was well known at the time and is covered in grisly detail in Theatrum Europaeum IX, 514 ff. The historical Schrammhans was member of a gang which consisted of Hans Liehmann (called "Wein-Hans"), also from Wohlau, and Liehmann's wife, son, and brother-in-law, Georg Wilde (called

"Wampe Georg"). In 1660 the authorities in Silesia arrested the three Liehmanns and, after interrogating them (both with and without the use of torture) seven times between December 21, 1660, and April 1, 1661, charged Wein-Hans with 34 counts of petty and grand theft, five counts of adultery and lechery (with four different persons), 25 counts of homicide, and four counts of arson; his wife and son were indicted as conspirators and also charged with incest, and the son with bestiality. All three were convicted as charged and condemned to torture and death; the sentence was carried out on April 27, 1661. Wampe-Georg and Schramm-Hans, whom Wein-Hans had implicated during interrogation, eluded the authorities for a while, apparently by fleeing across the border to Poland, but on Pentecost Sunday of 1661 they were apprehended when they, together with Schramm-Hans' wife, were recognized while taking communion at the church in Wohlau. After all three were interrogated (with and without the use of torture) on June 24 and 25, Schamm-Hans was indicted on 12 counts of petty and grand theft committed together with Wampe-Georg and thefts too numerous to mention which he committed alone, with six counts of lechery and rape (three together with Wampe-Georg), 28 counts of homicide (some of them particularly grisly), and three counts of arson. Schramm-Hans was, of course, convicted on all counts, and he was executed on July 11, 1661. While Grimmelshausen could not possibly have read the account in Theatrum Europaeum (Volume IX did not appear until after the publication of Simplicissimus), he may well have read the broadside on which the Theatrum Europaeum account is probably based; in any event, Schramm-Hans' alleged crimes were so numerous and so heinous that they must have been common knowledge at the time.

48.   Jo. Wierus: Johannes Wier (1515-1588), a pupil of Cornelius Agrippa and personal physician to the Duke of Cleves; his most famous work is De praestigiis daemonum (Basel, 1563), which was translated into German under the title De praestigiis. Von den teuffeln/zaubrern, schwartzkünstlern, teuffels beschwerern/hexen oder unholden vnd gifftbereitern (Frankfurt am Main, 1575)

49.   Callisto: an Arcadian nymph who was one of the many lovers of Zeus (Jupiter); he metamorphosed her into a she-bear, and when his wife arranged for the bear to be killed in a hunt, he placed her among the stars under the name Arctos (the Bear). Cf. Ovid, Metamorphoses II, 409 ff. The anecdote in German can be found in Acerra philologica II, 54 (p. 271 f.), where Jupiter's abduction of Europa is also told.

50.   Jupiter: chief of the Greek gods. He changed himself into a bull in order to kidnap Europa, the daughter of King Agenor of Phonecia; in the form of a bull he mingled with the king's herd while Europa and her maidens were playing by the seashore, and he seemed so tame to her that she climbed up onto his back, whereupon he rushed to the water and swam over to Crete with her. Cf. Ovid, Metamorphoses II, 847 ff.

CHAPTER 9: *Perverse praise for a fair lady*

51.   Perverse praise: Borcherdt (p. 376) conjectures that this satire was inspired by the Scherzgedichte of Johann Lauremberg; a similar "perverse praise" occurs in Sorel's Francion (p. 413).

52.   Ulm: city in Swabia on the Danube.

CHAPTER 10: *Tells of nothing but heroes and famous artists*

53.   Nabuchodonesar: Babylonian king who, according to Daniel 4, was turned into an ox as punishment for his arrogance.

54.   Alexander the Great: (356-323); king of Macedonia and the foremost ruler and military leader of his era. The anecdotes concerning him were quite popular from the Middle Ages on. Grimmelshausen's immediate source, Kissel (p. 17) asserts, was Boaistuau-Launay's Theatrum mundi (four-language version), p. 996 (Alexander sweating blood), p. 1022 (Alexander's breath like balsam), and p. 940 ff. (Alexander's tears).

55.   Quintus Curtius: Quintus Curtius Rufus (1st century AD), a Roman historian and author of a biography of Alexander the Great in ten books. Borcherdt (p. 377) notes that Grimmelshausen's citation comes not from Curtius but from stories by Johannes Freinsheim (1608-1660) which are based on Plutarch's Life of Alexander, cap. 4.

56.   Julius Caesar: (Pliny VII, 25) gives the total number killed as 1,192,000. Boaistuau-Launay mentions 1,152,00 (p. 944 ff.).

57.   Pompey: Gnaeus Pompeius Magnus (106-48 B.C.), Roman general and one of the triumvirate. Pliny (VII, 25) mentions 846 ships, not 940. Here again Grimmelshausen's number agrees with that given by Baoistuau-Launay (p. 944 ff.)

58.   Marcus Sergius: Pliny (VII, 28) recounts in some detail the heroics of this warrior, who fought valiantly in the wars against Hannibal.

59.   Lucius Siccius Dentatus: Pliny (VII, 28) mentions 120 battles rather than 110.

60.   Spurius Turpeius and Aulus Eternius: Roman consuls in 454 B.C.

61.   Manlius Capitolinus: a Roman consul (died 384 B.C.) who in 390 B.C. saved Rome from the Gauls. Pliny (VII, 28) mentions only 23 wounds. Manlius Capitolinus "diminished" his honor at the end of his life by plotting—or so it was alleged—to restore the monarchy, for which crime he was hurled from the Tarpeian Rock in 384 B.C.

62.   Hercules: most famous of the classical demigods and heroes; his many labors and adventures demonstrated his valor and strength.

63.   Theseus: the legendary hero of Attica (cf. above).

64.   Zeuxis: Greek painter (flourished 424-380 B.C.).

65.   Apelles: Greek painter (4th century B.C.); a contemporary of Alexander the Great, whom he alone was permitted to paint.

66.   Plutarch: Greek biographer and philosopher (1st century A.D.).

67.   Archimedes: (287-212 B.C.); most famous of the ancient mathematicians and natural philosophers, he was also a famous inventor; his war machines, which were employed in the siege of Syracuse, were widely praised.

68.   Sapor: Sapor I (reigned 241-272 A.D.), one of the first rulers of the house of Sassinids.

69.   Ptolemy: Claudius Ptolomaeus (flourished 127-148 A.D.), famous astronomer, mathematician and geographer.

70.   Ceres: Roman goddess (Greek: Demeter) who was the protectress of agriculture.

71.   those terrible things I saw...: he means the cannons on caissons described above.

72.   that holy man: meant, as Konopatzki (p. 64) recognized, St. Anthony (see above, Notes to Book I, Chapter 6), whom Konopatzki considers to be the role model which Grimmelshausen had in mind for both the Hermit and for Simplicissimus.

CHAPTER 11: *About the onerous and perilous life of a regent*

73.   the onerous and perilous life of a regent: a favorite topic of the time; the list of famous men scorned or even persecuted by their fellow citizens is a nearly verbatim reproduction of similar lists in Boaistuau-Launay's Theatrum mundi (four-language version), p. 467 ff, and Zanach's Historische Erquickstunden III, 162 ff. (doubtless copied verbatim, and without attribution, from Launay). The best-known such list in classical antiquity was provided by Plutarch in his essay on "Precepts

of Statecraft" in his Moralia (800 D-E), where he mentions the public carping at Cimon, Scipio, and Pompey. Resnaissance polyhistors were, of course, quick to expand the list.

74.   Orb...Braunfels...Staden: Orb, a village in the northeast Spessart Forest, taken from the Imperials by protestant forces on December 7, 1634 (Könnecke I, 163, citing Theatrum Europaeum III, 383); Braunfels, a town located in Hesse, about 3 miles up the Mühlbach, a left tributary of the Lahn River; it was taken back from the Imperials on January 18, 1635 (Könnecke I, 160, citing Theatrum Europaeum III, 403-04); Staden, a village in upper Hesse was not taken until May 15, 1635 (Könnecke I, 163 f., citing Theatrum Europaeum III, 458); as Könnecke points out, the inclusion of Staden in the list of towns taken violates the chronology of the novel.

75.   Simonides: not Simonides, the Greek lyricist, as Borcherdt (p. 370) and others assume, but Cimon (died 449 B.C.), an Athenian general and statesman; Plutarch (Moralia 800 D-E) reports that the Athenians criticized him because he drank too much wine.

76.   The Thebans complained about their Paniculus...: the statement makes no sense. Surely the reference is not to "Panniculus," one of the stock comic figures in the Roman mimes (he was the stupid one who always got slapped by his comrade, Latinus). The only figure in Theban history with a name even vaguely similar to "Paniculus" is Polyneices, and I find no reference that the Thebans were critical of his expectoration.

77.   Lycurgus: not the legendary law-giver of Sparta (9th century B.C.), but rather a Lacedaemonian who was chosen king in 220 B.C. and died about 210 B.C.

78.   Scipio: P. Cornelius Scipio, called Africanus the Younger (died 129 B.C.).

79.   Pompey: see above, Notes to Book II, Chapter 10.

80.   Cato: M. Porcius Cato Uticensis (95-46 B.C.), sometimes called Cato the Younger.

81.   Hannibal: most famous of all Carthaginian generals (247-c. 183 B.C.) and military commander in the Punic Wars.

82.   Demosthenes: greatest of the Athenian orators (c. 384-322 B.C.).

83.   Socrates: (469-399 B.C.); first of the great Athenian philosophers.

84.   Solon: (639-c. 559 B.C.); greatest of the Athenian lawgivers.

CHAPTER 12: *About the intelligence and knowledge of mindless beasts*

85.   the intelligence and knowledge of mindless beasts: despite the fact that such enumerations are frequently found in polyhistorical works of the time, Grimmelshausen's immediate source has been determined, for the observations here are taken verbatim from Boaistuau-Launay's Theatrum mundi (four-language version), p. 92 ff, or perhaps from Zanach's Historische Erquickstunden III, 26 ff., where Launay's text was reproduced unchanged (and, of course, without attribution).

86.   chelidonio: common ceclandine, also called "swallow-wort," presumably because swallows used its thick yellow juice.

87.   affectionibus: affects.

88.   philosophi: philosophers.

CHAPTER 13: *Contains all manner of things; anyone who desires to know about them must read it himself, or have someone read it to him*

89.   the Pater noster: the Lord's Prayer.

90.   We read of a man who...: the following six anecdotes are "exempla melancholicorum." A favorite topic in the seventeenth century was psychological aberration in the form of an overwhelming fixation (a person who suffered from one was called a "melancholicus"—in German a "Phantast"), and identical, similar, or partly similar examples abound in the literature of the time. Kurz (p. 388) found the first two of Grimmelshausen's examples in Galen and the first three in both Beyerlink's Magnum theatrum vitae humanae (XI 397 f.) and Goulard's Schatzkammer (I, 324 ff.). Bechtold (p. 63 ff.) found three of the examples in the Moscherosch—the first, third and sixth—and four in Johann Praetorius' Eine neue Weltbeschreibung— the first, third, fourth and fifth (and Praetorius himself cited both Zeiller and Redschor as his sources). Borcherdt ("Miszellen zu Grimmelshausens Simplicissimus," Euphorion 23, 291 f.) reported on the occurrence of the first and fifth example in Remigius' Daemonolatria (II, 5, p. 267 f.). More recently Weydt (p. 69 f.), suggested that Grimmelshausen's source was a list of "madmen" ("Die Wahnsinnigen") in Harsdörffer's Der große Schauplatz Lust- und Lehrreicher Geschichten, in which examples only remotely similar to Grimmelshausen's first, fourth and sixth "melancholicii" are given; Weydt emphasized that Harsdörffer, in his version of the first example, the so-called "homo vitreus," cited Cervantes' "El licenciado vidriera," thus providing a link between Cervantes and Grimmelshausen. Inasmuch as none of the sources suggested thus far include identical examples of all six "melancholicii" in the same order and with demonstrable verbatim borrowings by Grimmelshausen, it would seem that the real source of the list has not been established.

CHAPTER 14: *What a noble life Simplicius continued to lead, and how the Croats spoiled it for him when they took him as part of their spoils*

91.   Cardinal Richelieu: (1585-1642); French statesman; he concluded an alliance with Sweden in 1636, despite the fact that France was a Roman Catholic country and the Swedes were leaders of the Protestant cause in this phase of the Thirty Years' War, which from this point on became less and less a religious struggle and more and more a contest between the French and the Habsburgs of Austria and Spain.

92.   Duke Bernhard of Weimar: see above, Notes to Book I, Chapter 19.

93.   comoedia: comedy, farce.

94.   Mee vameh....: the faultily written Croatian is supposed to mean: "We'll take this fool with us, we'll take him to our colonel. By God, yes! he understands German, he'll have fun with him."

CHAPTER 15: *Simplicius' life with the troopers and what he saw and experienced with the Croats*

95.   Budingen: town in upper Hesse at the edge of the Wetterau region.

96.   Fulda: town in Hesse situated on the right bank of the Fulda River between Vogelsberg Mountain and the Röhn.

97.   s. v.: salva venia, with your indulgence, i.e. if you'll pardon my language.

98.   convent of Hirschfeld: the Benedictine monastery in Hersfeld, to the northeast of Budingen.

99.   Colonel Corpes: (died 1638); commander of a Croatian light cavalry unit in the Imperial army led by Ottavio Piccolomini; Corpes' immediate superior was the Imperial general Count Isolani. In late January 1635, at a time when

the water in the moat at Hanau was frozen, he was sent there on a scouting mission in order to determine whether Duke Bernhard of Weimar was in the fortress. Corpes' men seized some youngsters who were playing on the ice—among them, perhaps, Grimmelshausen himself. Könnecke (I, 171 ff.) presents the ascertainable facts in exhaustive detail.

100.   Melander: Peter Melander Reichsgraf zu Holzappel (1585-1648); between 1633 and 1640 he was the commander-in-chief of the army of Hesse-Cassel; he was not in Hesse at this time, as Grimmelshausen mistakenly assumed, but in Westphalia (cf. Könnecke I, 181 f.).

101.   Cassel : principal city in Hesse, situated on the Fulda; at the time it was the capital of Hesse-Cassel.

102.   to puff up...: the German ("aufblasen") is unclear, but the context seems to support my interpretation.

CHAPTER 17: *How Simplicius went to the witches' dance*

103.   the witches' dance: the episode, as critics have noted, represents a sudden break in the action; Simplicissimus himself intimates at the end of the chapter that it is a literary device to shift the scene of the action from Hesse to Magdeburg.

104.   nota: note.

105.   a blue flame: it was commonly believed that a blue flame was the necessary light for unholy doings involving the devil; in Grimmelshausen's Vogelnest I the blue flame plays an important role in a robbery attempt by persons in league with the devil.

106.   harmoniam: harmony.

CHAPTER 18: *Why it should not be thought that Simplicius is a teller of tall tales*

107.   Simon the Magus: the famous sorcerer (Acts 8, 9-24) who, when he saw that "through laying on of the apostles' hands the Holy Ghost was given,...offered them money." The story of Simon's disastrous attempt to fly was widespread at the time. Garzoni tells it in Discourse 41 (p. 335), as Konopatzki (p. 13) pointed out, and Zeiller refers to it in the commentary to Rosset's Traurige Geschichten (p. 98), which seems to be the source of two other passages in this chapter (see below).

108.   Nicolaus Remigius: Nicolaus Remi (1530-1612), author of Daemonolatriae libri tres (1595), which was translated into German in 1598 under the title Nicolai Remigii Daemonolatria, oder Beschreibung von Zauberern und Zauberinnen; the work was widely read during the seventeenth century. Borcherdt ("Miszellen zu Grimmelshausens Simplicissimus," Euphorion XXIII, 292 f.) presented parallel texts which demonstrate that the German translation of Remigius is the source of the passage on Johann von Hembach and Catherina Praevotia and that quoted from Olaus Magnus and cited from Torquemada.

109.   Majolus: Simeone Maiolo (1520-1597?), Bishop of Volturara and Monte Corbino from 1572 to 1597; his most famous work (and the source of the anecdotes recounted here) was Dies caniculares, a German translation of which appeared in 1650. In one of his commentaries to his translation of Rosset's Traurige Geschichten Zeiller (p. 99) gives the second and third examples, which agree almost verbatim with Grimmelshausen's account: S: "Majolus in besagtem Colloq. 3. p. 212 setzet zwey Exempel von einem Ehebrecher / so der Ehebrecherin Büchsen genommen / sich mit Salben geschmiert / vnd sie also beyde in der Zauberer Zusammenkunfft kommen seynd. Und wird es diesem schier ergangen seyn / als jenem Knecht / in einem wolbekandten Land und Ort / (daselbsten es mir von etlichen glaubwürdigen Leuten erzehlt worden /) welcher / vor wenig Jahren / früh auffgestanden ist / und die unrechte Büchsen in der Finstere erwischt / und den Wagen geschmiert / der sich mit sampt den Rädern übersich in die Lufft soll erhebt haben / also / daß man ihn wieder herab hat ziehen müssen."; ST : "Majolus setzet zwey Exempel / von einem Ehebrecher / so sich an sein Frau gehängt / und von

eionem Ehebrecher / so der Ehebrecherin Büchsen genommen / sich mit deren Salben geschmiert / und also beyde zu der Zauberer Zusammenkunfft kommen seyn. So sagt man auch von einem Knecht / der frühe auffgestanden / und den Wagen geschmiert / weil er aber die unrechte Büchs in der Finstere erdappt / hat sich der Wagen in die Lufft erhoben / also daß man ihn wieder herab ziehen müssen." Zeiller's commmentary (p. 99) also contains the anecdote attributed to Ghirlandus: S : "Obgedachter Majolus schreibt d.col. 3. p. 211. auß Paul. Grillandi Buch / de sortileg. von einem vornehmen Mann / welcher / als er gemerckt / daß sein Weib sich salbe / und darauff auß dem Hauß fahre / hab er sie gezwungen / ihn einsmals mit ihr su der Zauberer Sabbat zunemmen. Als man nun daselbst aß / und aber kein Saltz verhanden war / habe er solches begehrt / und mit harter müh auch erhalten / und darauff gesagt: Gott sey es gelobt / jetzt kompt das Saltz. So bald er dieses redt / sezy alles verschwunden / und seyen die Liechter erloschen; (sintemal die Zauberer nicht allein kein Saltz by ihren Conventen sollen leiden / sondern auch den Namen Gottes nicht hören können. Vid. Bodinus lib. 2. cap. 2. de Daemonomania.) Als es nun Tag worden / habe er von den Hirten oder Haltern verstanden / daß er nahend der Stadt Benevento, im Königreich Neapolis / und also 100. Meil wegs von seiner Heimat sey. Derowegen / ob er wol sonst reich gewesen / habe er doch nach Hauß betteln müssen / und so bald er heim kommen / habe er sein Weib / als eine Zauberin bey der Obrigkeit angeben / die auch gerichtet worden sey."; ST : Ghirlandus schreibet auch von einem vornehmen Mann / welcher als er gemerckt / daß sich sein Weib salbe / und darauff auß dem Hauß fahre / habe er sie einsmals gezwungen / ihn mit sich auff der Zauberer Zusammenkunfft zu nehmen; Als sie daselbst assen / und kein Saltz vorhanden war / habe er dessen begehrt / mit grosser Mühe auch erhalten / und darauff gesagt: Gott sey gelobt / jetzt kompt das Saltz! Darauff die Liechter erloschen / und alles verschwunden. Als es nun Tag worden / hat er von den Hirten verstanden / daß er nahend der Statt Benevento, im Königreich Neapolis / und also wol 100. Meil von seiner Heimat sey; Derowegen ob er wol reich gewesen / habe er doch nach Hauß betteln müssen / und als er heim kam / gab er alsbald sein Weib vor eine Zauberin bey der Obrigkeit an / welch auch verbrennt worden." Grimmelshausen was familiar with the Latin version of Grillandi's name from Garzoni, where it is cited repeatedly.

110.   Olaus Magnus: (1490-1558); Archbishop at Upsala and Swedish historian, author of Historia de gentibus Septentrionalibus (1555), which was translated into German under the title Beschreibung allerley Gelegdenheite, Sitten, Gebräuchen vnd Gewohnheiten der Mitnächtigen Völcker (Strasbourg, 1567).

111.   Hading: mythical king of Denmark whose exploits were described by Saxo Grammaticus in his Gesta Danorum I, 23 ff.

112.   Odin: Wotan, the chief Nordic god.

113.   Torquemada: Antonio de Torquemada (16th century), author of Iardin de flores curiosas , which was translated into from the French version of Gabriel Chappuys into German with the title Hexamereon; oder Sechs Tagezeiten (Cassel, 1652).

114.   Ghirlandus: Paulo Grillando (late 16th century), a jurist whose chief work, which dealt with witches and the punishment of them, was entitled Tractat de hereticiis: sortilegiis omnifariam coitu: eorum penis (1536).

115.   Doctor Faust: the story of Faust's flight through the air was well known, for it was told in the very first Faust book and retold in all later versions, including Widman's Faust of 1599 (II, 10, p. 61 ff.). Grimmelshausen was doubtless familiar with it, but he may have been reminded of it by Zeiller's references to Faust in the commentary to Traurige Geschichten (p. 83).

116.   Archbishopric of Magdeburg: region around Magdeburg in Saxony.

CHAPTER 19: *Simplicius comes to be a fool once more, just as he had been before*

117.   Zerbst beer: the beer brewed in Zerbst, a village on the Nuthe River, some 24 miles southeast of Magdeburg, was not only much praised, it was furnished to both sides in the war indiscriminately.

118.   the armies of both the Emperor and the Prince Elector of Saxony: the siege began in late April of 1636; Könnecke (I, 187 ff.) notes how accurate Grimmelshausen's account is and presumes that he was indeed present at the siege.

119.   master-of-horse: the officer in charge of the care of the horses of staff officers.

CHAPTER 20: *A rather long chapter dealing with dice-playing and what goes with it*

120.   dice-playing: sermons on the evils of gambling abound in medieval and later literature; no source for this lecture has been found, but it does seem likely that Grimmelshausen did not write this chapter as an original treatise based on his own experience.

121.   physiognomiam: physiognomy, the art of telling a person's character and fortune from the person's facial features.

122.   chiromantia: chiromancy, palmistry, the art of telling a person's character and fortune by reading the person's palm.

123.   fatum: fate, fortune.

124.   materi: matter, subject matter.

CHAPTER 21: *A chapter somewhat shorter and more amusing than the previous one*

125.   inventio: invention, device.

126.   materi: subject matter, material.

127.   Dicis non facis: You talk but you do not act (you don't practice what you preach).

128.   pater: priest.

129.   cavaliers a la mode: men of fashion, men of the world.

130.   galantes dames: elegant ladies.

131.   Diana: goddess of the hunt.

132.   conjured larger horns onto their husbands' heads: made cuckolds of their husbands, betrayed their husbands.

133.   Acteon: legendary huntsman who while roving about one day saw Artemis (Diana) and her nymphs as they were bathing; as punishment for observing them, Acteon was turned into a stag and torn to pieces by his own hunting dogs. Cf. Ovid, Metamorphoses III, 138-252. The tale is told in Acerra philologica II, 4 (p. 184 f.) and Moscherosch (I, 875). Richard Trueheart : in German "Ulrich Hertzbruder." The name is actually employed by Grimmelshausen as a tag-name; the word "Herzbruder" has the sense of "bosom buddy," "very best and most loyal friend." Könnecke (I, 151 f.) conjectures that Grimmelshausen's friendship with another steward named Ulrich Bruder, together with the fact that Count von Götz' secretary was named Ulrich Lauttenmayer, inspired the name.

CHAPTER 22: *A scoundrelly thief's trick to do another man in*

134.   provosts: in seventeenth-century armies the provost was the chief military police officer.

135.   specter-cavalrymen: a common superstition of the time was that some practitioners of black magic could conjure up spectre cavalrymen in order to turn the tide of a battle.

136.   as impervious to musket balls...: it was believed that by entering into a pact with the devil a person could make himself "shotfree" and thereby safe from wounds by bullets.

137.   Saturn...scythe: Saturn was frequently depicted as an old, bent-over man with grey hair and a long beard; in his right hand he held a crutch or a scythe; Weydt (p. 375) reproduces a contemporary depiction of Saturn.

138.   conjunctio of Saturnus and Mercurius: in astronomy and astrology a "conjunctio" was the alignment of two planets; here the reference is to the alliance of the provost (Saturn) and the clerk (Mercury); Grimmelshausen employs a similar turn of phrase in the title of Chapter 2 of The Singular Life of Heedless Hopalong ("Conjunctio Saturni, Martiis & Mercurii") to describe the meeting of Simplicissimus (Saturn), Hopalong (Mars), and the scribe Philarchus (Mercury). Grimmelshausen's use of astronomical parlance in this manner has inspired some scholars (Rehder, Weydt, and Weydt's students) to develop a "planetary god" theory (see in particular Weydt, 243-301 and appendix). It should be pointed out that Moscherosch, who obviously exerted a great influence on Grimmelshausen as a writer, makes use of the same device (he speaks of the conjunctio Saturni et Martis) in I, 634.

139.   large gold-plated goblet: the misuse of the goblet is reminiscent of Joseph's ruse to require that his brothers leave Benjamin behind in Egypt with him while they returned home (Genesis 44). A similar incident occurs in Grimmelshausen's Vogelnest I when a stolen object is planted in the quarters of Simplicissimus' own son by his enemies, with the result that the son is compelled to leave the court where he had been held in high esteem. It is thus difficult to agree with the suggestion of Bechtold (p. 502 f.) that Grimmelshausen was inspired by a passage in the "Somnium" (Book VI).

CHAPTER 23: *Richard Trueheart sells himself for a hundred ducats*

140.   burdened him down with a pike: see above, Notes to Book I, Chapter 16.

141.   this summam: this sum of money.

142.   buy his way free: in the seventeenth century it was possible and quite legal for a soldier to buy his freedom from the army or from the unit to which he had been assigned.

143.   a freebooter: a soldier—of any rank—who fought with a military unit to which he was not officially attached; because plunder and spoils were the freebooter's major incentive, the term soon took on the pejorative meaning it has today.

CHAPTER 24: *Two prophecies fulfilled simultaneously*

144.   mathematicus: mathematician.

145.   chiromanticus: reader of palms.

146.   the battle of Wittstock: Wittstock was a town in the Prignitz in Brandenburg; in the battle fought there on September 24, 1636, the Imperial army defeated the forces of the Prince Elector of Saxony.

147.   Magdeburg...: city in Saxony located on the middle course of the Elbe, where the old overland trade routes crossed the river; Könnecke (I, 187) surmises that Simplicissimus arrived at Magdeburg in May of 1636; the city was finally taken on July 13, 1636.

148.   the Prince Elector of Saxony: Johann Georg I (1585-1658); since the Peace of Prague (1635) he had sided with the Imperial cause.

149.   von Hatzfeld: Melchior von Hatzfeld (1593-1658), general of the Imperial army, which together with the Saxon army of the Prince Elector, was besieging Magdeburg.

CHAPTER 25: *From a lad Simplicius is transformed into a lass and acquires divers lovers*

150.   Simplicius is transformed into a lass: Bloedau (p. 52 f.) assumed that an episode in Sir Philip Sydney's Arcadia, which was translated into German from the French version in 1629 and was revised and republished by Martin Opitz in 1638, inspired this episode: a young lover, Pirocles, dons women's clothes in order to be near the object of his desire, a maiden named Philocles, but the maiden's father, King Basilius, becomes smitten with him, while her mother, Gynecias, who sees through the disguise, also begins to lust for him. Walter Holzinger ("Der abentheurliche Simplicissimus and Sir Philip Sidney's Arcadia," Colloquia Germanica 1969, pp. 189 ff.) made a careful comparison of the two works, which Bloedau had omitted to do, and attempted, without much success, to point out verbal agreements between them. Weydt (p. 88), noting that the motif of disguise as a member of the opposite sex is a widespread motif, believes that Grimmelshausen's inspiration for the episode is to be found in an anecdote entitled "Virtue Preserved" ("Die gerettete Keuschheit") in Harsdörffer's Der große Schau-Platz Lust- und Lehrreicher Geschichte (Anecdote LXXXIII), in which a maiden dresses as a youth in order to preserve her virtue. While the maiden's situation bears some slight resemblance to that of Courage before she came to the army, it merits no consideration as the model for Simplicissimus' plight; Bloedau's suggestion is far more convincing.

151.   histori: story, tale.

152.   von Wallenstein...at Eger: Albrecht von Wallenstein, Duke of Friedland (1583-1634), the most important field marshal on the Imperial side, was assassinated at the fortress of Eger on February 25, 1634, because it was feared that he would defect with his forces to the other side.

153.   secretarius: company clerk.

154.   Achilles...Lycomedes: Achilles, the greatest of the heros who fought in the Trojan war, was the son of Peleus and the Nereid Thetis; in an attempt to prevent him from participating in the war, Thetis disguised him as a maiden and sent him to the court of Lycomedes, the king of the Dolopians on the island of Scyros. The king was taken in by the disguise, but not the king's daughter, Deidamia, who bore Achilles two sons. The anecdote appears in one of Grimmelshausen's sources, Cerda's Weiblicher Lustgarten (p. 14).

155.   Werberschanz...Havelberg...Perleberg: Werberschanz refers to fortifications thrown up at Werben, a village on the Elbe; taken by the Imperials on August 27, 1636 (Könnecke I, 190, citing Theatrum Europaeum III, 690); Havelberg, a town in the Magdeburg region not far from the mouth of the Havel River, was taken by Imperial forces on August 25, 1636 (Könnecke I, 190, citing Theatrum Europaeum III, 690); Perleberg, a town in the Westprignitz, was taken by the Imperials on Septermber 14, 1636 (Könnecke I, 191).

156.   Fortuna: goddess of fortune.

157.   the two armies...: the Imperial army under von Hatzfeld and the army of the Prince Elector of Saxony.

158.   General Banier: Johan Baner (1593-1641), a Swedish general; he was the victor at the battle of Wittstock (see above, Notes to Book II, Chapter 24). Chapter 26 turned me over to the stableboys: in army camps and garrisons it was customary to punish loose women by turning them over to the boys who were too young to fight but not too young to commit rape; this fate also very nearly befalls Courage (The Runagate Courage, Chapter 12).

CHAPTER 26: *How he is imprisoned as a traitor and sorcerer*

159.   Domine, non sum dignus: Lord God, I am not worthy.

CHAPTER 27: *How the provost fared at the Battle of Wittstock*

160.   the battle of Wittstock: see Notes to Book II, Chapter 24 above.

161.   battaglia: battle.

162.   In the battle itself, however,...: Bechtold (p. 502) suggested that the following battle description was inspired by a rather brief description in Moscherosch, "Complementum" (p. 693). H. Geulen ("'Arcadische' Simpliciana," Euphorion 63, 427 ff.) and Walter Holzinger ("Der abentheurliche Simplicissimus und Sir Philip Sidney's Arcadia," Colloquia Germanica 1969, 186 ff.) presented parallel texts from Simplicissimus and the German translation of Arcadia (III, 7, 5), in which a number of verbatim agreements occur. Despite these findings the stylistic analyses of the passage by Richard Alewyn (Johann Beer: Studien zum Roman des 17. Jahrhunderts, Leipzig: 1932, pp. 200ff.) and M. E. Gilbert ("Simplex and the Battle of Wittstock," German Life and Letters 18, 264 ff.) remain valid.

163.   Summa summarum: In sum.

164.   So that's the sort of fellow you are!: "So you are one of those who are in league with the devil!" (because he is impervious to bullets); Borcherdt (p. 389) suggests that the episode may have been inspired by an account in Theatrum Europaeum III, 99 of another battle (at Phillipsburg in 1633): "Among the dead was a chasseur and village-mayor who could not be killed by any rifle or fire-arm, but rather had to be beaten to death with battle axes."

CHAPTER 28: *Concerning a battle in which the victor is captured whilst vanquishing his foes*

165.   strategemata: stratagems, ruses, plans.

166.   armada: army.

167.   cavalcada: a detachment of cavalry.

168.   Gemmer March: Gemmer Mark; Könnecke (I, 212) suggests that Grimmelshausen meant the Günner Mark, a part of the Arnsberg Forest, which lies somewhat south of Hamm-Soest.

169.   Hamm: town in Westphalia; situated in a broad level valley south of the Lippe River.

170.   Soest: Town in the fertile Soester Börde; c. 15 miles southeast of Hamm and 13 miles southwest of Lippstadt.

171.   rencontre: encounter, battle, skirmish.

172.   dragoon: see Notes to Book I, Chapter 20.

CHAPTER 29: *How well a pious soldier fared in Paradise, till he died, and how after his death a chasseur took his place*

173.   the battle of Pavia: the coat must inded have been old, for the battle of Pavia, in which the army of Emperor Charles V defeated that of King Francis I of France, took place on February 15, 1524.

174.   Lippstadt: town in Westphalia situated on the Lippe River; despite the fact that it was a Hansa city and thus technically neutral in the war, it was occupied in December of 1633 by Swedish and Hessian troops, who then heavily fortified it; together with Soest, Lippstadt is the scene of most of Simplicissimus' adventures in Westphalia.

175.   a furrier...a mastersinger: the members of the furriers' guild were renowned as mastersingers; their guild had the third largest number of mastersingers, even more than the shoemakers' guild, to which the most famous mastersinger of them all, Hans Sachs, belonged (cf. Bert Nagel, p. 17).

176.   orthographice: orthographically, spelled correctly.

CHAPTER 30: *How the chasseur started out when he fell to plying the soldier's trade, from which a young soldier can learn a few things*

177.   refusing to let me pass for a grown man....: Bechtold (p. 506) points out that in Guzman (I, 13) the hero finds himself in the same situation, but he does not succeed in becoming a soldier.

178.   Count von Götz: (1595-1645); after serving with Mansfeld he became an officer in the Imperial army, then transferred to the allied army of the Prince Elector of Bavaria. Götz was in charge of the Imperial campaign launched in 1636 to retake Westphalia from the Protestant forces; Könnecke (I, 14 ff., esp. 223 ff.) adduced evidence which makes it seem plausible that Grimmelshausen served as a stableboy with one of Götz' regiments during 1636 and 1637.

179.   Dorsten: town in Westphalia, on the lower course of the Lippe River; Könnecke (I, 216) notes that it remained, despite Count von Götz' efforts, in protestant hands.

180.   Lippstadt: Lippstadt likewise remained a Protestant stronghold.

181.   Coesfeld: town in Westphalia, on the Berkel, west of Münster; the Hessians controlled it throughout this period (cf. Könnecke I, 216).

182.   siege...at Ostende: a harbor city in East Flanders; it was besieged by the Spaniards under Ambrose Spinola in 1601 and finally taken by them in 1604.

CHAPTER 31: *How the devil stole the parson's bacon and how the chasseur got himself into a trap*

183.   the parson's bacon: the theft of bacon by a person who, when apprehended, pretends to be the devil, was an old an popular tale, as Bechtold (p. 508) noted. Anton Birlinger ("Zu Grimmelshasens Simplicissimus," Alemannia X, 79-81 and XIV, 79-101 and 252-256) cited a number of collections of tales in which the anecdote appeared; Johannes Bolte ("Studien zu Grimmelshausens Simplicissimus," Alemannia XV, 62-63) cited a similar tale in Memel's Lustige Gesellschaft ; Bloedau (p.61) believed the source to be Anecdote 52 in Parival's Histoires facetieuses; Josef Trostler ("Zur Quellengeschichte des Simplicissimus," Euphorion 21, 695-702) found the same motif in Hans Sachs, Thünger's Facetien, Wendunmuth, Talitz von Liechtensee's Kurtzweilige Reyse-Gespan, and Erasmus Francisci's Lustige Schaubühne ; and Bechtold (p. 508 f.) pointed to the same anecdote in Johann Praetorius' Wünschelruthe. Whatever Grimmelshausen's immediate source was, it seems indisputable that Bechtold was correct in asserting that the first treatment which makes the thief a musketeer and thus places the action in a military context was that of Thisabo von Redtschorn (the pseudonym of Christoph Schorer), whom Praetorius himself cited as his source of the anecdote. In Schorer's work, Allmodische Sitten-Schule (Magdeburg, 1660), the anecdote is entitled "Wunderlicher Speck-Fall" (pp. 110-113). It might be noted that another item in Schorer's book (pp. 292-296) about the "torment and usefulness of flax" ("Von des Flachses Marter und Nutzen") might well have inspired the so-called "Schermesser-Episode" which Grimmelshausen included in the first Continuatio to Simplicissimus.

184. Recklinghausen: city in Westphalia, on the northern edge of the Ruhr territory; in 1636 Imperial forces co-occupied it in order to keep the Hessians under surveillance.

185. caravana: caravan, wagon train.

186. re vera: as a matter of true fact.

187. convivium: repast, convivial meal.

188. O mirum!: O wonder!

189. Acteon: see Notes to Book II, Chapter 21.

190. Hopalong: in German "Springinsfeld"; the name is actually a tag-name, since "Springinsfeld" is the word for a heedless madcap, which fairly well characterizes Simplicissimus' partner in crime during his days in Soest. In the second of the Simplician novels, The Runagate Courage, we are told how he got his name. In the contract which Courage demanded he enter before she would agree to live with him as his common-law wife, the seventh point stipulated, in her words: "that I call him by a special name, which name was to be formed from the first words of the command by which I should the first time order him to do something." (p. 109) As it turned out, Courage, in order to send him off so that she might take her pleasure with a young officer, ordered him to "hop along and catch our piebald," which the officer was ostensibly interested in purchasing (p. 111). Hopalong later becomes the principal narrator of The Singular Life Story of Heedless Hopalong. Könnecke (I, 150) notes that in 1665 a drummer named Jacob Springinsfeld is documented as living in Oppenau, a village quite near Gaisbach, where Grimmelshausen resided.

191. Interim: In the meanwhile.

192. Rheine: town in Westphalia; situated on the Ems.

193. Münster: main city of Westphalia; located in the middle of the Westphalian plain.

194. Vale: Farewell!

Simplicissimus, The German Adventurer

BOOK III

How the chasseur strayed too far from the right path

Gracious Reader, you will probably have gathered from the previous book how ambitious I had become in Soest, and that I sought and found honor, fame, and favor in deeds which for others would have merited punishment. Now I am going to relate how I let my folly lead me further astray, and how as a result I lived in constant peril to life and limb. I was, as I have already mentioned, so intent upon garnering honor and fame that I could not sleep for thinking of it, and when my head was teeming with fanciful notions, and many a night when I was lying in bed devising new tricks and wiles, I had wondrous ideas. Thus I invented a kind of shoe which could be put on backwards so that the heel was under one's toes; at my own expense I had nigh on to thirty pair of them made, and when I distributed them amongst my men and went on a raiding party with them, it was impossible to track us, for sometimes we wore these shoes and sometimes our regular shoes, carrying the others in our packs, and when anyone came to the spot where I had commanded the shoes be changed, the tracks looked precisely as if two raiding parties had come together there and had both disappeared together; if, however, I kept the backwards shoes on, then it looked as if I were going towards where I had already been, or as if I were coming from the spot towards which I was in fact going. And so any time I left tracks, they were far more confused than a maze, so that it would have been impossible for anyone who attempted to follow or chase me by means of my tracks to do so. I was often directly alongside of men from the other side who were looking for me far away, and even more often several miles away from the very thicket which they were surrounding and searching in order to capture me there. And I did the same thing when I was abroad on horseback that I did with raiding parties on foot, for it was not uncommon for me to have my men dismount at a crossroads or a fork in the road and have the horses' shoes changed so that they were backwards. And the usual ruses which are employed when a small raiding party desires to be thought from its tracks to be a large one, or when a large one desires to be taken to be a small one, were so commonplace with me, and I hold them to be so trifling, that I do not hold them to be worth talking about. Also, I devised an instrument with which I could hear, at night when there was no wind, a trumpet being blown three hours' walk distant from me, a horse neighing or a dog barking two hours' walk away, and people talking an hour's walk away, which trick I kept very secret, and with it I made a reputation for myself because it seemed to everyone to be impossible. By day this same instrument (which I usually kept in my pocket along with a spyglass) was not as useful, except at a lonely and quiet place, for one could not but hear every single thing in the entire area that so much as moved and made a sound, from horses and cattle down to the smallest bird in the air or frog in the water, so that it sounded precisely as if one (as in the middle of a marketplace) were surrounded by many people and animals, all of them making sounds, so that one's cry made it impossible to understand the other's.

I well know, of course, that to this very day there are people who do not believe this, but whether they believe it or not, it is still the truth. With this instrument I can recognize, at night, a person talking at normal volume by his voice, even if he is as far away from me as a person with a spyglass, by day, can recognize him from his clothes. I cannot blame anyone, however, if he do not believe what I am now writing, because not one of those would believe me who saw it with their own eyes, when I employed this instrument and said: "I hear troopers of horse coming, for the horses are shod"; "I hear peasants coming, for the horses are not shod"; "I hear draymen, but they are peasants; I can tell by the way they speak"; "Musketeers are coming, about so and so many, for I can tell that by the rattling of their bandoliers"; "There is a village in this or that region; I hear cocks crowing, dogs barking, etc."; "There goes a herd; I hear sheep bleating, cows lowing, swine grunting," and so forth. My own comrades at first held these things I said to be idle boasting, but when they found out by what then happened that my prophecies were always right, they could not but believe that it was all witchcraft, and that what I told them had been revealed to me by the devil and his grandmother. And you, fair Reader, will also think the same thing, I believe. Nevertheless, in this way I often made wondrous escapes from the enemy when they got report of me and came to take me prisoner. And I contend that if I had revealed this science, it would have since become commonplace, because it would have come in very handy for them in time of war, particularly in sieges. But I shall go on with my *histori*.

When I was not allowed to go out on a raiding party, I went out stealing anyway, and then neither horses, cows, swine, nor sheep in their stalls were safe from me, all of which I fetched from several miles around. I knew how to put boots, or shoes, onto cattle and horses till I got them to a much-traveled road, so that they could not be tracked. Then I put the horseshoes on pointing the wrong way, or if the animals were cows and oxen I put on them shoes which I had made for that purpose and brought them to safety that way. The big, fat hog-folk, who because of their sloth do not like to travel by night, I was a master at taking away, even though they grunted and did not desire to go with me. With flour and water I made them a nice salted porridge which I let soak into a sponge to which I had tied a stout string; then I let those I had my eye upon gobble down the sponge full of food, whereupon, without any further exchange of pleasantries, they patiently went along with me, paying the account for me with hams and sausages. And when I brought back anything like that, I loyally shared it with both the officers and my comrades. Therefore, another time I was allowed to go out again, and when my theft was betrayed or found out, they helped me quite nicely. Otherwise, I thought myself to be much too good to steal from the poor, or to steal chickens[1] or other insignificant things. All the while I little by little fell to leading an epicurean life, glutting myself with food and drink, because I had forgotten my hermit's teachings and had no one to guide me in my tender years, no one whom I could look up to; for my officers themselves were participants when they caroused as my guests, and those who should have punished and admonished me instead goaded me on to all the vices, as a result of which I grew, in the end, so godless and wicked that no roguery was too great for me to perpetrate. At last I was also an object of envy, particularly by my comrades, because I had a luckier hand for stealing than anyone else had, and also by my officers, because I acted the madcap, had good fortune on raiding parties, and made a greater name and had greater fame for myself than they had. And I do believe for sure that in time one group or the other would have sacrificed me, had I not entertained them so often.

CHAPTER 2

The chasseur of Soest rids himself of the chasseur of Werl

Now as I was continuing to live in this manner and was in the process of having some devils' masks made and, to go with them, terrible costumes with horses' and oxen's hoofs, by means of which I meant to frighten the enemy and also to take from friends their possessions without being recognized, an idea which was prompted by the bacon-stealing incident, I got word that there was a fellow staying in Werl[2] who was an excellent raider, who dressed in green, and who had perpetrated under my name not only rape and pillage but all manner of excesses here and there in the countryside, and particularly amongst those who paid us tribute, with the result, therefore, that grievous complaints were lodged against me, such that I should have paid a pretty price, had I not expressly demonstrated that at those times when he did the one thing or the other in my name I was somewhere else. This I was not of a mind to gainsay him, much less to suffer that he make use of my name any longer, take booty in my guise, and thereby cause me such disgrace. I invited him, with the knowledge and consent of the commandant of Soest, to be my guest for a pass with a saber or a brace of pistols in the open field, and when he had not the courage to appear, I had it spread abroad that I desired to take my revenge upon him, even if it was in Werl at the headquarters of the commandant there, who was not punishing him for his misdeeds. Indeed, I said publicly that were I to encounter him upon a raiding party, he would be used by me like an enemy. This caused me to put aside my devils' masks, with which I had planned to undertake great things, and also to cut my green clothes up into little pieces and burn them in front of my quarters in Soest, for all to see, despite the fact that my clothes alone, not counting plumes and horse tack, were worth over a hundred ducats. Indeed, I swore in a rage that the next person who called me "the chasseur" must needs either murder me or die by my hand on the spot, even if it should cost me my head. Nor was I willing to lead any more raiding parties (which it was not my duty to do anyway, since I was not an officer), till I had first avenged myself upon my counterpart in Werl. And so I remained in the garrison and performed no soldierly deeds other than standing my watch, except when I was sent somewhere on special duty, which, however, I carried out quite lazily, like any other sluggard. Word of this soon spread through the neighborhood, and the raiding parties from the other side became so bold and were so reassured by it that they lay daily well nigh just outside our barrier-gates, which in the long run I too could not tolerate. But what I found most intolerable was that the chasseur of Werl kept on claiming to be me and kept on taking rather much booty.

Now in the meantime, when everyone thought I had lain down upon a bed of sloth from which I would not so soon arise again, I inquired into what my counterpart in Werl was doing and omitting to do, and I found that he was not only aping me in name and dress but was also wont to steal secretly, at night, anything he could lay his hands upon. For that reason I unexpectedly awoke again and made my plot accordingly. My two grooms I had little by little trained like spaniels, and they were therefore also so loyal to me that each of them would have run through fire for me if need be, because with me they had good food and drink on which to glut themselves, and they took excellent booty. One of them I sent to Werl to my counterpart. He pretended that because I, his erstwhile master, was beginning to live like any other *cujon* and had sworn never to go on any more raiding parties, he no longer desired to stay with me and instead had come to serve him, because he had put on the chasseur's garb in his master's stead; and he said that he would let him use him like an honorable soldier, that he knew all the highways and byways in the countryside, and that he could give him many a stratagem to take good booty, etc. This fine simpleminded fool believed my groom and let himself be persuaded to take him into his service and, on a certain night, to go with his comrade and him to a sheepfold to fetch some fat wethers, where Hopalong and I were lying in wait for them with my other groom, and I had bribed the shepherd to tie up his dogs and to let the new arrivals tunnel into the shed unhindered, in which shed I was of a mind to cook their mutton for them. Now when they had made a hole through the wall, the chasseur of Werl desired that my groom straightway creep in first. He, however, said: "No, someone might be lying in wait in there and give me a blow on the head. I well see that you do not rightly know how to pilfer. First of all, one must make sure it is safe." Then he drew his sword and, hanging his hat upon the point of it, pushed it through the hole several times, saying: "First of all, one must see whether or not the cat's away." When this had been done, the chasseur of Werl was himself the first to crawl in. And Hopalong straightway grabbed him by the arm in which he had his sword and asked him whether he desired quarter. His companion heard that and tried to run away, but because I knew not which of them was the chasseur and because I was fleeter of foot than this fellow, I hied myself after him and caught him in few strides. I asked: "What army are you with?" He answered: "The Imperials." I asked: "Which regiment? I'm an Imperial too. Any man who would deny his master is a rogue!" He answered: "We're with the dragoons in Soest and came to fetch a few wethers. I hope, my friend, that if you're an Imperial too, you will let us pass." I answered: "If you're from Soest, then who are you?" He answered: "My comrade in the stall is the chasseur of Soest." "Rogues are what you are!" said I. "Why are you plundering your own quarters? The chasseur of Soest is not such a fool as to let himself be trapped in a sheepfold!" "O, I meant to say, he is the chasseur of Werl!" the other one answered me in return. And while I was disputing with him this way, my groom and Hopalong came along too with my counterpart. "Look you here, my fine-feathered friend, so this is where we meet! Were it not for the fact that I respect the Imperial weapons which you have undertaken to bear against the foe, I should straightway put a bullet through your brain! I have been, till now, the chasseur of Soest, and you I shall hold to be a rogue till you take one of these two swords and duel with me like a soldier." With that my groom (who, like Hopalong, had on a frightful devil's costume with large billy goat's horns) placed between us at our feet two identical swords which I had brought with me from Soest and gave the chasseur the choice to take up one of them, at which the poor chasseur was so frightened that the same thing happened to him as had to me in Hanau when I ruined the dance, for he shat his breeches so full that well nigh no one could stay near him. He and his comrade trembled like wet dogs;

they fell to their knees and begged for mercy. But Hopalong growled as if out of an empty pot and said to the chasseur: "You must fight, or I'll break your neck!" "O, most esteemed Sir Devil, I did not come hither to fight. If you, Sir Devil, will spare me that, I'll do whatever you desire in return." During these confused utterances my groom handed him one sword and me the other, but he was trembling so much that he could not hold it. The moon was shining very brightly, so the shepherd and his servants could see everything from their hut. I called to him to come to us so that I might have a witness to this affair. He, when he came, acted as if he did not see the two in devil's costumes and asked why I was quarreling so long in his sheepfold with these fellows. If I had some bone to pick with them, he said, I should do it somewhere else; our arguments were none of his affair; he let the army take its monthly contribute out of him, and therefore he hoped to live in his sheepfold in peace. And the other two he asked why they let me plague them so and why they did not strike me down. I said: "You wretch! They were going to steal your sheep." The peasant answered: "Then I wish they were compelled to kiss my arse, and my sheeps' arses too." And with that he went away. Then I again insisted that we fight, but the poor chasseur was so frightened that he well nigh could not stand on his feet any more, so that I felt sorry for him. Indeed, he and his comrade uttered such moving words that I finally forgave and forgot everything. But Hopalong was not satisfied with that, but compelled the chasseur to kiss the arse of three sheep (for that is how many he was going to steal), and in the bargain scratched his face so terribly that he looked as if he had been in a fight with a cat, with which slight revenge I was satisfied. The chasseur, however, soon disappeared from Werl, because he was too ashamed to stay there, for his comrade spread abroad everywhere—and swore by all that was holy that it was true—that I in truth had two real live devils with me who were in my service. Therefore I was feared even more, but on the other hand loved all the less.

CHAPTER 3

The great god Jupiter is captured[3] and reveals the counsels of the gods

Of this I soon became aware; for that reason I put aside my former godless way of life and devoted myself to virtue and piety. Of course, I went on raiding parties once more as I had before, but I behaved towards friend and foe so affably and discreetly that all those who fell into my hands thought I was different from what they had heard about me. In addition, I desisted from superfluous and wasteful extravagances and gathered together many fine ducats and precious stones, which I now and again hid in hollow trees in the countryside on the Plain of Soest, because the well-known sibyl of Soest counseled me to do this and assured me that I had more enemies setting snares for me and my money in that city and amongst my regiment than outside the city and in enemy garrisons. And whereas they had news here and there that the chasseur had fled to foreign parts, before they knew it, I had by the throats those who were tickled at this, and before a town had even heard that I had done damage in another one, it perceived that I was present there, for I rode like the wind and was here one minute and there the next, so that there were more stories told about my exploits than when that other fellow was pretending to be me.

One time I was sitting with twenty-five flintlock not far from Dorsten,[4] lying in wait for a convoy with several draymen which was said to be going to Dorsten. I, as was my wont, was standing guard myself, because we were near to the enemy. There came a lone man strolling up, clad nice and honorably, and talking to himself and making feints like a dueler with the cane he was carrying in his hand.[5] I could only make out that he was saying: "I am really going to punish the world unless it concede that I am the great *Numen*!"[6] From this I presumed that he might perchance be a powerful prince who had been going about in disguise this way in order to inform himself about his subjects' lives and behavior,[7] and had now undertaken to punish them appropriately (perchance because he had not found them as he desired them to be). I thought to myself: "If this man is from the enemy, then there will be a good ransom for him. If not, you can use him so courteously and thereby so steal away his heart that he shall do you good in the future, your entire life long." Therefore I jumped out from the bushes in front of him, presented my weapon cocked and at the ready, and said: "Sir, be so kind as to precede me into this thicket, unless you desire to be used like an enemy." He answered very earnestly: "To such usage the likes of me is not accustomed." I, however, pushed him along politely, saying: "Sir, you surely will not be so contrary as to refuse on this occasion to reconcile yourself to the situation as it is." And after I had taken him into the bushes to where my comrades were and had assigned new watches, I asked him who he was. He answered, quite magnanimously, that it would be of little consequence to me, even if I already knew that he too was a great god! I thought he might perhaps be acquainted with me and might perchance be a nobleman from Soest and speaking in this manner to bait me, because people are wont to vex the citizens of Soest by teasing them about their great god and his golden apron;[8] but I soon discerned that instead of a monarch I had captured a madman who had addled his wits by studying too much and immersing himself too deeply into poetry, for when he warmed up to me a bit, he introduced himself as the god Jupiter.[9]

I wished, to be sure, that I had not made this catch, but because I had the fool in hand I was pretty much obliged to hold him till we moved away from there, and inasmuch as time was hanging rather heavy upon my hands anyway, I decided to humor this fellow and employ his gifts to good advantage. Therefore I said to him: "Well now, my dear Jove,[10] how is it that Your Divine Highness has left his throne and climbed down to us on earth? Forgive me my question, O Jupiter, which you might deem impertinent, for we too are related to the heavenly gods and are in fact *sylvani*,[11] born of *faunis*[12] and *nymphis*,[13] and we are thus folk to whom this secret may properly be revealed." "I swear to you by the River Styx," answered Jupiter, "that you would learn nothing of this matter from me if you did not so closely resemble my cupbearer, Ganymede,[14] even if you were Pan's[15] own son, but on Ganymede's account I shall communicate to you that the great hue and cry about the world's vices has penetrated through the clouds to me, in response to which it was resolved in a council of all the gods that I could, as in Lycaon's time,[16] wipe out life upon earth again with a flood. But because I am particularly partial to the human race and always prefer mild to harsh action anyway, I am now rambling about like a vagabond to inquire in person after what human beings are doing and omitting to do; and even though I find everything worse than I had expected, I am still not of a mind to extirpate all human beings alike and without distinction, but instead to punish only those who ought to be punished, and afterwards induce the rest to do my will."

I could not but laugh, of course, but I stifled my laughter as best I could and said: "Alas, Jupiter, your toil and labor, I fear, will surely be in vain unless you afflict the world, as before, with water or even fire; for if you send a war, then all the bad, bold lads will flock to it and will merely torment the people who are virtuous and peace-loving; if you send a famine, it will be just what the usurers have been praying for, because then the price of their grain will go up; and if you send death, then the skinflints and all other people will be the winners, because afterwards they will inherit a great deal. Therefore, you will be obliged to extirpate all mankind—lock, stock, barrel—if you are really of a mind to levy punishment."

Concerning the German hero who will conquer the entire world and establish peace amongst all peoples

Jupiter answered: "You speak of the matter like a natural- born human being, as if you did not know that it is possible for us gods to arrange it so that only the evil are punished and the good spared. I am going to rouse from his sleep a German hero who will accomplish all this with the blade of his sword. He will kill all who are wicked and spare and raise up those who are virtuous." I said: "Then such a hero must needs have soldiers too, and where soldiers are employed there is war, and where there is war the innocent as well as the guilty cannot but suffer!" "Are you earth-gods then of the same mind as the earth-humans," Jupiter then said, "so that you can understand nothing at all? I am going to send such a hero as has no need of soldiers, and yet is going to reform the entire world. At his nativity I shall endow him[17] with a well-formed and stronger body than the one Hercules[18] had, and endow him to excess with caution, wisdom, and understanding; in addition, Venus[19] is to give him a handsome face, so that he shall outstrip even Narcissus,[20] Adonis,[21] and my Ganymede himself; along with all his virtues she is to extend to him a special grace, delicacy, and demeanor and thus make him loved by all, because at his nativity I for these reasons shall look upon her with all the more fondness. Mercury,[22] however, shall endow him with incomparably sound common sense, and the inconstant Moon shall be not harmful but useful to him, because he will implant into him incredible celerity. Pallas[23] shall educate him on Parnassus,[24] and Vulcan[25] shall forge his weapons for him *in hora Martis*,[26] particularly a sword, with which he shall conquer the entire world and strike down all who are godless, without any further aid from a single human being who might assist him as a soldier. He will require no assistance. Every large city will tremble in his presence; every fortress, otherwise invincible, he will have under his command in a quarter-hour; finally, he will command the greatest rulers of the world, and he will institute a government over sea and earth so laudable that both gods and men shall take pleasure in it."

I said: "How can the striking down of all who are godless be achieved and put into effect without bloodshed—and command over the entire world without particularly great power and a strong arm? O, Jupiter, I candidly confess to you that I can no more conceive of this than can a mortal man!" Jupiter answered: "That does not surprise me, because you do not know what manner of rare power my hero's sword will possess. Vulcan will construct it from the same materials from which he makes my thunderbolts and will so direct its virtues that when my hero bares it and makes but one pass through the air with it, the heads of an entire army will be chopped off, even if they are behind a mountain an entire Swiss mile[27] away from him, so that the poor devils must needs lie there headless before they even know what has happened to them! Now when he then sets out upon his course and comes to a city or a fortress, he will behave as Tamerlane[28] did and raise a white flag as a signal that he is there in the cause of peace and to promote the commonweal. If they then come out and accommodate themselves, then all's well and good; if not, he will draw his weapon and with the power of this oft-mentioned sword chop off the heads of all the sorcerers and sorceresses who are in the entire city, and he will hoist a red flag. And if still no one appears before him, he will kill all the murderers, usurers, thieves, rogues, adulterers, whores, and knaves in that same manner, and show a black flag. And if those who are still left in the city do not come to him very soon and behave contritely, then he will extirpate the entire city and its inhabitants for being stubborn and disobedient folk, but he will execute only those who have held back the others and have been the reason why the people did not surrender earlier. And so he will move from one city to the next, giving each city the land around it to govern in peace, and taking unto himself from each city throughout all Germany two of the wisest and most learned men, and he will make of them a parliament, unite the cities with one another in perpetuity, abolish bonded servitude, along with all tolls, taxes, excises, rents, payments in kind, and duties, thus initiating changes so that people will no longer know the meaning of the words 'compulsory service,' 'mandatory guard duty,' 'tribute,' 'cash donation,' 'war,' and other tribulations, but instead will live more blessedly than in the Elysian fields.[29] Then," Jupiter said further," I shall often take the entire *chorum deorum*[30] and climb down to the Germans to enjoy their grapevines and fig trees. I shall put the Helicon[31] in the midst of their borders and plant the Muses upon it anew. I shall bless Germany more with superabundance than happy Arabia, Mesopotamia, and the region around Damascus. The Greek language I shall then foreswear and speak only German and, in a word, show myself to be such a good German that in the end I shall let them succeed, as the Romans did before, in ruling over the entire world." I said: "But most sublime Jove, what will the princes and lords say when the coming hero makes so bold as to subjugate their cities and deprive them, in an unlawful manner, of what is rightfully theirs? Will they not meet force with force, or at least protest before gods and men against it?" Jupiter answered: "To this the hero will pay little heed. He will divide all the rulers into three groups and punish those who live wickedly and provide a bad example, just as if they were commoners, because no earthly power can stand against his sword. The others, however, he will give the choice to stay in the country or not; those who stay and love their fatherland will be obliged to live like other common folk, but the private life of the Germans will be much more pleasant and much happier than is the life and estate of a king nowadays; and the Germans will then all be like Fabricius,[32] which ruler was unwilling to share his kingdom with King Pyrrhus[33] because he so ardently loved his fatherland, along with virtue and honor; and these are the second group. The third group, however, who do wish to remain masters and to continue to rule he will lead through Hungary and Italy into Moldavia, Wallachia, into Macedonia, Thrace, Greece, indeed, across the Hellespont to Asia, to win these lands for them, giving them all the lansquenets in Germany to take along, and there make kings of all of them. Then he will take Constantinople in one day and cut off the heads of all the Turks who refuse to be converted to Christianity and to be obedient, and put them next to their rumps. There he will re-establish the Roman Empire and betake himself back to Germany, and with his parliament lords (whom he, as I have already said, will collect in pairs from all the German cities and name as directors and fathers of his German fatherland) he will build a city in the middle of Germany which will be much larger than Manaoh in America[34] and far richer in gold than Jerusalem in Solomon's time, a city whose walls will be comparable to the Tyrolean Alps, and whose moats will be comparable in width to the sea between Spain and Africa. He will build in it a temple made of nothing but diamonds, rubies, emeralds, and sapphires. And in the art gallery which he will erect there, all the rare things in the entire world will be collected, from the rich gifts which will be sent to him by the kings in China, Persia, by the Great Mogul in oriental India, the great Tatar Khan,[35] Prester John[36] in Africa, and the great Tsar in Muscovy. The Turkish emperor would be more generous, had this same hero not taken his empire from him and given it in fief to the Roman emperor."

I asked Jove what role the Christian kings would play in this affair. He answered: "The ones in England, Sweden, and Denmark, because they are of German blood and origin, and the ones in Spain, France, and Portugal, because the old Germans in times of yore occupied and ruled these lands too, will receive their crowns, kingdoms, and incorporated lands in fief voluntarily, and then, as in the times of Augustus,[37] there will be perpetual peace amongst all the peoples in the entire world."

CHAPTER 5

How he will unite the religions with one another and pour them into one mold

Hopalong, who had been listening to us, very nearly made Jupiter indignant and almost spoiled the jest when he said: "And then things in Germany will be the way they are in the Land of Cockaigne, where it rains muscatel and one-penny pastries pop up overnight like mushrooms! There I'll needs eat like a day laborer, with both cheeks full, and drink malmsey till tears fill my eyes." "Yes indeed," answered Jupiter, "particularly when I visit upon you the plague of Erysichton,[38] because you, so it seems to me, are mocking my majesty." To me, however, he said: "I thought I was amongst true *sylvani,* but now I well see that I have run afoul of envious Momus[39] or Zoilus.[40] To think that one should reveal to these traitors what heaven has resolved and thus cast pearls before the swine, who are, in fact, so stupid that they cannot tell batshit from buckshot!" I thought to myself: "This is indeed a droll and nasty god, trafficking as he does in such lofty things and, at the same time, in such a soft *materi.*"[41] I well saw that he did not like to be laughed at, and therefore I choked back my laughter as best I could and said to him: "Most benevolent Jove, just because of an uncouth forest god's rudeness, you surely will not keep secret from your Ganymede what else will transpire in Germany?" "O no!" he answered. "But first I command this Theon[42] is to henceforth keep his Hipponax-tongue[43] in check, before I turn him into a stone (as Mercury did to Battus[44]). And you, sir! Confess to me that you are my Ganymede, and tell me whether my jealous Juno[45] did not in my absence chase you out of the heavenly realm!" I promised to tell him everything after I had first heard what I desired to know. Then he said: "My dear Ganymede (do not keep denying it, for I well see that you are my Ganymede), then gold-making will become as certain and commonplace in Germany as pottery-making, so that well nigh every stableboy will be dragging the *lapidem philosophorum*[46] about with him!" I asked: "But how can Germany have such long-lasting peace with such diverse religions? Will not the divers parsons incite their parishioners and once again instigate a war because of their faith?" "O no!" answered Jupiter. "My hero in his wisdom will prevent this eventuality and will first of all unite all the Christian religions in the entire world." I said: "O miracle of miracles! That would be a great achievement! How would it be accomplished?" Jupiter answered: "I am happy from the bottom of my heart to reveal that to you. After my hero has brought about universal peace in the entire world, he will address in a highly moving sermon the religious and secular leaders and heads of the Christian peoples and of the divers churches, and sharply remind them of the hitherto most damaging schisms in matters of faith and persuade them through the most sensible reasons and incontrovertible *argumenta*,[47] so that they, of their own accord, will desire a general unification of churches and will turn the entire task over to him to direct as his noble reason dictates. Then he will assemble from all the ends of the earth and from all religions the very wisest, most learned, and most pious *theologos*,[48] and he will prepare a place for them, as Ptolomaeus Philadelphus[49] did in olden times for the seventy-two translators, in a pleasing yet quiet spot, where they can ponder unhindered upon important matters; he will provide them with food and drink and all other necessities and will charge them first to settle, as soon as possible, but after most mature and diligent deliberation, the points of contention in their religions and, after that, with complete unanimity, to set forth in writing the genuine, true, holy, and Christian religion according to Holy Scripture, ancient tradition, and the recognized opinion of the Church Fathers. At this same time Pluto[50] will scratch his head mightily, because then he will fear the diminution of his empire; indeed, he will think up all sorts of schemes and plots to raise an objection, and he will labor mightily, if not to thwart it completely, at least to postpone it *ad infinitum* or *indefinitum*;[51] he will make so bold as to paint for every single *theologo* a glowing picture of his own interests, status, peaceful life, wife, child, esteem, and anything else which might move him to cleave unto his particular opinion. But my valorous hero will not rest either. As long as the *concilium*[52] is in session, he will have the churchbells rung in all Christendom and thereby admonish the Christian peoples to pray without surcease to the highest *Numen* and to beg Him to send them the spirit of truth. Whenever he sees, however, that the one cleric or the other has let Pluto take hold of him, he will torment the entire *congregatio*,[53] as in a conclave, with hunger; and if they are still unwilling to further so lofty a work, he will preach to all of them about a trip to the gallows, or he will show them his wondrous sword, and thus he will persuade them, first with mildness and in the end with severity and threats, to take strides *ad rem*[54] and no longer to confound the world, as in bygone times, with their stubbornly held false notions. After unity is achieved, he will hold a great feast of jubilation and make public to the entire world this purified religion, and anyone who believes otherwise he will then send to a martyr's death, burning him at the stake with sulphur and pitch, or pin a palm onto such a heretic and give him to Pluto as a New Year's present.[55] Now you know, my dear Ganymede, everything you desired to know. And now, in return, tell me what the reason is that you left heaven, where you have poured so many a goblet of nectar for me."

CHAPTER 6

What the legatio[56] of lice did with Jove

I thought to myself that perhaps the fellow might not be the fool he was pretending to be, but instead, as I had done in Hanau, was making a fool of others so as all the better to escape us. Therefore I resolved to test him with anger, because that is the best way to tell if a man is a fool, and I said: "The reason why I came from heaven was that I missed you there, and so I took the wings of Daedalus[57] and flew to earth to seek you: but wherever I asked after you, I found that at all ends of the earth they had scant praise for you, for throughout the world Zoilus and Moscus[58] have slandered you and all the gods,[59] calling you vile, wanton, and nasty, so that you have lost all credit with mankind. You yourself, they say, are a crablouse-ridden, adulterous whoremonger; what right have you to punish the world for such vices? Vulcan,[60] they say, is a timid cuckold who let Mars put horns onto him without taking any particularly noteworthy revenge; so what manner of weapons can that limping simpleton forge? Venus, they say, is herself the most detested slut in the world, because of her lewdness; so what manner of fame and fortune can she bestow upon someone else? Mars, they say, is a murderer and robber; Apollo a shameless whoremonger; Mercury a babbler, thief, and panderer; Priapus[61] a filthy pig; Hercules an addlepated bully; and, *in summa,* the whole host of the gods, they say, is so vile that they ought to be lodged nowhere but in the stable of Augias,[62] the stench of which is renowned throughout the world." "Aha!" said Jupiter. "Is it any wonder that I have put aside my mildness and pursued these damnable slanderers and blasphemous calumniators with thunder and lightning? What do you think, my loyal and most beloved Ganymede? Shall I torment these chatterboxes[63] with perpetual thirst, as I did Tantalus?[64] Or shall I have them hanged on Mount Thorax[65] alongside that arrant gossip, Daphitas? Or shall I grind them up with Anaxarchus[66] in a mortar? Or shall I stick them in to the red-hot ox of Phalaris[67] in Agrigento? No, no, Ganymede! These punishments and torments are all of them taken together too slight. I am going to fill Pandora's box[68] anew and have it emptied out upon these scoundrels' heads. Nemesis[69] is going to awaken Alecto, Megaera, and Tisiphone[70] and set them on them, and Hercules is going to borrow Cerberus[71] from Pluto and with him hound these naughty knaves like wolves. Not till then, when I have hexed and vexed them sufficiently in this fashion, shall I have them tied to a stake in the house of hell alongside Hesiod[72] and Homer[73] and mercilessly punished by the Eumenides,[74] throughout eternity."

While Jupiter was uttering these threats, in the presence of myself and my entire raiding party he took down his breeches without the slightest shame and shook out of them the lice which, as one could see from his blotched skin, had tormented him terribly. I could not imagine what was going to happen, till he said: "Get you gone, you little varmints! By the River Styx,[75] I swear to you that in all eternity you shall not receive what you are so intently soliciting!" I asked him what he meant by these words. He answered that the race of fleas and lice, when they heard that he was coming to earth, had sent their ambassadors to him to present him with their compliments. These had called it to his attention that though he had indeed assigned them to live on dogs' hides, some of them at times, because of certain characteristics which women had, had strayed from home and gotten into women's fur. These poor lost ninnies, however, were treated so badly by women—caught and not only murdered but beforehand even tortured and crushed so miserably between their fingers—that it would make a stone statue cry. "Indeed," Jupiter went on, "they presented their case to me so movingly and pitifully that I could not but feel sorry for them and promised them my assistance, but upon the condition that I first would also hear what the women had to say. But they objected that if the women were permitted to present their side of the case and contradict them, then they well knew that with their poisonous bitch-tongues they would either paralyze my kindness and goodness, or drown out the cries of the lice themselves, or with their lovely words and beauties they would delude me and mislead me to make a false judgment. They made the further plea that I permit them to enjoy the submissive loyalty to me which they had always shown me and intended to continue to show me, since they had always been nearest to my person and had known best what had transpired betwixt me and Io, Callisto, Europa,[76] and many others, but had never told tales out of school, or said a single word to Juno, even though they were wont to abide with her, in consequence of which they had exhibited such discretion that no human being to date (despite the fact that they were all too close at hand during all bouts of lovemaking) had found out anything from them, as Apollo had from the ravens.[77] Moreover, if I were ever to let women chase them in their territory, catch them, and slaughter them, as is the hunter's right, then it was their request that they might henceforth be executed in such wise as to meet a hero's death, and either be slain with an ax, like an ox, or felled like wild game, and no longer let women so dishonorably squash and draw them between their fingers, whereby the women made into hangman's tools those appendages with which they often touched something else, which was a disgrace to all men of honor. I said: 'You gentlemen must torment them terribly, else they would not tyrannize you so frightfully.' 'Yes indeed!' they gave me an answer. 'They are envious of us too, perhaps because they fear that we see, hear, and feel too much. As if they had not been sufficiently assured of our discretion! What's to become of us? They cannot even tolerate us in our own *territorio*,[78] which is clear from the fact that many of them use upon their lapdogs brushes, combs, soaps, bleaches, and other things, so that we are of necessity obliged to quit our fatherland and seek other domiciles, not to mention the fact that they could put their time to better use and perchance clean the lice off their own children!' Then I let them move in with me and make my mortal body feel that they were living upon it, and feel what they were doing and omitting to do. Then this pack of ragamuffins fell to so plaguing me that I am obliged, as you have seen, to rid myself of them again. I say 'Shit on the *privilegium*[79] I gave them!' Let women squash and crush them as much as they like! Indeed, should I lay hands upon one of these little beggars, he won't fare a whit better!"

CHAPTER 7

The chasseur once more wins honor and booty from the chase

We could not laugh out loud, both because we were obliged to keep silent and because the madman did not like it, as a result of which Hopalong very nearly burst. At just that moment our main watch, whom we had in a tree, reported that he saw something in the distance coming towards us. I climbed up the tree too and saw through my spyglass that it indeed must be the draymen for whom we were lying in wait. However, they had no foot soldiers with them, but some thirty or more horse, as a convoy. Therefore I could easily calculate that they would not come up through the woods where we were, but would instead avail themselves of the open field where we could not take anything away from them, since there was there a road of sorts, about six hundred paces from us, which cut through the plain some three hundred paces from the end of the forest or hill. I was not of a mind to have waited there for so long in vain and to have taken nothing but a madman as booty, so I quickly made a different plan, and it worked, too.

From the spot we were occupying, a rill of water ran down into the plain through a gully which was easy to ride through. At the end of the gully I place twenty men and took up my position with them, and I left Hopalong to hold his vantage point where we had lain before, and I commanded that when the convoy came, each of my lads should make sure to take his man, and I told each of them who was to fire his weapon and which ones were to keep shots in reserve in the barrel. Some old fellows asked what I was about and whether I really thought that a convoy would come into this place, where they had no business being, and to which probably not a single peasant had come in a hundred years. Others, however, who believed that I could perform witchcraft (for which I at that time stood in great repute) thought that I would conjure the enemy into our hands. But for this purpose I had no need of devilish deeds, but only of Hopalong, for when the convoy, which was riding in rather close formation, was about to go directly past us, Hopalong, at my command, fell to bellowing like an ox and neighing like a horse so loudly that the entire forest echoed with the sounds, and, anyone would have sworn by all that is holy that there were horses and cattle in there. As soon as the convoy heard that, they thought to take good booty and in this place to lay hands upon something which was not to be found in all the rest of the region, because the countryside had been turned into a wasteland. All of them rode without discipline and as quickly as if each desired to be the first to receive the best of our blows, which indeed came so fast and furious that straightway after the first welcome we gave them, thirteen saddles were emptied and a few more troopers were squashed out of theirs. Then Hopalong ran down the gully towards them screaming "Chasseur! Over here!" at which the fellows were frightened even more and grew so confused that they could ride neither forwards, nor backwards, nor to the side, and they jumped off their mounts and attempted to escape on foot. And I took all seventeen of them prisoner, together with the lieutenant who had commanded them, and with that I headed for the wagons, unhitched twenty-four horses, but got only some silkware and Dutch cloth, for I durst not take the time to plunder the dead, much less to search the wagons thoroughly, because the draymen had taken to their heels as soon as the skirmish began, and by them I could have been betrayed in Dorsten and captured on the way back. Now when we had packed up the booty, Jupiter came running out of the woods too and screamed after us, asking whether his Ganymede was really going to forsake him. I answered "Yes," unless he were willing to restore to his lice the *privilegium* they desired. "I'd sooner see them lying together in Cocytus!"[80] he answered. I could not but laugh out loud at this, and because I had an empty horse anyway, I let him mount it, but inasmuch as he could ride no better than an old maid, I was obliged to have him tied onto the horse.[81] Then he said that our skirmish reminded him of the battle which the Lapithae had begun in olden times against the Centaurs at the wedding feast of Pirithous.[82]

Now when it was all over and we were galloping away with our prisoners as if we were being pursued, the captured lieutenant realized for the first time what a grave blunder he had made, namely, that he had so rashly led such a fine unit of horse into the hands of the enemy and had delivered up thirteen such fine lads to slaughter, and he therefore began to despair, and he gave me back the quarter which I had granted him. In fact, he attempted to compel me, as it were, to shoot him dead, for the thought occurred to him that this oversight, for which he would be held responsible, was not only a great disgrace to him, but also that it would be an obstacle to his further advancement, were it not, in fact, to turn out that he must needs pay with his head for the harm he had done. I, however, spoke to him and called it to his attention that fickle Fortuna had shown many an honest soldier her spite, but I had never yet seen anyone who was so disheartened or even desperate on that account. His behavior, I said, was a sign of faintheartedness, whereas brave soldiers, by contrast, would resolve to repay on another day the damage done them. He would never bring me to the point, I told him, where I would violate the rules of war or commit such a disgraceful deed, contrary to all fairness and to the usage and tradition of honorable soldiers. Now when he saw that I would not assist him, he fell to vilifying me, thinking to goad me to anger, and he said I had not fought fair and square with him, but instead had behaved like a rogue and assassin, and had stolen like a thief the lives of the soldiers he had with him, at which his own lads whom we had captured were mightily frightened, and my own lads so enraged that they would have filled him as full of holes as a sieve, had I but permitted it, for which reason I had my hands full to prevent it. But I did not pay any heed to what he said, but instead took both friend and foe as witnesses of what was taking place there, and I had him, the lieutenant, bound and kept under guard like a madman. I also promised him, the lieutenant, as soon as we came to our post, and if my officers would permit it, to outfit him with my own horse and weapons, from which he should have his choice, and to show him publicly with pistol and saber that to practice deceit in wartime against the opposite side is by rights allowed; and why had he not stayed with his wagons, to which he had been assigned, or, if he had wished to see what was there in the woods, why then had he not had them first properly reconnoitered, which would have behooved him better than that he now started with such tomfoolery as no one would really pay any heed to. In this, friend and foe alike agreed that I was right and said that not one in a hundred raiding party soldiers they had encountered but would have not only shot the lieutenant dead for such vilification, but would also have sent all the other prisoners to join his corpse. And so the next morning I brought my booty and prisoners safely back to Soest and garnered more honor and fame from this raiding party than ever before. Everyone said: "This fellow is a young Johann de Werdt!"[83] which tickled me mightily. But a fight or exchange of shots with the lieutenant the commandant was not willing to permit, for he said that I had already bested the lieutenant twice. Now the more my reputation increased in this manner, the greater grew the envy of those who did not grant me my good fortune anyway.

CHAPTER 8

How he found the devil in a trunk, and how Hopalong seized some fine horses

Of my Jupiter I could not rid myself, for the commandant did not desire him, because there were no more feathers to be plucked from him, and he said he would give him to me. So I got my own fool and had no need to buy me one, even though I, the year before, had been obliged to let them use me myself as their fool. So strange is Fortune, and so changeable is Time! Shortly before, the lice had tribulated me, and now I had in my power the god of fleas and lice; six months before, I had served as the page of a simple dragoon, and now I had under my command two servants who called me their master; it was not yet a year ago that the stableboys had chased after me to make me a whore, and now the time was at hand when all the maidens would fall head over heels in love with me. So I became aware betimes that there is nothing more constant in the world than Inconstancy. Therefore I could not but fear that when Fortuna would one day turn against me, she would make me pay mightily for the good life I was now leading. At that time Count von der Wahl,[84] the commander-in-chief of the Westphalian district, drew together some troops from all the garrisons to form a *cavalcada*[85] to go through the bishopric of Münster against Vecht, Meppen, Lingen,[86] and such places, and particularly to capture two Hessian companies of horse in the bishopric of Paderborn[87] which were located two German miles from the city of Paderborn and were making things uncomfortable for our troops there. I was ordered out along with our dragoons, and after some troops had assembled at Hamm, we advanced quickly and blockaded the headquarters of those two companies of horse, which was an ill-fortified little town, till our forces arrived. They made an effort to escape, but we chased them back into their nest again; we offered to let them pass without horses and weapons but with all their possessions which they could carry upon their backs, but they were unwilling to agree to these terms, but instead desired to defend themselves like musketeers with their carbines. So it came about on that same night that I was obliged to test what manner of luck I had in storming towns, because the dragoons led the assault. I was so successful there that I, together with Hopalong, got into the little town unharmed with the first of our troops. We soon cleared the streets, because anyone under arms was slain, and the townsmen had no desire to defend themselves; and so we fell to searching the houses. Hopalong said we must needs choose the house which had the largest dunghill, for it was in such houses that the richest birds were wont to roost, and that they generally quartered officers. Then we attacked such a house, in which Hopalong undertook to search the stables and I the house, with the understanding that each would share whatever booty he took with the other. So each of us lit a wax taper; I called to the master of the household but got no answer, because everyone had hidden. Meanwhile I came upon a chamber but found in it nothing but an empty bed and a locked trunk. I hammered the trunk open in hopes of finding some valuables in it, but when I raised the lid, a pitch-black thing raised up towards me which I took to be Lucifer himself. I can swear that I have never in all my live-long days been as frightened as at that moment, when I so unexpectedly caught sight of this black devil. "I'll dispatch you to hell!" I straightway said in my fright and brandished the hatchet with which I had opened the trunk, and yet I had not the courage to strike him in the head with it. He, for his part, knelt down, lifted his arms up to heaven, and said: "My dear sair! I pray ye to Gawd, don' take me life!"

Thus I first heard that it was not a devil, because he spoke of God and pled for his life. Then I said that he should get out of the trunk in a hurry; this he did, and he went with me, as naked as the day God created him. I cut off a piece of my taper and gave it to him to light the way for me; this he did obediently and led me into a little room where I found the master of the house who, together with his servants, looked at this diverting spectacle and with fear and trembling begged for mercy. This he was easily granted, because we were not permitted to do anything to townsmen anyway and because he handed over to me the baggage of a captain of horse, amongst which was a nicely stuffed locked valise, reporting that the captain and his men, except for one servant and this blackamoor here, had gone to their posts to defend themselves. Meanwhile Hopalong had also caught the aforementioned servant in the stable with six fine saddled horses. Then we brought into the house, locked them in, and had the blackamoor get dressed; and we gave the master of the house orders as to what he must needs do concerning his captain of horse. But when the town gates were opened, the guards posted, and our major general of ordnance, Count von der Wahl, permitted to enter, he took up lodgings in the very same house we were in; therefore we were obliged, by dark of night, to seek other quarters. These we found with our comrades, who had also come into the town during the assault; with them we made ourselves comfortable and passed the remainder of the night glutting ourselves with food and drink, after Hopalong and I had shared our booty with one another. I took as my share the blackamoor and the two best horses, one of them a Spanish one upon which a soldier would never be ashamed to let the opposite side see him, with which horse I afterwards made no little show; from the valise, however, I got divers costly rings and a portrait of the Prince of Orange[88] in a golden box set with rubies, because I left everything else to Hopalong. And it all came, had I been of a mind to give it away, what with the horses and all, to over two hundred ducats; but for the blackamoor, who had been the most trouble for me to get, I was presented with no more than two dozen sovereigns by the major general of ordnance, to whom I gave him as a gift. From there we quickly moved on to the Ems River but accomplished little, and because it just so happened that we were going towards Recklinghausen, I took leave to pay a visit, along with Hopalong, to the parson from whom I had earlier stolen the bacon; with him I made merry, and I told him that the blackamoor had paid me back for the fright which he and his cook had recently suffered. I also presented to him, in amicable *valete,*[89] a beautiful chiming pendant watch which I had got out of the valise of the captain of horse, and thus I was everywhere wont to make friends of those who otherwise would have had good reason to hate me.

CHAPTER 9

An unequal fight in which the weaker party wins and the winner is taken captive[90]

As my good fortune increased, so did my pride, which, in the end, could not but lead to my downfall. We were camped about a half hour from Rheine when I, together with my best comrades, requested leave to go into that town to have something on our weapons repaired, which leave we were granted. But because it was our intent to finally make properly merry with one another, we turned in at the best inn and bade players come, who were obliged to fiddle our wine and beer down our gullets. Things were *in floribus,*[91] and nothing was left undone which might cause pain to our money; indeed, I invited lads from other regiments to join us and comported myself exactly like a young prince who disposes over land and subjects and has a great deal of money to waste every year. We therefore received better service than a party of troopers of horse who were likewise taking their meal there, because they were not throwing their money about so madly; this vexed them, and they began to rail at us. "How is it," they said to one another, "that these mosquitos (they took us to be musketeers, since there is no beast in the world that looks more like a musketeer than a dragoon,[92] and when a dragoon falls off his horse, what gets to its feet is a musketeer) are spending so much?" Another one answered: "That infant is for sure a country bumpkin to whom his mother gave the milk money, which he is now using to wine and dine his comrades so that some time in the future they will pull him out of the mud somewhere or maybe carry him over a ditch." These words were aimed at me, for I was regarded by them to be a young nobleman. This was passed on to me by the serving-maid, and because I had not heard it myself, I could do nothing but pour a large beer-glass full of wine and have it passed around for everyone to drink a toast to the health of all good musketeers, and I caused such a commotion to be made at each toast that you could not hear yourself think. This vexed them even more. They therefore said for all to hear: "What a hell of a life these musketeers lead!" Hopalong answered: "Of what concern is that to bootblacks?" He got by with that because he looked at them with such a terrible mien and made such a horrible and threatening face that no one wished to rub him the wrong way. But it did arouse them again, and in particular one imposing fellow, who said: "If these shitty armchair soldiers can't strut around on their own dung heap, then where can they show their faces? (He thought we were in garrison there, because our clothes were not as weatherbeaten as those of musketeers who are in the field day and night). It is a well-known fact that in the open field every one of them would assuredly fall prey to us, just as a dove does to a falcon!" I answered him: "We are the ones who are obliged to take towns and fortresses, and they are entrusted to us to defend, whereas you horse troopers, by contrast, cannot lure even a dog out into the open from the smallest rat's nest. So why should we not be permitted to make merry in a place that is more ours than yours?" The trooper answered: "The army that is master of the battlefield will be master of the fortresses, and we are the ones who must needs win pitched battles; consequently, not only do I have no fear of three youngsters of your stripe, together with your muskets; I'd dispatch two of you and ask the third where there are more like you. And were I sitting at your table," he said quite scornfully, "to show you that that is true, young squire, I'd box your ears for you!" I answered him: "Even though I am of the opinion that my brace of pistols is as good as yours, even though I am not a trooper of horse but only a sort of cross between one of them and a musketeer, look you, this youngster here, armed but with his musket and on foot, in fact has the courage to meet in the open field a braggart like you, on horseback and armed with all your weapons." "Ah, you *cujon!*" said the fellow. "I'll deem you a scoundrel if you do not forthwith, as behooves a man of noble blood, back up your words with deeds." Then I threw down the gauntlet to him, saying: "Look you here, if I do not, with my musket and on foot, take this gauntlet back from you in the open field, then you will have sufficient right and might to deem me and to proclaim me to all to be what you have had the audacity to call me." Then we paid the innkeeper, and the trooper made his carbine and pistols ready, and I my musket, and as he was riding away from us with his comrades to the appointed place, he said to my trusty Hopalong that he should go ahead and arrange a grave for me. Hopalong, however, answered that he might take the precaution of charging his own comrades to arrange one for him. Me, however, he reprimanded for my frowardness and said bluntly that he feared I should soon be singing my swan song. I, in reply, laughed, because I had long since bethought myself what I must needs do if I were to meet a well-mounted trooper who attacked me as a foe in the open field when I was on foot and armed only with my musket. Now when we came to the spot where this tussle was to take place, I had already loaded my piece with two musket balls, stirred up fresh tinder, and smeared the touchpan with tallow, as cautious musketeers are wont to do when, in rainy weather, they desire to protect the touchhole and the gunpowder in the pan from water.

Now before we had at one another, comrades on both sides stipulated that we should attack one another in the open field, and to this end one of us should enter a fenced-in field from the east and the other from the west, and then each was to do his best against the other, as a soldier should do when in this wise he catches sight of his foe. And neither before, during, nor after the fight was anyone from either side to assist his comrade or avenge his death or injury. When they had promised one another this in words and by handshake, my opponent and I also shook hands and each pardoned the other for being the cause of his death. Is that not the utterly absurdest folly that ever a reasonable human being can commit! Each of us hoped to uphold the *prae* for his branch[93] of the soldiery; as if the honor and *reputatio*[94] of the one or the other branch depended upon the outcome of what we, in such a devilish manner, were setting out to do! Now when I entered the appointed field at the end assigned to me, with my fusecord burning at both ends, and caught sight of my opponent, I acted as if I were shaking out the old tinder as I walked, but I did not do that; instead I merely stirred the tinder on the lid of my touchpan, blew it off, and with two fingers on the pan kept my eyes upon the opponent, as is customary. And before I could see the whites of the eyes of my opponent, who was also keeping a careful eye upon me, I took aim at him and burned off the false tinder on the lid of the pan, with the result that nothing happened. My opponent thought that my musket had misfired and that my touchhole was stopped shut, and therefore, with pistol in hand, he galloped all too eagerly *recta*[95] up to me, intent upon making me pay for the way I had insulted him; but before he knew what was happening, I had the pan open, had taken aim again, and indeed bade him welcome in such wise that he and my shot fell at the same instant.

I then retired to my comrades, who were so happy to see me that they very nearly kissed me, whereas his comrades freed him from his stirrup and used him and us like honorable fellows, in consequence of which they also returned my gauntlet to me with full praise. But just when I esteemed my honor to be at its zenith, twenty-five musketeers came from Rheine and took me and my comrades prisoner. In fact, I was forthwith chained and shackled and sent to the general staff, because dueling was forbidden under penalty of punishment, both corporal and capital.

CHAPTER 10

The major general of ordnance spares the chasseur's life and otherwise gives him cause to hope for the best

Inasmuch as our major general of ordnance[96] was wont to maintain strict military discipline, I feared I might lose my head. On the other hand, I still had hopes of being spared, because even in this first blossoming of youth I had already behaved well in the face of the foe and had earned a great name and reputation for bravery. But this hope was still uncertain, because on account of the daily occurrence of such fights, necessity dictated that an example be made of me. Just at that time our forces had blockaded a rat's nest and had sent a demand that it surrender but had received a refusal because the enemy knew that we had no heavy artillery with us. Therefore our Count von der Wahl moved with his entire *corpo*[97] up to the town, again sent a trumpeter to demand that it surrender, and threatened to take it by storm; but this resulted only in the following response:

> Most noble and esteemed Count, etc.
>
> From the message which Your Royal Excell. has dispatched to me I have learned what Your Ex. plans to undertake against me in the name of His Maj. the Emp. of the Holy Rom. Emp. Now Your Esteemed Excell., by virtue of your great intelligence, must know how unbefitting, indeed irresponsible, it would be for a soldier to hand over a town such as this to the enemy without duress, for which reason Your Excell., it is to be hoped, will bear me no ill will when I endeavor to hold this town till Your Excell. addresses it with weapons. If, however, your most humble servant can be of any assistance to Your Excell. in any other way, I shall of course be
>
> Your Excel.'s most obedient servant,
>
> N.N.[98]

Sundry ways to take the town were then discussed in our camp, for to leave it in the hands of the enemy was not at all advisable, but to storm it without having first breached the walls would have cost much blood, and it was still uncertain whether it could be conquered or not. However, if one were to fetch the cannons and other necessary equipment from Münster[99] or Hamm,[100] a great deal of effort, time, and money would be expended. Now as soldiers great and small were mulling over this problem, it occurred to me that I should make use of this occasion to gain my freedom. So I gathered my wits together and considered how we might trick the enemy, because all we were lacking were cannons. And because I straightway came upon an idea as to how this thing might be done, I had my lieutenant colonel informed that I had a scheme by which the town might be taken without effort and losses, which scheme I would carry out only if I should receive a pardon and be set free again. Some of the old and tested soldiers laughed at this and said: "Any port in a storm! The fellow is attempting to talk his neck out of the noose!" But the lieutenant colonel himself, and others who knew me, took what I said at face value, for which reason he personally went to the major general of ordnance and informed him of my assertion, telling him many things he knew about me. Now because the count had also already heard about the chasseur, he had me brought before him and relieved of my fetters for as long as I was in his presence. Just as I came in, the count was dining, and my lieutenant colonel told him that when I was standing guard duty for the first time this past spring at St. James' Gate in Soest and a cloudburst came unexpectedly, with much thunder and lightning, for which reason everyone ran from the fields and gardens into the town to take cover, and because the crowd of people both running and riding on horseback grew rather large, I at that time had had the presence of mind to call the watch to arms, because in such melees a city can be taken most easily. "Last fall," said the lieutenant colonel, "there came walking up an old woman who was dripping wet and said, just as she was walking past the chasseur: 'This rain has been a-stickin' in my backbone for two weeks now!' Now when the chasseur heard this, and he happened to have a stick in his hand, he beat on her backbone with it and said: 'You old witch! Why didn't you let the rain out earlier? Why must you wait till just when I am beginning to stand guard duty?' And when the officer told him to stop, he answered: 'It serves her right. The old crowbait has been hearing for a month how everyone has been crying for a good rain. Why didn't she grant it to them earlier? Then perhaps the barley and hops would have turned out better.'" At this the major general of ordnance, though he was otherwise a dour gentleman, laughed heartily. I, however, thought to myself: "If the lieutenant colonel has told the count of such pranks, then he has assuredly not kept from him what else I have done." And I was admitted to the count's presence.

Now when the major general of ordnance asked me what I had to report, I answered: "Your Excellency, etc. Even though I have been sentenced to death for my crime—and that in keeping with Your Excellency's lawful right to both bid and forbid—nevertheless, my most devoted loyalty (which I owe it to His Imperial Majesty, my most gracious lord and master, to manifest till my death) bids me do what little I can, one way or the other, to harm the enemy and thereby further the military aims and advantages of His Most Sublime Majesty, the Emperor of the Holy Roman Empire." The count interrupted me, saying: "Did you not recently bring me the blackamoor?" I answered: "Yes, most gracious milord." Then he said: "Well, your zeal and loyalty might perchance merit that your life be spared, but what manner of scheme do you have to remove the enemy from this town without particular loss of time and troops?" I answered: "Because the town cannot withstand fire from heavy artillery, your humble servant is of the opinion that the enemy would soon come to terms if he but believed that we had cannons with us." "Any fool could have told me that!" answered the count. "But who is going to persuade them to believe that?" I answered: "Their own eyes. I have seen their tower watch through my spyglass. They can be deceived. If some logs the size of the earthenware pipes used in fountains are simply loaded onto wagons and driven by a strong team of horses into the field, they will surely believe that they are heavy cannons, especially if Your Excellency has earthworks thrown up somewhere in the field as if we intended to plant our cannons behind them." "My dear little fellow," answered the count, "those folk in the town are not children. They will not believe this flummery, but instead will desire to hear these cannons too. And if the trick does not work," said he to the officers standing around us, "then we shall be a laughingstock for everyone." I answered: "Gracious milord, I shall cause the cannons to ring in their ears, all right, if I can have a few large muskets and a rather large barrel. Indeed, without the noise there would he no effect. Should we, however, contrary to our hopes, reap nothing but scorn, then I, as the deviser of this ruse, since I must needs die anyway, shall take this shame with me to my grave and thus put an end to it with my life." Now though the count was not of a mind to try it, my lieutenant colonel nevertheless persuaded him to agree to it, for he said that in such matters I was so lucky that he doubted not in the least that this trick would work too. Therefore the count commanded him to arrange the matter however he thought it could be done and said to him in jest that the honor he might reap from it would be his alone.

So three such logs were found, and to each were hitched twenty-four horses, even though only two would have sufficed. These we drove towards evening into full view of the enemy. Meanwhile, however, I had laid hands upon three large muskets and a powder keg, which we got from a castle, and set everything up the way I desired it to be. During the night the powder keg was brought up to where our strange artillery was. The large muskets I gave a double powder charge and fired them off through this keg (from which one end had been removed), so that it sounded just like three warning shots. It thundered so loud that anyone would have staked wife and life upon it that they were heavy howitzers or demi-cannons. Our major general of ordnance could not but laugh at the trick and again commanded that the enemy be offered the opportunity to surrender the town *per accord,*[101] adding that if they did not acquiesce to it this very evening, things would not go well for them on the morrow. Then hostages from both sides were dispatched, the accord concluded, and that same night a city gate turned over to us, which turned out very much to my advantage, for the count not only spared my life—which I had forfeited by doing something which he had forbidden— that very night he restored my freedom to me and commanded the lieutenant colonel in my presence to give me the first command which became available, which, however, did not suit him, the lieutenant colonel, for he had so many cousins and kinsmen who were waiting commands that I could not be given one before they were given theirs.

CHAPTER 11

Contains all manner of things of slight importance and considerable fancy

On this same march I encountered nothing else worthy of note, but when I came back to Soest, the Hessians[102] had captured upon the meadow and taken away with them my servant, whom I had left in camp with my baggage and a horse. Of him the other side inquired and found out about what I did and omitted to do; they therefore held me in greater esteem than before, because they had been persuaded before by common gossip to believe that I could perform witchcraft. He also told them that he had been one of the devils who had so frightened the chasseur of Werl at the sheepfold. When the just-mentioned chasseur learned of that, he was so ashamed that he once more took French leave and from Lippstadt[103] went over to the Dutch. But it was my greatest good fortune that this servant was captured, as will be discerned from what follows of my *histori.*[104]

I began to behave in a somewhat more seemly manner than before, because I had such high hopes that I would soon have a command. Little by little I began to consort with the officers and young noblemen who were intent on precisely that which I imagined I should soon receive. These were for that reason my worst enemies, and yet they behaved towards me as if they were my best friends; nor was the lieutenant colonel all that partial to me either, because he had orders to promote me before his kinsmen; my captain looked upon me with disfavor, because I had finer horses, clothes, and weapons than he did and because I no longer, as before, spent my money wining and dining the old skinflint: he would rather have seen them chop off my head a short while back than promise me a command, for he thought that he was going to inherit my fine horses; and my lieutenant hated me on account of one remark which I had heedlessly let slip recently. That came about like this: we were ordered on the last *cavalcada*[105] to keep a near-desolate guard post with one another. Now when it was my turn to do guard duty (which must needs be done lying down, despite the fact that it was pitch-black night) he, the lieutenant, crept up to me on his stomach like a snake and said: "Sentinel, do you mark anything?" I answered: "Yes, lieutenant." "What? What?" said he. I answered: "I mark that you're scared, sir!" From that time on I found no more favor with him, and wherever it was most perilous, I was the first man to be sent thither. Indeed, everywhere and every place he sought opportunity and reason to give me a good hiding before I became a squad leader, because I durst not defend myself against him. No less were all the non-commissioned officers my enemies, because I had been given preference over all of them. And as far as the common soldiers were concerned, they too began to waver in their friendship and love for me, because it had the appearance as if I held them in contempt, since I no longer associated particularly with them but instead, as already mentioned, associated with the higher-ups, who did not like me any the more for it. The very worst thing of all was that not a single soul told me how everyone felt towards me, and I could not perceive it because many a man who would have preferred to see me dead said the nicest things to my face! I simply lived from one day to the next like a blind man, feeling completely secure and growing more arrogant with each passing day, and even when I knew that it vexed the one fellow or the other that I outdid the nobility and the high officers in splendor, I still did not leave off doing it. I did not hesitate, after I had been made a lance corporal, to wear a necklace made of sixty sovereigns, hose of red scarlet, and white satin sleeves trimmed all over with gold and silver, which at the time was the way the highest officers dressed. Thus everyone's eyes were offended by it. I, however, was such a terrible young fool that I spent money like a drunken sailor, for had I behaved differently and used as palm-grease in all the right places the money which I so uselessly squandered to drape my body, I should not only soon have got my squad, I should also not have made so many enemies. But I did not leave off there, but so decked out my best horse, which Hopalong had got from the Hessian captain of horse, with saddle, tack, and arms that when I sat astride it I might very well have been taken for a second St. George. Nothing vexed me more than the fact that I was not a nobleman, so that I could not also clothe my servants and pages in my livery. I thought to myself: "Everything has a beginning. When you have a coat of arms, you will have your own livery, all right, and when you are a squad commander, you must needs have a seal, even if you are not a squire by birth." I had not gone about great-bellied with these thoughts for long when I had a *comitem palatinum*[106] bestow upon me a coat of arms. It had three red masques upon a field of white, and upon the crest a bust of a young fool in a calfskin habit, with a pair of hare's ears, adorned at the tips with bells: for I thought this best suited my name, because I was called Simplicius, and I wished to make use of the fool to remind me in my future exalted condition of what manner of fellow I had been at Hanau, so that I should not grow all too arrogant, because even now I deemed myself to be no swine. And so I became the first person of my name, family, and escutcheon, and had anyone attempted to make fun of me for it, I should without doubt have challenged him to a duel with saber or a brace of pistols.

Even though at the time I had no interest in womenfolk, I did go all the same with the noblemen when they visited any of the ladies, of whom there were many in the city, to let everyone see me and to show off my fine hair, clothes, and plumes. I must confess that on account of my appearance the ladies preferred me to all the others, but at the same time I could not but overhear how these spoiled bitches compared me to a beautiful and well-carved mannikin which had, except for external beauty, neither savor nor flavor, for there was nothing else about me which they liked. Nor could I do or say anything else which was pleasing to them, unless it be to play the lute, because as yet I knew nothing of love. Now when those who knew how to dally with women made fun of my gauche behavior and clumsiness so as to make themselves all the more popular and to display their eloquence, I said in reply that it was enough for me if I still found my pleasure in a gleaming saber and a good musket. And when the ladies expressed their approval of what I had said, it so vexed the gentlemen that they secretly swore to see me dead, even though there was not a one of them who had the courage to challenge me or to give me cause to challenge him, for which a few slaps in the face, or even a few rather offensive remarks, would have sufficed, particularly since I was cutting a rather dashing figure anyway. From this behavior the ladies assumed that I must needs be a resolute youth and candidly said that my mere good looks and laudable sentiments could speak more loudly to a maiden than all the compliments which Amor[107] had ever invented, which assertion embittered the gentlemen present even more.

CHAPTER 12

Fortuna[108] unexpectedly bestows a noble present upon the chasseur

I had two fine horses.[109] They were what I at the time enjoyed the most in the entire world. Every day I rode them to the riding school or on an excursion when I had nothing else to do—not, of course, that the horses had any need of learning anything; rather, I did it so that people might see that the beautiful creatures belonged to me. When I then went prancing along—or better, when the horse went dancing along under me, the foolish folk looked on and said to one another: "Look you, that is the chasseur! Ah, what a fine horse! Ah, what a beautiful plume in his cap!" or "Mygawd! what a fine laddie that 'un be!" Then I pricked up my ears mightily and was as flattered as if the Queen of Sheba[110] had compared me to wise Solomon sitting there in all his glory. But, fool that I was, I did not hear what sensible folk thought of me at the time, or what those who wished me ill said about me. The latter, without doubt, wished that I would break my neck, because they could not do it for me, but the others assuredly thought that if everyone got his just deserts, I would not be riding along so madly. *In summa*, the very wisest people of all, without any doubt whatsoever, must needs have considered me a young fool whose pride would soon bring him to a fall, because it was built upon a bad foundation and must needs be sustained by uncertain booty alone. And if I am to admit the truth, I must confess that these latter folk were not wrong in their judgment, though at the time I did not comprehend it, for the only thing that mattered to me was that I could have stood my ground and made it properly uncomfortable for my opponent if anyone had run afoul of me, so that I could have passed for a good common soldier, even though I was still no more than a child. But the reason I was so great was that nowadays the meanest stableboy can shoot dead the very bravest hero in the world; but had gunpowder not yet been invented, I should probably have been obliged to leave my pipe in my poke unplayed.[111]

It was my wont, when I was roaming about, to ride over all the highways and byways, through all the ditches, swamps, thickets, up all the hills, and along the banks of all bodies of water, in order to familiarize myself with them and to fix them in my memory, so that if there should perchance be in the future at one place or the other the occasion to skirmish with the enemy, I would be able to make use of the terrain of the spot both on offense and defense. To this end I was riding one time not far from the city along an old wall on which in bygone times a house had abutted. At first glance I thought this would be a good spot to lie in ambush or to retreat to, particularly for us dragoons, if we were to be outnumbered and chased by troopers of horse. I rode into the courtyard, the walls of which were rather dilapidated, to see whether one might take cover there on horseback, should the need arise, and how one might defend oneself on foot from there. Now when to this end I was about to inspect everything closely, and I attempted to ride past the cellar, the walls of which were standing all around, I could not, either with kind words or with curses, compel my horse, which otherwise never shied away from anything, to go in there. I raked its flanks with my spurs till I felt sorry for it, but to no avail! I dismounted and led it by the bridle down the caved-in cellar stairs at which it was shying back, so that I could rely upon it another time if I had need to go down them. But it pulled back with all its strength; but finally, with kind words and stroking I got it to come down, and as I was stroking it and caressing it, I discovered that it was sweating from terror, and kept its eyes directed towards one corner of the cellar, towards which it was least willing to go, and where I did not see the slightest thing at which the sorriest nag might have got upset. Now as I was standing there in this state of bewilderment and watching the horse as it trembled with fear, such a feeling of horror came over me, too, that I felt exactly as if someone were dragging me along by the hair and pouring a pailful of cold water over me, and yet I could see nothing. But the horse behaved much more strangely, so that I could imagine only that perchance I, together with the horse, must needs be under a magic spell, and that I must needs meet my end in that same cellar. I therefore desired to go back out of it, but my horse did not follow me; I therefore grew all the more frightened, and so confused that I well-nigh knew not what I was about. At last, I took a pistol in hand and tied the horse to a stout elder bush (which had grown up in the cellar), with the intent to walk out of the cellar and to seek people in the vicinity who could help my horse back up the stairs; and as I was engaged in this, it occurred to me that there might perhaps be a treasure hidden in these old walls, for which reason it might be so frightful there. I believed that my notion was true, and when I looked about more closely, and particularly in the corner towards which my horse was unwilling to go, I noticed a piece of the wall, about as large as an ordinary chamber-chest, which indeed did not look like the rest of the old wall in either color or workmanship. But when I attempted to walk towards it, I felt as I had before, namely, as if my hair were standing on end, which strengthened in me my surmise, namely, that a treasure must needs be buried there.

I should rather have exchanged fire with the enemy ten times, nay, a hundred times, than have found myself in such terror. I was tormented, and yet I knew not by whom, for I neither saw nor heard anything. I took the other pistol from my horse too and was about to flee with it and leave the horse there, but I could not walk up the stairs because, so it seemed to me, a strong draft of air was holding me hack. Then I really did feel cold chills run up and down my spine! Finally it occurred to me that I should fire my pistols so that the peasants who were working in the fields nearby would run to me and come to my assistance with word and deed. This I did, because I neither had, nor could I think of, any other means, counsel, or hope of getting out of this horrible enchanted place; also, I was so angered, or, rather, so desperate (for I no longer knew how I felt) that in firing I aimed my pistol straight at the spot where I thought the cause of this strange encounter lay, and I hit the above-mentioned piece of wall with two bullets so hard that they made a hole into which one might have stuck both fists. When the shots fell, my horse neighed and pricked up his ears, which greatly relieved me. I know not whether the monster or ghost then disappeared, or whether the poor beast was happy to hear shots fired. Anyway, I again took heart and walked quite unhindered and without any fear to the hole which I had just opened with the shots. Then I fell to breaking in the wall completely, and I found there a treasure[112] of silver, gold, and precious stones of such value that it would be doing me good to this very hour, had I but known how to preserve and invest it properly. There were, in fact, six dozen Old Franconian silver cups, a large gold goblet, some dice boxes, four silver saltcellars and one gold one, an Old Franconian gold chain, sundry diamonds, rubies, sapphires, and emeralds, set in both rings and other pieces of jewelry; *item,* a whole tray full of large pearls, but all spoiled and lackluster; and then, in a moldered leather pouch, eighty of the oldest thalers of fine silver from the Joachim Valley,[113] and 893 gold pieces with the French coat of arms and an eagle upon them, which coins no one could identify because, they said, the inscription upon them could not be read. These coins, the rings, and the jewelry I stuck into my pockets, boots, breeches, and pistol holsters, and because I had no pouch with me, since I had only gone out for a pleasure ride, I cut the cover from my saddle and packed into it (because it had a lining and could serve well as a pouch) the rest of the silver ware, hung the gold chain round my neck, cheerfully mounted my horse, and rode back towards my quarters. As I came out of the courtyard, however, I caught sight of two peasants, who attempted to run away as soon as they saw me. I easily overtook them, because I had six feet and a level field, and I asked them why they had attempted to take flight and why they were so terribly frightened. Then they told me that they had thought that I was the ghost which lived in that deserted courtyard and which was wont to use people horribly when they came too near to him. And when I asked further after its nature, they said in response that out of fear of the monster no human being had come to this spot in many years, except for strangers who lost their way and went thither by accident. The story went about that there was an iron chest full of money there which a black dog guarded, together with an enchanted maiden, and, so went the old legend, which they themselves had heard from their grandparents, a stranger who was a nobleman but who knew neither his father nor his mother would come to the country, deliver the maiden from her enchantment, open the iron chest with a fiery key, and take away the money hidden in it. They told me many other silly fables of that sort, but because they were of slight significance I shall, in the interest of sweet brevity, break off here. After that, I asked them what on earth they had been doing there, since they durst not enter the walls anyway. They answered that they had heard a shot and a loud scream, and then they had run up to see what there might be to do there. And when I told them that I had indeed fired the shots in the hope that people would come into the walls to assist me, because I was, in fact, rather frightened, but that I knew nothing about any scream, they then answered: "One could hear shots in this castle for a long time before anyone from our neighborhood would run in there, for, in truth, there is something so queer about the place that we would not believe Your Lordship when you said you had been in there, had we not with our own eyes seen you ride out of there." Then they desired to know many things of me, particularly what it was like in there, and whether I had not seen the maiden and the black dog on the iron chest, so that if I had been of a mind to cut a fine figure for them, I could have told them all manner of tall tales; but I told them nothing in the least, not even that I had discovered the precious treasure, but instead I rode on my way, to my quarters, and there examined my find, which filled my heart with joy.

CHAPTER 13

Simplicius' strange crotchets and castles in the air, and how he kept his treasure secure

Those who know the value of money and therefore hold it to be their god have no small reason for doing so, for if there is anyone in the world who has experienced its powers and well nigh divine virtues, it is I. I know how a man feels when he has a considerable amount of it, and I have experienced more than once how a man thinks when he does not have a penny to his name. Indeed, I might make so bold as to demonstrate that it has and possesses all virtues and strengths much more powerfully than any precious stones,[114] for it dispels all *melancholia,*[115] as the diamond does; like the emerald, it creates desire and love for the *studiis,* for which reason students at the university are more commonly the children of rich folk than of poor men; like the ruby, it takes away timidity and makes a man cheerful and happy; like garnets, it often hinders sleep; on the other hand, like the hyacinth, it also has great power to promote calm and sleep; like the sapphire and the amethyst, it strengthens the heart and makes a man joyous, well behaved, lively, and mild; like the sardus, it dispels bad dreams, makes one cheerful, sharpens the mind, and when someone quarrels with you, it makes you the victor, particularly when you employ it nicely to grease the judge's palm; and it quenches lewd and unchaste desires, particularly since beautiful women can be got for money. *In summa,* as I have written heretofore in my book *BLACK AND WHITE,*[116] what all money is capable of doing, if one but know how to make use of it and to invest it properly, cannot be put into words.

Insofar as my own money was concerned, both that which I had got together by stealing and that which I had got by finding this treasure, it had about it a curious quality, for, first of all, it made me more arrogant than I was before, so much so that it vexed me to the bottom of my heart that my name was just Simplicius. It hindered my sleep, like the amethyst, for many a night I lay awake speculating about how I might invest it and get even more of it. It made me a perfect master at reckoning, for I tallied up what my unminted silver and gold might be worth, added that to what I had lent out here and there and what I still had upon my person in my purse, and arrived, not counting the precious stones, at a sizable amount! It also gave me a taste of its own innate rascality and evil nature by showing me the meaning of the old saw "The more you have, the more you want!" and by making me so greedy that everyone could have become my enemy. It put really foolish schemes and curious crotchets into my head, and yet I did not pursue a single idea which I had. Sometimes the idea came to mind that I should quit the war, settle down somewhere, and peer out my window, smacking my lips. But then again I quickly rued the thought, particularly when I considered what a life of freedom I was leading and what hopes I had of becoming a great man. And then I thought: "Ha, Simplicius! Have yourself made a member of the nobility, and, if you recruit out of your own pocket your own company of dragoons for the emperor, you'll be accepted as a young gentleman, and then you'll go up in the world." But as soon as I recalled that I could fall from my lofty position as a result of a single unlucky battle, or else it would soon come to an end, along with the war, as a result of an armistice, I no longer let this scheme tempt me. Then I fell to wishing that I were completely of age: "For then," I said to myself, "you could take a beautiful, rich young wife, and then you would buy a royal manor somewhere and lead a life of peace and quiet." I planned to devote myself to raising cattle and thereby to be able to have an honest and ample income. But since I knew that I was still much too young for this, I was obliged to abandon this scheme too. I had many of these and such-like ideas, till I finally resolved to put my best things in safekeeping somewhere with a man of means, in a well-protected city, and to wait to see how Fortuna would further treat me. At the time I still had my Jupiter with me, for I could not rid myself of him again. At times he talked very subtly and for some weeks behaved quite sensibly, and he loved me beyond all measure because I had done so much good for him, and after he saw me always walking deep in thought, he said to me: "My dearest son, give away your filthy lucre, your gold, and your silver." I said: "Why, my dear Jove?" "For this reason:" he answered, "so that by so doing you make friends for yourself and rid yourself of your useless cares." I said that I would rather have even more money. Then he said: "So look you that you get more. But in this way you will find neither peace nor friends your entire life long. Leave greed to old skinflints. You, however, comport yourself as behooves a fine young fellow. You'll much sooner lack good friends than money." I pondered upon the matter and indeed found that Jupiter spoke well about the matter, but avarice had already so taken hold of me that I gave no thought at all to giving anything away, though in the end I did present my commandant with a pair of silver and gilded dice boxes, and my captain with a pair of silver saltcellars, by which actions I achieved nothing but that I made their mouths water for the rest of my things, because they were rare antique pieces. To my most loyal comrade Hopalong I gave twelve Imperial thalers; he, in return, counseled me to get rid of my riches or to be prepared to meet with misfortune because of them, for the officers looked with displeasure upon a common soldier who had more money than they did. Thus, in the past he had even seen one comrade secretly murder another on account of money. Till now, he said, I had been able to keep secret what manner of booty I had taken, for everyone believed I had spent it all again upon clothes, horses, and arms; but now I should no longer be able to hide anything from anyone, or make anyone think that I had no other money, for everyone now made the treasure I had found larger than it really was, and, anyway, I was no longer, as in the past, spending money entertaining others. Often, he said, he could not but hear what the lads were muttering to one another. Were he in my place, he would leave the war to its own devices, settle down somewhere safe, and leave the rule of the world to God. I answered: "Listen, Hopalong, how can I toss away so lightly the hopes I have for a command of my own?" "O yes!" said he. "May the you-know-who take me if you ever receive a command! The others who are hoping for it would sooner help break your neck a thousand times when they see that one is available than see you receive it. Don't tell me about the ways of sharks; my father was a fisherman. Take my word for it, Simplicius, for I have seen how things go in wartime longer than you have. Do you not see how many sergeants grow grey carrying a musket and yet merit command of a company more than many others who got one? Do you think they are not also fellows who have a right to hope for something? Moreover, by rights they are more deserving than you of such promotion, as you yourself recognize." I could not but remain silent, because Hopalong was so loyally telling me the truth from the bottom of his honest, upright heart, and he was not dissembling. However, I secretly clenched my teeth, for at the time I had great things in mind.

Still, I weighed very carefully these remarks and those my Jupiter had made, and realized that I did not have a single friend in the world who would stand by me in time of need, or who would avenge my death, should it happen either secretly or openly. Also, I could easily imagine how things really stood. But nevertheless, neither my ambition nor my avarice, much less my hopes of becoming a great man, let me quit the war and find a life of peace and quiet. Instead, I persisted in my first intent, and when an opportunity happened to present itself for me to go to Cologne[117] (when I, together with a hundred dragoons, was obliged to help convoy some merchants and wagons from Münster[118] thither), I packed up the treasure I had found, took it with me, and gave it in deposit to one of the most prominent merchants there, against the issuance of a specified certificate. That was forty-seven marks of unminted fine silver, fifteen marks of gold, eighty Joachim thalers and, in a sealed chest, sundry rings and pieces of jewelry which, with gold and precious stones, weighed eight and one half German pounds in all, together with 893 antique minted gold pieces, each of which was one and a half gold guilders in weight. My Jupiter I also took along, because he desired it and had wealthy kinfolk in Cologne. To them he praised the good deeds which had been done him by me and caused them to show me much honor. Me, however, he kept on counseling that I should invest my money better and buy myself friends with it who would be of more use to me than gold locked in a chest.

CHAPTER 14

How the chasseur is taken prisoner by the other side

On the way back I had all manner of thoughts about how I was going to comport myself in the future so that I might indeed incur everyone's favor, for Hopalong had put a flea into my ear and had persuaded me to believe that everyone envied me, which, in truth, was indeed the actual case. And so I also remembered what the famous sibyl of Soest had told me before, and I therefore burdened myself with even greater cares. With these thoughts I sharpened my wits excellently and became aware that a man who lives carefree from one day to the next is almost like a beast of the field. I excogitated the reasons why one person or the other might hate me and weighed how I might again incur his favor, and I was, at the same time, most greatly surprised that these fellows should be so false and should say nothing but sweet things to me when they did not love me! I therefore decided to behave the way the others did and to say whatever pleased each one of them, and to meet each one with deference, even though it was not heartfelt. Primarily, however, I clearly perceived that my own arrogance had burdened me with the most enemies. I therefore deemed it necessary to behave with modesty once more, even though I was not that way at all, and to lie once more with the common herd, below and above, and to meet the higher-ups with hat in hand, and to decrease somewhat the splendor of my attire till my rank perhaps changed. I had had the merchant in Cologne give me a hundred sovereigns, to be returned with interest when he handed my treasure back over to me; this money I resolved to spend on the way back entertaining the convoy, because I now recognized that avarice makes no friends. In such manner was I resolved to change my ways and to make a beginning of it upon this very journey. But I reckoned without my host. For as we were about to pass through the land of Berg,[119] eighty fire-lock and fifty horse ambushed us at a very advantageous spot, just as I and four others and a corporal were sent to ride on ahead and scout the road. The enemy kept silent when we came into their trap and let us pass, so that when they attacked us the convoy would not be warned till it too had come into their vise. But they sent a cornet with eight horse after us and they kept us in sight till their soldiers had attacked our convoy itself and we turned back to return to the wagons. Then they rode up to us and asked if we desired quarter. I, for my part, was well mounted, for I had my best horse under me, and I did not desire to take flight anyway; so I wheeled around upon a small, level spot to see whether honor might not be garnered there. Meanwhile, from the salvo which our troops received I heard right off for whom the bell was tolling and therefore endeavored to take flight, but the cornet had already thought everything out and had already cut us off at the pass, and when I was about to hew my way through, he again, because he took me to be an officer, offered me quarter. I thought to myself that to get away with one's life is better than to take an uncertain risk, and therefore I asked whether he would keep his promise of quarter like an honest soldier. He answered: "Yes, assuredly!" So I presented my sword to him, thereby giving myself up as a captive. He straightway asked me who I was, for, he said, he saw me to be a nobleman and an officer also. But when I answered that I was the chasseur of Soest he answered: "Well, you're in luck that you did not fall into our hands four weeks ago, for at that time I should not have been permitted to offer you quarter or to keep my promise of quarter, because then they took you to be a proven sorcerer."

This cornet was a valiant young cavalier, and not over two years older than I. He was exceeding happy that he had the honor of capturing the famous chasseur; therefore he kept his promise of quarter in an honorable way and in the manner of the Dutch, whose wont it is to take from their captured Spanish foes nothing which their belt encircles. Indeed, he did not even have my person searched. I myself, however, was so kind as to take the money from my pouches and turn it over to them when they fell to dividing up the booty, and I told the cornet in private that he should see to it that my horse, saddle, and tack fell to him, for in the saddle he would find thirty ducats, and besides, the horse scarce had its equal anywhere. For these reasons the cornet was as kind to me as if I were his own brother, and he mounted my horse and let me ride his. From the convoy, however, no more than six had died, and thirteen were taken prisoner, of whom eight were wounded; the rest escaped and had not the courage to take the booty away from the enemy in the open field, which they could easily have done, because they were all on horseback.

That very evening, after the booty and the prisoners had been divided up, the Swedes and the Hessians (for they were from different garrisons) separated. Me, the corporal, and three more dragoons the cornet kept, because he had taken us prisoner. Therefore we were taken to a fortress which was not even two full German miles[120] from our garrison. And because I had performed all manner of exploits before at that same town, my name was well known there, and I myself was more feared than loved. When we had the city in sight the cornet sent a trooper on ahead to announce his arrival to the commandant and also to report how things had gone and who the prisoners were. At that, there was a running hither and thither in the city such as cannot be described, because everyone desired to see the chasseur. One person told one tale about me, the other another one, and it really looked as if a great potentate were making his entry into the city.

We prisoners were taken directly to the commandant, who was very surprised at my tender years. He asked me whether I had ever served on the Swedish side and from what region I came. Now when I told him the truth, he desired to know whether I did not wish to remain on their side again. I answered him that it would be all the same to me but for the fact that, because I had sworn an oath to fight for the Holy Roman Emperor, it seemed to me that it behooved me to keep it. Then he charged that we be taken to the provost marshal, but he did let the cornet, at his request, have us as guests at his table, because this was how I had used my prisoners heretofore (among whom had been the cornet's brother). Now when evening came, divers officers, both soldiers of fortune and gentlemen by birth, came to the quarters of the cornet, who had me and the corporal fetched too. There, to tell the truth, I was used exceeding courteously by them. I made as merry as if I had not lost a thing and conversed as amicably and openly as if I were not with enemies who had captured me, but with my very best friends. Thereby I maintained discretion as best I could, for I could easily imagine that the commandant would be apprised of my behavior, which did indeed happen, as I later found out.

The next day we prisoners were taken before the regimental magistrate, who interrogated us; the corporal was the first to be questioned, and I the second. As soon as I entered the hall he too expressed surprise at my tender years and told me to step closer: "My child, what has the Swede done to cause you to make war upon him?" This vexed me, particularly since I had seen amongst their troops soldiers as young as I was, and therefore I answered: "Swedish soldiers took away my marbles and aggies. I was of a mind to take them back." Now when I had repaid him in this manner the officers sitting with him were embarrassed, for which reason one of them began to say in Latin that he should speak to me of serious matters, for he surely heard that he had no child before him! I remarked thereby that his name was Eusebius, because this officer called him by that name. Then he asked me my name, and when I told it to him, he said: "There's not a devil in hell named Simplicissimus!" Then I answered: "And there isn't one named Eusebius there either!" So I repaid him as I had our company clerk, Cyriacus, which was not very well received by the officers, for which reason they told me that I should remember that I was their prisoner and had not been brought there to make jests. I was not embarrassed by this reprimand, nor did I beg for pardon; instead I answered that because they had taken me prisoner as they would a soldier, and had not let me go free again as they would a child, I had taken care that they not question me like a child either. I had answered, I said, as their questions deserved to be answered, and I hoped that I had not erred in doing so. Then they asked me about my nationality, origin, and birth, and particularly whether I had ever served on the Swedish side before; *item,* how things were in Soest, how large the garrison was, and more of the like, etc. I answered every question quickly, succinctly, and well, and indeed, as concerned Soest and the garrison there, as much as I deemed I might answer for, but I was able to keep silent about the fact that I had played the role of a fool there, because I was ashamed of that.

CHAPTER 15

Under what conditionibus[121] the chasseur was released once more

Meanwhile they learned at Soest what had happened to the convoy and that I, along with the corporal and some others, had been taken prisoner, and also whither we had been taken. Therefore, the very next day a drummer was sent to fetch us. The corporal and the three others were turned over to him, together with a letter which read as follows and which the commandant sent me to read:

Monsieur, etc.

From the bearer, this tambour, your letter was handed over to me, and in response I herewith send back to you, in return for the ransom received, the corporal and the three other prisoners. Insofar as concerns Simplicius, the chasseur: this person, because he has heretofore served on our side, cannot be permitted to return to you. If, however, I may be of service to Your Lordship in any way save as regards Simplicius' obligation to serve on our side, you will find in me your obedient servant, who is and remains

Your Lordship's most obedient

N. de S. A.[122]

This letter did not please me in the least, and yet I was obliged to express my gratitude for this communication. I requested to speak with the commandant but received the answer that he would be sending for me himself as soon as he had first dispatched the drummer, which was to be tomorrow morning. Till then I should be patient.

Now when I had waited the interval stipulated, the commandant sent for me, just at mealtime. Then, for the first time, I had the honor of dining with him at his table. As long as we were eating he had me drink up and gave me neither subtle nor blunt hints of what he had in mind to do with me, and it did not behoove me, either, to broach the matter. But after we had eaten our fill and I had grown rather tipsy, he said: "My dear chasseur, you have learned from my letter upon what pretext I am holding you here. And in fact, I do not have in mind anything illegal or contrary to common sense and military etiquette, for you yourself confessed to me and the regimental magistrate that you had once served in our main army. Therefore you must needs resolve to enter service in my regiment. And in time, and if you acquit yourself well, I shall accommodate you in such wise as you would never dare hope for in the Imperial forces. If you will not, then you will not take it amiss if I send you back to the lieutenant colonel from whom the dragoons captured you before." I answered: "Most honored colonel (for at that time it was not customary to address soldiers of fortune[123] by the title "Your Grace," even though they were colonels), because I never obligated myself by an oath of allegiance to the Crown of Sweden, nor to its confederation, much less to the lieutenant colonel, but was, rather, merely a stableboy, I trust that for that reason I am not bound to accept Swedish service and in so doing to break the oath which I swore to the Holy Roman Emperor, for which reason I most obediently request you, my most honored colonel, to be so kind as to refrain from making this demand of me." "What?" said the colonel. "Do you despise Swedish military service? You must know that you are my prisoner, and before I let you return to Soest to serve the other side, I shall put you on trial again and leave you to rot in prison. I know how such matters are done!" I did indeed take fright at these words, but I did not yet give up because of them but instead answered that God would protect me, both from such contemptuous usage and from perjuring myself. Otherwise, I said, I remained respectfully hopeful that the colonel, in keeping with the discretion for which he was renowned far and wide, would use me like a soldier. "Indeed!" said he. "I know quite well how I could use you if I were to proceed with severity, but give my offer better consideration, so that I shall have no cause to use you differently." Then I was taken back to the jail.

One can imagine without difficulty that I did not sleep much that night, but instead had all manner of thoughts teeming in my head. In the morning, however, some officers and the cornet who had taken me prisoner came to visit me under the pretext of helping me while away the time, but in truth to make me believe that the colonel was of a mind to have me tried as a sorcerer if I would not change my mind. In this wise they meant to frighten me and to see what my situation really was. But because I had the consolation of a clear conscience, I accepted all they said with great equanimity and did not talk much, but I did see that the colonel was interested in nothing except that he did not desire to see me in Soest, and he could also easily imagine that if he released me I would probably not leave that town, because I hoped for promotion there and still had two fine horses and other valuables there. The following day he had me brought to him again and asked me whether I had reached a decision one way or the other. I answered: "This is my decision, colonel: that I shall die before I break my word. If, however, you, my most honored colonel, will set me free and will be so kind as not to burden me with any military duties, I shall promise you, upon my word of honor, that for six months I shall neither bear nor employ arms against the Swedes and the Hessians." To this the colonel was immediately agreed, offering me his hand on the bargain and at the same time forgiving me my ransom: and he also commanded his *secretario*[124] to set forth, for that purpose, an agreement *in duplo*[125] for us both to sign in which he promised me safety, security, and complete freedom as long as I remained in the fortress entrusted to his care. I, on the other hand, agreed to the limitations in the two points mentioned above, namely, that for as long as I remained in that fortress I would undertake no action detrimental to that same garrison and its commandant, nor would I conceal anything which might be undertaken to its disadvantage and harm, but, rather, I would act to its benefit and profit and prevent harm to it wherever possible. Indeed, if the town were attacked by the enemy I should and would assist in its defense.

Then he kept me with him again for the noonday meal and did me more honor than I had ever dared hope to receive from the Imperials. In this way he little by little so won me over that I should not have gone back to Soest even if he had let me and had absolved me of my promise to him.

CHAPTER 16

How Simplicius became a gentleman

If a thing is meant to be, then all things conspire to bring it about. I thought that Fortuna[126] had taken me as her bridegroom, or had at least so closely allied herself with me that even the worst possible events must needs turn out for the best for me, since while I was sitting at the commandant's table I heard that my manservant had come from Soest with my two fine horses to join me. I did not know, however (as I later found out when the tables were turned), that fickle Fortuna has the character of the sirens, who wish the most ill to those to whom they show themselves the most partial, and that she lifts a man up all the higher so that he will afterwards fall all the further.

This manservant (whom I had captured before from the Swedes) was loyal to me beyond all measure, because I had done him many kindnesses. Therefore he saddled my horses every day and, as long as he was out, rode a good piece of the way out from Soest to meet the drummer who was supposed to fetch me, so that I should not be obliged to walk so far alone, or come to Soest naked or in rags (for he thought that they had stripped me of my clothes). And so he met the drummer and his prisoners, and he had packed up my best clothes. But when he did not see me, but learned instead that I was being importuned by the other side to enter into their service, he put his spurs to his horse, saying: "Adieu, drummer and corporal! Wherever my master is, there will I be too!" And so he escaped and came to me just when the commandant had pronounced me free and was doing me great honor. He, the commandant, then stabled my horses at an inn till I myself might find lodgings which suited me, and he praised me as fortunate because of my manservant's loyalty and was surprised that a common dragoon, and such a young fellow to boot, should have at his disposal such fine horses and should be so well equipped; and he so highly praised the one horse when I said *valet*[127] and went to the aforementioned inn that I saw straightway that he would have liked to buy it from me, but because he, for reasons of discretion, did not make me an offer for it, I said that if I durst desire the honor that he be so kind as to keep it on my account, then it was at his service. But he outright refused to accept it, more because I had grown rather tipsy and he did not desire to have people saying behind his back that he had talked a drunken man out of something which he might perchance regret when he was sober, than because he was content to do without that splendid horse.

That same night I pondered how I ought to arrange my life in the future. I then resolved to remain for six months where I was and thus to spend in peace and quiet the winter, which was now at hand, for which, then, I knew that I had enough money, even if I did not touch my treasure in Cologne. "During this time," I thought to myself, "you will finish growing up and achieve your full strength, and afterwards, the following spring, you can betake yourself all the more boldly into the field with the Imperials."

Early the next morning I dissected my saddle, which was far better stuffed than the one which the cornet had received from me. After that I had my best horse brought to the door of the colonel's quarters, and I told him that inasmuch as I had resolved to spend the six months during which I was not permitted to fight in the war in peace and quiet here under the colonel's protection, my horses were of no use to me, and it would be a shame if they were to go to wrack and ruin, for which reason I begged him to be so kind as to grant this soldier's nag a place amongst his horses, and to accept it from me as a token of my grateful acknowledgement of favors received of him. The colonel expressed his thanks with great courtliness and very courteous words, and that afternoon he sent me his steward with a fattened live ox, two fat swine, a hogshead of wine, four hogsheads of beer, and twelve cords of firewood, all of which he had them bring to me for my new lodgings, which I had rented for half a year; and he sent word that because he saw that I was of a mind to set up housekeeping in his city, and he could easily imagine that in the beginning I would not be well provided with victuals, he was sending me as a contribution to my household something to drink and a piece of meat, together with the wood with which to make the fire to cook it, adding that if there were any other way in which he might be of assistance to me, he would not hesitate to do so. I expressed my gratitude as courteously as I could, made the steward a present of two ducats, and asked him to commend me as best he could to his master.

When I saw how highly honored I was by the colonel because of my generosity, I resolved to earn the fine praise of the common herd too, so that they might not hold me to be a miserable sluggard. Therefore, in the presence of my landlord I had my manservant appear before me. To him I said: "My dear Nicholas, you have shown me more loyalty than a master dare expect from his servant, but since I am now unable to pay my debt to you, because I have, for the time being, no master and thus no war to fight either, in which to take anything with which to reward you as it behooves me to do, and particularly since, because of the life of peace and quiet which I intend to lead henceforth, I am not planning to keep a manservant any longer, I am hereby giving to you, as your reward, the other horse, together with the saddle, tack, and pistols, with the request that you be satisfied with them and for the time being seek yourself another master. If I can be of any service to you in the future, you may request it of me any time." Then he kissed my hand and well nigh could not speak for crying, and he was not at all willing to take the horse, but instead thought it better that I should turn it into silver and use the money to support myself. Finally I did persuade him to take it, after I had promised to take him back into my service as soon as I had need of anyone. At the sight of this leave-taking my landlord was so moved that his eyes too filled with tears, and just as my manservant praised me amongst the *soldateska*,[128] so too my landlord, because of my actions, singled me out for great praise amongst the townsfolk, calling me a man unlike any other. The commandant held me to be such a resolute fellow that he was willing to take my word as gospel, because I, in order to loyally keep all the more strictly not only the oath of allegiance I had sworn to the Emperor but also what I had agreed to with him in writing, had divested myself of my fine horses, my weapons, and my loyal manservant.

CHAPTER 17

Wherewith the chasseur thought to pass the six months, and also something concerning the sibyl of Soest

I believe that there is not a person in the world who is not at heart a bit of a fool, for we are all cut from the same cloth, and by watching my own pears I can tell when my neighbor's are ripe. "O, you coxcomb!" someone might answer. "Do you think that just because you are a fool, others are fools too?" No, don't say that, for that would be an exaggeration. But I do contend that some people conceal the fool within them better than others do. A person is not a fool merely because he has foolish notions, for in our tender years we all generally have them; but a person who gives voice to them is held to be a fool, because some do not let the fool within them be seen at all, and others let him be seen only halfway. Those who suppress the fool within themselves completely are true killjoys; but those who, when the right opportunity presents itself, let the fool within them poke his ears out a bit and catch his breath so that he not be stifled to death within them, these people I hold to be the best and most sensible. But I let the fool within me go too far. When I saw myself in such a state of personal freedom and knew that I still had money, I took on a boy whom I dressed like a nobleman's page, indeed, in the most foolish colors, namely, violet-brown and yellow, which was obliged to serve as my livery, because I liked it that way. He was obliged to wait upon me as if I were a, nobleman, not the dragoon I was shortly before, or the stableboy I had been a half a year before.

This was the first folly I committed in that city, which folly, though it was a rather large one, no one noticed, much less censured. But what difference does that make? The world is so full of that folly that no one pays any heed to it anymore, or derides it, or is surprised by it, because they have grown accustomed to it. And then too, I had the reputation of a clever and good soldier, not of a fool not yet dry behind the ears. I contracted with my landlord for meals for me and my page, and gave him in payment-on-account the meat and wood which the commandant had given me on account of my horse, but I insisted that my page have a key to the spirits cabinet, because I liked to give something to drink to those who called upon me, for since I was neither a soldier nor a townsman, and thus had no one of my own kind to keep me company, I consorted with both groups and therefore had comrades enough whom I did not let call upon me without being served something to drink. Of the townsfolk the organist become my closest friend there, because I loved music and (to be honest about it, and not to boast) I had an excellent fine voice which I desired not to let grow moldy. This man taught me how to compose music, *item*, how to play that instrument better and also the harp; and I was a master on the lute anyway, and therefore procured a harp of my own and well nigh daily amused myself with it. Then, when I was tired of making music, I called to me the furrier who had instructed me in Paradise in the use of weapons; with him I practiced in order to become even more proficient in the use of arms. I also received permission from the commandant to let one of his cannoneers teach me, for a price, the gunsmith's trade and something about how to handle fireworks. Otherwise I lived very quietly and withdrawn, so that people were surprised when they saw me sitting over my books like a university student, since I, after all, had been accustomed to rapine and bloodshed.

My landlord was the commandant's bloodhound and my watchdog, and I perceived that he reported to him everything I did and omitted to do, but I was able to adapt myself nicely to this, for I never gave a single thought to things military, and when people talked about them, I acted as if I had never been a soldier and was but there to attend to the daily exercises which I just mentioned. I wished, to be sure, that my six months were over, but from what I said no one could tell which side I was then going to serve. Every time I waited upon the colonel he kept me to dine with him. Then, every time, there would begin a discourse which was meant to elicit from me my plans, but every time I answered so cautiously that they could not determine of what mind I was. One time he said to me: "How do things stand with you, chasseur? Are you still willing to be Swedish? One of my ensigns died yesterday." I answered: "My most highly honored colonel, if it behooves a woman that she does not marry again right after her husband's death, then why should I not be patient for six months?" In this wise I escaped every time and with each passing day rose in the colonel's esteem, so much so that he granted me the privilege of taking walks both inside and outside the fortress. Indeed, in the end I was permitted to stalk hares, partridges, and birds, which his own soldiers were not permitted to do. And also I fished in the Lippa River[129] and was so lucky at it that it had the appearance as if I could conjure both fish and crayfish out of the water. For that reason I had a simple hunter's suit made for myself; dressed in it I roamed by night into the fertile plain of Soest (for I knew all the highways and byways there) and on one occasion and the other gathered together my hidden treasure, dragged it to the aforementioned fortress, and gave the impression that I was going to stay with the Swedes forever.

By the same way the sibyl of Soest came to me and said: "Look you, my son, did I not counsel you well before when I told you to keep your money outside the city of Soest? I assure you that your greatest good fortune was that you were taken prisoner, for had you come back home, some fellows who had sworn to kill you, because the ladies preferred you to them, were going to strangle you to death when you were hunting." I answered: "How can anyone be jealous of me when I paid no attention to the ladies?" "Assuredly," said she, "if you stay of the same mind as you are now, the ladies will make you an object of scorn and disgrace and chase you out of the country. You have always derided me when I prophesied something about you. Would you again refuse to believe me, were I to tell you more? Do you not find in the town where you now are people more partial to you than those in Soest? I swear to you that they love you all too much and that this excessive love will redound to your harm if you do not accommodate yourself to it." I answered that if she really knew as much as she claimed to know, then she would tell me instead how things stood with my parents and whether I should ever in all my days be reunited with them, and, I said, she should not speak in riddles but tell me bluntly. Then she said that I should ask after my parents when I unexpectedly met my foster-father leading my wet nurse's daughter along by a rope. Then she broke out into loud peals of laughter and added that she, of her own accord, had told me more than she did others who implored her to do so. After that, just because I fell to making fun of her, she quickly left me, after I had first made her a present of a few thalers, because I was finding silver money heavy to carry. At the time I had a goodly sum of money and many precious rings and pieces of jewelry collected together, for in the past, whenever I had known some precious stones to be in the possession of soldiers, or had came upon them on raiding parties and elsewhere, I had acquired them, and for less than half what they were worth too. These precious stones kept screaming at me that they would like to go back into polite society, and I was all too glad to acquiesce; and, because I was rather puffed up with pride, I made a show of my possessions and without hesitation let my landlord see them, and in talking with others he made more of them than they were. They, however, wondered where I had taken all these things from, for it had been sufficiently bruited about that I had deposited in Cologne the treasure which I had found, because the cornet had read the merchant's receipt when he took me prisoner.

CHAPTER 18

How the chasseur turns wooer and makes a trade of wooing

My resolve to learn completely the gunsmith's trade and the art of fencing during these six months was a good one, and I knew that it was. But it was not enough to stave off idleness, which is the root of much evil, primarily because there was no one to command me to keep busy. To be sure, I pored over all manner of books and learned many good things from them, but some which fell into my hands did me about as much good as grass does a dog. The incomparable *ARCADIA*,[130] from which I desired to learn eloquence, was the first work which drew me away from genuine histories to love stories and away from true stories to romances full of derring-do. Works of these sorts I procured wherever I could, and when I got hold of one of them, I did not stop till I had read it through to the end, even if I was obliged to pore over it day and night. These taught me not eloquence but the art of whispering sweet nothings into women's ears. But at that time this weakness in me was not so violent and pronounced that one could have called it, in the words of Seneca, a divine rage or, as it is termed in Thomas Thomäus' *WORLD GARDEN*,[131] a troublesome ailment, for wherever my love was directed, I achieved easily and effortlessly what I desired, so that I had no cause to complain, as other swains and wooers do,[132] who are full of fanciful notions, tribulations, desires, secret sorrows, anger, jealousy, lust for vengeance, rage, tears, bombast, threats, and a thousand such-like follies and are so short of patience that they wish they were dead. I had money and was not afraid to spend it, and a good voice in the bargain, and I was always practicing on all manner of musical instruments. Instead of dancing, to which I was never partial, in order to display my fine figure I showed it off when I engaged in swordplay with the furrier. In addition, I had a fine smooth face and through practice became cordial and amiable, so that on their own accord women, even though I took no particular interest in them, chased after me more than I desired, as Aurora did[133] after Clitus, Cephalus, and Tithonus;[134] as Venus did after Anchises, Atidus, and Adonis;[135] as Ceres did after Glaucus, Ulysses, and Jason;[136] and as even chaste Diana did after her beloved Endymion.[137]

At this very time Martinmas came round, and then we Germans fall to glutting ourselves with food and drink, and this lasts with some folks till Shrovetide.[138] Then I was invited to sundry places, to the homes of both townsmen and members of the garrison, to help devour Martinmas goose. At such times then some things fell to happening, because on such occasions I made the acquaintance of some women. My lute-playing and my singing compelled each of them to look upon me, and when they were thus observing me, I was able to perform my new love songs, which I wrote myself, with such charming looks and gestures that many a pretty maid lost her head and before she knew it became enamored of me. And so that I might not be thought a skinflint, I, too, held two parties, one for the officers and the other for the most distinguished townfolk, by means of which I acquired the good graces of both groups and obtained access to both, because I had expensive delicacies served them. And the object of all this for me was the dear ladies, and even though I did not find in one of them or the other what I was seeking (for there were indeed still some who could refuse it to me), I nevertheless paid visits to them as to the others, so that they would not bring into ill repute those who showed me more favor than befits a modest maiden, but would instead believe that I tarried with them solely for the sake of their conversation. And of this I persuaded each one individually, so that she believed it of the others and could not but believe that she was the only one who was enjoying my person.

I had an even half-dozen of them who loved me, and I them in return, but not one of them possessed my heart completely or me alone. In one of them, only her dark eyes pleased me; in another her golden hair; in a third her lovely grace; and in the others something else of that sort, which the others did not have. And when I paid a visit to someone other than them, it was only either for the above-stated reason or because it was strange and novel and because I did not scorn or reject any woman anyway, since I did not intend to stay in this town forever. My page, who was a rogue of the first order, had his hands full arranging rendezvous and carrying love letters back and forth, and he knew how to hold his tongue and to keep secret my lewd doings with the one maiden or the other, so that no one found out about them. For that he received from these sluts a heap of favors which, however, were most costly for me, as a consequence of which I tossed away a considerable sum this way and could well say "If you are going to dance, you must pay the piper." In so doing I kept my affairs so secret that not one person in a hundred would have taken me to be a libertine, except for the parson, from whom I was not borrowing as many religious books as before.

CHAPTER 19

By what means the chasseur made friends, and what devoutness he displayed during a sermon

im whom Fortuna desires to plunge into the depths she first raises up to the heights, even though the good Lord warn each and every man of his fall. I had my warning too, but I paid no heed to it! I was persuaded in my mind that my position at the time was built on such a firm foundation that no ill fortune could cast me down from it, because everyone, particularly the commandant, wished me so well. Those whom he held in high esteem I won over by all manner of deferential actions. His loyal servants I brought over to my side with presents; and with those who were somewhat above my station I drank brotherhood and pledged to them my undying loyalty and friendship. The common townfolk and soldiers were partial to me because I was amiable to everyone. "Ah, what a friendly man the chasseur is!" they often said to one another." He passes the time of day with every child on the street and never has a harsh word for anyone." When I caught a young hare or some partridges, I sent them to the kitchens of those whose friendship I sought, thereby inviting myself to dine with them, and I had a drop of wine fetched, which was costly in that term. Indeed, I arranged it so that I bore well nigh all the expenses. When, at such feasts, I fell into a conversation with someone, I praised everyone but myself and was able to behave as modestly as if I had never known arrogance. Now because I thus curried favor with everyone and everyone held me in high esteem, I did not think that any misfortune could befall me, particularly since my money pouch was still rather well stuffed.

I often went to visit the oldest parson of that city, which gentleman loaned me books from his library; and when I brought one back to him, he discussed all manner of things with me, for we got along so well with one another that each of us was genuinely fond of the other. Now when not only the Martinmas goose and the hog-slaughter soup[139] had come and gone, but also the feast days of Christmas were over, I gave him as a New Year's present a bottle of Strasbourg brandy, which he liked to sip in the Westphalian manner, with sugar candy in it, and after that I went to visit him, arriving just as he was reading my *JOSEPH*,[140] which my landlord had lent him without my knowledge. I grew pale when I saw that my work had fallen into the hands of such a learned man, particularly since it is claimed that in a man's writings he is best seen for what he really is. He, however, bade me sit down with him and in fact praised my invention, but he faulted me for devoting so much time to the love affairs of Suleika (who was Potiphar's wife):[141] "What really interests you is what you feel bound to talk about." And he added: "If you did not know what goes on in the heart of a person in love, you would not have been able to depict and present to our eyes this woman's passion so well." I answered that what I had written was not my own invention, but, rather, I had extracted it from other books in order to practice writing a little. "Yes, yes!" he answered. "I'm happy to believe that *(scil.),*[142] but rest assured that I know more about you than you imagine." I was frightened when I heard these words and thought to myself: "Did Old Nick tell you that?" And because he saw that I changed color he went on, saying: "You are young and healthy, you are handsome, and you have time on your hands. You live without a care in the world and, so I hear, with more than enough of everything. Therefore I beseech and implore you, in the name of the Lord, to consider what a dangerous situation you are in. Beware of the beast which braids its hair if you desire to keep an eye to your happiness and salvation. You may, of course think: 'Of what concern is it to this parson what I do or omit to do?' ('you have guessed correctly,' I thought to myself) or 'What right has he to tell me what to do?' It is true, I am a spiritual counselor by profession! But be assured that as concerns you, my benefactor, your welfare in this world is, because of the Christian love I bear you, as important to me as if you were my own son. It is always a shame, and you can never in all eternity answer for it to your Heavenly Father, if you bury the talent which God has given you, and let your noble *ingenium,*[143] which I recognize in this book here, go to wrack and ruin. My loyal and paternal counsel would be that you devote your youth and your means, which you are wasting here so uselessly, to studying, so that now or some day you can be of service both to God and to mankind and yourself; that you leave off soldiering, for which, I hear, you have such a great hankering; and that you remain as you are now, before you suffer reverses and learn from your own fate the truth of the old saying 'If you go a-soldiering when you're young, you'll go begging when you're old.' "[144] I listened to these *sententiae*[145] with great impatience, because I was not accustomed to hearing these sorts of things. However, I behaved quite differently than I felt in my heart so that I might not lose the reputation that I was a fine man. I even expressed my gratitude to him for the true interest which he had taken in me, and I promised to consider his advice; but to myself I thought what the goldsmith's boy in the story[146] said—"Kiss me arse!"; and "What business of the parson's is it how I arrange my life?"; because at the time I had reached my zenith and was unwilling to any longer do without the delights of love I had tasted. That is simply the way it is with such warnings when youth has already grown accustomed to bridle and spur and is rushing full tilt to its perdition.

CHAPTER 20

How he gave the parson other grist for his mill, so that he would forget to correct his Epicurean life

was not yet, however, so mired in these delights, or so stupid, that I did not keep in mind to retain everyone's friendship for as long as I was still willing to remain in the fortress (namely, till winter was over). And I also clearly recognized what trouble a person can be in if he has acquired the enmity of the clergy, which has great credit with all folks, no matter what the religion may be. Therefore I took the bull by the horns and the very next day went prancing in to see the parson, and in erudite words I told him such a pack of lies about how I had resolved to follow his counsel that he was delighted to the bottom of his heart, as I could see by his reactions to them. "Yes," said I, "for some time now, even when I was still in Soest, I have been in need of nothing so much as an angelic counselor such as I have encountered in you, most honored sir. If only the winter were soon over, or else the weather were pleasant, so that I might depart!" At the same time I begged him to assist me further with good counsel about which *academiam*[147] I should betake myself to. He answered that as far as he personally was concerned, he had studied at Leyden,[148] but he would counsel me to go to Geneva because I, to judge by my accent, was a South German. "Jesus, Mary, Mother of God!" I answered. "Geneva is further from my homeland than Leyden is!" "What do I hear?" he then said with great consternation. "I hear quite well, sir, that you are a papist! O, my Lord! How I find myself deceived!" "How so? How so, parson?" said I. "Must I needs be a papist because I do not wish to go to Geneva, the seat of Calvinism?" "O no," said he, "rather, because I hear you invoking the Virgin Mary as Catholics do." I said: "Is it improper for a Christian to utter the name of the mother of our Saviour?" "That is all right," said he, "but I beg and implore you, as urgently as I can, to give all honor to God and to confess to me which church you belong to, for I very much doubt that you are of the Evangelical faith (though I see you in my church every Sunday), because you did not come to our just-past feast of the birth of Christ, or to the Lutherans' table of the Lord either." I answered: "Parson, you can hear that I am a Christian, and if I were not one, I should not have attended church so often. But for the rest, I admit that I am an adherent of neither Peter nor Paul;[149] instead, I believe *simpliciter*[150] what is contained in the twelve articles of faith[151] of the universal holy Christian faith, nor shall I bind myself completely to one confession till the one or the other of them persuade me by sufficient proofs to believe that it, instead of the others, is the one genuine true religion which alone can bring salvation." "Now," said he, "I really believe that you do have a valiant soldier's courage to boldly risk your life, since you live from one day to the next, without a care in the world, almost without regard for religion and worship, and with no thought of tomorrow, and so blasphemously hurl your salvation into the breach! Good Lord, how can a mortal man, who must needs be either damned or delivered, ever be so audacious? Were you brought up in Hanau and not instructed any differently in Christianity? Tell me why you did not follow in the footsteps of your parents and espouse the pure Christian religion? And why are you just as willing to follow another one as to follow this pure Christian one, whose *fundamenta*[152] are laid out as clear as day, both in *natura* and in Holy Writ, so much so that neither papist nor Lutheran will ever in all eternity be able to overturn them?" I answered: "Parson, everyone says that about his own religion, but whom am I to believe? Do you, sir, think it is a matter of little consequence that I entrust the salvation of my soul to one confession, which reviles the other two and accuses them of propagating false doctrine? Just look (but with my impartial eyes) at what Conrad Vetter and Johannes Nass have spread abroad, in published writings, against Luther;[153] and Luther and his followers, on the other hand, against the pope; and, in particular, Spangenberg[154] against St. Francis,[155] who was held for several hundred years to be a saintly and divine man. Which party should I join, seeing that each is proclaiming that there is not a decent bone in the other's body? Do you think, sir, that I do wrong if I wait till my mind is more fully developed and till I know how to tell black from white? Ought anyone really counsel me to jump in blindly, like a fly into a bowl of hot porridge? O no! Certainly, parson, you cannot, I hope, do that with a clear conscience. One religion, inevitably, must be right, and the other two wrong. Now if I were to commit myself to one of them without most careful reflection, I might just as easily seize the wrong one as the right one, which I would repent afterwards through all eternity. I would rather stay off the road completely than take one which will but lead me astray. Besides, there are yet more religions than just those in Europe, such as the Armenian, the Abyssinian, the Greek, the Georgian,[156] and the like; and no matter which one I might choose, I, with all my fellow-believers, must needs declare all the other ones to be wrong. Now sir, if you are willing to be my Ananias,[157] then I shall follow you with great gratitude and accept the religion which you profess."

Then he said: "Sir, you are much in error, but I hope that God will enlighten you and lift you from the muck and mire, to which end I shall henceforth, from Holy Writ, so authenticate our confession that it shall prevail, even against the portals of hell!" I answered that I would look forward to that with great longing, but to myself I thought: "If you will but reproach me no more about my lady-loves, I shall be well content with your faith." From this the reader can deduce what manner of godless youth I was at that time, for I caused the good pastor to labor in vain, so that he would leave me alone to pursue my lewd life unhindered, and I thought to myself: "By the time you are finished with your proofs, sir, I shall perhaps be over the hills and far away!"

CHAPTER 21

How the chasseur unexpectedly came to be a bridegroom

Across from my lodgings lived a retired lieutenant colonel. He had an exceeding beauteous daughter whose bearing was quite noble. I had long since desired to make her acquaintance, despite the fact that in the beginning she did not seem to me to be of the sort that I could not only love but desire to possess forever, and I did take many a walk on her account, and I cast even more lovelorn glances in her direction, but she was so carefully guarded from me that I could not once speak to her alone, as I desired to, and I durst not brazenly pop in to wait upon her, because I had no acquaintance with her parents, and their circle of acquaintances seemed to me much too exalted for a fellow of such humble origins as I knew mine to be. I got closest to her when we happened to be entering or leaving church. Then I eagerly took advantage of the opportunity to approach her so that I might heave a few sighs, which I could do masterfully, even though they all came from a perfidious heart. For her part, she received them with such coolness that I could not but imagine that she would not let herself be seduced so easily as a simple townsman's daughter, and when I thought how she was well nigh unattainable for me, my yearnings for her grew all the more violent.

The lucky star which brought me together with her for the first time was the one which schoolboys carry about at that time of year as a constant reminder that the three wise men were guided to Bethlehem by such a star, which I took at the outset to be a good omen, because one such star lighted my way into her house when her father himself sent for me. "Monsieur," he said to me, "the neutrality which you maintain betwixt the townsfolk and the members of the garrison here is the reason I have asked you to come to me, because I have need of an impartial witness in a matter in which I intend to pass judgment betwixt two parties." I thought that he must have something of great import in mind, because writing materials and paper were on the table; therefore I offered him my most humble service in any honorable business transaction, and made him a special compliment by saying that I should in fact deem it a great honor for me if I were to be so fortunate as to render him the service he desired. The service, however, was nothing more than "creating a kingdom" (as is the custom in many places, since it was just then the Eve of the Three Rings. I was to see to it that everything went fairly and that the offices were distributed by lot, without regard for person. During this business, at which the colonel's *secretarius*[158] was also present, the lieutenant colonel had wine and sweetmeats served, because he was a first-rate toper, and it was after dinner anyway. The *secretarius* wrote down the names, I read them out, and the young ladies drew lots while their parents looked on. And I do not wish to tell in detail how it all went; suffice it to say that I made their acquaintance there for the first time. They complained about the long winter nights and thereby gave me to understand that in order to pass them all the more pleasantly I might pay them visits of an evening, since they had nothing important to do anyway. This was precisely what I had long since been yearning for.

From that evening on (since I had made but few advances towards the maiden) I once more fell to playing the ardent lover and to playing the fool, so that both the girl and her parents could not but imagine that I had taken the bait, though I was but half in earnest. Like the witches, I dressed in my finery only towards evening when I was going to see her, and throughout the day occupied myself with books about love, which I used in order to write love letters to my beloved, just as if I were living a hundred miles away from her, or would not come to visit her for many years. Finally I became quite intimate with the family, because her parents did not particularly object to my wooing of her; instead it was expected of me that I should teach their daughter to play the lute. So I now had free access to her both by day and, as before, in the evening, so that I changed my usual rhyme, "The bat and I, By night we fly," and composed a little song in which I praised my good fortune, because after so many a pleasant evening it was also granting me such days filled with joy, during which I could feast my eyes upon my beloved and comfort my yearning heart; but on the other hand I lamented in that same song my misfortune and accused my fortune of making my nights bitter and not letting me spend them, as I did my days, in pleasurable dalliance; and even though it was a bit forward of me, I sang the song to my beloved, accompanying it with sighs of devotion and a charming melody, during which the lute did its part extremely well and begged the maiden, as it were, to be complaisant, so that my nights might come to be as happy as my days. But I received a rather cool response, for she was extremely clever and knew how to turn aside most politely the requests which I devised and from time to time made in a most charming manner. I was very careful to say nothing about matrimony;

indeed, when it cropped up in our conversations I was really very finicky in my choice of words, which my beloved's sister, who was already married, soon noted, and she therefore blocked all the passes between me and my darling maiden, so that we should not be alone together as often as before, for she clearly saw that her sister loved me from the bottom of her heart and that in the long run the affair would end badly for her.

It is not necessary to relate in detail all the tomfoolery I engaged in during my wooing, because all love stories are full of such nonsense anyway. Suffice it to say, dear Reader, that things finally progressed so far that I durst make so bold as to kiss my little darling and, in the end, to engage in other such foolishness. I pursued the desired goal with all manner of inducements, till finally I was permitted to come to my beloved's room by night, and I whisked into her bed with her as if I were her husband. Because everyone knows what is generally wont to transpire when such games are being played, you, dear Reader, might well imagine that I committed some impropriety. Not at all! For all my efforts were in vain. I was met with such resistance as I could never have imagined I should encounter in a woman, because she had but two things in mind: wedlock and the preservation of her honor. And even though I promised her these, thereby swearing the most terrible oaths, she was nevertheless simply not willing to let anything happen, before the *nuptialia*;[159] but she did let me remain lying in her bed next to her, upon which bed I, quite exhausted from frustration, did in fact fall gently asleep. I was awakened, however, quite ungently, for at four in the morning the lieutenant colonel was standing at the bedside with a pistol in one hand and a torch in the other. "Croat!"[160] he screamed at the top of his lungs to his servant, who was standing next to him with saber drawn. "Quick, Croat! Fetch the parson!" at which I then awoke and saw in what peril I found myself. "O, woe is me!" I thought to myself. "You surely should say confession before he kills you dead!" My head was spinning like a top, and I knew not whether I should open my eyes or not. "You ruttish rascal!" he said to me. "Must I discover that you have brought disgrace upon my house? Would I do you wrong if I were to break your neck, and this slut's too, who has become your whore? Ah, you *bestia*,[161] how ever can I keep myself from tearing your heart out of your breast and hacking it into pieces and throwing them to the dogs?" With that he gnashed his teeth and rolled his eyes like a beast gone out of its wits. I knew not what to do, and my bedmate could do nothing but weep. Finally, when I got my wits about me a little, I attempted to say something to the effect that we had done nothing wrong, but he told me to shut my mouth and fell to reproaching me anew, saying that he had trusted me to behave much differently, but that I, for my part, had in mind to commit against him the greatest perfidy in the world. Meanwhile his wife came into the room too. She set forth on a brand-new sermon, which made me wish that I were lying in a hedge of thorns somewhere; and I do believe that she would not have left off for two hours if the Croat had not come in with the parson.

Before he arrived I made several attempts to get out of bed, but the lieutenant colonel, with threating grimaces, compelled me to remain lying there, so that I was obliged to find out how completely devoid of courage a fellow is who is caught red-handed and how a thief feels when he is seized breaking into a house, even though he has not yet stolen anything. And I thought of that happy time when, had the lieutenant and two such Croats come upon me, I would have ventured to chase all three of them off. But now I lay there like any other sluggard and did not have the heart to properly open my mouth, much less clench my fist. "Look you, parson," said he, "at this fine spectacle to which I am obliged to call upon you as a witness to my disgrace?" And scarce had he uttered these words when he fell into a rage again and so jumbled up his words that all I could understand of what he said was "breaking necks" and "bathing my hands in blood": he foamed at the mouth like a wild boar truly behaved as if he were about to take leave of his wits, so that I thought to myself every moment: "Now he is going to put a bullet through your brain!" The parson, however, struggled with all his might to see to it that no murderous act occurred which he might later regret. "What?" said he. "Colonel, use your common sense and remember the old proverb: 'What's done is done, and one must simply put the best face on it'; this fine young couple, which scarce has its equal in the entire country, is not the first, nor will it be the last either, to let the invincible power of love overcome them. The mistake which these two have committed together can also be easily corrected by them again, since it can truly be termed no more than a mistake. Of course, I do not praise this way of marrying, but nevertheless, this young couple does not merit the gallows or the wheel for what they did; nor should you, colonel, expect any disgrace on account of it, if you will but forgive and keep secret this mistake (which no one knows about anyway) and give your consent for these two to marry and have this marriage publicly confirmed by the customary church service." "What!" said he. "Am I, instead of punishing them as they deserve, to actually pay court to them and do them all honor? I'd rather bind the two of then together tomorrow and have then drowned in the Lippe River! You must marry them this instant, which is why I had you sent for, or I'll wring both their necks as if they were chickens!"

I thought to myself: "What are you to do now? As the old saying goes, 'Eat crow or die!' Moreover, she is the sort of maiden of whom you need not be ashamed. Indeed, when you consider your own origins, you are scarce worthy to kiss the ground she walks on." But I swore and attested by all that was holy that we had had nothing improper to do with one another, but I was told by way of an answer that we should have behaved in such wise that no one could have suspected ill of us, but as things now stood, we could not persuade anyone that the suspicions which they now held were false. Then, sitting in bed, we were given to one another in holy wedlock by the parson, and after this had happened, we were compelled to get up and leave the house together. At the door the lieutenant colonel said to me and his daughter that we should never again in all eternity let him lay eyes upon us. I, however, as soon as I had got my wits together and had a saber at my side, answered, as if in jest: "I know not, father-in-law, why you are arranging everything in such an unreasonable manner. When other bridal couples are joined in wedlock their next of kin escort them to the bridal chamber, but you, after our wedding, not only chase me out of the bed, you even chase me out of the house, and instead of wishing me good fortune as you should, you wish me to be so unfortunate as to not see my father-in-law face to face and to be of service to him. Truly, if this custom were to become the norm, marriages would form the foundation of few friendships in the world any more."

CHAPTER 22

How things went at the wedding feast, and what else he undertook to do

The people in my lodging house were all surprised when I brought the maiden home with me, and even more so when they saw that without so much as batting an eye she went to bed with me, for even though this prank which had been played upon me had put vexatious notions into my head, I was nevertheless not so foolish as to reject my bride. Of course, I had my beloved in my arms but, on the other hand, a thousand different thoughts in my head as to how I might improve and arrange my affairs. At times I thought to myself: "It serves you right!"; and at other times I was of the opinion that the very worst insult in the world had been dealt me, one which I could not get over with honor unless I took my just revenge. But when I considered that this revenge must needs be directed against my father-in-law and thus also against my innocent and virtuous beloved, all my schemes collapsed. I was so very ashamed that I resolved to withdraw from the world and let no human being ever see me again, but I decided that then I should be committing the greatest folly of all. Finally my resolve was that I should first of all win back my father-in-law's friendship and otherwise behave towards everyone as if nothing untoward had befallen me and that I had well taken care of everything in regard to my marriage. I said to myself: "Because all this came to pass and took its beginning in a strange and unusual way, you must needs put a good face on it. Should people find out that you are annoyed about your marriage and were bound into holy wedlock against your will, like a poor young maiden to a rich old cripple, you will be no more than a laughingstock for it."

With these thoughts in mind, I began my day early, though I should rather have remained in bed longer. First of all I sent for my brother-in-law, who was married to my wife's sister, and represented briefly to him how closely related to him I had become, and at the same time I requested him to have his beloved join us to help prepare some food, so that I could give the people at my nuptial feast something to eat. And if he would be so kind as to mollify my father-in-law and my mother-in-law, I would meanwhile go out to invite the guests, who would then make peace between me and him completely. This he took upon himself to do, and I betook myself to the commandant, whom I told in a diverting and charming manner how I and my father-in-law had instituted a new way of making marriages, which new fashion progresses so quickly that in one hour I was betrothed, wedded, and bedded, but because my father-in-law had spared himself the expense of a wedding breakfast, I had in mind to act in his stead and to apprise honorable folk of the feast which I humbly desired to invite him to attend. At my diverting account the commandant laughed till he well nigh split, and because I saw that his heart was in the right place, I grew more candid and excused myself for it by saying that I necessarily must needs be not very sensible now, because other bridegrooms are not possessed of all their wits for a month before and after the wedding; other bridegrooms, I said, had, of course, a month's time in which they little by little could let their follies slip out unnoticed and thus could conceal fairly well their lack of wit, but because this entire bridegroom business had taken me completely by surprise, I must needs let foolish jests fly in throngs, so that afterwards I might embark upon married life all the more sensibly. He asked me how the marriage contract was set up and how many of my father-in-law's gold pieces, of which the old skinflint had many, were in the dowry. I answered that our marriage contract consisted of but one point, which stipulated that his daughter and I should never in all eternity let him lay eyes upon us again, but since neither notaries nor witnesses had been present, I hoped he would revoke it, particularly since all marriages are made for the purpose of assuring continued good friendship, unless he had married his daughter to me the way Pythagoras did his,[162] which I could never believe, because I had never consciously offended him.

Through these jests, which they were not wont to hear from me in this town, I obtained the commandant's promise that he would appear at my feast together with my father-in-law, whom he would assuredly persuade to come. He also straightaway sent a barrel of wine and a stag to my kitchen. I, for my part, had such good food prepared as if I were going to entertain a prince, and I also got together a considerable number of guests, who not only nicely made merry with one another, but also, and more importantly, so reconciled my father-in-law and my mother-in-law with my wife and me that they heaped upon us more best wishes for good fortune than they had curses the night before. In the entire city, however, the rumor spread that our wedding had been arranged in such a strange way on purpose, so that no prank could be played upon us by malicious people. And for me this quick marriage was a very good thing, for if I had been married in the normal manner, with the reading of bans from the pulpit, as is common usage, I fear that there would have been some sluts who would have made so bold as to raise objections to prevent it, for from amongst the townsmen's daughters I had a full half-dozen who knew me more than all too intimately.

The next day my father-in-law entertained my wedding guests, but by far not so well as I had, for he was parsimonious. Then, for the first time, I was asked what manner of trade I intended to pursue and how I was going to set up my household; and then I realized for the first time that I had lost my noble freedom and was now to live under another's dominion. I began with complete humility and desired first to hear, and to follow, the counsel of my father-in-law, a sensible gentleman, which answer the commandant praised, saying: "Because you are a hale young soldier, it would be folly if in these times of war you were to set your hand to any trade but that of the soldier. It is far better to stable your horse in another's barn than to be compelled to feed another's horse in your own. So far as I am concerned, I shall give you command of a company if you desire it." My father-in-law and I expressed our gratitude, and I did not refuse it as I had before, but I did show the commandant the receipt signed by the merchant who had my treasure in safekeeping in Cologne. "This," said I, "I must needs first fetch before I take service with the Swedes, for should the people in Cologne learn that I am serving on the other side, they would give me the sign of the fig[163] and keep my treasure, which is not the sort of thing you find just lying by the wayside." They both agreed that I was right, and so betwixt the three of us it was agreed, promised, and resolved that in a few days I should betake myself to Cologne to fetch my treasure there, and afterwards I should report back to the fortress and assume command of a company. At the same time a day was set, upon which a company was to be turned over to my father-in-law, together with the post of lieutenant colonel in the commandant's regiment, for since at that time Count von Götz[164] was in Westphalia with many Imperials and had his headquarters in Dortmund,[165] the commandant expected a siege the next spring and was therefore recruiting good soldiers, though this fear was bootless, since Count von Götz, because Johann de Werdt[166] had been defeated in the Breisgau,[167] was obliged to quit Westphalia that spring and, because of the fortress of Breisach,[168] to campaign against the Prince of Weimar on the upper Rhine.

CHAPTER 23

Simplicius goes to a city which he calls pro forma Cologne[169] to fetch his treasure

There are many ways in which things come to pass. One person's misfortune comes gradually and step by step, and another's overtakes him on a sudden. Mine, however, had such a sweet and pleasing beginning that I reckoned it to be not misfortune but great good fortune. Scarce more than a week had I spent with my dear wife in the state of matrimony when, dressed in my hunter's clothes, with a flintlock upon my shoulder, I took leave of her and her friends. I slipped safely through the enemy lines, because all the roads were known to me, so that I encountered no hazard on the way. Indeed, I was not seen by a single soul till I came to the turnpike to Deutz,[170] which lies across from Cologne on this side of the Rhine. But I did see many people, particularly a peasant in the Berg country[171] who in fact reminded me of my Pa in the Spessart Forest and whose son closely resembled my Pa's Simplicius. This peasant boy was herding swine as I was about to go past him, and because the sows got wind of me they fell to grunting, and the boy to cursing at them, saying he wished thunder and hail would strike them dead and that they would "ga ta tha divil." The maidservant heard that and screamed to the boy that he should leave off cursing or she would tell his father. To her he replied that she could kiss his arse and "fock 'er muther too." The peasant was likewise listening to his son, and he therefore came running out of the house with his cudgel, screaming: "A thousand rogues take you, etc. I'll learn ya to cuss! May the hail strike ya daid yaself, so the divil get in ya!" With that he seized the boy by the nape of the neck, cudgeled him like a dancing bear, and with every blow said: "Ya evil scamp, ya, I'll learn ya to cuss, the divil take ya! I'll learn ya to kiss me arse, I'll learn ya to fock yar muther, etc." This chastisement naturally reminded me of myself my Pa, and yet I was not so honorable or God-fearing that I thanked God for drawing me out of this darkness and ignorance and for leading me to better knowledge and understanding. Why should the good fortune which He had sent me every day necessarily persist in the long run? Now when I got to Cologne I went to the house of my Jupiter, who was, at the time, quite rational. When I now confided to him why I was there, he straightway told me that he feared I would be beating a dead horse, because the merchant whom I had given my belongings to keep had gone bankrupt and had absconded. To be sure, my things had been put under seal by the authorities, and the merchant had been cited to appear before them, but they doubted very much that he would return, because he had taken with him the best things he could carry off. Now by the time the matter was decided, Jupiter said, much water would have flowed down the Rhine. How pleasing this news was to me, anyone can easily assess. I cursed worse than a sailor, but to what avail? I did not get my things back by cursing, and moreover I had no hopes of getting them back; and I had not brought along with me more than ten thalers expense money, so I could not remain there as long as was demanded. Moreover, to remain there for so long was also hazardous, for I could not but fear that because I was attached to an enemy garrison, I would be found out and thus not only lose my property but also fall into even worse straits in the bargain. But to go back without having accomplished anything, impetuously leaving behind my property, and having made the trip for nothing, did not seem advisable to me either. Finally I resolved that I would remain in Cologne till the matter was decided, and I would report to my beloved the cause of my continued absence. Accordingly, I betook myself to a public prosecutor who was a *notarius*[172] and told him what I was doing in Cologne, and I bade him assist me in word and deed, in return for a fee. If he would speed up my case, I would present him, along with the regular fee, a sizable sum of money. Because he then hoped that there might be something which he could fish out of me, he obligingly took my case, and took me as a boarder into his house too. Then he went with me the next day to see those gentlemen who are responsible for deciding bankruptcy cases, submitted to them a certified copy of the merchant's receipt, and presented the original, whereupon we were given the answer that we must needs wait patiently till the case had been completely decided, because the things spoken of in the document were not all on hand.

Thus I once more prepared for a period of idleness during which I would see how life was in large cities. The man with whom I boarded was, as you have heard, a *notarius* and public prosecutor; in addition, he had about a half-dozen boarders and always kept eight horses in his stable which he was wont to rent to travelers; in addition, he had a German and a French manservant who let him use them as both riders ad coachmen and who tended the horses, through which three or three and a half trades he not only earned his daily bread and much more, but also without doubt engaged in moneylending, for because no Jews were permitted to move into that same city, he could all the better carry on usury with all sorts of things.

I learned much in the short while I was in his house, particularly to diagnose all illnesses, which is the greatest skill a *doctor medicinae*[173] possesses, for they say that if an illness can be correctly diagnosed, the patient is half cured. Now the reason I acquired this skill was my landlord, for after examining him and his complexion, I fell to looking at others and theirs. Then I found many a mortally ill man who himself did not even know about his illness and who was thought by others, indeed even by *doctoribus,*[174] to be hale and hearty. I found people who were ill with anger, and when this illness came over them they contorted their faces so that they looked like devils, they roared like lions, they clawed like cats, they lashed out like bears, they hit like dogs, and, so that they might behave worse than the raging beasts, like madmen they hurled in all directions everything they could lay their hands on. They say that this illness comes from gall, but I believe that it arises when a fool is arrogant, for which reason when you hear an angry man raging, particularly about something of no consequence, then go right ahead and believe that he is more proud than intelligent. This illness led to innumerable misfortunes, both for the sick man himself and for others, and in fact, for the sick man it led in the end to paralysis, gout, and a premature, if not eternal death! And you can in good conscience call these sick people patients, even though they are not dangerously ill, because what they most of all lack is patience. I saw some of them fall ill with envy, of which people it was said that they were "eating their heart out," because they always went about so pale and disconsolate. This illness I hold to be the most dangerous one of all, because it has its origin with the devil, though it stems from nothing more than the good fortune which the sick man's enemy enjoys; and anyone who cures such a person completely may well nigh boast that he has converted a lost soul to the Christian faith, because this illness does not attack any true Christian, which sort of person detests sins and vices. Gaming-fever I also hold to be an illness, not only because the name itself indicates it to be one, but also because those who are saddled with it are as taken with it as if they had been poisoned. This has its origin in sloth, not in avarice, as some opine, and if you take away lust and sloth, this illness will go away by itself. And I found that gluttony is also an illness and that it comes from habit and not from superabundance; poverty, of course, is a good remedy for it, but it is not completely cured by that, for I have seen beggars carouse and rich men go hungry; it brings its own medicament with it, which is called want, if not want of goods then want of physical health, so that in the end these sick folk generally cannot but become healthy again when, either because of poverty or some other sickness, they can no longer partake of food and drink. Pride I also took to be a kind of madness which has its origin in ignorance, for if a person knows himself and knows whence he came and whither, in the end, he is going, then it is impossible for him to be a proud fool any longer. Whenever I see a peacock or a guinea hen spread out its tail feathers and go strutting along, I cannot but feel how ridiculous it is that these mindless beasts are able to so charmingly mock poor man in his great illness. I have not been able to find any specific medicament with which to treat it, because those who lie ill with it can no more be cured without humility than can other fools. I found too that laughter is an illness, for Philemon[175] died of it, and Democritus[176] remained infected with it till the end of his life. And thus, to this very day, our women say they will "die laughing." They say laughter has its origin in the liver, but I believe rather that it comes from folly, since much laughter is not the mark of a sensible man. It is not necessary to prescribe a medicine for it, because not only is it a merry ailment, many a person recovers from it before he would wish to. No less did I remark that curiosity is also an illness and is well nigh inborn, to the female of the species particularly. To be sure, it seems to be of slight import, but it is in truth very dangerous, particularly when one considers that we are still paying for the curiosity of the mother of us all. Of the other illnesses, such as sloth, vindictiveness, passion, blasphemy, love sicknesses, and other illnesses and vices of that sort I shall remain silent for the time being, because I never intended to write anything about them anyway. Instead I shall return to the subject of my boardinghouse keeper, who gave me cause to ponder upon ailments of that sort, because he was possessed and consumed by avarice, right down to his fingertips.

CHAPTER 24

The chasseur catches a hare, right in the middle of the city

This Man, as noted above, had sundry trades by which he scraped together money. He feasted upon his boarders, but his boarders did not feast with him;[177] and yet, he could have fed himself and those in his house quite well with what they brought in for him, if the skinflint had but used some of his income to do it; but he fed us like a Scotsman and kept most of the income for himself. In the beginning I did not eat with his boarders but with his children and servants, because I did not have much money with me. The portions were very small, which seemed strange to my stomach, which had now grown accustomed to Westphalian fare. We did not get a single good piece of meat upon the table, only what was left over from the students' meals the week before, already well gnawed all over by them, and now grown as grey as Methuselah. Then his wife (who was obliged to do the cooking herself, for he would not hire her a maid) would pour sour black broth over it and pepper it like the devil; then the bones were licked so clean that you could well nigh have turned chess pieces out of them on a lathe, and yet they were still not completely used up; they went into a container specified for this purpose, and when our miser had collected a large number of them, they were first chopped up fine and then the rest of the fat, down to the very last drop, was boiled out of them. I know not whether the soups were larded with this fat or whether it was used to polish shoes. On fast days, of which there were more than enough and all of which were observed *solenniter*,[178] because in this regard the master of the house was quite punctilious, we were obliged to chew around on stinking kippers, oversalted codfish, rotten stockfish, and other sorts of putrid fish, because he always bought what was cheapest and even went to the trouble of going to the fish market himself for this purpose, and he snatched whatever the fishermen had in mind to throw away.[179] Our bread was usually black and stale and our drink a thin beer that like to have cut my gut, and yet he insisted upon calling it "well-lagered Marchbeer." Moreover, I learned from his German manservant that it was even worse in the summertime, for then the bread was moldy, the meat full of maggots, and the best food on the table was perchance a few radishes at the noonday meal, or a handful of lettuce in the evening. I asked him why he continued to tolerate it, and he answered that most of the time he was away on trips and was therefore obliged to be more attentive to the travelers' gratuities than to his scurvy Jew. He did not trust his wife and children in the cellar, because he scarce granted himself a drop of wine, and he was, *in summa* such a money-hound as can scarce be found. What I had seen before, said the manservant, was nothing, however. If I remained a while longer I would learn that he was not ashamed to flay an ass for a farthing. One time he brought home six pounds of chitterlings or tripe; this he put into his food cellar, and because, to his children's great good fortune, the cellar window was open, they tied a fork onto the end of a stick and with it fished out all the tripe, which they forthwith devoured, half-cooked, in great haste, and then claimed the cat had got it, but the old pea-counter was unwilling to believe that, and so he caught the cat, weighed it, and found that with all its hide and hair it was not as heavy as the tripe had been. Thus, because he behaved so very shamelessly, I no longer desired to eat with his family but rather, no matter what the cost, at the students' table, at which, in fact, the food was somewhat better; but it did me little good, for all the dishes they served us were but half-done, which suited our host well in two ways: first, in the firewood which he saved, and, second, because we could not digest as much of it. Moreover, it seemed to me that he counted every mouthful we took and looked daggers at us when we fell to heartily. His wine was somewhat watered down and not of the sort that aids digestion. The cheese, which was served at the end of every meal was usually as hard as a rock, and the Dutch butter was so salty that no one could eat more than a half ounce of it at a meal. The fruit was green and hard, and he obliged his servants to bring it to the table and remove it again till it was soft and ready to eat; then, when one guest or the other complained about it, he fell to quarrelling terribly with his wife, so that, we could hear what he said, but privately he commanded her to keep up the same old tune. One time one of his clients brought him as a present a hare, which I saw hanging in the larder, and I thought we would finally get to eat some game, but the German manservant told me that we were not going to lay a tooth onto it, for his master had decreed that no such delicacy be served the boarders. I should simply go to the old market that afternoon, the servant said, and see whether I did not find the hare for sale there. Then I cut a little piece out of the hare's ear, and when we were sitting over the noonday meal I related that our miser had a hare to sell which I planned to cheat him out of, if one of them were willing to follow me; thus, I said, we would not only devise a diversion, for ourselves but also get the hare itself. Everyone said yes, for they would have long since liked to play on our host a prank of which he could not complain. So that afternoon we betook ourselves to the place where, as I had learned from the manservant, our host was wont to stand whenever he was offering anything like that for sale, so that he might keep a careful eye upon how much the vendor sold it for, so that he might not perchance be cheated of so much as a farthing. We saw him in the company of distinguished people with whom he was discoursing. I had hired a fellow who went to the peddler who was supposed to sell the hare and said: "Friend, that hare is mine, and I am taking it away as stolen property, as is my right. It was fished out of my window last night, and if you do not let me take it voluntarily, then I'll go with you wherever you will, at your own peril and court costs." The peddler answered that he would see what he must do; there stood the distinguished gentleman, he said, who had given him the hare to sell, which gentleman without doubt had not stolen it. Now as these two were thus exchanging words, a crowd of people collected around them, which our miser straightway noted, and he saw which way the wind was blowing and therefore gave the peddler a signal that he should let the hare be taken away, because, on account of the fact that his many boarders were there, he feared yet more disgrace. And the fellow whom I had hired for this purpose was cleverly able to show the bystanders the missing piece of the hare's ear and to fit it into the notch, so that everyone agreed that he was in the right and awarded the hare to him. Meanwhile, I too approached with my companions, as if we were coming along by chance, and we went up to the fellow with the hare and fell to haggling with him about buying it; and after we had agreed upon a price, I turned the hare over to our host with the request that he take it home with him and have it prepared for our meal; and to the fellow whom I had hired for this purpose I gave instead of payment for the hare a gratuity of two tankards of beer. Thus our miser was obliged, against his will, to serve us the hare, and he could not say anything about it either, at which we had enough to laugh about. And had I remained in his house any longer, I should have played more pranks of that sort upon him.

END OF THE THIRD BOOK

NOTES — BOOK III

CHAPTER 1: *How the chasseur strayed too far from the right path*

1.　　to steal chickens: see Notes to Book I, Chapter 16.

CHAPTER 2: *The chasseur of Soest rids himself of the chasseur of Werl*

2.　　Werl: village near Soest; it too was in the hands of Count von Götz' troops.

CHAPTER 3: *The great god Jupiter is captured and reveals the counsels of the gods*

3.　　The great god Jupiter is captured...: like several other "episodes" in Simplicissimus, the so-called "Jupiter Episode" extends over several chapters (3 through 7) and consists of fairly clearly defined segments: 1) The Meeting of Jupiter and Simplicissimus (Chapter 3); 2) Jupiter's Prophecy of a German Hero and Secular Reform Leading to a Utopia (Chapter 4); 3) Jupiter's Argument with Hopalong (Chapter 5); 4) Jupiter's Prophecy of Religious Reform Leading to a Utopia (Chapter 5); 5) Jupiter's Argument with Simplicissimus (Chapter 6); 6) Jupiter's Battle with the Lice (Chapter 6); and 7) Jupiter after the Skirmish (Chapter 7). The structure of the episode (and Bechtold failed to note this) is somewhat similar to that of Moscherosch, "Phantasten-Spital." Philander, the narrator, encounters a number of "Phantasten," but there are only two lengthy episodes: 1) his encounter with a "sehr ehrbarn / köstlich bekleidten und gravitätischen Mann" (Grimmelshausen describes Jupiter as "fein ehrbar gekleidet"), whom Philander at first takes to be a doctor but then discovers to be an inmate who believes he is God and who embarks upon a description of how he will treat the Pope, Luther and Calvin on Judgment Day; and 2) a poor gardner who is convinced that he is a general in the French army and explains why a German would wish to serve in the French army rather than in a German one. The "General" and "God" episodes are thus satires on matters religious and secular, as are Jupiter's two prophecies about his German Hero.

The Jupiter Episode has been of prime importance for Grimmelshausen scholarship and for the interpretation of Simplicissimus since the 1960s, for it is the starting point for those who have advanced the "astrological" interpretation: Weydt, in 1965 in a paper entitled "Planetensymbolik im barocken Roman. Versuch einer Entschlüsselung des Simplicissimus aufgrund der astrologischen Tradition" given at the third Internationaler Germanisten-Kongress in Amsterdam and in 1968 in Nachahmung, in a chapter with the same title (pp. 243-279); and Helmut Rehder, in 1968 in an essay entitled "Planetenkinder: Some Problems of Character Portrayal in Literature" (The Graduate Journal 8, Nr. 1, 69-97). That Grimmelshausen was interested in astrology is indisputable—his Eternal Calendar (Deβ Abentheurlichen Simplicissimi Ewig-währender Calender) contains long passages on the subject which were taken verbatim from Garzoni's Discourse 40 and Johannes ab Indagine's Natürliche Stern-Kunst. At the time astrologists, soothsayers, and casters of horoscopes still relied on the Chaldean-Ptolomaic (geocentric) view of the universe, which conceived of a fixed earth around which rotated seven planets, traditionally arranged in the following sequence, beginning with the planet furtherest from the earth (the one which took the longest to complete one full revolution): 1) Saturn, 2) Jupiter, 3) Mars, 4) Sol (the sun), 5) Venus, 6) Mercury, and 7) Luna (the moon). Astrologers maintained that these seven, which were conceived of as "planetary gods," influenced mortals, and everything else on earth, with the influence depending on 1) their momentary relationship to one another and 2) the prevailing "mansion" (sign of the Zodiac, of which there were twelve: the "midnight," i.e. northern mansions—Aries, Taurus, Gemini, Cancer, Leo, and Virgo—and the "midday," i.e. southern ones—Libra, Scorpio, Saggitarius, Capricorn, Aquarius, and Pisces). The astrological interpreters of Simplicissimus believe that Grimmelshausen intentionally and consciously structured his novel according to the "astrological" cycle, with each of the seven planetary gods at some point the dominant force. Rehder, focusing on the figure of Simpicissimus, discerned seven "stations" in his life (as depicted in Books I-V), corresponding to the following seven planetary gods: 1) Saturn (god of solitary and base occupations) - childhood and stay with the hermit; 2) Mars - from the death of the hermit to the end of the sojourn in the Paradise Cloister; 3) Jupiter (master of the hunt, bestower of good fortune) - Simplicissimus' adventures as the Chasseur of Soest; 4) Sol (god of leisure, of the arts and sciences) - the sojourns in Lippstadt and Cologne; 5) Venus - the adventures in Paris; 6) Mercury (the changeable god, sometimes bestowing good fortune and sometimes bad) - up to the beginning of the Lake Mummer episode; 7) Luna (goddess associated with water) - up through the end of the novel, which returns to Saturn (withdrawal to a life of solitude). Rehder realized that the Jupiter and Mars "stations" were the reverse of the accepted sequence but noted that "such reversion of sequence is not disturbing, judging from similar instances in astrological and moralizing literature" (p. 90).

Weydt considered both the first five books and the first Continuatio (Book VI) and examined not only the hero but 27 other factors which the seven planetary gods are traditionally described as controlling or being associated with, and he arrived at the following structure, in which the dominant planetary gods overlap (cf. Weydt, p. 301): 1) Saturn - up to Book I, Chapter 18; 2) Mars - from the beginning to the end of Chapter 5/6 in Book II; 3) Sol - Book I, Chapter 20/21 to Book II, Chapter 29; 4) Jupiter - Book II, Chapter 26 to Book III, Chapter 23; 5) Venus - Book III, Chapter 17 to Book 4, Chapter 6/8; 6) Mercury - Book III, Chapter 23 to Book 5, Chapter 18; 7) Luna - Book V, Chapter 8 to the middle of Book VI; and 8) Saturn (beginning a new cycle, as would astrologically be expected) - middle of Book VI to its conclusion. In each instance the planetary god is most dominant, according to Weydt, midway through its cycle (Book I begins and Book VI ends at mid-cycle). Weydt's sequence, it will be noted, does not agree with the traditional sequence either.

The astrological theory, Weydt argues, is supported in part by the fact that there are two pieces of evidence which indicate that Grimmelshausen was immersed in the study of astrology at the very time he must have been composing Simplicissimus (the mid-1660s): 1) his citation of Hildebrand's Planetenbuch in the "Gegensatz" of The Satyrical Pilgrim I, 10; and 2) his use of the 1664 edition of Johann ab Indagine's Natürliche Stern-Kunst as a source for the so-called "fifth materia" in his Perpetual Calender. The citation of the Planetenbuch, which first appeared in 1613 and was re-issued in a revised edition in 1625, is meaningful only a) if one assumes (as many scholars do) that Grimmelshausen wrote—compiled would be a better word—The Satyrical Pilgrim I immediately before its publication in the fall of 1666 and b) if he in fact took the citation directly from the Planetenbuch and not from another source which cited and quoted the Planetenbuch —which the form of the citation renders quite probable: "Wolfgang Hildebrand meldet Generaliter im teutschen Theil seines Planetenbuchs auß Gu: H: R: & Mathem: da er von der Phisiognomiae handelt / ..." (in virtually every other instance when Grimmelshausen is so specific in citing a source, he has borrowed both the information and the citation from another source). The second piece of evidence (cf. Weydt, pp. 308 ff. in an Exkurs entitled "Die Indagine-Ausgabe von 1664 als Vorlage für die Fünfte Materie des <Ewigwährenden Kalender>") is at first glance far more persuasive, for a) it supplies a terminus a quo—1664, b) one must presume only that Grimmelshausen was working on The Perpetual Calender, which did not appear until the fall of 1671, at about the same time he was writing Simplicissimus, the editio princeps of which appeared in the spring of 1668, and c) there appear to be some borrowings from Indagine in Simplicissimus, Book III, Chapter 4 (see below). The evidence seems to indicate conclusively that Grimmelshausen must have used Indagine sometime between 1664, when it appeared, and 1668, when Simplicissimus was first published. There were, however, earlier editions of Indagine's work. It was first published (in Latin) in Strasbourg in 1522 under the title Introductiones apotolesmaticae elegantes in chiromantium, phisignomiam, astrologiam naturalem, complexiones hominum, naturas planetarum...; a year later a German version appeared under the title Die kunst der Chiromantzey..., but neither this edition nor a second German version published in 1540 represented a translation of the complete Latin text (Scholte, p. 68, nevertheless believed that the 1523 edition was the source). Weydt is probably correct when he argues (p. 308) that Grimmelshausen did not use a sixteenth-century German version of the work. There is, however, at least one indication that Grimmelshausen used not the 1664 edition but an earlier German one which appeared in 1630. The full title of the 1664 edition is Natürlicher Stern-Kunst / Oder Gründlicher Bericht wie auß Ansehen des Gesicht / der Händ / vnd gantzer Gestalt des Menschen Wahr gesagt werden könne: Lateinisch beschrieben durch Johann von INDAGINE, Ins Teütsch übersetzt vnd erklärt von Johann Freridrich Halbmeyer Der Stern-Kunst Liebhabern.; the title of the 1630 edition is slightly different: Deß hochgelehrten Ioannis Indagine Astrologia naturalis; das ist, Gründlicher Bericht, wie man Chiromancia, Physiognomia vnd Astrologia leichtlich erlehrnen .... The heading to the fifth "materia" in the Perpetual Calender reads "Simplicii Discurs mit Ioanne Indagine / darinnen er unterrichtet wird, wie vermittelst der Astrologia Naturali er einem jeden Menschen ohne Kopfbrechung die Nativität stellen könne...." This heading contains two elements which agree with the title of the 1630 edition and are at variance with that of the edition of 1664: the term "Astrologia naturalis" (translated as "Natürliche Stern-Kunst' in the 1664 edition); and the form of the author's name ("Ioannis Indagine" in the 1630 edition, but translated into German as "Johann von Indagine" in the 1664 edition). On the basis of the titles and the heading, it surely seems more likely that Grimmelshausen copied out of the 1630 edition, and if that were the case he could have used the book any time before 1668, when borrowings from it appear in Simplicissimus. Weydt's two arguments are thus far from persuasive proofs.

4.   Dorsten: see above, Book II, Chapter 30.

5.   There came a lone man strolling up...: Grimmelshausen begins the Jupiter Episode by employing a favorite technique of Moscherosch: the narrator describes a person whom he observes but does not know and cannot identify—or identifies incorrectly; the narrator and the person then begin to converse, and the person's identity is revealed. In at least three instances—in addition to the encounter with the man with the "God" complex mentioned above—Moscherosch' stranger is in some respects similar to Grimmelshausen's Jupiter: in the "Todtenheer" one dead person who "was walking along gravely" approaches Philander and introduces himself as "the first King of the Old Franconians" (I, 188 f.), and another, whose appearance is such that Philander takes him for a "wild man" and regards him with a mixture of fear and awe, introduces himself as "Herr Lug ins Land, the most accurate astrologus and prophet who can be found today" (I, 211 f.). The astrologer, like Jupiter, is quick to take offense and flies into a rage when Philander speaks of "foolish prophecies" attributed to him which one now and again hears in Germany. In a later vision, "Alamode Kehrauß," Philander encounters a figure who introduces himself as "King Ariovistus" and who not only rails against those who are ruining the German language by introducing foreign words into it, but even goes so far as to predict the total destruction of Germany unless a "Hero" appears who can restore German to its original purity (I, 684 f.)

6.   Numen: Latin for god, godhead, divinity.

7.   a powerful prince who had been going about in disguise this way in order to inform himself about his subjects' lives and behavior: the idea of having Jupiter come to earth to investigate man's doings may have been inspired by the assertion of Diodorus Siculus (I, 12, 9-10), who cited Homer (Odyssey XVII, 485-87) as his authority, that the gods, Jupiter of course among them, visited the cities of men in disguise in order to observe their good and evil ways; Grimmelshausen was probably familiar with Herold's German translation of the passage (p. vi: "...die Gütter ziehen offtermals in frembder gestalt in den stätten hin und wider / und nemmen acht was böses oder guttes die menschen thuen.").

8.   vex the citizens of Soest by teasing them about their great god and his golden apron: the "great god" of Soest was a crucifix with a five-foot long figure of Christ on it; it reposed in St. Patroclus Cathedral in Soest.

9.   he introduced himself as the god Jupiter: Grimmelshausen scholars have suggested a number of figures as the model for Jupiter: 1-2) Bloedau (p. 119 f.) pointed out 1) an episode in Quevodo's Buscon in which two madmen, one an engineer and the other a poet, expound their bizarre ideas and theories; he also cited 2) Fischart's Flohhatz as possible inspiration for Jupiter's problems with lice. 3-4) Bechtold (pp. 514-18) cited 3) one of Philander's visions (in "Phantasten-Spital") in which a melancholicus who thinks he is God plans to do away with religious strife among the Christian confessions; he also pointed out that 4) in Guzman there is a description of Jupiter presiding over an assembly of the gods which is considering whether to extirpate mankind as punishment for its vices. 5) Koschlig (pp. 45-87) believed the model for Jupiter was Hortensius, a character in Charles Sorel's Histoire comique de Francion, which was translated into German

in 1662 and 1668; Koschlig emphasized (p. 67 f.) that Hortensius, like Jupiter, is a writer who has studied too much, who suffers from "morbus poetarum," and who is greatly interested in fleas and lice (he intends to write a poetic work about them). While the similarities between Jupiter and Hortensius are superficial, at best, Koschlig does make the very good point that Grimmelshausen, in The Satyrical Pilgrim II, 1, expressly singles out Francion for praise (in one of the few passages not taken from Garzoni, I might add). 6-9) Weydt, in an essay entitled "Don Quijote, Der Wahnsinnige Schäfer und Jupiter Teutsch" (revised and reprinted in Weydt, pp. 138-154), cited as sources four works written by Harsdörffer and members of his circle: 6) the renarration of Sorel's Le berger extravagant under the title of "Der wahnwitzige Schäfer" in the Frauenzimmer-Gesprächspiele of 1647 (CCL VII); 7) the "Hylas Episode" in the continuation of the Pegnitz-Schäferey (1645), written by Harsdörffer's friends Sigmund von Birken and Johann Klaj; 8) the "Pamela Episode" in the first Pegnitz-Schäferey (1644); and 9) the "Neptune-Jupiter Anecdote" recounted by Harsdörffer in his list of melancholicii referred to above in the Notes to Book II, Chapter 13. Weydt points out the following similarities to Grimmelshausen's Jupiter: Lysis, the "mad shepherd," addled his pate by reading too much; Hylas suffers from the same delusion as Lysis, is introduced to the reader in the way Jupiter is, and includes names of figures from mythology in his tirades; Pamela, an equally "mad shepherdess," believes that she is "poor Germany lying in her death throes"; and the two melancholicii are poor souls who are convinced that they are Neptune and Jupiter respectively. No verbatim borrowings by Grimmelshausen are established, but Weydt does discuss what he takes to be a borrowing in another part of Simplicissimus (Book I, Chapter 3): the peculiar idiom "to poison toads" ("den Kröten vergeben"), which is also found in the continuation of the Pegnitz-Schäferey ("... und könde man mit seinen Schwanken zur Noht einer Kröten vergeben.") However, as indicated above (Notes to Book I, Chapter 3), Grimmelshausen is here quoting Garzoni nearly verbatim: Simplicissimus I, 3: "Da fienge ich an mit meiner Sackpfeiffen so gut Geschirr zu machen / daß man den Krotten im Krautgarten damit hätte vergeben mögen /..."; Garzoni, Discourse 42 (p. 348), in discussing the flaws of musicians: "Und damit wir auch deß dritten / oder wol vierdten Mangels nicht vergessen / so finden sich auch etliche Sudeler unter ihnen / welche sich zwar auch understehen / beydes zu singen vnnd zu componiren / wollen auch hoch darfür abgesehen seyn / machen aber solch jämmerlich Geschirr / daß man den Krotten im Krautgarten damit vergeben möchte / ..." In fact, Garzoni employs the same idiom a second time, in Discourse 103 (p. 575, recta 574): "Ihre inventiones sind daß man wol den Kröten darmit vergeben möchte...."

Not all suggested models for Jupiter are literary; both Julius Petersen and Scholte suggest historical personalities: 10-13) Petersen ("Grimmelshausens Teutscher Held," Euphorion 17, 5 ff.) believed Grimmelshausen may have met one "mad prophet" well known in his time, 10) Bartholomäus Holzhauser (died 1658), and may have been familiar with the chiliastic writings of two others, 11) Johann Warner and 12) Philippus Ziegler; he also found it probable that Grimmelshausen read in Theatrum Europaeum about a mad prophet who called himself 13) Albrecht von Adelgreiff and who claimed to be the "Prince of Peace" and the "Judge of the Quick and the Dead" (Adelgreiff—who was plagued by lice, by the way—first gained notoriety in 1636, about the time, Petersen notes, that the Jupiter episode occurs, and was executed on October 12, 1637). 14) Scholte, in an essay first published in 1946 entitled "Der 'Simplicissimus Teutsch' als verhüllte Religionssatire" (reprinted in Scholte, Der Simplicissimus und sein Dichter, pp. 15-48), attempted to demonstrate that the Jupiter figure, with his utopian visions and overwhelming knowledge of classical mythology, was actually a) a satirical portrayal of Jesaias Rompler von Löwenhalt, who was a poet and the theorist and leader of the Tannengesellschaft in Strasbourg, and b) a parody of Rompler's disciple, Count Friedrich von Württemberg-Mompelgard; Scholte was convinced that the actual model for Jupiter was Grimmelshausen's contemporary, Count Georg von Württemberg-Mompelgard, whose behavior and views were quite out of the ordinary (p. 40). Scholte goes to some lengths to demonstrate Grimmelshausen's dislike for Rompler and concludes that only Rompler and his friends could have been the language reformers whom Grimmelshausen attacked in Der teutsche Michel, but he neglects to consider that in The Satyrical Pilgrim II, I—again in a passage not taken from Garzoni and presumably Grimmelshausen's own composition— poets are linked to language reformers who coin new words, use them both in writing and in speech, and attempt to prescribe new rules for grammar and orthography for the German language: "so giebts auch etliche / und zwar nicht wenig / die sich als Sprachhelden unterstehen / ganz Nagelneue Wörter uff die Bahn zu bringen / deren sie sich nicht allein in ihren Schrifften gebrauchen / sonder auch in ihren täglichen Reden vernemmen lassen; und ob sie zwar deßwegen offt so kahl damit bestehen / daß sie auch die Wald-bauern verlachen und corrigiren, so vermeinen sie iedoch / das Vaterland sey ihnen umb solcher ihrer närrischen Witz halber hoch verbunden; Andere wollen eine neue Grammatica und Orthographicam der teutschen Sprach vorschreiben / die so Phantastisch beschaffen / daß die Schüler Knaben / wann sie darmit ufgezogen kämen / bey den Schulmeistern übel anlauffen würden; und dennoch schämen sie sich nicht / sich solcher Thorheit halber zu rühmen." Surely Rompler was one of the persons Grimmelshausen had in mind when he penned this diatribe (see also below, Note to Helicon).

To these possible historical models I might add two more: 15) Simon Morin, a French "mad prophet" who was executed in Paris on 4/14 March 1653, i.e. roughly at the time Grimmelshausen was embarking upon his literary career. Morin had preached that the king should turn over to him all church properties and that the church should be completely reorganized; he claimed, moreover, that he was Christ returned to earth to pass judgment and to establish the "realm of the Holy Ghost." Morin's views and fate were dutifully reported in Theatrum Europaeum IX, 1077, and while Grimmelshausen could not have used this report (the volume did not appear until 1672), it seems quite likely that Morin's "heresy" was well known at the time and possibly described in broadsides. 16) Tomaso Garzoni, the polyhistorian and encyclopaedist to whom Grimmelshausen owed so much. Although Garzoni was not a poet but a scholar, in Discourse 153 he assumes the role of a poet and writes a parody of an invocation (p. 719): "Auff solche weise wil ich nun / wie ein nachfolger der Poeten / aber doch in Prosa / den Mercuriuim anruffen / daß er mir seine talaria wölle leyhen / oder auch wo müglich / grössere wölle verschaffen / daß ich so hoch fliegen wie Iupiter als er vnter der gestalt eines Adelers den Ganimedem hinweg geföhret. Oder den Phoebem, daß er mir seine güldene Cythat, als er den Plutonem vnnd die Proserpinam auß der Höllenm hinweg föhrete: oder aber die / wie Penthasilea gewapnete Mineruam, daß sie mich so muthig mache / wie Bacchus gewesen / als er auff einem langohrichten Esel in den Krief wider die Centauros gezogen. Deßgleichen die Cytheram, daß meine Lippen mit lieblichem Honig wol bestreichen: Chloridem und Galatheam, daß sie mich auch in den Arcadischen Wälden angenehm machen. Nereidam und Thetin, daß sie mich bey den Meergüttern commendiren / Pomonam und Cererem, daß sie mich Handthaben / vnnd daß Laub vnd Graß zu mir neygen. Und damit ich ja niemandt vergesse / ruffe ich auch Pythonem an, daß sie mich als eine Göttin der Wolredenheit mit gebührlicher Eloquentz wölle begaben / die Camoenas, als Göttin des Gesangs / vnnd Stimulam, daß sie mich zu diesem lustigen Discurs wöllen aufmuntern / Heben die Göttin der Jugend / daß sie Muth un Krafft darzu wölle verleyhen / auff daß ich mich im Namen der schönen Doridis im Meer / der holdseligen Tochter Latone in der Lufft / Promethei deß Gottes des Fewers / Florae der Göttin der Erden / mit dem Thyrso Bacchi, mit dem Schmidthammer Vulcani, mit dem Tridente Neptuni, mit dem eisernen Kühriß Martis, mit dem Kolben Herculis, unnd dem fulmine oder Blitzstralen Iovis in diesem meinem Dioscurs die gantze Ehrliche Gesellschafft der Edelen / vnd mit Lorberblätter gekröneten Poeten nach ihren Würden müge rähmen vnnd ehren." This horrendous peroration is precisely the sort of thing Grimmelshausen must have had in mind when he, in The Satyrical Pilgrim II, 1, lamented that the average person could barely understand poets unless he had studied intensively classical mythology: "Jetziger Zeit findet man viel / die in ihren Poematis sich mit Untermengung der alten Poetischen Grillen dermassen schleppen und versteigen / daß mancher gelehrter und erfahrner Kerl geschweige ein gemeiner Mann / beynahe nichts daraus verstehet / er habe dann sich zuvor auch in dergleichen Thorheiten geübt / und der alten Poeten schrecklich Einfäll und Wundergedichte gelesen / und ihre Phantastische und Närrische Träume im Kopff behalten /..." The passage, furthermore, links Garzoni to Jupiter twice, once at the beginning, where the rape of Ganymede is alluded to, and once at the end, where Garzoni requests, among other gifts from the gods, the "lightning bolts of Jupiter." The conclusion of the passage could not but have reminded Grimmelshausen of the beginning of Garzoni's Introduction, where Momus explicitly compares Garzoni to Jupiter, among others, in much the same terms: "...hie schlägt er einen mit deß Herculis Kolben / dort einen andern mit deß Neptuni Trident / hie lähmet er einen mit Jupiters Blitz / dort erschreckt er einen andern wie ein Meerwunder / als einer / so ihm vorgenommen / die gantze Welt zu ersäuffen /..." Finally, it should be noted that Jupiter's threat to punish his detractors as Tantalus and others were punished (see below) is taken from Garzoni's response to his calumniators in his Introduction, perhaps an indication that Grimmelshausen in his own mind associated his Jupiter with Garzoni.

While the concensus has been that Grimmelshausen first created his Jupiter figure and then embellished his dialogue with material borrowed from Garzoni, it seems possible that Garzoni's Discourse 153, together with his Introduction, could have been the starting point. In any event, Grimmelshausen's intimate knowledge of Garzoni and Moscherosch, together with his experiences with the poetic circle in Strasbourg and his awareness of various historical "mad prophets" with ideas of utopian reform, would be sufficient for him to create in Jupiter a figure in which he satirizes a number of human types: the overly erudite, classically educated scholar and polyhistor who relishes recondite classical allusions; the poet who is similarly intent upon displaying his knowledge of classical mythology; the madman; the mad prophet; the astrologer, soothsayer, and caster of horoscopes; the language reformer; and the totally impractical utopist.

10.   Jove: Jupiter.

11.   sylvani: divinities of the fields and forests, defined by Grimmelshausen's source for information on classical mythology (Acerra philologica I, 85, p. 156, and Moscherosch VI, 299) as "forest spirits, or gods, patrons of peasants and farmers; of just the same appearance as satyrs, with horned heads and with goats' feet." Grimmelshausen's inspiration to have Simplicius adopt the role of Silvanus, however, may have been Garzoni's definition (in Momus' Tirade against Garzoni, in the Introduction): "the father of herdsmen of swine and cattle." Considering Simplicissimus' first occupation as a boy, the appellation Silvanus is quite appropriate.

12.   faunis: fauns (in Roman mythology the equivalent of the Greek satyrs); rural deities associated with Pan; defined (loc. cit.) exactly the same as "sylvani."

13.   nymphis: nymphs; female deities believed to dwell in groves, on mountain tops, in rivers and streams, and in grottoes (similarly defined in Grimmelshausen's sources).

14.   Ganymede: in Greek legend he was the most beautiful of all mortals and was carried off to Mount Olympus to serve as Jupiter's cupbearer. Cf. Apollodorus, Library III, 12, 2. Grimmelshausen's sources for information on classical mythology (Acerra philologica I, 85, p. 155 f., and Moscherosch VI, 299) describe him as "a little lad...taken up to heaven by Jove on an eagle; there he was given the post of waiting upon the gods when they dined and pouring them nectar, that is the drink of the gods, and ambrosia, that is the food of the gods." It might be noted that in Garzoni's Introduction, in two passages lifted by Grimmelshausen, the "rape of Ganymede" is mentioned (and both times Grimmelshausen deletes it from his text).

15.   Pan: Greek god of flocks and shepherds. Grimmelshausen's sources (op. cit. I, 85, p. 155 and VI, 299) lump Pan together with satyrs, calling them "gods of herdsmen and bagpipers, wondrous in form, with goats' feet, thick fur, horns on their heads, long ears, and ugly faces...."

16.   in Lycaon's time: Lycaon, the king of Arcadia, served Jupiter a dish of human flesh, whereupon Jupiter turned him and all his sons except Nyctimus into wolves; during Nyctimus' reign Jupiter sent the great flood, which only Pyrrha and Deucalion were able to survive. Cf. Apollodorus, Library III, 8, 1-2. Grimmelshausen may have been reminded of the "flood" by a remark in Momus' Tirade against Garzoni in Garzoni's Introduction in which Momus alludes to "wielding Jupiter's lightning bolt" and "undertaking to inundate the world...."

CHAPTER 4: *Concerning the German hero who will conquer the entire world and establish peace amongst all peoples*

17.   I shall endow him...shall conquer the entire world: this passage, which is deemed by proponents of the astrological interpretation to be of the greatest significance, reads as follows in the original: "in seiner Geburt-Stund will ich ihm verleyhen einen wolgestalten und stärckern Leib / als Hercules einen hatte / mit Fürsichtigkeit / Weisheit / und Verstand überflüssig geziert / hierzu soll ihm Venus geben ein schön Angesicht / also daß er auch Narcissum, Adonidem und meinen Ganymedem selbst übertreffen solle / sie soll ihm zu allen seinen Tugenden ein sonderbare Zierlichkeit / Auffsehen

und Anmütigkeit vorstrecken / und dahero ihn bey aller Welt beliebt machen / weil ich sie eben der Ursachen halber in seiner Nativität desto freundlicher anblicken werde; Mercurius aber soll ihn mit unvergleichlich-sinnreicher Vernunfft begaben / und der unbeständige Mond soll ihm nicht schädlich / sondern nützlich seyn / weil er ihm eine unglaubliche Geschwindigkeit einpflantzen wird; die Pallas soll ihn auff dem Parnasso aufferziehen / und Vulcanus soll ihm in Hora Martis seine Waffen / sonderlich ein Schwerd schmiden / mit welchem er die gantze Welt bezwingen / ...” Weydt (p. 244 ff.) asserts that this passage proves that Grimmelshausen meant Jupiter and the other gods mentioned to be regarded as planetary gods. Haberkamm (p. 44 ff.) pointed out, as yet further proof, that the gifts of some of the gods are evidently patterned on remarks which are found in Grimmelshausen's Perpetual Calendar and which were taken verbatim from Indagine (the underlinings are Haberkamm's): “Venus hat gar nahe mit dem Jove gleiche Eigenschafften / doch etwas geringer / und was der Planet Jupiter von Tugenden / Künsten / Geschicklichkeiten und allem Guten im Thun und Lassen inflösset / demselben gibt Venus hinzu eine Zierlichkeit besonders Auffsehen und Anmuth; und solches umb so viel destomehr / wann Jupiter sie freundlich anblickt;...”; “Jupiter hat ein unsträfflich anmuthige Influentz / sintemahl kein Gab noch Ruhm der Rathgebung / Weißheit / Fürsichtigkeit /Kunst / Wohlredenheit noch Schönheit ist / die nit seiner Geburt mit allem Fleiß verleyhen solte.”; and “Mercurius ist / wie etliche Authores wollen / ein zweiffelhafter Planet / bey guten Planeten gut / und bey bösen böß / sonsten für sich selbst ist er ein erwehlter guter Planet / bevorab Vernunfft und Sinnreichen Verstand zu verleyhen....” Haberkamm also points out that in the same text the moon is described as inconstant, but in the proper astrological configuration it can be beneficial, and celerity (“Schnelligkeit”) is one of its attributes. Haberkamm cites no verbal reminiscences in Jupiter's remarks concerning Mars, but points out that Mars' role is consistent with the astrological view and that the phrase “Hora Martis” points towards astrology rather than mythology. Both Haberkamm (p. 46, footnote 23 et passimi) and Weydt (p. 248) suspected that Grimmelshausen meant Pallas Athena to be construed as the sun and Vulcan as Saturn, in which case the passage would list all seven planetary gods.

Left unanswered by Weydt and Haberkamm is one important question: What prompted Grimmelshausen to have Jupiter give this horoscope of his German Hero, i.e. was there a model for the passage in terms of form rather than content (partially)? Several possibilities might be considered: 1) In Moscherosh, “Phantasten-Spital” (I, 411 f.) there is a satire on casters of horoscopes which involves exaggerated predictions. The wealthy parents of the most hideous looking child imaginable call in the “most distinguished Professores of things to come,” and when these gentlemen saw “what was to their advantage,” they declared that “from the Genesi, Horoscopo, lineamenten and all other circumstances they could only conclude that this child would surpass Nestor in length of life, Aristotle in high intelligence, Hercules in strength, Alexander the Great in good fortune and Croesus in wealth, and Julius Caesar in heroic deeds, Octavius Augustus in fame and praise....” Doubtless other satires on casters of horoscopes, many of whom were frauds, could be cited. 2) Garzoni, Discourse 153, which deals with poets and poetry, includes scathing remarks about the tendency of poets to flatter their friends and benefactors: “Wenn aber die Poeten einen wollen loben / so müssen ihm auch die Planeten weichen / die himlische Spheren sich für ihm beugen / Sonn vnnd Mond ihn ehren / vnd himlische Götter ihn zu sich nehmen / so bald sie seiner ansichtig werden; dannenhero Horatius sagt: Dignum laude virum Musa vetat mori. Das ist: Einen Mann der is lobens werth /Der Poet mit ewigen namen ehrt. Item: Caelo Musa beat. Die Musae ihn in den Himmel heben.

Wenn du einen Poeten zum freundt hast vnd behelst / so bistu in weißheit gleich wie ein Athlas, in vorsichtigkeit / wie ein Iuppiter; in wolredenheit / wie ein Mercurius, in ehren glantz wie ein Phoebus, in stärcke vnd tapfferkeit wie ein Mars, in herrlichkeit wie eine glantzende Sonne. Der Poet macht dich mit seinen Versen so schön / wie ein Rose / die Charites theilen dir ihre freundtlichkeit vnd holdseligkeit mit / der Chorus Aphius zieret dich mit allen Tugendten vnd Gaben / die Venus muß ihre anmühtigkeit mir dir theilen. In summa, es müssen alle Götter mit dir zu thun haben / daß du zu einem Außbundt genugsam auß gebutzt seyest: vnnd kompt alles / was du gutes an dir hast / von den Gratiis, oder von deß Athlantis Enckel / oder von dem Superno choro, oder von dem weisen Motore der gantzen Welt. Ein Poet kan dich / wie Iupiter Europam in einem huy vber das wilde Meer führen / ja biß in den Himmel führen; kan dich wie eine Ariadnam zwischen die Sterne setzen; wie eine Mineruani zu den öbersten oder höchsten Chor deß templi Honoris setzen: wie einen Ganimedem vber

265

alle frewde der Götter erheben. Dieweil ein Poet deine laudes beschreibet / gewinnst du Flügel wie ein Adeler / schwingest dich in die höhe wie ein anderer Pegasus, badest dich in dem fonte Cabillino, vnd kompst eines mals auff die spitze des Parnassi oder Heliconis. In summa, wo wolte man grössere wunderwerck sehen / als bey einem Poeten / welcher mit seiner Federn einen in den abgrundt der Erden kan störtzen / vnd also bald widerumb biβ vber den Olympum erheben?" Garzoni's satire on poets' exaggerated praise mentions nine of the fourteen classical figures or planetary gods named in Jupiter's horoscope (only Hercules, Narcissus and Adonis, and Vulcan are missing); and it contains three clearly identifiable groups of figures: planetary gods (the sun and the moon, mentioned in the introduction); classical figures which can only be mythological (Atlas, Phoebus, the Charites, the Graces, Europa, Ariadne, Minerva, Ganymede, Pegasus, the Parnasasus, the Helicon, and Mount Olympus); and figures which could be either gods from mythology or planetary gods (Jupiter, Mercury, Mars, and Venus)—their qualities, derived as they are from Greek mythology, fit both mythic and planetary gods. 3) Grimmelshausen first exploited the above passage from Garzoni in The Satyrical Pilgrim II, 1 ("On Poetry"), where the revision reads as follows: "Wan du einen Poeten zum Freunde hast / so erhebt er dich über den Athlantem: die Planeten müssen dir weichen / Sonne und Mon mueβ dich ehren / und die gantze welt mueβ sich über dich vorwundern; Alsdann bistu tapfferer als Mars; stärcker als Hercules; ohnerschrockener als Minos; klüger als Minerua; beredter als Mercurius; vorsichtiger als Juppiter; höher erhaben als Phoebus; schöner als Narcissus; anmutiger als Venus; holdseeliger als die Charites selbsten; und alles was du ahn dir hast / seind lauther seltene Gaben der Gratien; Ein solcher Poet erhebt dich biβ ahn den Himmel / und setzet dich wie ein andere Ariadnae zwischen die Stern / oder wie eine Palladem in den höchsten Orth des Templi Honoris! oder gar wie einen Ganimedem über alle Freud der Himlischen Götter; da kriegstu Flügel wie ein Adler: schwingst dich in die Höhe wie Pegasus! badest dich in fonte Caballino und kömst einsmals uff die Spitze des Parnassi oder Heliconis." As in Garzoni's satire, exclusively planetary gods (the sun and the moon, and the planets) are mentioned in an off-hand manner in the introduction, and figures which are exclusively mythological and those which could be either mythological or planetary gods are intermingled. Grimmelshausen not only deletes several purely mythological figures, he adds three not found in Garzoni (Hercules, Narcissus, and Minos), and two of them (Hercules and Narcissus) appear in Jupiter's Horoscope; thus eleven of the thirteen figures (or places) in the horoscope appear in Grimmelshausen's first re-working of Garzoni's satire—only Vulcan and Adonis (who is a logical addition to Narcissus and Ganymede, both also paragons of male beauty) are missing. Having included Minerva (Athena) by that name in the opening list of gods, he changes Garzoni's Minerva to Pallas, the form of the name employed in Jupiter's Horoscope (apparently Pallas cannot be construed to be the Sun after all). Finally, the entire opening section of this satire is cast in the same form as the satire on casters of horoscopes in "Phantasten-Spital": the person being praised is said to excel in virtue the mythological paragon of that particular virtue.

In light of the above it would seem that Grimmelshausen thought of his Jupiter figure not as a planetary god but as a mad poet and visionary and that Jupiter's Horoscope or the German Hero is meant to be just what its model and Grimmelshausen's first reworking of that model is: a satire on the tendency of poets, prophets, soothsayers, astrologers, and casters of horoscopes to indulge in excessive praise (for a variety of reasons). The encomium itself, like its model in Garzoni's discourse and its predecessor in The Satyrical Pilgrim, presents an intermingling of mythological gods, planetary gods, and figures which could be either, with some characteristics for Venus, Jupiter, Mercury and the Moon borrowed from Indagine.

18.   Hercules: strongest and boldest of the classical mythological figures. Lauremberg's Acerra philologica I, 43 (p.76 ff.) presents a survey of his more important feats, and Herold describes no fewer than 32 heroic "deeds of Hercules" (Diodorus Siculus rendering, clxxv-cxci).

19.   Venus: goddess of love and beauty, termed in Acerra philologica I 85 (p. 157) and Moscherosch VI 301 f. "the most beautiful goddess."

20.   Narcissus: a beautiful youth, inaccessible to the feeling of love, rejected Echo, who pined for him; as punishment Nemesis caused Narcissus to become so enamored of his own reflection in the water that he pined away and died. Cf. Ovid, Metamorphoses III, 339-510. Following Ovid, Lauremberg tells the tale in Acerra philologica I, 67 (p. 122 f.).

21.   Adonis: a youth of such beauty that Aphrodite (Venus), the goddess of love herself, fell in love with him. Cf. Ovid, Metamorphoses X, 503-739.

22.   Mercury: Roman god of commerce and financial gain; defined in Acerra philologica I, 85 (p. 155) as "the messenger of all the gods, with wings on his feet and head, in his hand a rod with which he leads souls to hell; is the patron of merchants,... Eloquence is his province."

23.   Pallas: surname of Athena, the foremost goddess of the Roman Pantheon; she was patroness of the arts and sciences. Acerra philologica I, 85 (p 156 f.) and Moscherosch (VI, 300f.) list her as "Minerva or Pallas. Goddesses (sic) of wisdom and intelligence, and of studying...."

24.   Parnassus: mountain in Greece, in legend the home of Apollo (god of art and poetry, among other things) and the Muses (goddesses of song and different kinds of poetry). It is also so defined, together with the Helicon, in Acerra philologica I, 85 (p. 157) and Moscherosch VI, 301.

25.   Vulcan: Roman god of fire (equivalent to Greek Hephaestus); defined in Acerra philologica I, 85 (p. 153) as "the limping god, and smith of all the gods."

26.   in hora Martis: in the hour of (under the sign of) Mars, the Roman god of warfare. Haberkamm (p. 39 f.) discusses the astrological import of the phrase; more important, in a footnote (p. 39-40) he identifies two possible sources for it: Harsdörffer's Gesprechspiele and Johann Staricius' Heldenschatz.

27.   an entire Swiss mile: like the "German mile," it was about 7.5 kilometers.

28.   Tamerlane: see above Notes to Book I, Chapter 17; the source of this anecdote has not yet been determined.

29.   Elysian fields: Elysium, the part of the afterworld where the shades of the blessed reside.

30.   chorum deorum: choir of the gods; the phrase is used several times by Garzoni in his Introduction.

31.   Helicon: mountain range in Boetia which was sacred to Apollo and the Muses. The notion that the Helicon should be moved to Germany may be a sly dig at Jesaias Rompler von Löwenhalt which Scholte failed to note in his argument that this poet inspired in part the Jupiter figure. To Rompler's only published volume of poetry, Des Jesaias Romplers von Löwenhalt erstes gebüsch seiner Reim-getichte, were appended seven congratulatory poems—one in French, two in Latin, and four in German. Inasmuch as one of the German poems is by Johannes Küeffer, it seems quite likely that Grimmelshausen, who worked for Küeffer as a steward for several years and was presumably during that time either considering or already embarking upon a career as a writer, was familiar with it and the volume in which it appeared. Of the three other congratulatory poems in German, which were written by Balthasar Venator, Harsdörffer, and Johann Matthias Schneuber, Venator's is particularly interesting: it begins with the assertion that the Helicon had moved to Germany, that the Muses were German and that Apollo and Venus and her son were beginning to use the German language; there follows a description of the ravages of the Thirty Years' War which put an end to this removal of Greece to Upper Germany, and the poem ends with the claim that Rompler, despite the war, had preserved "our Helicon" and kept it in high esteem. If Grimmelshausen is indeed alluding to Rompler, then the figure in Rompler's poem which would correspond to Jupiter would be Rompler himself, the man who allegedly created the Helicon in Germany.

32.   Fabricius: Gaius Fabricius Suscinus, consul in Rome in 282 and 278 B.C. and one of the most popular heros in the annals of Rome because of the steadfastness with which he resisted the efforts of Pyrrhus to subvert him.

33.   King Pyrrhus: (318-272) king of Epirus.

34.   Manoah in America: city in Dorado, Venezuela renowned for its wealth in gold.

35.   Tatar Khan: title of the Mongolian rulers of Persia.

36.   Prester John: during the Middle Ages it was believed that he ruled over a Christian empire deep in Asia.

37.   in the times of Augustus: Gaius Julius Caesar Octavianus (63 B.C.- 14 A.D.), given the name Augustus when he became the first Roman emperor in 27 B.C. Although only the last five years of his reign were free of war, he did establish the so-called pax Augusta, which despite the ineptitude of his successors became the pax Romana, the longest period of peace and prosperity ever known to mankind.

CHAPTER 5: *How he will unite the religions with one another and pour them into one mold*

38.   the plague of Erysichton: Erysichton cut down trees in a grove sacred to Demeter (Ceres), and he was punished with a ravening hunger which compelled him to devour his own flesh. Cf. Ovid, Metamorphoses VII, 725-884.

39.   Momus: god of mockery and censure.

40.   Zoilus: a grammarian from Amphipolis who flourished during the reign of Philip of Macedon; his harsh treatment of Homer's works caused posterity to regard him as the epitome of the carping critic and incorrigible fault-finder.

41.   materi: substance.

42.   Theon: presumably Aelius Theon of Alexandria, a sophist and rhetorician who apparently lived during the reign of Augustus, is meant.

43.   Hipponax-tongue: a sharp or biting tongue; Hipponax of Ephesus (flourished 546-520 B.C.) was famous for his bitter satires.

44.   Battus: a shepherd of Neleus; when he saw Hermes (Mercury) driving away cattle he had stolen from Apollo, he promised to say nothing of what he knew, but he broke this promise and as punishment was turned into a stone. Cf. Ovid, Metamorphoses II, 676-707. In Garzoni's Introduction he is one of the participants and presents his defense of his actions, and in Garzoni's Discourse 88 (p. 511), which deals with calumniators, his actions and fate are described (see above).

45.   Juno: wife of Jupiter.

46.   lapidem philosophorum: philosophers' stone.

47.   argumenta: arguments.

48.   theologos: theologians.

49.   Ptolomaeus Philadelphus: Ptolomaeus II (309-247 B.C.), king of Egypt from 285 until his death; according to tradition it was at his command that the Holy Scriptures of the Jews were translated into Greek. The story of the "72 translators" was wide-spread; it appeared, among other places, in Garzoni, Discourse 127 (p. 644).

50.   Pluto: Pluton (at first a surname of Hades), god of the lower world; so defined in Grimmelshausen's sources for classical mythology.

51.   ad infinitum or indefinitum: indefinitely.

52.   concilium: council.

53.   congregatio: congregation, group, persons assembled.

54.   take strides ad rem: to get down to business.

55.   to pin a palm onto such a heretic and give him to Pluto as a New Year's present: to flay a heretic with thorns (cf. Borcherdt, "Miszellen zu Grimmelshausens Simplicissimus," Euphorion 23, p. 294).

CHAPTER 6: *What the legatio of lice did with Jove*

56.   legatio: legation, group of deputies sent on a mission.

57.   Daedalus: a mythological craftsman of renown who procured wings for himself and his son and flew across the Aegean Sea. Cf. Apollodoris, Epitome I, 12 f. and Ovid, Metsmorphoses VIII, 183-235. The tale of Daedalus and his son Icarus was well known; Acerra philologica II, 7, p. 185 f., among other works, made it available to Germans who knew little or no Latin or classical mythology. Grimmelshausen may have been prompted to use Daedalus' flight by the last sentence in the Response and Judgment of the Assembled Gods, in Garzoni's Introduction: "And if it is deemed appropriate that you do...something useful and in accord with the dignity of the Author, then you should forthwith put on the wings of Daedalus and bring the happy message to us." : Garzoni: "Und wann ihr in gemeltem Hoff etwas nützliches / nach Würden deß Authoris verrichtet / solt ihr also bald deß Daedali Flügel anziehen / und uns die früliche Bottschafft bringen."; ST: "... die Ursach / daß ich auß dem Himmel kommen / ist / daß ich dich selbst darinn manglete / nam derowegen deß Daedali Flügel / und flog auff Erden dich zu suchen /..."

58.   Zoilus and Moscus: for Zoilus, see above, Book III, Chapter 5; Moscus is not, as Borcherdt (p. 397) suggested, intended to be "Momus"; Moscus is the name of the arrogant pedant who speaks against the author in Garzoni's Introduction (his tirade is entitled "Moscus redet von wegen deß gantzen Collegii der Schulfüchse und Naßweisen Magistellis, welche alles verbessern / und das Magnificat corrigiren wöllen"). The name is apparently derived from the Italian "mosca" (Latin "musca": literally "fly" and figuratively "pest").

59.   the slander of the gods: this diatribe is modeled very closely on two tirades in Garzoni's Introduction: that of Zoilus, which excoriated Jupiter, Apollo, and Mercury and ended with the comparison of the gods to the stalls of Augias—interestingly enough, a reference to Jupiter's rape of Ganymede is omitted (parallel texts in Scholte, p. 131—the Garzoni passage will be repeated here, in this instance); and that of Minerva (overlooked by Scholte), in which she cites the calumnies of Momus concerning Venus, Vulcan, Mars and Priapus (again reference to Jupiter's rape of Ganymede is omitted). Garzoni 1: "Wer ist Jupiter / oder was ist er mehr / als sin Filtzläusiger Hurenhängst? Und Läst sich darbey noch nicht benügen / wie man an dem raptu deß Ganymedis gnugsamb mag abnehmen? Was ist der schöne Jungfrawenknecht Apollo, mit seinen Krausenlettich umb den Halß / mehr / als ein vnverschämpter Hurenbul / wie ihr dann solches / so wol als ich / in allen Historien gelesen? Was ist Mercurius mehr / als ein beschwätzter Hurenmackeler und Ruffian / der beydes den Göttern und den Göttinnen in ihren unzimblichen Bulschafften zu Hauß und zu Handt gehet? Was ist / damit ich es kurtz zusammen fasse / dieser gantze chorus oder Hauffe mehr / alß deß Augei Viehe / dessen Stall durch die gantze Welt hindurch stincket?"; Garzoni 2): "Wer hat den Ehebruch Veneris mit dem Marte außgebracht? Hat es nicht Momus gethan? Wer hat Mercurium für einen Gott und Fürsteher der Diebe außgeschrien? ...von Momo kompt es her / daß ...Priapus für einen Unflat gehalten wirdt." ; ST: "du selbst / sagen sie / seyest ein Filtzläusiger Ehebrecherische Hurenhengst / mit was für Billichkeit du dann die Welt wegen solcher Laster straffen mögest? Vulcanus sey ein gedultiger Hanrey / und habe den Ehebruch Martis ohne sonderbare nahmhaffte Rach müssen hingehen lassen / was der hinckende Gauch dann vor Waffen werde schmiden können? Venus sey selbsten die verhaßte Vettel von der Welt / wegen ihrer Unkeuschheit / was sie denn vor Gnad und Gunst einem andern werde mittheilen können? Mars sey ein Mörder und Rauber; Apollo ein unverschämter Huren-Jäger; Mercurius ein unnützer Plauderer / Dieb und Kuppler / Priapus ein Unflat / Hercules ein Hirnschälliger Wüterich / und in Summa die gantze Schaar der Götter so verrucht / daß man sie sonst nirgends hin als in deß Augei Stall logiren solte / welcher ohne das durch die gantze Welt stinckt." Garzoni, Discourse 74 (p. 465), probably also contributed to

the passage: "Ich will auch der alten Poeten geschweigen / welche von den alten Göttern vorgeben / dz sie auch außbündige Hurenmaklern gewesen / wie den Mercurius ir Bott / beynah nichts anders zu thun hatte als dz er die Hurenbottschaft verrichtet /... Venus is eine Göttin / welche alle Hurenliebe befördert /... Mars setzt dem Vulcano hörner auff/..."

60.   Vulcan...Mars...: Mars is said to have seduced Vulcan's wife, Venus. The tale was retold in several of Grimmelshausen's favorite sources: Moscherosch I, 120; Cerda's Weiblicher Lustgarten, p. 273; and Garzoni, Discourse 74 (p. 465).

61.   Priapus: fertility god, protector of sheep and goats, of bees, of viniculture and agriculture. Acerra philologica (I, 85, p. 156) and Moscherosch (VI, 299) define him as "the wooden god, with his abominable large members....a protector of gardens, into which he is put so that he can protect them and their fruits from thieves." Garzoni, Discourse 146 (p. 701) describes him in a similar manner. Herold (p. cllxxii) gives Diodorus Siculus' description of him.

62.   the stable of Augias: according to legend, Augias had a herd of 3,000 oxen, and the stalls had not been cleaned out for 30 years, until Hercules accomplished the task on a single day (the "fifth labor of Hercules"). Cf. Apollodorus, Library II, 5, 5. The tale appears in Acerra philologica I, 43, p. 77, and Herold, p. clxxix (where it is the "tenth deed").

63.   Shall I torment these chatterboxes...Anaxarchus in a mortar: Jupiter's "threatened punishments" are taken from Garzoni's Response to the Chorus of the Gods in his Introduction; Scholte (p.131 f.) reproduces parallel texts.

64.   Tantalus: as punishment for divulging secrets entrusted to him by Zeus (Jupiter) Tantalus was afflicted with a great thirst and placed in the middle of a body of water which always receded before him when he attempted to drink from it. Garzoni, Discourse 88 (p. 511), describes the punishments of Tantalus and of the next two figures, Daphitas and Anaxarchus.

65.   Mount Thorax...Daphitas: Daphitas, a grammarian from Telmesus in Asia Minor, was celebrated for his slanderous disposition, which ultimately moved the ruler of Pergamon to have him crucified on Mount Thorax.

66.   Anaxarchus: a philosopher of Abdera, of the school of Democritus; Nicocreon, the king of Cyprus, whom Anaxarchus had offended, had him pounded to death in a stone mortar.

67.   Phalaris: ruler of Agrigentum in Sicily; his name was synonymous with cruel tyranny. At his command Perillus created a brazen bull into which the tyrant forced his victims; he then lit a fire underneath it and roasted the man in it till he was dead. Polybius (XII, 25) noted that the screaming of the victim caused a sound to come from the machine which was very like the bellowing of a bull. Phalaris used Perillus himself to test the device (it worked as planned). The anecdote appears in Acerra philologica (II, 54, p. 274) and at the end of Garzoni, Discourse 87 (p. 508), i.e. just before the tales of the punishments of Daphitas, Anaxarchus and Tantalus in Discourse 88.

68.   Pandora's box: in Greek legend Pandora, the first woman on earth, was destined by her beauty to bring misery upon the entire human race; her box contained all the ills of the world, but also Hope, which might make them bearable. Cf. Hesiod, Works and Days, 60-105. Grimmelshausen could have read the story in Acerra philologica I, 85, p. 158 and III, 21, p. 398 f.

69.   Nemesis: Greek goddess who meted out to mortals both misery and happiness and made sure that those with too many blessings were sooner or later visited with losses and suffering.

70.   Alecto, Megaera, and Tisiphone: see above Notes to Book II, Chapter 6.

71.   Cerberus: the many-headed dog which guarded the entrance to the underworld, defined in Acerra philologica (I, 86, p. 160) and Moscherosch as "the dog...with three heads and spitting fire" which guards "the house of the god of hell." Grimmelshausen may have been inspired by a passage in Minerva's Oration in Garzoni's Introduction in which she compares Cerberus to Momus and then links Cerberus with the dogs of Acteon.

72.   Hesiod: early Greek poet and cosmogonist from the Boetian school (flourished c. 735 B.C.).

73.   Homer: most famous of the Greek epic poets (flourished c. 850 B.C.).

74.   the Eumenides: see above Notes to Book II, Chapter 6.

75.   the River Styx: the river which flows around the underworld seven times; mentioned as one of the three rivers in the underworld in Acerra philologica I, 86, p. 159, and Moscherosch VI, 305.

76.   what had transpired betwixt me and Io, Callisto, Europa...: for Jupiter's affairs with Callisto and Europa see above, Notes to Book II, Chapter 8; Io, the daughter of King Inachos of Argos, was loved by Jupiter, who turned her into a heifer in order to protect her from his jealous spouse. Cf. Apollodorus, Library II, 1, 3, and Ovid, Metamorphoses I, 568 ff. The story of Jupiter and Io may have been familiar to Grimmelshausen from Cerda's Weiblicher Lustgarten, p. 150.

77.   Apollo...the ravens: the raven, one of Apollo's servants, reported to him that his mistress Coronis had been unfaithful, whereupon Apollo railed at the raven so violently that it turned black. Cf. Apollodorus, Library III, 10, 3, and Ovid, Metamorphoses II, 531 ff. The punishment is referred to in Garzoni, Discourse 88 (p. 511).

78.   territorio: territory, domain.

79.   privilegium: privileges.

CHAPTER 7: *The chasseur once more wins honor and booty from the chase*

80.   Cocytus: a river in the underworld, the so-called "river of wailing."

81.   inasmuch as he could ride no better than an old maid...: in The Satyrical Pilgrim II, 1, Grimmelshausen points out that a poet's head is so full of strange things that no room is left for him to engage in practical matters—which is surely Jupiter's state here: "...daß alsdann ihr Hirn mit Poetischen Dünsten der Thorheit solcher gestalt übernäbelt und angefüllt sey / daß beynahe kein Platz mehr übrig bleibt / dahin sich die Gedanken uff Verrichtungen anderer nötigen Gefshäfften logiren könten;..."

82.   the Lapithae...the Centaurs...the wedding feast of Pirithous: during the feast, in which Pirithous, king of the Lapithae, was celebrating his marriage with Hippodamia, an intoxicated centaur carried off the bride, which led to a celebrated war between the Lapithae and the Centaurs, in which the latter were defeated. Cf. Ovid, Metamorphoses XII, 210-535. The battle between them became a simile for a heated and bloody military encounter—it is used this way, for example, in Arcadia, p. 320 (cf. H. Geulen, p. 435). In Garzoni's Introduction Momus, in his Tirade against Garzoni, specifically refers to the gods hurling thunder and lightning down upon the Centaurs and Lapithae. Grimmelshausen could have read about the battle in Herold (p. ccxx), where the account of Diodorus Siculus (IV, 70 2) was rendered into German.

83.   Johann de Werdt: see above, Notes to Book I, Chapter 17.

CHAPTER 8: *How he found the devil in a trunk, and how Hopalong seized some fine horses*

84.   Count von der Wahl: Johann Christian von der Wahl (died 1644) was an artillery general in the army of the Duke of Bavaria; in 1637, his army marched from the Upper Palatinate into Westphalia, where he was commander-in-chief of Imperial troops.

85.   cavalcada: cavalcade, military unit.

86.   Vecht, Meppen, Lingen: Vechte (a village on the Vechta, a tributary of the Haase) was attacked by von der Wahl's troops June 10-13, 1637 without result (cf. Könnecke I, 252); equally unsuccessful was an attack on Meppen, a town in

Hannover in Lower Saxony at the confluence of the Haase and the Ems (Könnecke I, 252). Lingen was a town in Lower Saxony on the Ems.

87.　the bishopric of Paderborn: region whose capital was the city of Paderborn, which was situated in Westphalia at the western foot of the Egge Mountains.

88.　the Prince of Orange: the Dutch stadtholder Friedrich Heinrich von Oranien (1584-1647) is probably meant; in 1634 he sent a Dutch army of 5,000 men to help the Swedes and the Hessians in their struggle with the Imperials. Bechtold (p. 512 f.) explains that the Dutch soldiers insisted on being paid in coin of their own realm, and he suggests that if the Hessian officer had taken part in the campaign with them, his possession of such a coin would be quite reasonable.

89.　valete: farewell present.

CHAPTER 9: *An unequal fight in which the weaker party wins and the winner is taken captive*

90.　An unequal fight...: Weydt (p. 70 ff.) suspects that the inspiration for this episode may have been an anecdote entitled "Fatal Imagination" ("Die tödtliche Einbildung"), which appeared in Harsdörffer's Heraklit und Demokrit (as Anecdote CXCIX) and which was reprinted with minor editing in the 1671 Europäischer Wundergeschichten-Kalender (Weydt attributes this publication to Grimmelshausen; Koschlig disputes it). In the anecdote two soldiers who are mortal enemies are compelled by their commanding officer to stop feuding with each other; they follow orders, but one of them, using an unloaded weapon, pretends to attack the other and fire the weapon at him, with the result that the target of the feigned attack dies of heart failure; the attacker is punished as if he had in fact attacked his foe with a deadly weapon. Weydt (p. 74) notes that if this anecdote was Grimmelshausen's starting point, as Weydt believes, he reshaped it in a masterly fashion. It would seem more likely, however, that the fight between Simplicissimus and the trooper of horse is based on a ruse which was doubtless much discussed amongst soldiers at the time and in fact has probably been in use since wars began (feigned incapacitation in order to take by surprise a foe who has been lulled into a false sense of security).

91.　Things were in floribus: The party was in full swing; in floribus is also used by Moscherosch in describing drinking bouts (see "Höllenkinder," p. 358, and "Hanβ hinuber Ganβ hinuber," p. 791); Moscherosch also uses the abbreviated form "in flor." ("Hofschule," p. 409 and 552).

92.　musketeers...dragoons: see above, Book I, Chapters 16 and 20.

93.　the prae of his branch: the honor of his branch.

94.　reputatio: reputation, good name.

95.　recta: directly

CHAPTER 10: *The major general of ordnance spares the chasseur's life and otherwise gives him cause to hope for the best*

96.　major general of ordnance: Count von der Wahl.

97.　corpo: army; the use of the wrong case in Latin here, according to Weydt (Nachahmung, p. 24), does not prove that Grimmelshausen knew little or no Latin, but rather represents an attempt to give the flavor of the Latin military terms as they were used during the Thirty Years' War; the term "corpo" does indeed occur repeatedly in Grimmelshausen's two favorite historical sources, Wassenberg and the Theatrum Europaeum.

98.   N.N.: abbreviation for "nomen nescio" (I do not know the name) or "nomen nominandum" (the name is yet to be given), used by Grimmelshausen and others at the time when they wished not to give a name.

99.   Münster: see above, Notes to Book II, Chapter 21.

100.   Hamm: see above, Notes to Book II, Chapter 28.

101.   surrender...per accord: surrender conditionally ; during the Thirty Years' War this generally meant that a besieged garrison was permitted to withdraw from its fortress without risk of attack, leaving the stronghold to be occupied by the enemy; those vacating the fortress were usually permitted to take their personal effects with them—in the worst cases at least as much as they could carry on their own person.

CHAPTER 11: *Contains all manner of things of slight importance and considerable fancy*

102.   the Hessians: the Lippstadt garrison.

103.   Lippstadt: see above, Notes to Book II, Chapter 29.

104.   histori: story, tale.

105.   cavalcada: here in the sense of "military mission."

106.   comitem palatinum: the Count Palatine, who at that time was responsible for bestowing coats of arms and the like.

107.   Amor: the god of love

CHAPTER 12: *Fortuna unexpectedly bestows a noble present upon the chasseur*

108.   Fortuna: goddess of fortune.

109.   I had two fine horses....: Bechtold (p. 506 f.) points out a similar description in the Guzman (I, 24).

110.   Queen of Sheba...Solomon: I Kings 10.

111.   nowadays the meanest stableboy...: Grimmelshausen makes the same point in The Satyrical Pilgrim (Part II, Section 2 : "On Guns") and in The Singular Life Story of Heedless Hopalong, Chapter 15 (p. 64). The thought is not original with him, of course; Moscherosch, among others, makes the same point in his "Soldatenleben."

112.   the discovery of the buried treasure: Bechtold (p. 509) asserts that motifs from this episode come from Goulart and Praetorius, where (p. 104) the discovery of a treasure in Soest in 1622 is reported; he also notes that Praetorius describes the unusual behavior of horses and other animals in the presence of spirits and ghosts (Neue Weltbeschreibung II).

113.   Joachim Valley: actually St. Joachim's Valley (St. Joachimsthal), a town in northwestern Bohemia which was the center of silver mining; the "Joachimsthaler" (the word dollar derives from the suffix -thaler, from Thal: valley), a silver coin, was first struck in 1517.

CHAPTER 13: *Simplicius' strange crotchets and castles in the air, and how he kept his treasure secure*

114.   virtues and strengths (of) precious stones: Kurz (p. 400 f.) noted that many of the examples also appear in Konrad von Megenburg's Das Buch der Natur.

115.   melancholia: melancholy, sadness.

116.   my book BLACK AND WHITE: see above, Notes to Book II, Chapter 1.

117.   Cologne: a major German city since medieval times, it is located on the Rhine in the so-called Cologne Basin, the region between where the Sieg and the Wupper flow into the Rhine.

118.   Münster: see above, Book II, Chapter 31.

CHAPTER 14: *How the chasseur is taken prisoner by the other side*

119.   the land of Berg: in the seventeenth century Berg was a duchy situated on the right bank of the lower course of the Rhine; its capital was Düsseldorf.

120.   German miles: a German mile was about 7.5 kilometers.

CHAPTER 15: *Under what conditionibus the chasseur was released once more*

121.   conditionibus: conditions.

122.   N. de S.A.: Daniel de St. Andräe, the then commandant of Lippstadt (see Notes to Book I, Chapter 17).

123.   soldiers of fortune: during the Thirty Years' War a "soldier of fortune" was a man of common birth who as a consequence of uncommon valor and very good luck had been able to rise to a military rank ordinarily reserved for men of noble birth.

124.   secretario: secretary, clerk.

125.   in duplo: in dupicate, in two copies.

CHAPTER 16: *How Simplicius became a gentleman*

126.   Fortuna: the goddess of good fortune.

127.   valet: farewell, goodby.

128.   soldateska: soldiery.

CHAPTER 17: *Wherewith the chasseur thought to pass the six months, and also something concerning the sibyl of Soest*

129.   the Lippa River: tributary of the Rhine which arises in the western part of the Egge Mountains and flows in a westerly direction for more than 200 miles through Westphalia until it empties into the Rhine at Wesel.

CHAPTER 18: *How the chasseur turns wooer and makes a trade of wooing*

130.   ARCADIA: famous pastoral romance (1590) by Sir Philipp Sidney (1554-1586) which was translated into German by Valent. Theocritus in 1630 and by Martin Opitz in 1638.

131.   Thomas Thomäus' WORLD GARDEN: Thomaeus was a physician and author from Ravenna; his Idea del giardino del mondo appeared in German translation in 1620 under the title Hortulus mundi, i.e. Welt-Gärtlein.

132.   as…swains and wooers do…: Scholte (p. 132 f.) suggests Garzoni, Discourse 96, as the source of the "catalogue of lovers' woes" which follows and presents parallel texts; the sequence of the woes is not identical, however, and such catalogues doubtless abounded in satirical and homiletic works of the time.

133.   as Aurora did…Endymion: the passage, not noted by Scholte, is taken, with one exception (discussed below), verbatim from Garzoni, Discourse 96 (p. 543): Garzoni: "Sie würden sich nicht also Tag vnd Nacht vmb ein leichtfertiges / boβhafftiges vnd betriegliches Weib grämen / welches / wenn sie ihre Reputation wüsten zu halten / vnd sich ein wenig theuwer zu machen / ihnen selbst würden nachlauffen / wie die Aurora dem Clito, Cephalo, vnd Vitoni, Venus dem Anchisae, Atidi vnd Adoni, Ceres dem Iasoni, vnd die Diana oder Luna irem lieben Endimioni"; ST: "…also daβ mir das Frauenzimmer / wann ich mich dessen schon nicht sonderlich anname / wie Aurora dem Clito, Cephalo, und Vitoni, Venus dem Anchise, Atidi, und Adoni, Ceres dem Glauco, Ulysse und Jasoni, und die keusche Diana selbst ihrem Endimione, von sich selbst nachlieffe / mehr als ich dessen begehrte."

134.   Aurora…Clitus, Cephalus, and Tithonus: Aurora, the goddess of the dawn, carried off several youths renowned for their beauty; those usually mentioned are Orion, Cephalus, and Tithonus.

135.   Venus…Anchises, Atidus, and Adonis: Venus had two mortal lovers, Anchises and Adonis; her union with Anchises produced Aneas (for Adonis see Notes to Book III, Chapter 4). Atys (Attis), a Phrygian shepherd, was the beloved of Cybele, not of Venus; when he betrayed her he was changed into a fir tree. A slightly different version, with which Grimmelshausen was probably familiar, appeared in Herold's version of Diodorus Siculus (p. clv). When it became known that Cybele was with child by Atys her father had Atys and all Cybele's handmaidens killed, and Cybele fell into madness and wandered distraught around the kingdom.

136.   Ceres…Glaucus, Ulysses, and Jason: here the text departs from Garzoni, who mentions only Ceres and Jason; either Grimmelshausen or one of his publisher's editors inserted Glaucus and Ulysses, who had no connection whatsoever with Ceres. The misunderstanding apparently arose because Jason was taken to be the famous seafarer and leader of the argonauts. In fact, the figure in classical mythology who is meant is not Jason but the hero Jasion, who was the beloved of Demeter (Ceres)—cf. Hesiod, Theogony, 969 f. Ulysses and Glaucus were perhaps interpolated in the phrase because they, like Jason, were famous seafarers. Ulysses, by far the better known of the two, is, of course, the hero of Homer's Odyssey. Glaucus, a fisherman from Anthedon in Boetia, ate part of a divine herb which Chronos had sown and thereby became immortal; he was said to have built the Argo and sailed with Jason. It is also possible that Ceres was confused with Circe, who had designs on both Ulysses (Homer, Odyssey X, 133 ff.; Ovid, Metamorphoses XIV, 247 ff.) and Glaucus (Ovid, Metamorphoses XIV, 10 ff.); she bewitched the the crew of Ulysses, and when Glaucus rejected her overtures, she disfigured his beloved, Scylla. Herold's description of Medea, the wife of Jason, as "the Circe of Colches" (p. cciii), could have linked the two women in Grimmelshausen's mind. In producing a German version of Diodorus Siculus, Herold of course reproduced the story of Jason and the Argonauts (pp. cc ff.), including Jason's encounter with Glaucus.

137.   Diana…Endymion: see above Notes to Book I, Chapter 2.

138.   Martinmas…Shrovetide: Martinmas is the feast of St. Martin, traditionally on November 11; Shrovetide is the three days before Ash Wednesday, the beginning of Lent.

CHAPTER 19: *By what means the chasseur made friends, and what devoutness he displayed during a sermon*

139.   hog-slaughter soup: in German "metzelsuppe"; defined by Grimm as the soup in which sausages are cooked during the slaughter of hogs, o r sausage soup, and also the festive meal which was held during the slaughtering of hogs.

140.   my JOSEPH: Chaste Joseph (Der keusche Joseph), which centers on the biblical hero's problems with Potiphar's wife, actually was a work of Grimmelshausen, who gave as his name on the title page Samuel Greifnson vom Hirschfeld (an anagram of Grimmelhausen's own name); it appeared in 1666 for the first time.

141.   Suleika (who was Potiphar's wife): in Chaste Joseph Grimmelshausen calls her "Selicha"—a name he gleaned from Adam Olearius' Persianisches Rosenthal (1654), Book I, Chapter 40, footnote a (p. 40); for Grimmelshausen's defense of his work against what he took to be criticism, see Vogelnest I.

142.   scil.: see above, Notes to Book II, Chapter 4.

143.   ingenium: mind, mental abilities.

144.   If you go a-soldiering when you're young, you'll go begging when you're old": this old saw is the topic of another of the Simplician novels, The Singular Life Story of Heedless Hopalong.

145.   sententiae: words of wisdom, sententious remarks.

146.   the goldsmith's boy in the story: see above, Notes to Book II, Chapter 7.

CHAPTER 20: *How he gave the parson other grist for his mill, so that he would forget to correct his Epicurean life*

147.   academiam: university, institution of higher learning.

148.   Leyden: Leiden was a town in the Netherlands in the province of Holland; the University of Leyden was founded in 1575, three years after the Spaniards were expelled from there, and it soon became one of the major universities in Europe.

149.   an adherent of neither Peter nor Paul: neither Catholic nor protestant.

150.   simpliciter: simply.

151.   the twelve articles of faith: precisely what Grimmslhausen has in mind here is unclear; he may be referring to the basic principles of Christianity as stated by Jesus in the Sermon on the Mount.

152.   fundamenta: fundamentals, basic principles.

153.   what Conrad Vetter and Johann Nass have spread abroad...against Luther: Conrad Vetter (died 1622), a jurist from Munich, wrote polemics against Luther. The major work of Johannes Nass (1534-1590), bishop of Brixien, is Sechs Centurien Evangelischer Wahrheiten (Ingolstadt, 1569).

154.   Spangenberg: Cyriacus Spangenberg (1528-1604), theologian and historian.

155.   St. Francis: St. Francis of Assisi (1182-1226), founder of the Franciscan order.

156.   religions...the Armenian, the Abyssinian, the Greek, the Georgian...: variants of Christian catholocism.

157.   Ananias: a disciple of Christ in Damascus, he was one of the men who converted Saul of Tarsus (later St. Paul) to the Christian faith (see Acts 9, 10-31).

CHAPTER 21: *How the chasseur unexpectedly came to be a bridegroom*

158.   secretarius: secretary.

159.   nuptialia: nuptials.

160. Croat: the officer's servant was a Croation whose name the officer had not even bothered to learn.

161. bestia: beast.

CHAPTER 22: *How things went at the wedding feast, and what else he undertook to do*

162. unless he had married his daughter to me the way Pythagoras did his: reference is to the anecdote that when Pythagoras was asked why he had married his daughter to his enemy, he answered: "I had nothing worse to give him." The anecdote appeared in Cerda's Weiblicher Lustgarten (p. 278).

163. give...the sign of the fig: make an obscene gesture (the sign of the fig, which was made by sticking the thumb between the index and middle finger).

164. Count von Götz: see above, Notes to Book II, Chapter 30.

165. Dortmund: city in Westphalia; in the eastern part of the Ruhr region, on the upper course of the Emscher; Götz made his headquarters there from December 1637 until March 1638 (Könnecke I, 285).

166. Johann de Werdt: see above, Notes to Book I, Chapter 17.

167. the Breisgau: the southern part of the Black Forest; i.e., the territory between the upper Rhine and the Black Forest.

168. the fortress of Breisach: Breisach, on the right bank of the upper Rhine, was the site of fortresses from Caesar's time on, because of its location and terrain (mons Brisiacus); the fortress was besieged in 1633 and again in 1638, at which time it was in Imperial hands.

CHAPTER 23: *Simplicius goes to a city which he calls pro forma Cologne to fetch his treasure*

169. a city which he calls pro forma Cologne: precisely why Grimmelshausen is chary about openly naming the city is unclear; it is, of course, indeed the city of Cologne. Weydt (p. 247) points out that in astrology Cologne, where the Jupiter figure has relatives, is under the dominance of the planetary god Jupiter, and he believes that Grimmelshausen's wording here is tantamount to a "fingerprint"; Grimmelshausen may also have been acting out of deference to Franz Egon von Fürstenberg, who was ambassador of the Prince Elector of Cologne before assuming the post of Bishop of Strasbourg in 1663 (see below, Notes to Book IV, Chapter 4).

170. Deutz: town on the right bank of the Rhine, across the river from Cologne; there was a Benedictine abbey there founded in 1002 by St. Heribert.

171. the Berg country: see above, Book III, Chapter 14.

172. notarius: notary, lawyer.

173. doctor medicinae: doctor of medicine.

174. doctoribus: doctors.

175. Philemon: (360-265 B.B.); the first author of the New Comedy; he is said to have died laughing at one of his own jokes.

176. Democritus: (c. 460-361 B.C.); Greek philosopher; Seneca (On Anger II, 10) reports that Democritus could never observe the actions of his fellow-citizens of Abdera without laughing (and perhaps rightly so, for the people of Abdera were famous in classical antiquity for their absurd behavior and slowness of mind).

CHAPTER 24: *The chasseur catches a hare, right in the middle of the city*

177.   he feasted upon his boarders....: the skinflint landlord or innkeeper, as Bechtold (p. 519) pointed out, is a stock figure in the picaresque novel of the time and appears in Sorel's Francion, Quevodo's Buscon, in Guzman, in Lazarillo des Tormes and even in Moscherosch, "Phantasten-hospital." Garzoni, in Discourse 66, is similariy critical of their behavior.

178.   solenniter: solemnly, ceremoniously.

179.   we were obliged to chew around on stinking kippers...in mind to throw away: Scholte (p. 133) believes Garzoni, Discourse 66, to be Grimmelshausen's source.

Simplicissimus, The German Adventurer

BOOK IV

CHAPTER 1

How and for what reasons the chasseur was tricked into going off to France[1]

The sharper the blade, the sooner it's nicked, and if you pull a bow too tight, in the end it cannot but break. The prank with the hare which I played upon my host was not enough for me; rather, I made so bold as to punish his insatiable greed even more. I taught his boarders to soak his salted butter in water so that the excess salt was drawn out of it, and how to grate the hard cheeses like Parmesan and moisten them with wine, which was like plunging a dagger into the old miser's heart. With my tricks I extracted the water from his wine right at the table and made a song in which I compared the greedy man to a sow, from which nothing worthwhile can be expected till the butcher has it lying dead upon the trestle. By acting this way I caused him to pay me back nicely with the following act of treachery, because he had not taken me into his house in order that I play such pranks upon him.

Two young noblemen there received a bill of exchange and the command from their parents to betake themselves to France and to learn the French language—this just when our host's German manservant was elsewhere on a journey, and, so said our host, he durst not trust the French manservant to take the horses to France, because he did not know him well; for he feared, so he alleged, he might forget to come back and thus cost him his horses. Therefore he asked me whether I might not be able to do him a great service and take the two noblemen to Paris with his horses, because my case was not to be argued for another month anyway. He, in return, was willing to conduct my business affairs, if I would give him complete power to do so, as faithfully as if I were personally present. The noblemen urged me to do this too, and my curiosity to see France likewise counseled me thus, because now I should be able to do it at no expense to myself, and I would be obliged to be idle for a month anyway and would be spending money in the bargain. So, taking the place of the postillion, I set out with these noblemen on the journey, on which nothing worth mentioning befell me. But after we came to Paris and went to our host's correspondent, from whom the noblemen also received their allowance for the term, not only were both I and the horses taken into custody the very next day, but a man who claimed that my host owed him a *summa* of money seized the horses, with the approval of the *commissarius*[2] of his borough, and turned them into silver despite everything I said. So I sat there like a bump upon a log and knew not how to help myself, much less to devise a plan by which I might go back such a long and, at that time, very uncertain road. The noblemen evinced great sympathy for me and presented me all the more decently with a sizable gratuity; and they were not willing to let me leave them till I had acquired either a good master or a good opportunity to get back to Germany. They rented lodgings, and I stayed some days with them so that I might care for the one of them, who had fallen somewhat ill as a result of the long journey, to which he was not accustomed. And since I was so nice to him he gave me his suit, which he put aside when he had clothes in the newest fashion made for himself. Their counsel was that I stay in Paris a few years and learn the language. What I had in Cologne, they said, would not run away from me. Now while I was attempting to make a choice and had still not made up my mind what I was going to do, the *medicus*[3] who came to our lodgings every day to treat my young squire heard me playing the lute, and singing a little German song to its accompaniment, which pleased him so well that he offered me a good salary and board at his table if I would be willing to move into his house and give instruction to his two sons, for he already knew better than I how my affairs stood and that I would not reject a good master. So we soon came to an agreement with one another, because both noblemen spoke their best to it and highly recommended me, but I did not hire myself out for longer than from one quarter-year to the next.

This doctor spoke German as well as I did, and he spoke Italian as if it were his mother tongue. Therefore I was all the happier to serve him. Now when I ate the farewell meal with my noblemen he was also present, and my head was teeming with perturbing thoughts, for I had in mind the wife I had recently taken, the command which had been promised me, and my treasure in Cologne, from all of which I had so foolishly let myself be persuaded to part, and when we came to speak of our former host's greed it occurred to me, and indeed I said during the meal: "Who knows whether perchance our host did not purposely dupe me into coming hither so that he might withdraw and keep for himself the things in Cologne which are mine?" The doctor answered that this could well be the case, particularly if he believed I was a fellow of mean birth. "No," answered one of the noblemen, "if he has been sent here to the end that he remain here, then it was done because he caused the host so much vexation on account of his greed." The sick nobleman began: "I, for my part, believe there is another reason. When I was standing in my room of late and our host was carrying on a loud conversation with his French manservant, I listened to find out what it was all about and finally made out from the manservant's broken German that the chasseur was overshadowing him with the ladies and was saying that he did not attend to the horses properly, which, however, the jealous fool, because of his poor German, did not understand correctly but took to be a statement which impugned a man's honor, and therefore the host assured the Frenchman that he ought to remain there and that the chasseur must needs soon leave. He had also the whole while been looking askance at his wife and had quarreled with her much more seriously than before, which I myself observed the fool doing."

The doctor said: "No matter what the reason, I would guess that the matter was arranged so that you could not help but remain here. But do not let that disturb you. I shall assuredly help you get back to Germany when a good opportunity to do so presents itself. Simply write him that he should keep a careful eye upon your treasure, or he will assuredly be held sharply to account. What makes me suspicious that it was arranged in advance is that the man who claimed to be his creditor is a very good friend of your host and his correspondent here, and I believe, in fact, that you yourself brought along with you the *obligatio*[4] on the basis of which he seized and sold the horses."

CHAPTER 2

Simplicius acquires a better host than he had before

Monsieur Canard[5]—that was the name of my new master—offered to be of assistance to me with word and deed so that I should not be deprived of the things in Cologne which were mine, for he clearly saw that I was downcast. As soon as he had me in his home he desired that I tell him in what state my affairs were, so that he might come to grips with them and be able to arrive at counsel as to how I might best be helped. I thought for sure that I should not count for much if I were to reveal my origins and therefore claimed to be a poor German nobleman who had neither father nor mother, but only some relatives still alive in a fortified town occupied by a Swedish garrison, which information, however, I had been obliged to conceal from my host at Cologne and the two noblemen, who were partisan to the Imperials, so that they would not take unto themselves what was mine as goods properly belonging to the enemy. It was my opinion, I said, that I should write the commandant of that fortress, in whose regiment I held the position of a company commander, and not only report to him how I had been duped into coming hither, but also request of him that he be so kind as to take possession of what was mine and put it at the disposal of my friends till I should again find an opportunity to rejoin the regiment. Canard found my plan advisable and promised to get the letter to its destination, even if that be to Mexico or some place in China. Accordingly, I composed letters to my darling wife, to my father-in-law, and to Colonel de S.-A., the commandant in L.,[6] to whom I also addressed the envelope and included the other two letters. The contents were that I would return as soon as I laid hands upon the means to complete so long a journey, and I requested both my father-in-law and the colonel that they, by means of the *militiae*,[7] undertake to get possession of what was mine before it went to pot, and I also reported how much it amounted to in gold, silver, and jewelry. This letter I made *in duplo*;[8] one copy Mons. Canard took care of, the other I posted, so that if one did not arrive the other would. So I became of good cheer again and gave instruction all the more easily to my master's two sons, who were being brought up like young princes, for because Mons. Canard was very rich, he was also extremely proud and desired people to esteem him, which illness he had caught from great lords, because he consorted well nigh every day with princes and imitated them in all things. His house was like a count's court in every way, except that he was not addressed as "Your Lordship," and he fancied himself so great that he did not even treat a marquis, whenever one chanced to visit him, with any more deference than one of his own station. Of course, he gave of his means to common folk too, and he did not accept modest fees but instead forgave them what they owed him so that he might make a great name for himself. Because I was rather curious and knew that he made a show of my own person when I walked along behind him with his other servants when he was visiting his patients, I also helped him in his *laboratorio*[9] to concoct medicines. From this I became rather familiar with him, since he liked to speak German anyway, and I therefore asked him one time why he did not take the title of the noble manor house which he had recently bought in the environs of Paris for twenty thousand crowns; *item*, why he thought to make of his sons nothing more exalted than doctors and why he had them study so hard; and whether it would not be better if he (since, after all, he already did have a patent of nobility) were to buy them positions as noble gentlemen somewhere, thus making it possible for them to enter into the estate of the nobility completely. "No," he answered, "when I come to a prince he says: 'Doctor, won't you sit down?' But to a nobleman he says: 'You must stand and wait a while.'" I said: "But Dr. Canard, do you not know that a doctor has three faces: the first that of an angel, when the sick man first lays eyes upon him; the second that of a god, when he helps him; and the third that of a devil, when the patient is well and rids himself of the doctor again. Thus, this honor will last no longer than the sick man has gas in his gut, and when it is out and the rumbling stops, then the honor is at an end, and then they say: 'Doctor, wait outside!' Accordingly, the nobleman has more honor when he is standing than the doctor does when he is sitting down, namely, because the nobleman waits upon his prince constantly and has the honor of never leaving his side. Recently you, Dr. Canard, put something from the prince into your mouth and were obliged to determine his condition from how it tasted. I would rather stand and wait upon a prince for ten years than taste another man's excrement,[10] even if they gave me a bed of roses for doing it." He answered: "I was not obliged to do that; rather, I was happy to do it, so that when the prince sees what pains I take to diagnose his condition correctly, the sum he pays me will be all the larger. And why should I not taste the excrement of a man who gives me as payment several hundred pistoles for it, while I pay him nothing when he has to eat something I have concocted which is completely different? You speak of the matter like a German—if you were from another nation, I should have said that you spoke of it like a fool." This *bon mot* I had to swallow, because I saw that he was on the point of growing angry, and so that I might put him into a good mood again, I begged him to take my simplemindedness into account, and I changed the subject to something more agreeable to him.

CHAPTER 3

How he let himself be used as an actor and acquired a new name

Even as Mons. Canard had more wild game to throw away than many a man who has his own game preserve has to eat, and more domesticated fowl and beasts were presented to him than he and his household could ever possibly devour, so in his home it looked as if he were holding open house. One time the king's master of ceremonies and other distinguished personages from the court were visiting him, which people he served a royal *collatio*,[11] because he well knew whom he must needs keep as friends, namely, those who were always about the king or were in his good graces. Now so that he might show them how very much he was devoted to them and might afford them every pleasure, he expressed the desire that I, to honor him and to please the considerable number of guests, let them hear me sing a little German song to my own accompaniment on the lute. I was happy to oblige, for I was in the mood to do it[12] at that moment (you know how oddly capricious *musici*[13] generally are). Therefore I endeavored to do my very best and as a consequence so pleased those present that the master of ceremonies said that it was indeed a shame that I did not know the French language, else he would procure me an exceeding good position with the king and queen.[14] My master, however, who feared that I might be snatched away from his service, answered that I was of the nobility and did not intend to stay in France for long, and, accordingly, I would scarce let myself be used as a common musician. Then the master of ceremonies said that in all his days he had not found such rare beauty, such a clear voice, and such skillful lute playing in a single person. He said that in the near future a *comoedia*[15] was to be played in the Louvre for the king, and if he were able to use me in it, he hoped to reap great honor with me. Mons. Canard explained this to me. I answered: "If they will tell me what manner of person I am to represent and what melodies to play on my lute and sing, I could, of course, learn both the melodies and the words by heart and accompany myself on the lute, even if the songs were in French." Certainly, I said, my mind was easily as good as that of schoolboys, whom they generally used for this purpose, despite the fact that they were obliged first to learn by heart the words and gestures. When the master of ceremonies saw how willing I was, I was obliged to promise him to come to the Louvre[16] the next day to try out in order to see if I was suited to the task. So I appeared there at the appointed time. The melodies of sundry songs that I was to sing I straightway played perfectly on the instrument, because I had the notes before me. After that, I received the French songs to learn by heart and with the correct pronunciation, which songs were at the same time rendered into German for me so that I could make the appropriate gestures while I sang. This was not difficult for me to do, so I was able to do it sooner than they expected and, in fact, in such fashion that when they heard me sing (as Mons. Canard said in praise of me) not one person in a thousand but would have sworn that I was a born Frenchman. And when we came together to rehearse the *comoediam* the first time, I was able to act so downcast with my songs, melodies, and gestures that they all thought that I must needs have played the role of Orpheus,[17] whom I was then representing, many times and that I must needs be acting so sad because of my Eurydice. My entire life long I have never had as pleasant a day as the one on which this *comoedia* was presented. Mons. Canard gave me something to swallow to make my voice even clearer, but when he attempted to enhance my beauty with *oleo talci*[18] and to powder my half-curly hair, which was glistening with black dye, he found that he merely disfigured me by doing so. I was crowned with a laurel wreath and put into a sea-green costume like those worn in Antiquity, with the upper part of my chest, my arms up to above the elbow, and my legs from halfway up the thigh to the lower calf bare and naked. Around my body I wore a flesh-colored mantle of taffeta which rather resembled a sash. In this costume I wooed my Eurydice, called, in a beautiful song, upon Venus for assistance, and finally took my beloved away, in which *actu*[19] I was able to strike a wonderful pose and to look upon my beloved with yearning sighs and flashing eyes. After I had lost my Eurydice, I put on a completely black costume of the same type as already described, from which my white skin shone forth like snow; in it I lamented my lost wife and imagined the situation to be so lamentable that in the midst of my mournful songs and melodies tears welled up in my eyes and sobs very nearly prevented me from going on singing, but I kept on singing beautifully till I reached Hades and stood before Pluto and Proserpina.[20] To them I painted, in a very moving song, a picture of the love which they bore for one another and then pled with them to deduce from that with what great pain Eurydice and I had been separated from one another, and after that I pled, with gestures of the utmost devotedness—singing all this, of course, to the accompaniment of my harp—that they let her come back to me. And after I had received their answer of "Yes" I expressed my gratitude in a happy song I sang to them and was able to make my visage and my gestures and voice so happy that all of the spectators present were astonished by it. And when I unexpectedly lost my Eurydice again, I imagined in my mind the greatest peril into which a person could fall and from that grew as pale as if I were about to fall into a faint, for because I was all alone upon the stage at the time and all the spectators were looking at me, I devoted myself all the more zealously to my task and as a result received the honor of being acclaimed the person who had acted his role best. After that I sat down upon a rock and fell to lamenting the loss of my beloved in heart- rending words and a mournful melody, and to calling upon all creatures for their sympathy; at that all manner of tame and wild beasts, rocks, trees, and the like came up to me, so that in truth it appeared as if everything had been arranged by magic in some supernatural way. The only mistake I made was at the end when I renounced all womankind, was strangled by the *bacchis*[21] and thrown into the water (which was arranged so that only my head was visible, for the rest of my body was in complete safety under the stage), and when the dragon was supposed to gnaw upon me, and the fellow who was inside the dragon to control it could not see my head and therefore caused the dragon's head to graze next to mine. That seemed to me so ridiculous that I could not keep from pouting about it, which the ladies, who were looking at me very intently, well remarked.

From this *comoedia* I not only received, along with the praise which many bestowed upon me, excellent payment, I also acquired another name, since the French from then on never called me anything but "Beau Aleman."[22] Yet more plays and ballets of that sort were given, because Shrovetide was being celebrated, in which plays I likewise let myself be used; but at last I found that I was envied by others because I caused the spectators, particularly the ladies, to turn their eyes to me, so I left off doing it, particularly after one time I was dealt some rather sharp blows when I, playing Hercules and nearly naked in a lion skin, struggled with Achelous for Deianira,[23] since they struck me harder than is customary in a stage-play.

CHAPTER 4

Beau Aleman is taken against his will to the mountain of Venus[24]

Through this I became known to high personages, and it seemed as if good fortune were about to smile upon me once again, for I was even offered the opportunity to enter into the service of the king, which does not happen to many a man of high rank. One time a lackey came; he spoke to Monsig.[25] Canard and brought him a letter concerning me, just as I was sitting with him in his *laboratorio* and working with the reverberatory furnace (for to divert myself I had already learned from the doctor how to perulate, insolulate, sublimate, coagulate, assimilate, calcinate, filtrate,[26] and all the other innumerable alchemical tasks of that sort by which he was wont to prepare his medicaments). "Monsieur Beau Aleman," he said to me, "this letter concerns you. A distinguished gentleman is sending for you. He desires that you come to see him immediately; he desires to speak to you and to hear whether you will be so kind as to teach his son to play the lute. He asks me to urge you not to refuse him this trip, making the courteous promise that he will reward you for your trouble with friendship and gratitude." I answered that if I could be of service to anyone for his (Mons. Canard's) sake, I should spare no effort to do so. Then he said I should just change my clothes in order to go with the lackey; meanwhile, by the time I was finished, he would have something ready for me to eat, for I had, he said, a rather long way to go, so that I should scarce arrive at the appointed place before evening. So I decked myself out somewhat and in haste bolted down some of the *collatio*,[27] particularly a few delicate little sausages which, so it seemed to me, strongly smacked of the apothecary. After that I walked with the lackey for an hour on a curious detour till, towards evening, we came to a garden door which was ajar. This the lackey pushed wide open, and after I had stepped in behind him he slammed it shut again, then led me into a pavilion which was in one corner of the garden, and, after we had walked through a rather long passageway, knocked at a door which was forthwith opened by an aged noblewoman. Speaking in German she very politely bade me welcome and bade me come all the way into the room, and the lackey, who knew no German, made a deep bow and took his leave. The old lady took me by the hand and led me completely into the room, which had precious tapestries on all the walls and was in other regards beautifully appointed. She bade me sit down so that I might catch my breath and at the same time learn for what reason I had been brought to this place. I was happy to comply and sat down in an overstuffed chair which she had placed for me by the fire which was burning in the room, because it was rather cold, and she sat down next to me in another chair and said: "Monsieur, if you know anything about the powers of love, namely, that it generally overpowers and dominates the very bravest, strongest, and wisest men, then you will be all the less surprised that love also assumes mastery over the weaker sex. You have been charged to come to me not by a gentleman, because of your lute, as they persuaded you and Dr. Canard was the case, but in fact by the most worthy lady in Paris, because of your unparalleled beauty, which lady believes she will surely die if she does not soon look upon your divine figure and if she should not have the good fortune to refresh herself with it. Therefore she has charged me to apprise you, my dear fellow countryman, of this and to beg you more fervently than Venus did her Adonis[28] that you come to her this evening and let her look upon your beauty to her heart's content, which you will, let us hope, not deny her, a lady of distinction." I answered: "Madame, I know not what to think, much less say, to this! I know full well that I am not by nature such that a lady of such high quality should be desirous of one of such low estate as myself. Moreover, it comes to mind that if the lady who desires to see me were of such excellence and such distinction as you, my most honored fellow countrywoman, have asserted, she would probably have sent for me earlier in the day and would not have commanded me to come hither to such an isolated spot so late in the evening. Why did she not command that I come to her directly? What am I doing in this garden? You, my most honored fellow countrywoman, will forgive me if I, a stranger all alone, grow fearful that someone is trying to dupe me, particularly since I was told that I should be coming to see a gentleman, which now turns out to be in fact not the case. And should I note that anyone were about to treacherously attack my person through some knavery, I should be capable of using my saber to protect myself from death!" "Gently! Gently! My esteemed fellow countryman! Put such bootless thoughts out of your mind!" she answered. "Women are so queer and curious in their wiles that it is not so easy to accommodate oneself so easily to them right off. If the lady who loves you more than anything in the world desired you to have any knowledge of her person, she would of course not have had you come hither first, but rather straight to her. There (she pointed to the table) lies a hood which you must put on when you are taken from here to her home, because she does not wish you to know even the place where you are, much less the identity of the person you are with. Accordingly, I beseech and admonish you, sir, as urgently as I can, to use this lady as both her high estate and the inexpressible love she bears you merit, else you will find yourself in a position to learn that she is powerful enough to punish, this very instant, your arrogance and contemptuousness. If, however, you act towards her as is fitting, you may rest assured that even the tiniest step you have taken on her account will not go unrewarded."

Gradually it grew dark, and I had all manner of cares and anxieties, so that I sat there like a man carved of stone; and I could well imagine that I would not be able to escape from this place so easily unless I agreed to everything demanded of me. Therefore I said to the old woman: "Well then, my most honored fellow countrywoman, if things are as you have described them to me, I shall entrust myself to your innate German rectitude, in the hope that you will not permit, much less yourself arrange, that an innocent German fall prey to treachery. Carry out what you have been charged to do concerning me. The lady of whom you told me assuredly will not have the eyes of a basilisk[29] to strike me dead with!" "Heaven forbid!" said she. "It would be a shame if such a body, of which our entire nation can be proud, were to perish now. You will find more delight than you ever in all your life dreamed of." When she had my consent she called Jean and Pierre; they forthwith stepped forth from behind the arras, each in a polished full-length cuirass, armed from head to toe, with a halberd and a pistol in hand, at which I was so frightened that I turned pale as a ghost. The old woman remarked this and said with a smile: "A man must know no fear when he goes to a woman."[30] Then she commanded them both to take off their armor, to take the lantern, and to accompany me armed only with pistols. After that she slipped the hood, which was made of black velvet, over my head, carried my hat under her arm, and led me by the hand on a curious journey. I well remarked that I was going through many doors, and also over a plastered street; finally, after about ten minutes, I was obliged to climb some narrow stone stairs; then a little door opened, whence I walked into a carpeted passageway and was obliged to go up a circular staircase, and after that several steps downwards again, where, after about six paces further, a door opened. When I finally walked through it the old woman took the hood off again. Then I found myself in a hall which was decorated with extreme daintiness: the walls were adorned with beautiful paintings, the buffet with silver services, and the bed which stood there with curtains of gold cloth. In the middle of the room was a table splendidly set, and by the fire was a bathtub which was pretty, all right, but which, to my way of thinking, desecrated the entire room. The old woman said to me: "Now, my fellow countryman, welcome! Can you still say that you are being duped by treachery?

If you will just put aside all ill humor and act as you did recently upon the stage when you got your Eurydice back from Pluto, I assure you that you will find a more beautiful woman here than you lost there."

CHAPTER 5

How he fared there, and how he got out of there again

From these words I could tell that at this place I was not only to let someone feast her eyes upon me, I was supposed to do something else too. Therefore I said to my old fellow countrywoman that it would do a thirsty man little good to sit by a spring from which he was forbidden to drink. She, however, said that in France folks were not so spiteful that they would deny a thirsty man water, particularly where there was a superabundance of it. "Indeed!" said I. "You would be right if I were not already married!" "Nonsense!" this godless woman answered. "They will not believe you if you tell that tale tonight, for married cavaliers seldom come to France, and even if it were true, I really cannot believe that you are so foolish that you would sooner perish of thirst than drink from a strange spring, particularly when it is perhaps more diverting and has better water than your own." This was our discourse, during which a noble maiden who was tending the fire took off my shoes and stockings, which I had soiled all over in the dark, for Paris is a very dirty city anyway.[31] Straightway after that the command came that they should bathe[32] me before I dined, for the aforementioned maiden went back and forth and brought things to bathe with, all of which smelled like musk and aromatic soaps; the linens were of the purest cambric, and edged with fine Dutch lace. I was ashamed and did not wish to let the old woman see me naked, but it was to no avail; I was compelled to do it and to let her dry me off. The maiden, however, was obliged to go outside while this was going on. After the bath I was given a soft shirt, and a precious fleece of violet taffeta was put about my shoulders, together with a pair of silk stockings of the same color; and the nightcap and the slippers were embroidered with gold and pearls, so that after my bath I sat there looking as splendid as the King of Hearts. Now while the old woman was drying and combing my hair, for she attended to me as if I were a prince or a small child, the maiden brought in food, and after the meal was served, there came into the hall three young ladies who looked like demigoddesses and who were wearing gowns which rather much left their alabaster breasts bare, and they wore masks which covered the entire upper part of their faces. All three of them seemed to me to be exceeding beauteous, but one was much more beauteous than the others. Without saying a word I made a deep bow to them, and they expressed their thanks to me in the same ceremonious way, which naturally made it appear as if a group of mutes had come together who were acting the roles of people who could speak. All three sat down at the same time, so I could not divine which of them was of the most exalted birth, much less which one I was there to serve. The first question was whether I spoke French. My fellow countrywoman said "No!" Then the second lady replied that she should tell me to be so good as to sit down. When this was done, the third one commanded my interpretress to sit down too, from which I again could not deduce which amongst them was the most noble. I sat next to the old woman, directly across from these three ladies, and accordingly my beauty without doubt shone forth all the more, next to such an old bag of bones. They all three looked at me very intently, and I could swear that they let a hundred sighs of yearning pass their lips. Their eyes I could not see sparkle, on account of the masks they wore in front of them. The old woman asked me (no one else was able to talk to me) which of the three I held to be the most beautiful. I answered that I could not choose amongst them. At this she fell to laughing so that one could see all four of the teeth she still had in her mouth, and she asked why. I answered, because I could not rightly see them, but from as much as I could see, all three of them were not exactly ugly. The ladies desired to know what the old woman had asked and what I had answered; the old woman translated it, and in the bargain she lied, saying that I had said that each had a mouth which merited a thousand kisses, for I could see their mouths clearly below the masks, particularly that of the one who was sitting directly across from me. With this piece of flattery the old woman gave me to understand that this one was of the most noble birth, and I regarded her all the more intently. This was our entire discourse at the table, and I acted as if I did not understand a word of French. Now because everything was so quiet we got up from the table all the sooner. Then the ladies bade me good night and went their way, which ladies I was allowed to escort no further than the door, which the old woman straightway bolted behind them. When I saw that, I asked where I was to sleep. She answered that I must needs make do with sleeping with her in the bed there. I said that the bed was good enough, if only one of those three ladies were in it too! "Indeed," said she, "you'll assuredly not have any one of them tonight." As we were chatting this way, a beautiful lady who was lying in the bed pulled back the bedcurtains a little and told the old woman she should leave off chattering and go to bed. Then I took the candle from her and was about to look to see who was lying in the bed, but she extinguished it, saying: "Sir, if you value your life, then do not make so bold as to do what you just had in mind to do. Lie down, and be assured that if you make an effort to see this woman's face against her will, you will never leave this place alive!" With that she fled and locked the door behind her. And the maiden who was tending the fire extinguished it completely and also went away, through a door concealed behind the arras. Then the lady who was in the bed said: "Allez, Mons.[33] Beau Aleman! Gom clozer to mee, my cheri,[34] gom, gom clozer to mee!" This was all of my mother tongue that the old woman had taught her. I betook myself to bed to see what there might be there to do, and as soon as I was there, she threw her arms about my neck, welcomed me with a host of kisses, and in her ardent desire well nigh bit off my lower lip. In fact, she fell to unbuttoning my fleece robe and to almost tearing my shirt to shreds, and she drew me to her and acted so insane with love that there are no words which can express it. She knew not a word of my native tongue except "Gom clozer to mee, my cheri!" Everything else she conveyed to me by means of gestures. I, to be sure, thought secretly of my beloved wife, but to what avail? I was, unfortunately, a human being, and I found in bed with me a creature of such fine proportions and indeed of such loveliness that I must needs have been a clod, had I escaped with my virtue intact.

In this manner I passed eight days and as many nights in this place, and I do believe that the other three lay with me too,[35] for they did not all talk like the first one, nor did they act as madly in love either. Now though I was with these four ladies for eight entire days, I still cannot say I was ever permitted to look at any one of them except through a veil or, unless it was dark, straight in the face. After the eight days were at an end they took me blindfolded to a courtyard and put me into a closed carriage together with the old woman, who on the way unbound my eyes and took me to the home of my master; then the groom drove away again quickly. My reward was two hundred gold pieces,[36] and when I asked the old woman whether I should not give someone part of it as a gratuity, she said: "Certainly not! For if you were to do such a thing, it would vex the ladies. Indeed, they would think that you imagined you had been in a whorehouse, where everything must be paid for." Afterwards I acquired more customers of this sort who took things so far that I finally, because I could no longer perform, grew quite jaded with this foolishness.

CHAPTER 6

Simplicius secretly steals away, and how his tables were turned when he thought he had the *mal de Naples*[37, 38]

Through this pursuit of mine I accumulated so many presents in money and other things that I began to grow afraid, and I was no longer surprised that women betake themselves to a brothel and make a trade of this bestial lewdness, because it does bring in such a goodly sum of money. But I fell to looking into myself, not, to be sure, from godliness or from pangs of conscience, but for fear that I might sometime be caught red-handed and given my just deserts. Therefore I pondered how to get back to Germany, and this all the more because the commandant in L. had written me that he had seized several merchants from Cologne whom he was not going to let out of his hands till my effects were first turned over to him; *item*, that he was still keeping in reserve the company whose command he had promised me and desired to have me there well before spring, for otherwise, should I not come betimes, he must needs fill the position with someone else; and my wife also enclosed a letter filled with sweet protestations of her great yearning for me; but had she known what an honorable life I was leading, she would probably have included greetings of another kind.

I could well imagine that I would scarce get away with Monsig. Canard's consent, and I therefore planned to slip away secretly as soon as I had the opportunity, which opportunity, to my great misfortune, did indeed present itself. For one time when I encountered some officers from the army of the Duke of Weimar I gave them to understand that I was an ensign in Colonel de S.-A.'s regiment and had been in Paris for a time attending to personal affairs, but had now decided to return to my regiment; and I made the request that they take me into their company and along as a traveling companion. And they revealed to me the day of their departure and willingly accepted me. I bought a nag and outfitted myself for the journey as secretly as I could, packing up my money (which amounted to about five hundred doublons, all of which I had earned from those godless women), and set out with them without Mons. Canard's express permission; but I did write a letter back to him and gave Maastricht[39] as the place where it had been written so that he would think that I was going to Cologne, in which letter I took my leave of him, announcing that it was impossible for me to remain with him any longer because I should not have been able to tolerate his aromatic sausages any longer.

When we stopped the second night after leaving Paris, I broke out in red blotches like a person who has St. Anthony's fire, and my head ached so terribly that it was impossible for me to get out of bed. It was in a quite small village in which I could not have a *medicum*,[40] and what was worst was that I had no one to wait upon me, for early the next morning the officers continued their journey on towards Alsace, leaving me, who meant nothing to them, lying there sick unto death; but upon their departure they did commend me and my horse to the innkeeper and leave word with the village magistrate that he should keep an eye upon me, since I was an officer who had served the king.

So I lay there a few days, quite out of my wits and babbling like a madman. They brought a priest, but he could make no sense of what I was saying. And because he saw that he could not give me remedies to cure my soul's ills, he pondered upon means to come to the aid of my body as best he could, for which reason he opened one of my veins, gave me a drink to make me perspire, and had me put into a warm bed to sweat. This did me so much good that I remembered that night where I was and how I had got there and had fallen ill. The following morning the priest came to visit me again and found me quite desperate, since not only had my money been stolen, I could not but think that I had (*s.v.*)[41] the "fine French malady,"[42] because I deserved it more than my many pistoles, and over my entire body I was covered with spots, like a leopard. I could neither walk, stand, sit, nor lie still. There was no patience within me, for just as I had been unable to believe that God had bestowed upon me the money which was now lost, now I was so annoyed that I said that the devil had taken it away from me again! Indeed, I behaved precisely as if I were about to despair completely, so that the good priest had difficulty consoling me, because the shoe was pinching me so painfully in two different places. "My friend," said he, "do behave like a sensible man. If you cannot bear your cross like a good Christian, what will you do if, in addition to your money, you were to lose your life too, and, what is more, eternal salvation also?" I answered: "I should not be perturbed about the money at all if I were only not saddled with this abominable, accursed disease, or if I were but somewhere or other where I could be cured!" "You must be patient," answered the clergyman. "How must the poor children feel, of whom more than fifty of them in the village are in bed sick with it?" When I heard that children too were afflicted with it, I forthwith grew more resolute, for I could easily imagine that they could not contract that noxious plague. Therefore I took my valise to hand and looked to see what it might still contain, but except for my linen there was nothing of value in it but a little box with a lady's portrait, set with rubies around it, which a woman in Paris had bestowed upon me. I took the portrait out and turned the rest over to the clergyman with the request that he turn it into silver in the next town, so that I might have something to live on. It ended up that I got scarce a third of what it was worth, and because it did not last long, my nag was obliged to go also, With that money I scarce managed till the pustules began to dry up and I felt better again.

CHAPTER 7

How Simplicius reflected upon his past life and learned to swim when he was up to his neck in water

The thing which causes us to sin is generally the instrument by which we are punished. This smallpox so disfigured me that henceforth I was left in peace by the women. I got so many pockmarks on my face that I looked like a barn floor upon which peas have been threshed. Indeed, I became so ugly that my beautiful curly hair, in which so many a woman had become entangled, grew ashamed of me and left home. In its place I got other hairs, which might be compared to hog bristles, so that I was of necessity obliged to wear a periwig, and just as I was left with no external beauty to my skin, my beautiful voice also departed, for my throat had been full of pox too. My eyes, which before had never been found to lack the fire of love in them with which to kindle the flame in every woman, now looked as red and rheumy as those of an eighty-year-old crone who has the *cornelium*.[43] And in addition to all that, here I was in a strange land. I knew neither man nor beast who might have had my best interests at heart; I did not understand the language; and I had no money left.

Then I fell to thinking of times gone by and to bewailing the splendid opportunities which had heretofore presented themselves to me to promote my welfare, which opportunities, however, I had so carelessly let pass me by. For the first time I looked back and realized that my extraordinary good fortune in the war and in finding the treasure had been nothing more than the cause and preparation for my ill fortune, which could nevermore have brought me so low if Fortuna had not first looked upon me with false eyes and raised me so high. Indeed, I found that the good things which had befallen me and which I took to be good had been evil and had led me into the depths of corruption. There was no hermit any more to look to my best interests, no Colonel Ramsey to take me in in my misery, no parson to give me good counsel, and, *in summa*, not a single soul to do me a good turn. Instead, now that my money was gone, they told me to get myself gone too and to seek my fortune elsewhere, even if it must needs be amongst the swine, like the prodigal son. Then I thought for the first time of the good counsel of the parson who thought that I should apply my means and my youth to *studiis*,[44] but it was much too late to lay on the shears to clip the bird's wings, for it had long since flown the coop. Alas, how quickly things change for the worse! A month ago I was a fellow who moved princes to admiration, delighted the ladies, and seemed to the folk one of nature's masterpieces, aye, an angel; but now I was so vile that the dogs did not hesitate to piss on me. I had thousands upon thousands of different notions about what I should undertake to do, for the innkeeper threw me out when I could no longer pay. I would have liked to sign on with a regiment, but no recruiter was willing to accept me as a soldier because I looked like a cuckoo with scabies. I could not work because I was still too weak, and not accustomed to any kind of labor anyway. The only thing that consoled me was that it was getting on towards summer, and if need be, I might make do with a hedgerow as lodgings, for no one was willing to suffer me in their house any more. I still had the fancy clothes which I had had made for the journey, together with a valise full of costly linen, which, however, no one was willing to buy from me because everyone feared I might saddle him with the disease along with it. These things I took onto my back, took my saber in hand, and took to the road, which led me to a small town which boasted its own apothecary shop. I went into it and had them prepare a salve which was supposed to rid one of pox scars on the face, and because I had no money, I gave a beautiful soft shirt to the apothecary's assistant, who was not so fastidious as the other fools who were unwilling to have any cloths from me. I thought: "If you are but rid of these shameful blotches, your lot will assuredly begin to improve too." And because the apothecary assured me that after a week people would see little more of the deep scars which the pustules had eaten into my skin, I was already of much better cheer. It was market day there just then, and at the market was a huckster who was making excellent money by foisting rubbish off onto people. "You fool!" I thought to myself. "Why do you not set up a booth like that too? If you lived so long with Mons. Canard and did not learn enough to cheat a simpleminded peasant and earn your feed that way, then you really are a wretched booby!"

CHAPTER 8

How he came to be a mountebank and a charlatan[45]

At that time I was probably eating like a horse, for my stomach was not to be sated, even though I had nothing on hand but a single gold ring with a diamond in it, which was worth about twenty crowns. It I pawned for twelve crowns, and since I could easily imagine that this would soon be gone if I did not earn something to go with it, I resolved to become a doctor. I bought me *materialia*[46] for a *Theriaca Diatessaron*[47] and prepared some of it. Then I made from herbs, roots, butter, and some oils a green salve for all manner of wounds, with which one could also cure a galled horse; *item*, from calamine, crushed pebbles, crab's eyes, emery, and *terra Tripolitana*[48] I made a powder to make the teeth white; and, further, from lye, copper, *sal ammoniacum*,[49] and camphor I made a blue liquid for scurvy, trench mouth, toothaches, and eye-aches; and I acquired a heap of little tin and wooden boxes, paper, and little glass jars to smear my wares into. And so that they might look legitimate, I had a slip of paper drafted and printed in French which told what the one and the other medicine was good for. In three days I was finished with my work and had spent scarce three crowns in the apothecary shop and for equipment when I left that little town. So I packed up and undertook to wander from one village to the next, towards Alsace, peddling my wares along the way, and then, in Strasbourg, a neutral city, to sail down the Rhine when the opportunity arose and to betake myself, in the company of merchants, back to Cologne and from there to make my way to where my wife was. My intentions were the best, but my well-laid plans surely went awry!

The first time I stopped at some church steps with my quack medicines and offered them for sale, my earnings were quite meager, because I was too shy, and also because I could master neither the language nor the brash demeanor of a mountebank. From that I straightway saw that I must needs take a different tack if I desired to take in any money. I went into an inn with my wares and at the meal heard from the innkeeper that in the afternoon all manner of people would be gathering outside under the linden tree in front of his place; there, he said, I might sell such things if I had good wares, but there were so many charlatans in the land that people were mighty slow to spend their money if they did not see with their own eyes that the *theriac*[50] was uncommonly good. When, in this wise, I heard what was wanting, I got a drinking glass full of Strasbourg brandy and caught a kind of toad they call a "rana" or a "portentosa," which in spring and summer sits in stagnant pools of water and sings; they are golden-yellow or almost reddish-yellow, with black check-spots at the bottom of their bellies, quite unappetizing to look upon. One of these I put into a wine glass full of water and placed it next to my wares on a table under the linden tree. Now when the people began to foregather and to stand about me, some of them thought that I was going to pull teeth with the tongs I had borrowed from the kitchen of the innkeeper's wife, but I said: "Gentleman and goode friends! (for I could still speak very little French), I be no pull-your-tooth man, but I do have this goode eyewash, it tak' all runniness and redness out of the eyes." "Yes," answered one of them, "one can see that by the looks of your eyes all right. They do look like two will-o'-the- wisps!" I said: "That be true, but if I not 'ave this liquid, I 'ave probablement go completement blind. And I no sell this eyewash; the *theriac* and the powder for the white tooth and the salve for the wound I sell, and give the wash for free with them. I be no hawker or shit-on-you-folks fellow. My *theriac* I no offer to sale if I not try her, and if you don' like her, you don' buy her from me." Then I had one of them choose one of my little boxes of *theriac*. From it I put a pinch the size of a pea into my brandy, which the people took to be water, crushed it up in it, and then with the tongs I took the croaker out of the glass filled with water and said: "Regardez, my goode friends, if this poisonous worm be able drink my *theriac* and no die, then this thing be no good, you don' buy her from me!" With that I thrust the poor toad, which was born and bred in the water and could not tolerate any other element or liquor, into my brandy and held it in the glass with a piece of paper so that it could not jump out. Then it fell to raging and writhing in there, indeed, to acting much worse than if I had thrown it onto glowing coals, because the brandy was much too strong for it, and after it had kept this up for a little while, it croaked and its legs went rigid and straight. The peasants looked on with their mouths and purses agape, since they had seen this so certain proof with their very own eyes; to their way of thinking there was no better *theriac* in the world than mine, and I had all I could do to wrap the rubbish in the slips of paper and take in the money for it. There were some amongst them who indeed bought three, four, five, and six times the regular amount, so that in case of need they would be well supplied with this so precious antidote; indeed, they also bought it for their friends and kinfolk who lived elsewhere, so that with this tomfoolery, even though it was not market day, I took in ten crowns that same evening and yet still had more than half my wares left. That night I made off to another village, because I feared that a peasant might perchance be so curious as to put a toad into water to test my *theriac* and then, when the experiment failed, beat me black and blue. However, so that I might also prove the excellence of my antidote in another way, I made up two poisons: from flour, saffran, and *gallus* a yellow *arsenicum*;[51] and from flour and *victril*[52] a *mercurium sublimatum.*[53] And when I desired to do the test, I had two identical glasses of fresh water set upon the table, one rather strongly laced with *acquam fortis*[54] or *spiritum victril,*[55] into which I dissolved a little of my *theriac;* and then I poured into both glasses as much as necessary of my two poisons; the result was that the water which had no *theriac* in it, and therefore no *aquam fortis* either, turned as black as ink, while the other one, on account of the acid in it, remained the way it was. "Aha!" said the people. "Look you there, that is surely a fine *theriac* for so little money!" When I then mixed the contents of the two glasses together, then all the liquid turned clear. As a result of that, the good peasants took out their purses and bought my wares from me, which not only did my empty belly good, it also made it possible for me to buy myself a mount again, and in the bargain I prospered and earned much money on my journey, and I came safely across the German border. Therefore, dear peasants, do not be so quick to believe hawkers you do not know, lest you be swindled by them, since these persons are interested not in your health but in your wealth.

CHAPTER 9

How the doctor was given a musket and put into the service of Captain Rumblygut

Now as I was going through Lorraine my wares ran out, and because I avoided garrisoned towns I had no opportunity to prepare more. Therefore I was obliged to do something else till I could make some more *theriac.* I bought me two measures of brandy, colored it with saffran, poured it into little half-ounce bottles, and sold it to people as precious gold-water which was good for fevers, thus making the brandy worth thirty guilders. And when I was about to run out of little bottles, I heard about a glassworks which was located in the Fleckenstein district[56] and betook myself thither to equip myself again; but as I was looking for a back road I chanced to be captured by a raiding party from Philippsburg[57] which was staying at Wagelnburg Castle.[58] So I lost all that I had swindled from the people on my journey, and because the peasant who went along to show me the way had told the fellows that I was a doctor, I was taken, against my will, to Philippsburg as a doctor.

There I was interrogated and did not hesitate for a moment to say who I was, which, however, they did not believe, but instead attempted to make more of me than I ever could have been, for I was obliged and compelled to be a doctor. I was obliged to swear that I had been one of the Imperial dragoons at Soest, and I further told them upon my word of honor what all had befallen me from that time to the present, and what I planned to do now. But they said that the Emperor needed soldiers in Philippsburg as much as he did at Soest. I could remain with them, they said, till a good opportunity presented itself for me to return to my regiment; if, however, this suggestion did not suit me, then I could content myself with a place in the jail, and till I got away again, I would be treated as a doctor, which is what I had been taken prisoner as.

Thus I went from bad to worse and was obliged, against my will, to be a musketeer again. That seemed to me bloody awful, because John Rumblygut was in charge there and the rations were frightfully meager. I mean "frightfully meager" literally, for every morning when I received them I felt fright, because I knew that I would have to make do with them the entire day, whereas I could really have finished them off all at once without any difficulty. And to tell the truth, a musketeer who must pass his life this way in garrison and make do with nothing but dry bread, and not even half enough of that to still his hunger, is indeed a miserable creature, for in garrison no one is any different from a prisoner who is prolonging his wretched life with a diet of bread and water; in fact, a prisoner is better off, for he is not permitted to stand watch, make rounds, or stand guard duty; instead, he lies there in peace, and he has as much hope as a poor garrison soldier of one day, sometime, getting out of this prison. To be sure, there were some who fared a little better, and, in fact, sundry categories of such people, but not one of these ways of life appealed to me and seemed to me to be a decent way to earn my keep. For in this misery some of them took women as wives (even if they were runaway whores), for no reason other than that they might be supported by them, either by their labor, such as sewing, washing clothes, and spinning, or haggling and hawking wares, or even stealing. Amongst the women one was a commanding officer of the women; she had her pay just like a soldier. Another woman was a midwife, and through her work she brought to pass many a good feast for her husband and herself. Another knew how to starch and wash clothes. Some washed shirts, stockings, night shirts, and I know not what else for the unmarried officers and soldiers, from which tasks they got their special names. Others sold tobacco and provided pipes to fellows who lacked them. Others sold brandy, and of them it was reported that they adulterated it with water which they distilled in their own bodies so that it would not lose its proof. Another one was a seamstress and could do stitches and make patterns to earn money. Another one was able to support herself solely from fruits of the field; in the winter she dug snails, in the spring she harvested salad greens, in the summer she found birds' nests, and in the fall she knew how to get thousands of other kinds of delicacies. Some, like pack asses, carried wood to sell. And others also dealt in other things. To be provided for in this manner was not for me, for I already had a wife. Some fellows supported themselves by gaming, at which they were better than any cheats, and with loaded dice and marked cards they could pinch away what belonged to their simpleminded comrades, but this profession filled me with revulsion. Others worked like beasts on the fortifications and elsewhere, but I was too lazy to do that. Some knew and pursued a trade, but I, booby that I was, had not learned any trade. To be sure, if they needed a musician, I could have easily passed the test, but this famine-ridden land made do with drums and fifes. Some stood guard duty for others and never left the guardposts, night and day, but I would rather have starved to death than to so abuse my body. Some kept body and soul together by going on raiding parties, but I was not even trusted to go outside the city gates. Some were better at mousing than a cat, but I hated this handiwork like the plague. *In summa*, no matter where I turned, there was nothing I could grasp which might have stilled my hunger. And what vexed me most of all was that in the bargain I was obliged to let the fellows make sport of me by saying: "You're supposed to be a doctor, and the only thing you're expert at is starving!" Finally my plight compelled me to lure some fine carp out of the moat up to me on the wall, but as soon as the colonel got wind of it, I was obliged to ride the wooden horse,[59] and I was forbidden, under penalty of death by hanging, to further practice my craft. In the end the ill fortune of others was my good fortune, for after I had cured some people (who must have had special faith in me) of jaundice and a few of the fever, I was permitted to go outside the fortress to gather roots and herbs (that was my pretext). There, however, I set snares and traps for hares and had the good fortune to get two of them the first night. These I took to the colonel and thereby received not only a thaler as a reward but also permission to go out to trap hares whenever I did not have the watch. Now because the countryside was rather barren and there was no one who was catching these animals, and particularly since they had multiplied splendidly, this was also grist for my mill, inasmuch as it appeared that the hares were falling like snowflakes, or as if I could conjure them by magic into my snares. When the officers saw that they could trust me, I was permitted to go out on raiding parties with the other soldiers. Then I began to live again as I had at Soest, except that I was not permitted to lead and command raiding parties as before in Westphalia, for to do that it was necessary first to know all the highways and byways and to be acquainted with the Rhine.

CHAPTER 10

Simplicius survives an unpleasant bath in the Rhine

I shall relate a few more of my adventures before I tell how I was delivered from my musket once more: one about great peril to life and limb, from which I escaped through the grace of God; the other about peril to my soul, in which state I stubbornly persisted, for I am no more willing to conceal my faults than my virtues, not only so that my *histori*[60] will be fairly complete, but also so that the untraveled reader can find out what manner of strange fellows there be in this world.

As reported at the end of the preceding chapter, I was permitted to go out on raiding parties with the other soldiers, which in garrisons is not granted to just any old reprobate, but only to honorable soldiers. Now one time nineteen of us were going together up through the Lower Margravate[61] to lie in wait up-river from Strasbourg for a ship from Basel in which there was supposed to be hidden some of the Duke of Weimar's officers and goods. Up-river from Ottenheim[62] we got a fisherman's skiff to cross the river with and to put into a river island there which was advantageously situated for compelling approaching ships to put in to shore, in accordance with which plan ten of us were safely ferried over by the fisherman. But when one of us, who was usually able to handle a boat well, fetched the other nine, amongst whom was I, the skiff capsized unexpectedly, so that on a sudden we were all in the Rhine. I did not pay much heed to the others but thought of myself instead. Now even though I flailed away with all my might and used all the advantageous moves of a good swimmer, the river played with me as if I were a ball, tossing me up into the air one moment and down into the water the next. I strove valiantly to take a breath as often as my head came above the water. Had it been somewhat colder, I should never have held out so long and been able to escape with my life. I attempted repeatedly to reach the river bank, but the eddies prevented it by hurling me from one side to the other, and even though I shortly came down to below the village of Goldscheuer,[63] as more and more time passed, I well nigh despaired of my life. But after I had passed the region near Goldscheur and had already resigned myself to the fact that I must needs make my way, either dead or alive, down to the bridges over the Rhine at Strasbourg, I espied a large tree whose branches reached out of the water not far in front of me. The river went straight and *recta*[64] towards it, and therefore I used all the strength I had left to reach the tree, which I was indeed quite fortunate to do, so that as a result of the current and my own efforts I ended up sitting upon the largest branch, which I had initially taken to be a tree; but it was so agitated by the eddies and waves that it was compelled to whip me up and down without surcease and therefore so shook my stomach that I thought I was going to vomit up lungs and liver. I could scarce hold onto it because my head fell to spinning; I would have liked to let myself back into the water again, but I well remarked that I was not man enough to withstand even a hundredth part of the sort of the labor I had already performed, and so I was obliged to remain where I was and to hope for whatever uncertain salvation God might chance to send me, since otherwise I would not come away from this alive. But my conscience gave me slight consolation in this regard, representing to me that I had been so frivolously forfeiting such merciful assistance for a year now; however, I hoped for something better than I merited and fell to praying as devoutly as if I had been brought up in a cloister. I made up my mind to live more virtuously in the future and made divers vows: I renounced the life of a soldier and foreswore foraging sorties forever, tossed away my bullet bag and my knapsack, and fell to acting precisely as if I were going to become a hermit again, expiate my sins, and thank the mercy of God till my dying day for my hoped-for deliverance. And when I had spent two or three hours like this on the tree branch, hovering betwixt hope and fear, there came down the Rhine the very ship which I had been supposed to be lying in wait for. I raised my voice in heart-rending cries and screamed for help in the name of God and all His archangels, and since they were obliged to sail past not far from me and therefore saw all the more clearly what a wretched situation and what peril I was in, everyone in the boat was moved to pity, for which reason they straightway put in to shore in order to discuss how they might help me.

Now since, because of the eddies which were on all sides of me and which were caused by the roots and branches of the tree, it was impossible, without peril to life and limb, either to swim out to me or to sail to me with a boat large or small, a long while was required to think over how to help me, and how I felt in the meanwhile is easy to imagine. Finally they sent two fellows upstream from me in a rowboat, and they let a rope float down to me and held onto one end of it while with great effort I laid hold of the other end and tied it round my body as best I could, so that I was then pulled by it, like a fish hooked onto a line, to the rowboat and taken onto the ship.

Now since I had escaped death in this manner, I should by rights have fallen to my knees upon the shore and thanked Divine Mercy for my deliverance, and I should have made a beginning at improving my life otherwise, as I had indeed, in my extremest need, promised and vowed to do. Ah, good intentions! When they asked me who I was and how I got into this perilous predicament, I fell to telling these fellows such lies as might have made the heavens turn black, for I thought to myself: "If you tell them that you were going to help plunder them, they will forthwith throw you back into the Rhine." And so I claimed to be an organist who had been driven from his homeland, and I said that while I was attempting to go to Strasbourg to seek service in a school or some other institution on the other side of the Rhine, I was captured by a raiding party, stripped of my clothes, and thrown into the Rhine, which had carried me to that same tree. And because I was able to flesh out these lies of mine, and particularly since I swore by all that was holy that they were true, they believed me and gave me food and drink to restore myself, which I assuredly had great need of.

At the tollhouse in Strasbourg most of them went ashore, and I with them, where I then thanked them profusely, and amongst them I espied a young merchant whose countenance, gait, and bearing led me to believe that I had seen him often somewhere before, but I could not recollect where; but from his voice I perceived that he was the very same cornet who had taken me prisoner before, but I could not make out how he had turned from such a fine young soldier into a merchant, particularly since he was a gentleman by birth. The desire to know whether or not my eyes and ears were deceiving me drove me to go to him and say: "Monsieur Schönstein, is it you or is it not?" He, however, answered: "I am not a member of the von Schönstein family; I am a merchant." Then I said: "Then I am not the chasseur of Soest; rather, I am an itinerant beggar." "O, my dear friend!" said he in return. "What the devil are you doing? Where are you rambling about?" I said: "My friend, if you are foreordained by Heaven to help me preserve my life, as has now happened for a second time, then my *fatum*[65] without doubt requires that I not be very far away from you." Then we took one another by the arm, like two true friends who had before mutually promised to love one another till death part them. I was obliged to put up in his lodgings and to tell him everything which had befallen me since I had left L.[66] to go to Cologne to fetch my treasure; nor did I keep from him the truth about how I, with a raiding party, was lying in wait for their ship, and what happened to us thereby. But about how I had lived in Paris I kept quiet as a mouse, for I was afraid that he might bruit it about in L. and thereby get me into hot water with my wife. He, for his part, confided to me that he had been sent by the Hessian general staff to Duke Bernhard, the prince of Weimar, to report to him on all manner of matters of great import concerning the war and to confer with him about the coming campaign and military plans, and, he said, as I could see with my very own eyes, he was on the return journey disguised as a merchant. He also told me, besides, that when he had departed, my beloved was big of belly and, along with her parents and kinfolk, was still in good financial condition; *item*, that the colonel was still keeping a command open for me; and in the bargain he teased me because the pox had so disfigured me that neither my wife nor any other women in L. would take me to be the chasseur any more, etc. Then we agreed that I should stay with him and go back to L. at this occasion, which was what I desired to do. And because I had nothing on but rags, he lent me some money so that I might outfit myself to look like a storekeeper.

They say that what is not meant to be will not transpire, and I found that out; for when we were sailing down the Rhine and the ship was boarded at Rheinhausen[67] by an inspection party, the Philippsburg soldiers recognized me, seized me once more, and took me back to Philippsburg, where I was obliged to play again, as before, the role of a musketeer, which did sorely vex my good cornet as much as it did me, because we were obliged to part again, and he durst not take my part too much either, for he himself was hard put to get himself through safely.

CHAPTER 11

Why clergymen should not eat hares caught with snares

So now, dear Reader, you have heard in what peril to life and limb I was, but as concerns the peril to my soul, it should be known that with a musket upon my shoulder I was the sort of wild man who does not trouble himself about God or His word. No wickedness was too great for me. All the mercy and beneficence I had ever received from God was, of course, forgotten, and I also heeded nothing in this world or the next, but instead lived, like a beast in the field, from one moment to the next. No one would have believed of me that I had been brought up by a pious hermit. I seldom went to church, and I did not go to confession at all; and inasmuch as the salvation of my own soul meant nothing to me, I tormented my fellow men all the more. Whenever I could cheat someone I did not fail to do it; indeed, I desired to have fame for it in the bargain, and thus well nigh no one who had dealings with me went unscathed. On account of that, I was oft dealt heavy blows and got to ride the wooden horse[68] even more often; in fact, they threatened me with torture and the gallows, but nothing helped; I continued my godless behavior, so that it appeared as if I were acting like a desperate man and was intentionally running headlong to hell. And though I did not commit any crimes by which I might have forfeited my life, I was nevertheless so wicked that one could scarce have encountered a more degenerate person (except for those who practice black magic and sodomy).

This our regimental chaplain remarked, and because he was a right pious soul-saver he sent for me at Easter to hear why I had not reported for confession and communion. But after his many true-hearted exhortations to me, I used him as I had the parson in L. before, so the good gentleman could do nothing with me. And when it seemed as if Christ and baptism had been wasted upon me, he said in conclusion: "Alas, you wretched man! I thought that you were erring from ignorance, but now I see that you are continuing to sin out of pure wickedness, premeditatedly, as it were. Alas, who do you think will have pity upon your poor soul when it is damned? I, for my part, protest before God and the world that I have no guilt as regards your damnation, because I have done, and I should be happy to unflaggingly continue to do, what would be necessary to achieve your salvation. But in the future, I fear, no more will be required of me than to refuse to let your body, after your poor soul leaves it in this state of damnation, be buried together with other virtuous departed Christians, but instead to have it dragged to the carrion pit with the carcasses of dead beasts, or to that place where they put other people who are forgetful of God and who die in a fit of despair!"[69]

This earnest threat was just as fruitless as the earlier admonitions, and, in fact, solely for the reason that I was ashamed to go to confession. O, what a fool I was! I often recounted my misdeeds in the presence of large groups of people, and I even made them out to be worse than they were, but now, when in order to receive forgiveness I ought to have mended my ways and contritely confessed my sins to a single mortal, acting in God's stead, I remained stubbornly silent! I say "stubbornly" with good reason, and I remained stubborn, for I answered: "I serve the Emperor as a soldier and if I now die like a soldier, then it will not be a miracle if I must needs be content with a grave outside the churchyard like other soldiers (who cannot always be buried in consecrated ground, but must make do somewhere on the battlefield, in trenches, or in the bellies of wolves and carrion crows)."

Thus I parted from the clergyman, who for his holy zeal to save my soul got nothing from me in return, except that one time I refused to give him a hare which he urgently begged of me, on the pretext that because the hare had hanged himself on a piece of cord in a snare and thus had taken his own life, it was therefore not fitting that the hare, having died in a fit of despair, should be buried in consecrated ground.

CHAPTER 12

Simplicius is unexpectedly relieved of his musket

And so there was no improvement in me; instead I grew worse with each passing day. The colonel once told me that if I did not behave myself, he was going to send me away from the company burdened with disgrace, but because I well knew that he was not in earnest about that, I said that this could be done easily if he but compelled me to leave carrying as my burden one of the provost's men upon my shoulders. So he let me stay, because he could well imagine that I would consider it not a punishment but a favor if he were to let me go. Accordingly, I was obliged to remain, against my will, a musketeer and to suffer hunger till it was well into the summer. But the closer Count von Götz approached with his army,[70] the closer came my deliverance, for when he had his headquarters in Bruchsal,[71] my friend Trueheart, whom I had loyally assisted with my money in the camp at Magdeburg, was sent by the general staff on some official business to our fortress, where they treated him with the greatest deference. I was just then standing guard in front of the colonel's quarters, and even though Trueheart was wearing a black velvet coat I nevertheless straightway recognized him at first glance, but I had not the heart to address him immediately, for I could not but fear that in accordance with the way of the world he might be ashamed of me, or otherwise not desire to let on that he knew me, because to judge by his clothes he was of high rank, whereas I was but a louse-ridden musketeer. But after I was relieved of duty I inquired of his servants about his name and rank, so that I should be assured that I would not perchance be addressing another instead of him, and yet I had not the heart to speak to him, but instead wrote this note and had his valet-de-chambre hand it to him the next morning:

> Monsieur, etc.
>
> If you, most esteemed sir, would be so kind as to now, through your excellent good name, release me, whom you heretofore through your valor delivered from fetters and bonds in the battle of Wittstock, from the most wretched condition in the world, into which I, like a plaything of fickle Fortuna, have fallen, it would not only not be difficult for you to accomplish, rather, you would also gain as a faithful servant forever
>
> Your ever loyal but now most wretched and forlorn
>
> S. Simplicissimus

As soon as he had read this he had me brought to him and said: "Friend, where is the man who gave you this letter?" I answered: "Sir, he is a prisoner in the fortress here." "All right," said he, "go to him and say that I desire to help him get out, even if he were to already have the rope round his neck!" I said: "Sir, that will not require such effort. I myself am poor Simplicius, who has now come hither, not only to thank you for my deliverance at Wittstock, but also to beg you to deliver me once more from the musket which I am being compelled to bear against my will." He did not let me finish what I was saying but, by embracing me, demonstrated how inclined he was to help me. *In summa*, he did everything which one loyal friend ought to do for another, and before he asked me how I had got into the fortress and into this servitude, he sent his servant to the Jew to buy a horse and clothes for me. In the meantime I told him how I had fared since his father died in the camp at Magdeburg, and when he heard that I was the chasseur of Soest (about whom he had heard many a glorious tale of military derring-do), he lamented that he had not known this before, for at that time he could most assuredly have helped me obtain the command of a company.

Now when the Jew came in with enough military clothing of all sorts to weigh down a porter, Trueheart picked out the best for me, had me put them on, and took me with him to the colonel, to whom he said: "Sir, in your garrison I have come upon this fellow here, to whom I am so deeply indebted that I cannot leave him in such a lowly station, even if his qualities merited no better one. Therefore, colonel, I beg you to do me a favor and either to accommodate him better or to permit me to take him with me in order to help him advance in rank in the army, which you, colonel, perhaps do not have the opportunity here to do." The colonel crossed himself in astonishment when he heard someone finally praise me and said: "Most honored sir, forgive me if I assume that you desire to test me in order to determine whether I am willing to serve you as you indeed merit, and if this be the case, then if you demand something else of me which it is in my power to do, you will see from my deeds how willing I am to comply. But as far as concerns this fellow, he does not belong under my command but, as he himself attests, to a dragoon regiment. Besides, he is such a bad apple, who since he has been here has given my provost more work than a whole company of men ever did, that I cannot but believe of him that there is no body of water in which he can drown!" With that he ended his speech with a laugh and wished me good fortune when I went to the field of battle.

This, however, did not satisfy my friend Trueheart; rather, he asked the colonel not to refuse to let me dine at his table, which request he was granted, and he did this to the end that he might tell the colonel in my presence what he, while discoursing with Count von der Wahl[72] and the commandant of the garrison in Soest, had heard about my exploits in Westphalia, all of which he now laid forth in such wise that all who heard him were obliged to hold me to be a good soldier. I behaved so modestly during the conversation that the colonel and his men, who had known me before, could not but believe that in different clothing I had also become a completely different person. And when the colonel desired to know where I had gotten the name "Doctor," I told him all about my journey from Paris to Philippsburg and about how many peasants I had duped in order to win my daily bread, at which tales they laughed heartily. Finally, I confessed candidly that I had been of a mind to so perturb and wear him, the colonel, down that he might finally be obliged to turn me out of the garrison if he desired to live in peace and not be plagued by the many complaints about me.

Then the colonel told of the many knavish tricks which I had played upon people for as long as I had been in the garrison, namely, how I had boiled peas, poured lard over them, and sold them for pure lard; *item*, how I had passed off a sack of sand as a sack of salt by filling the bottom of the sack with sand and putting a layer of salt on the top; and then how I had played a practical joke upon one person here and another there, and had vexed the men with pasquilles; so that during the entire meal they talked only about me. But had I not had such an important friend, all my deeds would have been worthy of punishment. This I took to be an example of how it must be at court when a wicked knave has acquired his prince's favor.

After dinner was over the Jew had no horse which my friend Trueheart deemed good enough for me, and because he was held in such high esteem that the colonel could scarce do without his patronage, the colonel made me a present of one, with saddle and tack, from his own stable, which steed Mr. Simplicius mounted and rode happily out of the fortress with his friend Trueheart. Some of his comrades called after him: "Good luck, friend, good luck!" But some, out of envy, cried: "The greater the rogue, the better his luck!"

CHAPTER 13

Concerns the Brotherhood of Merode[73]

On the way Trueheart arranged with me that I should claim to be his cousin, so that I might be regarded all the more highly. He, for his part, was going to procure me a horse, together with a groom, and assign me to the Neuneck regiment,[74] where I could remain as a freebooter[75] till an officer's post came available in the army, which post he could help me obtain.

And so, in a trice, I was once more a fellow who looked like a good soldier, but I did few deeds that summer, except that I now and again helped steal some cows in the Black Forest and made myself rather well acquainted with the Breisgau[76] and Alsace. For the rest, I still lived under an unlucky star, for after my groom, together with his horse, was captured from me by the Weimar troops at Kenzingen[77] I was obliged to wear out another horse escaping and finally to ride it to death, so that I was therefore compelled to join the Order of the Brotherhood of Merode. My friend Trueheart, of course, would have gladly procured me another mount, but because I had so quickly used up the first two horses, he held back and thought to leave me dangling till I learned to look out for myself better. But I did not demand anything of him anyway, for I found in my new comrades such a pleasant company that I could have wished for no better trade till time to go to winter quarters.

I must tell just a little about what manner of folk Meroders be, because without doubt there are some people, particularly those unversed in warfare, who know nothing about them; nor have I thus far come upon any author who has incorporated into his writings anything about their usages, customs, rights, and privileges, despite the fact that it is well worthwhile that not only present-day generals but also today's peasantry know what manner of guild it be. Now first of all, as concerns their name, I surely hope it will not be construed as an insult to the valiant cavalier under whom they received it, for I would he unwilling to publicly pin a label onto anyone. I have seen a kind of shoe which had twisted seams instead of holes, so that one could tramp through the mud in them all the better, but if anyone were, for that reason alone, to call General Mansfeld[78] a pitch-fart (as we are wont to call cobblers), just because those shoes were devised by his troops and were therefore called "Mansfelders," I should hold him to be a madman. This name "Meroders," which will not perish as long as Germans make war, must be understood in just the same way. Now it came about as follows: One time a gentleman named "Merode"[79] brought a newly recruited regiment to the army, and the fellows in it were as weak and physically infirm as the Frenchmen from Brittany, with the result that they could not tolerate marching and other strenuous activities which a soldier in the field must needs endure, for which reason their brigade soon became so small that it could scarce cover a single company; and whenever one came upon one or more sick and lame men at a market place, in houses, and behind fences and hedges and asked "What regiment are you from?" the answer was usually "We're Meroders!" From that it came about that finally all those men—whether sick or well, wounded or not—who straggled along outside the column of march or did not take up quarters in the field with their regiments, were called "Meroders," which fellows had before been called "sow-swipers" and "honey-snatchers," because they are like the bees in beehives which, when they have lost their stingers, can no longer make honey and do nothing but eat. When a trooper loses his horse or a musketeer his health, or his wife and child fall sick and he desires to stay behind, then that already makes two and one half Meroders, a small rabble which resembles no one more than gypsies, because they not only ramble about in front of, behind, to the side of, and in the midst of the army; they are also like gypsies both in customs and habits, since one sees them together in packs (like partridges in the wintertime) lying about behind the hedges in the shade or, depending upon the time of year, in the sun, or somewhere around a campfire, smoking and lounging about, while elsewhere, at that same moment, a proper soldier is enduring heat, thirst, hunger, frost, and all manner of misery. Outside the column of march goes a horde of them foraging, while at that same moment many a poor soldier is well nigh collapsing from fatigue under his weapons. In front of, to the sides of, and in back of the army they despoil everything they come upon, and what they cannot use, they destroy, so that the regiments, when they come to quarters or pitch camp, often do not find a single decent drink of water; and when a serious effort is made to keep the Meroders with the baggage train, one often finds that it is almost larger than the army itself. And when they march, take quarters, camp, and plunder, they have no sergeant major to command them, no sergeant to thrash them, no corporal to assign them guard duty, no drummer to remind them of tattoo, squad watch or day watch, and, *in summa*, no one to send them into battle as an adjutant does, no one to assign them quarters as a quartermaster does—rather, they live like princes. And when rations are distributed to the *soldateska*[80] they are first in line to fetch their share, though they do not merit it. On the other hand, the greatest plague for them was the regimental and chief provost marshals, who at times, when the Meroders went too far, put bracelets made of iron onto their wrists and ankles, or even adorned their necks with hempen collars and had them hanged by their fine necks.

They don't stand watch, they don't build fortifications, they don't storm fortresses, nor do they get into any pitched battles; yet they are fed. And the damage they do to the general, the peasant, and the *armada*[81] itself, amongst which there is so much of this rabble, simply cannot be described. The most godforsaken trooper's stableboy, who does nothing but forage, is of more use to a general than a thousand Meroders, who make foraging their trade and lounge about when they are not plying it. They are captured by opposing armies and in some places given a rap upon the knuckles by the peasantry; as a result, the army grows smaller and the enemy stronger, and even if such a dissolute rascal (I do not mean the poor folk who are sick, but rather the mountless troopers of horse who have let their horses perish from neglect and have joined the Meroders so that they can spare their hides) does survive the summer, the only thing one has as a result is that one must equip him again at great expense for the winter, so that he has something to lose in the next campaign. Meroders should be harnessed in teams like whippets and taught in garrison how to make war, or even shackled to galleys if they are unwilling to do their part as foot soldiers on the battlefield till they get a horse again. I shall pass over in silence here how many a village is burned down by them, either through carelessness or intentionally, how many a man from their own army they remove, plunder, secretly rob, and even do in, and how many a spy can hide amongst them so long as he can mention by name but one regiment and company from the *armada*. Now at that time I too was one of these fine fellows, and I remained one till the day before the battle of Wittenweier,[82] at which time headquarters were in Schuttern;[83] for when I then went with my comrades to the Geroldseck region[84] to steal some cows and oxen, as was our wont, I was captured by Weimar troops, who knew how to use us much better, for they loaded us down with muskets and pushed us into the one regiment and the other, and I went to Colonel Hattstein's.[85]

CHAPTER 14

Single combat with peril to life and limb in which each combatant nevertheless escapes with his life

At that time I came to comprehend that I had been born doomed to misfortune, for about four weeks before the aforementioned engagement occurred I heard some of Götz's low-ranking officers discussing the war, and one of them said: "This summer will not pass without a fight! If we beat the enemy, we'll most likely take quarters in Freiburg[86] and the forest towns[87] this coming winter. But if we get the worst of it, we'll go to winter quarters nonetheless." From this prophecy I drew my own conclusions and said to myself: "Well, be of good cheer, Simplicius. This coming winter you'll be drinking wine from the Neckar and the lake district,[88] and you'll share in whatever the Duke of Weimar's forces win." But I was greatly deceived, for because I was now a soldier in the Duke's army I was thus predestined to help besiege Breisach,[89] since this siege was laid down right after the oft-mentioned battle of Wittenweier, with the result that I, like the other musketeers, was obliged to stand watch and build fortifications night and day, and the only profit I had from it was that I learned how approach-trenches to a besieged fortress must be laid out, an art to which I had paid scant attention when I was in the camp outside the walls of Magdeburg. For the rest, however, I fared quite badly, because two or even three of us were crowded in together in cramped quarters, my purse was empty, wine and beer and meat were a rarity, and the best game I could snatch was apples and a half-loaf of bread.

This left a sour taste in my mouth, particularly when I thought back upon the fleshpots of Egypt, by which I mean the Westphalian hams and the knockwursts in L.[90] I never gave a thought to my wife any more, except when I was lying in my tent and frozen half stiff; then I often said to myself: "Ha, Simplicius! Do you really think you would be done wrong if someone were to repay you in kind for what you did in Paris?" And with such thoughts I tormented myself like any other jealous cuckold, even though I could impute to my wife nothing but honor and virtue. Finally I grew so impatient that I revealed to my captain how my affairs stood and also wrote by post to L. and succeeded in having Colonel de S.-A. and my father-in-law bring it to pass, through letters of the Duke of Weimar, that my captain was obliged to give me a pass to leave the regiment.

About three or four weeks before Christmas I marched out of camp with a good firelock and went down the Breisgau, with the idea in mind to receive in Strasbourg, at the time of the Christmas fair, twenty thalers which my father-in-law had made over to me, and then to betake myself down the Rhine in the company of some merchants, since there were, after all, many Imperial garrisons along the way. But as I was passing by Endingen[91] and came to a house standing alone, a shot was fired at me[92] in such wise that the musket ball put a hole through the brim of my hat, and immediately after that a strong, stocky fellow sprang out of the house and upon me, screaming that I should lay down my musket. I answered: "No, by God, friend, not just to please you!" and I readied the trigger. He, however, whisked out of its sheath a thing that looked more like a hangman's sword than a saber and hurried towards me with it. Now when I saw that he was in earnest, I fired at him and hit him in the forehead in such wise that he spun around and finally fell to the ground. In order to take advantage of this, I quickly wrested the sword from his fist and attempted to plunge it into his body, but when it refused to go through, he suddenly sprang to his feet again, snatched me by my hair, and I snatched him by his. His sword, however, I had already tossed away. Then we fell to such serious sport with one another as made sufficiently clear the strength born of bitterness which each of us possessed, and yet neither could master the other. I was on top of him one instant, he on top of me the next and in a trice we were on our feet again, but that did not last long, for each of us was attempting to kill the other. The blood which gushed from my nose and mouth I spat into my opponent's face, inasmuch as he was after my blood so passionately. That was good for me, for it prevented him from seeing. In this manner we pulled one another about in the snow for nigh onto an hour and a half, from which labors we grew so fatigued that, to all appearances, with naught but fists the weakness of the one could not have vanquished completely the fatigue of the other, nor could one of us have brought death to the other with the strength he had left and without weapons.

The art of wrestling, which I had often practiced in L., then stood me in good stead indeed, else I should without doubt have paid with my life, for my foe was much stronger than I and, besides that, as impervious to musket balls as steel.[93] When we had fatigued one another till we were both almost dead, he finally said: "Stop, I give up!" I said: "You should have right off let me pass!" "What good will it do you," he answered, "if I should straightway die?" "And what good would it have done you," I asked, "if you had shot me dead? I have not a farthing on me!" Then he begged for quarter, and I relented and let him stand up, after he had first sworn to high heaven that he would not only keep the peace but would also be my loyal friend and servant. But I would not have either believed or trusted him if the wicked deeds he had done had been known to me.

Now when we were both on our feet, we pledged with a handshake that everything which had happened was to be forgotten, and each expressed his astonishment that he had met his match in the other, for he believed that through magic my hide had been rendered as invincible as his own had, in fact, been made. And I let him labor under that delusion, so that when be got his rifle he would not attack me again. He had a large knot upon his forehead from my shot, and I had lost much blood, but neither of us complained about more than our necks, which were so battered that neither of us could hold his head upright.

Because it was then on towards evening and my opponent told me that I would not encounter so much as a dog or a cat, much less any human being till I came to the Kinzig River,[94] whereas he had a good piece of meat and something to drink in an isolated cottage not far from the highway, I let him persuade me to go with him, and on the way he attested with frequent sighs as to how sorry he was that he had offended me.

CHAPTER 15

How Olivier[95] thought to excuse his wicked brigandage

A resolute soldier who has resigned himself to risking his life and to paying slight heed to it is indeed a stupid beast! Not one man in a thousand could be found who would have had the heart to go to an unfamiliar place as the guest of a man who had just attacked him with murderous intent. On the way I asked him what army he belonged to; to that he said that for the time being he had no master but was instead waging war for himself, and at the same time he asked what army I was with. I said that I had been with the army of the Duke of Weimar but now had my discharge and was of a mind to betake myself to my home. Then he asked what my name was, and when I answered "Simplicius," he turned round (for I had him walk in front of me because I did not trust him) and peered into my face. "Are you not also called 'Simplicissimus'?" "Yes," I answered, "no one but a rogue would refuse to admit to his own name. But what is your name?" "Ah, my friend," he answered, "I am Olivier, whom you knew very well in the camp at Magdeburg." With that he hurled his flintlock away and fell to his knees to ask my forgiveness for his having meant to do me harm, saying that he could well imagine that he would find no better friend in the world than he had in me, because, according to old Trueheart's prophecy, I was to avenge his death so valiantly. I, for my part, was astonished at such an unexpected meeting, but he said: "It's not so strange. It's a small world. But what is strange to me is that we have both changed so, since I have turned from a *secretario*[96] into a highwayman, and you from a fool into such a valiant soldier. Be assured, my friend, if there were ten thousand men like us, we would capture Breisach tomorrow and in the end make ourselves masters of the entire world." In such discourse, since night had just fallen, we went into a small, isolated day laborer's cottage, and though I do not like to boast, I nevertheless agreed with him, principally because his scoundrelous and perfidious character was well known to me; and though I really did not trust him in the least to behave himself, I nevertheless went into the aforementioned cottage with him, in which a peasant was just heating the room. To him he said: "Have you cooked anything?" "No," said the peasant, "but I do still have the roast leg of veal which I brought from Waldkirch[97] today." "Well then," answered Olivier, "go and fetch what you have, and at the same time bring along a keg of wine."

When the peasant was gone I said to Olivier: "My friend (I called him that so that I might be all the safer from him), you have a willing host." He said: "The rogue has the

316

devil to thank for it, for I feed him, together with his wife and child, and in the bargain he takes good booty for himself. I leave him all the clothes I take, to put to his own use." I asked Olivier where he kept his wife and child, and Olivier said that he had moved them to Freiburg, where he visited them twice a week and brought him victuals from there, as well as powder and shot. He further reported to me that he had been carrying on this freebooting for a long while and that it suited him better than serving a master; nor did he intend to stop till he had nicely stuffed his purse. I said: "My friend, you're plying a perilous trade, and if you were to be caught during such a robbery, how do you think they would use you?" "Ha!" said he. "I see that you are still the same old Simplicius. I know that if you wish to dance you must pay the piper, but you must know that the gentlemen in Nuremberg[98] cannot hang a man unless they have hold of him." I answered: "But my friend, let us assume that you are not caught, which seems quite unlikely, since the pitcher goes to the well till it finally breaks; nevertheless, such a life as you lead is the most vile one in the world, and so I do not believe that you desire to die living like that." "What!" said he. "The most vile life in the world? My dear Simplicius, I assure you that robbing others is the most noble *exercitium*[99] a man can have in this world! Tell me, how many kingdoms and principalities have not been acquired and stolen from another by force? Where in the whole wide world is it taken amiss when a king or a prince enjoys the income from his properties, which were usually acquired by main force by his forefathers? What could with more right be termed noble than the very trade which I am now plying? I can tell from the look upon your face that you would like to remind me that many of them have been drawn and quartered, hanged and beheaded, for murdering, robbing, and stealing. I already know that quite well, for that is what the law requires. But the only people you'll see hanged are poor and petty thieves,[100] which they do merit, because they ought never have undertaken this splendid profession, which is, after all, proper and reserved for none but stouthearted men. When did you ever see Justice punish a noble person of rank for having been too great a financial burden upon his lands? And what is more, no usurer is punished who practices this noble art in secret, under the guise, indeed, of Christian love for his fellowman. So why should I be punishable when I do it openly, in the good old-fashioned German way, without flummery and deceit? My dear Simplicius, you have not yet read your Machiavelli.[101] I am of a right upright character, and I choose to live this way freely, openly, and without any skittishness. I fight and, in doing so, risk my life like the heroes of olden times, and I also know that those trades whose practitioners put themselves in jeopardy are permitted, and because I put my life in jeopardy, it follows, incontrovertibly, that it is right and permissible for me to practice this art."

I then answered: "Even assuming that you are permitted to rob and steal, I nevertheless know that it is against the law of nature, which does not permit that one do unto another what one would not wish done unto himself. And this iniquity is also against the laws of the world, which command that the thief be hanged, the robber beheaded, and the murderer broken upon the wheel. And, finally, it is also against the laws of God, which is the most important thing of all, for He leaves no sin unpunished." "It is as I said before," answered Olivier. "You are still the same old Simplicius and have not studied Machiavelli. But were I able to found a *monarchiam*[102] of sorts, I should like to see who would then preach much against it." We would have disputed much more with one another, but because the peasant came with food and drink, we sat together and stilled our hunger, which I indeed had great need to do.

How he interprets Trueheart's prophecy to his own advantage and therefore loves his worst enemy

Our meal was white bread and a cold roast leg of veal. With it we had a goodly drink of wine and a warm room. "Well, Simplicius," said Olivier, "it is better here than in the trenches outside the walls of Breisach, is it not?" I said: "That is true, even though one might enjoy life there with some safety and more honor." At that he laughed loudly and said: "Are the poor fellows in the trenches, who must needs fear an attack at any moment, any safer than we are? My dear Simplicius, I do well see that you have put off your fool's cap but have still retained your foolish head, which cannot comprehend what is good or bad, and were you anyone but that same Simplicius who, according to old Trueheart's prophecy, is destined to avenge my death, I should teach you to confess that I lead a nobler life than a lord." I thought to myself: "What is he about? I must choose different words than before, else this monster, who now has a peasant to help him nicely, might now do me in." And therefore I said: "Who has ever in his live-long days heard it said that the apprentice understands his trade better than his master? My friend, if you have as noble and happy a life as you contend, then let me share your happiness, since I am in great need of good fortune." Then Olivier answered: "My friend, be assured that I love you as much as I do myself, and that the offense I gave you today hurts me far more than the musket ball with which you struck me in the forehead when you defended yourself against me like a brave and proper fellow. How, then, could I deny you anything? If it please you, stay with me. I shall care for you as I do for myself. But if you have no desire to be with me, I shall give you a goodly sum of money and accompany you whither you will. And so that you believe that these words come from the heart, I shall tell you the reason why I hold you in such high esteem. You will surely recall how rightly old Trueheart hit the mark with his prophecies. Look you, in the camp outside Magdeburg he told me my future in these words, which I have ever kept firmly in mind: 'Olivier, say what you will about our fool. He will nevertheless one day frighten you with his valor and play the greatest prank upon you that you will ever experience your entire life long, because you will give him cause to do it at a time when you two have not recognized one another. Yet he will not only spare your life, which is in his hands, he will also come sometime later to that place where you will be slain, at which place he shall happily avenge your death.' On account of this prophecy, my dear Simplicius, I am prepared to share with you the very heart in my body, for inasmuch as a part of the prophecy was fulfilled when I gave you cause to behave like a brave soldier and shoot me in the head and take my sword from me (which, in fact, no one had ever done before), and also to spare my life when I was lying under you and well nigh choking to death on my own blood, I therefore have no doubt that the rest of it, the part concerning my death, will go not awry in the least. Now, my dear friend, from this revenge I cannot but conclude that you are my loyal friend, for were you not, you would not take such vengeance on my account. Now there you have the *concepta* of my heart,[103] so now tell me what you are of a mind to do." I thought to myself: "May the devil trust you! But not I! Were I to take money from you and depart, you might then do me in; but were I to remain with you, I could not but fear that I might be drawn and quartered along with you." Accordingly, I resolved to pull the wool over his eyes by remaining with him till I should have an opportunity to escape from him, and so I said that if he were willing to tolerate me I would stay with him a week or so, to see whether I could accustom myself to this sort of life. If it pleased me, he would have in me a loyal friend and good soldier; if it pleased me not, there would always be time to part from one another. Then he importuned me to drink one glass after the other, but I did not trust him and pretended to be full with drink before I really was, in order to see whether he would perchance attack me when I was apparently no longer able to defend myself.

Meanwhile the lice, of which I had brought a goodly number along with me from Breisach, were tormenting me right sharply, for in the warmth of the room they were no longer willing to make do with my rags but instead came strolling out to make merry. This Olivier observed, and he asked me whether I had lice. I said: "Yes indeed! More than all the ducats I hope to have my entire life long." "You must not talk that way," said Olivier. "If you remain with me you can surely get more ducats than you now have lice." I answered: "That is as impossible as my being able to get rid of my lice now." "O, no," said he, "both things are possible." And he straightway commanded the peasant to fetch me some clothes which were hidden in a hollow tree not far from the house; they were a grey hat, a doublet of elk leather, a pair of red scarlet breeches, and a grey coat; stockings and shoes he was going to give me the next day. When I saw this beneficence on his part, I began to trust him somewhat more than before, and I cheerfully went to sleep.

CHAPTER 17

Simplicius' thoughts are more pious when he goes robbing with Olivier than they were when he was in church

In the morning towards dawn Olivier said: "Get up, Simplicius! We're going out, by God, to see what may perchance be got." "O Lord!" I thought to myself. "Am I then going to go out robbing now, taking Thy most hallowed name in vain, whereas before, after I came from my hermit, I was not even so bold as to hear without astonishment one man say to another: 'Come, friend, let us guzzle a measure of wine together, by God!' because I held it to be doubly sinful to get drunk whilst taking Thy name in vain. O, Heavenly Father, how I have changed! O, dear God, what is finally to become of me if I do not mend my ways? O, check my course, which will lead me straight into hell if I do not do penance!" With such words and thoughts I followed Olivier into a village in which there was not a single living creature. There we climbed up to the top of the church tower,[104] on account of the view into the distance it afforded. Up there he had the stockings and shoes hidden which he had promised me the evening before, along with two loaves of bread, several pieces of dried pickled meat, and a small demi-keg full of wine, with which provisions he alone could easily have made do for a week. Now when I put on the gifts he had presented me, he told me that he generally lay in wait at this spot whenever he desired to take good booty, for which reason he had laid in such goodly provisions there, adding that he had yet several other places which were stocked with food and drink, so that if the man he wished to see was not in one place, he might find him at another. I, of course, could not but praise his cleverness, but I did give him to understand that it was really not right to desecrate in this wise such a holy place as a church, which was dedicated to God. "What!" said he. "Desecrate? Churches, were they able to speak, would admit that they could not but deem what I commit in them to be very slight compared to the vicious acts which have been committed in them before. How many men and women, do you really think, have entered this church since it was built under the pretext of worshiping God, but have in reality but come here to display their new clothes, their fine figures, their *praeeminence*, and the like? Here comes a fellow into church like a peacock and takes a place in front of the altar as if he were going to pray the saints' feet off; there stands a fellow in the corner to sigh like the publican in the temple, which sighs, however, are directed solely to his beloved, upon whose visage he feasts his eyes and for whose sake alone he appears in church at all. Another comes to the church door or, if all goes well, right into the church with a packet of letters, like a man who is collecting fire-taxes, more to dun his debtors than to pray, and had he not known that his debtors must needs go to church, he would have remained comfortably at home poring over his balance sheets. Indeed, it sometimes happens that when the authorities of a parish have something or other to proclaim in a village, the messenger must needs do it on Sunday at the church service, for which reason many a peasant fears church more than a poor sinner does the courthouse. Do you really not know that amongst those who are buried in the church there are some who merited the executioner's sword, the gallows, the stake, and the rack? Many a man could not have carried out a seduction if the church had not been of assistance to him. When anything is to be sold or leased, in some places notice is affixed to the church doors. While many a usurer takes no time the entire week to ponder upon his skinning of others, he sits in church during the service and plots how to play the Jew. Here and there they sit, carrying on conversations with one another during mass and during the sermon, just as if the church had been built solely for that purpose; often matters are discussed there which they would not dare even think in private places. Some sit there and sleep, as if they had rented their pews. Some do nothing but pillory other folks, saying: 'Ah, how nicely the preacher hit upon this person and the other person in his sermon!' Others pay strict, heed to what the preacher has to say, but not to the end that they improve themselves as a result of it, but rather so that they may berate and belabor their clergyman if he in the least offend (as they understand it). I shall pass over in silence[105] here those tales which I have read about what manner of love affairs now and again have their beginning and their end through pandering in the churches; nor do I now recall all of what I might yet have to say about this *materia*.[106] But this you really must know, namely, that people defile the churches with blasphemy, not only in their lifetimes—they fill them with vanity and folly even after their deaths. As soon as you enter a church, you will see by the gravestones and *epitaphia*[107] how those whom the worms have long since devoured still vaunt their grandeur. If you then look up at the walls, you will see more shields, helmets, armor, swords, standards, boots, spurs, and things of that sort than in many an armory, so that it is no wonder that during this war in some towns the peasants have defended their belongings from inside churches, as if they were fortresses. Why, pray tell me, should I, a soldier, not be permitted to ply my trade in a church when in a bygone time two spiritual fathers of the church, simply because of a dispute over primacy, caused such a bloodbath[108] that the church looked more like a butcher's slaughterhouse than a house of God? I, to be sure, would still refrain from using the church if people came hither but to perform the church service, since I am, after all, a secular person; but they, the clergymen, simply do not respect the exalted majesty of the Holy Roman Emperor. Why should I be forbidden to seek my daily bread in the church when so many other people get theirs from it? Is it right that so many a wealthy man, in return for a goodly sum of money, is buried in the church, to attest to the pride of the deceased and his kith and kin, whereas, on the other hand, the poor man who has nothing to give to the church (and who is just as much a Christian as the rich man—indeed, perhaps an even more devout one than he is) must needs be buried outside the church, in some far corner of the churchyard? It is what you make of it. Had I known that you had reservations about lying in wait in a church, I should have considered answering you differently. Meanwhile, let this answer suffice for a while, till I can some other time persuade you that I am right." I should have liked to reply to Olivier that those folks who brought dishonor to churches were wicked people like himself, and that they would assuredly get their just deserts, but because I did not trust him anyway and would not have liked to fight with him again, I did not contradict him. After that he demanded that I tell him how I had fared since we parted from one another at Wittstock, and then why I had on fool's clothes when I arrived in the camp outside Magdeburg. But because I was quite morose because of a sore throat, I declined, asking that he do tell me first his life story, which would assuredly contain some merry pranks. This he granted me, and he fell to describing his wicked life as follows.

CHAPTER 18

Olivier tells of his origins[109] and of how he behaved in his youth, particularly in school[110]

My father," said Olivier, "was born of common folk not far from the city of Aachen, for which reason he was obliged in his youth to enter the service of a wealthy merchant who dealt in copper. In his employ he behaved so well that he let him learn to read, write, and cipher and put him in charge of his entire business, as Potiphar did Joseph.[111] This profited both parties well, for because of my father's industriousness and circumspection the merchant grew richer with each passing day, while my father, as a result of these good times, grew prouder with each passing day, so much so that he became ashamed of his parents and despised them, which they often lamented, but in vain. Now when my father attained his twenty-fifth year the merchant died and left behind his old widow, together with their daughter, who had recently kicked over the traces and got herself a baby boy by some bed-chamber stud, which baby, however, soon followed his grandfather into the ranks of the deceased. Now when my father saw that the daughter was bereft of father and child but not of money, he paid no heed to the fact that she would never more wear upon her head the virginal wreath, but instead weighed her wealth and paid court to her, which her mother was happy to grant, not only so that her daughter might regain her honor, but also because my father had full knowledge of the entire business and could, moreover, ply the Jew's trade excellently well. And so through this marriage my father instantly became a wealthy merchant, and I was his first heir, whom he, because of his affluence, had tenderly brought up. I was dressed like a nobleman, fed like a prince, and in other respects used like a king, which I owed more to copper and zinc than to gold and silver.

"Before I had completely finished my seventh year it was already evident what sort of person I would become, for if you are destined to be a nettle, you will sting betimes. No rascality was too great for me, and whenever I could play a trick upon anyone, I did not omit to do so, since neither my father nor my mother punished me for it. I went about on the streets with other bad boys of my ilk, through thick and thin, and indeed had the courage to fight with boys who were stronger than I was; if I then got a beating, my parents would say: 'What is this? Should such a big lout be fighting with a child?'[112] If I won the fight (especially since I scratched, bit, and threw things at my opponent), they would say: 'Our little Olivier is going to grow up to be a fine fellow!' In consequence of this, my courage grew greater. I was still too young to pray, and when I cursed like a sailor they would say that I knew not what I was saying. And so I grew worse and worse, till they sent me to school. What other bad boys thought up but did not dare put into practice, I did. When I soiled or tore up my books, my mother bought me new ones, so that my penny-pinching father would not grow angry.[113] I made my schoolmaster's life miserable, for he durst not use me severely, because he received rather expensive gifts from my parents, whose unbecoming and fond love for me was well known to him. In the summer I caught field crickets and sneaked them into school, where they sang lovely songs for us; and in the winter I stole hellebore and dusted it upon the place where they were wont to castigate the boys; when a recalcitrant one then chanced to resist, my powder dusted up into the air and provided me with a pleasant diversion, because everyone could not but fall to sneezing.[114] Later on I deemed myself much too good to play such common practical jokes, but instead all my deeds were of the sort I mentioned above. I often stole something from one boy or the other and put it into the schoolbag of another one whom I desired to see receive a beating, and I was able to play such-like tricks so cleverly that I was almost never caught doing then. Of the wars which we fought back then, during which I was generally the commander, *item*, of the beatings which I often received (for I always had a face full of scratches and a head covered with lumps) I shall say nothing for the time being; everyone knows quite well anyway the sort of pranks which schoolboys often play. And so, from the things which I have just told you, you can easily see how I started to develop in my tender years.

CHAPTER 19

How he studied at Liège[115] and how he behaved there

Because my father's wealth grew greater with each passing day he acquired all the more flatterers and spongers, who were fulsome in their praise of my fine mind for studying, but they passed over in silence my character flaws, or at least were able to make excuses for them, for they saw quite well that anyone who did not do so could not remain in the good graces of my father and mother. Therefore my parents took more joy in their son than a crow does in a nightingale it chances to bring up. They hired for me my own *praeceptor*[116] and sent me with him to Liège, more in order that I might learn French than that I should study, because they desired to educate me to be a merchant, not a theologian. The *praeceptor* was charged not to be too strict with me, lest I acquire a cringing and servile character. He was to let me mingle nicely with the other youths, so that I should not become timid, and he was to bear in mind that they desired to make of me not a monk but a man of the world, who must needs be able to tell black from white.

"This aforementioned *praeceptor*, however, had no need of these instructions, for he was by nature given to all manner of rascality; how could he have forbidden me such or punished me for my minor transgressions when he himself committed much worse ones? He was most given to drinking and wenching, while I by nature was given to fighting and brawling; and so at night I prowled the streets with him and his ilk and in a short while learned from him more vices than Latin. As concerns studying,[117] I relied upon my good memory and keen mind and was therefore all the more neglectful of my studies and instead immersed myself in all manner of vices, rascalities, and wantonness.[118] The gate of my conscience was already so far from strait that you could drive a hay-wagon through it. It did not perturb me that in church during the sermon I read Bernius,[119] Burchiellus,[120] or Aretinus[121] and heard nothing of the entire church service except when they said 'Ita[122] missa est.'[123] At the same time I did not consider myself a swine in the least; rather, I behaved like a dandy.[124] For me every day was Martinmas[125] or Shrovetide, and because I behaved in this manner, like a man of means, and let slip through my fingers not only the ample funds which my father sent me for my sustenance but also my mother's milk money,[126] the wenches too lured us unto themselves, particularly my *praeceptor*; from these bawds I learned to flirt,[127] to pay court to the ladies, and to gamble; wrangling, brawling, and fighting I could already do; and my *praeceptor* did not deny me the right to glut myself with food and drink either, for he himself was happy to assist me in my gluttony. This splendid life lasted a year and a half before my father found out about it, which his *factor*[128] in Liège, with whom we boarded at first, reported to him; he, for his part, received orders to pay all the closer heed to us, to get rid of the *praeceptor*, to keep me under tighter rein henceforth, and also to be more sparing in giving me money. This vexed us both, and even though he had been dismissed as my *praeceptor*, we nevertheless stuck together day and night, treading one and the same path; but inasmuch as we could no longer spend money as before, we joined forces with a gang of fellows who at night snatched people's coats away from them,[129] or even drowned them in the Meuse River; what we snatched in this manner, at the greatest risk to our persons, we squandered upon food and drink with our whores and let studying fall almost completely by the wayside.

"Now one time when we, as was our wont, were sneaking about at night in order to fall upon students like wolves and steal their coats, we were overpowered, my *praeceptor* was stabbed to death, and I and five others, who were true rogues, were caught and put into jail. Now when we were questioned the following day and I gave the name of my father's *factor*, who was a reputable man, they sent someone to him, asked him about me, and let me go free on his recognizance, but on the condition that I remain under arrest in his house till further notice. Meanwhile my *praeceptor* was buried, the five others were punished as rogues, robbers, and murderers, and my father was informed how things stood with me. He came hurrying up to Liège himself, straightened out my affairs by means of his money, read me the riot act, and scolded me for the pain and unhappiness I had caused him; *item*, for the fact that my mother was behaving as if she were about to despair because of my wicked ways; and he threatened to disinherit me and send me packing to the devil if I did not mend my ways. I promised to mend my ways and rode home with him. And so my studies came to an end.

CHAPTER 20

The homecoming and departure of the honorable studiosus[130] and how he sought to make a career in the war

When my father brought me home he found that I had been spoiled till I was rotten to the core.[131] I was not an honorable *domine*,[132] as he had hoped I would be, but a nitpicker and braggart who thought that he knew just about everything. I had scarce warmed up a little at home when he said to me: 'Hark you, Olivier, the more you talk, the more I see your ass's ears protruding. You are a useless burden upon the earth, a scoundrel who will never amount to anything. You are too old to learn a trade, and you are too churlish to serve any master, and you are too good-for-nothing to learn and carry on my business. Alas! What have I accomplished with all the great expenditures I made upon you? I had hoped to take joy in you and to make a man of you, and instead I have been obliged to buy you free from the hangman's hands! O, the shame of it! It would be best if I were to put you to work as a scribe in some quill-mill[133] and let you melt *miseriam cum aceto* till, after you have atoned for your evil deeds, a better fortune befalls you!'[134]

These and such-like *lectiones*[135] I was obliged to listen to daily, till at last I grew impatient and said to my father that not I, but he and my *praeceptor*, who had led me astray, were responsible for all I had done, and it served him right that he had no joy in me, since his parents, whom he had abandoned to starve as beggars, had found no joy in him either. He, for his part, snatched up a cudgel and was of a mind to reward me for my words of truth, swearing loud and long that he was going to have me put into the penitentiary in Amsterdam. So I ran away and betook myself that very night to a farm which he had recently purchased, espied there my advantage, and rode off to Cologne with the best stallion which the farmer had in his stable.

"The horse I turned into silver, and again I joined a company of rogues and thieves like the one I had left in Liège. They straightway recognized me for what I was when I gambled with them, and I recognized them because both they and I were so adept at cheating. I went straightway into their guild and helped break into houses by night whenever I could; but since shortly afterwards one of us was captured when he attempted to filch a heavy purse from a lady of quality on Old Market Square, and particularly since I saw him obliged to stand for half a day in the stocks wearing an iron collar and saw them cut off one of his ears too, and beat him with rods—this caused me to lose my taste for that trade. Therefore I let myself be recruited as a soldier, because at just that time our commander,[136] with whom we were in the camp outside Magdeburg, was taking on men in order to bring his regiment up to strength. Meanwhile my father had found out whither I had gone and therefore wrote to his *factor* that he should inquire after me; this happened just after I had accepted the money to sign on with the regiment; the *factor* reported this to my father, who charged him to buy me free, no matter what it might cost. When I heard that, I feared that he was going to put me into the penitentiary in Amsterdam, and I had no desire to be bought free. In this way my commanding officer learned that I was the son of a wealthy merchant and therefore raised the ante so high that my father left me where I was, with the idea in mind of letting me dangle in the war for a while to see if I might mend my ways.

"After that, before very long, it happened that my commanding officer's scribe got his discharge by dying, in whose stead he took me, as you know. At that time I began to have delusions of grandeur, hoping to rise higher, from one rank to the next, and finally even to become a general. I learned from our *secretario* how I should comport myself, and my resolve to become a great man caused me to behave honorably and reputably and to no longer, as had been my wont before, involve myself in rascalities; but I made no progress at all till our *secretarius* died; then I thought to myself: 'You must see to it that you get his post.' I entertained with food and drink whenever I could, for when my mother learned that I was beginning to do well, she kept sending me money. And because young Trueheart was the apple of my commanding officer's eye and was preferred to me, I plotted to get him out of the way, particularly when I became aware that the commanding officer's mind was quite made up to give him the secretary's post. As a result of this delay in my promotion, which I so eagerly sought, I grew so impatient that I had our provost make me as impervious to musket balls as steel,[137] because it was my intent to duel with Trueheart and dispatch him with a saber; but I could never rightly get at him, and our provost also argued against my plan, saying: 'Even if you kill him, it will do you more harm than good, because you will have murdered the commanding officer's favorite.' And he counseled me to steal something while Trueheart was present and turn it over to him, and he would be willing to arrange it so that Trueheart lost favor with the commanding officer. I followed this counsel, took the gold-plated goblet at the christening of the commanding officer's child, and gave it to the provost, with which goblet he then got rid of young Trueheart, as you will doubtless recall, when he conjured your clothes full of puppies in the commanding officer's great-tent."

CHAPTER 21

How Simplicius fulfilled Trueheart's prophecy concerning Olivier when neither recognized the other one

I saw red when I was obliged to hear from Olivier's own lips how badly he had used my most valued friend and yet durst not take any vengeance; in the bargain I was obliged to choke down my feelings so that he not notice them, and therefore I said to him that he should tell me how he had further fared after the battle of Wittstock.[138]

"In that engagement," said Olivier, "I behaved not like a quill-sharpener, who is hired solely to man the inkwell, but like a proper soldier, for I was well mounted and as impervious to musket balls as iron and, moreover, not assigned to any particular squadron; and I therefore let my valor be seen, like anyone who means to achieve preferment by the sword or to die by it. I rushed about our brigade like the Wild Huntsman,[139] so as to exercise myself and to show our side that I was better suited to the sword than to the quill, but it was to no avail; the fortune of the Swedes prevailed,[140] and I was obliged to share our side's misery, since I was obliged to accept quarter, even though shortly before I had been unwilling to grant quarter to anyone.

"So now I, like the others who were captured, was put into a regiment of foot which was sent back to Pomerania[141] to restore itself, and since there were in it many raw recruits, and because I had exhibited exceeding courage, I was made corporal; but I did not intend to remain on that dunghill for long, but instead to soon go back to the Imperials, whose side was more to my liking, even though I should without doubt have found better preferment with the Swedes. My escape I set about in the following way: I was sent out with seven musketeers to collect by force some outstanding tributes in our more remote outposts.[142] Now when I had got together over eight hundred guilders, I showed my men the money and made their mouths water for it, so that we were soon in accord with one another to divide it up amongst ourselves and to abscond with it. When this was done I persuaded three of them to help me kill the other four, and after this was accomplished we divided up the money again, namely, two hundred guilders for each of us, with which money we marched towards Westphalia. On the way I talked one of the three into helping me shoot down the other two, and when we were about to divide up the money again with one another, I strangled the last one to death and with the money came safely to Werl, where I settled in and made right merry with this money.

"When it was well nigh all gone, I should have liked to continue to feast in one way or another, and particularly since I had heard much praise of a young soldier in Soest—what excellent booty he was taking and what a great name he was making for himself by doing so—I was inspired to emulate him. Because of his green clothes they called him 'the chasseur'; I therefore had such clothes made for myself and in his name stole things in his and our quarters, and I perpetrated all manner of things which were so outrageous that both of us were going to be prohibited from going out upon forays. He, to be sure, remained home, but I continued to snatch in his name as much as I could, so that the chasseur, on account of this, challenged me to a duel; but I thought to myself, if the devil (with whom, so I was told, he was in league too) were to be fighting on his side, he would nicely deprive me of my imperviousness to musket balls.

"But I could not escape his cunning, for with the aid of his servant he tricked me, together with my comrade, into going into a sheepcote, and he attempted to compel me to brawl with him there in the moonlight, in the presence of two real-life devils whom he had with him as seconds. And because I was unwilling to do it, they forced me to do the most despicable thing in the world, which act my comrades bruited about amongst the folk and of which act I was so ashamed that I ran away from there and to Lippstadt, and there took service with the Hessians; but I did not remain there long, because they did not trust me; instead I trotted on further and into service with the Dutch,[143] where I found, to be sure, better pay but a war that was, to my way of thinking, boring, for we were penned up like monks and were supposed to live as continently as nuns.

"Now because I now durst not show my face amongst either the Imperials or the Swedes or the Hessians, unless I were of a mind to brazenly place my person in jeopardy, since I had deserted from all three armies, and particularly since there was no remaining with the Dutch any longer, because I had dishonored a maiden by force, which to all appearances would soon become evident to all, I resolved to take refuge with the Spaniards,[144] in the hope of going home from them to see what my parents were doing. But when I went out to set about doing this, my compass was so thrown awry that I unexpectedly fell amongst the Bavarians,[145] with whom I marched, amongst the Brotherhood of Merode, from Westphalia to the Breisgau,[146] sustaining myself by gambling and stealing. Whenever I had any money, then by day I was at the gaming blankets and by night in the sutler's tent; and whenever I had nothing, I stole whatever I could lay my hands upon. Often I stole two or three horses in one day, both from pasture and from quarters, sold them, and gambled away again what I had sold them for; and then, by night, I sneaked into people's tents and snatched away the best things they had from right under their noses. Were we on the march, however, then when we came to narrow passes I kept a weather eye on the knapsacks which the women carried upon their backs and cut them off; and in this manner I managed to stay alive till the battle of Wittenweier[147] was over, in which action I was taken captive, thrust back into a regiment of foot, and thus made a soldier in the army of the Duke of Weimar.[148] But the camp outside the walls of Breisach[149] was simply not to my liking, so I quit it betimes and from there went to waging war for myself, as you now see that I do. And be assured, my friend, that since then I have laid low many a proud fellow and have prospered with many a fine sum of money; nor do I intend to stop till I see that I can get nothing more. And now it is your turn to tell me your life history."

CHAPTER 22

How a man fares, and what it means, when he "goes to the cats"

When Olivier had in this wise finished his discourse, I could not wonder enough at the ways of Divine Providence! I could well understand that our dear Lord had not only preserved me from this monster before, in Westphalia, but had also seen to it that he was terrified of me. Only then did I see what manner of prank I had played upon Olivier, a prank which old Trueheart had prophesied to him, a prophecy which Olivier himself, as can be seen in the sixteenth chapter, interpreted differently, to my great advantage; for had this *bestia*[150] known that I was the chasseur of Soest, he would certainly have repaid me in kind for what I did to him before in the sheepcote. I also considered in what a wise and obscure manner old Trueheart had uttered his prophecies, and I thought to myself that even though his prophecies were generally fulfilled without fail, it would nevertheless be difficult, and must needs occur in a wondrous way, if I were to avenge the death of a man like this, who deserved to be drawn, quartered, and hanged. I also found that it had been exceeding healthy for me that I had not told him my life history first, for in that event I should have indeed told him myself in what manner I had done him injury before. Now while these thoughts were going through my mind I became aware of some scars upon Olivier's face which he had not had in the camp at Magdeburg; I therefore imagined that these scars were made by Hopalong when he, disguised as a devil, had scratched his face before. Therefore I asked him whence these marks came, adding that even though he was telling his entire life history, I could not but see, nevertheless, and could easily apprehend, that he was keeping the best part of it secret from me, because he had not yet said who had so marked him. "Ah my friend," he answered, "if I were to tell you all my roguish tricks and rascalities, it would take too long for both you and me. But so that you may indeed see that I am concealing from you nothing which has befallen me, I shall tell you the truth about this too, even though it seems as if it redounds to my disparagement.

"I believe full well that from the time I was in my mother's womb I was predestined to have a countenance marked with scars, for even in my tender years I was scratched up this way by my schoolmates when I tussled with them; and one of the devils who attended the chasseur of Soest also used me most severely, so that for a full six weeks the marks of his claws could be seen upon my face, but it healed again completely, leaving no scars. The streaks which you still see upon my countenance, however, are of a different origin, and, in fact, of the following one: When I was still lying in quarters with the Swedes in Pomerania I had a beautiful doxy, and my host was obliged to give up his bed let us lie in it. His cat, which was accustomed to sleep in that same bed and every evening, came every night and caused us great inconvenience, because it was not as willing to give up the spot where it had usually slept as its master and mistress had been. This vexed my doxy (who could not tolerate cats anyway) so much that she swore by all that was holy that in no event was she going to give proof of her love for me till I had first got rid of that cat for her. Now I desired to continue to enjoy her favors, so I resolved not only to comply with her demand, but also to take vengeance upon that cat in such wise that I too might take pleasure in it. Therefore I stuck it into a sack, took my host's two large farm dogs (who were rather averse to cats anyway, but liked me well enough) with me and the cat in the sack to a broad and lovely meadow; and there I thought to divert myself, for I believed that because there was in the vicinity no tree up which the cat could retreat, the dogs would chase it back and forth upon the plain for a while, the way they do hares, and would thus afford me excellent sport. But 'ods blood! Not only did my handsome countenance go to the dogs, as the saying goes, it also went to the cats (which is a thing that befalls few people, else they would without doubt long since have coined the phrase 'going to the cats'), because when the cat, as soon as I opened the sack, saw before it only a broad field and upon it its two worst enemies and nothing high enough to climb up upon to take refuge, it was unwilling to run about miserably upon the ground and let its fur be torn off, and instead it jumped upon my head, because it could not find any higher spot; and when I pushed it away my hat fell off; now the more I attempted to tear it off my head, the more firmly it dug in its claws to hold on to it. The two dogs were not of a mind to sit idly by and watch this struggle for long, but instead intervened in the fray; they leaped up the front of me, up the back, and up the sides, snapping at the cat, which, however, was not willing to depart from my head, but instead clung to it as best it could by digging its claws into both my head and my face. When it took a swipe at the dogs with its thorny glove and missed, it of course scratched me; and because it occasionally raked the dogs on their noses, they made every effort to knock it off with their paws and thereby gave me many an unfriendly blow to the face; and when I groped for the cat with both hands, to pull it off me, it bit and scratched me to the best of its ability. And so I was attacked by both the dogs and the cat at the same time, and I was scratched and abused so terribly that I scarce looked like a human being any more; and what was worst of all, when they snapped at the cat I was of necessity in danger of having one of them accidentally lay hold of my nose or my ear and bite it off completely. My collar and doublet were as bloody as a smith's vice on St. Stephen's Day,[151] when horses are locked into it to be bled; and I could not think of any way to deliver myself from this frightening situation. Finally I was obliged to fall to the ground of my own accord, so that the two dogs could lay hold of the cat, unless I were willing to let them continue to use my *capitolium*[152] as their battleground. The dogs, of course, wrung the cat's neck, but I had by no means such an excellent diversion from it as I had hoped, but instead only ridicule, and a countenance the likes of which you see with your very own eyes. As a consequence I grew so enraged that I afterwards shot the two dogs dead and beat the tar out of my doxy, who had prompted me to this folly, and she ran off from me, because of this and because, without doubt, she could no longer love anyone whose face looked so loathsome."

CHAPTER 23

A little tale which gives an example of the trade which Olivier plied, at which he was a master and Simplicius was to be his apprentice

I should have liked to laugh at this tale of Olivier's, but I was obliged to evince sympathy for him, and just as I fell to telling my life history we saw a coach convoyed by two troopers of horse coming up across the countryside. We therefore climbed down from the church tower and took a position in a house which was at the side of the road and very well suited to attacking the travelers. My flintlock I was obliged to hold at the ready, but with his shot Olivier straightway laid low one trooper and his horse before they saw us, for which reason the other trooper straightway took flight, and when I, with both barrels primed, made the coachman halt and climb down, Olivier sprang up to him and with his broad-sword cleaved his skull in two right down to his teeth and was then about to slaughter the women and children who were in the coach and who were already so pale with fear that they looked more like dead bodies than living human beings. I, however, roundly refused to permit it, saying instead that if he were of a mind to do that, he must needs kill me first. "Ah!" said he. "You're a fool, Simplicius! I should never in my life have thought that you were such a hapless fellow as you are now behaving like!" I answered: "Friend, why do you desire to punish innocent children? If they were men who could defend themselves, that would be another matter." "What!" he answered. "If you break eggs into a pan, they won't hatch chickens.[153] I know these young bloodsuckers well. Their father, the major, is a real mean cur and the worst martinet in the world to his men." And with these words he was about to go on with his killing, but I prevented him till he finally relented. The people in the coach were a major's lady, her maids, and three beautiful children, whose plight touched my heart. These, so that they might not so soon betray us, we locked in a cellar in which they had nothing to eat but fruit and turnips till they were again set free by someone. After that we plundered the coach and rode with seven beautiful horses to where the forest was the thickest.

When we tethered the horses and I looked about a little bit, I saw not far from us a fellow standing stock-still next to a tree. I pointed him out to Olivier and suggested that we ought to take care. "O, you fool!" he answered. "It is a Jew. I tied him there. The fellow has long since frozen to death and given up the ghost." And, walking up to him, he chucked him under the chin with his hand, saying: "Ha! You dog, you brought me many fine ducats too!" And when he moved his chin that way, there rolled out of his mouth several more doubloons, which the poor rogue had managed to hold onto even in death. Olivier then reached into his mouth and brought out twelve doubloons and a precious ruby. "This booty," said he, "I have you to thank for, Simplicius." Then he gave me the ruby, put the money into his purse, and went to fetch his peasant, commanding me to remain with the horses and to take care that the dead Jew not bite me, by which he meant to reproach me for not having as much courage as he had.

Now when he had gone for the peasant I fell to having worrisome thoughts and to considering what a perilous situation I was in. I resolved to mount one of the horses and ride away, but I feared that Olivier might catch me in the act and then shoot me down, for I suspected that this time he was merely putting my steadfastness to the test and was standing somewhere keeping an eye upon me. Then I thought about running away on foot, but I could not but fear that even if I escaped from Olivier, I might nevertheless not be able to run away from the peasants in the Black Forest, who at that time had a reputation for knocking soldiers in the head. "However," I thought to myself, "if you were to take the horses with you so that Olivier has no means of chasing after you, and if you were then captured by Weimar troops, you would be strapped to the rack as a convicted murderer." *In summa*, I could not think up any safe way to take flight, particularly since I found myself in a wild forest and knew neither highway nor byway there. Moreover, my conscience was also pricked and was tormenting me, because I had stopped the coach and had been the reason why the coachman had been so wretchedly deprived of his life and the women and the innocent children had been locked in the cellar, in which they might perchance, like this Jew, remain till they wasted away and passed away. On the other hand, I consoled myself with my innocence, because I had stopped the coach against my will, but my conscience insisted to me that, considering the many other wicked things I had done, I had long since deserved that I fall into the hands of Justice in the company of the arch-murderer and get my just deserts, and perhaps righteous God had ordained that I should be punished in this way. Finally I fell to hoping for better things and begged God in His goodness to deliver me from my plight, and when such devoutness came over me I said to myself: "You fool! You are not locked up or tied down. The entire world is before you. Do you not have enough horses to undertake your escape? Or, if you do not desire to ride, your feet are surely swift enough to carry you away from here." Now while I was thus torturing and tormenting myself and yet could not arrive at any decision, Olivier came up with our peasant, who led us, together with the horses, to a farm, where we foddered and by turns slept for a few hours. After midnight we rode on, and towards noon we came to the outermost border of the Swiss, where Olivier was well known and commanded that we be served a sumptuous meal; and while we were making merry the innkeeper sent for two Jews, who haggled for the horses at about half their value. It was all arranged so neatly and nicely that there was little exchange of words. The main question the Jews had was whether the horses had belonged to the Imperials or to the Swedes, and when they heard that they had come from Weimar troops they said: "Then we must not take them to Basel but ride them into Swabia to the Bavarian army."

We feasted like kings, and I enjoyed the good mountain trout and delicious crayfish there. Now when it got on towards evening we set out upon our way again. We had our peasant laden like an ass with roasts and other victuals; with these we came the next day to an isolated farm house, where we were welcomed as friends and taken in, and where we remained for a few days because of the inclement weather. Following that, we came, by way of nothing but forests and trails, to that very same little house to which Olivier had taken me the first time he got his hands on me.

CHAPTER 24

Olivier bites the dust, taking six men with him

Now as we were sitting there, resting up and attending to our bodies, Olivier sent the peasant out to buy some food, together with powder and shot. When the fellow was gone he took off his coat and said to me: "My friend, I do not wish to carry all this infernal money about by myself anymore." And, accordingly, he took off two rolls of money, or money-belts, which he had strapped round his belly under his clothes, next to his skin, threw them down onto the table, and continued: "You must needs trouble yourself with these till I finally retire and we both have enough. The damned money has rubbed me raw." I answered: "My friend, had you as little money as I do, it would not rub you the wrong way." "What?" he interrupted. "What's mine is yours, and whatever else we take while we are together we will split half and half." I picked up the two money belts and found them exceeding heavy, because they were filled with all gold coins. I said that it was all quite uncomfortably packed, and if it please him, I would sew it into his clothes, so that carrying it would not be half so sour a burden. When he turned it over to me I went with him to a hollow oak tree, where he kept scissors, needle, and thread. Then from a pair of breeches I made for him and myself a scapulary, or vest, and lined them with many a fine red coin; and when we then put them on under our shirts it was just as if we were wearing armor of gold upon our breasts and backs. And since I was astonished and asked him why he had no silver money, I was told in reply that he had, hidden in a tree, more than a thousand thalers, from which he paid the peasant his living expenses, never demanding a bill for them because he did not highly prize such horseshit.

When this was done and the money was packed away, we went back to our lodgings, in which that entire night we cooked our food and warmed ourselves by the stove. And then, an hour after midnight, when we least expected it, six musketeers, together with a corporal, with muskets at the ready and fuses in the firing pans, pushed open the door and screamed that we should surrender. But Olivier (who, like myself, always kept a cocked musket lying beside him and who at all times had his sharp sword at his side, and at that moment was sitting at the table, while I was standing behind the door by the stove) answered them with a pair of musket balls, with which he straightway felled two of them. I, for my part, slew the third one and wounded the fourth with similar shots. Then Olivier whisked out of its sheath his trusty sword, which was so sharp it could split a hair in two and might well be compared to Caliburn, the sword of King Arthur[154] of England, and he split the fifth one from brisket to belly button, so that his guts fell out onto the ground and he fell beside them, while I struck the sixth one upon the head with the stock of my flintlock so that he fell to the floor dead. By the seventh one Olivier was dealt such a blow, with such force, that his brains spewed forth from out of his skull, but I hit the one who had done that to him such a blow that he could not but join his comrades in the ranks of the dead. When the one whom I had wounded when I hit him with my first shot saw these blows and realized that I was about to attack him with the butt-end of my flintlock, he threw his piece away and ran off as if the devil himself were after him. And this battle lasted no longer than it takes to say the Lord's Prayer, in which short time seven bold soldiers bit the dust.

Now when, in this wise, I remained master of the place, I examined Olivier to see if he had any breath left in him, and when I found that he had quite given up the ghost, it seemed senseless to me to leave a corpse so much money, of which it really had no need; therefore I took off him the golden fleece which I had made for him only yesterday, and I put it round my neck with the other one. And since I had smashed my flintlock to pieces I took Olivier's musket and sword; with then I was prepared for my emergency, and I shook the dust from my heels and of course went down the road where I knew that our peasant must needs be coming towards me. I sat down beside the road to wait for him and at the same time to consider what I should do next.

Simplicius comes away rich; Trueheart, on the other hand, appears in very wretched condition

I had been sitting there deep in thought for scarce half an hour when our peasant came along, huffing and puffing like a bear. He was running as fast as his legs could carry him and did not see me till I touched him. "Why the great haste?" said I. "What are the tidings?" He answered: "Quick! Both, of you get away from here! A corporal is coming with six musketeers. They are to apprehend you and Olivier and bring you to Lichteneck[155] dead or alive. They had me taken captive so that I should lead them to you, but I got away from them and came hither to warn you!" I thought to myself: "O, you rogue! You betrayed us so that you might take Olivier's money which is in the tree." But I did not let him notice anything, because I wished to use him as a guide, and instead I told him that both Olivier and the men who were supposed to capture him were dead, and when the peasant would not believe it, I was so good as to go inside with him so that he might see for himself the wretched sight of seven dead bodies. "The seventh of the men who attempted to capture us," said I, "I let run away; and would to God, if I could make these men here alive again, I should not fail to do so!" The peasant was petrified with fright and said: "What are we to do?" I answered: "What we are to do has already been resolved. Of three things I give you your choice: either lead me forthwith, by safe paths, through the forest and out to Villingen, or show me Olivier's money which is hidden in the tree, or die here and keep the other dead men company! If you lead me to Villingen,[156] then Olivier's money will be yours alone. If you will show it to me, however, I shall share it with you. But if you do neither of these things, I shall shoot you dead and go my way anyway." The peasant would have liked to run away, but he was afraid of my musket, so he fell to his knees and offered to lead me through the forest. And so we rambled hastily along, walking that day and the entire following night, because it was, as luck would have it, quite bright, without food, drink, or any rest, till towards dawn we saw the city of Villingen lying before us, where I let the peasant leave me. On this journey the peasant was driven by the fear of death and I by the desire to get myself and my money away from there; and I cannot but believe that gold imparts great strength to people, because though I was in fact carrying a heavy load of it, I nevertheless did not feel any particular fatigue.

I took it to be a good omen that they were just opening the city gates as I came to Villingen. The officer of the watch questioned me, and when he heard me claim to be a freebooter from that regiment into which Trueheart had put me when he delivered me from the musket at Philippsburg, and also that I was coming from the camp outside the walls of Breisach, from the army of the Duke of Weimar, by which I had been captured at Wittenweier and pressed into service, and that I now desired to return to my regiment in the Bavarian army, he turned me over to a musketeer who took me to the commandant of the city. This man was still lying abed, because he had been awake on military matters for more than half the night, so I was obliged to wait outside his quarters for a good hour and a half, and because people were just coming from early mass, a large number of soldiers and townsmen gathered about me, all of whom desired to know how things stood at Breisach, from which clamor the commandant awoke and had me brought to him.

He fell to questioning me, and I answered as I had at the city gate. After that he asked me detailed particulars of the siege and so on, and with that I confessed everything: how I had stayed a week or two with a fellow who had also deserted, and with him had attacked and plundered a coach, with the idea of taking from Weimar troops so much booty that we should be able to purchase horses and return decently equipped to our regiments, but that only yesterday we were fallen upon by a corporal and six other fellows who attempted to take us prisoner, during which struggle my comrade and six of the enemy had died upon the field of battle, while the seventh one and I had escaped, each to rejoin his own side. But about the fact that I had resolved to go to see my wife in L.[157] in Westphalia, and that I had such well-lined scapulars fore and aft, I kept quiet as a mouse; and it caused me no pangs of conscience that I concealed these things, for what business of his were they anyway? Nor did he ask me about them either; rather, he was astonished and found it hard to believe that Olivier and I should have laid six men low and chased the seventh one off, though my comrade did lose his life too. During this conversation there was occasion to speak of Olivier's sword, which I spoke of with praise and had at my side; it so well pleased him that I was obliged to hand it over to him in return for a sword which he gave to me, if I was to get away from him amicably and receive a pass. And it was truly an exceeding beautiful and good sword; there was an entire perpetual calendar[158] etched upon it, and I refuse to be persuaded that it was not forged by Vulcan himself[159] *in hora Martis*[160] and was in fact made like the one which is described in the *HERO'S TREASURE CHEST*[161] and which in combat cannot but break all other blades in two and cause the doughtiest foes, who are lions in the fight, to flee like faint-hearted hares. Now after he had dismissed me and commanded a pass to be issued for me, I went down the next street to an inn, not knowing whether I should first eat or sleep, for I was in need of both: but first off I resolved to placate my stomach and thus had them bring me something to eat and drink, and I fell deep in thought, pondering how I might arrange my affairs so that I should get to L. and my wife safe and sound and with my money, for I no more meant to go to my regiment than to cut off my own head.

Now while I was speculating in this manner a fellow limped into the room, a cane in his hand. His head was bandaged up, one arm was in a sling, and he had on such wretched clothes that I would not have given a farthing for them. As soon as the servant saw him, he attempted to drive him out of the room, because he stank so bad and had so many lice crawling over him that the entire Swabian heath[162] could have been covered with them. He, however, begged that he for God's sake be permitted to stay just to warm himself a little, but to no avail, and so I felt sorry for him and requested that he in his distress be allowed to approach the stove. He, so it seemed to me, looked on with greedy appetite and great intensity while I was digging into my meal, and several times he heaved sighs; and when the servant went to fetch me a piece of roast, he came up to my table and stretched out his hand with a cheap earthenware cup in it, so that I could well imagine why he was coming. I therefore took my tankard and filled his cup before he requested it. "Ah, my friend," said he, "for the sake of Trueheart, give me something to eat!" When he said this, it went straight to my heart, and I discovered that the man was Trueheart himself. I well nigh swooned when I saw him in such a woebegone state, but I collected myself, threw my arms round his neck, and sat him down at my table, where the eyes of both of us filled with tears, mine with tears of compassion and his with tears of joy.

CHAPTER 26

The end of this Fourth Book, because there is not any more of it

Our unexpected meeting made it almost impossible for us to either eat or drink, since each of us was asking the other how he had fared since we were last together, but because the innkeeper and his manservant were forever coming and going, we could not confide in one another. The innkeeper was surprised that I would suffer such a louse-ridden fellow in my presence, but I said that this was the custom in wartime amongst honest soldiers who were comrades. Since I also understood that Trueheart had till now been in the hospital, surviving on alms, and that his wounds had been bandaged carelessly, I rented a separate room from the innkeeper, put Trueheart into bed in it, and had the best surgeon I could find fetched for him, and also a tailor and a seamstress to make him new clothes and to rid him of his lice. I happened to have in my purse the doubloons which Olivier had got out of the mouth of the dead Jew; these I slapped down onto the table and said to Trueheart so that the innkeeper could hear: "Look you, my friend, here is my money. I'll use it for you and spend it up with you!" so that as a consequence the innkeeper waited upon us all the more attentively; and to the barber I showed the ruby, which had also been the property of that Jew and was worth about twenty thalers, and I said that because I must needs spend the little money I had for clothing for my comrade and for sustenance for us both, I was willing to give him the ring if he would cure, completely and quickly, my comrade, at which he was indeed well contented and made his best effort to effect the cure.

And so I cared for Trueheart as if he were my other self and had a simple garment of grey cloth made for him, but before that I went to the commandant about my pass and reported to him that I had come upon a badly wounded comrade whom I desired to wait upon till he be completely healed, for were I to leave him behind, I doubted if I could answer for it to my regiment. The commandant praised my resolve and granted me permission to remain there as long as I desired, and further offered to provide us both with proper passes whenever my comrade could follow me.

Now when I went back to Trueheart and was sitting with him at his bedside, I requested of him that he candidly tell me how he had fallen into such a heart-rending state, for I imagined that on account of important reasons or some inadvertence he might have been stripped of his former dignities, declared dishonored, and set in his present misery, but he said: "My friend, you know that I was the *factotum*[163] and most beloved and intimate friend of Count von Götz,[164] and it is sufficiently well known to you how wretchedly the most recent campaign under his command and generalcy ended, since we not only lost the battle of Wittenweier, we were also unable to relieve the besieged fortress of Breisach either. Now because differing opinions about this defeat have now and again been expressed in public, and particularly since the count has been ordered to Vienna to defend himself, I am voluntarily, out of shame and fear, living this mean existence; and I often desire either to die in this wretchedness or at least to keep myself hidden till the count will have demonstrated his innocence, for so far as I know, he has always been loyal to the Holy Roman Emperor, and the fact that he had no good fortune at all this past summer is in my opinion to be attributed more to Divine Providence (which bestows victories upon whomever it will) than to any mistakes committed by the count.

"When we were at work attempting to relieve Breisach and I saw that our troops were moving so sluggishly, I armed myself and went out onto the pontoon bridge as if I were going to finish it all by myself, even though at the time it was neither my profession nor my obligation to do so. I did it rather, to set an example for others, and because we had accomplished nothing whatsoever last summer. As luck, or rather ill luck, would have it, I was amongst the first wave of troops upon the bridge to see the white of the enemy's eyes; there the battle was heated, and just as I was the first in the attack, I was also the last to retreat where we could no longer withstand the furious onslaught of the French, and I was the first to fall into the hands of the foe. At the same time I was hit by one musket ball in my right arm and by another in the leg, so that I could neither run away nor use my sword, and since the spot upon which we were fighting was so narrow and the extreme tenacity of the struggle did not allow much parleying about giving quarter or accepting it, I received a blow to the head which knocked me to the ground, and because I was dressed in fine clothes, in the fury of battle I was stripped by enemy soldiers and thrown into the Rhine for dead. In this moment of need I cried to God and left everything to His holy will, and as I was making various vows, I felt Him come to my aid. The Rhine tossed me onto shore, where I staunched my wounds with moss, and though I was well nigh freezing to death, I nevertheless felt within me enough strength left to crawl away, whereupon God helped me so that I (grievously wounded, to be sure) came upon some Meroders and some soldiers' wives, all of whom had pity for me, even though they did not know me. These folk had already despaired of any success at relieving the fortress, which hurt me more than did my wounds; they refreshed me and dressed me by their fire, and before I had bound up my wounds a little, I must needs see that our troops were preparing to retreat in disgrace and had given the battle up for lost, which caused me the utmost pain. I therefore resolved to myself to reveal my identity to no one, so that I would not expose myself to ridicule, whereupon I joined the company of some wounded from our army who had their own surgeon; to him I gave a little gold cross which I had escaped with round my neck, in return for which he has till now been dressing my wounds. Now in this wretched condition, my worthy Simplicius, I have till now made shift to live, nor do I mean to reveal my identity to a single living soul either, till I see how Count von Götz' affair turns out. And since I see your loyalty and tenderheartedness, it gives me such great consolation that our dear God has not yet forsaken me, wherefore this morning, when I came out of early mass and saw you standing in front of the commandant's quarters, I imagined that God had sent you to me in the stead of an angel to come to my aid in my hour of need." I consoled Trueheart as best I could and confided to him that I had more money than the doubloons he had seen, all of which was at his disposal; and thereby I told him also of Olivier's demise and of how I could not but avenge his death, which news so refreshed his spirits that it was also of advantage to his body, as a consequence of which all his wounds daily improved.

END OF THE FOURTH BOOK

NOTES - BOOK IV

CHAPTER 1: *How and for what reasons the chasseur was tricked into going off to France*

1.   the chasseur was tricked into going off to France: Martin Erich Schmid (p. 280) points out that the transition here is almost as abrupt as that in Book II, Chapters 17 and 18, where Grimmelshausen arbitrarily transports his hero from Fulda to Magdeburg. Schmid (p. 280) also correctly discerns that the so-called "Beau Alman Episode" which follows consists of three segments: 1) Simplicissimus in the home of Dr. Canard (part of Chapter 1 and all of Chapter 2); 2) Simplicissimus as the singer Beau Alman at the royal court (Chapter 3); and 3) Simplicissimus' erotic adventures and conquests (Chapters 4 and 5).

2.   commissarius: commissioner.

3.   medicus: doctor, physician.

4.   obligatio: seizure order.

CHAPTER 2: *Simplicius acquires a better host than he had before*

5.   Monsieur Canard: "canard" in French literally means "duck" but it soon came to mean "an absurd story spread abroad as a hoax"; Weydt (p. 28) states that "canard" suggested, even in Grimmelshausen's time, boastfulness. Bechtold (Johann Jacob Christoph von Grimmelshausen und seine Zeit, Munich: 1919, p. 112 f.) and many other Grimmelshausen scholars presume that the model for Dr. Canard was Dr. Johann Küffer der Jüngere of Strasbourg, by whom Grimmelshausen was employed as a steward from 1662 to 1665.

6.   L.: Lippstadt.

7.   militiae: military authorities.

8.   in duplo: in duplicate, in two copies.

9.   laboratorio: laboratory.

10.   taste another man's excrement: in Moscherosch, II, 105, doctors are derided for tasting patients' excrementa.

CHAPTER 3: *How he let himself be used as an actor and acquired a new name*

11.   collatio: collation, repast, meal.

12.   I was happy to oblige, for I was in the mood to do it: the sentence is apparently derived from Garzoni, Discourse 40 (p. 347 f.): Garzoni: "...daß sie (singers) so seltzam und Fantastisch seynd / daß man nit kan wissen / wenn sie im Laun seynd zu singen oder nicht; und wenn man irer begehret / muß man sie so lang bitten / daß man müdt und uberdrüssig wird / ehe sie anfangen. Hergegen / wenn sie selbst anfangen / können sie nicht nachlassen / und machen abermals deß guten Geschirs so viel / daßman ihrer auch uberdrüssig wird:..."; ST: "ich folgte gern / weil ich eben im Laun war / wie dann die Musici gemeiniglich seltzame Grillenfänger sind / beflisse mich derhalben das beste Geschirr zu machen /..."

13.   musici: musicians.

14.   he would procure me an exceeding good position with the king and queen: if the opera Grimmelshausen had in mind was indeed one which was performed for the French court in 1647 (see below), then Grimmelshausen is possibly guilty of an anachronism here: "king and queen" seem to refer to the monarch and his wife, but in 1647 Louis XIV, who had officially become King of France at the age of five upon the death of his father in May, 1643, was only nine years old, and the Queen of France was his mother, Anne of Austria (Louis was not to marry until fourteen years later).

15.   comoedia: theatrical performance.

16.   the Louvre: the French royal palace in Paris which, of course, contained a court theatre.

17.   the role of Orpheus...: the tale of Orpheus and Eurydice was well known and often retold, in Acerra philologia III, 18 (p. 392 ff.) and Cerda's Weiblicher Lustgarten (p. 146), among other works Grimmelshausen probably consulted. Schmid, after examining all the Orpheus operas he could find, decided that the version in which Simplicissimus stars was L'Orfeo (music by Luigi Rossi, libretto by Francesco Buti), which was performed (in Italian with an Italian cast) at the Palais Royal in Paris immediately before and after Lent, 1647 (Schmid, 290 ff.). The performance of March 6 (mardi gras) was described in detail in the house organ of the French royal court, the Gazette de Paris (March 8, 1647: Issue No. 27, pp. 201-212). Whether Grimmelshausen had access to this review or a German description based upon it has not been determined. While L'Orfeo was extremely well received by the French court, it has fared less well with modern critics: Romain Rolland (Histoire de l'opera en Europe avant Lully et Scarlatti, Paris: 1895, p. 246) called it "un cortüge d'äpisodes insipides et niais." I should add that Schmid was unaware that a French Orpheus music drama was being presented in Paris at about the same time (see below).

18.   oleo talci: a facial creme made of tallow.

19.   actu: performance, action.

20.   Pluto and Proserpina: the ruler of the underworld and his wife; so defined in Acerra philologica I, 86 (p. 160 f.) and Moscherosch, VI, 306.

21.   the bacchis: priests or priestesses of Bacchus, the god of wine and revelry.

22.   "Beau Alman": "handsome German."

23.   Hercules...Achelous...Deianira: Hercules and Achelous, the river god, were rivals for the hand of Deianira, the daughter of Oeneus, and fought in single combat in order to win her; despite the fact that Achelous turned himself first into a snake and then into a bull, Hercules vanquished him and took the fair Deianira as his wife. Cf. Ovid, Metamorphoses IX, 4-88.

While no opera with Hercules as its hero was performed in 1647, one was given in Paris in 1662. In 1659 Cardinal Mazarin, intent upon properly celebrating the political marriage which he had arranged for Louis XIV, decided to have a new Italian opera performed as part of the nuptial festivities. With characteristic energy and guile he set about having a proper theatre built (by the famous Italian architect Vigarini) and presuaded one of the most famous Italian composers of the time, Pietro Francesco Cavalli, to relinquish his post in Venice and come to Paris. Cavalli arrived with one new opera, Serse (Xerxes) complete, and a second one, to be composed to a libretto by Buti, in preparation. The second one, which was premiered in the theatre in the Tuilleries after many delays and only after Louis XIV himself set a deadline for the performance, was entitled Ercole amante. The first performance, given before the king and his bride, the Infanta of Spain, was sung on February 7 and repeated twice more before Lent and six times after Lent was over; the libretto was in Italian, not French, but a French translation of the text was published that same year. Anyone familiar only with the title might well conclude that Ercole amante must have dealt with the contest of Hercules and Achelous for the hand of Deianira. In fact, it presented the story of Hercules' last love affair, in which his passion for Iole, who loves and is loved in return by Hercules' own son, Hyllus, leads to Hercules' death when Deianira gives him the cloak of the Centaur Nessus (Demuth, p. 88 ff., gives a synopsis of the plot). Ercole amante thus in no way resembles the opera to which Simplicissimus briefly alludes. It is nevertheless a striking coincidence that the two operas in which Simplicissimus sings treat the very two mythological figures who were heros in two very expensive operas presented at the court of France under the aegis of Cardinal Mazarin.

Yet another remarkable coincidence: In 1662, at the time when Ercole amante was being performed in Paris, a music drama in French treating the Orpheus legend was also being presented. The Rossi-Buti L'Orfeo, despite its success with the French nobility, was never played again in France after its last performance in May of 1647 (Demuth is in error when he asserts that it was revived for the King's nuptials). The production, requiring a complete cast of Italian singers and extremely complex stage settings and machinery, was simply too expensive and too difficult to cast—no one but a king (or a venal prime minister) could afford to put it on. The spectacular stage affects, however, made a profound impression on French audiences, and the Parisian theatre of the time was quick to capitalize on the reputation of L'Orfeo and on public interest in this new kind of spectacle. In 1639, well before the premiere of L'Orfeo, the troupe royale had presented at the Hôtel de Bourgogne a play by de Chapoton entitled La descente d'Orfäe aux Enfers, which included some songs (cf. Deierkauf-Holsbeer, p. 28). When the directors of the Thââtre du Marais saw how successful L'Orfeo was, they hired a stage machinist, Denis Buffequin, to construct stage machines for their theatre, and they revived de Chapoton's play, now with a somewhat altered title: La Grande Journäe des Machines ou Le Mariage d'Orfäe et d'Euridice. This piüce @ grand spectacle was apparently quite successful (see Deierkauf-Holsbeer, p. 29 for contemporary reactions). When, in 1661, the Parisian theatres learned that Cardinal Mazarin was planning to present Ercole amante for the court, they immediately revived Le Mariage d'Orfäe et d'Euridice. The comädiens de Madmoiselle d'Orleans included it in their repertoire in 1661 and performed it to enthralled audiences in Brussels during the carnival season, or so the gazette Relations veritables reported (cf. Liebrecht, p. 59). During the carnival season of 1662 the Thââtre du Marais performed in Paris its revival of this music drama, which played to packed houses; it was apparently played again in 1663 (Deierkauf-Holsbeer, p. 143 and 150).

Thus, in 1662 operas devoted to both Hercules and Orpheus, the latter in French, were presumably the talk of Paris. It is impossible do determine whether Grimmelshausen became aware of the two operas, perhaps through Dr. Küffer, who as a member of the patriciate in Strasbourg probably followed political and cultural events in France (i.e. Paris) fairly closely—given the situation of Strasbourg at the time, a free city, surrounded by territory under French control, the Strasbourg patriciate had every reason to keep a close eye on France, particularly since Louis XIV's political marriage had apparently put to an end the hostility between Spain and France which had previously prevailed. In any event, it is a remarkable coincidence that in Paris during the carneval season of 1662 two operas or music dramas, Ercole amante and Le Mariage d'Orfäe et d'Euridice, were being performed which treat somewhat the same subject matter as the two operas in which Simplicissimus performs during the carneval season in Paris.

CHAPTER 4: *Beau Aleman is taken against his will to the mountain of Venus*

24.   the mountain of Venus: the basic motif of this third part of the Beau Aleman Episode is an old one: the amorous encounter between a handsome young man and a woman who takes every precaution to keep her identity from becoming known to him, for if the young man is able to identify her, he will lose his life or be separated forever from her. Kurz (p. 405) thought one of Bandello's novellas (Part IV, No. 26) might be the source, but he also saw some similarities in one of the anecdotes in the Mämoires du Maräschal de Bassompierre (presumably the very anecdote which supplied material to both Goethe and Hofmannsthal). Felix Bobertag, in his Habilitationsschrift (Ueber Grimmelshausens Simplicianische Schriften, Breslau: 1874) noted that it was Novella 25 rather than 26 and suggested that Grimmelshausen's source was actually a French translation of the tale which was included as No 96 in Volume V of Histoires tragiques, extractes des oeuvres Italiennes du Bandel, et mises en langue Françoise (Rouen: 1604); Bobertag stressed that the intermediary between the "demoiselle, qui n'auoit le don de continence" and her young lover was an "apothicaire" (p. 19). In Bandello's novella a young widow who has no wish to marry again has a cavalier in whom she has become enamored brought to her home by dark of night and by a circuitous route, and the trysts continue without the cavalier ever discovering either the identity of his mysterious beloved or the location of her residence.

Bloedau (p. 54 f.) thought Simplicissimus' amatory adventures were based on the similar experience of a young German knight in Italy which was recounted in Balthasar Kindermann's Die unglückselige Nisette (1660). In this story the hero does know where the lady lives, but when he points to her balcony and boasts of his conquest, she sends six armed ruffians after him who straightway do him in.

In 1952 Leonard Forster (pp. 161 ff.) suspected he had found Grimmelshausen's model in an episode in Brantôme's Le Beau Escuyer Gruffy.

Finally, Weydt (pp. 49 ff,) maintained that the true link to the Bandello novella and thus Grimmelshausen's prime source for the episode was to be found in Harsdörffer's Großer Schauplatz Lust- und lehrreicher Geschichte in Part V of the 1651 edition in an anecdote (No. CII) entitled "Das gefährliche Vertrauen" ("Dangerous Trust"). In this story Adonis, an exceedingly handsome young man in Paris, becomes the lover of an unknown lady, spends five nights in her company, and receives for his services a large diamond, of which he is then robbed while returning home from the adventure. Despite a number of dissimilarities between this tale and Simplicissimus' adventure, and the complete absence of any verbal borrowings, Weydt was so sure that Harsdörffer was the source that he made the "Beau Alman Episode" the "comparative motif test case" ("motivgeschichtlicher Probefall") in his effort to prove that Harsdörffer was one of Grimmelshausen's prime sources and also represented a link between Grimmelshausen and French, Spanish and Italian literature.

No critic, to my knowledge, has yet pointed out a possible source for the sequence of events which lead to Simplicissimus' transformation into a male whore: his transformation into a fool, described in Book II, Chapters 5 and 6. Immediately before each transformation he is given a drug—in Hanau the pastor gives him an ointment to smear on himself to protect him, and in Paris Dr. Canard gives him "a few delicate little sausages which...strongly smacked of the apothecary." In both transformations the attempt is made to trick him: in Hanau the four men in devil's masks try to make him think he is being taken to hell; in Paris he ls led to believe that he is being taken to see a gentleman who wishes him to give music lessons. In both instances he is then taken blindfolded to another location, and in each case he is escorted by soldiers, in Hanau by soldiers disguised as devils, in Paris by men dressed as soldiers. In each episode Simplicissimus is bathed by a member or members of the opposite sex, in each instance by old crones whose teeth he describes. In Hanau he is put to bed after his bath and awakens to see two "angels," who are meant to convince him that he has left hell and is in heaven; in Paris he dines after his bath with three beautiful masked women. In Hanau he is then put to sleep yet again and awakens in the goose coop to find himself dressed in fool's garb; in Paris he spends a week with the lady (or ladies) and is then returned, blindfolded, to Paris, where he continues to ply the trade of a male whore, and when, after escaping Paris, he comes down with small pox, he awakens to find himself a penniless and pock-marked wretch, robbed of both his wealth and his beauty.

The two transformations are clearly contrapuntal, and the stark contrasts between them underscore the irony of the second one. In Hanau Simplicissimus is still a naive boy, while in Paris he is a worldly, materialistic and sensual young man who has already strayed from the path of righteousness. Whereas he permits the pastor in Hanau to help him and is thus prepared for the experience to which he is subjected, he rejects the attempts of the pastor in Lippstadt to help him and is thus unprepared for the direction his life takes. In Paris he is deceived, in part at least, by external appearances: the three French ladies whom he sees are beautiful and desirable, and with little resistance he falls prey to them, whereas in Hanau the physical ugliness of the three old crones causes him to realize the dangers of temptations to the flesh and remark: "Truly a frightening sight, which might have served no purpose other than as an excellent antidote against the mindless lust of lewd billy goats." This insight of the young and naive Simplicissimus, inspired by the sight of one of the old hag's "pendulous breasts," which he compares to "two shrunken cow-udders drained of two-thirds of their milk" with "at the bottom of each...a dark brown teat a half-finger long," is completely forgotten when Beau Alman gazes at the three Parisiennes, whose gowns "left their alabaster breasts rather bare." One would think that the presence of the old German woman, whose function is similar to that of the three old hags in Hanau, should have reminded Simplicissimus of what he had already realized as a child, but Beau Alman is as blind as the Calf was clear-sighted.

25.   Monsig.: Monsieur, Mister.

26.   to perulate, insolulate...: a similar series of alchemical terms—all ending in the same suffix (-irt in German) is found in Moscherosch I, 412.

27.   collatio: meal, repast.

28.   Venus...Adonis: see above Notes to Book III, Chapter 4.

29.   the eyes of a basilisk: the basilisk was a legendary reptile whose breath and gaze killed anyone they struck. The creature is described in Acerra philologica II, 17 (p. 224 f.).

30.   A man must know no fear when he goes to a woman: this remark is quite similar to a bon mot which Hoffmann puts into the mouth of his heroine, Mme. de Scudery: "An amant, qui craint les voleurs, n'est point digne d'amour." Hoffmann's source was an anecdote in De Sacri Rom. Imperii Libera Civitate Noribergensi commentatio (pp. 561-563) by Johann Christoph Wagenseil (1633-1705), who tells how Mme. de Scudery wrote the aphoristic statement after courtiers had implored Louis XIV to do more to protect them from robbers and brigands who were attacking them when they went out in Paris in the evening to see their beloveds. It is possible to determine approximately when the bon mot was the talk of Paris, for Wagenseil indicates that at about the same time Philippe Quinault (1635-1688) had completed the first three acts of his comedy Astrate, roi de Tyr, which was first played in Paris between December 27, 1664 and January 6, 1665 (it received "privelüge" on February 10, 1665). Wagenseil, who accompanied as preceptor the son of Count Ernst von Traun on his grand tour of Europe, which included, of course, the then obligatory sojourn in Paris, must have heard about Scudery's clever remark sometime in 1664 or earlier. Inasmuch as Wagenseil's written account of the bon mot, its cause, and its results for Mme. de Scudery, did not appear until 1697, it would seem that if Grimmelshausen was indeed inspired by it, he must have learned of it by word of mouth, presumably sometime during his tenure as steward for Dr. Küffer, i.e. from 1662-1665.

CHAPTER 5: *How he fared there, and how he got out of there again*

31.   for Paris is a very dirty city anyway: Weydt (p. 28) believes that this is a paraphrase of the etymological witticism which branded Paris ("Lutetia") a dirty city (Lutece @ Luto, de la boue"—"Luto," from "lutum," which meant "mud, excrement, filth"); if F. J. L. Meyer (Briefe aus der Hauptstadt und dem Innern Frankreichs, Tübingen: Cotta, 1802, 2 vols.) is to be believed, the city was still noted for its filthiness at the end of the eighteenth century (I, 75).

32.   Simplicissimus' bath: of all the sources suggested for this episode, only Die unglückselige Nisette contains a similar scene: Albertus, a young German nobleman, is taken to the lady's house and led to an opulently furnished room. The lady is quite beautiful, but when she genteely makes her desires known to him, he temporizes, and only after she assures him that he has no cause to be afraid does he permit himself to be taken to another room, while the lady retires; in this room, which is equipped with a bath tub, described in some detail, and various oils and perfumes, Albertus is required to undress and permit the maidservant to bathe him, as this is the "custom of the country"; after his bath Albertus is led to a bed, where the lady is waiting to receive him, and after the maidservant withdraws, the lady overcomes Albertus' scruples and the two pass the night in lovemaking.

33.   Allez, Mons.: Let us go , sir.

34.   my cheri: my darling.

35. I do believe that the other three lay with me too: While none of the suggested models for this episode portray the hero as the lover of four ladies of high station, in the early 1660s one of the juicier morsels of scandalous court gossip linked a well-known opera singer to four ladies with close connections to the court of Louis XIV. The ladies were sisters, the nieces of Cardinal Mazarin, and were referred to in Paris as "les Mazarinettes." In 1647, the very year in which L'Orfeo was first performed in Paris, the Cardinal began to bring members of his family to Italy to live with him in his palace in Paris. His nieces were given as a governess Mme. de Senüce, the same lady who had earlier been the governess of young Louis XIV; and it is reported that Anne of Austria dircted personally the nieces' devotions. Les Mazarinettes, it seems, were reared like princesses and treated like royalty.

Of the five daughters of Mazarin's sister, Baroness Mancini, only the eldest, Laura, was destined to remain untainted by scandal. She was married in 1651 to the Duke of Mercoeur and died six years later (her husband so adored her that upon her death he renounced his wealth, took orders, and withdrew from the world). Laura's four sisters were equally beautiful; they were also the talk of Paris and other European cities from the 1650s on. The oldest of the four, Olympe, was married to the Count de Soissons in 1657, and soon thereafter court gossips noted that young King Louis XIV was spending most of the evenings at soiräes held at the home of the young Countess, apparently with the full blessing of the Count. Within a year, however, Louis had transferred his affection from Olympe to her younger sister Marie. Their romance, perhaps the only genuine one Louis was ever to experience, and certainly the only innocent one, very nearly frustrated Cardinal Mazarin's carefully laid plans to bring about a political marriage between Louis and his cousin, the Infanta of Spain Maria Theresia. It appears that Louis ardently desired to marry Marie Mancini and live happily ever after. Mazarin succeeded in breaking up the affair when he duped the young king into believing that Marie had jilted him in favor of Charles of Lorraine (who was, in fact, smitten with her). The third Mazarinette, Hortense Mancini, was generally conceded to be the most beautiful of the four girls. Mme. de Lafayette described her as "non seulement la plus belle de niüces du cardinal, mais aussi une des plus parfaites beautäs de la cour"; and for St. Evremond—a connoisseur of feminine beauty—Hortense was simply "la plus belle femme du monde." The fourth and youngest of the Mancinis, Marie-Anne, was only 15 in 1661, when her uncle died, and was the least conspicuous one at the time, her only claim to fame then being that she was one of the Mazarinettes; twenty years later, as the Duchess of Bouillon, she achieved notoriety when she and her sister Olympe were exiled because of their alleged involvement in the celebrated Affair of the Poisons.

The opera singer to whom gossips linked the Mazarinettes in the early 1660s was a castrato named Atto Melani (the name is almost an anagram of "Alman"). He was born on March 31, 1626, in Pistoia, Italy, the son of a humble bellringer. When the beauty of the lad's voice was discovered, it was decided to perform on him that operation by which, at the time, it was customary to attempt to preserve permanently a boy-soprano voice. When Melani was later sent to Rome he was immediately admitted to the circle of elite musicians whom Luigi Rossi had assembled there, and the boy soon found a wealthy patron in Grand Duke Matthias of Tuscany. When Cardinal Mazarin decided in 1644 to import Italian opera to France, and with it Italian singers, he was able to prevail upon the Grand Duke to let Melani come to Paris. Within weeks of his arrival at the French court he had become the favorite of the regent, Anne of Austria, and in so doing he aroused, as Simplicissimus also did, the envy and jealousy of the other singers who had access to the court. Melani's letters have been preserved, and in them he boasts, in much the same way Simplicissimus does, of his inordinate success and fame (cf. Pruniüres, p. 60, footnote 4). In the spring of 1645 Melani returned to Italy, but when Cardinal Mazarin decided to establish a permanent Italian opera troupe in Paris, he again succeeded in procuring Melani's services, and again the castrato was the darling of the French court (cf. Pruniüres, p. 90 and Anne of Austria's letter quoted by him, p. 141). In the 1647 performance of Buti-Rossi's L'Orfeo Atto Melani was cast, of course, in the title role. He again returned to Italy, but in 1657, when Cardinal Mazarin, having defeated for once and for all the Fronde, again turned to his favorite project, a permanent Italian opera in Paris, Melani again came back to France, this time to stay. Louis XIV, now no longer a child but a young monarch, rewarded him well; he appointed Melani a "gentilhomme de la Chambre" and bestowed upon him the revenues of the Abbey de Beauhä in Normandy, about 1800 livres (Pruniüres, p. 189 and p. 237). These tokens of royal esteem, of course, rendered Melani de facto a servant of the crown, just as Simplicissimus claims was nearly the case with him. Melani did not perform, however, in Ercole amante in 1662, for by then he had fallen into disfavor with the king—as a direct result, according to Hortense Mancini, of rumors of his liaison with her and her sisters (Mämoires, p. 519).

In a very real sense, Cardinal Mazarin, who was responsible for Melani's honored position at court, was also the cause of his downfall, which began shortly after the Cardinal's death in early February of 1661. The Cardinal had spent his last months attempting to achieve two objectives: to protect the marriageable but as yet unmarried Mazarinettes by marrying them off to suitable husbands, and to ensure that the name Mazarin would be perpetuated and that the fortune which he had amassed, sometimes by rather unethical means, should for the most part accompany the name. His one surviving nephew he considered unfit to carry on the family name, so he suggested to Armand-Charles, Marquis de la Meilleraye, that he marry Marie, give up his own fine family name, and become after his marriage "Duke Mazarin." The Marquis rejected the proposal, perhaps because he felt that no former beloved of the King of France would make a very good spouse, but when the Cardinal then proposed Hortense as his bride (with the same conditions), the Marquis was quick to agree, for he had literally fallen in love with Hortense the first time he laid eyes on her. The wedding took place only ten days before the Cardinal's death; a month after his death a second marriage which he had arranged took place: Marie Mancini and Connetable Colonna, an extremely wealthy Italian nobleman, were married by proxy in Paris, after which Marie left France for Italy to join the spouse she had never seen. With Cardinal Mazarin's disappearance from the political scene, the animosities became evident which Frenchmen of all classes had felt, but had feared to express openly, towards him and towards the Italians he had brought to Paris. The Mazarinettes, now married into French and Italian aristocracy, were unassailable, but the other Italians were not, and with Mazarin dead and Marie in Italy, so Hortense asserts in her memoires, the Cardinal's enemies began to make war on Melani and spread vicious rumors about him in an attempt to drive him from the court and from France. One such rumor accused him of being the lover of all four of the Mazarinettes. As Hortense put it in her memoires: "Ce (Duc Mazarin) ne fut pas la seule Personne, @ qui j'eus le Malheur de plaire. Un Eunuque Italien, Musicien de M. le Cardinal, Homme de beaucoup d'Esprit, fut accusä de la même chose; mais, il est vrai que c'ätoit ägalement pour mes Soeurs et pour moi." (Mämoires, p. 509). The "eunuch" was, of course, Atto Melani.

It would seem at first glance highly improbable that a man of Grimmelshausen's station and position in the world should be privy to such court gossip—surely there were no printed accounts of the scandal—but certain unusual circumstances render it quite possible and perhaps less improbable. From about mid-summer 1662 until 1665 Grimmelshausen was the steward of a man who certainly had access to such knowledge and may have spoken about the affair to Grimmelshausen or in his presence: Dr. Johannes Köffer the Younger (his name is also found spelled Küeffer and Kieffer). Küffer's connection to Strasbourg literary circles has been noted above (Notes to Book III, Chapter 4), but in regard to the matter under consideration his professional life is more relevant. Küffer was the "Leibmedicus" (personal physician) for a number of members of the nobility, among them Margrave Wilhelm of Baden, the count of Nassau-Saarbrücken, Duke Eberhard of Wörttemberg and his brother Duke Ulrich, and Franz Egon von Fürstenberg, Bishop of Strasbourg from 1663 until his death (cf. Bechtold, Grimmelshausen und seine Zeit, p. 107). It was through Duke Eberhard that Küffer acquired the Ullenburg, a run-down castle and lands which had formerly belonged to the Bishop of Strasbourg and had been mortgaged to the Duke. Küffer received the property on the condition that he put it in good order and maintain it; and to this purpose he hired Grimmelshausen as steward and overseer. Bechtold (Ibid.) assumes that Küffer spent most of the warm summer months at the Ullenburg and that Grimmelshausen was therefore in daily contact with him and with any guests who may have come to visit. Of all Köffer's noble patients, however, it was Franz Egon von Fürstenberg who undoubtedly knew everything going on in Paris. Before becoming Bishop of Strasbourg in 1663 he had for years been "the guest and agent of the Archbishop of Cologne" (cf. F. L. Ford, p. 51), and the French strongly supported his candidacy for Bishop of Strasbourg because they were intent upon maintaining and extending their influence in Alsatia (G. Livet, pp. 275 ff.). Franz Egon could not have been unaware that the policy forged by Cardinal Mazarin and Colbert de Choissy was designed to annex ultimately the free city of Strasbourg, a policy which proved to be astonishingly successful—in 1681, three years after Grimmelshausen's death, France annexed the city and turned it into a near unassailable fortress. Thus Franz Egon, who did not always act in accord with the French, had every reason to keep a careful eye on the court of Louis XIV, and on the governor of Alsatia whom it appointed to administer French territories and cities there.

Franz Egon was not only probably aware of the Melani-Mazarinettes scandal, he may have met socially one of the ladies in question: Hortense, Duchess Mazarin. Duke Mazarin proved to be an ever watchful husband, and whenever his official duties obliged him to leave Paris, he took her along. After five years of this life—"cette Vie vagabonde," Hortense called it—she demanded a legal separation from her possessive spouse, and when, in 1668, she realized that the courts would not accede to her request, she donned men's clothing and fled to Italy to join her sister Marie, who was also unhappy in her marriage (Hortense later went to England, where she became the mistress of Charles II, to whom there had once been plans to affiance her; she never set foot on French soil again). The travels in the "provinces" which Hortense so detested included at least three sojourns in Alsatia, if we are to believe Hortense's lament: "Pendant les trois ou quatre premiüres annäes de notre Mariage, je fis trois voyages en Alsace...."; for Cardinal Mazarin, wishing to assure that the man who was to perpetuate his name have not only money and prestige but also a position of responsibility in the government, had seen to it before his death that Duke Mazarin was appointed the new governor of Alsatia. On the first visit, in 1661, the Duke (and perhaps the Duchess) received a number of important visitors at the governor's administrative headquarters in the fortress of Breisach, among them several who were patients or acquaintances of Dr.Küffer: the two dukes of Württemberg, the Margrave of Baden-Durlach, and Count Georg of Württemberg-Mompelgard and his wife, the former Anne de Coligny-Chatillon (see above, Notes to Book III, Chapter 4); the magistrates of the city of Strasbourg also came to pay their respects and subsequently acted as hosts at two formal dinners (deux repas bien ordonnes) given for the Duke and his entourage (G. Livet, p. 96). The second sojourn of the Duke and Duchess in Alsatia, from September 1662 to January 1663, was of particular diplomatic importance, for the Duke's main efforts were devoted to assuring that the French candidate for the post of bishop of Strasbourg, Franz Egon von Fürstenberg, be appointed to the position. The Duke's mission, as already noted, met with success. I might add that from 1667 until his death Grimmelshausen served as mayor-administrator of Renchen, the property of the Bishop of Strasbourg; his ultimate superior was thus that same Franz Egon von Fürstenberg, to whom, however, he did not report directly.

It is also quite possible, indeed very probable, that Franz Egon knew Atto Melani personally, and it is certain that he knew much about him. Melani was not merely a singer whose beautiful voice, pleasing appearance and ingratiating manner quickly captivated members of the nobility, particularly the ladies; he was also a master of intrigue, and until Cardinal Mazarin's death a secret agent who operated under the Cardinal's direction. Whether he was already serving as Mazarin's spy during the Fronde, as Pruniüres (p. 148) believes, is not certain, but it is known that he carried out a delicate secret mission for the Cardinal in Germany in 1657. In 1653 Melani had gone to Munich and, as always, had immediately become a court favorite. In this instance his patroness was the Prince Electress of Bavaria, Henriette Adalaide, a former princess of Savoy who was a devotee of the opera (Rudhart, p. 179 ff., lists those presented during her reign and later—L'Orfeo was not among them). When Emperor Ferdinand III died on April 1, 1657, Cardinal Mazarin saw an opportunity to deal the Austrian Habsburgs a blow, for if he could persuade Ferdinand Maria, Prince Elector of Bavaria, to seek the post, and if he were indeed to become emperor, the balance of power on the continent would shift radically in favor of France. Melani was dispatched to Munich to convince the Prince Electress to cajole her husband into announcing his candidacy. Details of the intrigue can be found in the memoires of one of the participants in the plot, Marächal de Gramont (Collection des Mämoires relatifs a l'histoire de France, Second series, Paris: Foucault, 1826, volume 56, pp. 464 f.), who also emphasizes that at the time very few persons were aware of Melani's mission to

Munich: Melani and Mazarin, of course, and de Gramont, Franz Egon von Fürstenberg, and one or two others. Melani soon discovered that the Prince Electress was using every power at her command to persuade her husband to make her an empress, and Melani reported that he was convinced that the Prince Elector in his heart of hearts yearned for the position but felt he dared not let his desire be known. Meanwhile, the Prince Elector, in his official correspondence with Louis XIV, was giving the impression that he was quite content with his lot and had no desire to rise any higher. Mazarin simply did not know whom to believe. From September of 1657 on, de Gramont relates, the matter of the Bavarian Prince Elector was the subject of prolonged secret discussions which he and de Lionne held with the Prince Elector of Mainz and with Franz Egon von Fürstenberg, who was acting as the ambassador of the Prince Elector of Cologne. Finally it was decided to send Franz Egon to Munich as an independent observer, in the hopes that the Prince Elector would speak more openly with him. Franz Egon returned from Bavaria completely convinced that Atto Melani's assessment was correct, but the matter then became even more complex and protracted and ultimately led to naught. A Habsburg, Leopold, the second son of the late emperor, succeeded to the Imperial throne. The wisdom of Mazarin's efforts to prevent another Habsburg from becoming Emperor was demonstrated later when Leopold intervened in the Dutch War (1672-1679) and the War of the Palatine Succession (1688-1697) and thereby frustrated France's expansionist aims. Given Franz Egon von Fürstenberg's role in "Melani's mission to Munich," it seems quite probable that he knew Melani personally, and it is hard to believe that he would not have been intensely interested in Melani's later misadventures, including the accusations linking him to the Mazarinettes. Whether Franz Egon, after Melani's fall from grace, ever discussed the scandal with his personal physician, Dr. Küffer, and whether Grimmelshausen ever heard of it from his then employer cannot, of course, be determined, but it is possible, and if he did, Simplicissimus' adventure with the four noble ladies in Paris might well be a "conte @ clef."

36.   My reward was two hundred gold pieces: this is in stark contrast to the "rewards" which Harsdörffer's Adonis and Kindermann's Albertus receive. Each is given by his unknown beloved a precious jewel, a token of love and gratitude for love returned; Simplicissimus is given, as he clearly realizes, a whore's wages.

CHAPTER 6: *Simplicius secretly steals away, and how his tables were turned when he thought he had the mal de Naples*

37.   Simplicissimus' illness: this could have been inspired by an actual historical event, Christian Ernst Margrave of Kulmbach's bout with smallpox in 1660. That Dr. Küffer and his circle, and in fact members of the Strasbourg patriciate in general, were aware of Christian Ernst's dangerous illness appears not only possible but highly probable, for Christian Ernst had close ties to Strasbourg. When, at the age of eight, he lost both parents, his cousin, Friedrich Wilhelm the Great Elector, had himself appointed the lad's guardian and undertook to give him an education which would prepare him to assume his obligations as a ruler. After attending school in Halberstadt and in Berlin under Friedrich Wilhelm's watchful eye, Christian Ernst was immatriculated, in the summer of 1657, in the University of Strasbourg, where he studied various subjects, including the French language, until April of 1659, when he embarked upon his "grand tour." The following year, while in France, he contracted smallpox but survived the illness. Sigmund von Birken, using the diaries of some of the members of Christian Ernst's retinue and perhaps notes made by the young man himself, described in loving detail the young prince's experiences and travels in a work entitled, with customary Baroque hyperbole, Der Brandenburgische Ulysses. This work, which mentions Christian Ernst's bout with smallpox prominently, was published in 1668 and thus could not have been read by Grimmelshausen while he was writing Simplicissimus, but it is difficult to believe that he could remain unaware of the young prince's illness.

Dr. Küffer was almost certainly aware of the young prince's illness, and it is not impossible that Küffer had earlier had occasion to act as a consulting physician to the young prince. In 1658 Christian Ernst, while a student at Strasbourg, suffered a prolonged illness "von einem beschwer- und verdrißlichen affect" and went "auf vielfältiges Einrathen der

Leib- und anderer Medicorum, den 17. Juli / nach Griesbach / die Sauerbrunnen Cur daselbst zu gebrauchen" (Der Brandenburgische Ulysses, p. 33). He returned from his cure strong and healthy. There is some reason to believe that Dr. Küffer may have been one of the "other physicians," for in July of 1657, while on his way to Strasbourg, Christian Ernst visited the courts and was entertained by several noblemen who retained Dr. Küffer as their personal physician: Duke Johann Friedrich and Duke Ulrich of Württemberg, and Albrecht Margrave of Baden-Durlach. These men could well have recommended their personal physician to the young prince.

One interesting coincidence might also be noted. In 1662, the year after Christian Ernst had officially taken over the government of his principality, he married the daughter of Johann Georg II of Saxony and his wife Magdalene Sybille, the very couple whose nuptial celebrations twenty-four years earlier had included a performance of the Buchner-Schütz Orpheus opera ballet. Unfortunately, von Birken concludes his description of Christian Ernst's exploits with the prince's trimuphant entry into his capital, Bayreuth, in 1661 and thus provides no information concerning the prince's wedding celebration.

38. the mal de Naples: syphillis.

39. Maastricht: capital of the province of Limburg in the Netherlands; situated on the Meuse (Maas in German) where it is joined by the Jeker.

40. medicum: doctor, physician.

41. s.v.: salva venia, i.e. with your indulgence, i.e. if you'll pardon my language.

42. the fine French malady: syphillis.

CHAPTER 7: *How Simplicius reflected upon his past life and learned to swim when he was up to his neck in water*

43. cornelium: cataract.

44. studiis: studies.

CHAPTER 8: *How he came to be a mountebank and a charlatan*

45. How Simplicissimus came to be a mountbank and a charlatan: Bechtold (p. 521) suggests that this episode is modeled on a similar depiction in Guzman (III, Chapter 8).

46. materiala: materials, ingredients.

47. Theriaca Diatessaron: a poison antidote.

48. terra Tripolitana: Tripoli, Tripoline powder (a fine earth used at the time as a polishing powder, named after the area in North Africa where it was found; it consisted mainly of decomposed siliceous matter, for which reason it is alsi called rotten-stone or infusorial earth).

49. sal ammoniacum: sal-ammoniac.

50. theriac: nostrum, cure-all.

51. gallus of yellow arsenicum: risigallum, i.e. yellow arsenic; it is made by heating metallic (gray) arsenic and then rapidly cooling its vapor.

52.   victril: sulfuric acid.

53.   mercurium sublimatum: mercuric chloride (bichloride or perchloride of mercury), a white crystalline powder which acts as a deadly poison.

54.   acquam fortis: nitric acid.

55.   spiritus victril: sulfuric acid.

CHAPTER 9: *How the doctor was given a musket and put into the service of Captain Rumblygut*

56.   the Fleckenstein district: area in the Vosges Mountains around Fleckenstein Castle, which is situated at the head of the Sauertal.

57.   Philippsburg: an important fortress on the Rhine; about 11 miles from Bruchsal.

58.   Wagelnburg Castle: Könnecke (I, 283) assumes that the summer palace of the bishop located in the hamlet of Waghäusel is meant (it is only a few miles northeast of Phillipsburg); it seems more likely, however, that Grimmelshausen had in mind the Wegelburg (Wegelburg Castle), a fortress situated near Fleckenstein on a mountain top from which one can see not only the Vosges Mountains but the Black Forest and the Odenwald; like Fleckenstein castle, the Wegelburg is on the border of the Palatinate.

59.   ride the wooden horse: a type of corporal punishment meted out in the Bavarian army at that time; the victim's arms and legs were tied together around a wooden beam which was then moved up and down quickly and vigorously.

CHAPTER 10: *Simplicius survives an unpleasant bath in the Rhine*

60.   histori: life story.

61.   the Lower Margravate: the Baden-Durlach territory.

62.   Ottenheim: village on the right bank of the Rhine near the mouth of the Lahr; it is somewhat more than 20 miles from Offenburg.

63.   Goldscheuer: a village on the Rhine, some ten miles north of i.e. downstream from) Ottenheim.

64.   recta: directly, straight.

65.   fatum: fate.

66.   L.: Lippstadt.

67.   Rheinhausen: village on the Rhine, several miles north of Phillipsburg.

CHAPTER 11: *Why clergymen should not eat hares caught with snares*

68.   ride the wooden horse: see Notes to Book IV, Chapter 9.

69.   die in a fit of despair: euphemism for "commit suicide."

CHAPTER 12: *Simplicius is unexpectedly relieved of his musket*

70.   the closer Count von Götz approached with his army: Duke Bernhard of Weimar's threat to take the key fortress of Breisach compelled the Imperial high command to order von Götz to withdraw his army from Westphalia and march it to the upper Rhine and engage Duke Bernhard's forces in battle.

71.   Bruchsal: town in northern Baden; General von Götz used it as his headquarters from June 4 to 10, 1638 (Könnecke I, 290).

72.   Count von der Wahl: see above, Notes to Book III, Chapter 8.

CHAPTER 13: *Concerns the Brotherhood of Merode*

73.   the brotherhood of Merode: as Könnecke (I, 297 f.) determined, Grimmelshausen found much of his information about these folk in Theatrum Europeaeum III, 796.

74.   the Neuneck regiment: such a regiment, that of Alexander von Neuneck, was indeed at that time part of Götz' Bavarian army (see Könnecke I, 296), but it was a regiment of harquebusiers, not of dragoons, as Simplicissimus indicates (the harquebus was an early type of portable gun which could be pulled along behind a carriage by its hook; later the term referred to any sort of portable gun).

75.   freebooter: see above, Notes to Book II, Chapter 23.

76.   the Breisgau: see above, Notes to Book III, Chapter 22.

77.   Kenzingen: town in Baden in the Breisgau; situated on the Elz River, it is some 20 miles northeast of the fortress of Breisach; the Imperials had a large garrison there in the summer of 1638, and General von Götz made it his headquarters for one day (June 26) on his march to Breisach to relieve the embattled garrison there.

78.   General Mansfeld: see above, Notes to Book I, Chapter 22.

79.   a gentleman named "Merode": there was a Swedish colonel named Werner von Merode whose troops rebelled during a miltary action and dispersed in all directions; when news of the incident spread, this Merode soon became mistaken for the Imperial general Johann Graf von Merode (died 1633), who was in fact a valiant cavalry officer (cf. Borcherdt, p. 414, who cites A. Bechtold's article in Zeitschrift für Wortforschung XII, 230 f.). The English equivalent of "Meroder" derives from the French "Marauder" (from "maraud": rogue, vagabond), and although the earliest citation in the Oxford English Dictionary is 1698, the word could well have come into German much earlier. Interestingly, Grimms (under "Marode" rather than "Merode") cites Grimmelshausen as its source for the definition of the word.

80.   soldateska: soldiery, troops.

81.   armada: army.

82.   the battle of Wittenweier: in the battle, which took place on August 9, 1638, Duke Bernhard of Weimar defeated Count von Götz and Duke von Savelli.

83.   Schuttern: an abbey located on the Schutter, a left tributary of the Kinzig which arises in the Black Forest and flows into the Kinzig above Kehl; Count von Götz' forces arrived there on August 7; Götz used it as his headquarters during the battle at Wittenweier.

84.   the Geroldseck region: area around Geroldseck Castle, which is situated in the northern Vosges Mountains some ten miles south of Offenburg.

85. Colonel Hattstein: Philipp Eustachius Hattstein (died 1644); a colonel in the army of Duke Bernhard of Weimar whose regiment, as Simplicissimus states, participated in the taking of the bridge (see Könnecke I, 305, who cites the passage from Theatrum Europaeum III, 991 which may have been Grimmelshausen's source).

CHAPTER 14: *Single combat with peril to life and limb in which each combatant nevertheless escapes with his life*

86. Freiburg: a fortified town in Baden situated on the Dreisam at the foot of the Schlossberg, some 40 miles north of Basel.

87. the forest towns: Rheinfelden, Säckingen, Laufenburg and Waldshut.

88. the lake district: the Lake of Constance is meant.

89. besiege Breisach: Duke Bernhard of Weimar's forces completely encircled the fortress, with the idea of either taking it by storm or starving it into surrender.

90. L.: Lippstadt.

91. Endingen: village in Baden northwest of Freiburg and seven or so miles from Breisach.

92. a shot was fired at me: the beginning of the "Olivier Episode," which continues through the end of Chapter 24 and includes, among other things, a satire on "robbers as the equivalent of noblemen" (Chapter 15), Olivier's misinterpretation of old Trueheart's prophecy (Chapter 16), a satire on the abuse of churches by clergy and worshipers (Chapter 17), the complete life-story of Olivier (Chapters 18 through 22), an example of Olivier's ruthlessness (Chapter 23) and Olivier's death, in which Old Trueheart's prophecy for him is finally fulfilled (Chapter 24).

93. as impervious to musketballs as steel: see above, Notes to Book II, Chapter 22..

94. the Kinzig River: right tributary of the Rhine; it originates on the eastern slope of the Black Forest and flows in a westerly direction, reaching the Rhine River Valley at Offenburg, and joining the Rhine below Kehl.

CHAPTER 15: *How Olivier thought to excuse his wicked brigandage*

95. Olivier: Könnecke (I, 152) notes that Grimmelshausen was well acquainted with the fate of one Antoni Oliver, a soldier in Bärthel's dragoon regiment who was involved in a mutiny against Colonel Bäarthel and was condemned to death. Grimmelshausen has Hopalong give an account of the mutiny in Chapter 20 of The Singular Life of Heedless Hopalong, supplying some details which were not given in Theatrum Europaeum.

96. secretario: secretary, company clerk.

97. Waldkirch: village in the Black Forest at the foot of the Kandel Mountains.

98. the gentlemen in Nuremberg...: a well-known saying, in German: "Die Nürnberger hängen keinen, sie haben ihn denn zuvor"; Kurz (p. 408) gives as a variant "Nach dem Nürnberger Recht hängt man keinen, bis man ihn hat."

99. exercitium: exercise, trade, pursuit.

100. The only people you'll see hanged are poor and petty thieves: Kurz (p. 408 f.) lists several German proverbs which assert that "petty thieves are hanged, thieves on a grand scale go Scot free": "Kleine Diebe hängt man, die großen lässt man laufen"; Kleine Diebe hängt man, vor großen zieht man die Kappe ab"; Ei kleiner Dieb an Galgen muß; Von großen nimmt man Pfennigs Buß"; and "Kleine Diebe henk man ins Feld, Große ins Geld."

101. Machiavelli: Niccolo Machiavelli (1469-1527) expounded in his famous treatise The Prince (1513/1514) on the ruthless political actions which could be employed by a regent.

102. monarchiam: monarchy.

CHAPTER 16: *How he interprets Trueheart's prophecy to his own advantage and therefore loves his worst enemy*

103. the concepta of my heart: the truth about my innermost feelings.

CHAPTER 17: *Simplicius' thoughts are more pious when he goes robbing with Olivier than they were when he was in church*

104. we climbed up to the top of the church tower: Bechtold (p. 527), notes that according to local legend the church was in the village of Langendenzlingen near Freiburg.

105. I shall pass over in silence...: Bechtold (p. 525, Note 1) believes that this is an allusion to an episode in Guzman in which the hero's father begins his wooing in a church.

106. materia: matter, subject.

107. epitaphia: epitaphs.

108. two spiritual fathers of the church...caused such a bloodbath...: Borcherdt (p. 415 f.) suggests that the reference may be to the quarrel which broke out in the Cathedral fo Goslar in 1063 between the followers of Bishop Wetzel of Hildesheim and Abbot Widerad of Fulda.

CHAPTER 18: *Olivier tells of his origins and of how he behaved in his youth, particularly in school*

109. Olivier's life story: Bobertag (p. xix) noted that a robber named Olivier plays a fairly significant role in Sorel's Francion, but, as Bobertag's plot summary indicates, Sorel's Olivier is quite different from Grimmelshausen's (he longs to break with his fellow robbers and put his life of crime behind him). Bechtold (p. 524 f.) suggested that a tale in Moscherosch, "Complementum," about a famous robber named "der kleine Jacob" might have been the model for Olivier's life story. Weydt (pp. 123-129) suggests that an anecdote in Harsdörffer's Jammer- und Mord-Geschichten (No. CIV), concerning the life of the then famous robber Guillery) is the basis for it. The story of Guillery's life, crimes, exploits and death was indeed popular, and it appeared in far greater detail in several works, one of which, Rosset-Zeiller's Trawrige Geschichten, Grimmelshausen demonstrably knew and borrowed from for his Simplician novels (see above, Notes to Book II, Chapter 18). In Zeiller's learned commentary on the story of Guillery (it is No. 30, entitled "Von der grossen Rauberey / so einer / Namens Guillery, in Frankreich verübt / unnd was er vor ein End genommen": pp. 1037 ff.), he remarks (p. 1050 f.) that many times parents start their children off wrong by spoiling them and that the children behave all the worse when they are given their freedom at a university and fail to "shun evil companions." Zeiller also laments that many who have fought valiantly as soldiers choose in peace time to turn to robbery and violence rather than to an acceptable profession.

If Grimmelshausen did use the Guillery story as a model, he took from it only a few main points: the wealth of the hero's family, his misspent university days, his preference of life as a soldier to a return home, and his life as a robber and bandit after he quit soldiering. The specifics of Olivier's life story seem to have been dictated not so much by any model as by Grimmelshausen's conscious attempt to present in Olivier a figure which would be in stark contrast to Simplicissimus but whose path in life could remind Simplicissimus of what was happening to him. Thus, Olivier is born to well-to-do parents who give him everything that money can buy, while Simplicissimus grows up in abject poverty. While Simplicissimus' foster parents are poor farmers and his real parents are clearly noble both by birth and in character, Olivier's father and mother are of the merchant class and totally devoid of nobility of character; in fact, Olivier is technically illegitimate, while Simplicissimus, as it turns out, was born in wedlock. Whereas Simplicissimus receives no formal education at all, only religious instruction and the basics of reading and writing from the hermit, Olivier is exposed to an excellent formal education, both at home as a boy and later at the university. The most telling contrast, of course, is apparent in the Olivier Episode: The life of a bandit and murderer suits Olivier perfectly, because he has become totally devoid of moral scruples, but this sort of life causes Simplicissimus to contemplate seriously for the first time how far he has strayed from the path of virtue.

110. how he behaved in his youth, particularly in school: Olivier's behaviour is modeled on remarks in Garzoni, Discourse 101, about schoolboys and their teachers, and university students and their professors.

111. Potiphar...Joseph: Genesis 39, 1-6.

112. I went about on the streets with other bad boys of my ilk...: Garzoni: "Sonderlich aber sollen sie (young schoolboys) sich höchstes fleisses hüten für böser Gesellschaft...."; ST ich terminirte mit meines gleichen bösen Bube durch dinn und dick auff der Gassen herumb /..." Garzoni: "Hergegen aber sollen sie wissen / daβ es ihnen ubel anstehet / wann sie allerhandt Mutwillen in den Schulen anstellen in deβ Praeceptoris Abwesen / sich miteinander schlagen..." ; ST: "und hatte schon das Hertz / mit stärckern als ich war / herumb zu schlagen..."

113. When I soiled or tore up my books...: Garzoni: "wann sie...ihre Bücher verhönen / verklettern / zerreissen / oder mit Esels Ohren zeichnen..."; ST: "Wenn ich eine Bücher verklettert oder zerrisse /..."

114. In the summer I caught field crickets...: Garzoni: "wann sie...Grillen auff dem Feldte fangen / und dieselbe in die Schul setzen / daβ sie anfangen zu singen..."; ST: "Im Sommer fieng ich Feldgrillen / und setzte sie fein heimlich in die Schul / die uns ein lieblich Gesang machten /..."

CHAPTER 19: *How he studied at Liège and how he behaved there*

115. how he studied at Liège...: Garzoni, Discourse 101, also supplied much material for this description.

116. praeceptor: tutor; wealthy students were accompanied to the university by private tutors who also functioned as valets, companions, and sometimes, as in Olivier's case, as instructors and fellow participants in less laudable pursuits.

117. As concerns studying...: Garzoni: "...daβ sie (university students) sich nicht sollen verlassen auff ihre Geschwindigkeit / auff die Schärpfe ihres Verstandes /..auff ihre gute Gedächtnu~ /..."; ST: "So viel das Studirn anbelangt / verlieβ ich mich auff mein gut Gedächtnus und scharpfen Verstand /..."

118. and immersed myself in...: Garzoni: "Es geschicht aber heutiges Tages fast allenthalben / gantz das Widerspiel / und ist kein Laster / kein Mutwillen / kein Bubenstück / da man nicht die heutigen Studenten meistentheils gleichsam innen ersoffen findet."; ST: war deβwegen desto fahrlässiger / im übrigen aber in allen Lastern / Bubenstücken und Muthwillen ersoffen / ..."

119. Bernius: Francesco Berni (c. 1497-1535), Italian poet and translator, best known for his burlesques and satires.

120. Burchiellus: Domenico Burchiello (1404-1449), Italian poet best known in his own time for his sonnets.

121. Aretinus: Pietro Aretino (1432-1556), Italian author known for his unconventional language, colorful style and treatment of the sensual aspects of life.

122. Ita missa est: The mass is over.

123. in the church during the sermon...Ita missa est: taken verbatim, with a large excision, from Garzoni, Discourse 101; parallel texts presented by Scholte (p. 133).

124. I behaved like a dandy: Garzoni: "Die Freygebigkeit unnd Verschwendung zu allerhandt unnötigen ja uppigen Sachen / ist bey diesen gemachten Herren und Stutzern eine Adeliche und Heroische Tugendt; ..."; ST: "Darneben bedänckte ich mich keine Sau zu seyn / sondern hielte mich recht Stutzerisch / .. und weil ich mich dergestalt hielte wie ein gemachter Herr / ..."

125. For me every day was Martinmas...: Garzoni: "Im ubrigen halten sie alle Tage so lang ihr Geldt währet / Martins-Abendt / unnd Fastennacht / ..."; ST: "alle Tag war mirs Martins-Abend oder Faßnacht / ..."

126. my mother's milk money: Garzoni: "Unter dessen haben sie wol anders zu gedencken / als zu studiren / biß ihr Bott kommet vnnd ihnen von den armen Eltern / die ihnen ihr Brodt lassen Blutsawr werden / daß ihre Söhnlein bey den studiis mögen erhalten / das Geldt beneben einem Guten Mutter-Pfennig bringen / welches alsdann seinen gewissen Mann weiß / vnd gehet gemeinlich zu der Isabella oder der Iacomina zu"; ST: "und nicht nur das / so mein Vatter zur Nothdurfft reichlich schickte / sonder auch meiner Mutter fette Milchpfennig dapffer durchgehen liesse / lockte uns auch das Frauenzimmer an sich / ..."

127. from these bawds I learned to flirt...: Garzoni: "leffeln / bulen / spielen / ist ihre beste Kunst die sie zu Hauß bringen / frühe vnnd spat mit fressen vnd sauffen außhalten / ..."; ST: "bey diesen Schleppsäcken lernte ich leffeln / bulen und spielen; hadern / balgen und schlagen konte ich zuvor / und mein Praeceptor wehrte mir das Fressen und sauffen auch nicht / ..."

128. factor: business representative.

129. at night snatched people's coats away from them: Bechtold (p. 52) pointed out that "der kleine Jacob," whose career is described in Moscherosch, "Von den Lastern der Welt" (V, 325), and Guzman (Guzman I, Chapter 59) also engaged in this sort of crime.

CHAPTER 20: *The homecoming and departure of the honorable studiosus and how he sought to make a career in the war*

130. studiosus: student.

131. When my father brought me home...: the entire passage is also based very closely on the concluding paragraph of Garzoni, Discourse 101: Garzoni: "Wann sie aber hernach zu Hauß kommen / vnnd die arme Eltern meynen / sie werden einen wolgelerten züchtigen Ehrbaren Domine zu Haußbekommen / darvon ihr gantzes Geschlechte sol Ehre haben / so kommet inen ein anfangliches ein sauber Gesellchen /ein Disputirer unnd Schnarcher / der trawn auch will wissen / was die Rüben geldten / unnd was weiß oder schwartz ist. Wann es aber eine kleine Zeit gewähret / so wirdt man gewahr / wie die EselsOhren mit gewalt herfür stossen / daß man einen groben unwissenden Schlingel / unnd ein inutile terrae pondus, eine unnütze Last der Erden / hat mit so grossem Kosten auffgebracht / dann der gute Dominus tauget nirgendt mehr zu: Ein Handwerck zu lernen ist er zu groß / einem Herrn zu dienen / ist er zu steiff / müssen sich derhalben die Eltern mit Betrübnuß bedencken / was sie mit dem Schlingel wöllen anfangen / .. Unnd wol dem der noch die Gabe hat / daß er kan ein Schulmeister / ein Schreiber / ein Corrector oder Lector, oder sonsten etwas werden / daß er den hungrigen Bauch möge stillen."; ST: "Da mich mein Vatter heim brachte / befand er / daß ich in Grund verderbt war; Ich war kein ehrbarer Domine worden / als er wol gehofft hatte / sonder ein Disputirer und Schnarcher / der sich einbildete / er verstehe trefflich viel. Ich war kaum ein wenig daheim erwarmt / als er zu mir sagte: Höre Olivier, ich sihe deine Esels-Ohren je länger le mehr herfür ragen / du bist ein unnütze Last der ERden / ein Schlingel / der nirgends zu mehr taug! ein Handwerck zu lernen bistu zu groß / einen Herrn zu dienen / bistu zu Flegelhafftig / und meine

Handierung zu begreiffen und zu treiben / bistu nichts nötz. Ach was hab ich doch mit meinem grossen Kosten / den ich an dich gewendet / außgericht?"

132.   domine: cleric, churchman (the vocative form gradually came to be used as a nominative); Grimmelshausen, in adapting the Garzoni passage, obviously forgot that Olivier was not sent to the university to become a cleric (see above, Chapter 19).

133.   quill-mill: slang term for a room full of scribes or copyists.

134.   let you melt miseriam cum aceto...: Heining (p. 81) suspected that the Latin phrase might be a fairly well-known and common one; Weydt (p. 26) nevertheless thought it indicated Grimmelshausen's solid knowledge of Latin. In fact, it is taken verbatim from Garzoni's Discourse 101 (p. 567): Garzoni: "Da wir ihn (the lazy university student) lassen sitzen / schwitzen unnd miseram cum aceto schmeltzen, biß ihme ein besser Glück aufstösset."; ST: "Das beste wirds seyn / daß ich dich in eine Kelmüß-Mühl thue / und Miseriam cum aceto schmeltzen lasse / biß dir ohne das ein besser Glück auffstösst / wenn du dein übel Verhalten abgebüst haben würdest."

135.   lectiones: lectures.

136.   our commander...in the camp outside Magdeburg: General von Hatzfeld (see above, Book II, Chapter 24).

137.   as impervious to musket balls as steel: see above, Notes to Book II, Chapter 22.

CHAPTER 21: *How Simplicius fulfilled Trueheart's prophecy concerning Olivier when neither recognized the other one*

138.   the battle of Wittstock: see above, Notes to Book II, Chapter 24 and Chapter 27.

139.   the Wild Huntsman: "der wilde Jäger," in German folk superstition the spirit who rides in howling winds during storms.

140.   the fortune of the Swedes prevailed: see above, Notes to Book II, Chapter 27.

141.   Pomerania: province of Germany on the Baltic; the Swedish forces had their bases on the continent there.

142.   My escape I set about...: Weydt (Bp. 133 f.) suggests that an anecdote in Harsdörffer's Jammer- und Mord-Geschichten (Tale No. LXXX) might have inspired this episode.

143.   service with the Dutch: the army of Frederick Henry of Orange, who was allied with the French against the Cardinal Infante of Spain, whose army occupied the Spanish Netherlands.

144.   refuge with the Spaniards: the Cardinal Infante's army.

145.   the Bavarians: the army of General von Götz occupied much of Westphalia in 1637 and the first few months of 1638.

146.   from Westphalia to the Breisgau: see above, Notes to Book IV, Chapter 12.

147.   the battle of Wittenweier: see above, Notes to Book IV, Chapter 13.

148.   the Duke of Weimar: see above, Notes to Book I, Chapter 19.

149.   the camp outside the walls of Breisach: see above, Notes to Book IV, Chapter 14.

CHAPTER 22: *How a man fares and what it means, when he "goes to the cats"*

150. bestia: beast, wild animal.

151. St. Stephen's Day: August 3; horses were fed hay which had been blessed and then they were bled, and their blood was kept as a cure for various diseases (Borcherdt, p. 417).

152. capitolium: head.

CHAPTER 23: *A little tale which gives an example of the trade which Olivier plied, at which he was a master and Simplicius was to be his apprentice*

153. If you break eggs into a pan, they won't hatch chickens: Kurz (p. 410) lists several German proverbs to the same effect, among them "Eier in die Pfanne geben Kuchen abker keine Küken."

CHAPTER 24: *Olivier bites the dust, taking six men with him*

154. Caliburn, the sword of King Arthur: in English Arthurian tradition the sword is named "Excaliber."

CHAPTER 25: *Simplicius comes away rich; Trueheart, on the other hand, appears in very wretched condition*

155. Lichteneck: a fortress several miles from Endingen; at the time it was occupied by troops of Duke Bernhard of Weimar.

156. Villingen: town on the eastern edge of the Black Forest; situated on the Brigach River; in 1638 it was in fact in the hands of the Imperials.

157. L.: Lippstadt.

158. an entire perpetual calendar: a perpetual calendar was a numerical table by which the date of any given day in any given year could be reckoned. Grimmelshausen, of course, included one in his own Perpetual Calendar.

159. forged by Vulcan himself: Vulcan (Hephaestus) was the smith of the gods who forged their weapons and devices.

160. in hora Martis: in the hour of Mars (literally), under the sign of Mars (figuratively); see above, Notes to Book III, Chapter 4.

161. HERO'S TREASURE CHEST: in German "Heldenschatz"; critics long interpreted it to be the much better-known Heldenbuch, but the work in question is in fact Johann Staricius' Heldenschatz.

162. the Swabian heath: Schwäbischer Alb; i. e. that part which is called the "Rauhe Alb" (a high plateau).

CHAPTER 26: *The end of this Fourth Book, because there is not any more of it*

163. factotum: right-hand man.

164. Count von Götz...the most recent campaign under his command and generalcy: in December of 1638, after the utter failure in the campaign in the Breisgau to succour the fortress of Breisach, Götz was arrested by the Emperor and brought to Ingolstadt; in August of 1640 he was cleared of all charges and returned to the army.

Simplicissimus, The German Adventurer

BOOK V

CHAPTER 1

How Simplicius becomes a pilgrim and makes a pilgrimage with Trueheart

After Trueheart had regained his strength and his wounds were healed, he confided to me that in his direst need he had vowed to make a pilgrimage to the Cloister of Einsiedeln.[1] Because he was now so close to Switzerland anyway, he resolved to do it, even if he were obliged to beg his way thither. I was very pleased to hear this; therefore I offered him my money and my company; indeed, I was prepared straightway to buy two nags upon which to make this journey—not, of course, because devoutness drove me to it, but in order to see the Swiss Confederation, the only land in which sweet Peace was still flourishing. So it pleased me no little bit either that I had the opportunity to serve Trueheart on this journey, since I loved him almost more than myself. He, however, rejected both my aid and my company, under the pretext that his pilgrimage must needs be made on foot, and with dried peas in his shoes. Now if I were to be in his company I should not only hinder him in his devotions but also take upon myself a great burden because of his slow pace. But he said this to drive me from him, because it bothered his conscience to live on such a holy journey from money which was got by robbery and murder. Moreover, he did not wish to cause me all too great an expense, and he said candidly that I had done more for him than I owed him, and more than he could ever hope to repay. At this we fell into a friendly quarrel which was so heartwarming that I have never heard squabbling like it, for our arguments consisted only in each of us saying that he had not yet done for the other what one friend should do for another one, indeed, that each had not repaid the other for the good deeds the other had done him. But all this did not succeed in moving him to tolerate me as a traveling companion, till I finally realized that he found both Olivier's money and my godless life odious; therefore I resorted to lies and persuaded him that my resolve to convert to Catholicism was what was drawing me to Einsiedeln; should he prevent me from carrying out such a good work, and were I to die before, then he could scarce answer for it. In this way I persuaded him to let me visit the holy place with him, particularly because I (though it was all a lie) exhibited great remorse over my wicked life, and then I also persuaded him that I had imposed upon myself the penance of walking to Einsiedeln like him, with peas in my shoes.

The tiff was scarce over when we fell into another one, for Trueheart was far too scrupulous. He was scarce willing to concede me a pass from the commandant for return to my regiment. "What!" he said. "Do we not have it in mind to mend our ways and to go to Einsiedeln? And now, look you, for God's sake, you desire to begin with a deceit and by pulling the wool over others' eyes through duplicity! 'But whosoever shall deny me before men, him will I deny before my Father Which is in heaven,' said Christ.[2] What manner of fainthearted ninnies are we? And if all the martyrs and converts to Christ behaved in like fashion, there would be few saints in heaven! Let us go, in God's name, and commending ourselves to His protection, wherever our holy intent and desires take us, and otherwise let God prevail; then God will assuredly lead us to where our souls will find peace." Now when I put it to him that one must not tempt God, but instead we should adapt ourselves to the times in which we live, and employ the only means available to us, primarily because going on pilgrimages is an unusual thing for the *soldateska*[3] to do, and if we were to divulge our plan, we would be taken to be deserters rather than pilgrims, which might then greatly discommode and imperil us, and particularly since even St. Paul, to whom, of course, we should in no wise be compared, adapted himself wondrously to the age in which he lived and to the customs of this world, then he finally let me get a pass to go to my regiment; with it and a trusty guide we went out of the city gates as they were being closed, making as if we were going to Rottweil;[4] but soon we turned down a side road and that same night crossed the Swiss border and came the following morning into a village, where we outfitted ourselves with long black cloaks, pilgrim's staffs, and rosaries; and we sent the messenger back after paying him well.

To me this country, compared to other German lands, seemed as foreign as if I had been in Brazil or China. There I saw the people living and working in peace; the stables were full of cattle; farmyards were full of chickens, geese, and ducks running about; the roads were safe and full of travelers; the inns were full of people making merry; there was no fear of an enemy at all, no worry about being plundered, no anxiety about losing life, limb, or property; every man lived secure in his vineyard or under his fig tree[5] and, compared to other German lands, in sheer delight and joy, so that I held this land to be a paradise on earth, even though it seemed to be rough enough in character. That was the reason I stared at everything the entire way, while Trueheart, by contrast, was telling his rosary, for which reason I received many a reprimand from him, for he desired that I pray the same way he was doing, which activity, however, I could not get accustomed to.

At Zürich he discovered what I was really about, and therefore he told me quite bluntly what he truly thought of me, for when we were spending the previous night in

Schaffhausen[6](where my feet hurt a great deal from walking on the dried peas in my shoes), because I feared walking on the peas again the next day, I had them cooked and put back into my shoes, for which reason I then got to Zürich on foot without pain, whereas his feet were terribly sore, and he said to me: "My friend, God has bestowed great grace upon you by letting you walk along so easily, despite the peas in your shoes." "Well, my dear Trueheart," said I, "I cooked them, else I could not have walked far on them." "God have mercy!" he answered. "What have you done? You should rather have not put them into your shoes at all, if all you desire to do is to make a mockery of our pilgrimage. I cannot but fear that God will punish you, and me too. Do not take it amiss, my friend, when I tell you bluntly, out of brotherly love, how I feel in my heart, namely, that if you do not change your attitude towards God, your salvation will be in direst peril. I assure you that I love no human being more than you, but I also cannot deny that if you do not mend your ways I must needs have scruples about continuing to love you." I fell silent in such fright that I could well nigh not recover from it; finally I candidly confessed to him that I had put the peas in my shoes not because of devotion but solely to please him, so that he would take me along on the journey. "Alas, my friend," said he, "I see that you are far from the path which leads to eternal bliss, even if there were not this business with the peas. May God grant that you mend your ways, for unless you do, our friendship cannot endure."

From this time on I followed him quite downcast, like a man who is being led to the gallows. My conscience fell to bothering me, and when I fell to thinking all sorts of thoughts, there passed before my mind's eye all the knavish deeds I had done my entire life long; then, for the first time, I lamented my lost innocence, which I had brought with me out of the forest and had trifled away in the world in so many ways; and what increased my anguish was the fact that Trueheart no longer conversed with me and merely sighed whenever he looked at me, which seemed to me to reveal nothing except that he knew I was damned, and he was bemoaning it.

CHAPTER 2

Simplicius is converted after he has first been frightened by the devil

In this wise we reached Einsiedeln and entered the church just as a priest was exorcising a man who was possessed.[7] Now to me this was something new and wondrous; therefore I left Trueheart to kneel and pray as long as he liked, and I went, out of curiosity, to observe this spectacle. But scarce had I drawn a little near when the evil spirit screamed out of the poor man: "Aha, my fine fellow, what brings you here? I had thought to encounter you in our infernal abode, in the company of Olivier, when I arrived home, but I see that you can be found here, you murderous, adulterous whoremonger! You probably think that you can escape us. O, ye men of the cloth, do not accept him! He is a hypocrite and a worse liar than I am. He is merely jeering and he makes a mockery of both God and religion!" The exorcist commanded the spirit to be silent, because since the spirit was a liar of the first order, no one believed him anyway. "Yes, yes!" the spirit answered. "Ask the traveling companion of this renegade monk! He will assuredly tell you that this atheist went so far as to cook the peas upon which he vowed to walk hither." I knew not whether I was standing upon my feet or upon my head when I heard all this and everyone began to stare at me. The priest, however, punished the spirit and made it be silent, but that day he could not drive it out. Meanwhile Trueheart came over also, just when I, out of fear, was looking more like a dead man than a live one and, hovering betwixt fear and hope, knew not what I ought to do. He consoled me as best he could, assured those who were standing there, particularly the padres,[8] that I had never in all my days been a monk, but was rather a soldier who might perchance have done more wicked things than good ones, adding that the devil was a liar, inasmuch as he had made the business with the peas out to be much worse than it had really been. But I was so confused in my mind that it seemed to me just as if I were already experiencing the pain of hell, so that the clergymen had all they could do to console me; they admonished me to confess and to take communion, but the spirit screamed out of the possessed man: "O, yes, he'll make a fine confession! He does not know what confession is; and what do you expect to do with him anyway? He is of the heretical sort and belongs to us; his parents were more Anabaptist than Calvinist," etc. The exorcist again commanded the spirit to be silent, saying to it: "Then it will vex you all the more if we snatch this poor little lost lamb from the jaws of perdition and put it back into Christ's flock." At that the spirit fell to roaring so horribly that it was terrible to hear, from which dreadful song I took my greatest consolation, for I thought to myself that if I could not achieve God's grace any more, the devil would not be behaving so badly.

Though at the time I had not prepared myself for confession, nor had it ever occurred to me my entire life long to confess my sins, but instead I had always, out of shame, been as afraid of confessing as the devil is of a crucifix, I nevertheless felt within me at that moment such remorse for my sins and such a yearning to do penance and to mend my ways that I forthwith requested a father confessor, at which abrupt conversion and mending of my ways Trueheart was most happy, because he had perceived and well knew that I had hitherto belonged to no church; then I publicly proclaimed myself a member of the Roman Catholic church, went to confession, and, after receiving absolution, took communion, whereupon I felt so relieved and so good that I cannot describe it; and what was most astonishing of all was that the spirit in the possessed man thenceforth left me in peace, whereas before my confession and absolution it had as severely reproached me as if it had been assigned no other task to do than to reveal my sins; but those who heard it deemed it a liar and believed nothing it said, particularly since my pilgrim's garb presented a different picture of me to their eyes.

We remained fourteen entire days in this divinely blessed place, where I thanked God for my conversion and observed the miracles which took place there, all of which inspired me to considerable devoutness and godliness; but this did not last as long as it might have, because inasmuch as my conversion had its origin not in love for God but in the anxiety and fear of being damned eternally, I little by little grew lukewarm and indolent, because I gradually forgot the terror which the evil fiend had inspired in me. And after we had looked to our heart's content at the relics of saints, the vestments, and other things worth seeing, we betook ourselves to Baden[9] in order to pass the entire winter there.

CHAPTER 3

How the two friends passed the winter

There I rented for us a lovely parlor and bedroom which at other times, particularly in the summertime, the spa guests were wont to occupy, which guests are generally wealthy Swiss who go thither more to divert themselves and to display their wealth than to take the baths for some physical ailment. And at the same time I arranged for board for us, and when Trueheart saw how I was setting us up like noblemen, he admonished me to be frugal and reminded me of the long harsh winter which we still had to survive, since he did not know that my money would go that far. I would need my reserves for the spring, he said, when we made ready to leave from here; much money is soon gone when one only takes from it and adds nothing to it; it disappears like smoke, he said, and promises never to return, etc. After such well-meant exhortations I could no longer conceal from Trueheart how full of wealth my purse was and that I was of a mind to do both of us good with it, since its origin and provenience were so unworthy of the slightest blessing that I gave no thought to buying a farm with it; and even if I were not using it to maintain my best friend on earth with it, it would be fair and right anyway for Trueheart to lead a pleasant life on Olivier's money, to make up for the harm he had been done by him before in the camp at Magdeburg. And when I knew I was completely safe, I took off my two scapulars, cut the ducats and pistoles out of them, and told Trueheart that he might now dispose over all this money as he saw fit, and use it and give it out as he thought most useful for us both.

When he saw both the trust I bore him and so much money that I, even without him, could have lived the life of a rather well-to-do gentleman, he said: "My friend, as long as I have known you, you have done nothing but demonstrate the love and loyalty you have for me. But tell me, how do you think I shall ever be able to repay you? It is not merely a matter of money, for in time money might perchance be paid back; rather, it is a matter of your love and loyalty, and especially of the great trust you place in me, which is incalculable. In a word, my friend, your virtuous soul makes me your slave, and what you do for me is so admirable that it cannot be recompensed. O, honest Simplicius! In these godless times in which the world is so full of perfidy, it does not occur to you that poor and most needy Trueheart might abscond with such a large sum of money and thrust you into penury in his place! I assure you, my friend, this proof of true friendship binds me more closely to you than a rich man could bind me if he presented me with many thousand ducats. But I beg of you, my friend, remain master, guardian, and distributor of your own money. It suffices me that you are my friend!" I answered: "What strange words be these, most honored Trueheart? By your words you give me to understand that you are bound to me, and yet you are in favor of my not wasting my money, to the harm of both me and yourself!" Thus we talked foolishly enough to one another, because each of us was intoxicated by the other's love for him. And so Trueheart became at one and the same time my guardian, my count of the exchequer, my servant, and my master; and during this period of inactivity he told me the story of his life and by what means he had become acquainted with and had been promoted by Count von Götz, whereupon I told him how I had fared since his late father died, for we had never since then had so much time together. And when he heard that I had a young wife in L., he reproached me for betaking myself to Switzerland with him instead of first going to her, for that would have been the more proper thing for me to do, and it was my obligation too. And after I made the excuse that I simply could not bring myself to forsake my very best friend in his misery, he persuaded me to write to my wife and to make my circumstances known to her, promising to betake myself back to her at the earliest opportunity, and also saying, by way of apology for having stayed away so long, that on account of all manner of untoward events I could not have returned to her sooner, much as I had desired to. And when Trueheart learned from the newspapers that things were going well for Count von Götz, specifically that he was about to be vindicated in the eyes of His Imperial Majesty, released from custody, and even put back in command of an army, Trueheart reported his condition to the count in Vienna and wrote to the army of the Prince Elector of Bavaria concerning his personal effects, which he still had there, and he fell to hoping that fortune was smiling upon him again; therefore we made the decision to part from one another the next spring, he to go to join the count, and I to betake myself to L. to my wife. But so that we should not pass this winter in idleness, we learned from an engineer more on paper about building fortifications than the kings of Spain and France could ever make use of; along with that I struck up an acquaintance with some alchemists who, because they saw that I had gold coins behind me, were willing to teach me how to make gold, if I would but advance them some of mine for it; and I believe they would have persuaded me, had Trueheart not given them their walking papers, for he said that anyone who really knew this art would not go about so like a beggar, asking others for money.

Now whereas Trueheart received from Vienna a pleasant reply and splendid promises from the count, I heard not a word from L.,[10] despite the fact that I had written *in duplo*[11] on different post-days. This made me indignant and was the reason I did not set out upon a journey to Westphalia that spring, but rather prevailed upon Trueheart to take me with him to Vienna to let me enjoy his anticipated good fortune. So we outfitted ourselves with my money like two gentlemen, with clothes, horses, servants, and weapons, went by way of Constance[12] to Ulm,[13] where we took a boat down the Danube, and from there arrived in Vienna in a week. On that journey I observed nothing, except that the women who lived on the banks of the Danube did not answer in words to those who sailed past and called out to them, but instead replied by baring their buttocks, which manner of greeting folks can afford a man many a fine sight.

CHAPTER 4

How Trueheart and Simplicius go to war again and leave it again

Wondrous things do happen in our ever-changing world! People are wont to say "A man who knew everything would soon be rich" but I say "A man who always strikes when the iron is hot will soon become great and powerful." Many a penny pincher, or skinflint (for both these fine names are given to men who are greedy), will probably soon be rich, because he understands and exploits the one or the other advantage, but that does not make him great; rather, he is and mostly remains a man of even slighter esteem than he was before when he was poor. But a man who knows how to make himself great and powerful will find wealth dogging his heels. Fortuna,[14] who is wont to provide power and wealth, was looking upon me with such exceeding favor and, when I had been in Vienna a week or so, put into my hands opportunity enough to climb through the ranks to the heights without any hindrances, but I did not do it. Why? I believe, because my *fatum*, namely, the one towards which my *fatuitas*[15] was leading me, had decided differently.

Count von der Wahl,[16] under whose command I had made a name for myself before in Westphalia, was also in Vienna when I arrived there with Trueheart. At a banquet attended by divers Imperial military councillors, together with Count von Götz and others, when they were talking about all manner of odd fellows, divers soldiers, and famous adventurers, Count von der Wahl made mention of the chasseur of Soest and told some tales about him in such laudatory words that some of his listeners were astonished at so young a fellow and expressed regret that the cunning Hessian colonel, S.-A.,[17] had shackled him with ball and chain so that he should either lay down his sword or else bear weapons for the Swedes, for

370

the esteemed Count von der Wahl had collected all the information about how that same colonel had tricked me in L. Trueheart, who happened to be standing there and would have liked to help me to preferment, begged pardon and permission to speak and said that he knew the chasseur of Soest better than any other man in the world, that he was not only a good soldier who knew well the smell of powder but also a very good horseman, a perfect fencer and excellent maker of firearms and fireworks, and, more important than all this, a man who was every bit as good as any engineer. He said that chasseur had left behind in L. not only his wife, because by means of her he had been so despicably duped, but also everything he owned, and had sought service with the Imperials once more, as a result of which he had served under Count von Götz in the recent campaign, and when he had been captured by troops of the Duke of Weimar's army and had desired to betake himself back to the Imperials, he and his comrade had laid low a corporal and six musketeers who were supposed to hunt them down and bring them back, and had taken considerable booty from them, for which reason the chasseur had come to Vienna with him, with the desire to let himself be used once more against the enemies of His Roman Imperial Majesty, but only insofar as he could enjoy such *conditiones*[18] as he deemed proper, for he desired to play no longer the role of a common soldier.

This eminent company was then already so enthusiastic with strong drink that they desired to have their curiosity to see the chasseur satisfied, for which reason Trueheart was sent to fetch me in a carriage. On the way he instructed me how I should comport myself amongst these eminent men, because my future fortune depended upon it. Therefore, when I arrived there I made brief and apothegmatic reply to everything I was asked, so that they fell to wondering at me, for I said nothing but things which were prudent and to the point. *In summa*, I behaved in such wise that I was pleasing to everyone, because I had been praised as a good soldier by Count von der Wahl anyway. In the process I grew tipsy, and I do believe that I then let it be seen that I had been but little at court. In the end, the result was that a colonel promised me a company in his regiment, which I did not at all refuse, for I thought it child's play to be a captain! But Trueheart reproached me the next day for my heedlessness and said that had I but held out even longer, I should indeed have arrived at a higher rank.

So I was introduced to a company as its captain, which company, even though its officers' corps was, counting me, *in prima plana*[19] quite complete, had in it no more than seven common soldiers, and in the bargain most of my non-commissioned officers were old croaks; at the sight of this company I scratched my head in bewonderment, and so I was soundly thrashed all the more easily in the bitter engagement which occurred not long after that, in which battle Count von Götz lost his life[20] and Trueheart his *testiculos*,[21] when he was hit by a musket ball. I got in mine in the leg, which was, however, a very minor wound. Then we betook ourselves to Vienna to have ourselves cured, because we had money there anyway. Despite the fact that these wounds soon healed, another dangerous malady befell Trueheart which the *medici*[22] were not able to straightway identify at first, for his arms and legs became paralyzed, like those of a *cholericus*[23] whom gall has laid low, and yet his complexion did not reflect anger in the least; nevertheless he was counseled to take the waters at a spa, and for this purpose Griesbach[24] in the Black Forest was suggested to him.

Thus our fortunes suddenly changed. Shortly before Trueheart had been of a mind to wed a distinguished noblewoman and to this end to make himself a member of the landed gentry and make me a nobleman, but now he was obliged to entertain other thoughts, for because he had lost that with which he might propagate a new generation, and particularly since he was threatened by his paralysis with a protracted illness, during which he would have need of good friends, he made his last will and testament and made me sole heir to all he might leave behind, especially because he saw that for his sake I was tossing my own good fortune to the winds and quitting my company so that I could accompany him to the spa and remain there till he could regain his health.

CHAPTER 5

Simplicius rides courier and in the guise of Mercury learns what Jupiter actually has in mind as regards war and peace

Now when Trueheart was once more able to ride, we transferred our cash (for we had but one purse betwixt us) to Basel per letter of exchange, outfitted ourselves with horses and servants, and betook ourselves up the Danube to Ulm and from there to the aforementioned spa, because it was just then May and delightful to travel. There we rented lodgings, and I rode to Strasbourg, not only, in part, to get our money, which we had transferred thither from Basel, but also to look about for experienced *medicos*[25] who could prescribe for Trueheart *recepta*[26] and a regimen at the baths; they betook themselves to the spa with me and determined that Trueheart had been poisoned, and because the poison had not been strong enough to do him in straightway, it had settled in his limbs and must needs be evacuated again by means of *pharmaca*,[27] *antidota*,[28] and sweet-baths, and this cure would take a month or two. Then Trueheart straightway recalled when and by whom he had been poisoned, namely, by those who would have liked to have his position in the army; and because he was given to understand by the *medicos* that his cure did not require a visit to a spa, he firmly believed that his *medicus*[29] in the field had been bribed with money by these same rivals of his to counsel him to go far away; however, he resolved to complete his cure at the spa, because not only was the air healthful there, there were also all manner of charming social groups amongst the guests at the spa.

I did not wish to waste this time, because I had the desire to finally see my wife again, and because Trueheart had no particular need of me, I revealed my wishes to him. He praised the plan I had in mind and counseled me to visit her; he also gave me several valuable pieces of jewelry which I was to present to her as gifts from him and thereby beg that she forgive him for having been the cause of my not visiting her sooner. And so I rode to Strasbourg and not only equipped myself with money but also inquired how I might arrange my journey so that I should travel the safest way; and I found that it could not be done alone on horseback, because it was rather unsafe because of the raiding parties betwixt so many garrisons of the opposing forces. Therefore I obtained a pass for a Strasbourg post-rider and wrote several letters to my wife, her sister, and her parents, as if I were going to send the courier with them to L.;[30] but then I acted as if I had changed my mind, and I tricked the courier out of the pass, sent my horse and servant back again, disguised myself in the red and white livery of a post-rider, and sailed off on a ship down to Cologne, which at that time was a neutral city betwixt the warring parties.

Before anything else, I went to visit my Jupiter, who had declared me his Ganymede before, to find out about the disposition of my effects which were deposited there; but at that time he had once again gone quite mad and was indignant at the human race. "O, Mercury," he said to me when he saw me, "what news do you bring from Münster?[31] Do the folk there believe that they can make peace without my consent? Never! They had a peace. Why did they break it? Were not all vices in full swing when they provoked me to send the war to them? What have they done since then to deserve that I give peace back to them again? Have they since that time turned over a new leaf? Have they not grown worse, and do they not run to the war as if it were a country fair? Did they even turn over a new leaf after the famine which I sent them and in which so many thousands died of hunger? Did even the terrible plague (which carried off so many millions) frighten them so that they would mend their ways? No! No, Mercury, the survivors, who saw that wretched misery with their very own eyes, have not only not mended their ways, they have grown much worse than they ever were before! If they have not turned over a new leaf after so many terrible disasters, but instead, amidst so many difficult trials and tribulations, have not ceased to live godlessly, what will become of them if I send blissful and golden peace back to them? I cannot but fear that they would do to me what the giants did heretofore and make so bold as to storm the heavens. But I am going to avert these impudent plans betimes and leave them wallowing in war!"

Now because I knew how one must approach this "god" if one desired to put him into the right frame of mind, I said: "But my great god, the entire world is sighing for peace, and they promise to greatly mend their ways. Why then do you desire to continue to deny it to them?" "Yes," Jupiter answered, "they sigh all right, but not for my sake or yours, not in hopes that everyone may praise God in his own vineyard or under his own fig tree,[32] but rather so that they may enjoy their fruits at their leisure and in all delight. I recently asked a mangy tailor whether I should give mankind peace, and he answered me, what difference did it make to him; in peacetime as well as in wartime he must needs ply his needle. Such an answer I also got from an iron caster who said that if he had no bells to cast in peacetime, he had in wartime enough to do casting cannons and mortars. And a smith also answered me that way, saying: 'Though I have no plow shares or wagonwheel rims to forge in wartime, I still lay hold of enough troopers' horses and army wagons so that I can easily make do without peace.' Look you now, Mercury, why should I bestow peace upon them? O yes, there are some few of them who wish for it, but only for the sake of their bellies and their pleasures; there are others, on the other hand, who desire the war to keep on—not, of course, because I desire it, but because it earns them money. And whereas the masons and carpenters wish for peace, so that they may earn money rebuilding the houses which have been burned to ashes, others, who doubt that they can maintain themselves in their trades in peacetime, demand the continuation of the war so that they may continue to steal while it is going on."

Now because my Jupiter was preoccupied with these matters, I could easily imagine that in his confused state he could give me little news about my loved ones, and therefore I did not discover myself to him but rather took hold of myself and made my way to L. by side roads, all of which were indeed well known to me, and inquired there after my father-in-law, as if I were a stranger, of course, bearing a message for him; and I learned straightway that he and my mother-in-law had gone on to a better world six months ago, and then that my beloved wife, after she had given birth to a baby boy, whom her sister now had with her, had likewise, straightway after she took to her childbed, gone the way of all flesh. Then

I delivered to my brother-in-law the letters which I had written to my father-in-law, my beloved wife, and him, my brother-in-law. He then insisted upon putting me up so that he might learn from me, in my capacity as a messenger, what had become of Simplicius and how I was faring. To that end my sister-in-law conversed with me for a long while, and I said about myself whatever laudable things I knew about, for the pox had so ruined my looks and changed me that no one recognized me any more, except von Schönstein, who, as my most loyal friend, held his tongue.

Now when I told in great detail how Mr. Simplicius had many fine horses and servants and walked abroad in a black velvet hat embroidered all over in gold, she said: "Yes, I always thought that he was not of such humble origins as he claimed to be. The commandant here persuaded my late parents, by making promises to them, to saddle him to their advantage with my late sister, who was indeed a devout and virtuous maiden, from which plot I never did expect any good to come; but he did nevertheless make a promising beginning and resolved to accept Swedish, or rather Hessian, service here in the garrison, for which reason he to this end resolved to go fetch his effects, which he had in Cologne, which effort then came to a standstill and during which effort he was most scurvily tricked into going to France, leaving behind my sister, who had been his wife scarce four weeks, and at least a half-dozen other maidens in town, all of them with child; and in fact, all of them (my sister last of all) gave birth to baby boys. Now inasmuch as my father and mother were dead and my husband and I have no hopes of having children together, we adopted my sister's child and made it heir to all we shall leave behind; and, with the aid of the commandant here, we laid hold of what his father had in Cologne, which may amount to three thousand guilders, so that this young lad, when he comes of age, will have no cause to reckon himself amongst the poor. And my husband and I love the child so much that we would not give him to his father, even if he were to come in person and wish to fetch him. Moreover, he is the prettiest of all his half-brothers and is the spitting image of his father; and I know that if my brother-in-law knew what a fine son he had here, he could not refrain from coming hither, just to see the little darling (even though he might shun his other, illegitimate children).

This and such-like things my sister-in-law brought forth, from which I could easily discern how much she loved my child, who was then running about there in his first pair of breeches and who delighted me; therefore I took out the pieces of jewelry which Trueheart had given me to present with his compliments to my wife. These, I said, Mr. Simplicius had given to me to bring along and to hand over to his beloved wife with his greetings, but since she was dead, I esteemed it would be proper for me to leave them behind for his child, which jewels my brother-in-law and his wife were happy to receive, and from which they concluded that I must needs have no lack of means, but must needs be a different fellow than they had before imagined me to be. Then I implored them to give me leave to depart, and when I received it, I requested permission, in the name of Simplicius, to kiss young Simplicius, so that I could tell his father about it. Now when, with the consent of my sister-in-law, this transpired, both my nose and that of the child fell to bleeding,[33] at which I thought my heart would break; but I concealed my feelings, and so that they would not have time to ponder upon the cause of this *sympathia*[34] betwixt me and the child, I forthwith shook the dust from my heels and after fourteen days, through much effort and peril, came back to the spa dressed in beggar's rags, because on the way I had been attacked and plundered.

CHAPTER 6

Story of a prank which Simplicius played at the spa

After my arrival I grew aware that Trueheart's condition had taken a turn for the worse rather than for the better, even though the *doctores*[35] and the apothecaries had plucked him cleaner than a fat goose; moreover, he seemed to me to be quite childish too, and he could walk straight only with difficulty. I, of course, cheered him up as best I could, but he was in a bad way. He himself had clearly perceived from the dissipation of his strength that he could not last much longer; his greatest consolation was that I should be at his side when he closed his eyes for the last time.

I, for my part, made merry and sought my pleasure wherever I thought I might find it, but in such wise that Trueheart lacked for nothing in terms of care. And because I knew myself to be a widower, the good times and my youth once more tempted me into going a-wooing, which avocation I then did eagerly pursue, because the terror which had been struck in me at Einsiedeln had of course been forgotten again. There was at the spa a beautiful lady who claimed to be of the nobility[36] but who was, in my opinion, more *mobilis* than *nobilis*.[37] This same man-trap, because she was rather sleek in appearance, I courted most diligently, and in a short while I gained not only free access to her but also all the pleasure which I might have wished and desired; but because of her wantonness I straightway felt disgusted by her, and I therefore pondered how I could rid myself of her again in good fashion, for it seemed to me that she was more intent upon milking my purse than upon getting me for a husband. Moreover, wherever we met she bestowed upon me ardent and adoring glances and other tokens of her burning affection in such an exaggerated manner that I could not but feel ashamed, for her sake as well as my own.

Besides that, there was also a rich Swiss at the baths; he was robbed not only of his money but also of his wife's jewelry, which consisted of gold, silver, pearls, and precious stones. Now because such things are as sorely missed as they are difficult to obtain, this Swiss therefore sought every way and means by which he might get his hands upon them again, for which reason he sent for the famous conjurer Geißhut,[38] who by his conjuring so tribulated the thief that he was obliged to return personally what he had stolen to the place from which he had taken it, as a result of which the conjurer was presented with ten Imperial sovereigns.

The necromancer I should have liked to see and confer with, but to my mind this could not be done without damage to my reputation (for I thought myself at that time to be no part of the common herd); therefore I arranged for my manservant to tope with him that evening, because I had heard that he was supposed to be a wine bibber of the first order, to see whether I might perchance in this wise make his acquaintance, for I had been told so many wondrous things about him, which I could not believe unless I should hear them from his own lips. I disguised myself as a mountebank who had salve for sale, sat down at the table with him, and waited to hear whether he would divine, or the devil would inform him, who I was. But I could not tell the least thing about him, for he kept on toping and took me to be the sort of person my clothes proclaimed me to be, so that he also drank several glasses in my honor and yet showed my servant more respect than he did me; to him he confided that if the person who had robbed the Swiss man had thrown even the slightest part of what he had taken into the water and in that way given the devil his *partem*,[39] it would have been impossible either to name the thief or to lay hands again upon what had been lost.

All of this foolishness I listened to and was astonished that the malicious and thousandfold cunning fiend can get his claws into a poor mortal through such petty things. I could easily infer that this little piece of information was part of the pact he had struck with the devil, and I could well imagine that this trick would be of no avail to the thief if another conjurer, in whose pact this clause was not included, were to be fetched to reveal a theft. I therefore commanded my servant (who was a worse thief than any Bohemian) that he should drink him under the table and afterwards steal his ten Imperial sovereigns and forthwith toss a few farthings from the sum into the Rench River.[40] This the fellow did quite adroitly. Now when the exorcist found his money missing early the next morning, he betook himself to the Rench wasteland and into a copse, without doubt in order to conjure up his *spiritum familiarem*[41] on that account, but he was so evilly dispatched that he came back with his countenance black and blue and all scratched up, for which reason I felt so sorry for the poor old scoundrel that I had my servant give him back his money and in so doing tell him that because he could now see what a deceitful and wicked fellow the devil is, he should henceforth quit his service and company and turn back to God. But this admonition profited me the way eating grass does a dog, for from that time on, I had neither good fortune nor any luck, as a consequence of which my fine horses straightway after that perished as a result of magic. But why should they not have anyway? I lived as godlessly as an Epicurean[42] and never commended what was mine to God's protection, so why then should this magician not have been able to take vengeance upon me in turn?

CHAPTER 7

Trueheart dies and Simplicius goes a-wooing again

The spa suited me better with each passing day, not only because the number of guests was increasing, but also because the place itself and the way of life there seemed delightful to me. I made the acquaintance of the merriest folk who came thither, and I began to learn courtly speech and compliments, to which I had otherwise never in all my days paid any heed. I was taken to be a man of noble birth because my servants called me "captain," for no soldier of fortune[43] achieved that rank so easily at the tender age in which I then found myself. Therefore the wealthy fops not only made acquaintance with me, we also became close friends; and diversions, gambling, wining, and dining were my foremost task and care, which deprived me of many a fine ducat without my particularly noticing or paying heed to it, for my purse was still quite heavy with what I had inherited from Olivier.

Meanwhile Trueheart grew worse with each passing day, till he was finally obliged to pay the debt of nature, when the *medici*[44] and the apothecaries forsook him, after they had first grazed away upon him sufficiently; he again confirmed his last will and testament and made me heir to all that he had received from his late father's estate. I, for my part, had him given a splendid funeral and let his servants go their way with the mourning clothes and a sum of money.

His departure grieved me greatly, particularly because he had been poisoned, and though I could not do anything about it to change it, it did change me, for I fled all society and sought only solitude, in order to give audience to my sorrowful thoughts. To that end I hid myself somewhere or other in some bushes and considered not only what manner of friend I had lost, but also that never again in my life would I have another one like him either. In addition, I made all manner of plans about arranging my future life, and yet I resolved nothing for certain. One minute I was of a mind to go back to the war, and before I knew it I was thinking to myself that the meanest peasant in this region had a better life than a commanding officer, for no raiding parties came into these mountains, nor could I imagine, either, to what purpose an army would feel obliged to spoil this land's way of life, since all the farms were excellently cultivated, just as in peacetime, and all the stalls were filled with cattle, despite the fact that in the villages in the flatlands not a dog or a cat was to be found.

Now while I was taking delight in listening to the loveliest songs of the birds and was imagining that the nightingale in her loveliness was casting a spell upon the other birds so that they must needs keep silent and listen to her, either from shame or in order to steal from her some of her charming notes, there approached the shore on the other side of the water a beauteous maiden who (because she was wearing the garb of a peasant girl) affected me more than a fine lady might have. She took down from atop her head a basket in which she was carrying a clump of fresh butter to sell at the spa; this she moistened with water so that it would not melt from the great heat; at the same time she sat down in the grass, threw off her kerchief and peasant hat, and wiped the perspiration from her countenance, so that I could observe her as much as I desired, and so that my foolish eyes could feast upon her. It seemed to me that I had never in all my days seen a more beautiful creature; the proportion of her body seemed perfect and beyond reproach, her arms and hands snow white, her countenance fresh and lovely, and her black eyes full of fire and alluring glances. I called over to her: "Ah, fair maiden, you have, to be sure, cooled your butter in the water with your beautiful hands, but you have set my heart afire with your bright eyes!" As soon as she saw and heard me, she ran away as if she were being chased, without answering me with a single word, leaving me behind laden with all those foolish feelings by which fond lovers are wont to be tormented.

And my desire to bask further in this sun did not let me remain in the solitude which I had chosen for myself, but caused me to esteem the song of the nightingale no more highly than the howl of the wolf. Therefore I trundled back to the spa and sent my boy out to stop the maiden selling the butter and to haggle with her till I arrived. He did his part, and after my arrival I did mine, but I found such a heart of stone and such indifference towards me as I never expected to encounter in a peasant lass, which of course made me all the more smitten with her, despite the fact that I, as one who had been in that school more than once, could easily reckon that she would not be so easily deluded.

At that time I should have had either an implacable enemy or a bosom friend: an enemy so that I would have been obliged to focus my thoughts upon him and forget this foolish love, or a friend who would have counseled me not to do it and who would have admonished me to leave off this folly I was set upon committing. But alas, I unfortunately had nothing but my money, which blinded me; my carnal desires, which seduced me, because I gave them free rein; and my gross heedlessness, which ruined me and plunged me into misfortune. Fool that I was, I should have judged from our clothes, as from a bad omen, that her love would turn out badly for me, for because I had just lost my Trueheart and she her parents, we were both wearing mourning clothes when we saw one another the first time, so how could our love affair have brought us happiness? In a word, I was properly hooked, with a ring in my nose, and therefore as blind and devoid of common sense as a little Cupid himself; and because I knew no other way to satisfy my carnal lust, I resolved to marry her. "Why not?" I thought to myself. "After all, you are merely a peasant's son and will never in all your days own a castle; this is a splendid land which, compared to other places, has got through this terrible war unscathed and is prospering and flourishing. Moreover, you have enough money to buy the best farm in the area. You can marry this honest peasant lass and get yourself a fine peaceful manor in the midst of the other peasants. Where could you ever find a more interesting place to live than near the spa, since what with the guests coming to take the baths and leaving them, you can see an entire new world, as it were, every six weeks, and from that you can form judgments about how the world is changing from one *saeculo*[45] to the next. These and a thousand such-like thoughts I turned over in my mind, till I finally asked my beloved to be my wife and got her (though not without effort) to say yes.

CHAPTER 8

Simplicius embarks upon a second marriage, encounters his Pa, and learns who his parents were

made excellent preparations for the wedding, for my head was in the clouds. The farm upon which my bride had been born I not only took sole possession of, I even set to building a fine new house upon it, just as if I were going to live the life of a country squire there instead of the life of a farmer; and before I completed the nuptials, I already had more than thirty head of cattle there, because that many could be kept on that farm year round. *In summa*, I arranged everything in the best possible way, even down to expensive household goods, spending whatever my folly prompted me to. But I was brought back down to earth again soon enough, for whereas I had thought that with fair winds I would sail my ship up a cozy narrows, hugging both shores, I found myself instead, despite this certainty, sailing up a wide broad, a waterway which others had so thoroughly dredged out that my little boat was seldom in sight of shore; and only then, but much too late, did I become aware of the reason why my bride had been so loath to take me; but what pained me most was that I durst not complain to anyone about this ridiculous situation in which I found myself. I, of course, could well recognize that fairness dictated that I pay for the deeds which I had done, but recognizing this made me no more patient in the least, much less more virtuous; rather, because I found myself deceived, I resolved to deceive the woman who deceived me, for which reason I fell to grazing on any pasture I could get onto; besides, I was more often in good company at the spa than at home. *In summa*, I let my household go its merry way for a good year; my wife, on the other hand, was just as negligent of it. An ox which I had slaughtered she pickled in brine; and one time when she was supposed to prepare a suckling pig, she went so far as to pluck it as if it were a fowl; and, similarly, she attempted to broil me a crayfish upon a grill and a trout upon a spit. From these few *exempla*[46] one can easily tell how I was otherwise provided for by her, and what is more, she liked to take a nip of my wine, and she shared it with others too, which seemed to me to be a prognostication of my impending financial ruin.

One time I was ambling down the valley with some dandies to visit the lower spa, which was in a village that is called "Nannygoatbrook,"[47] when we encountered an old peasant leading a nanny goat on a tether, which animal he desired to sell; and because it seemed to me that I had seen this man somewhere before, I asked him whence he was coming with this nanny goat. He then doffed his cap and said: "Yer Grayece, I really cain't be a-tellin' ye that." I said: "Surely you did not steal it?" "Nay," the peasant answered, "but I'm a-bringin' it from the little town down in the valley which I jest cain't mention by name to ye in front of this here nanny goat." This moved my companions to laughter, and because my countenance grew pale, they thought that I was vexed or ashamed because the peasant had given me tit for tat. But I had other thoughts in mind, for by the large wart which the peasant, almost like a unicorn, had upon his forehead, I was in fact certain that this man was my Pa from the Spessart Forest; and therefore I was of a mind to play the fortune-teller before I revealed my identity to him and delighted him with such a fine son as the clothes I was wearing showed me to be. Therefore I said to him: "My good old man, is your home not in the Spessart Forest?" "Aye, yer Grayece!" answered the peasant. Then I said: "Did not troopers of horse plunder and burn down your house and farm eighteen years ago?" "Aye, God 'elp us!" answered the peasant. "But 't was not so long ago." I further asked: "Did you not have two children: a full-grown daughter and a young boy who tended the sheep for you?" "Sir," answered my Pa, "the daughter was me own child, but not the boy. I was just a-bringing' 'im up as me foster child." From this I well understood that I was not this uncouth clodhopper's son, which made me happy on the one hand, but also distressed me, because it had fallen my lot that I must needs be a bastard or a foundling. Therefore I asked my Pa where he had come upon this boy, or what reason he had for bringing him up as a foster child. "Ah," he answered, "'t was curious enough how I come to him; the war give him to me, and the war took him away from me again." Because I feared that point might well be made regarding my birth which might redound to my disadvantage, I turned the conversation back to the nanny goat and asked whether he had sold it to the innkeeper's wife for use in her kitchen, which would surprise me, because the guests at the spa were not wont to dine on tough old goat meat. "O no, sir," answered the peasant, "the innkeeper's wife has nanny goats enough herself and won't pay nothing for this here thing. I'm a-bringin' it to the countess who's takin' the waters at the spa, and Dr. Whats-'is-name prescribed for her some herbs that the nanny goat must eat, and the milk she then gives from 'em the doctor takes and puts some other sort of medicine in for the countess, and then she must drink the milk and get well again from it; they say that the countess has no guts, and if the nanny goat helps 'er she'll be a-doin' more for 'er than the doctor and his a-bother-carriers[48] put together." During this narration I reflected upon how I might talk further with the peasant and therefore offered him a thaler more for the nanny goat than the doctor or the countess were willing to give him for it. To this he straightway agreed (for slight profit soon makes people change their minds), but upon the condition that he first give the countess notice that I had offered one thaler more for it; if she were willing to give as much for it as I, then she should have purchase of it; if not, then he would let me have the nanny goat and he would notify me that evening how the business stood.

And so my Pa went his way, and I and my companions ours too, but I could not and would not remain longer with my companions, but instead went back to where I found my Pa again. He still had his nanny goat, because the others were not willing to give as much for it as I was, which astonished me about such rich folks but made me no more niggardly. I took him to the farm which I had just bought, paid him for his nanny goat, and after I had got him half drunk I asked him whence he had got the boy of whom we had talked today. "Ah, sir," said he, "Mansfeld's war[49] gave him to me, and the battle of Nördlingen[50] took him away from me again." I said: "That must be a diverting *histori*!"[51] And I asked him, because we had nothing else to talk about, to tell it to me to while away the time. Then he began, saying: "When Mansfeld lost the battle of Höchst,[52] his fleeing soldiers were scattered far and wide, because they knew not whither they ought to retreat. Many came into the Spessart Forest, because they were seeking woods in which to hide themselves; but while they escaped death upon the plain, they found it with us in the mountains, and because both warring parties deemed it permissible to rob one another and to do one another in upon our land and soil, we were out for their hides too. At that time 't was seldom a peasant went into the woods without a flintlock, and we could not stay at home with our hoes and plows. In that same tumult I came upon a beautiful young noblewoman upon a magnificent horse, in a huge and wild forest not far from my farm, just after I had heard some musket shots not far from that spot. At first I took her to be a man, because she was not riding along sidesaddle but astride the horse, but when I saw her lift both her eyes and her arms heavenwards and heard her cry out in French to God in a pitiable tone of voice, I lowered my flintlock, which I was about to fire off at her, and uncocked it, because her cries and gestures assured me that she was a lady in distress. And so we drew nearer to one another, and when she saw me she said: 'Alas! If you are a Christian, I beg you in the name of God and His mercy, aye, in the name of the Last Judgment, at which we must all account for what we have done and omitted to do, to take me to honorable women who with God's help will deliver me of the burden my body bears!' These words, which reminded me of God in His greatness, together with the sweet way in which she said them and the clearly distressed but still exceeding beautiful and gracious figure of the lady, compelled me to take pity upon her, and I took her horse by the reins and led her through the hedge and shrub to the very densest part of the forest, whither I had fled with my wife, child, hired hands, and cattle. There she gave birth less than a half-hour later to the boy about whom we talked with one another today."

With this my Pa concluded his tale and accepted another drink, for I kindly urged him to; but when he had emptied his glass I asked: "And what happened to the lady after that?" He answered: "When she had in this wise become a mother, she asked me to be the child's godfather and to take the child to be baptized as soon as possible. She also told me her husband's name and hers, so that they might be writ down in the baptismal book, and in doing so she opened her knapsack, in which she indeed had precious things, and gave me, my wife and child, the housemaid, and one other woman there so many presents that we could be well satisfied with her. But while she was doing this and telling us about her husband, she died, right there in front of us, after having first commended her child to our care. Now because there was such turmoil in the country at the time that no one could stay in his home, we were scarce able to find a clergyman to conduct the funeral and to baptize the child; but when both things were finally done, I was commanded by our mayor and our pastor to bring up the child till it was full grown and to take for my effort and expense everything which the lady had left behind, except some rosaries, precious stones, and some jewelry, which I was to keep for the child. And so my wife nursed the child with goat's milk, and we were glad to keep the boy and thought we would give him our girl as a wife when he was full grown. But after the battle of Nördlingen I lost both the girl and the boy and everything we owned."

"You have told me a pretty story," I said to my Pa, "but you have forgotten the best part of it, for you have not said what the names of either the woman or her husband or the child were." "Sir," he answered, "I did not think you would have desired to know them. The noblewoman was named Susanna Ramsey;[53] her husband was Captain Sternfelß von Fuchsheim; and because my own name is Melchior, I had the boy christened Melchior Sternfelß von Fuchsheim and so entered into the baptismal book."

From this I came to understand that I was the son of my hermit and of Governor Ramsay's sister, but alas, much too late, for my parents were both dead, and of my uncle Ramsay[54] I could find out nothing except that the people of Hanau had expelled him and the Swedish garrison, for which reason he went quite mad from anger and frustration.

I well nigh drowned my foster father in wine, and the next day I had his wife fetched too. Now when I revealed my identity to them, they did not believe me till I showed them a black hairy mole which I had upon my chest.

CHAPTER 9

How he suffered the pangs of childbirth and once more came to be a widower

Not long after that I took my foster father along with me and took a ride with him down into the Spessart Forest to collect official papers and documents concerning my family origin and legitimate birth, which I easily obtained from the baptismal book and from my foster father's testimony. I also went straightway to the parson who had been at Hanau and had taken my part there; he gave me, to take with me, proof in writing about where my father had died and that I had been with him up till his death, and later for a time with Mr. Ramsay, the governor of Hanau, under the name Simplicius. Indeed, I had a *notarium*[55] draft from the testimony of witnesses a legal instrument concerning my entire *histori*,[56] for I thought to myself: "Who knows but what you might need it some day?" This journey cost me over four hundred thalers, for on the way back I was seized by a raiding party, robbed of my horse, and plundered, so that my Pa, or foster father, and I got off stripped naked, but scarce with our lives.

Meanwhile things at home were going badly too, for when my wife learned that her husband was to the manor born, she not only played the role of the *grande dame*, she let everything in the house go to wrack and ruin, which I bore in silence because she was big with child. In addition, ill fortune befell my stalls, carrying off the most and the best of my cattle.

All of this I might have been able to tolerate, but, *o mirum*,[57] misfortunes come not singly. At the hour at which my wife gave birth, our maidservant also came down with child. And, in fact, the child which she had looked like me, while the one my wife had was the spitting image of the hired man. In the bargain, that very night the lady whom I mentioned above also left a baby upon my doorstep, with a written report that I was its father, so I suddenly had got three children, and to my mind it appeared as if other ones were going to come crawling out of every corner, which gave me no few grey hairs![58] But it cannot be otherwise when a man follows his bestial lusts in such a godless and reprehensible life as I was leading.

Well, what could I do about it? I was obliged to let them be christened and to let the authorities fine me heavily in the bargain; and because at just that time we were under Swedish rule, whereas I had before served the Emperor, the bills were all higher for me, which bills were outright *praeludia*[59] to my second complete financial ruin. Now whereas so many unfortunate incidents greatly depressed me, my little wife, for her part, simply shrugged them off; indeed, she tormented me day and night in the bargain, because of the fine discovery that had been made upon my doorstep, and because I had been fined so much money. But had she known how things stood with me and the housemaid, she would probably have tortured me all the worse; but that good slut was so honest as to let herself be persuaded, in return for as much money as I should have otherwise been obliged to pay in fines on account of her, to name as the father of her child a dandy who had visited me once in a while the year before and had been at my wedding, but otherwise had no knowledge of her. And she was obliged to leave the house, for my wife suspected of us what I suspected her and the hired man of, and yet she durst not do anything about it, else I should have represented to her that I could not have been with her and the maidservant at one and the same time. Meanwhile I was pained and haunted by the thought that I must needs bring up my hired man's child, and my own children were not going to be my heirs, and that I must needs keep silent in the bargain and be happy that no one else knew aught of it.

With these thoughts I daily tormented myself, but my wife treated herself hourly to wine, for since our wedding she had grown so accustomed to the wine tankard that it was seldom far from her lips, and almost nary a night went by that she did not go to sleep fairly well in her cups. By so doing she soon swilled the life out of her child and caused her innards to grow so inflamed that they soon afterwards failed her and made me a widower once more, which so touched my heart that I almost laughed myself sick at the thought of it.

CHAPTER 10

Tales of sundry peasants about wondrous Lake Mummer

Now when in this wise I found my freedom restored to me again, but my purse pretty well emptied and my large household burdened with many hired hands and cattle, I took in my foster father Melchior as my father, my foster mother (his wife) as my mother, and the bastard child, Simplicius, who had been left upon my doorstep, as my legal heir; and I turned over to the two old folks my house and home, together with my entire estate, except for a few gold coins and trinkets which I had saved and put by in case of direst emergency, for I had found an aversion towards living with or consorting with any woman; so I resolved, because I had fared so ill with them, never again to marry. This old couple, who had scarce their equals *in re rusticorum*,[60] straightway poured my household into a different mold; they got rid of the servants and animals which were of no use and instead got onto the farm what would bring in some money. My old Pa and Ma held out to me hopes of good times and promised that if I simply let them run the place, they would always keep a good horse in the stable for me and would take in so much money that I could at any time drink a measure of wine with one of the honorable townsmen. I straightway saw what manner of folk were now managing my farm; my Pa tilled the fields with the hired hands and chaffered in cattle and wood and pine pitch worse than a Jew, and my foster mother attended to the herd and was able to get and keep together more milk money than ten women of the sort which I had formerly had. In this wise my farm was in a short while sufficiently stocked with all manner of provisions and with animals large and small, so that it was soon esteemed to be the best one in the entire region. I, for my part, spent my time going for walks and devoting myself to contemplating all manner of things, for since I saw that my foster mother was making more money from the wax and honey she got from the bees than my wife had earned before from the cattle, swine, and other livestock, I could easily imagine that she would not miss any other opportunities to turn a profit.

One time I was taking a walk to the spa, more to get a drink of fresh water than to make the acquaintance of the dandies there, as was earlier my wont, for I was beginning to imitate the stinginess of my old parents, who counseled me not to associate with people who uselessly squandered their own and their parents' money. But I fell in with a group of burghers anyway, because they were discoursing upon an unusual thing, namely, Lake Mummer,[61] the bottom of which had never been fathomed, which lake was situated in the vicinity of one of the highest mountains. They had also sent for sundry old peasants who were obliged to tell what the one or the other of them had heard about this wondrous lake, which tales I listened to with great pleasure, though I held them to be so many fables, for they sounded as full of lies as some of the tales of Pliny.

One of them said that if a man take an odd number of things, be they peas or pebbles or something else, and tie them into a handkerchief and lower them into the lake, he would find an even number of things when the handkerchief was opened. Another one, and, in fact, most of these peasants, contended, and supported by examples too, that if a man threw one or more stones into the lake, then no matter how beautiful the day had been before, a terrible storm would straightway come up, with frightful rain, hail, and storm winds.

From this they came to all manner of strange stories about what had happened upon such occasions, and what manner of wondrous *spectra*[62] of earth and water sprites were to be seen then, and what they had talked about with the people. One related that one time, when some herdsmen were tending their herds near the lake, a brown bull rose up out of it and joined the rest of the cattle, but straightway there came a little man following after it to drive it back into the lake, but it had not been willing to obey till the little man had uttered the wish that all man's ills should befall it if it did not return to the lake, at which words the bull and the little man betook themselves back into the lake. Another said that one time, when the lake was frozen over, a peasant drove over the lake with his oxen and some big logs from which planks are cut without any harm befalling him, but when his dog attempted to come along after him, the ice gave way under it and the poor dog fell into the lake and was never seen again. Yet another one maintained, swearing that it was true, that a hunter on the track of some game came by the lake and saw a water sprite sitting upon it who had his whole lap full of sundry kinds of gold coins which he was playing with, and when he attempted to fire at it, the sprite ducked and was heard to say: "If you had asked me to come to your aid in your poverty, I should have been willing to make you and yours rich enough!"

These and other stories of the same sort, all of which seemed to me to be fairy tales with which to amuse children, I listened to, laughed at, and not once did I believe that there could be such a bottomless lake atop a high mountain. But there were yet other peasants, and in fact trustworthy old men, who related that in their and their fathers' time personages of high and noble birth had come up to view that lake and that, for example, a reigning duke in Württemberg had had a raft made and sailed out onto the lake in order to measure its depth, but after the lines with the sounding lead on them had already been lowered nine twine-nets (a measure of length which peasant women in the Black Forest understand better than I or any *geometra*)[63] and had nevertheless still not touched bottom, the raft, contrary to the nature of the wood from which it was made, had begun to sink, so that those who were on it were obliged to abandon their project and save themselves by going ashore, for which reason to this very day pieces of the raft can be seen upon the banks of the lake, as can the royal Württemberg coat of arms and other things carved in stone to commemorate this event. Others proved, citing many witnesses, that an archduke of Austria, etc., had even meant to dig out the lake, but he was counseled by many people not to, and his plans were brought to naught by the pleas of the country folk, for fear the entire country might perish and drown. Moreover, very prominent noble personages had had several barrels full of trout emptied into the lake, but in less than an hour all of them had died before their very own eyes and had floated out the mouth of the lake, despite the fact that the water which flows below the mountain (atop which the lake is situated) and through the valley (from which the lake takes its name) brings forth those fish by nature, and indeed, at the mouth of the lake pours into that same water.

Unheard-of thanks uttered by a patient, which rouses almost holy thoughts in Simplicius

The testimony of these last men almost caused me to give full credence to them and pricked my curiosity so that I resolved to go see this wondrous lake. Of those who had heard all the stories along with me, some expressed one judgment about them and others another one, from which their divers and contradictory opinions were then sufficiently clear. I, to be sure, said that its very name, Lake Mummer, gave it sufficiently to be understood that it was, like a mummer in a masquerade, a creature so disguised that not everyone could fathom its character or its depth, neither of which had been found out either, even though personages of such high station had deigned to concern themselves with it; and with that I went back to that spot where a year before I had seen my late wife for the first time and had sucked in all the sweet poison of love.

There I laid me down in the shade in the green grass, but I paid no heed, as I had before, to what the nightingales were piping; rather, I considered what manner of changes I had undergone since then. Then I saw in my mind's eye that at this very spot I had taken the first step which turned me from a free man into a slave of love; that since then I had turned from an officer into a peasant, from a wealthy peasant into an impoverished nobleman, from Simplicius into Melchior, from a widower into a husband, from a husband into a cuckold, and from a cuckold back into a widower; *item*, that I turned from a peasant's son into the son of a proper soldier, and forthwith back into the son of my Pa. Then I recollected how my *fatum*[64] had robbed me of Trueheart and in return for him had provided me with an old married couple; I thought about the God-fearing life and death of my father, about the pitiable death of my mother, and also about the manifold changes to which I had been subjected my entire life long; and I could not refrain from weeping. And when I recollected how much fine money I had possessed and had squandered all the days of my life, and was indeed beginning to regret it, two fine topers, or wine bibbers (who had got the *cholica*[65] into their limbs and were using both the baths and the spa), came along and sat down quite close to me, because it was a good place to rest; and each complained to the other about his need, because they thought that they were alone. The one of them said: "My doctor sent me hither, because he despaired of curing me, or because, among other things, I was to repay the innkeeper for the keg of butter he recently sent the doctor. I wish that I had never in my life laid eyes upon him, or that he had straightway in the beginning counseled me to come to this spa; then I should have either more money or better health than I do now, for this spa is really doing me good." "Ah," the other one answered, "I thank God that He did not give me more money than I have, for had my doctor known that I still had more in reserve, he would have waited a long while to send me to the spa; rather, I should have been obliged first to share my money with him and his apothecaries (who for that reason grease his palm every year) even if I should have laid me down and died in the process. These swindlers do not counsel folks like us to go to a healthful place till they either do not think that they can help us any more, or do not think that we have anything left of which they can fleece us. To tell the truth, anyone who becomes involved with them and whom they know to have money in reserve must needs pay them to keep him from getting well."

These two heaped much more abuse upon their *doctores*,[66] but I shan't tell all of it, for otherwise the *medici*[67] might grow hostile towards me and in the future give me a purgative which might drive my soul out of my body. I relate this tale only because the last patient, with his expression of thanks that God had not given him more money, so consoled me that I put out of my mind all the trials and tribulations which I was suffering at that time on account of money. I resolved to seek neither honor nor money any more, nor anything else which the world loves. Indeed, I resolved to philosophize and to make an effort to lead a God-fearing life, and particularly to repent of my unwillingness to do penance, and to make so bold as to climb to the highest stages of virtue, like my late father.

CHAPTER 12

How Simplicius journeys with the sylphis[68] into the centrum terrae[69]

The desire to see Lake Mummer increased within me when I learned from my foster father that he too had been there and also knew the way thither; but when he heard that I, moreover, also desired to go thither, he said; "And what will you bring back from there, even if you go thither? You and I will see nothing but a body of water which is the spitting image of a pond lying in the middle of a large forest. And when you have found out that what it is now your pleasure to do brings you, in fact, displeasure, then you will have, for all your pains, nothing but remorse, sore feet (for one assuredly cannot go thither on horseback), and as far to walk hither as it was to walk thither. No one could have brought me to go thither, had I not been obliged to flee thither when Doc Daniel (he meant *le duc d'Anguin*) marched down to Philippsburg with his troops."[70] My curiosity, however, was such that I ignored his admonition and instead hired a fellow to lead me thither. Now when my Pa saw that I was in earnest, he said that since the oats were already planted and there was neither hoeing nor reaping to do on the farm, he would go with me and show me the way, for he loved me so much that he was loath to let me out of his sight; and because the folks thereabouts believed that I was his real son, he took great pride in me and behaved towards me and everyone else the way a poor and common man might behave towards a son whom fortune, with or without any assistance from him, had made into a great lord.

And so we rambled with one another over hill and dale and came to Lake Mummer before we had been walking six hours, for my foster father was as hale and hearty of foot as a youth. There we devoured what food and drink we had taken with us, for the long distance and the height of the mountain upon which the lake lies had made us fatigued and famished. After we had restored ourselves, however, I went to look at the lake and straightway found in it divers pieces of hewn wood which my Pa and I took to be the *rudera*[71] of the Württemberg raft. I took, or measured, the length and breadth of the water by means of geometry, because it was quite difficult to walk around the lake and measure it by paces or feet, and I sketched its shape, reduced in scale, in my notebook; and when I was finished with that, particularly since the sky was still bright and the air completely still and comfortable in temperature, I set about testing the truth of the tale that a storm would arise if a man threw a stone into the lake, since I had already found, by the mineral taste of the water, that the allegation was true that no trout could live in the lake.

And in order to make this test I walked down along the lake to the left to that spot where the water (which was otherwise as clear as crystal) seemed to be as black as pitch, because of the enormous depth of the lake there, and therefore looked so terrifying that one is horrified by the mere sight of it. There I proceeded to throw into it the largest stones I could carry; my foster father, my Pa, not only did not help me, he warned me and begged me as much as he could to desist from doing it; but I diligently continued my labor, and whatever stones were too large and too heavy for me to carry, I rolled to the water's edge, till I had dropped over thirty of them into the lake. Then the sky became covered with black clouds in which frightful thundering was heard, so that my foster father, who was standing on the other side of the lake at its mouth and was lamenting over my labors, cried out to me that I really should rescue myself, so that the rain and the terrible storm not overtake us or an even greater misfortune befall us. But I answered him in return: "Pa, I am going to remain and await the end, even if it should fall to raining halberds!" "O yes," said my Pa, "you're behaving like all rash youths, who do not care a fig if the entire world be destroyed!"

Now while I was listening to his scolding, I did not take my eyes off the depths of the lake, thinking that I might perchance see some bubbles or air pockets rise up from the bottom of it, as generally happens when stones are thrown into deep waters, both still ones and free-flowing ones. But I espied nothing of the sort; rather, I saw far away in the *abyssum*[72] some creatures, which in shape reminded me of frogs, fluttering about in the water and spinning round like fireworks from a Roman candle which has risen up into the air and is successfully achieving its desired effect. And as these things came nearer with each passing moment, they seemed, to my eyes, to grow larger with each passing moment and all the more similar in shape to human beings, for which reason there came over me, first, great astonishment and, finally because I had them so near to me, a feeling of horror and terror. "O!" I then said to myself in fright and astonishment, and yet so loud that my Pa, who was standing on the other side of the lake, could hear it clearly (even though it was thundering frightfully), "How great are the Creator's wondrous works, even those in the bowels of the earth and the depths of the waters!" I had scarce uttered these words when one of these *sylphis* was already on top of the water and answered: "Look you, you are acknowledging this before you have even seen anything of it. Whatever would you say, were you ever to be *in centro terrae* and see our dwelling, which your curiosity has disturbed?" Meanwhile even more water sprites of this sort came up here and there, just like little diver-geese, all of which creatures were looking at me and bringing back the stones which I had thrown in, at which I was quite astonished. And the first and foremost of them, whose clothing gleamed like pure gold and silver, threw to me a shiny stone as big as a pigeon's egg and as green and transparent as an emerald, saying: "Take this jewel, so that you will be able to tell something about us and this lake!" And I had scarce picked it up and put in into my pocket when I felt precisely as if the air were about to stifle me to death or to drown me, for which reason I could no longer hold myself upright and tumbled around like a skein of yarn unwinding and finally fell into the lake. But as soon as I got into the water, I recovered again, and from the power of the stone which I had on me I breathed the water as if it were air. I was also straightway able, with slight effort, to move about in the water as well as the water sprites, for which reason I went down into the abyss with them, which sprites reminded me of nothing more than a flock of birds letting themselves down, in a roundabout way, from the uppermost part of the air to earth.

Since my Pa had seen this wonder in part (namely, what happened above the water) and my abrupt disappearance, he trundled away from the lake and homewards as if his head were on fire. There he told everyone what had transpired, principally that at the height of the thunderstorms the water sprites had carried the stones which I had thrown into the lake back up again and had put them back where they had been before, but, on the other hand, had taken me down into the lake with them. Some believed him, but most took it to be a fable; others imagined that I had drowned myself in the lake, like a second Empedocles of Agrigento (who leaped into Mount Aetna so that everyone would think, when he was nowhere to be found, that he had flown up into heaven),[73] and that I had commanded my father to give out such fables about me in order to make an immortal name for myself. They said they had for some while seen clearly by my melancholy humor that I had been half desperate. Others would have liked to believe, had they not known about my great physical strength, that my Pa had murdered me himself, so that he, greedy old man that he was, would be rid of me and might be sole master of my farm, so that at this time, in both the spa and in the countryside thereabouts, folks could talk and conjecture about nothing but Lake Mummer, me and my disappearance, and my foster father.

CHAPTER 13

The prince of Lake Mummer tells of the nature and origin of the sylphs

Pliny writes at the end of the second book about the *geometra* Dionysius Dorus[74] that his friends found in his grave a letter which he had written and in which he reported that he had gone from his grave to the midmost *centrum* of the earth and had found that the distance thither was 42,000 *stadia*.[75] However, the prince of Lake Mummer, who was accompanying me and had fetched me from the surface of the earth as described above, told me for sure that from the *centro terrae*[76] to the air, through one half the earth, it was exactly 900 German miles,[77] whether they desired to go to Germany or to its *antipodibus*,[78] and that these journeys they were obliged to take through lakes of that sort, of which there were as many in the world as there are days in the year, and the ends, or abysses, of all of them converge at the residence of their king. Now this great distance we traversed in less than an hour, so that with our rapid journey we ceded very little, or nothing at all, to the moon's journey round the earth, and yet this happened without any difficulty at all, so that I not only felt no fatigue but could discuss, during this gentle downward-journey, all manner of things with this prince of Lake Mummer; for when I perceived that he was friendly, I asked him to what end they were taking me with them such a long, perilous, and, for all human beings, unusual way. He then answered me quite diffidently that a way was not long which one could walk in an hour, and that it was not dangerous because I had him and his companions along, together with the stone which they had given me to hold, but the fact that it seemed unusual to me was in no way surprising; were it otherwise, he would not only not have fetched me, at the command of his king, who desired to talk with me about something; rather, he said, I should straightway look at the strange wonders of nature under the earth and in the waters, at which I had been astonished even before, when I was upon the earth's surface, before I had scarce seen anything of them. Then I further asked him if he would report to me to what end the generous Creator had made so many wondrous lakes, since they, it seemed to me, were of no use to anyone, but, much rather, could bring harm. He answered: "It is right that you ask about what you do not know or understand. These lakes were created for three reasons. For, firstly, all seas as have names, and particularly great *Oceanus*,[79] are affixed to the earth by them, as if they were nails. Secondly, the waters are moved by us (for this is our task), out of the *abyssu*[80] of the *Oceanus* and into all the springs upon the earth's surface, through these lakes (just as water is pumped through pipes, hoses, or cylinders in the fountains which you human beings use), from which then all the springs in the entire world flow, and large and small bodies of flowing water arise, by which the earth is moistened, plants are refreshed, and both man and beast are given to drink. Thirdly, that as God's reasonable creatures we are supposed to live in them, carry out the tasks assigned to us, and praise God, the Creator of all things, in His great and wondrous works. It is to this end that we and these lakes were created and will continue to exist till Judgment Day. And when, towards the end of time, we are obliged, for one reason or another, to cease our work, which we were created and commanded to do by God and Nature, then the world must needs perish through fire, which, however, cannot occur till, and unless, you first lose the moon (*donec auferatur luna, Psal. 71*),[81] Venus, or Mars, and the morning and evening star, for the *generationes fructu- & animalium*[82] must first perish and all waters disappear, before the earth can be spontaneously ignited by the heat of the sun, then burn to cinders, and regenerate. But it does not behoove us to know this, and it is known to God alone, except for what we assume and what your *chymici*[83] prattle about on the basis of their art."

When I heard him talk this way and cite Holy Scripture, I asked him whether they were mortal creatures who had hopes for a future life after departing this world, or whether they were spirits who would simply perform their assigned duties for as long as the world existed. To this he answered: "We are not spirits but mortal folk who are indeed endowed with rational souls which, however, must needs perish and die together with our bodies. God is indeed so wondrous in His works that no creature can put it into words, but I shall tell you *simpliciter*[84] as much concerning our nature as you need to know, so that you may grasp from that how far we are to be deemed different from God's other creatures. The holy angels are spirits made in God's image—just, reasonable, free, chaste, bright, clear, swift, and immortal—created to that end that they laud, exalt, honor, and praise God in eternal joy; but in this temporal world they serve God's church here upon earth, carrying out commands most hallowed and divine, for which reason they are sometimes called *nuntii*,[85] and as many hundred thousands of thousand millions of them were created at one time as was pleasing to Divine Wisdom; but after from amongst their great number indescribably many of them who had become vain about their high nobility had, on account of pride, fallen from grace, your earliest ancestors were created by God in His own image, with a reasonable and immortal soul, and were endowed with bodies, so that they might multiply amongst themselves till their race replaced the number of fallen angels. Now to this end the world was created, with all the other living creatures, so that man—till his race had sufficiently increased so that the number of fallen angels could be replaced by it—might live upon it, praise God, and avail himself of all the other things which God had created upon the entire earth (over which God had made man master) to God's honor and for the preservation of his, man's, body, which required sustenance. At that time man differed from the holy angels in that he was burdened with an earthly body and knew not what was good and what was evil, and therefore could not be as strong and swift as an angel; on the other hand, man had nothing in common with the mindless beasts of the field either; but after he subjected his body to death through his fall from grace and in the Garden of Eden, we esteemed him to be in the middle betwixt the holy angels and the mindless beasts, for while a holy disembodied soul of an earth-bound but heaven-minded man had about it all the properties of a holy angel, the soulless body of an earth-bound man (after it putrefies) is like any other carcass of a mindless beast. We ourselves, however, we esteem ourselves to be in the middle betwixt you and all other living creatures in the world, since, though we have reasonable souls like you, they nevertheless die off straightway with our bodies, just as the living spirits of mindless beasts disappear at their deaths. To be sure, we have been informed that you have been most highly ennobled by the eternal Son of God, by Whom we too were created, since He espoused the cause of your race, satisfied Divine Justice, appeased the wrath of God, and gained for you eternal blessedness once more, all of which makes your race superior to ours. But I am talking about eternity here, and I understand nothing about it, because we are not capable of enjoying it, but enjoy instead only this temporal world, in which the most generous Creator has blessed us sufficiently, as, for example, with common sense; with the ability to recognize God's most holy will, insofar as we are in need of it; with healthy bodies, long life, noble freedom; and with sufficient knowledge, art, and understanding of all natural things; and, finally, what is most important of all, we are not subject to any sin, and therefore not to any punishment or to the wrath of God either, indeed, not even to the slightest illness of the body, all of which I tell you in such detail, and for which reason I have also made mention of the holy angels, the earth-bound humans, and the mindless beasts, so that you might understand me all the better." I answered that I could nevertheless not get it through my head. Since they were not guilty of misdeed and were therefore not subject to any punishment either, for what, then, did they have need of a king? *Item*, how could they boast of freedom if they were subject to a king? *Item*, how could they be born and die if they were so constituted as not to suffer any pain or illness? Then the little prince answered that they did not have a king in order that he should administer *justitiam*[86] or that they should serve him, but rather that he directed their work the way the queen bee in a beehive does. And whereas their wives felt no pleasure *in coitu*,[87] they were not subject to any pain when they gave birth either, which I could to some extent adduce and believe from the example of cats, which, of course, suffer pain when they conceive but sensual pleasure when they give birth. Nor did they die in pain either, or from the infirmities of old age, much less from illness, but rather as a light is extinguished when its time to burn is over; and indeed, both their bodies and their souls then disappeared. Compared to the freedom which he claimed to possess, the freedom of the very greatest monarch was to be accounted as nothing at all, indeed, not so much as a shadow, for they could not be killed, either by us or by other creatures, or be compelled to do what they did not desire to do, much less be taken captive, because they could go through fire, water, air, and earth without effort or fatigue (of which they knew nothing). Then I said: "If that is your condition, then your race has been blessed and ennobled by our Creator far more than ours." "Alas, no!" answered the prince. "You commit a sin if you believe that, for you are accusing God in His goodness of something which is not true; for you are far more blessed than we are, since you are created for eternal blessedness, and to look without surcease upon the countenance of God, in which blessed state one of you who is blessed enjoys in a single instant more joy and bliss than our entire race, from the beginning of creation till the Day of Judgment." I said: "Well, what does that profit those who are damned?" He answered me with a question of his own: "What can God in His goodness do if one of you forgets himself, becomes like the other creatures of the world, gives free rein to his carnal desires, and thereby makes himself no more than a mindless beast of the field—indeed, makes himself, by his disobedience towards God, more like the infernal spirits than the blessed ones? Those damned souls' eternal torment, into which they plunged themselves, does not in the least diminish the grandeur and nobility of their race, since in their temporal life they could have just as well achieved eternal bliss as others, had they but been willing to tread the prescribed path which leads to it."

CHAPTER 14

What further matters Simplicius discussed on the way with this prince, and what wondrous and strange things he heard and saw

I told the little prince that because I had more occasion upon earth anyway to hear about this *materia*[88] than I had made use of, I should like to ask him if he would tell me instead the reason why a great storm arose at the times when a man threw stones into these lakes, for I remembered having heard the very same thing about Lake Pilatus[89] in Switzerland and having read such-like about Lake Camarina in Sicily, from which originated the saying *camarinam movere*.[90] He answered: "Because anything which is heavy does not stop falling towards the *centrum terrae* when it is thrown into the water, unless it hit bottom on the way where it can remain, and since all these lakes are bottomless and open all the way down to the *centrum*, the stones that are thrown into them necessarily and naturally fall into our dwelling place and could not but remain there if we did not get them away from us and back to the place whence they came; and so we do this with violence so that mischief-makers who are wont to throw them into the lakes may be frightened and held in check, which is one of the principal tasks for which we were created. Were we, however, to let stones be tossed in and got out again without thunderstorms of that sort, it would finally come to the point where we would have to do solely with mischief-makers who, to amuse themselves, would daily be sending stones down to us from all parts of the world. And from this single task which we have to perform, you can perceive the necessity for our race, because if the stones were not carried out by us, as described above, and yet every day so many of them were put into so many divers lakes located here and there in the world, and dropped to the *centrum terrae* where we dwell, then in the end the structures by which the sea is affixed to the earth could not but be destroyed, and the passages through which the springs are led from the abyss of the sea back and forth to the earth's surface would also be stopped up, which would then bring with it nothing but chaos and the end of the entire world."

I expressed my thanks for this communication and said: "Because I understand that through these lakes your race supplies water to all the springs and rivers upon the entire earth, you could doubtless also report as to why not all waters are the same, either in smell, taste, etc., and in power and effect, despite the fact that all of them (as I understand it) take their substance originally from the abyss of the great *oceanus*, into which all waters pour back; for some springs are lovely mineral springs and beneficial to the health; some are, of course, sour and unpleasant, and harmful to drink; and others are even deadly and poisoned, like the spring in Arcadia, with whose waters Jolla is said to have poisoned Alexander the Great;[91] some springs are lukewarm, some boiling hot, and others ice cold; some have water which eats through iron like *aqua fort*,[92] such as the one in Zepusio, and county of Zips[93] in Hungary; other, by contrast, have water which heals wounds, like one which is said to be in Thessaly;[94] some waters turn to stone, others to salt, and some to vitriol. The lake at Zircknitz in Corinthia[95] has water only in the wintertime and is, in fact, dry in the summer; the spring in Aengstlen[96] flows only in the summertime, and then only at certain hours, when cattle are being watered; the Schändle Brook at Ober-Nähenheim[97] does not flow till a misfortune is about to befall the land; and the *Fluvius Sabbaticus*[98] ceases to flow every seventh day; which things I could not but find most extremely wondrous when I thought about them and could not determine a cause for them."

Then the prince answered that all these things, without exception, had their natural causes, which had been sufficiently surmised, deduced, and revealed by natural scientists of our race from the divers smells, tastes, powers, and effects of the waters. When a stream of water flowed out through all manner of stone from their dwelling place to its mouth (which mouth we call a 'spring'), then, to be sure, it remained cold and sweet; but if it passed on the way through *metalla*[99] (for the great belly of the earth is inwardly not of the same character in one place as in another), since there is gold, silver, copper, tin, lead, iron, quicksilver, etc. there, or through the *semi-mineralia*,[100] namely, sulphur, salt in all its varieties, such as *sal naturale*,[101] *sal gemmae*,[102] *sal nativum*,[103] *sal radicum*,[104] *sal nitrum*,[105] *sal ammoniacum*,[106] *sal petrae*,[107] etc., white, red, yellow, and green colors, vitriol, *marchasita aurea, argentea, plumbea, ferrea*,[108] *lapis lazuli*,[109] *alumen*,[110] *arsenicum*,[111] *antimonium*,[112] *risigallum*,[113] *Electrum naturale*,[114] Chrysocolla,[115] *sublimatum*,[116] etc., then it took unto itself their taste, smell, character, strength, and effect, so that it was either beneficial or harmful to human beings. And for just that reason, he said, we have such divers salts, for some are good and some bad. "In Cervia[117] and Commachio[118] the water is rather black, in Memphis reddish in color, in Sicily snow white; Centuripean water[119] is purple in color, and Cappadocian[120] yellow-hued.[121] As concerns the warm waters," he said, "they take their heat from the fire which burns in the earth and which, like our lakes, has its air holes and chimneys here and there, as one can see from the famous Mount Aetna in Sicily, Hekla in Iceland, Gunung-Api on the Banda archipelago, and many others. As regards Lake Zircknitz, however, its water is seen in the summertime at the *antipodibus* of Corinthia, and the Aengstlen spring can be encountered at other places upon the earth's surface at certain hours and times of the year and day, doing precisely the same thing it performs for the Swiss; the same holds true for Schändle Brook in Ober-Nähenheim. These divers springs are led and directed this way by our race of people, in accordance with the will and command of God, so that His praise may thereby be increased amongst you human beings. As far as the *Fluvius Sabbaticus* in Syria is concerned, in our dwelling place we are wont, when we celebrate the seventh day, to rest and repose in its source and channel, since that is the most delightful spot in our entire *aequatoris*,[122] for which reason, then, that river cannot flow as long as we are tarrying there to honor the Creator."

After this conversation I asked the prince whether it might also be possible for him to take me back to the world through a lake other than Lake Mummer, to another spot upon earth. "Of course." he answered. "Why not, if it be God's will? For in this wise our ancestors in ancient times took to America some Canaanites who were fleeing the sword of Joshua and had in desperation thrown themselves into such a lake, for which reason their descendants, to this very day, are able to point to the lake from which, in the beginning, their first ancestors originated." Now when I saw that he was astonished at my astonishment, just as if he knew not that his tale was astonishing enough, I asked him if they were not also astonished when they saw something strange and unusual in the behavior of us human beings. Then he answered: "Nothing astonishes us more about you than the fact that you, who have been created to enjoy after death eternal blessedness and unending heavenly joys, let yourselves be so deluded by temporal and earthly sensual delights (which are, in fact, no more without pain and displeasure than the rose is without thorns) that you thereby lose your right to heaven, rob yourselves of the opportunity to look with joy upon the most hallowed countenance of God, and plunge down to join the fallen angels in eternal damnation! Ah, if our race were but in your place, how each of us would strive to pass better than you the test in this instant of your vain and fleeting temporal existence! For the life that you have is not life; rather, your life, or death, is given you only when you leave this temporal existence, and what you call life is, as it were, but a moment or instant which is granted you, in which to recognize God and draw nigh to Him, so that He may take you unto His bosom. Therefore, we hold the world to be God's touchstone, for just as the rich man uses a touchstone to test gold and silver, God uses fleeting temporal existence to test men; and after He has measured their value, or after He has purified them by fire, He places the good and genuine pieces of gold and silver into His heavenly treasure chest and throws the evil and false ones into the eternal fire, which divine judgment your Saviour and our Creator has sufficiently revealed and preached to you in the parable of the wheat and the tares."

CHAPTER 15

What the king said to Simplicius and Simplicius said to the king

This was the end of our conversation, because we were drawing near the seat of the king, into whose presence I was brought without ceremony or any waste of time at all. Now there I indeed had cause to be astonished at His Majesty, since I saw there neither a well appointed royal court nor any pomp and circumstance, indeed, no chancellor or privy councillors, or any interpreters, or any gentlemen-at-arms and royal guardsmen, indeed, not even a court fool, or cook, steward, page, or any court favorite or toady; rather, there hovered about him the princes of all the lakes there are in the entire world, each dressed in the native costume of the land into which the lake under their command emptied from the *centro terrae*; thus I saw together figures which were the spitting images of Chinese and Africans, of troglodytes[123] and folk from Nova Zembla,[124] of Tatars and Mexicans, of Samoyedes[125] and Moluccahs,[126] indeed, even of those who dwell under the *polis arctico* and *antarctico*,[127] which was indeed a strange sight to behold. The two who were inspectors for Wild Lake[128] and Black Lake[129] were, to be sure, clad like the one escorting me, because their lakes were situated nearest to Lake Mummer, and the one who had jurisdiction over Lake Pilatus appeared with a fine beard and a pair of wide breeches, like any respectable Swiss; and the one who had responsibility for Lake Camarina was in both clothing and gesture so like a Sicilian that one would have sworn by all that is holy that he had never set foot outside Sicily and did not know a word of any language but Italian. And I also saw, as in a book of costumes, figures who looked like Persians, Japanese, Muscovites, Finns, Lapps, and members of all other nations in the entire world.

I had no need to stand upon ceremony, for the king himself addressed me in my own language, his first words to me being the question: "For what reason did you make so bold as to send in quite impudent manner a pile of stones down to us?" I answered succinctly: "Because in our land anyone may knock upon a closed door." Then he said: "And what if you were to reap the rewards of your importunate curiosity?" I answered: "I can receive no greater punishment than death, and because I have seen and experienced, since I threw the stones into the lake, so many wonders which not one out of many millions of men has ever had the good fortune to witness, my dying would be of slight consequence to me, and my death could not be accounted a punishment at all." "Alas! What wretched blindness!"

said the king in reply, thereby lifting up his eyes like one who is looking heavenwards in astonishment, and continued: "You human beings can die but once, and you Christians ought not to be able to go through death with good cheer till you are assured that, as a result of your faith in and love for God, you may hope beyond any doubt that your souls will really look upon the countenance of the Almighty as soon as your dying body has closed its eyes. But for the nonce I have something far different to talk to you about."

Then he said: "It has been asserted to me that mortals, and particularly you Christians, foresee in the immediate future the Day of Judgment, because it will not only fulfill all prophecies, particularly those which the sybils left behind, but also because all who live upon the earth are so terribly given to vice that Almighty God will no longer hesitate to put an end to the world. Now because our race must needs perish together with the world and be consumed by fire (even though water is our element), we are no little horrified by the approach of this terrible time; we have therefore had you brought to us to hear what we might perchance have to hope or fear in this regard. To be sure, we have as yet been unable to deduce anything of the sort from the stars, nor have we noted anything upon earth that portends such imminent change. We must therefore seek reports from those to whom their Saviour Himself has heretofore left behind some portents of His future; we therefore most humbly request of you that you be so kind as to tell us whether or not there still exists upon the earth that faith which the future Judge will scarce find any longer when He arrives." I answered the king that he had asked me things which were much too lofty for me to answer; much less did I know the future; and in particular, the time of the arrival of the Lord was known to God alone. "Well then," answered the king in return, "tell me how the estates of the world are plying their trades, so that from that I may conjecture either that the world and our race are about to perish, or that, as I have said, I and mine are to enjoy a long life and happy reign. In return I shall let you see what till now few men have got to see, and I shall afterwards let you leave with a present which will make you happy your entire life long, if you but tell me the truth." Now when I then kept silent and was considering what to say, the king continued: "Commence now, commence with the highest estate and conclude with the lowest one! You really must, if you desire ever to return to the surface of the earth again!"

I answered: "If I am to commence with the highest estate, then I should by rights begin with the clergy. They are now generally all, no matter what church they may belong to, as Eusebius described them in a sermon:[130] namely, they uprightly scorn sloth and shun sensual pleasure; in their profession they are filled with the desire to labor; they are patient of disdain, impatient of worldly honor, poor in earthly goods and wealth, rich in conscience, humble when praised for their merits, and proud when they confront vice. And just as they endeavor to serve God alone and to bring others into the Kingdom of God, more by their own example than by words, so also the mighty rulers and supervisors in the secular realm are intent upon sweet *Justitiam*[131] alone, which they most fairly, without regard to person, dispense and bestow from the bench of justice to everyone, rich and poor alike. The *theologi*[132] are veritable Jeromes[133] and Bedes,[134] the cardinals genuine Borromaeuses,[135] the bishops Augustines,[136] the abbots the equals of Hilarion[137] and Pachomus,[138] and the other clerics altogether like unto the congregations of hermits in the Theban wilderness. Merchants engage in trade not because of greed or for the sake of profit, but so that they may provide their fellowmen with the wares which they bring from distant lands to this end. Innkeepers do not keep their hostelries in order to become rich, but so that the hungry, the thirsty, and the traveler may find refreshment in them, and so that they may provide accommodations, as a work of charity, to those who are tired and fatigued. And the *medicus* seeks not his own profit, but the health of his patient, which is the goal of the apothecary too. Artisans know nothing of cheats, deceits, and lies, but rather make every effort to supply their customers as best they can with lasting and honest work. Tailors blanch at the thought of stealing, and weavers remain so impoverished as a consequence of their honesty that they have scarce a pot to piss in or a window to throw it out of. Usury is unknown, and the well-to-do, out of Christian charity and quite unbidden, come to the aid of the poor; and when a poor man cannot pay without noticeable harm and diminution to his subsistence, the rich man voluntarily forgives him his debt. One detects no pride, for everyone knows and keeps in mind the fact that he is mortal. One sees no envy, for each knows and acknowledges his fellow man as one who is made in God's image. No one grows angry at another, because they know that Christ suffered and died for the sake of all mankind. One never hears of any unchasteness or inordinate carnal lusts; rather, whatever of the like transpires is done because of the desire and love of begetting children. One finds no sots or drunkards; rather, when one man drinks to another's health they are both content with no more drink than it takes to achieve the tipsiness which befits a good Christian. There is no sloth about attending church service, for everyone exhibits true zeal and eagerness by attempting to honestly serve God before all others, and for just that reason are there now such burdensome wars on earth, because each side believes that the other is not serving God properly. There are no misers, only folk who are frugal; no spendthrifts, only generous souls; no raiders who rob and ruin people, only soldiers who are protecting their fatherland; no wanton lazy beggars, only folks who scorn riches and love voluntary poverty; no hoarders of wine and corn, only cautious men who amass superfluous stores of wine and grain for use by the people in a possible future emergency."

CHAPTER 16

Some new tidings from the depths of the unfathomable sea which is called the Mare del Zur,[139] or the peaceful, quiet sea

I paused for a bit and considered what else I might bring up, but the king said that he had already heard so much that he desired to know nothing further; if I desired, he said, his minions would take me directly back to the place where they had found me, but ("for I well see," said he, "that you are rather curious") if I desired to view one thing or another in his realm which creatures of my ilk would without doubt seldom see, then I would be escorted safely in his jurisdiction to wherever I desired to go, and then he was going to give me leave to go and in parting give me a present with which I should be well satisfied. Now since I could not come to any decision and answer him, he turned to some of his subjects who were about to betake themselves to the bottom of the Mare del Zur and fetch food from there, as from a garden or from a hunt, and he said to them: "Take him along and bring him back soon, so that he may be put back onto the earth's surface before the day is out." To me he said, however, that in the meantime I might think about something which it was in his power to give me in recompense and as a lasting memento to take back with me to earth. And so I whisked away with the *sylphis* through a hole which was several hundred miles long, till we came to the bottom of the peaceful ocean mentioned above; upon it stood coral spikes as tall as oak trees, from which they took along what coral was not yet hard and colored, for it was their wont to eat this, as we eat young stags' antlers. Then we saw snails' shells as high as a good-sized turret and as wide as a barn door; *item*, pearls as large as your fist, which they ate instead of eggs; and too many other much stranger wonders of the sea to tell about. The bottom of the ocean was bestrewn everywhere with emeralds, turquoises, rubies, diamonds, sapphires, and other such stones, generally as large as the large stones on earth that lie here and there in flowing brooks; here and there one saw enormous bluffs rising many miles in height, which protruded out of the water and formed lovely islands in the sea; these were adorned all round with all manner of pretty and wondrous sea growths and were inhabited by many kinds of strange crawling, standing, and moving creatures, just as the earth's surface is with men and animals, whereas the fishes, of which we saw a great many, large and small and of innumerable different kinds, drifted about above us and reminded me, in fact, of the many kinds of birds which on earth fly merrily about in the air in the springtime and in the fall. And because there was just then a full moon and a clear sky (for the sun was at the time over the horizon, so that I and the antipodes at the time had night, and the Europeans day), I could see through the water up to the moon and the stars, and to the *polo antarctico*,[140] at which I could not but be astonished. And the one into whose care I had been placed told me that if we were to have day as well as night, then everything would be even more wondrous to me, for then one could see from afar how there were at the bottom of the sea, as there are on land, beautiful mountains and valleys, which, however, are more beautiful than the most beautiful landscape on the earth's surface. And when he saw that I wondered at him and at all who were with him, because they were dressed like Peruvians, Brazilians, Mexicans, and folk from the isles *de los latronos*[141] and yet spoke my mother tongue so well, he said that they could speak no more than one language, which language, however, all people upon the entire earth understood in their own language, as they understood them in turn, which was because their race had had no part in the great folly which had transpired at the Tower of Babel.

Now when the convoy had been sufficiently provendered, we returned through another cave from that sea to the *centrum terrae*; on the way I told some of them that I had thought that the center of the earth was hollow in the inside, in which hollow part the *pygmaei*[142] ran about, as on a treadmill, and thereby turned the entire globe so that all of it would be beshone by the sun, which, in the opinion of Aristarchus and Copernicus,[143] stood motionless in the midst of the heavens, for which simplemindedness I was heartily derided and told that I should put out of my mind as an idle dream both the opinion of those two learned men and what I myself had imagined. Instead of these thoughts, they said, I should consider what manner of gift I was going to desire of their king, so that I might not come back to the surface of the earth empty-handed. I answered that the wondrous things which I had hitherto seen had so completely put me beside myself that I could think of nothing, and I asked them to be so kind as to counsel me what I ought to ask of the king. My idea would be (since he had all the springs of the world under his direction) to ask him for a mineral spring for my farm, like the one which had recently sprung up on its own in Germany and which likewise produced only sweet water. The prince, or regent, of the quiet ocean and its caves answered that this would not be in his king's power, and even if he could, and were gladly willing to gratify my desire, springs of that sort would not remain in existence for long anyway, etc. I asked him if he would candidly tell me the reason for this; then he answered: "Here and there upon the earth there are empty places which little by little fill up with all manner of metals, because they are generated there by an *exhalatione humida*;[144] *viscosa & crassa*; and when such generation occurs, sometimes water from the *centro*, from which all springs are driven, is pressed through the cracks in the *Marchasitae aureae vel argentae*,[145] which water then remains for many hundreds of years in and around the *metallis*[146] and acquires the metals' noble character and healing properties; then, when the water from the *centro*, with passing time, increases more and more and through its strong pressure seeks and finds an outlet on the earth's surface, then the water which has been locked for so many hundreds and thousands of years betwixt the metals and has acquired their powers is pushed out first and then exerts upon human bodies that wondrous effect which one sees in such new medicinal springs; now as soon as this water, which was kept so long amongst the metals, has flowed out, ordinary water follows, which of course goes through the same passageways, but in its rapid flow cannot acquire any of the virtues or powers of the metals, and therefore cannot be as healthful as the first water was either." If I (he said) was so interested in good health, then I should request of his king that he recommend me for a cure to the king of the *salamandrae*,[147] with whom he was on good terms; this king could treat the *corpore* and equip them with a precious stone, so that they could not burn up in any fire, like a strange cloth which we had on earth[148] and were wont to cleanse by fire when it had got dirty. Then one put such a person, like a slimy, stinking old tobacco pipe, into the midst of the fire, and then all the evil humors and noxious vapors are eaten up, and the patient comes out as young, lively, healthy, and new-created as if he had taken the elixir of Theophrastus.[149] I knew not whether the fellow was chaffing me or whether he was in earnest, but I thanked him for the confidential communication and said that I feared this cure would be too hot for me, since I was a *cholericus*.[150] Nothing would be more to my liking than if I could bring to earth with me a rare healing spring for my fellowmen, which would be of use to them and do honor to their king, and which would make my name immortal and forever remembered. Then the prince answered me that if I were seeking such a spring, he would say a good word on my behalf, though the king's character was such that he paid equally little heed to whether honor or disgrace was his lot upon earth. During this we came back to the center of the earth and into the king's presence, just as he and his princes were about to dine. It was a repast like a Greek *nephalia*,[151] since they drank neither wine nor strong drink, but instead they drank out pearls like raw or soft-boiled eggs which had not yet hardened and which bestowed or provided excellent strength, so the peasants say.

Then I observed how the sun beshone one lake after another and cast its rays down through them into this frightful depth, so that these *sylphi* never wanted for light. One saw them shine in this abyss as cheerfully as on earth, so that they too cast shadows, so that for them, the *sylphi*, the lakes served as portholes, or windows, through which they received both light and heat, and while this was not everywhere the case, because some lakes went down quite crooked, this was made up for by reflexions, because here and there nature had arranged entire rocks of crystal, diamonds, and carbuncles which sped the light downward.

Journey back from the center of the earth, strange crotchets, castles in the air, schemes, and a reckoning without the host

Meanwhile the time when I was supposed to go back home had grown nigh; for that reason the king commanded that I let him hear wherewith he might favor me. And I said that no greater favor could be bestowed upon me than if he would have a genuine medicinal mineral spring come up on my farm. "Is that all?" answered the King. "I should have thought that you would have taken some large emeralds out of the American Sea[152] with you and would have requested that you be permitted to take them back to the earth's surface. Now I see that there is no avarice in you Christians." With that he handed me a stone of strangely varying colors and said: "Take this with you, and wherever you put it down upon the earth's surface, it will set to seeking out the *centrum* again and pass through the most convenient *mineralia*,[153] till it comes back to us and sends back to you, on our account, a magnificent mineral spring which will be as good and healthful for you as you have merited of us for revealing the truth to us. Then the prince of Lake Mummer forthwith took me back by way of the lake through which we had come, etc.

This journey home seemed to me much longer than the journey thither, and I reckoned it to be two and a half thousand fully measured German-Swiss miles;[154] the reason, however, that time hung so heavy upon my hands was assuredly because I did not speak a word to my convoy, except that I learned from them that they would live to be three, four, or five hundred years old, and this span they lived without any illness. Otherwise, I was, in my mind's eye, so wealthy with my mineral spring that it was all my mind and wits could do to decide where I was going to put it and how I was going to make use of it for myself. I already had my plans made for the fine buildings which I must needs erect near it, so that the guests at the spa might be properly accommodated, and so that I, for my part, might take in a large sum in rents. I was already calculating what manner of bribes I was going to give to the *medicos*[155] to persuade them to give my mineral spring preference over all others, even over the one in Schwalbach,[156] and to send me a flock of wealthy spa guests; I was already leveling entire mountains, so that the people traveling to and from the spa should not complain about arduous travel; I was already hiring cunning house servants, miserly cooks, cautious chambermaids, watchful stable hands, fine and honest stewards for the spa and spring; and I had already decided upon a place in the mountain wilds near my farm onto which I was going to plant a beautiful level garden park and grow in it all manner of rare plants and shrubs, so that the ladies and gentlemen from abroad who had come to take the waters could promenade there, so that the sick could be refreshed, and the hale could delight and recreate themselves with all manner of diverting games. And the *medici*[157]—for a price, of course—must needs commit to paper a glowing treatise about my mineral spring and its priceless qualities, which I was then going to have printed, with a beautiful copper etching of my farm, from which treatise any sick person not at the spa could read himself and hope himself halfway well, as it were. I would fetch all my children from L.[158] and have them taught all manner of things which would be appropriate for my new spa, but not a one of them was ever to be a spa guest, for I had undertaken to bleed my guests unmercifully, not with leeches, of course, but with exorbitant rates.

Amidst such thoughts of riches and such superb and delightful castles in the air I reached the earth's surface again, where the oft-mentioned prince had put me out of Lake Mummer onto dry land, with dry clothes, of course; but I was obliged to cast away immediately the jewel which he had given me in the beginning when he fetched me away, for otherwise I would have drowned in the air or I would have been obliged to stick my head back into the water in order to catch my breath, because this stone had that effect. Now when this was done and he had taken the stone back into his possession, we wished one another God's blessing and protection, like people who were never going to see one another again; he submerged and dived back into the abyss with his retinue, and I walked away with the *lapide*[159] which the king had given me, as full of joy as if I had carried off the Golden Fleece from the Island of Colchis.[160]

But alas! My joy, which was based upon the vain notion that things will remain ever unchanged, did not last long at all, for I had scarce got away from this wondrous lake when I began to lose my way in the enormous forest, because I had not paid heed to the way to the lake which my Pa had led me. I walked on a good ways before I became aware that I was lost, and I was still scheming about how I would put the priceless mineral spring onto my farm, situate it well, and thusly create for myself a steady business. In this wise, without noticing it, the further I walked, the further away I went from the spot to which I most desired to go, and, worst of all, I did not become aware of it till the sun was setting and I no longer knew how to help myself. There I stood, in the middle of a wilderness, like a bump on a log, without either food or firearm, both of which I might well be in need of against the coming night; but my stone, which I had brought forth from the innermost bowels of the earth, consoled me: "Patience! Patience!" I said to myself. "This will more than make up for all the trouble you suffer. Anything that is worthwhile takes a while, and things of value are not won without great effort and labor, else any fool, without working up a sweat or mopping his brow, could make a fine mineral spring like the one you have in your pocket any time he wished to."

Now when I had in this wise cheered myself up, I acquired, along with my new resolve, new strength at the same time, for which reason I strode along far more boldly than before, even though night had overtaken me as I was doing so. The full moon lit my way nicely, to be sure, but the tall fir trees prevented its light from being as agreeable to me as the deep sea had been that same day; but I walked on this way till at midnight I espied a fire in the distance, towards which I walked by the most direct path, and from a distance I saw that some woodsmen were there who were working with resin. Now though such fellows are not always to be trusted, my straits compelled me and my own courage counseled me to accost them. I slipped up upon them without their seeing me and said: "Good night, or good day, or good morning, or good evening, gentlemen! Tell me straight off what time it is, so that I may greet you accordingly." There stood and sat all six of them, trembling with fear and not knowing what answer to give me, for because I am one of those very large fellows and at that particular time had on black mourning clothes, because of my late wife, who had died but a short while before, and particularly because I was carrying in my hands a terrible cudgel, upon which I was leaning like a wild man of the woods, my appearance seemed to terrify them. "What?" said I. "Will no one answer me?" They remained in a state of astonishment for a good while, till finally one of them collected his wits and said: "Who be ya, suh?" Then I realized, from his accent, that they must be Swabians, who are thought (though erroneously) to be dim-witted, and therefore I said that I was a wandering scholar who had only just now come from the mountain of Venus, where I had learned a whole heap of wondrous tricks. "Aha!" answered the oldest peasant. "Now, praise God, I do believe I'll live to see peacetime, because the wandering scholars have set to traveling about again."

CHAPTER 18

Simplicius loses his mineral spring by planting it in the wrong spot

So we fell to talking to one another, and they were so civil to me as to bid me sit by the fire, and they offered me a piece of black bread and thin cow cheese, both of which I indeed accepted. Finally they grew so familiar that they expected me, as a wandering scholar, to tell them their fortunes; and because I knew a bit about both *physiognomiam* and *chiromantiam*[161] I told one after the other of them whatever pack of lies I thought might please them, so that I should not lose credit with them, for I was not, in fact, completely at ease with these wild woodsmen. They demanded that I teach them all manner of curious tricks, but I put them off by promising to do that the next day, and I demanded that they let me rest a little. And after I had thus played the gypsy, I laid me down a little ways off to the side, more in order to hear and learn what their intentions were than because I had any great desire to sleep (though I was not wanting in appetite to do so). Now the more I snored, the alerter they showed themselves to be. They put their heads together and fell to attempting to guess who I might be. They were not of a mind to take me for a soldier, because I was wearing black clothes, and they could not deem me to be a burgher, because I had come trudging into Mückenloch[162] (that was the name of the forest), so far from any towns or villages, at such an unusual hour. At last they decided that I must be a student who had lost his way, or a wandering scholar, as I purported to be, because I was such an excellent fortune-teller. "Aye," another one of them then began, "that is not why he knew all that. Perhaps he is a knavish soldier and has but dressed that way in order to spy out our cattle and our secret trails in the forest. If we but knew for sure, we'd put him so soundly to sleep that he'd never wake up!" Another one, who was of a different opinion, quickly replied and took me to be someone else. Meanwhile I lay there and pricked up my ears, thinking to myself that if these clodhoppers were to attack me, two or three of them were going to bite the dust before they did me in.

Now while they were deliberating this way and I was worrying and fearing for my life, it on a sudden seemed to me as if there was lying next to me someone who had pissed in the bed, for before I knew it I was completely wet, *O mirum!*[163] Troy was lost, and all my fine plans had gone awry, for I could tell from the smell that it was my mineral spring. I then fell into such a rage of anger and indignation that I, all by myself, was on the verge of attacking and fighting with all six of them. "You God-forsaken oafs!" I said to them after I had leaped up with my terrible cudgel. "You can tell what I am from this mineral spring which is gushing forth from where I was lying. It would be no wonder if I were to punish all of you so that the devil would take you, because you harbored such wicked thoughts about me!" And then I made such threatening and terrifying faces that they were all horrified at the sight of me. But I forthwith came back to my senses and realized what a folly I was committing. "No," I thought to myself, "it is better to have lost your mineral spring than to lose your life, which you may be deprived of if you get into a fight with these louts." Therefore I spoke civilly to them again and said, before they could come to any other decision: "Get up and taste of this magnificent mineral spring which, on account of me, you and all other resin gatherers and woodcutters shall henceforth have in this wilderness for your enjoyment!" They could not follow my drift; rather, they looked at one another like living dummies, till they saw that I was nice and calmly taking the first drink out of my hat. Then they one after another got up from by the fire around which they had been eating, examined the miracle, and tasted the waters, but instead of thanking me for it, they fell to reviling me, saying that they wished that I and my mineral spring had wandered into some other spot, for were their master to find out about this, the entire Dornstett district[164] would be pressed into statute labor, to make a road leading to it, which would then be a great burden to them. "On the other hand," said I, "you will all be able to enjoy it; your chickens, eggs, butter, cattle, and other produce you will be able to market better." "No, no!" said they. "No! Our master will put a steward in, and he alone will get rich, and we must needs play his fools, maintaining the roads and trails for him, and we'll get no thanks for it either." In the end they fell into a disagreement, and four of them demanded that I remove it again, which, had it been in my power, I should have been happy to do, whether it pleased them or not.

Now because day had then dawned and I had nothing more to do there, and particularly since I could not but fear that, since the wrangling went on and on, we would soon fall to fighting, I said that if they did not desire all the cows in the entire Baiersbronn valley[165] to give red milk for as long as the spring gushed forth, they should forthwith show me the way to Seebach,[166] which they were indeed content to do, and to this end they sent two of them to accompany me, because one of them by himself was afraid of me.

And so I departed from that spot, and though this entire region was unfruitful and bore nothing but pinecones, I would have liked to put a curse upon it, making it even more barren, because I had lost all my hopes there. But I walked silently on with my guides till I came to the crest of the mountain range, from which vantage point I could recognize the lay of the land again a little. There I said to them: "You gentlemen can make excellent use of your new mineral spring: namely, if you were to report the origination of it to your authorities, it will bring you a fine reward, because then the prince will build it up in order to embellish and profit the land and will make its existence known far and wide in order to enhance his own stature." "Aye," said they, "we'd indeed be fools if we furnished the rod with which to cane our own bodies. We had rather the devil took you and your mineral spring. You've heard right enough why we hate the very sight of it!" I answered: "O, you ninnies! I ought to brand you traitorous wretches for straying so far from the ways of your virtuous ancestors! They were so loyal to their prince that he could boast of them that he would venture to lay his head into the lap of any one of his subjects and sleep there safe and sound. And, because you are afraid of a little work, for which, in time, you would be repaid and the fruits of which your descendants would richly enjoy, you brigands are so dishonorable as to refuse to report this healthful mineral spring, which would profit both your most royal prince and the health and welfare of many a sick person! What difference does it make if each of you must needs do a few days statute labor?" "What!" they said. "We'd sooner kill you, so that your mineral spring stay a secret." "You dolts!" said I. "It would take more than two of you to do that!" And then I shook my cudgel and chased them to hell and gone. Following that I walked downhill towards the south and west and, after much effort and labor, came back home towards evening to my farm, finding that what my Pa had told me before this was true, namely, that from this pilgrimage I would return with nothing but sore feet and as far to walk hither as it was to walk thither.

CHAPTER 19

Some few facts about the Hungarian Anabaptists[167] and their way of life

After my return home I lived a very reclusive life. My greatest joy and delight was to sit over my books, of which I had procured many which treated of all manner of things, and particularly over those which required a good deal of mulling over.[168] What the *grammatici*[169] and pedants must needs know I soon grew tired of, and I was likewise soon surfeited with *arithmetica*;[170] and as concerns *musicam*[171] I had long since come to hate it like the plague, which is why I smashed my lute into a thousand pieces. *Mathematica*[172] and *geometrica*[173] were still of interest to me, but as soon as I was led by them a little into *astronomia*[174] I laid them aside and devoted myself for a time to it and to *astrologia*,[175] in which I then took great delight. In the end they too began to seem to me false and uncertain, so I did not burden myself with them any longer either, but instead seized upon the "art" of Raymundus Lullus,[176] but I found in it much sound and fury and little substance, and because I deemed it a *topicam*[177] I left off and turned to the *cabbalam* of the Hebrews[178] and the *hieroglyphicas*[179] of the Egyptians; but I found that as the ultimate of all my arts and sciences there was no better art than *theologia*[180] when, by means of it, one loves God and serves Him. Following its guides to conduct I divined a way for mankind to live which is more angelic than human, namely, if a society was formed, of both married and single folk, of both men and women, who in the fashion of the Anabaptists were intent only upon providing for their bodily needs by the labor of their hands, under the guidance of an understanding supervisor, and upon spending the rest of their time in the praise and service of God and in the effort to achieve salvation for their souls. For I had once seen such a life upon the farms of the Anabaptists in Hungary, so that, if these good folk had not been so immersed and entangled in other false doctrines, which the Christian churches deem to be repugnant and heretical, I should have voluntarily thrown in my lot with them, or at least esteemed their life to be the most blessed in the entire world, for in their lives and deeds they appeared to me to be like the Jewish sect called the Essenes, whom Josephus and others describe.[181] First of all, they had great treasures and food in abundance, with which, however; they were in no way wasteful; no curses, complaints, or impatience could be noted amongst them; indeed, one heard amongst them no idle talk. I saw their craftsmen toil in their workshops as if they were bound there as apprentices. Their schoolmasters instructed the youth as if they were their own children. Nowhere did I see men and women intermingled with one another, but instead, at each place each sex performing its appointed chores. I found rooms in which there were only mothers who had just given birth and who, together with their children, were amply provided with all necessary care by their fellow-women, without any interference from their husbands. Other special rooms had nothing in them but many cradles with babies in them who were tended to, diapered, and fed by women appointed to do this, so that their mothers were not obliged to further trouble themselves with them, except when they came daily at three specific times to put them to their milk-laden breasts; and this task of caring for new mothers and infants was entrusted only to widows. Elsewhere I saw women doing nothing but spinning, so that in one room one encountered more than a hundred distaffs; there one of them washed the clothes, the second made the beds, the third tended the flocks, the fourth washed the dishes, the fifth tended the pantry, the sixth was in charge of the linen, and so it was with all the others; each one knew what she was supposed to do. And just as the tasks were allotted in an orderly manner to the women, so too each of the men and boys knew his task. When a man or a woman fell ill, he or she had a special man or woman to serve as a nurse, and both sexes had a common *medicum*[182] and apothecary, though because of their laudable diet and good regimen they seldom took sick; and I saw amongst them many a fine man who was very old but still hale and hearty, of the likes of which one encounters very few elsewhere. They had their appointed hours to eat, their appointed hours to sleep, but not a single minute for playing and promenading, except for the youth, who for reasons of health took a half-hour walk with their preceptor after each meal, during which, however, they were obliged to pray and sing hymns. There was no anger there, no passion, no vengefulness, no envy, no enmity, no desire for worldly goods, no pride, no remorse! *In summa*, there was throughout a lovely *harmoniam*,[183] which seemed to be attuned to nothing but increasing the human race and the kingdom of God in every honorable way. No man saw his wife except at the appointed time when he was together with her in his sleeping quarters, in which he found his bed made up but nothing else except his chamber pot, together with a washbowl, a pitcher, and a white hand towel, so that with clean hands he could go to bed and get up the next morning to go back to his work. Moreover, they all addressed one another as "brother" and "sister," and such a decent familiarity was really no cause to be unchaste. Such a blessed life as these Anabaptist heretics led I should also have liked to achieve, for as far as I could see, it surpassed even the monastic life. I thought to myself: "If you could achieve such honorable and Christian behavior under the protection of your secular authorities, you would be a second St. Dominick[184] or St. Francis. "O," I often said, "if you could but convert the Anabaptists so that they could teach their way of life to members of our faith, you would be indeed such a blessed person! Or if you could persuade your fellow-Christians to lead such a (to all appearances) decent and Christian life as these Anabaptists lead, what a great work you would have wrought!" I said to myself, of course: "You fool! What do other people mean to you? Become a Capuchin monk! You are surfeited of women anyway." But then I thought to myself: "You will not be the same man tomorrow that you are today. Who knows what means you may need in the future to walk properly the path of Christ? Today you are leaning towards chastity, but tomorrow you may be burning with passion."

With these and such-like thoughts I long occupied my mind, and I would have gladly given my farm and my entire fortune for such a united Christian society, in order that I might be a member of it. But my Pa prophesied me straight off that I would probably never bring such a group of people together.

CHAPTER 20

Contains a diverting stroll from the Black Forest to Moscow in Russia

That same fall the French, Swedish, and Hessian armies approached in order to replenish their supplies in our land and at the same time to keep under blockade an Imperial city in our vicinity which had been built by an English king and named after him,[185] for which reason everyone rushed off into the upland forests with his cattle and most valued possessions. I did the same as my neighbors, and in my house, which I left rather empty, a Swedish colonel was lodged. In my study he found some few of my books, since in my haste I could not carry everything away, and amongst other things some mathematical and geometrical sketches and some work on military fortifications with which engineers are principally concerned; therefore he concluded that his quarters must not have belonged to a common peasant, and he fell to inquiring after my condition and attempting to make my acquaintance, in consequence of which he persuaded me, through courteous invitations intermingled with veiled threats, to betake myself to visit him at my farm, where he used me most civilly and prevented his servants from ruining or needlessly destroying any of my property. With his friendliness he brought it to pass that I confided to him everything concerning my condition, principally about my family and my origins. Then he expressed surprise that in the midst of war I preferred to dwell amongst peasants and sit idly by while a stranger tethered his horse to my hitching post, when with better honor I could be tethering mine to someone else's. I, he said, should put my saber back on and not let my gifts, which God had bestowed upon me, go to wrack and ruin while I was huddling by my stove and plodding along behind my plow. He knew, he said, that if I were to accept service with the Swedes, my qualities and knowledge of the arts of warfare would soon earn me a high post. I reacted to this with great indifference, saying that any promotion would be a long ways off if one did not have a friend who would give one a leg up. He, on the other hand, replied that my character and abilities would assuredly procure for me both friends and preferment; moreover, he did not doubt that I should encounter in the main Swedish army some of my relatives who counted for something too, since there were many a distinguished Scots of noble blood serving with the Swedes. In fact, he continued, he had been promised a regiment by the General Torstenson,[186] and when he received it, which he had no reason to doubt he would, then he would forthwith appoint me his lieutenant colonel. With these and such-like words he got my mouth to watering, and because hopes for peace were slight and for that reason I would be subjected not only to further billeting of Swedish troops, but also to complete financial ruin, I resolved to join up again and promised the colonel to go along with him, if he would keep his word and give me the post of lieutenant colonel in the regiment which he was soon to be given.

And so the die was cast. I sent for my Pa, or foster father; he was still with my cattle at Bairischbrunn;[187] to him and his wife I signed over my farm for them to own, but under the condition that after their death my natural son, Simplicius, should inherit it and everything upon it, because I had no heirs born in wedlock. Following that I fetched my horse and what money and valuables I still had, and after I had put all my affairs into order and arranged for the upbringing of my son out of wedlock, the blockade was suddenly lifted, so we were obliged to set forth and march to join the main army before we expected to. I served as a "steward" to this colonel and provided for him, his men and horses, and his entire household by stealing and pilfering, which is called "foraging" when soldiers do it.

Torstenson's promises, of which he had made so much at my farm, were by far not so grand as he had alleged, and it seemed to me that he was pretty much ignored. "Alas!" he then said to me. "What scurvy dog has blackened my name with the general staff? I shan't be able to stay here for long." And inasmuch as he suspected that I would not patiently remain with him for long, he concocted a tale to the effect that he had a new regiment he was going to recruit in Livland,[188] where his home was, and with that he persuaded me to immediately mount up in Wismar[189] and go with him to Livland. Now there, too, it all came to naught, for not only did he have no regiment to recruit, he was, though a nobleman, as poor as a churchmouse, and what he did have was from his wife.

Now even though I had let myself be deceived twice and led so far away from home, I nevertheless put in with him a third time, for he showed me letters which he had received from Moscow in which he was offered high military posts, so he alleged, for that is how he translated them into my native tongue; and he boasted loud and long about how prompt and good the pay was that was being offered. And because he immediately set forth with wife and child, I thought to myself: "He surely can't be going on a wild-goose chase this time." And therefore I, filled with high hopes, set out with him, because I saw no means or opportunity to return to Germany at this time anyway. But as soon as we came across the Russian border and encountered sundry German soldiers who had been discharged, mainly officers, I began to get the wind up and said to my colonel: "What the devil are we doing? We leave a country where there is a war going on, and go to one which is at peace and in which soldiers are of no value and are being discharged!" But he continued to cozen me, saying that I should leave everything to him, he knew better what should be done than these fellows, who were not of much use anyway.

Now after we arrived in the city of Moscow I straightway saw that things had gone awry. To be sure, my colonel conferred daily with the magnates,[190] but far more often with metropolitans than with princes, which behavior did not seem all that odd to me, but did seem to savor too much of religion, which fawning over Russian priests aroused in me all manner of crotchets and musings, though I could not divine what his goal and purpose was. Finally he notified me that the business with the war had come to naught and that his conscience compelled him to convert to the Russian Orthodox church; his candid advice was that I should do likewise, since he could not help me as he had promised anyway. His Majesty the tsar, he said, already had good report of my person and good qualities; if I would agree to convert, His Majesty would be so gracious as to make me a nobleman and bestow upon me a royal estate and many subjects, which most gracious offer should not be rejected, since it was more advisable for anyone to have in a great monarch a most generous master rather than a hostile grand prince. I was completely taken aback at this and knew not what answer to give, because if I had had the colonel somewhere else I would have seen to it that he felt rather than heard my answer; but I was obliged to sing a different tune and adapt myself to the situation in which I found myself, a prisoner, as it were, for which reason I held my tongue for a long while before I could resolve upon an answer. Finally I told him that I had of course come hither with the intent to serve His Majesty the tsar as a soldier, which he, the colonel, had occasioned me to do. Now if His Majesty were no longer in need of my services, I could not alter that, much less blame His Majesty for my having traveled such a long way in vain on his account, because His Majesty had not written me to come into his service; however, the mere fact that His Majesty should so graciously deign to bestow upon me such high favor was for me a far greater glory, in which to glory before the entire world, than it would be if I were to most submissively accept it and merit it, because at present I could not yet make up my mind to change my religion and wished only that I were back in the Black Forest on my farm, so that I should cause no one concern or inconvenience. Then he said: "Do as you see fit, sir, but I should have thought that when God and good fortune greet you, you would properly thank them both. If, however, you do not desire to let anyone help you, or to live like a prince, as it were, I nevertheless hope that you will bear in mind that I have spared no effort to do for you everything in my power." Then he made a deep bow, went his way, and left me sitting there; nor was he willing that I escort him to the door.

Now as I sat there quite perplexed and considered my present situation, I heard two Russian coaches outside our lodgings; then I looked out the window and saw my good colonel and his sons climb into one of them and his lady and his daughters into the other one. They were the coaches and livery of the grand prince, and some clergymen were along who were waiting upon this couple, as it were, and were showing them all deference and good will.

CHAPTER 21

How Simplicius further fared in Moscow

From this time on I was placed under guard, not openly but secretly, by some *strelitzi*,[191] without my ever knowing it, and the colonel and his family I did not lay eyes upon a single time again, so I could not know whither he had gone. At that time, as can be easily imagined, my head was filled with strange thoughts and, without doubt, with many grey hairs too. I made the acquaintance of some Germans, both merchants and craftsmen, who resided *ordinari*[192] in Moscow, and I complained to them about my troubles and how I had been duped. They gave me words of consolation and instructions on how I might, upon a good opportunity, get back to Germany again. But when they got wind that the tsar had resolved to keep me in the country and was going to compel me to stay there, they all acted as if the cat had got their tongues. Indeed, they excluded me from their company, and it grew difficult for me even to find a place to lay my head, for I had already used up the money I got by selling my horse, together with saddle and tack, and there went one ducat today and another one tomorrow, which coins I had before wisely sewn into my clothes for a rainy day. Finally I even began to turn my rings and valuables into silver, in hope of maintaining myself till I should finally have a good opportunity to get back to Germany. Meanwhile a quarter of a year passed, after which the oft-mentioned colonel, together with his family, was baptized into his new religion and was provided with a large royal estate and many subjects.

At that time a mandate was issued to the effect that, under severe and unfailing penalty, no idlers, be they Russians or foreigners, would any longer be tolerated, since they were merely taking bread from the mouths of those who did work; and foreigners who were unwilling to work were to leave the country within one month, and the city within twenty-four hours. So well nigh fifty of us banded together, with the idea in mind to make our way as best we could back to Germany together by way of *Podoliam*;[193] but not quite two hours outside the city we were overtaken and taken into custody by some Russian horse, under the pretext that His Majesty the tsar was highly displeased that we had so wickedly made so bold as to gather together in a mob and traverse, without passes and at our own pleasure, His Majesty's lands, with the addendum that His Majesty was not disinclined, in consequence of our crass behavior, to send us to Siberia. On the way back I learned how matters stood with me, for the man who was leading the troop of horses told me expressly that His Majesty the tsar would not let me leave the country; his candid counsel was that I should accommodate myself to His Most Gracious Majesty's will, adopt their religion, and, like the colonel, not refuse a large royal estate; and he assured me that if I were unwilling to live amongst them as a master, then I must needs serve, against my will, as a slave; and, he said, no one would find His Majesty to blame, either, for being unwilling to let such a highly experienced man, as the colonel had described me to be, leave the country. I then belittled myself and said that the colonel had perchance attributed to me more talent, virtue, and knowledge than I in fact possessed. To be sure, I said, I had come to the country to serve His Majesty the tsar and the estimable Russian nation, prepared also to shed my own blood in the struggle against their enemies, but I could not yet decide to change my religion; however, if there were any way at all in which I could be of service to His Majesty the tsar without burdening my own conscience, then I would do everything in my power to do so.

I was separated from the others and given lodgings in the home of a merchant, where I was now openly placed under guard, but in spite of this I was provided every day with magnificent food and delicious drink, which were sent to me from the royal court; and every day I had people who visited me and now and again invited me to be their guest. There was one in particular, a sly man, to whom I had without doubt been particularly recommended and who entertained me every day with friendly conversation, for I had already learned to speak Russian fairly well. On repeated occasions he spoke with me about all manner of mechanical arts; *item*, about war machines, fortifications, and artillery, etc.; at last, after he had on sundry occasions beat about the bushes to see whether I was finally willing to accede to His Majesty the tsar's intent and could find no hope that I would be willing to change my mind in the least, he asserted that if I were really not going to become a Russian, I should at least impart and communicate to the great tsar, by way of doing homage to their nation, something of my knowledge. The tsar, he said, would bestow upon me high royal favor in recognition of my compliance. Then I answered that it had always been my desire to most devotedly serve His Majesty the tsar, for which reason I had come to His Majesty's country to that purpose, and this was still my intention, though I saw that they were detaining me just as if I were a prisoner. "O, not at all, sir!" he answered. "You are not a prisoner here; rather, His Majesty the tsar loves you so much that he scarce knows how he can part with you." "Why then," I asked, "am I placed under guard?" "Because," he answered, "His Majesty the tsar fears that some harm might befall you."

Now when he understood my offer, he said that His Majesty the tsar would be interested in having saltpeter mined and gunpowder manufactured in His Majesty's land; and because there was no one amongst them who could do it, I would be doing His Majesty a great service if I were to undertake the task; they would put at my disposal, he said, sufficient means and men to do this, and he, for his part, desired to beg me most forthrightly not to refuse this most gracious request, because they already had sufficient report that I understood these matters quite well. Then I answered: "Sir, I say to you as I have before, if I can in any way be of service to His Majesty the tsar, with the understanding that you permit me to retain my faith, I shall devote all my energies to it." Then this Russian (who was one of the most distinguished princes) grew quite merry, with the result that he urged more drinks upon me than a German would have.

The next day there came to me from the tsar two princes and an interpreter who made the final arrangements with me and on behalf of the tsar presented me with a costly suit of Russian clothes. And so, some days later, I forthwith set to searching for saltpeter deposits and to teaching the Russians who were assigned to me how to separate it from the earth and refine it. And during this same time I completed the plans for a powder plant and taught other Russians how to burn coal in order to make charcoal from it, so that in a very short while we manufactured a goodly quantity of the finest gunpowder, both for hunting muskets and for cannons, for I had men enough and, besides them, my own particular servants who were supposed to attend to me, or, more accurately, to guard and watch over me.

Now after I had made such a good beginning, the oft-mentioned colonel came to me in great splendor, dressed in Russian clothes and attended by many servants, without doubt to persuade me by this ostentatious display that I too should let myself be baptized into the Russian Orthodox Church. But I well knew that the clothes were from the tsar's clothes closets and had but been lent to him to make my mouth water, because this is the most common practice at the court of the tsar.

And so that you, dear Reader, may understand how things are done there, I shall tell, by way of example, something which happened to me. One time at the powder plants which I had had built outside Moscow on the river, I was busy giving orders what work the one man or the other assigned me was to do that day and the next; on a sudden there was an alarm, because the Tatars,[194] one hundred thousand horses strong, were already within four miles of us, plundering the land and steadily advancing towards us. I and my men were obliged to betake ourselves forthwith to the court, where we were equipped from the tsar's armory and stables. I was clothed in quilted silk armor instead of a cuirass, which silk armor could stop any arrow but could afford no protection against a bullet; and I was given boots, spurs, and a royal helmet adorned with heron plumes, together with a saber which was so sharp that it could split a hair and which was plated with gold and embedded with precious stones; and of the tsar's horses I was mounted upon one, the likes of which I had never in my entire life seen, much less ridden. I and the horse's tack gleamed with gold, silver, precious stones, and pearls. I had on my belt a steel mace which glittered like a mirror and was so well made and heavy that I could easily kill anyone I struck with it, so that the tsar himself could not have ridden off better equipped. Behind me came a white standard with a double-eagle insignia, towards which the people rushed like snowflakes from all sides and from all villages, so that before we had ridden two hours we were forty thousand horse strong, and before four hours, well nigh sixty thousand horse strong, with which army we advanced to meet the Tatars. Every quarter-hour I received a new verbal command from the grand prince, which consisted of nothing but the demand that I should today prove myself to be a soldier (because I had claimed to be one), so that His Majesty could recognize and hold me to be one. Every instant our army was augmented by persons great and small, by troops as well as peasants from the countryside, and yet, in this haste, I could not recognize anyone who was in command of this entire *corpus*[195] and in charge of the order of *battaglia*.[196]

I shan't recount everything that happened, for this battle is not very important for my *histori*.[197] I shall only say that on a sudden we came upon the Tatars, who were burdened by tired horses and much booty, in a valley, or rather a deep hollow, and we attacked them from all sides with such fury that their forces were straightway split. In the first charge I said in Russian to the men following me: "Let us go! Everyone do as I do!" This they all screamed to one another, and with that I raced at full gallop towards the enemy and split in two the head of the first one I encountered, who was a *mirsa*,[198] so that his brains stuck to my steel mace. The Russians followed my heroic example, in consequence of which the Tatars could not withstand their attack and a general rout ensued. I behaved like a man gone stark raving mad, or rather, like a man who in desperation is seeking his own death and cannot find it. I struck down everyone I came upon, no matter whether he was a Tatar or a Russian. And the Russians whom the tsar had sent to guard me pressed on after me so eagerly that my back was always safely covered. The air was as full of flying arrows as if bees or honeybees had swarmed, one of which struck me in the arm, for I had rolled up my sleeve so that I might be all the more unhindered in using my saber and my mace to kill and slaughter. Before I was struck by the arrow my heart was leaping for joy at the sight of such bloodshed, but when I now saw my own blood flowing, my laughter turned into blind rage. And after these fierce enemies had been put to rout, I was commanded by several princes in the name of the tsar to bring their emperor tidings of how we had defeated the Tatars, so at their behest I turned back and had about a hundred horse following me. I rode through the city towards the residence of the tsar and was received by everyone with cheers and jubilation. But as soon as I had made my report about the battle, though the grand prince had already been apprised of all that had happened, I was obliged to take off my royal clothes, which were then put back into storage in the tsar's garderobe, even though they and the horse's tack were soiled and splattered all over with blood and thus almost completely ruined; and though I had thought for sure that because I had acquitted myself in such chivalric fashion in the battle, they would at least let me keep them, together with the horse, as recompense, from this I could well see how things stood with the splendid Russian clothes which the colonel was wearing, because they were all borrowed goods which, like everything else in all of Russia, were the property of the tsar, and no one else.

CHAPTER 22

By what direct and pleasant route he came back home to his Pa

For as long as my wound was healing I was indeed used like a prince. I was always dressed in a fleece adorned with golden buttons and lined with sable, even though my wound was neither mortal nor dangerous, and I have never in my life enjoyed such sumptuous meals as I did then. But these were all the booty I had for my labors, except the praise which the tsar bestowed upon me, which was made bitter for me by the envy of some of the princes.

But when I was completely hale I was sent by boat down the Volga to Astrakhan[199] to set up a powder plant there, as I had in Moscow, because it was impossible for the tsar to supply the frontier fortresses at all times with good fresh gunpowder, which must needs have been transported such a long way by water and through many perils. I was happy to comply because I had assurances that after I had completed this task the tsar would send me back to Holland and would give me, in keeping with his majesty and my merits, a goodly sum of money to take with me. But alas! When we believe that our hopes and well-laid plans are most sure and certain to come true, along comes an unexpected puff of wind and destroys the house of cards which we have been so long a-building. The governor of Astrakhan used me as his tsar had, and in short while I put everything on a good footing. His stored munitions, which were, in fact, spoiled and moldy and could no longer be fired, I recast anew, as it were, like a tinker who makes new tin spoons out of old ones, which at that time was an unheard-of thing amongst the Russians, for which reason, and because of other things I knew, some of them took me to be a sorcerer, others to be a saint and prophet, and yet others a second Empedocles or Gorgias Leontinus.[200] But while I was hard at work and found myself outside the fortress overnight in a powder plant, I was stolen and taken prisoner by a horde of thievish Tatars, who took me with them, together with some others, far into their country, so that I not only had the opportunity to see boromace, the sheep plant,[201] growing but was also permitted to eat some of it. They traded me for some Chinese merchant wares to the Ninchi Tatars, who afterwards gave me as a special present to the King of Korea, with whom they had just signed an armistice. There I was held to be of value because no one else of my kind was to be found in Dusesck and because I taught the king how to hit the bull's eye with his musket on his shoulder and his back to the target, for which reason he then, at my most respectful request, also gave me back my freedom and sent me by way of Japan to the Portuguese in Macao, who, however, paid me little heed. Therefore I went about with them like a sheep which has strayed from its flock, till I finally was captured in wondrous manner by some Turkish or Mohammedan pirates and (after they had dragged me about for well over an entire year amongst the strange, foreign folk who inhabit the East Indies) I was traded by them in Egypt to some merchants from Alexandria. They took me along, together with their wares, to Constantinople, and because the Turkish emperor was just then outfitting some galleys to fight the Venetians and seemed to want for galley slaves to row them, many Turkish merchants were obliged to turn over—in return for cash payment, to be sure—their Christian slaves, amongst whom was I, a stout young fellow. So I was obliged to learn how to row, but this harsh servitude did not last for over two months, for our galley was gallantly overpowered in the Levant by Venetians, and I, together with all my comrades, was rescued from Turkish captivity. Now when this galley put in at Venice with rich booty and some royal Turkish captives, I was set free, because I desired to make a pilgrimage to Rome and Loreto,[202] in order to see these cities and to thank God for my deliverance. To this end I quite easily got a pass, and from honest folk, particularly from some Germans, a tidy sum, so that I was able to outfit myself with a long pilgrim's cloak and set out upon my journey.

After that I betook myself by the most direct route to Rome, where things went exceeding well for me, because I begged a good piece of money from folks both great and small; and after I had remained there for about six weeks I made my way to Loreto with other pilgrims, amongst them Germans and, particularly, some Swiss who were about to go back home again. From there I went over the Gotthard through Switzerland and back to the Black Forest to my Pa, who had kept my farm and had taken the best possible care of everything; and I brought home with me nothing special but a beard which I had grown since I was away from home.

I had been away for three years and some months, during which time I had sailed across divers oceans and had seen all kinds of peoples, but had generally been done more ill than good by them, about which adventures a long book could be written. Meanwhile the Turkish peace had been concluded, so I could live with my Pa in peace and quiet; to him I left the care and management of my farm, and I sat down with my books once more, which then constituted both my vocation and my avocation.

CHAPTER 23

A right fine and short chapter which deals with Simplicius

I once read in what manner the Oracle of Apollo, when the Roman ambassadors asked what they must needs do so that their subjects might be ruled in peace, gave the following answer: *Nosce te ipsum*, that is: Know thyself. This caused me to reflect upon my past and to desire of myself an accounting of the life which I had led, because I was then idle anyway. Then I said to myself: "Your life has been no life at all, but death. Your days have been grievous shades, your years a grievous dream, your sensual pleasures grievous sins, your youth a fantasy, and your possessions an alchemist's treasure which can go up the chimney in smoke and abandon you ere you know it! You have followed the war through many perils and have experienced in it much good fortune and misfortune. You have been exalted one moment and abased the next, great one moment and small the next, rich one moment and poor the next, happy one moment and sad the next, loved one moment and hated the next, honored one moment and scorned the next. But now, poor soul, what do you have from this entire journey? This is what you have accomplished: I am poor in worldly goods; my heart is burdened down with care; I am too lazy, slothful, and spoiled to do anything worthwhile; and, what is worst of all, my conscience is heavy laden with anxiety and sorrow, and I myself am overwhelmed and wretchedly defiled with sins! My body is weary; my mind is confused; my conscience is lost; the best years of my youth are wasted; precious time has been lost; there is nothing which gives me joy; and, most important, I am at war with myself. When I came into this world, after my blessed father's death, I was simple and pure, upright and honest, truthful, humble, retiring, moderate, chaste, modest, devout, and virtuous; but I soon became malicious, false, mendacious, proud, restless, and quite godless generally, all of which vices I learned without any teacher. I prized my honor, not for its own sake, but in order to achieve preferment. I watched the time, not in order to make use of it to achieve salvation for my soul, but in order to make use of it for my body. I put my life in peril many times, and yet I never made any effort to mend my ways so that I could die happy and consoled. I looked only to the passing moment, and to my profit in this world, and thought not once of the next world, much less that some day I must needs give an accounting of myself before God. With these thoughts I tormented myself daily, and at just that time the writings of Guevara[203] fell into my hands, from which writings I must here set down some words, because they were so powerful that they made the world completely odious to me. They were as follows:

CHAPTER 24

The very last chapter, which reports why and in what wise Simplicius once more withdrew from the world

Farewell, World, forasmuch as one cannot and may not trust of thee or in thee.[204] For in thy house, O World, that which is past is vanished, and that which is present goeth soon away, and that which is to begin cometh wondrous late; that which seemeth most firm doth soonest fall, that which is most strong doth soonest break, and perpetuities soonest decay; in such wise that thou art a dead man amongst the dead, and of a hundred years thou dost not let us live an hour.

"Farewell, World, for thou takest us captive and renderest us not free again, thou bindest us and dost not loose our bonds again; thou worriest but comfortest not, thou robbest but makest no restitution, thou accusest us but without cause, thou condemnest us but wilt hear no testimony, and thus thou killest us without sentence to death, and buriest us before we are dead. By thee there is no joy without sorrow, no peace without discord, no love without suspicion, no rest without fear, no abundance without want, no honor without reproach, no riches without burdened conscience, no high estate without complaint, and no friendship without perfidy.

"Farewell, World, for in they palace promises are made and never kept, man serves and hath no reward, man is caressed so that he may be killed, raised to the heights so that he may be cast into the abyss, helped so that he may be felled, honored so that he may be disgraced, deprived of his fief so that he never again have it, and punished without that he ever be forgiven.

"God save thee, World, for in thy house great lords and favorites are cast down, the unworthy are given preferment, traitors are looked upon with favor, the loyal are dismissed, the guilty are set free, and the innocent are condemned; the wise and well qualified are given leave to depart, and the incompetent are retained and given great reward; the deceitful are believed, and the upright and honest have no credit; everyone doth what he will, and no one what he should.

"Farewell, World, for in thee no one is called by his right name. The foolhardy are called valiant, the cowardly cautious, the impetuous diligent, and the indolent peace-loving; a prodigal is called generous and a miser thrifty; a wily chatterbox and babbler is called eloquent, and a quiet man a fool or madman; an adulterer and despoiler of maidens is called a swain; a libertine is called a courtier; a vengeful man is called a zealous one, and a gentle man is called a fool; and thus thou sellest the good for the bad and the bad for the good.

"Farewell, World, for thou leadest all men astray. To the ambitious thou promisest honor; to the discontent, change; to the proud, royal favor; to the indolent, sinecures; to skinflints, many treasures; to gluttons and whoremongers, joy and sensual delights; to enemies, revenge; to thieves, safety from discovery; to the young, a long life; and to court favorites, thou promisest that royal favor hath constancy.

"Farewell, World, for in thy palace neither veracity nor fidelity findeth refuge; whoever speaketh with thee is misled; whoever trusteth in thee is deceived; whoever followeth thee is led astray; whoever feareth thee is most ill used of all; whoever loveth thee is ill rewarded; and whoever dependeth most of all upon thee is ruined most of all. With thee no gift helpeth which one giveth thee; no service which one performeth for thee; no kind words which one speaketh to thee; no fidelity which one giveth thee; and no friendship which one showeth thee. Rather, thou deceivest, undoest, defamest, despoilest, threatenest, consumest, and forgettest everyone. And for that reason everyone weepeth, sigheth, lamenteth, waileth, and spoileth; and everyone doth die. By thee one doth see and learn naught but to hate one another till one murdereth the other; to speak till one telleth lies; to love till one despaireth; to deal and trade till one cheateth; to beg till one deceiveth; and to sin till one doth perish.

"God save thee, World, for in following thee one passeth one's time in forgetfulness, one's youth in romping, running, and jumping over fence and hedge, down highway and byway, over hill and dale, through wood and wild, over sea and ocean, in snow and sleet, in heat and cold, in wind and weather. The years of manhood are spent mining ore and smelting it, quarrying stone and dressing it, hewing lumber and carpentering it, planting fields and tilling them; plotting and scheming, weighing conflicting counsels, worrying and wailing, buying and selling, arguing, quarreling, fighting, lying, and deceiving. Old age one passeth in wretchedness and misery; the mind groweth weak, the breath groweth short, the face groweth wrinkled, the straight back cometh to be bent, and the eye groweth dim, the limbs fall to trembling, the nose falleth to running, the pate groweth bald, the hearing faileth, the smell disappeareth, the taste goeth away; then man doth sigh and groan, grow ill and weak, and hath, *in summa*, naught but toil and travail, down to his dying day.

"Farewell, World, for in thee no one desireth to be virtuous. Daily are murderers executed, traitors drawn and quartered, thieves and brigands and highwaymen hanged, killers deprived of their heads, sorcerers burned, perjurers punished, and rebels sent into exile.

"God save thee, World, for those who serve thee have no vocation or avocation but to idle away the time, to vex and calumniate one another, to pay court to maidens, to wait upon beautiful women and flirt with them, to game at dice and cards, to entertain whoremongers, to fight with neighbors, to tell the latest tidings, to think up new things, to play the Jew, to invent new fashions, to devise new wiles, and to introduce new vices.

"Farewell, World, for no one is content and satisfied with thee. If he be poor he desireth wealth; if he be rich he desireth to count for more; if he be held in contempt he desireth to rise in the world; if he be insulted he desireth to avenge himself; if he be in favor he desireth more power; if he be vice-ridden he desireth but to be of good cheer.

"Farewell, World, for nothing in thee possesses constancy. High towers are struck down by lightning; mills are swept away by the waters; wood is eaten up by worms, corn by mice, fruits by grubs, and clothes by moths; livestock perisheth of old age and poor men of disease. One man hath scabies, the second cancer, the third ulcers, the fourth syphilis, the fifth podagra, the sixth gout, the seventh dropsy, the eighth gallstones, the ninth kidney stones, the tenth phthisis, the eleventh the fever, the twelfth leprosy, the thirteenth palsy, and the fourteenth is feeble-minded. In thee, O World, one man doth not what the other doth, for when one weepeth, the other doth laugh; when one sigheth, the other is of good cheer; when one fasteth, the other doth glut himself; when one feasteth, the other doth suffer hunger; one rideth on horseback, the other goeth on foot; one speaketh, the other remaineth silent; one gameth, the other toileth; and when one is born, the other doth die. And also, one doth not live like the other: one reigneth, the other doeth service; one tendeth men, the other swine; one followeth the court, the other the plow; one saileth upon the sea, the other traveleth over land to market; one toileth in the fire, the other in the bowels of the earth; one fisheth in the water, and the other catcheth birds in the air; one performeth hard labor, the other doth steal and rob the land.

"O World, God save thee, for in thy house one neither leadeth a virtuous life, nor doth one die a uniform death. The one doth die in the cradle, the second in his youth in bed, the third by the hangman's noose, the fourth by the hangman's sword, the fifth on the rack, the sixth at the stake, the seventh in the wine glass, the eighth in flowing waters; the ninth is stifled a-glutting at the trough; the tenth is strangled by poison; the eleventh dies on a sudden, the twelfth in battle, the thirteenth through sorcery; and the fourteenth doth drown his soul in his own inkwell.

"God save thee, World, for thy conversation vexeth me. The life which thou givest us is a wretched pilgrimage, an inconstant, uncertain, hard, harsh, fleeting, and unclean life, full of poverty and error, which should be called death rather than life; a life in which we every instant die from many frailties of inconstancy and from all sorts of deaths. Thou art not content with the bitterness wherewith thou hast surrounded us and imbued into us; rather, in the bargain thou deceiveth most men with thy flattery, charm, and false promises; from the golden chalice which thou hast in thy hand thou givest unto them bitterness and falseness to drink of, and makest them blind, deaf, mad, full, and senseless. Ah, how well be those who foreswear thy companionship, who scorn thy swift, transitory, and fleeting joys, who reject thy company and go not to wrack and ruin with such a deceitful, forsaken fraud as thou art! For thou makest of us a dark abyss, a wretched realm, a child of wrath, a stinking carrion, an unclean vessel in the offal pit, a vessel of putrefaction full of stench and horror. After thou hast long abused and tormented us with flattery, caresses, threats, blows, torments, tortures, and agonies, thou dost turn our ravaged bodies over to the grave and place our souls into uncertainty. For though nothing is more certain than death, yet man is not assured how, when, and where he will die, and, what is most lamentable of all, whither his soul may wander and how it will fare at its destination. Woe then, woe be unto the poor soul which hath served and obeyed thee, O World, and hath pursued thy lusts and luxuriance; for after such a sinful and reprobate soul hath departed the wretched body with swift and unexpected terror, it will not, like the body in life, be surrounded by servants and friends, but will be led by a horde of its most horrible enemies to the particular seat of judgment of Christ. Therefore, O World, God save thee, for I am assured that someday I shall forsake and depart thee, not merely, to be sure, when my poor soul must needs appear to face stern Judgment, but also when the most terrible of all judgments is felled and pronounced: 'Get ye hence, ye accursed ones, into the eternal flames!' etc.

"Farewell, O World, O vile and wicked World, O stinking, wretched flesh, for on thy account and forasmuch as thou hast been followed, served, and obeyed, the godless, unprepared for penance, are condemned to eternal damnation, in which there is to be expected in all eternity naught but sorrow without comfort instead of joy, thirst without refreshment instead of drink, hunger without assuagement instead of food, darkness without light instead of magnificence and splendor; instead of carnal delights, pain without surcease; instead of dominion and triumph, howling and weeping and wailing of woe; heat which cannot be made cool; fire which cannot be made not to burn; cold which cannot be measured; and misery which hath no end.

"God save thee, O World, for instead of thy promised joys and delights, the evil spirits will lay hand to the damned unshriven soul and tear it in a trice into the abyss of Hell; there it will see and hear naught but the terrifying forms of devils and of the damned, darkness and mist, fire which doth not glow, screams, howls, the gnashing of teeth, and horrid blasphemies. Then all hope of grace and alleviation will be past; rank will have no privilege; the higher a man hath climbed and the more grievously he hath sinned, the deeper will he be cast down and the harsher will be the torment he must suffer. Of him to whom much was given, much will be demanded; and the more magnificence a man hath attained in thee, O World, the more torment and suffering will be meted out unto him, for this Divine Justice doth demand.

"God save thee, O World, for though the body remain lying in the earth with thee for a while, it will arise again on Judgment Day and after the Last Judgment must needs be in eternal hellfire. Then the poor soul will say: 'Accursed be thou, World, for through thy contrivance I did come to be forgetful of myself and of God, and I followed thee in all lust, wickedness, sin, and shame, all the days of my life. Accursed be the hour God created me! Accursed be the day I was born into thee, O vile and wicked World! O ye mountains, hills, and cliffs, fall upon me and hide me from the grim wrath of the Lamb, from the countenance of Him Who sitteth upon the seat of Judgment! Alas! Woe is me! Woe is me in all eternity!

"O World! O unclean World! I conjure thee, I pray thee, I entreat thee, I admonish and protest against thee, that thou have no more part of me, and instead I demand and desire naught which is in thee, for I have determined with myself that *possui finem curis, spes & fortuna valete.*"[205]

All these words I weighed carefully and pondered upon constantly, and they moved me to leave the world and become a hermit once more. I should have liked to live near my mineral spring in Mückenloch, but the peasants there would not suffer it to be, though it would have been a pleasant wilderness for me; they feared that I would betray the secret of the spring and cause their ruler to make them build roads and trails to it, now that peace had come. Therefore I betook myself to another wilderness and took up again a life such as I had led in the Spessart Forest. But whether I, like my blessed father, shall remain there till the end of my life, I cannot say.[206] May God have mercy upon us all, that we may receive from Him that upon which we are most intent, namely that we attain salvation in

THE END

NOTES - BOOK V

CHAPTER 1: *How Simplicius becomes a pilgrim and makes a pilgrimage with Trueheart*

1.　the Cloister of Einsiedeln: town and cloister in Switzerland in Canton Schwyz; the Benedictine Monastery there is actually named "Maria-Einsiedeln" (after a painting of the Holy Virgin there); from medieval times on it has been the goal of pilgrimages by devout Roman Catholics.

2.　But whosoever shall deny me...: Matthew 10, 33.

3.　soldateska: soldiers, soldiery.

4.　Rottweil: a town situated between the Black Forest and the Swabian Alb; on the left bank of the upper course of the Neckar River.

5.　under his vine or under his fig tree: although the phrase occurs repeatedly in the Bible (I Kings 4, 25 and Zechariah 3, 10, among others), the allusion here is probably to Micah 4, 3-4: "He shall judge between many peoples, and shall decide for strong nations afar off; and they shall beat their swords into plowshares, and their spears into pruning hooks; nation shall not lift up sword against nation, neither shall they learn war any more; but they shall sit every man under his vine and under his fig tree, and none shall make them afraid; for the mouth of the Lord of hosts has spoken."

6.　Schaffhausen: town in Switzerland in Canton Schaffhausen; located on the right bank of the Rhine, just above the Rhine Falls.

CHAPTER 2: *Simplicius is converted after he has first been frightened by the devil*

7.　a man who was possessed: Bechtold (p. 529) pointed out that there is a depiction of such a man in Moscherosch, "Schergenteuffel," which appeasrs in revised form later in Moscherosch, "Somnium" (p. 252).

8.　the padres: the priests.

9.　Baden: town in Switzerland in Canton Aargau; on the Limmat where it breaks through the Lägern Range.

CHAPTER 3: *How the two friends passed the winter*

10.　L.: Lippstadt.

11.　in duplo: in duplicate, in two copies.

12.　Constance: town on the Lake of Constance; situated on the strip of land which separates the upper part of the lake from the lower one.

13.　Ulm: city in Württemberg, situated on the left bank of the Danube at the foot of the Swabian Alb.

CHAPTER 4: *How Trueheart and Simplicius go to war again and leave it again*

14.　Fortuna: the goddess of fortune.

15.　fatum...fatuitas: fate...fatuousness; Heining (p. 83) and Weydt (p. 26 f.) cite this play on words as an indication that Grimmelshausen possessed a fairly good command of the Latin language.

16.　Count von der Wahl: see above, notes to Book III, Chapter 8.

17.   the cunning Hessian colonel, S. A.: Daniel St. Andräe; see above, Notes to Book I, Chapter 17.

18.   conditiones: conditions.

19.   in prima plana: "on the first page" (the page of a unit's roster which listed the commissioned officers); Simplicissimus' unit thus has a full complement of officers but not of common soldiers.

20.   the bitter engagement...in which battle Count von Götz lost his life: Count von Götz was killed in a battle at Jankau on March 6, 1645; as Borcherdt (p. 420) points out, Grimmelshausen is guilty of an anachronism here, since the action in the novel must be taking place in 1640.

21.   testiculos: testicles.

22.   medici: doctors, physicians.

23.   a cholericus: an irascible sort of person; choler was, in the medical theory of the time, bile, one of the four "humours," and those who had a superabundance of it were thought to be prone to irascibility.

24.   Griesbach: village and then-famous spa in the northern part of the Black Forest, in the Rench River valley.

CHAPTER 5: *Simplicius rides courier and in the guise of Mercury learns what Jupiter actually has in mind as regards war and peace*

25.   medicos: doctors, physicians.

26.   recepta: recipes, prescriptions.

27.   pharmaca: drugs.

28.   antidota: antidotes.

29.   medicus: doctor, physician.

30.   L.: Lippstadt.

31.   Münster: see above, Notes to Book II, Chapter 21.

32.   under his own vine or under his own fig tree: see above, Notes to Book V, Chapter 1.

33.   both my nose and that of the child fell to bleeding: Bächtold-Stäubli, Handwörterbuch des deutschen Aberglaubens, mentions no popular superstition of this sort.

34.   sympathia: sympathy, bond.

CHAPTER 6: *Story of a prank which Simplicius played at the spa*

35.   doctores: doctors, physicians.

36.   a beautiful lady who claimed to be of the nobility: the lady is Courage, who gives her version of their affair in The Runagate Courage, Chapter 24 (164 ff.).

37.   more mobilis than nobilis: "more lax than lady-like." Weydt (p. 27) terms this Grimmelshausen's own word play, citing it as one of the indications that Grimmelshausen was indeed quite capable in Latin; Heining (p. 83) expresses some doubt that the word play is original. The inspiration for the word play is, in fact, found in Garzoni, Discourse 108 (p. 598):

Garzoni: "Item ein andrer / der von einem leichtfertigen Edelmann sagte: er were nicht weniger mobilis als nobilis."; ST: "eine schöne Dame / die sich vor eine Adel ausgab / und meines Erachtens doch mehr mobilis als nobilis war /..."

38.   Geißhut: Borcherdt (p. 421) conjectures that "Haus an der Geishut" (a little over a mile from Gengenbach) is meant.

39.   partem: share.

40.   the Rench River: a right tributary of the Upper Rhine; it originates at the Kniebis in the Black Forest and empties into the Rhine at Helmlingen; a number of spas with mineral springs lie on the Rench, among them Griesbach, Peterstal, and Sulzbach.

41.   spiritum familiarem: the "spiritus familiaris" was an evil spirit which one could acquire, by making a pact with the Devil, as an ever-present and willing personal servant; Courage was temporarily the master of one such spirit (see The Runagate Courage, Chapter 18).

42.   an Epicurean: one who pursues sensual pleasure.

CHAPTER 7: *Trueheart dies and Simplicius goes a-wooing again*

43.   soldier of fortune: see above, Notes to Book I, Chapter 17.

44.   medici: doctors, physicians.

45.   saeculo: saeculum, epoch.

CHAPTER 8: *Simplicius embarks upon a second marriage, encounters his Pa, and learns who his parents were*

46.   exempla: examples.

47.   "Nannygoatbrook": Geißbach, in German, from Geiß (nanny goat) and Bach (brook); the play on words is no more effective in the original than it is in English translation.

48.   a-bother-carriers: Pa's mangling of "apothecaries" (in German: "Abdecker" instead of "Apotheker").

49.   Mansfeld's war: the campaign of the summer of 1622, which began with Mansfeld's defeat of the Catholic forces under Tilly at Wiesloch and ended with Tilly's decisive victory over the protestant league at Höchst.

50.   the battle of Nördlingen: see above, Notes to Book I, Chapter 18.

51.   histori: story, tale.

52.   the battle of Höchst: see above, Notes to Book I, Chapter 22.

53.   Susanna Ramsay: no evidence has been found to indicate that Governor Ramsay had a sister, or that she was married to a German nobleman.

54.   my uncle Ramsay...went quite mad from anger and frustration.: in December of 1637 Ramsay refused to return Hanau to its rightful master, Count Philipp Moritz of Nassau. He was then taken prisoner on February 22, 1638, and popular report had it that he had died in prison a madman; in point of fact, he died at Dillenburg Castle on June 25, 1639, of a serious wound he had received at Hanau (see Könnecke I, 184).

CHAPTER 9: *How he suffered the pangs of childbirth and once more came to be a widower*

55.   notarium: notary.

56.   histori: life story.

57.   o mirum: O wonder!

58.   the lady whom I mentioned above also left a baby...: Courage's version, in The Runagate Courage, p. 163, is as follows: "I left Sauerbrunnen in great vexation and anger, pondering on revenge, because I had been both insulted and scorned by Simplicius. And my maid had been just as busy at Sauerbrunnen as I, and (because the poor ninny could not take a joke) she had been left with a baby boy instead of the usual fee, which child she brought safely into the world on my farm outside town. She was obliged to have it baptized 'Simplicius,' though Simplicius had never in all his life laid a finger on her. Now as soon as I found out that Simplicius had married a farmer's daughter, my maid was obliged to wean her child, and after I had fitted it out with soft diapers, indeed with silken blankets and swaddling bands, to make my deceit more complete and decorous, she, in the company of my farmhand, was obliged to take it to Simplicius' house, where she left it by night on his doorstep, with a written note that he had begot it with me." In The Singular Life of Heedless Hopalong, Chapter 5 (p. 17) Simplicissimus is apprised of Courage's revenge, but it turns out that it was she who was deceived, for Simplicissimus reveals: "'If I still found pleasure in that sort of foolishness, as I once did, it would greatly amuse me to hear that this foolish woman imagines that she pulled the wool over my eyes in this matter, since actually she has done me the greatest service while to this day deceiving herself with vain dreams; for at the time when I was making up to her I lay more often with her chambermaid than with her herself; and it is much more agreeable to me that this same chambermaid and not that wanton gypsy woman is the mother of my son, Sinmplicius, whom I cannot disown since he takes after me in both mind and body.'"

59.   praeludia: preludes.

CHAPTER 10: *Tales of sundry peasants about wondrous Lake Mummer*

60.   in re rusticorum: in matters concerning farming.

61.   Lake Mummer: in German, "der Mummelsee", a cirque lake situated on the southern slope of the Hornisgrinde (the highest peak in the northern part of the Black Forest). Bechtold (p.533 ff.) describes the similarities and differences between Simplicissimus' adventures and those of Elia Georgius Loretus, who depicted them in a report to Athanasius Kircher.

62.   spectra: spectres.

63.   geometra: geometer.

CHAPTER 11: *Unheard-of thanks uttered by a patient, which rouses almost holy thoughts in Simplicius*

64.   fatum: fate.

65.   cholica: gout.

66.   doctores: doctors, physicians.

67.   medici: doctors, physicians.

CHAPTER 12: *How Simplicius journeys with the sylphis into the centrum terrae*

68.   sylphis: usually spirits of the air, here the equivalent of water spirits.

69.   centrum terrae: center of the earth.

70.   when Doc Daniel (he meant le duc d'Anguin) marched down to Philippsburg with his troops: Duc d'Enghien was the title borne by Louis II of Bourbon (1621-1686) until the death of his father in 1646, at which time he took the family title, Prince de Conde. He marched his forces to Philippsburg in early August, 1644 (Hopalong describes the ensuing battle in Chapter 18 of The Singular Life Story of Heedless Hopalong). Since Simplicissimus' narrative has at this point reached only the year 1642, it is obvious that Grimmelshausen included the remark without paying any particular attention to his chronology.

71.   rudera: oars.

72.   abyssum: abyss.

73.   like a second Empedocles of Agrigento...up into heaven): this bit of erudition is taken verbatim from Momus' excoriation of Garzoni in Garzoni, Introduction (p. 2): Garzoni: "ein andrer Empedocles Agrigentinus, welcher sich in den Fewerberg Aetnam stürtzet / auf daß man meinen solte / dieweil man in nirgendt gefunden / er were gehn Himmel gefahren."; ST: "Andere bildeten sich ein / ich hätte mich wie ein anderer Empedocles Agrigentinus (welcher sich in den Berg Aetnam gestürtzt / damit jedermann gedencken solte / wenn man ihn nirgend finde / er wäre gen Himmel gefahren) selbst im See ertränckt / ..." Empedocles (c.490-430 B.C.), a Greek philosopher and statesman who resided in Sicily, killed himself, according to legend, by hurling himself into the crater of Mount Aetna; in fact, he died in exile somewhere in the Peleponesus.

CHAPTER 13: *The prince of Lake Mummer tells of the nature and origin of the sylphs*

74.   Dionysius Dorus: Dionysodorus, a geometer from Cydnus is meant; the classical source of this comment is Pliny, Historia Naturalis 2, 48. In this instance Grimmelshausen was misled by his source. Garzoni refers to the geometer, in the nominative case, as "Dionysius Dorus"; in Grimmelshausen's text the name appears in the dative case ("vom Geometra Dionysio Doro". Acerra philologica III, 20 (p. 397) gives the name nearly correctly (also in a dative case construction): "Es ist nur eine erdichtete und Griechische Lügen was Plinius schreibet l. 2. c. ult. vom Dionysiodoro, welcher nach dem er gestorben / vnd von seinen Verwandten ins Grab geleget war / hat man wenig Tage hernach im Grabe gefunden einen Brieff / welchen er Dionysiodorus aus der Hellen hätte an die Lebendigen auff Erden geschrieben: darin er angezeiget / daß von dannen bis zu vns weren 42000 Stadia, das ist / 1312 ein halb Meile: ...";

75.   Pliny writes...: the passage, as Scholte (p. 134 f.) demonstrates, was lifted from Garzoni, Discourse 24 (p. 147).

76.   42,000 stadia...centrum terrae: 42,000 stadia...center of the earth; since a Roman stadia was 607 feet, the radius of the earth would be 4,751 miles, or 7,644.35 kilometers; taking the figure of 1,312.5 German miles (given in Acerra philologica), the radius would be a little over 6,601 miles, or 9,843.75 kilometers.

77.   900 German miles: according to this, the radius of the earth would be about 4,185 miles, or 6,750 kilometers; of the two estimates, this is the closer one, for the radius (on average) is now calculated at about 3,959 miles, or 6,371 kilometers.

78.   antipodibus: antipodes.

79.   Oceanus: ocean.

80.   abyssu: abyss.

81.   donec auferatur luna, Psal. 71: "as long as the moon endureth" (actually Psalms 72, 7).

82.   generationes fructu- & animalium: the procreation of fruits (plants) and animals.

83.   chymici: chemists (alchemists at this time).

84.   simpliciter: simply, in simple terms.

85.   nuntii: messengers, ambassadors.

86.   justitiam: justice.

87.   in coitu: in sexual intercourse.

CHAPTER 14: *What further matters Simplicius discussed on the way with this prince, and what wonderous and strange things he heard and saw*

88.   materia: subject, matter.

89.   Lake Pilatus: a small mountain lake on Mount Pilatus (bordering Lake Lucerne).

90.   camarinam movere: Camarina was (in ancient geography) a city on the southern coast of Sicily, about 45 miles southwest of Syracuse.

91.   the spring in Arcadia, with whose waters Jolla is said to have poisoned Alexander the Great: the spring was the Styx; Jolla was Alexander's cupbearer.

92.   aqua fort: aqua fortis, i.e. nitric acid.

93.   county of Zips...: in Czech "Szepes" and Slovak "Spish"; a gold and silver mining area on the southeastern foot of the Hoher Tatra and in the Slovakian Erzgebirge, in what was then Hungary and is now Czechoslovakia.

94.   one which is said to be in Thessaly...: Thessaly is the northern part of Greece.

95.   The lake at Zircknitz in Corinthia: Zirknitz (in Slovenian Cerknica) is situated in what is now the Peoples Republic of Sovenia, Yugoslavia; the lake periodically drains through sinkholes and gorges into subterraneous passageways which empty into the Unz River.

96.   the spring in Aengstlen...: Aengstlen is in Switzerland in the Bernese Highlands.

97.   the Schändle Brook at Ober-Nähenheim : Ober-Nähenheim (in French Obernai) is a village in the Lower Alsace at the foot of Odilie Mountain.

98.   the Fluvius Sabbaticus: a river in Palastine which, according to Josephus, De bellico Judaico (VIII, 24) flows only on the sabbath, and according to Pliny (31, 18, 3) fails to flow only on the sabbath. Despite the fact that he used Josephus as a source for Chaste Joseph andMusai, Grimmelshausen here obviously is copying from someone whose source was Pliny.

99.   metalla: metals.

100.   semi-mineralia: semi-minerals. all the metals and "semi-minerals" (a classification no longer used) mentioned are also listed by Garzoni in Discourse 69 (p. 439), the metals in a slightly different order, the semi-minerals in the exact order in which Grimmelshausen lists them: Garzoni: "Halb Mineralien sind Schwefel / Saltz mit allen seinen Sorten / als naturale, sal gemma, sal natiuum, sal radicum, sal nitru (sic), sal armoniacum (sic), sal petrae, weisse, rothe, gelbe Farben / Spangrün / Victrill / marchasita aurea, argentea, plumbea, ferra, lapis Lazuli, alumen, arsenicum, antimonium, risigallum, Electrum naturale, Chrisocolla: Sublimatum, aber minium, cerusa, Sandaraca, Sandix, Suicum, vnnd Thutia, werden also

bereitet. // Die Metallen sind / Mercurius, Quecksilber / Bley / Zinn / Silber / Kupffer / Eisen vnd Gold / ...”; ST: “... zwischen die Metalla passire,...als da sey Gold / Silber / Kupffer / Zinn / Bley / Eisen / Quecksilber / & oder durch die halbe Mineralia, nemlich Schwefel / Saltz mit allen seinen Gattungen / als naturale, sal gemmae, sal nativum, sal radicum, sal nitrum, sal armoniacum (sic), sal petrae, &c. weisse / rothe / gelbe und grüne Farben / Victril, marchasita aurea, argentea, plumbea, ferrea, lapis lazuli, alumen, arsenicum, antimonium, risigallum, Electrum naturale, Chrisocolla, Sublimatum, &c. ...”

101.   sal naturale: natural salt (derived from brine).

102.   sal gemmae: crystalline salt.

103.   sal nativum: uric acid salts.

104.   sal radicum: “root salt” (apparently salt derived from root vegetables is meant).

105.   sal nitrum: saltpeter (usually potassium nitrate, but also possibly sodium nitrate or calcium nitrate).

106.   sal ammoniacum: sal ammoniac (ammonium chloride).

107.   sal petrae: rock salt.

108.   marchasita aurea, argentea, plumbea, ferrea: marcasites (iron pyrites) which had the color of gold, silver, lead, iron; they were used in the seventeenth and eighteenth century in the manufacture of ornaments.

109.   lapis lazuli: a semiprecious stone which is azure blue in color and is actually a complex silicate, often with iron pyrites intermixed.

110.   alumen: alum.

111.   arsenicum: arsenic (now recognized as an element; probably what is meant here is either gray arsenic or “arsenides”—the form of arsenic found in many sulfide ores).

112.   antimonium: antinomy (now recognized as an element; probably gray or metallic antinomy is meant).

113.   risigallum: yellow arsenic, which is obtained by heating gray (metallic) arsenic and then rapidly cooling its vapor.

114.   Electrum naturale: amber, which is neither a mineral nor an element, but rather a fossil resin.

115.   Chrysocolla: a mineral which is green or blue (also brown or black in its impure form), it is actually a hydrous silicate of copper.

116.   sublimatum: presumably mercuric chloride is meant (see above, Notes to Book IV, Chapter 8).

117.   Cervia: town in Italy in the province of Ravenna, on the Adriatic Sea between Ravenna and Rimini.

118.   Commachio: actually spelled Comacchio, a town in Northern Italy kin the province of Ferrara, situated on 13 islands and a promontory between the Adriatic and the inlet of Comacchio, some 29 miles southeast of Ferrara.

119.   Centuripean water: Centuripe was, in antiquity, a city in Sicily near Mount Aetna; according to Pliny 31, 7, much salt was found there.

120.   Cappodocian water: Cappadocia is an area in Asia Minor.

121.   In Cervia...yellow-hued: Scholte notes that these facts are taken virtually unchanged from Garzoni, Discourse 151 (p. 135).

122.   aequatoris: equator.

CHAPTER 15: *What the king said to Simplicius and Simplicius said to the king*

123.   troglodytes: cave-dwellers.

124.   Nova Zembla: see above, Notes to Book I, Chapter 5.

125.   Samoyedes: members of Uralic tribes living in Siberia.

126.   Moluccahs: inhabitants of the Moluccas (the Spice Islands, the islands of the Malay archipelago).

127.   the polis arctico and antarctico: the North and South Poles.

128.   Wild lake: presumably the "Wildsee" (in the Black Forest near the Enz River).

129.   Black Lake: presumably the "Schwarzer See" (also called the "Bistritzer See"), located in the Bavarian Forest, and 142 feet deep.

130.   as Eusebius described...in a sermon: the passage was taken from Garzoni, Discourse 3; Scholte (p. 135) presents parallel texts.

131.   Justitiam: Justice.

132.   the theologi: the theologians, churchmen, clergy.

133.   Jerome: St. Jerome (Eusebius Hieronymus, c. 347-420 A.D.), church father and biblical scholar; he produced the standard Latin translation of the Bible which is known as the Vulgate.

134.   Bede: usually termed "the Venerable Bede" (c. 673-735), Northumbrian monk and author of the Ecclesiastical History of the English People.

135.   Borromaeus: St. Borromaeus (Carlo Borromeo, 1538-1584); as archbiship of Milan and cardinal he worked for church reform, particularly at the third session of the Council of Trent (1560-1563).

136.   Augustine: St. Augustine (Augustine of Hippo, 435-530), bishop of Hippo, church father, and most important theologian of his epoch.

137.   Hilarion: St. Hilarion (c, 291-371 A.D.), monk and mystic who, following the Egyptian tradition, founded Christian monasticism in Palestine.

138.   Pachomus: St. Pachomius (c. 290-346 A.D.), the founder of Christian communal monasticism.

CHAPTER 16: *Some new tidings from the depths of the unfathomable sea which is called the Mare del Zur, or the peaceful, quiet sea*

139.   the Mare del Zur: the Pacific Ocean, the South Seas.

140.   polo antartico: South Pole.

141.   the isles de los latronos: the Marianas (should read "de los ladronos")

142.   pygmaei: pygmies.

143.   Aristarchus...Copernicus...: Aristarchus of Samos (c. 310-230 B.C.), Greek astronomer who was the first to theorize that the earth moved around the sun; Nicolaus Copernicus (1473-1543), Polish astronomer and proponent of the view that the earth rotates around the sun. Grimmelshausen could have learned this from Garzoni, Discourse 39 (p. 294), where the "error" of both astronomers is discussed.

144.   exhalatione humida, viscosa & crassa: humid, thick and tenacious vapors; in Garzoni's Discourse 69 (p. 439), where the phrase occurs in conjunction with a description of Aristotle's theory of the origin of metals, the words are afterwards translated into the vernacular: Garzoni: "Aristoteles schreibt lib. 3. Meteoror. daß sie (metals) vnter der Erden von einer exhalatione humida viscosa, & crassa, das ist / von einem feuchten dicken vnd zähen Dunst generirt werden / ..."; ST: "da antwortet er / es befinden sich hin und wieder in der Erden läre stätte / die sich nach und nach mit allerhand Metallen außfüllen / weil sie daselbst auß einer exhalatione humida, viscosa & crassa, generirt werden / ..."

145.   Marchasitae aureae vel argentae: marcasites (iron pyrites) which were the color of gold and silver.

146.   metallis: metals.

147.   the king of the salamandrae: the king of the salamanders (fire sprites).

148.   a strange cloth which we had on earth: asbestos fiber.

149.   the elixir of Theophrastus: Theophrastus is Paracelsus, whose full name was Philippus Aureolus Theophrastus Paracelsus von Hohenheim—called Bombastus (1493-1541) and who was said to have produced an elixer which cured all ills.

150.   cholericus: see above, Notes to Book V, Chapter 4.

151.   a Greek nephalia: a feast or celebration at which no alcoholic beverages are drunk.

CHAPTER 17: *Journey back from the center of the earth, strange crotchets, castles in the air, schemes, and a reckoning without the host*

152.   the American Sea: presumably the Pacific Ocean is meant.

153.   mineralia: minerals.

154.   German-Swiss miles: presumably the mile which equals about 7.5 kilometers.

155.   medicos: doctors, physicians.

156.   Schwalbach: town and mineral springs (Langenschwalbach) in a side valley of the Aar River, in the Taunus Mountains in Hesse.

157.   medici: physicians.

158.   L.: Lippstadt.

159.   lapide: lapis, i.e. stone.

160.   the Golden Fleece from the Island of Colchis: see above, Notes to Book I, Chapter 26.

CHAPTER 18: *Simplicius loses his mineral spring by planting it in the wrong spot*

161.   physiognomiam...chiromantiam: see above, Notes to Book II, Chapter 20.

162.   Mückenloch: a hamlet in the northernmost part of the Black Forest.

163.   O mirum! Troy was lost.: O wonder! Troy was lost.

164.   the Dornstett district: the area around Dornstetten, in the Black Forest east of Freudenstadt.

165.   the Baiersbronn valley: Baiersbronn is a town on the Murg in the northern part of the Black Forest, at the head of the Murg Valley.

166.   Seebach: Black Forest village on the Acher, to the southwest of the Mummelsee; the Acher itself was called the Seebach in the seventeenth century, and the construction in German leads one to believe that Grimmelshausen has the river in mind rather than the village.

CHAPTER 19: *Some few facts about the Hungarian Anabaptists and their way of life*

167.   the Hungarian Anabaptists: A. J. F. Ziegelschmid ("Grimmelshausens ungarische Wiedertäufer," PMLA 54, 1939, pp. 1033 ff.) identified this group as "Hutterer," members of Anabaptist communes (called "Bruderhöfe") which were established in Moravia in the sixteenth century; in 1622 the Hutterer fled to Hungary, where they settled and remained until 1763, when they migrated to Transylvania, Wallachia, the Ukraine and the North American continent. In 1654 one such group, from Sobotishte in Hungary, was permitted by Count Palatine Carl Ludwig to settle in Mannheim, where they stayed until 1684; because there is no evidence that Grimmelshausen ever visited Hungary, Ziegelschmid assumed that it was through this group that Grimmelshausen became acquainted with the life style of the Hungarian Anabaptists, which he dscribes with great accuracy.

168.   My greatest joy and delight...: all the subjects which Simplicissimus lists are treated by Garzoni in individual discourses.

169.   grammatici: grammarians.

170.   arithmetica: arithmetic.

171.   musicam: music.

172.   mathematica: mathematics.

173.   geometrica: geometry.

174.   astronomia: astronomy.

175.   astrologia: astrology.

176.   the "art" of Raymundus Lullus: Lullus (properly Ramon Llull, c. 1235-1316) was a Catalan mystic; the "art" is his major work, Ars magna, in which he interpreted all reality as the embodiment of some aspect of the divine and regarded art, science and nature as analogues of each other.

177.   because I deemed it a topicam: the sentence, of course, makes little sense, either in the original German ("und weil ich sie vor eine Topicam˘ hielte, ließ ich sie fahren") or as I have translated it; it does make better sense when Grimmelshausen's source, Garzoni, Discourse 21, is taken into account, where the passage reads: "Was mich aber anlangt / halt ich sie für eine Topicam, welche aber nicht so vollkommen / wie sich Raymundus bedunken läst..." (But as for me, I deem it a topicam which is, however, not so complete as Raymundus imagines); either Grimmelshausen or his printer dropped out the clause which qualifies the word topicam.

178.   the cabbalum of the Hebrews: Kabbala, esoteric Jewis mysticism; its major text was the Sefer ha-bahir, or Book of Brightness (12th century).

179.   hieroglyphicas: hieroglyphics.

180.   theologia: theology.

181. the Essenes, whom Josephus and others describe.: Flavius Josephus (first century A.D.); Grimmelshausen used his *De bellico Judaico* as a source for his first novel, *The Chaste Joseph*.

182. medicum: doctor, physician.

183. harmoniam: harmony.

184. St. Dominick: (1170-1221), founder of the Dominican Order of Preaching Friars.

CHAPTER 20: *Contains a diverting stroll from the Black Forest to Moscow in Russia*

185. an Imperial city...built by an English king and named after him: Offenburg, according to legend, was founded around 600 A.D. by an English king named Offo; the city was blockaded by the Duke of Weimar's troops from February till September 1643.

186. General Torstenson: Lennart Torstenson, Count of Ortala (1603-1647) was commander-in-chief of Swedish armies in Germany from 1641 until 1646, and he led them to victories in the second battle at Breitenfeld (1643) and in the battle at Jankau (1645).

187. Bairischbrunn:Baiersbronn (see above, Notes to Book V, Chapter 18).

188. Livonia: in German "Livland"; the lands now called Latvia and Estonia.

189. Wismar: seaport on the Bay of Wismar in the Baltic Sea, some 65 miles northeast of Hamburg.

190. magnates: high-ranking noblemen.

metropolitans: archbishops of the Russian Orthodox Church.

CHAPTER 21: *How Simplicius further fared in Moscow*

191. strelitzi: members of the tsar's royal guard.

192. ordinari: normally (i.e., they wwere permanent residents rather than visitors from Germany).

193. Podoliam: a part of Poland.

194. the Tatars: Turkic nomads of the south Russian Steppe.

195. corpus: military unit, army corps.

196. battaglia: battle.

197. histori: life history.

198. mirsa: son of a prince.

CHAPTER 22: *By what direct and pleasant route he came back home to his Pa*

199. Astrakhan: province on the Caspian Sea.

200. Empedocles or Gorgias Leontinus: Garzoni also links these two figures in Discourse 21 (p. 142), where they are pictured as men who could discourse on any subject.

201.   boromace, the sheep plant: melons which are shaped like lambs. Olearius (p. 155) mentions the plant. The "fur" of the plant was used by the natives to make wool. Superstition had it that the plant devoured all other plants around it and then died. Olearius determined that the plant simply did not exist.

202.   Loreto: town in Ancona province in central Italy; the goal of the pilgrims who went there was the Santa Casa (Holy House of the Virgin), which according to tradition was saved from destruction by the Turks in 1291 when a band of angels carried it away from Nazareth and esposited it unchanged in Dalmatia, which where it was later miraculously transported to the Italian caost of the Adriatic and then to Loreto.

CHAPTER 23: *A right fine and short chapter which deals with Simplicius*

203.   the writings of Guevara: Antonio de Guevara (c. 1490-1545), a Spanish ascetic and author; in the early seventeenth century Aegidius Albertinus translated several of his works into German.

CHAPTER 24: *The very last chapter, which reports why and in what wise Simplicius once more withdrew from the world*

204.   Farewell, World...: adaptation and mostly verbatim redaction of a tirade found in Guevara's Contemptus Vitae Aulicae et Laus Ruris.

205.   posui finem curis, spes & fortuna valete: I put an end to my cares, Hope and Fortune farewell!

206.   But whether I, like my blessed father, shall remain there till the end of my life, I cannot say: this remark left open the possibility of having Simplicissimus return to the world and recount yet more of his adventures, and this does indeed occur in the first Continuatio (sometimes called Book VI of Simplicissimus).